WE faced each other, and the surf crashed near us—the waves lapped the horses' hoofs, and receded, to come again. He was like some phantom of my dreams, vague adolescent dreams of a man who would take the place of my grandfather, a man rich in looks and authority. He became all those things for me in those first few minutes, and as yet he had not even smiled at me.

Suddenly the man took the reins of both animals in his hand, and with his free arm gathered me to him. The first kiss of passion I had ever received had no flavor of sugar about it. It was hard, and warm and searching.

"I never thought it could happen," I said. "You're Richard Selwin, and I love you."

He still held the two horses. Now his free hand went to sweep the tangled hair back from my face.

"Hush, child," he said. "I shouldn't have done it. I should never have done it."

THE SUMMER OF THE SPANISH WOMAN

Catherine Gaskin

FAWCETT CREST • NEW YORK

THE SUMMER OF THE SPANISH WOMAN

THIS BOOK CONTAINS THE COMPLETE TEXT OF
THE ORIGINAL HARDCOVER EDITION.

Published by Fawcett Crest Books, a unit of CBS Publications, the Consumer Publishing Division of CBS Inc., by arrangement with Doubleday and Company, Inc.

ISBN: 0-449-23809-1

Selection of the Reader's Digest Condensed Book Club.
Alternate Selection of the Literary Guild.

Printed in the United States of America

10 9 8 7 6 5 4 3 2 1

AUTHOR'S NOTE

This novel could not have been written without the assistance of those whose lives are closely concerned with the making of sherry and whose names are part of the history of Jerez.

I would like, therefore, to acknowledge my deep indebtedness to all the members of the González family, of González, Byass & Co., Ltd., in particular to Sir Manuel González Gordon, Marqués de Bonanza, patriarch of the sherry shippers, the beloved "Tío Manolo." The family have been unstintingly generous of their time and expertise, endlessly patient in showing, explaining, and answering questions. They have spared no pains in trying to give me a true picture of Jerez, and my husband and I have had the unforgettable experience of Spanish courtesy and hospitality. Through their kindness we have been permitted to visit the famous, invaluable, and now endangered wilderness of the Coto Doñana.

I must also thank Fatima Ruiz-Lasaleta, of Zoilo Ruiz-Mateos, whose enthusiasm for and love of old Jerez were an inspiration. To the Marquesa de Tamarón, I wish again to extend my thanks for cold water on a hot afternoon, and a tour of her wonderful castle at Arcos. In both London and Jerez we have enjoyed the friendship and tapped the memories of Geoffrey Hawkins Byass.

This is a work of fiction; any resemblance to any person, living or dead, is entirely coincidental.

C.G.

My well-beloved had a vineyard in a very fruitful hill: and he made a trench about it, and gathered out the stones thereof, and planted it with the choicest vine, and built a tower in the midst of it, and also hewed out a winepress therein: and he looked that it should bring forth grapes. . . . What could I have done more to my vineyard, that I have not done in it?

Isaiah 5:1–4

PART ONE

Irish Morning

CHAPTER ONE

1

The Irish Sea crashed in breakers on the sand in the fury it still possessed from last night's storm, and the man and the horse came towards me like the thunder of the sea. I knew at once who he was, and I had been prepared to dislike him, even to hate him. But I saw now the man and the stallion almost as the one being, and I coveted them both.

Afterwards when I looked back on this moment I knew it was the time when the last of childhood dropped from me.

He drew in the stallion, needing all his strength to do it; the horse had to be a full seventeen and a half hands, I judged. It was milk-white, with mane and tail tinged with cream. A dream of a horse. A quiver ran through the mare I rode, as blood and beauty seemed to recognize each other. At the same time I looked at the man, and my own body quivered. He returned the stare. Then slowly he raised his hat.

"Miss Charlotte?"

I slid my hand along to pat the neck of the mare, in a vain attempt to calm us both. "And you are Richard Selwin—Lord Blodmore."

He was unsmiling, and seemed at that moment as handsome as the horse he rode. He had the Blodmore features, the Blodmore eyes. He had more than a passing resemblance to my grandfather, who had once been called the handsomest man in Ireland. It was hard to hate him. But because of him we had to go—we had to leave Clonmara, dispossessed like gypsies turned off their campsite because they did not own it. And still, now I saw him, it was hard to hate him.

All these months we had been waiting for him. We had been waiting for Richard Selwin, now Lord Blodmore, because my mother had not had the tact and good sense to have been born a boy. We had been waiting since the day my grandfather put his famous hunter, Wicklow Lad, at a bank which had proved too much even for that great heart and strength. For almost fifteen years my grandfather had hunted this, his best-loved horse, over some of the fiercest country in County Wicklow, but that high, nearly impossible bank had been the last for both of them. Wicklow Lad had broken a leg, and my grandfather had broken his neck. The hunter had been shot there on the hunting field. The body of my grandfather had been carried home on the five-barred gate which, if he had been sensible, he would have opened and gone through, instead of putting Wicklow Lad at the bank. But he had been a man of great courage and little caution in matters like that. So the earldom of Blodmore and its entailed estate had passed to this man whom no one at Clonmara had ever seen before.

Now I saw him, and the loss of everything I had ever known became more bitter, because I wanted him also. And yet at this moment some new, strange feeling stirred; the half-veiled suggestions of Nanny and my mother's much broader innuendoes of the last months became a faint hope in my own heart. In these first moments of looking at him, when we had spoken only each other's names, my mind flashed back over the months since that

9

morning of last January when the frost was still white on the north side of the hedgerows and I had seen my grandfather killed. Everything had seemed to die with him; I had loved my grandfather. I was never sure, at that time, whether I actually loved my mother, Lady Pat. Of course I admired her, as many people did, admired her spirit, her charm, her "way" with people. But there were many things I found hard to forgive her, as, irrationally, I also found it hard to forgive my grandfather for making that last, mortal mistake of putting Wicklow Lad at that bank which had proved too much for both of them. I found it hard to forgive him for having only one child, and that one a girl, who couldn't inherit Clonmara. I couldn't forgive my mother for having made that mad, disastrous marriage, the marriage which had lasted only long enough for one child to be conceived. And that child had been born here at Clonmara—myself. It was the only world I had ever known, and there was no man, no son of my grandfather, no brother of my mother, to inherit it. The Blodmore strain, it seemed, did not run to boys. Fondly, and sometimes a little sadly, my grandfather had called me Charlie, as he had called his daughter Pat. It was a poor world, I thought, in which to have been born a woman.

My mother had gone back to hunting that same winter, restless and unable to maintain the formalities of mourning, beyond the black band on her sleeve and the heavily black-draped top hat. She had ridden, and flirted, more recklessly than ever before. But I, halfway between the schoolroom and womanhood, hadn't been able to face the rather wild camaraderie of the Irish hunting field without the stabilizing influence of my grandfather. Without him as Master of Hounds the field had seemed strangely empty and vacant. So I had taken to riding alone, without even a groom—something my grandfather would have known of, and forbidden, but which my mother didn't seem to notice. It had been a lonely time, a time which bred strange and frightening thoughts about the future, thoughts which provoked me to things I had never done before. I had even started to read books from my grandfather's library, beginning one, laying it aside for the next, growing desperate at the realization of my own ignorance. I had, in spite of the fear and anger of the head groom, Andy, dared to mount Half Moon, that mare of beauty and still uncertain temperament who had already given us the best foal, my mother said, ever bred at Clonmara. The mare, underexercised and feeling the lightness of the creature on her back, had at once thrown me, as if to establish immediately her supremacy. Hurting, and more than a little afraid, I had mounted her again, and had again been thrown. She seemed to sense my own unease, my state of bewilderment, and it affected her. I had offered her sugar, and only the gentle, calming words learned from my grandfather, and I had mounted her once more.

"Is it wanting to kill yourself you are, then?" Andy had demanded, furious with me. "And what will I be telling her ladyship?"

"Nothing," I shouted, struggling to keep my seat as the mare wheeled wildly in the space of the stable yard. "Nothing at all! She'll settle to me, you'll see!"

"She'll be the death of you," Andy had insisted. "And me too, when I come before the magistrate for letting a child kill herself." He added coaxingly, "Ah, Miss Charlie, you'd never be putting me in prison, would you now?"

But I didn't answer him because Half Moon had headed out of the stable yard and down the continuation of the long avenue, the part that led to the break in the dunes where the sea glittered distantly. There was no choice for me; at the time I went where Half Moon chose.

But I went on with my efforts to win the mare, to steady her and to banish my own unsteadiness of mind. I spent hours with her each day. There was little else to do, except spend the time with the books in the library which only made me anxious again. I had had a governess but she, guessing the state of my grandfather's affairs and being offered a post, she said, elsewhere, had gone. The steward of the estate attended to everything, and except for the aching absence of my grandfather, life appeared to go on as before. But an awful uncertainty hung over us, mostly unvoiced, but always present.

The one person, however, who always spoke of it was Nanny. She had been a young nurserymaid when my mother was growing up, and had still been at Clonmara when Lady Pat returned to have her baby. She had a position of privilege at Clonmara, and strong views, which she never hesitated to air. "Well, child," she would moan softly to me, "it's the end for all of us. What can we do but go out to that place in Galway that the Earl settled on Lady Pat? And it with the roof falling in on it. And very poor land that goes with it. And the mice in possession of everything, and the tenants as hungry as the mice. Ah, well—it was the Earl who was too easy to ask for their rents this long time. Well, that's where we'll be going when Himself, the fine heir, shows up." Then she would usually rattle the poker briskly against the irons of the grate. "Unless . . . unless, Miss Charlotte, you would bestir yourself to be a little pleasant to Himself. It wouldn't hurt, now, to comb your hair once in a while and put on a decent dress. You're not half bad-looking, though not the beauty Lady Pat was at your age. But still . . ." Then she would shake her head as she looked at the child she had brought up. "If his lordship could see you in those . . . those breeches things you ride in, sure wouldn't he die all over again, God rest his soul. Now when this new man comes, if he could find a nice, decent quiet young lady, such as you'd expect the Earl's granddaughter to be, why there's no knowing what might come of it, and he unmarried still. . . ." And her voice would go on crooning, beckoning up visions of this life at Clonmara which might go on forever if only I would make myself pleasant to the new heir. Then she would add with bitterness, as the reality of the situation struck her again, "It isn't as if any of the gentlemen around here would have you—you without a penny to your name—and even that name your mother has made a scandal of. Ah, if only the Earl hadn't been so foolhardy with those investments of his that went awry. Only trying to make some provision for his poor foolish daughter, he was, and taking risks and being led astray by scoundrels. Just trying to see she had a bit more than that terrible place out west, which is where we'll all be going—"

"*You* don't have to go, Nanny," I answered. I was wearied of all this talk of money, which she understood even less than I did. "The new Lord Blodmore will need servants at Clonmara."

Nanny, at this point, would draw herself up stiffly. "If you think for a moment, Miss Charlotte, that I'd abandon you and your poor mother . . ." Her voice invariably trailed off in a keening whimper that I found infinitely trying. I avoided the old nursery, and Nanny, as much as possible.

I couldn't always avoid my mother, who put the matter of the new heir more bluntly, but still without much hope. "He's busy in London, they say, and somewhere down in the south of Spain, where, it seems, he had some business connections. So God only knows when he'll turn up here and turf us out. I wonder what sort he is?—never a letter from him, or anything saying what he intends to do. I feel, from what Siddons says—though why I should think a fusty old solicitor like him would have much notion of these things—that our fine new Lord Blodmore is scarcely considered a gentleman. He's been mixing in commerce all his life, Siddons says. No money. His only expectation was that Father would die without an heir closer than he. A second cousin of my father, or something even more remote—that's all he is, and yet he's to have the title and Clonmara. Oh, I tell you, Charlie, it's not fair. No, not at all. He's probably some miserable little inky-fingered clerk, but he's to get it all. Those laws they have . . . Women don't have a chance."

She was referring, of course, to the laws of primogeniture and entail which prohibited any but the male closest in line from inheriting the title and estate. "Just a second-odd cousin who left Ireland as soon as he could, got some schooling in England, and got himself into some sort of clerk's work. Then he went out to Spain and worked there for a while. Doing God knows what. I sometimes wonder if he wasn't trying to make Father give him some

13

introductions there. Father must have known a lot of people from the timé he spent in Spain . . . but that was quite a long time ago, when he was chasing after that woman who was here that summer. Oh, if only he'd married *her!* They used to say she was richer than the King of Spain." Then she would shrug. "Well, never mind that. If he'd only married *someone* and had a son. When I was old enough to realize what the situation was I used to keep on at him to marry again. But he never seemed to hear me. And, dear God, he was so good-looking! He could have had almost anyone. No money, of course, but still he was so wonderful—and the title. The title could still attract money. It wasn't as if he didn't know he needed a son—but he didn't do anything about it. And Uncle Bertie. *He* could have married and had children, but always said he wasn't the marrying kind. And then getting himself killed in the Boer War. Really, he could have been more thoughtful. If he'd married and had a son, then surely *we* wouldn't have to be turfed out of Clonmara. I mean, the heir would have been a first cousin. He'd have let us stay, somehow. But instead we've got this inky-fingered little clerk coming . . . oh, it's unbearable. . . ." My mother rambled on in this way often, and I tried not to take too much notice, not even to hear it. Uncle Bertie, my grandfather's only brother, had been killed in South Africa in 1900—nine years ago, but still my mother talked of what might have been. Always, at about this point, she would reach for the brandy decanter which stood ready at her hand in the little sitting room we mostly used.

"I'll tell you, though, Charlie—inky-fingered little clerk or not—if I weren't still tied to that wretched husband of mine I'd have a try for him myself. I'd do anything, Charlie—anything—not to have to leave Clonmara." And then as the brandy relaxed and soothed her, her tone would grow more speculative, a trifle more hopeful. "But there's you, Charlie. *You're* not tied to anyone. Pity you're still so young in your ways. He's only about thirty—or less. Not too old for you—or any girl." She would purse her lips and look hard at me. "Perhaps we

14

should go to Dublin and get you some new clothes—grown-up clothes." Then she would sigh and shrug. "But who'd make them? I owe money to every dressmaker and milliner in the whole town. They'd never give us more credit now—now that Father's dead. . . ." Then she usually brightened up: it was not in her nature to be pessimistic for long. "Well, they do say that Miss Doyle in Wicklow Town is quite clever with dresses. Perhaps we could try her. . . ." Then she would look at me, her head tilted, a look of slight reproach, but also of expectation. "You could try, Charlie. You *owe* it to us. You owe it to us to keep Clonmara. After all, it would only be fair of him to make the offer. . . . If he's only half a gentleman he'd make the offer. Yes, we should try Miss Doyle. . . ."

But she forgot about it, as she forgot about most things of a practical nature, and I was allowed to go my own way, forgetting about dresses and this unknown, unattractive-seeming man, and what might be expected of me, or what I might owe to whom. The coming of the heir with inky fingers and the clerk's manner was only what it had always been, a distant threat.

The winter was over, the hunting ended, and Half Moon was mine—or as much mine as any animal of her pride and will would ever belong to another. The mare accepted me as she accepted the sugar from my hand. I never took the acceptance for granted; it was a relationship which only love would hold together.

My mother, without the long days in the hunting field to tire her, grew more restless. Without my grandfather's restraint, the atmosphere at Clonmara grew uncontrolled and rather wild. I never seemed to pass through the hall without seeing the hats and riding crops of my mother's gentleman visitors, without hearing the loud laughter from the sitting room. The drawing room was scarcely used these days; its air of shabby formality did not suit the new laxness which had come with Grandfather's death. The servants hurried by constantly with decanters of port and brandy. The laughter and the talk went on late at night—sometimes I heard stifled voices in the passage

15

outside my bedroom, and pretended I didn't. The house grew dusty and unkempt. "This place needs a house-keeper," Nanny would say. "And there's your mother, God help her, thinking that the new Earl will ask her to stay and keep house for him and be his hostess—she who never kept an account straight in her life! His hostess, she says—wouldn't *that* be a pretty scandal to add to all the talk she's already got dragging after her name."

Only in the stables was discipline maintained—partly because my mother genuinely loved horses and partly because Andy himself would tolerate no slipping of standards. Sometimes I wished my mother cared about or noticed the needs of her daughter as she noticed a swollen fetlock or a poorly mucked-out loose box. But mostly I was content enough, content to hold these precious days when Clonmara was still ours. My mother would never change but only go further along the bent her life had taken so many years ago. My mother was simply my mother, beautiful, reckless, lovable if one could overlook all the things that went with her passionate nature. She was the affectionately tolerated scandal of the society in which she now mixed, and she was the coldly talked-of scandal of the society which would no longer receive her. An earl's daughter she might be, but she was a married woman living apart from her husband, who himself had been no good to begin with. She encouraged her gentle-man visitors, other women's husbands, and showed no sign of repentance for having disgraced herself and her name. At eighteen she had had a brilliant season in London on money my grandfather had had difficulty in raising; she had been presented at court, been pursued by the son of a duke, and then hustled back to Ireland because she had caught the eye of Edward, Prince of Wales. She had then run away with a quick-talking, seemingly charming rogue, the son of a Scottish farmer whose poor acres would support no more sons but who had managed to squeeze out the money to buy a commission for Thomas in an unfashionable regiment then stationed in Ireland. His name was Drummond, Thomas Drummond, and I had never seen him. The stories of

him still lingered, mulled over by the servants. He had
been suspected of cheating at cards, they said, though it
was never proved; how else, except by cheating, could a
man win so consistently—win enough to pay his mess
bills? He had won a very fine horse, and he had won,
briefly, an earl's daughter. It was even said, I knew, that
he had borrowed money from the Earl which he later
used to carry Lady Pat away. That story was one which
never had been proved either; my grandfather's lips were
sealed about my father. He had welcomed his daughter
back to Clonmara as a loved child, and no one had ever
heard him reproach her. She had refused to assume the
role of meek penitent for her sins, and her father had
supported and shielded her. "Ah, sure the Earl was
always butter in your mother's hands," Nanny said. My
father, Thomas Drummond, had served in India, and
remained there, stubbornly refusing either to divorce his
wife or to die conveniently of some tropical disease or a
rebel's bullet. He sent no money to support us. My mother
told me he had written the Earl, "They will have my
support when they come to live with me in the regiment."
And that was that.

And so I saw my grandfather, in the years when I was
old enough to observe such things, struggling futilely to
make some kind of fortune for us against the day when
he would die and we would have to leave Clonmara. He
had tried and failed disastrously. He had placed himself
in the hands of money men in London, and whatever
Clonmara yielded in profits had gone to them to specu-
late with. Safe investment would not make a fortune—
only great risks would make that kind of money. The
risks had not paid off. "I've no head for it," I once heard
him confess to a friend, "and, I suppose, no real heart
for it either, or I'd get in there and do something for
myself. The worst of it is that I've sold off the few farms
that were outside the entail. If I had them back again,
they'd see her through, though not in style. I don't say
I've been cheated. I've just not had very good advice."
As the years passed and I learned more of such things,
I knew he moved desperately from one venture to another

and, when he died on the hunting field, he had been old beyond his years, exhausted with the efforts and the worry of trying to provide some inheritance for my mother and me. Half the county, it seemed, had turned out to his funeral. He had been more popular with his tenants and small farmers than with his own class. He had supported the views of Charles Stewart Parnell and the Land Leaguers, which automatically made him suspect by his own people, the Protestant Ascendancy. He had been notoriously "soft" with his tenants, deferring rents when the harvests were bad and forgetting to demand the arrears the next year. He was the despair of every steward he ever had, and they had come and gone in my time, frustrated at being unable to carry out the work they were employed to do, which was to make the estate profitable. So everyone, except a few of his own class, had a good word for the Earl, and everyone had come to his funeral. But that was the end of it. There was no one to rescue my mother and me. Since his death we had lived in a kind of limbo, my mother making the most of every day left to her at Clonmara, refusing to face the inevitable future; me spending my days as I pleased, riding Half Moon, trying not to think of what would happen to us. The summer approached and it should have been a time of mild excitement for me. That year I was supposed to have been presented to the Viceroy at Dublin Castle—my grandfather no longer pretended that there could be money for a London season. But all those plans had ended with his death. Officially we were in mourning; and we were waiting.

Now the waiting was over. This day had brought with it the man and the horse, and a sharp new hunger in my heart for both of them.

We faced each other, and the surf crashed near us— the waves lapped the horses' hoofs, and receded, to come again. This was no inky-fingered clerk with pale face and hunched shoulders. He was like some phantom of my dreams, vague adolescent dreams of a man who would

18

take the place of my grandfather, a man rich in looks and authority. He became all those things for me in those first few minutes, and as yet he had not even smiled at me.

The afternoon light was opalescent on the rise to the Wicklow Hills to the west. The wide acres of Clonmara lay between the sea and the gentle slope to the hills, land that was boggy and water-logged near the sea, and rich and sweet as it rose to the height crowned by the house. It was good land that gave grazing to Clonmara's famous horses and sleek cattle, good arable land which yielded plentiful harvests of wheat and barley, potatoes, turnips, beets. Some of the best land in the county belonged to Clonmara but it was beginning to show the lack of money which should have been spent on it. Small things, but important. Drainage ditches were blocked and not cleared, walls tumbled and were not repaired, sheep, which were less demanding, grazed on land that had once fattened cattle, gorse took hold in places and spread unchecked. But it was still a fair and beautiful inheritance, and now this man had come to claim it. Through the turmoil of what I felt for him, a shaft of jealousy and pain stabbed me the way the long afternoon light pierced the dark little coppice on the road back to the house. I had never known a feeling like it. Thoughtlessly I had loved Clonmara, possessed it, taken it for granted. I had taken it as Half Moon took sugar from my hand. But this man offered no sugar. The days of sweetness and sugar were gone.

I could stand it no longer—the pain and bewilderment of this clash of feelings. I was astride Half Moon, wearing the breeches no lady should wear. I dug my heels suddenly into the mare's flanks, and she shot away with a swift motion which was half indignation, half delight at the chance of an all-out gallop. The mare was supremely suited to the soft going of the wet sand; I gave her her head. We moved easily, almost flying, it seemed to me. It was a sweet release from the tensions of these last minutes to feel the wind in my face, the wind of our own making

19

as we sped along the shore. Clonmara wasn't quite lost while there was even a single moment like this left. Suddenly I understood my mother better.

The thunder of the hoofs increased. Glancing back, I saw the man and the stallion were coming after me. But the mare was lighter, swifter, more used to the terrain. Even the mighty span of the stallion's legs was stretched to the limit to gain on us. I leaned forward in the saddle, rising on the stirrups, my head low to the mare's neck. We were ahead; we held our lead. I heard myself laugh aloud with the triumph of it. But the strand was very long, miles of pale sand still to be raced before we reached the headland. The mare had great stamina, but the stallion had more. Slowly he gained. I urged Half Moon on, but I knew that soon she must be spent and winded. Not for any race, nor for any man, would I knowingly ruin a horse. So gently, gently I began to rein Half Moon in, letting her stride drop naturally, letting the headlong gallop drop to a canter, a trot, an easy walk. The man had waited only until he was a clear length ahead of me before he too began to rein in. We fell into stride together, the horses moving smoothly side by side. It seemed as if they moved in some guided rhythm, like the sea itself. At last we halted, and I slid from Half Moon, contrite now to see the lather of dark sweat on her silken coat.

The man did the same thing. We turned back towards the place where the track to Clonmara House began in the dunes, each leading a horse. Then suddenly the man took the reins of both animals in his hand, and with his free arm gathered me to him. The first kiss of passion I had ever received had no flavor of sugar about it. It was hard, and warm and searching. It surprised me but, being my mother's daughter, I was not shocked that not just my lips but my whole body responded. For half a minute we were still, I clinging to the new, wondrous creature who had come into my life. A wave of pleasure—no, of happiness, caught me up, wiping out the pain I had experienced. It was, then, I thought, just as all the stories, all the poems I had only half read, had promised. It was possible to love in an instant, and to know it would last a lifetime. It was absurd—and true. Half Moon thrust her head between us, seeking attention, seeking the praise she believed she had earned for that wild race, seeking the sugar. I drew back, laughing, happy, believing that this was only the first of the many, many times I would taste the warmth and passion of this man's lips.

"I can hardly believe it," I said, knowing my tone was awed and hushed so that he had to stoop to hear it above the waves. "I never thought it could happen. You're Richard Selwin, and I love you."

He still held the two horses. Now his free hand went to sweep the tangled hair back from my face.

"Hush, child," he said. "I shouldn't have done it. I should never have done it."

I remember laughing, so confident I felt. "But why undo it? Why undo anything? We have this, and we have so much else. There's everything before us. . . ." I gestured widely. "This place, the horses, us. . . . We were made for each other. Why did I never believe it? They all said it might happen. It's so right. Grandfather would have been so happy . . ."

Afterwards, for all the years afterwards, I would remember how my words must have sounded—ingenuous, the words of a child, foolishly seizing on love like some new toy, certain it would be mine forever, certain it could not shatter, or pierce or wound. Love could have no cutting edge.

He touched my hair again, traced his finger along the line of my cheek. "Red hair you have, and eyes that are no particular color, like the sea. And I should never have kissed you."

"Have you to ask then—to wait until we know more than each other's names? Do we have to sit and talk in the drawing room before we may kiss again?"

"I may never kiss you. I have no right."

"But you *have*—and it's done. It's so perfect. It fits so perfectly together. *We* fit—"

"Hush, child," he said again. "It's—"

"*Don't* call me child. I'm not a child any more. Don't you know that!"

He shook his head. "Child—woman—whatever . . . It's too late."

"Too late?" I echoed, and already the first disillusionment of love was upon me.

He gave me back Half Moon's reins and turned and started to walk towards the break in the dunes where the road began.

"Wait!" I called. "Tell me why it's too late. *Why?*"

He looked back at me. The resemblance to my grandfather came and went everytime he turned his head. He had some of the Blodmore features, the high cheekbones, the strangely light eyes that changed color to reflect that about them. But he was darker than any of us, darker of skin and hair. I knew him so little that I was still discovering these things about him, obvious physical things: his height, which reached up well against the shoulders of the stallion, the springing, lithe power of his body as he walked on the soft sand. He was so strange to me, so unknown, and yet I did know him, and I loved him.

"Why? Better to have asked your grandfather why he would never let me come to Clonmara. Ask me why I hadn't the sense to come as soon as he died. I was trying, against my own inclinations, to be kind, to give you all time to get used to it. To make your plans. I didn't hurry because I wanted to be the gentleman he never thought I could be. If I had once seen you . . . If I had only known what was waiting here . . ."

I knew he was not speaking of the lands, the house, the inheritance of Clonmara. "It's all here," I said, but a coldness of fear and crushing disappointment was growing in me. It was not going to be as I had thought. "It's all here for you. I'm here—"

He cut off my words with a jerk to the stallion's reins. "We'll walk the horses until they've cooled. And then we'll go back to the house, and we'll never speak like this to each other again. When we get back to the house I will introduce you to my wife—my bride whom I married in Spain three weeks ago."

22

The new Lord Blodmore's arrival, unannounced, had thrown Clonmara into confusion. We met it first in the stable yard, where grooms were rubbing down four perfectly matched carriage horses and a little mare almost as beautiful as Half Moon, tossing clean hay into loose boxes, and, I guessed, congratulating themselves on the tone and style the new Earl set. There was an air of excitement after the lassitude of these last months which communicated itself to the horses, who stood with their heads thrust out of the boxes, enjoying the activity; the hounds bayed in the kennels. A look of reverence was on Andy's face as he took the reins of the white stallion, and it tore into my heart. So quickly were allegiances changed. Half Moon was already second to the stallion. "Sure they must breed fine horses down in that place in Spain, m'lord." I turned my back and started to walk to the house. This from Andy to whom, until now, Irish horses, and Clonmara's horses in particular, had been second to none.

Richard Blodmore was at my side as we came around the rhododendron-lined path to the south front of the house. While Clonmara wasn't as big as the largest of them, it was said to be one of the finest houses of its kind in Ireland, built in the early eighteenth century, pure and spare in line and style, belonging to the great Palladian age of Irish building. It was an almost square, balanced house of pale gray stone, with curving colonnades which had been added at a later date, each ending in an elaborate pavilion, some of whose windows now were broken, and whose walls were threatened with the devouring ivy. It was beautiful, and for the first time I was acutely aware that it looked to be decaying. Lichen was darkening the gray stone, and valerian was sprouting along the balustrade which crowned it. Involuntarily we both paused, as if Richard Blodmore looked clearly for the first time at his inheritance, and I was seeing it as if it was the last sight I would have of it. "Clonmara," I said quietly. "So much better a name in Irish—meadow by the sea. When it was built it was called Seafield House. That's forgotten now."

Inside the house, another kind of confusion from that of the stable yard had been let loose. My mother seemed to have gone into a mild state of shock at the unexpected arrival of two coaches, a string of horses, the Earl's bride, her personal maid, a valet, and two female servants. I learned later that of them all only Lady Blodmore spoke a careful, correct English. She sat now on a sofa in the little sitting room, and her eyes and ears seemed to miss nothing, to judge everything. The room was dusty and strewn with magazines and newspapers, old hunting fixture cards, dates of point-to-point meetings, a few half-chewed bones left by dogs, three of my grandfather's gun dogs themselves, and two gentleman friends of my mother's, who had chanced to call that afternoon and stayed on to see the fun.

It was obvious that my mother had had a little too much wine. Her talk rattled on, talk about things and people the Spanish bride could not have known of, desperate talk that strove to cover her shock, her disbelief in the fact that this day had actually arrived.

She seized on our entrance with a kind of relief. "Ah —so you found her then. More than most of us can do these days. Marvelous horse that of yours, Lord Blodmore. Comes from the Hispano-Arab breed, Lady Blodmore tells me. He looked so fresh you'd never imagine you'd just ridden him down from Dublin."

"We stopped overnight on the way, Lady Patricia. But I thought I said that in the telegram."

"Telegram? I didn't receive a telegram." My mother rounded on the maid who was trying to find a place on the littered table for a tray piled with teacups and plates of clumsily made sandwiches and big wedges of fruitcake. "Mary, was there a telegram? No one told me—no one ever tells me anything."

"Sure how would I know, m'lady? I've not charge of

24

things like that. Mr. Farrell always brings the post in here."

My mother was now feverishly searching the piles of papers and unanswered letters spread on the table and on the elegant little writing desk at which she was supposed to write her notes, which were seldom written. Her face grew long as she discovered the telegram form and read it. "Oh—how stupid of me! I—I don't bother much with the post any more. It's mostly bills. Farrell must have forgotten to tell me there was a telegram." She turned to Blodmore. "How unmannerly you must think us." She gestured at the confusion of the room, and then her voice cracked in a laugh of desperation. "But if you'd given us two weeks' notice instead of two days we still wouldn't have been ready for you. Isn't that so, Charlie? Charlie will tell you how hopeless I am."

I never admired her quite so much as at that moment —her life and immediate surroundings in total disarray, and still laughing, putting a good face on it all. The two men standing at the fireplace began to laugh also, and so, after a small hesitation, did Blodmore. Only Lady Blodmore remained silent. Perhaps the rapid exchange in English had been too much for her.

"Can you forgive me then?" my mother asked, and knew she was forgiven by Richard Blodmore at least. "Oh, and I've made things even worse, not even introducing my daughter. This is Charlie, Lady Blodmore."

"Charlie?" Lady Blodmore repeated with a small frown. "Is it not a boy's name?"

"Charlotte," Richard Blodmore said quickly. "Her name is Charlotte. Charlie is a . . . a . . ." He didn't know how to finish.

"A pet name," my mother said.

It might have helped, I thought, if she had been plain, or plump or insipid. It might have helped if she had had the kind of dark Mediterranean looks one might have expected in a Spaniard. She was none of these things. She was golden-haired, with vivid blue eyes strikingly outlined with brown lashes; she had delicately modeled features all seemingly perfectly proportioned; she had small

25

delicate hands, soft in my own as I took one of them and stumbled out some words of welcome. She had tiny feet in soft leather boots, and she wore a dark blue traveling costume. Her whole style was as elegant as the way she wore her hair. I was miserably conscious of my own breeches and shirt, with the dirt of the stables on them, my uncombed hair, the stiff feeling of my face where the salt spray had dried on it. I wished then that I remembered to wear gloves more often when riding, because my hand felt calloused and worn like a scrubwoman's, like sandpaper against the silk of the other's hand.

The Countess was young, hardly older than myself, but she had a far greater sophistication; I fancied that she knew not only Madrid but Paris and London and other great cities as well. Her lips faintly twitched in a smile that revealed perfect little teeth, but it was a smile of judgment, not of friendliness. I guessed at once that she thought she had been dropped suddenly into a land of barbarians, people with titles but no manners. One of the men standing at the mantel, holding a glass, gazing with admiration at the new Countess, was himself a viscount, but he was only half hiding his delighted appreciation of the whole hideous mess of the room, the chaos of the arrival, my mother's desperate but laughing acceptance of it. All the same, Lord Oakes, while admiring the looks of the new Countess of Blodmore, was withholding judgment, waiting to see if she could ever belong here, if she was a "sport." I knew that he was very fond of my mother, and he would not like to see her and, through her, our whole society condemned in the bright blue eyes of the exquisitely turned-out young Spaniard. As for myself, I wanted to slide out of sight, hide myself, do anything to remove myself from the scene and from the consciousness of Blodmore, whom I had not once directly looked at since we walked back from the shore. Never until, or since, the moment of my grandfather's death had I known such misery. But it was a different kind of misery, some new ache which I had had no experience of, and yet knew I must conceal. I lifted my head, stared straight at Blodmore, and found his gaze on me as if there was no one else in the room; then I turned away just in time to take the teapot from my mother's unsteady hand.

"Shall I pour, Mother? Do you take milk or lemon, Lady Blodmore?" There was, however, as I should have known, no lemon.

I knew my face blazed crimson. I was cruelly aware of that delicate golden creature seated on the sofa, and how graceless I must appear by contrast. And I was never, for a second of that terrible hour that followed, an hour in which my mother and her friends switched from tea to their brandy, and the laughter between them grew louder, the tales they told to Blodmore and his Countess ever more tall and uproarious, an hour in which both tea and brandy were spilled, a stack of newspapers was knocked off the table, taking the sandwiches and fruitcake with them, and shortly afterwards one of the dogs was sick from eating too much of both, never was I unaware of Blodmore's eyes on me, and the awful echo of his words, "too late . . ."

Somehow we managed to put together what passed for a formal meal that evening. My mother prevailed on her two friends to stay. "You'll never desert me!" she had uttered in a piercing whisper which everyone heard. So grooms were dispatched to their various homes with messages to their wives that they were detained, and they both settled, with a satisfaction which I recognized as being the forerunner of the wonderful story they would have to tell the whole county the next day, to witness the first evening of the new Lord Blodmore in his inherited kingdom.

Everyone was pressed into service in the next hours to do what they could; Nanny was brought out of the nursery to help Farrell clean silver. The maids scurried about, carrying hot water and linen, more anxious to catch a glimpse of the new Earl and his bride than to see to their comfort. There would be a story for *them* to tell across the countryside the next day, also. As my mother was about to show Richard Blodmore and his wife to the principal guest room, I abruptly checked her.

"Mother—don't you think . . . ? Well, shouldn't Lord and Lady Blodmore have Grandfather's room? After all . . ." The anguish on my mother's face halted me.

"Of course! How stupid of me." She turned and hurried across the passage. "I didn't think." The room had not been used since my grandfather died. It was a light, high-ceilinged room whose elaborate plaster decoration was touched with faded gilt. It smelled faintly of dust and damp. But its occupancy signified more than anything else that the new owner of Clonmara had finally come to take possession. My mother flung open a window, and the wind that followed last night's storm blew in, stirring the hangings of the big four-poster bed. "Lovely view of the sea from this room. My father preferred this side of the house—the other looks towards the mountains." Her voice was choking a little. She rushed to fling open the door to the dressing room and there her gaze fell on my grandfather's belongings still on the bureau—his brushes, his tray of shirt studs and cuff links, a silver-framed miniature of my grandmother, an elaborately wrought box which contained a pair of dueling pistols he had prized. She rushed to the bureau and swept all the things together. "Here, Charlie, take these. I must get the drawers emptied. I'll send hot water. . . . There's a bathroom across the hall, but we've had trouble with the boiler recently. The hot water's . . . erratic. The bed will need airing . . ." Richard Blodmore bent and helped me pick up the small, spilled mementos of my grandfather's life as my mother hurried from the room. I followed as quickly as possible, desperate to be out of there. As the door closed behind me a torrent of Spanish broke from Lady Blodmore, answered and cut short, also in Spanish, by her husband. I stood, clutching my grandfather's belongings, and watched my mother go downstairs. But instead of going to the kitchen to give the necessary orders she headed at once to the sitting room where her two friends waited. At the door she paused, and I saw her brush her eyes with her hand.

Then she lifted her head and entered, and a moment larer came the sound of laughter once more.

I left my grandfather's things in my own room where my mother would not see them; then I went to the kitchen and tried to organize generous amounts of hot water, kindling, and scuttles of coal to take the smell of damp from the unused rooms, hot water jars for the big bed. To do anything about the boiler, I knew, was hopeless; it had been out of repair for months, and no hot water would flow into the marble bathtub.

In the kitchen there had already been some sort of altercation between the Spanish maids and valet and the Clonmara servants. Since none of them understood what the other lot shouted, it was a standoff, with neither side willing to give way. Farrell should have been there to smooth things down, but he seemed to have gone into some state of shock himself and would concern himself only with the silver and the keys of the wine cellar. The cook glared balefully at the Spaniards and sullenly at me. Nanny stood in the middle of the big stone-flagged room, her face grim.

"Miss Charlotte, it is not *my* place to give orders in this kitchen or to straighten out the tangles. But someone must do *something* if we're not to be disgraced entirely."

And so I, for the first time, and unwillingly, began to give orders.

I had just time to scramble into the old green velvet dress, too tight now across my breasts, and beginning to split, I noticed, under the arms, before Farrell sounded the gong for dinner. The dining room looked presentable enough as the soft light shone from the candles on the newly polished silver and the Waterford glass; it was easy to overlook the worn carpet and chair covers, the stained silk wallpaper which some former Earl of Blodmore had brought from China. The Chinese Chippendale furniture was as beautiful as ever. I wondered then why I was suddenly so conscious of the shabbiness of Clonmara. It had been home, always—beloved, familiar. I saw it now with a stranger's eyes, and parts of the picture dismayed me. It was all, of course, the result of my grandfather taking too much money from the yield of the estate in his attempts to make provision for my mother and me. It was a long time since money had been spent on the house or its furnishings. What money there was to spare had gone on horses, always horses. But from now on the returns from the estate belonged to Richard Blodmore, and he only would decide how and where they would be spent. He would have hard decisions to make, I thought, among the many needs of Clonmara.

My mother looked beautiful, if somewhat disarrayed, in pale green satin, her famous dark red hair drawn up in an enchantingly precarious mass. Since she seldom wore anything but her dark riding habit, she had never worn black mourning clothes for my grandfather, and I had none either. I wondered if the lack of them made us seem unfeeling to Lady Blodmore. She couldn't know that for both of us my grandfather's death had gone deeper than the wearing of black clothes; we had neither spirit nor money to fuss with such things. Lady Blodmore wore blue again, a light blue which gave her the appearance of fragile china. In deference to the hacking jackets which our two guests still wore, Blodmore had not changed into a formal dinner jacket but wore a dark suit. It made him seem older, more somber. I flushed as I felt his eyes on me again, in the tight old green velvet. Didn't he know how dangerous it was to look at me like that—and how little poise I had to counter such looks? Those about us weren't entirely blind, though my mother and her friends had obviously decided that the way to get through this strained occasion was to wash it down with a great deal of wine.

Farrell had seen to it that the best wine was brought from the cellar, but beyond that the whole meal was a disaster. We ate a soufflé which had degenerated into something like scrambled eggs. There were potatoes roasted black and hard, and chicken, tough and underdone. I could not remember a dinner quite so bad at Clonmara, but had I ever really noticed the food we ate?

It had been adequate and had seemed all right—until now. Had the altercations in the kitchen unnerved Cook, or had things always been like this, with Farrell and Mary colliding with each other in the service, banging platters, forgetting serving spoons and forks? It was the first time we had entertained at Clonmara since my grandfather's death, but had things really gone downhill so quickly in those few months?

The wine had loosened their tongues, and Lord Oakes and George Penrose evidently thought it was time they could decently ask a few questions. After all, the Blodmores were going to be neighbors, Richard Blodmore would be Master of Hounds, and they both knew they were going to be closely questioned by their wives when they got home.

"And what part of Spain, may I ask, Lady Blodmore, are you from?" Oakes smiled hazily at her across the table. "Where was this chap Blodmore lucky enough to find you?"

She had taken very little wine, and the edge was not off her reserve. She answered quite coolly. "I was mainly brought up in Madrid, Lord Oakes. But during the holidays from the convent I usually went to whatever part of Spain my aunt was. Galicia, Cádiz, Valencia, Asturias . . ."

"Elena," Blodmore put in, "was orphaned very young. Her aunt is her only close relative."

"How sad," George Penrose said. "Awful shame not to have a bit of family around. No one to fight with, what? Doesn't your aunt have any family then?"

She answered as if she were relating the story of someone else's family, not her own. "My two uncles were killed before I was born in a climbing accident in the Alps. They were said to be great sportsmen, and they went to climb some impossible peak. My aunt's younger sister, who was my mother, was murdered with my father at their estate in Mexico. The aftermath of the revolution—bad feelings as well as bad men lingered. My brother was killed with them. I was only a year old at the

31

time. I remember nothing of it. I was sent back to Spain and placed in the charge of my aunt."

"Your aunt is not married?" George Penrose pressed. "She has no family?"

"My aunt is married to the Marqués de Santander. She has no family," Lady Blodmore confirmed quietly.

I could see that Richard Blodmore knew they would go on with the questioning until they had the whole story. The arrival of the Blodmores was, after all, the most interesting thing that had happened in the county since my grandfather's death. Lord Oakes and George Penrose meant to have their full measure since they had stayed to get it. So Blodmore gave up sawing at the chicken and said, "Elena's aunt once visited Clonmara—many years ago. She was then the Marquesa de Pontevedra. That particular title may descend through the female line, and she came here after her brothers were killed."

Oakes's mouth dropped open. He took a hasty gulp of his wine and almost choked in his excitement. "Good Lord! *I remember her!* The Spanish Woman! Just imagine that! The Spanish Woman! You remember her, Lady Pat? Penrose? You remember her. A long time ago. You would have been about . . . about . . .?" He was looking at my mother and suddenly fearing he was being ungallant.

My mother was staring at Elena. Her voice dry and flat. "I must have been about ten years old—yes, about ten."

"And I'd have been about sixteen—seventeen, thereabouts, a long time ago. About twenty-five years. Good Lord!" he repeated. "The Spanish Woman—" Then he corrected himself. "Oh, I say, I do beg your pardon, Lady Blodmore. Terribly rude of me to call her that. But y'see, I didn't remember her title. Nobody much does, I'd say. But we remember *her*. We remember the time she was here. Everyone expected Blodmore and she would be married. He followed her to Spain. Stayed out there quite a long time, and came back—unmarried. Must have broken his heart. He never remarried. And now you're here as . . . as Lady Blodmore. Romantic, what? Very romantic, eh, Lady Pat?"

"Yes," my mother said. She tapped her glass, and Farrell rushed to refill it. "Very romantic."

"Well then." Penrose lifted his own glass. "Well then, Lady Blodmore. Permit me a toast. To the return of the Spanish Wo—Lady," he corrected himself. I hardly dared look at my mother's face at that moment.

"Do you remember, Oakes . . . ?" They had started once again on the tale of the Spanish Woman, and although it was twenty-five years since she had been here, the way they told it, I could have believed it was yesterday. They enjoyed it, enjoyed the embellishments the years had given the story. They savored every detail, real or imagined. The years in between lent color and a kind of enchantment.

"You remember the string of magnificent horses she brought with her? But she found our own lot suited the hunting better. . . . Took a string of Irish horses away with her when she left. . . ."

I could almost have recited the story myself. Twenty-five years ago a Spanish lady whom my grandfather had met in London had come to visit Clonmara. She had been expected only to stay a few weeks, just until the end of the hunting season. She had been a great horsewoman, and much admired on the hunting field. She was also, it seemed, a great and very important lady. The Viceroy had given a special reception for her in Dublin Castle. She had been invited to stay at houses all over the country. She had gone, usually in the company of my grandfather, and she had lingered, returning often to Clonmara, all through the summer. People all around here remembered her; the details piled on as the years made them more obscure. They talked of her carriage, her horses, her clothes, her jewels. No one had ever said she was beautiful, but they had never forgotten her presence. And then in the autumn she had set off again for Spain, and my grandfather had followed her. Everyone talked with excitement of the marriage that would surely come. Blodmore was not only lucky, they said, but for once being sensible as well. The lady's fortune was far greater than his, but wasn't he the best-looking man in Ireland, they argued? Fair exchange. He had stayed a long time in

Spain and sent no news to friends. Then he had come back, alone. He had not married the Spanish Lady, and he had married no one else. It was then he had begun to plunge recklessly with whatever money he could squeeze from the estate. Twenty-odd years ago the rot had begun. The evidence of it was now all about us.

They had just about exhausted their memories of the Spanish Woman, during which time Lady Blodmore had remained perfectly silent, letting them say what they pleased, correcting them in no detail, though probably she knew the story from another point of view. That certain smugness that stamped her, that confidence which came from more than the knowledge of her own beauty, was now explained. It was very likely that she had brought with her a very handsome dowry, and that Richard Blodmore would not have to pick his priorities when he set about putting the house and estate of Clonmara in order. There would be, I thought, money for that, and a lot more. And still he looked at me in a way he should not have done.

So George Penrose returned to his first subject. "Then tell us, Blodmore, how you were fortunate enough to meet up with Lady Blodmore?" There was just the faintest tinge of envy. I thought of him comparing notes with Lord Oakes on the luck of Richard Blodmore in marrying not only a beautiful girl but one who had no family and was the closest relative of the Spanish Woman of local legend and fable. I could almost see them wondering why, indeed, a much more advantageous match had not been arranged for this one niece. Richard Blodmore was handsome enough, they probably conceded, but with the rundown state of Clonmara's finances, he was nothing out of the ordinary as a marriage catch. So they probed. And I could almost hear the story run through the county the next day, the excitement, the callers, the curiosity. It was all coming, and my mother knew it too. Her face was white and strained. She had had nothing to add to the tales the two men told.

Elena Blodmore then permitted herself her only indulgence. She answered for Richard. "My aunt has an estate

34

at Sanlúcar de Barrameda, in the province of Cádiz. Don Paulo—her husband, the Marqués de Santander, has sherry vineyards and a bodega and a house in Jerez, which is only a short ride from Sanlúcar. My husband and I met some years ago, at various social functions in Jerez, and then . . ."

"And then," Richard said, "I went back again early this year . . ." He sipped his wine gravely. "I may tell you, gentlemen, that I was employed for some years in a very humble capacity in the *bodega* of Díez, O'Neale. Then I was sent to work in their London office. Also in quite a humble position. Don Paulo was kind enough to invite me back to Jerez for a visit . . ." He straightened, as if determined to say what he wanted to be said. "No, I was invited back to Jerez when it became known that I had inherited the earldom of Blodmore." He held up his hand, as if to silence any objection. He refused, it seemed, to put a polite face on it. "Yes, they did know in Jerez that I was next in line to the title, but after all, Lord Blodmore was not an old man. He might have married. Produced a son. In fact, it was *expected* of him, one would have thought."

The two men were embarrassed by such frankness. Everyone had thought the same about my grandfather, but no one was supposed to say it this way.

"So . . . I had the good fortune to meet Elena again, and she consented to be my wife." It sounded so cold, a formal arrangement.

"Well then—" Lord Oakes strove to cover the silence. "That must be an interesting part of the world. Near Cádiz, eh? Old Wellington and all that. Nelson off Cape Trafalgar. Seville. Yes, lots of British connections down there. This town . . . Her . . . What did you call it, Blodmore?"

"It's pronounced *Hereth*—which is simply the Spanish name for what we call sherry. It's the center of a rather small, unique winegrowing region which produces the grape that becomes sherry. But they don't produce it the way any other wine is made. The system is unique, and is practiced only in this small region. The grapes for sherry

35

are grown only in the area outside Jerez itself, the Puerto de Santa María, and Sanlúcar de Barrameda, where my wife's aunt has her estate. Sherry is produced by something called the *solera* system. Something that gives a uniquely consistent, fortified wine. There are, therefore, no vintage years in sherry. The system is one of constantly renewing—" He gestured. "Forgive me. One tends to break into lectures on the subject, especially if one has ever worked for a sherry shipper."

"My grandfather . . ." I said. Everyone turned to look at me. Perhaps it was the first time I had spoken during the whole meal. "My grandfather used to have his sherry and brandy shipped in by the butt. Different kinds . . ."

"Uncommonly fine it is too," Lord Oakes affirmed. "First-rate sherry, always—and brandy that's better than any of the French stuff I've tasted. Perhaps a trifle sweeter, but excellent . . . Any rate, there's always been plenty of it on tap at Clonmara. Blodmore was always a very gracious host—"

My mother broke in, her voice still flat and too calm. "This Hereth—did you say? Is it spelled J-e-r-e-z?" She continued as Richard Blodmore nodded. "Then that was the place my father went when he went to Spain—at least, that was one of the places." She looked at Lady Blodmore. "He must have gone there with your aunt—to that estate near there."

"How do you know?" I asked. "Grandfather never said anything about that time in Spain."

She passed her hand across her forehead, as if striving to pull together her thoughts. "No, he never talked about it. But it was there he went, just the same. The solicitors told me after he was killed. There's some sort of property there. A house, and a small vineyard, which seems to be no longer in production. The information was in a letter he gave them only to be opened after his death. They had no more idea than I that he had actually bought property while he was in Spain. There's been no income from it all these years, or at least none that came here to Ireland. There are also some shares in some sherry company."

36

She turned to Blodmore. "Is there a company called Thompson?"

"Fernández, Thompson is the sherry firm headed by the Marqués de Santander."

"Yes, that's it. That's the name. Father's solicitor, Siddons, wanted to write at once to this Thompson place, inquiring about it. They asked if I wanted someone to go out there to investigate, but I hadn't made up my mind. Solicitors keep pushing these things at people at times when they don't want to think about them. You've no idea what those solicitors are like—two of them here within days of Father's death, worrying at me like terriers, urging me to do this and that. Telling me I had to leave. I had to pull myself together. Send someone out to look at this property in Spain and see what it could be sold for. Things like that. I wouldn't be pushed. Father hadn't meant it to be that way. After all, if he's had these shares and some sort of house there all these years, he kept them for some reason. They can't be worth much. Everyone knows he sold everything except what was entailed. But Siddons thought if he could get a decent price it might be enough to set us up in the place in Galway. Heaven help me, I'd as soon be in Spain as that place out in the bogs. Did you ever see it, Oakes?" She shuddered. "The back of nowhere. Miserably poor land, no society within about thirty miles traveling. The house falling down. The Blodmores owned a lot of land out there years ago, not all of it so bad. But they sold everything they could—the way they sold the other place down in Cork. No one would take what's left in Galway, or the house—a great damp horror of a place with buckets in the attics to catch the water from the leaks. It doesn't bring in any money. The tenants are so poor, and you can't get blood from a stone. . . ." She switched the subject abruptly. "And are all your horses from that part of Spain, Lord Blodmore?"

He nodded. "They claim, and with justice, that the finest horses in the world are bred in Andalucía, and in Jerez the conditions for breeding are perfect. The Andalucian Arab was bred by the Carthusian monks there, and I'd match it for grace and intelligence and stamina against any in the world. It was this strain which first supplied the Spanish Riding School of Vienna."

My mother was all attention now. The talk turned to the technicalities of horse breeding, as it did so often in my mother's circles. I let it flow past me while I pondered what I had just learned, and wondered why this was the first time I had ever heard of this place in Spain my grandfather had bought. Surely my mother should have told me—perhaps she had, and in those first days of shock and grief I hadn't heard her. It was possible she herself had barely registered the fact, and it had been too trifling in the opinion of Siddons to press my mother about it. But she rarely allowed herself to be pressed when she didn't want it. To talk of such things, to begin to make arrangements, even to tell me what she had learned would have been to admit that my grandfather was truly dead and we had come to the end of our time at Clonmara. We had, each of us in our own way, shut our eyes and refused to look towards the future.

Now the future was with us, and I wanted to know. I grasped at this frail straw.

"Tell me," I said, breaking into the sacred subject of horses, "about this place—Jerez. Did you know the house my grandfather bought?"

"The house has been pointed out to me, but I've never been inside it. It's been shut up all these years, I believe. Oh, there are caretakers there, but they don't open up to people like me. It's a large house, in the middle of town."

"And the town—what's it like?"

He considered for a moment. "Very pleasant. Very ancient. And, surprisingly, until you know its history, very English—or should I say a nice blend of English, Irish, and Scottish. England has traditionally been Jerez's best customer for sherry, though of course it goes everywhere in the world. But the trade brought the English there, and a lot of them liked what they saw. And a lot came because it seemed as good a place as any to start up in business when they'd been driven from their homes by religious persecution. It was a haven for the Catholics who fled these islands. Catholic Spain welcomed them, but they have evolved to this day into a close-knit little group, all of whom, I'd say, have some strain of English, Irish, or Scottish blood in them. Most of them speak English like their own language, and it's a custom to send boys to school in England, and for the girls to have English governesses. All of them have nannies, and some of them speak their first words with a distinct Scottish accent."

"I say, Lady Pat, sounds nice," Oakes said. "Biggish sort of place, is it, Blodmore?"

"Because of the bodegas—the places where they store the sherry—it *looks* big. It has, however, all the manners and preoccupations of any small town. It has a strain of old Spanish nobility there because it was once a border town between the Christian and Moorish kingdoms—hence its full name, which is Jerez de la Frontera. The monarchs demanded that certain nobles settle there to give the place some sense of permanence. They built great fortresses, and walls, to hold out the Moors. Medina Sidonia is up in the mountains near there, and the dukes hold huge estates in the region. It has rich and poor, of course. Some people live in what are truly palaces. And then, of course, there are the others . . . the poor who own nothing."

"The vineyard?" I demanded. "Do you know anything about the vineyard?"

He shook his head. He looked questioningly at his wife, who also shook her head. "No. But then as one sees the miles of vineyards outside these three towns where the sherry is born, it is impossible to say who owns what. In 1896 the disease *phylloxera,* which began in France and ruined the vineyards there, finally reached Jerez. Since then a good deal of the *albariza* soil, which is best for the sherry grape, has never been replanted. Many families of sherry shippers were bankrupted. Some who had other resources hung on. Slowly they are getting their vineyards back into production. It requires a full replanting, the grafting of an American rootstock, which is resistant to the phylloxera, onto the native vine. An expensive and slow business. You can never hurry the wine."

"Sherry wine and horses, eh?" Oakes said reflectively. "Marvelous combination."

"And beautiful women," George Penrose added, with heavy gallantry, nodding to Lady Blodmore.

She took this as coolly as she took everything else. She turned to my mother. "Perhaps you should investigate Jerez yourself, Lady Patricia."

At these words my mother jerked herself out of her dreaming state. They were the first words of banishment that had actually been spoken. Her voice was terse. "Oh, don't worry. We'll be taking ourselves off. But not to Spain." She turned to Richard Blodmore. "Do you remember that old saying they used to have when the Catholic landowners in Ireland were all either supposed to become Protestant or give up their land and go west of the Shannon? They used to say, 'To hell or Connaught.' Well, it's Connaught for Charlie and me, I suppose, and it surely will be hell. Father hadn't meant it to be that way. There was always a sporting chance that one of his fliers would come home. There would have been money. After all, no one expected him to die when he did. He wasn't old, just unlucky. That last bank . . ."

Then, for the benefit of the Blodmores, if they didn't already know it, the two men recounted once more the story of how my grandfather died. I didn't want to hear it again. Hadn't I followed him blindly, as I had followed him in everything, over that last bank and almost ridden down his fallen body? They kept on remorselessly. "Always led the field he did, by God . . ." The supreme tribute. "There never was a finer Master if you looked from here to Cork. . . ." They relived famous hunting days, days when the scent had been strong, the hounds keen, the horses unwearying, and the chase had lasted until almost the coming of the dusk. How many kills had I been in on myself, proudly at my grandfather's side? But was that all he'd taught me? I was acutely, belatedly conscious of how little I was ready for this life which had suddenly been thrust upon me. Why did they—the men—continue to leave girls in such ignorance?—always with the thought that some man would come along, marry them, and take charge? But as my mother's eyes grew more misty over her wine, as her speech grew more slurred, as more endless stories of the hunt were told, I began to realize that it was I who would have to take charge. The thought made me gulp down my wine in sudden fright. I coughed and spluttered, and they all turned to look at me. As I coughed the split under the arm of my dress became a long rent. Tears of breathlessness and humiliation stood out in my eyes.

And that cool little beauty, that well-endowed niece of the Spanish Woman of long ago, looked at me and barely concealed her smile.

The dessert was served; it was a heavy lump of sponge smothered in whipped cream; its only saving grace was that it had been soaked in my grandfather's best cream sherry. Lady Blodmore toyed with it. She would, I thought, be making plans for the changes that would come when we were gone. Cook and Farrell and Mary might look for other positions. Lady Blodmore was used to better than this. But she betrayed no impatience. She could afford not to. It was all hers; she had all the time in the world, and all the money too, I thought. And she had Richard Blodmore.

I tried to attract my mother's attention. If we didn't leave the table soon my mother wouldn't be able to stand. The hunting stories would go on forever. I tapped my finger lightly on the glass to get Farrell's attention, and he, understanding at last, went and whispered in my mother's ear. As the meaning of the words penetrated, she got to her feet so abruptly that the slender chair tipped over behind her. She didn't notice it. "Ladies, I think we might . . ."

She walked from the room with a serene dignity, not at all aware that she swayed.

"Coffee in the drawing room, Farrell," she said. "Gentlemen, don't be too long over the port." I doubted that the drawing room had been dusted in a month. "Come, Charlie dear," she said as she left the room, loudly

41

enough for the men to hear. "We must begin to make plans. We mustn't impose on Lady Blodmore longer than necessary. They do say the Galway Blazers are a very good hunt. We'll have to find out about that. . . ."

It was very late before my mother could be persuaded to go to bed. I helped her undress. When she lay back against the pillows, her hair tumbled down about her shoulders, she looked at me and then hiccuped. This seemed to bring on a fresh spell of weak, helpless laughter. "Well, Charlie, he's here at last *and* he's married. Rotten luck you and I have, don't we, darling?" The laughter left her voice, and the tears she had fought were back. "And he's so damned good-looking, isn't he? In so many ways he reminds me of Father. Would have been easy to fall in love with him. Quite easy. . . ."

Then she turned her head away from the light of the candle, and in a little while I heard her deep breathing and, later, a gentle snore.

Sleep came reluctantly for me. My nerves thrummed with the kind of exhaustion I had never known before—the strain of that terrible dinner, staying up to see our guests off, checking that more hot water and coal were brought to the Blodmores' rooms, waiting to see my mother into that merciful sleep. Even as I dozed, and woke, and dozed again, I heard once more the talk at the dinner table, and along with it remembered the silences of Richard Blodmore. He had said so little, except to give the information asked of him. But his very silence had been more telling than words. I woke finally from my few hours of sleep to escape my dreams of him, and with my waking he seemed to be more urgently present. The first twitters of the birds had begun about the house, the soft beginning that would swell to the full throat of the dawn chorus. I got up and went to the window. Yesterday's fresh wind had gone and as always when it was still, I could hear the crash of the waves on the long strand behind the dunes. There was the dewy fragrance of early summer on the air.

I went downstairs to the library, a room seldom used

since my grandfather's death. He liked this room, spent much time in it; his presence seemed to linger, as did the smell of his cigars. How typical it suddenly seemed of the chaos of our lives that it took me so long to find the dictionary. The painful knowledge that had come to me last night that I would have to go out and fashion a life for myself and my mother pressed upon me still harder. What had I been taught? Almost nothing except how to read and write and sit a horse. I didn't even have the traditional skills of a woman; I couldn't sew, I knew nothing about cooking or menus. Those sorts of things had meant little to my grandfather, and he had been foolishly indulgent of my reluctance to learn, just as he had been with my mother. I felt that I wasn't stupid, but I knew I was ignorant, and the time for easy learning was gone.

I couldn't spell the word whose true meaning I sought. How could one look up a word one couldn't spell? Because the early morning light had not penetrated as far as my grandfather's desk, I lighted a candle, and the light fell on the yellowed page as I hunted, and at last found the word. *Primogeniture*. There were several meanings, but one thrust itself from the page at me. *The principle, custom, or law by which the property or title descends to the eldest son.* Then I sought the other word, the more familiar one, the one so often used as I grew up and one which must have assumed nightmare proportions in my grandfather's mind so that he had taken enormous risks to try to secure something that stood outside its restrictions for his daughter to inherit. *Entail. Settlement of succession of landed estate, so that it cannot be bequeathed at pleasure by any one possessor.* Thus Clonmara and the title had been my grandfather's for his life, but no part of it could be sold to provide for his daughter. They were ancient laws by which the English had held together large estates so that they should not be broken into small pieces, and the power and wealth pass away from the man who held the title. That was how my grandfather had explained it, and never before had I troubled to look for its meaning in the dictionary. He had also explained that in penal times in Ireland its reversal had been used by the ruling English against the native Catholic families of the land: a special law was passed which determined that any inheritance must be evenly divided among all the children; thus, within a few generations, the Catholics, their land divided again and again, were reduced to the level of peasants, each owning only a few acres on which to raise yet another family among whom it must be divided. It was not unknown for the eldest son of a Catholic family to become a nominal Protestant, to take the oath of loyalty to the English Crown in order to escape this law. Most of the others had been driven off their lands and herded west of the Shannon. Thus they had the choice of turning Protestant or going to the poor and rocky land in the phrase my mother used last night, "To hell or Connaught." I knew the history of Ireland was strewn with the wreckage of families who had torn themselves apart for these reasons, sons who had turned Protestant and dispossessed their own Catholic fathers. There were bitter memories of rebellions which had failed, of leaders executed. Catholics were seldom now found among the landowning classes. For so long the right to sit in Parliament or even to vote had been forbidden them. They had been excluded from the bar, the bench, the university, the navy, and all public bodies. They had been forbidden to possess arms, or a horse worth more than five pounds. No Catholic could keep a school or send his children to be educated abroad. These laws had changed, of course, but the Blodmores were still very much Protestant, a part of the Anglo-Irish Ascendancy which had ruled this land for so long. My grandfather had ignored all this—the whole system by which the country was ruled—when he defied tradition and expectation and married the daughter of a small shipping merchant from Waterford. Her beauty and a true love of her could have been the only reasons, I thought, because she had had no fortune of her own, and she was a Catholic. My grandfather was very young and had only just inherited the title and Clonmara when that happened. A typical act, though, for one of the "mad" Blodmores. We

44

had never been a family noted for prudence. It was an academic point now to wonder, if a son had been born of the marriage, whether my grandfather would have insisted on his being brought up a Protestant. But there had been no sons, and my grandfather had honored his promise and the Catholic Church's demand that his daughter Patricia be brought up in her mother's faith. And so, in my turn, had I followed her. I was inclined to think it a lot of nonsense. My mother only attended Mass when she felt like it, and I scrambled through my "Hail Marys" without thinking there could be much difference between the God of one church or the other. But it meant, in Ireland, that my mother and I were hopelessly divided from those who ruled. Not only lack of money made me ineligible for, in Nanny's words, "any of the young gentlemen around here." I was also the wrong religion.

And Uncle Bertie too, I thought. He'd failed in his duty to marry and produce a son, to which the title and estate would have gone. Perhaps, though, families being what they are, my mother and I wouldn't have fared much better if he had. When money and property came in the door, I had noticed, sentiment and family feeling usually went out the window. But Uncle Bertie had died in the Boer War, and that point too was academic. The Blodmores seemed to have failed singularly to do what was expected of them.

I looked around the still shadowed walls of my grandfather's favorite room, and to the view he had so much loved. The windows faced the break in the dunes where the distant and now calm and shining light of the Irish Sea could be seen. It was here, opposite the desk, he had hung the portrait of his wife, who had lived only five years after their marriage. If the artist had not flattered outrageously, the beauty of the shipping merchant's daughter would have been enough to make many men act as madly as people considered my grandfather had done. My mother's portrait, painted when she was about fifteen years old, characteristically in hunting clothes, hung on the same wall. She had a strong measure of her mother's beauty, along with the red hair she had inherited from her father. My own portrait hung on the wall behind my grandfather's desk out of his direct gaze. Perhaps I had reminded him too strongly of the man who had stolen his daughter—my father, whom I had never seen.

I wondered if Elena Blodmore would pack away the portraits when we were gone. "When we are gone . . ." I said the words aloud, trying to force their reality into my tired brain. I thought of that strange revelation last night that my grandfather had property in a place called Jerez, a place he had never spoken of, and something my mother had shied away from speaking of because to do so would have acknowledged with too much finality the fact of the Earl's death. In those first frightening lonely weeks when I had shunned the company of the hunting field and my mother desperately sought it, she had thrust my grandfather's keys into my hands. "We must clear out his papers, darling. There are probably old letters and things . . . things we wouldn't want to leave." The task was beyond my mother at that time, perhaps at any time. So during the winter afternoons when the darkness came early and my mother entertained her friends in the little sitting room, I had come here and unlocked the drawers and the cupboards under the bookcases. The litter of a lifetime seemed to pour out. Most of the estate books of Clonmara were in the steward's office near the stables, and no concern of mine. Richard Blodmore would have the task of reading them and learning how the money had been drained away from Clonmara. But I found the jumbled accounts, going back over generations, of the place out in Galway. It did not now even pay the wages of a steward to administer it. I had wondered, but did not dare to speak of it to my mother, how it would support us. In one of the desk drawers, carefully preserved, I found the few letters that had been exchanged between my grandfather and the girl he married—few, because the courtship had been so brief and they had never been separated after marriage. My grandmother's letters surprised me. Passion I would have expected from my grandfather; he had never been a man of half mea-

46

sures, never lukewarm. But his letters had been answered with an equal, perhaps even a stronger passion by the woman he married. I was glad to find she had been no coy little girl, given to Victorian simperings. Her legacy was clearly evident in my own mother. Perhaps it had shown itself in me, yesterday with Richard Blodmore on the shore.

But along with the jumble of our life one set of papers was clear and separate. They had been tied with faded pink legal tape, each a separate sheet, and they went back more than twenty years. Each was dated on the first day of the year. Each contained the same words, each was headed *Jerez,* and each was signed, in the same words: *Ella está viva.*

The words puzzled me, and burned on my memory. Now the words "Jerez" and "Santander" had taken on a troubling familiarity, two words my grandfather had not spoken either to me or to my mother, and yet were in some way part of his life. I took the keys from the place I always left them in the top drawer and opened the one below it. It was quite a deep drawer, but it contained only this one ribboned sheaf of notes. I took them out, shuffled through them, stared at the words for a long time. *Ella está viva.* The handwriting had remained almost the same over the more than twenty years the single sheets of papers represented, handwriting firm and strong, with a hint of impatience in it. *Santander . . . Jerez.* I sat and stared at the words, growing chill in this early summer dawn, and then the candle beside me flickered in the draft as the door opened.

He didn't hesitate but came directly to me. I was forever to remember that this man always acted with almost unbearable directness towards me, as if the feeling of truth between us was not only harsh but inescapable as well, and that we had better do without formalities. If we had indeed fallen in love yesterday as we raced each other, and then walked beside the swollen sea, then how he acted with me had been the only way. It had not been the wise, the prudent way, but that was how it had been. I had an instant to wonder if he was possessed of that

47

seemingly fatal Blodmore flaw of having no caution in the way or the place they gave their hearts.

"I'm sorry, Charlie." He was close to me, leaning across the desk, his eyes fixing mine so that I could not look away. "God, how sorry I am. I can't be sorry that I love you. But I'm sorry I let you know it. If I hadn't kissed you . . . If I'd any streak of decency I'd never have let you know."

The warm blood mounted in my face; I was both angry and hurt. He had the power now to hurt. "You really think I'm such a child? The very last of being a child went out of me yesterday. Don't you think I would have known? I'd have known if you'd never touched me, never even spoken to me. The way you look at me—no one has to be very wise or old to understand *that*. Do you suppose the others didn't see it—didn't wonder and guess? You have a beautiful wife, but you don't love her. She's everything I'm not. She despises me because I'm poor and badly dressed, and I don't cut much of a figure in the drawing room. She thinks my mother's a disgrace, and that we're probably two of a kind. But still she knows. She knows now that you'd rather have had me. *Me*—a nobody!"

"It's only the truth she knows, Charlie. I can't help it if she's shrewd and can discern the truth. Elena is far from being a fool."

"But you don't love her, do you? You married her, but you don't love her. If you loved her you wouldn't even have *seen* me."

"Charlie, I never even asked myself if I loved her. Love has never seemed important to me until this time. I never believed in it. Romantic love was for fools and dreamers, and I didn't have any of that in my nature— that's what I thought. I just *wanted* Elena. I'm an opportunist, Charlie. I have been, all my life. I've had to be. Your noble, wellborn friends around here would probably describe me as a bounder and a cad, but they'd be more than half right. Elena is a glittering prize. She's rich and she's beautiful. And I didn't have a hope in the world of marrying her until your grandfather was killed."

"What are you saying?"

"I'm saying what everyone in Jerez knew. I was nothing. My hopes and prospects were nothing until Lord Blodmore died. And he died before his time. He could still have married and had a son . . ."

"Yes . . . yes. We knew that. My mother used to urge him, and it was the only time he seemed to get angry and upset with her."

"So, you see how it was. He sent me to school in England and paid for it, probably, because he didn't want Clonmara inherited by an ignorant buffoon. But there his patronage ended. I had to make my own way after that. I found out he had some slight connection with the sherry trade, so I hunted around in London, using his name, until I found a position as a clerk with the London office of Díez, O'Neale. *Not* Fernández, Thompson. That door seemed to be firmly closed. Then I was sent out to Jerez to learn the shipping side of the business. I wrote to your grandfather and asked for letters of introduction. He refused them. He said he had no acquaintances left in the sherry business. He knew no one in Jerez. So when I went out there I introduced myself to Don Paulo, the Marqués de Santander, because I knew it was in his bodega that Blodmore had some small interest still. Quite obviously he wanted nothing to do with me. I was nothing but a clerk working for a sherry shipper. The fact that I was possibly Blodmore's heir made no impression. So I was stuck there in Jerez, writing out bills of lading all day, and living on next to nothing. There were no blooded Arabian horses for me then, I can tell you. Sometimes, perhaps out of pity, someone would invite me to a social function. I got my riding by being willing to get up at dawn and exercise other men's horses and their polo ponies. Of course no one took me as being eligible for any of their precious, guarded daughters. *They* remembered Blodmore, although he claimed they would not. Twenty-five years isn't so long in the memory of a small community like that. They hadn't forgotten him, any more than your friends have forgotten the Spanish Woman, as they choose to call her. I may tell you, she bears one of the most ancient and noble titles in Spain, to which are attached many privileges. She outranks her husband, Don Paulo, the Marqués de Santander, and being the sort of woman she is, she is known by her own title, the Marquesa de Pontevedra. Sometimes I wonder if she even remembers she once married Don Paulo—"

"Richard, what is this? Why do you tell me these things? I don't *care* what happened before. I only know what's happened now."

He put his hand on mine as if to quiet me. "Be patient, Charlie. I want you to know how it happened. I want you to know the sort of person I was before—before yesterday."

I nodded, but half my attention was in feeling the warmth of his hand on the chill of my own. Had the hands which until now had been sensitive only to horses suddenly expanded to be able to respond to the sensual touch of a man? It had been a swift growing up.

"I was there in Jerez for a few years. I met Elena once or twice, but she was still a child, a young girl. You understand that her aunt has a number of estates apart from the one at Sanlúcar, and quite apart from the house where one would normally expect the wife of Don Paulo to be living, which is in Jerez. When the Marquesa de Pontevedra pays her husband a visit, the whole town knows it, it's so rare. She's a strange woman—very independent. Hardly a woman you'd expect in Spain— except that she's been so used to her own freedom, the freedom that her wealth and position give her. A grandee of Spain has a natural freedom that's not given to ordinary people, men or women. And believe me, if your friends around here expected Blodmore to marry the Spanish Woman, then so did the whole of the sherry district down there in Andalucía. They remember how she brought Blodmore to Sanlúcar. They came in the autumn for the hunting at Doñana. Then, quite suddenly, she married Don Paulo and Blodmore was left high and dry. He stayed on about a year in Jerez—bought that house. What he hoped to gain by it no one knows, since the Marquesa had married elsewhere. And then he went away and never came back. But he's remembered. Oh yes, he's remembered. They remember him as a very handsome man, someone who rode well and shot well. And they laugh a little, perhaps spitefully, to think that she dragged this handsome Irishman all over Spain and then, right under his nose, married someone else. The town still nods its head over that, believe me, because Don Paulo, although he's good-looking and of a noble family, was very hard pressed for money at that time. To marry the Marquesa de Pontevedra was something quite unexpected. He'd been married before—had a young daughter, sixteen or so, who died. His sherry business was floundering—which was probably why he permitted your grandfather to buy into it. He needed the money. Now he's rich in his own right. Being able to borrow from his wife gave him the chance to take the opportunities as they came. He's in many things beside the sherry trade. It was a lucky day for Don Paulo when the Marquesa threw over Blodmore and chose him instead."

"But Elena—"

"I'm coming to Elena. I told you I met her once or twice, no more. She wasn't often to be seen in Jerez society—too young, still at school. After a few years I was sent back to the London office. It was supposed to be a promotion, but I missed having even the few things I'd enjoyed in Jerez. I missed the climate, the horses, even the little bit of society I had there. London's a dreary place for someone who's hardly more than a clerk. I thought of chucking it, trying Australia or Canada. And then your grandfather was killed and everything changed."

"It changed here," I said.

"It changed for me. Almost at once I was invited by Don Paulo—just about commanded, you'd say, to visit Jerez. I went, rather gladly. I didn't want to appear here at Clonmara too soon. I wanted you and your mother to have time to adjust. Perhaps, if I really told the truth, I hoped you'd just pack up and go. So I accepted the invitation and found myself staying at Don Paulo's house —which I'd only been in once before—and finding the Marquesa and her niece, Elena, in residence. It was clear,

51

almost from the first day, that the Marquesa intended Elena and me to marry. Why, I'll never exactly understand. I wasn't rich—and Elena could have had her pick in Spain. But why should I question what most other men would envy me? Why—"

". . . look a gift horse in the mouth? Most impolite, I'd say." I managed a feeble laugh.

He smiled rather bleakly. "That was my reasoning. I took what was offered and asked no questions. Particularly I asked no questions about the huge dowry Elena brought with her. I had a fair idea of Clonmara's finances, and Elena's dowry weighed heavily there. I told you I was an opportunist, Charlie. I didn't just take, I *seized* what came my way. I thought we were suited enough. The question of love didn't occur to me. Why should it, since I didn't really believe in it?"

I nodded. I couldn't agree with his description of his own character, but the facts of his life would seem to have made his actions inevitable. Why should he have done anything else? But I couldn't stop myself saying, "If only . . ."

He knew at once what I had started to say. "Yes—if only Blodmore had even once invited me here. Then I would have known what to do. *That* would have seemed right—and inevitable. I, as his heir, and you as his only grandchild . . . If we'd married you and your mother could have stayed at Clonmara forever. Why didn't he do it, Charlie? It was the perfect solution."

"Perhaps . . . perhaps that was why. Because it would have been too perfect." Now the growing light had reached the place over the mantel where my grandfather's portrait hung. He had been painted, conventionally, in his pink hunting coat, with a couple of hounds at his feet. "He loved me, Richard. He would have wanted me to marry whomever I wanted, not where it was most convenient. Whatever he hoped for, he would never have pushed me into a marriage I didn't want just because it provided a solution to our problem. He wouldn't have wanted any pressure on me."

"Then he made a terrible mistake, Charlie. If he'd given you and me only half a chance . . . If I'd ever come here just once . . ."

I shook my head. "Grandfather thought of me as a child. After all, until he died I still had a governess. Perhaps he'd had it in mind to invite you after I'd come out—which was what I was going to do this summer. Perhaps then he thought I'd be old enough to make a choice. He wasn't the sort to marry off a child, Richard, no matter how convenient."

He sighed. "Then he left it too late. He wasn't a very practical man, was he?"

I shook my head. "No, I don't think anyone would ever have said he was a practical man. It doesn't seem to run in the family. When people around here talk about the 'mad' Blodmores, it doesn't just mean a little bit reckless. Look at my grandfather's own marriage. No one could say it was prudent, or practical." I nodded towards my grandmother's portrait on the wall. "But just look at her, Richard. I think my grandfather loved her madly. There would be no other reason why . . ."

He gazed at it. "You look just a little like her—but you have the Blodmore eyes, like your mother." He turned back to me. "Charlie, *why* didn't I come sooner? My own selfishness and greed have caught up with me. I'm an old man, as these things go, to have fallen in love for the first time. I'm awkward and clumsy with my words. I've hurt you by my words, and I've made a terrible mistake."

I laid my hand across his lips. "Let's not talk about it any more. There are too many 'ifs' and 'whys'—and no answers." I got up and took his hand. "I want to show you my grandmother's rose garden. It's a very special place at Clonmara. My grandfather had it made as a sort of wedding present for my grandmother. I want to be the one to show it to you. . . ." Leading him, I crossed to one of the long windows that led to a flagged terrace. The cool morning-scented air met us as I opened it.

"You've no slippers on," he said.

I laughed. "As if that matters."

The flags were still wet with the night's dew; I noticed that weeds had begun to appear in the cracks between the flags and along the base of the balustrade. At the end of the terrace, steps led down from this level to an elaborately wrought-iron gate bearing the crest of the Blodmores. In contrast to the general state of the house, the gate gleamed with new paint, and it opened easily at my touch.

It was the only place at Clonmara, besides the stables, which had never lacked care. It was a formal garden with high walls of mellow brick, on which climbing roses were trained. It had never needed my grandfather's urging to keep its beds weeded, its paths immaculate, its grassy spaces trimmed. Here the cultivation of roses had reached a high art, but now only the very earliest roses, those along the warm, south-facing wall, were beginning to bloom. "My grandfather," I told him, "brought a man, an expert, from England to lay out the garden and to teach the gardeners about roses. He taught them everything about pruning and grafting, so to this day the same rootstock of those first roses is still here. He wrote it all down, and illustrated it, and the book is still in the library. But the men he taught . . . well, most of them couldn't read easily, so they passed it on by word of mouth, one to the other. The man who came from England—his name was Mr. Goodbody, which seems very right—never went back. He just stayed on here until he died. He died just a little after my grandmother. He was an old man when he came, but they say he died of a broken heart because he loved her. I wonder if that's true. A sort of legend grew up around it—but then the Irish love to make legends, don't they? They called it a garden made for love of my grandmother, and they seem to think it will bring bad luck on the family if anything dies here. So they look after it very carefully." The central grass walk led to another wrought-iron gate, and a path beyond it was lined with dark Irish cypresses, their shapes rising formally and rigid from the forest of rhododendron and laurel which threatened to engulf them. We walked between the budding green of the roses. The sun was beginning to touch the top of the brick wall. We reached the further gate, and stopped.

Then we were in each other's arms. I thought too late that it had been a mistake to bring him here. But I had so craved his touch, to feel his mouth once more on mine. In a future that looked so bleakly empty, I had to have some memories.

"This is our own place, Richard," I said. "I will always think of you here—and on the shore. And you will never open the gate of this garden without thinking of me. That way we will always have some part of each other."

"Someday I'll be with you, Charlie," he said.

I shook my head in some newly acquired wisdom. "Let's make no promises for the future, Richard. This time yesterday we knew nothing about each other. Today everything is changed. We can't call back the time when we didn't know each other. I don't want to look into the time when we'll be apart."

"I'll be with you always, Charlie," he protested. But it was no good. We couldn't pretend, even for a few minutes. I wanted to weep, but I didn't. Instead I took his arm and turned and we walked back along the grassy path to the gate near the house, conscious that the sun was slipping further down the wall and that sounds were coming from the stables; the hounds had begun their early morning keening cry. The grass was wet and soft beneath my feet. At the gate we embraced once more, and kissed, not caring that each time it was more painful and that the bond grew stronger; I believe that we both thought, but did not say, that we were due this seemingly small thing, the simple contact of our bodies, to carry us through the empty time ahead. We didn't seem to recognize then that it was a need that would feed upon itself.

The well-oiled gate opened silently at my touch. We went up the steps together, our hands touching now only lightly. The hems of my thin gown and robe were wet and bedraggled. I looked along the length of the house,

55

the gray stone warmed now by the touch of the sun. Directly above us I caught a movement, as if a lace curtain had fallen closed behind a window. A breeze, perhaps?—but the morning was windless. I said nothing to Richard.

It had been one of the windows of my grandfather's room, the room now occupied by Richard and Elena.

We went back through the open window of the library. The forgotten candle had now burned down close to its stump. I went to the desk, the joy of being with Richard now giving place to a sadness I knew I must not let him see. I blew out the candle.

I made my voice as firm and practical as Siddons', the solicitor's.

"Richard, you speak Spanish, don't you?"

"Of course."

"What does this mean? It *is* Spanish, isn't it?"

His face tightened as he looked at the heading, *Jerez,* and the signature. His fingers flipped swiftly through the pages as he counted the dates.

"Tell me!" I demanded.

"It means, simply, 'She lives.' It means 'She is alive.' "

" 'She lives . . .' " I repeated. "She lives."

"What does it mean, Charlie? *Who* is alive? Surely Don Paulo can't have written all these years to taunt Blodmore about the Marquesa. It wouldn't be like him. . . ."

I shook my head. "What does it matter? My grandfather's dead now, and a lot died with him. Whatever it means, it probably doesn't matter any more." Suddenly I felt a terrible weariness, as if I were very old. A whole lifetime of loving and experiencing seemed to have washed over me since yesterday, and I wasn't used to it. I heard the familiar sounds of the house. A door banged somewhere in the kitchen regions. Clonmara was coming to life. I locked the papers again in the drawer, closed the dictionary. This time I took the keys with me. Even this small habit had changed.

56

3

"He has offered me the *back gate lodge!*" My mother whispered it to me as if she were in some sort of agony. "The gate lodge of my own home! Charlie, have you ever really noticed the size of that place?—Have you ever been inside it? It's like a dog kennel—for a small dog!" Her voice had been rising, and finally she broke into one of her wild, intense laughs. "Well, I can be thankful he had the tact not to offer the front lodge. Just imagine watching the carriages go by on the way to the house. Well, the man's no gentleman. I always knew it!"

"What did you say, Mother? Did he offer anything else with it?"

"A pittance. A tiny annuity. Use of the horses and stables. A girl to come from the house to do some cleaning and cooking."

"It's not nothing . . ." Already the tug of unreason was there, the hopeful thought that at least I would see him sometimes, we might ride on the shore, the rose garden could still be entered. "What did you say, Mother?" I repeated.

"Say? Nothing! What could I say? Insult the man as he had insulted me?" She shook her head; her tone changed. "To tell you the truth, Charlie . . . I didn't know what to say. For one second I was tempted to take it. Say yes quickly—before he could change his mind. Or before that clever little wife of his could change it for him. She wouldn't like us here, you know. She's Lady Blodmore, and she intends to be mistress of her house. No carry-overs from the old days. No—she wouldn't like our friends calling at the back lodge and forgetting to come to the house. . . ."

"You see, Mother," I said, "already you're beginning to think you *could* stay. You always said he owed something to you. The back lodge wouldn't be so bad. It's not really a kennel—it's a sort of doll's house. We'd be comfortable, you and I."

57

"He said he'd refurbish it, of course. And we could have furniture from here. . . ." The back lodge had not had occupants for some years, since the last of the family who kept it had emigrated, and my grandfather hadn't bothered to replace them. The gates were never closed, so they didn't need a keeper.

"Think of the horses," I continued. "And the stabling —all for no cost. A girl to come and cook and lay the fires. Your friends would always come. You know they'd come. You'd hunt, just as you've always done. People would still invite you to things. It wouldn't change very much. Not all that much. We'd still be at Clonmara."

My mother's face grew twisted with yearning. "Do you really think so, Charlie? Do you think so? Just not to have to leave. Not to have to go to the place out west. Not even to have to move, really. A fresh coat of paint and a few tiles mended. Running water, he said he'd put in. All we'd have to do is move over our clothes and a few boxes of things. It could be cozy. Charlie—just you and me. Do you think he'd give me some decent mounts, Charlie? Not just the poor old things we'd be ready to put out to pasture? If he'd do that . . ."

I caught her arm, trying to emphasize what I wanted to say. "I think he'd give *you* anything you wanted, Mother. He admires you. I think he's generous and kind and—"

My mother now looked at me sharply, as if trying to drag her thoughts out of a future that seemed suddenly not so dark or strange. "And you, Charlie? What about you? You don't say anything about what he might do for you."

I tried to turn my face away to hide from her both my hope and my misery. "I don't need much. I wouldn't ask anything of him." I tried to drop my mother's arm and found that surprisingly strong hand holding my own in place. She had come out of her dream to a sharp reality.

"No, don't look away! *Look* at me, Charlie. It's he, isn't it? It's Richard Blodmore you want. And he wants you. All these things he's suddenly offering me. They're

58

not for me at all. They're for you. They're to keep me here, and you with me. Isn't that what it is?"

I didn't answer. Her hand went to my chin, forcing my face around, forcing me to look into the sea-green eyes. They were no longer vague, far off. I felt as if those eyes had witnessed every moment on the shore, had recorded every second in the rose garden. Then, as I looked, they grew misty with the tears that could come as readily as the wild laughter. All at once her hold was released and her arms were about me, holding me, rocking me like a child.

"Oh, my poor darling . . . my poor little Charlie. Here I've been carrying on like a fool, feeling sorry for myself, and not noticing . . . not noticing that my little girl had grown up and fallen in love. And to think I was actually urging you before he came . . . He can never be yours, you know. Has he said he loves you, Charlie? It's no good, you know. It can't work out. He's married, and she'll never let him go. Has he said anything to you, Charlie?" she repeated, and still got no answer.

"Oh, Charlie, you *want* to stay, don't you? Darling, you can't imagine the hell it would be. Trying to cover up, trying to hide it. It wouldn't stay hidden, you know. You're not made for scheming and conniving, my darling. And I'll not have your heart broken, if I can help it. You'll give all your young life to loving him, and one day you'll wake up to find you're too old to marry anyone else, and you'll find it's all gone into a stale, sour routine. Love doesn't stay the way it begins, you know. In the beginning everything is beautiful and bright and wonderful. Everything seems possible. It will all work out, you tell yourself. Darling . . . darling, trust me. I know. I've been down that road. And look at me now, a foolish woman with no husband and no future, who takes a drop too much. I'm thirty-six, Charlie. Thirty-six years old—and I've got nothing. Nothing except you. You're the only treasure I've got laid up. Oh, Charlie dear, I've been so careless and neglectful. Not a real mother at all. But as long as Father was alive you were never lonely, or wanted anything. Wasn't that so? He was father and

59

mother to you. Now I have to try . . . and I've not had much practice."

"What shall we do?" I said dully. I didn't attempt to deny anything my mother had said. I didn't argue that my case was different, special—that it would turn out any differently than she predicted. The knowledge had already begun that morning in the library.

"We must go," she said. "We must leave at once."

"You mean, go out to Galway."

She shook her head. "No, not to Galway. There's no future for us in Galway, and we'd be forever thinking of coming back here. No, we'll cut our losses, Charlie. We'll go farther than Galway. We'll cut our losses on this one and gamble on the next throw. A sporting chance, Charlie, the way Father always played it. What's there to lose now? We'll go to that place he left me in Spain. We'll go to Jerez."

4

It was all done more quickly, it seemed to me, than anything had ever been done at Clonmara. It had the swiftness and brutal pain of my grandfather's death, and the finality.

My mother summoned the solicitors, Siddons and his junior, Taylor, from Dublin to Clonmara. They came with a slightly reproving air, wanting to know why my mother never answered letters. "What letters? There were hundreds after my father died. They're all piled up there. How am I supposed to know what's important?" They looked at each other, sighed, shrugged, and decided not to argue. Siddons turned to me.

"I sent a letter, precisely thirty-five days ago, Miss Charlotte, outlining what we had learned of the situation in Jerez concerning your grandfather's properties there. There had been a small income from his shares in the sherry business of Fernández, Thompson over the years, all paid into a bank in Jerez. We are at a loss to understand . . ."

"Then that's settled," my mother said. "There is an income, a house, the annuity Lord Blodmore has suggested to me. It will suffice. We will be very economical, Charlie and I. We will live quietly. And we will go."

For two hours they tried to persuade her against it, pointing out that she could rent a small house nearby until the property in Jerez had been sold. Then she might buy something, something modest, of course. . . . The Marqués de Santander was interested in purchasing the shares held in the sherry shipping firm. No, he had not made a definite offer, but surely Lady Patricia would rather remain in Ireland. . . . It did no good. "Charlie and I will try it," she said. "We can do worse than to try it. In the end perhaps we will sell and come back, but I'm willing to take a chance. The fact is we cannot stay much longer in this house. We cannot accept charity." She clearly didn't see Richard Blodmore settling an annuity on her in that light.

The solicitors departed to take their train back to Dublin from Wicklow Town, shaking their heads. I knew what they thought. The Blodmores had always been difficult, unpredictable clients, given to mad notions. They had been dealing with the firm of Siddons and Siddons for a hundred and thirty years. Siddons and Siddons should no longer be surprised at anything the Blodmores did.

So the announcement of my mother's decision was made, and greeted with ill-disguised approval and relief by Elena and silence by Richard Blodmore. My mother then set out on a round of farewell visits to her friends, leaving vague orders for packing to Nanny and Mary and me. She would return from these visits slightly tipsy, to dinners at Clonmara that each day grew better as Elena started to come to grips with the cook and Farrell. No one had said anything about liking the new Lady Blodmore, but she was obeyed.

Richard made one last attempt to stop us going. He caught my mother one morning before she started on her day's round, a time when her head was still clear, a time before Elena had yet appeared downstairs. He asked us both to come to the library. His face was tense as he made his plea, his words stiff as if he had difficulty in bringing them out. "For the last time, I beg you to think again. You don't know what you're going to . . ."

"There is a house, there's a vineyard, there's the money from the shares in this . . . this bodega place. My mind is made up. I'll go where Charlie has a chance—"

"A chance of what, Lady Pat? Of *what*? You are taking her into a situation you don't understand."

"I'm taking her *from* a situation I understand all too well, Lord Blodmore. I'm taking my Charlie out of harm's way."

He did not reply directly to that. For a long time he stood staring at nothing, and the silence was heavy. My mother tapped her riding crop impatiently against the desk. "If that's all you have to say, Lord Blodmore . . . ?"

He turned back to face us. "It's a strange land, strange customs, a language you do not speak. It's true that most of the educated people there speak English because of their long trade with England, but it's peasants you'll have to deal with finally. You have no man with you . . . that's a disadvantage in Spain which you yet don't understand. You'll find the—the gentry there full of courtesy and good manners and grace—and there still will be a streak of cruelty in them as ingrained as their pride. They will make you welcome, and still hold you at arm's length. You'll never understand the mind of a Spaniard, even if he speaks perfect English, and even bears an English name . . ."

"We'll take our chances, won't we, Charlie? Those who went before us seem to have done quite well, and your wife has promised us introductions to *everyone*. Her aunt's husband, Don Paulo, is, I understand, a very important man in Jerez."

"He is that. And no doubt you'll get all the introductions you need. But I think you may find Don Paulo less a friend than you suppose, despite what my wife says.

The only time I ever mentioned the Blodmore connection to him, he was distinctly cool."

"Then we'll manage without him. Now, I think we've talked enough."

He slammed his fist on the desk, his face anguished. "It's folly! It's utter folly! Go to Galway. Go anywhere in Ireland. Take Charlie away. But stay among your own people. They understand people like you, Lady Pat. You understand *them*. . . ."

"I must do what I think best—best for Charlie. For myself, as you see, there's not much hope, is there, Lord Blodmore? Oh, I don't need you to say any more. What is it—can't you bear the thought of Charlie in Jerez, and perhaps a suitable husband for her? You want her out there in the bogs where she'll see no one. Or you want her in your own back lodge where she's available—"

I didn't hear any more; I turned and left the room. A few minutes later I heard the front door slam and my mother's brisk footsteps as she headed for the stables.

But she did accept, formally, Richard Blodmore's offer of an annuity. "Conscience money," was how she described it. "The least he could do when it's our home he's taken."

"He didn't have to, Mother," I reminded her.

"A gentleman—"

"I don't think he claims to be a gentleman. That's what makes him different."

"Different, is it? Oh, he's different, all right. A bride of only a month at his side, but he wants you as well. But it'll all come to an end. You must believe me, Charlie. These mad flashes of romantic love are only that— flashes. I've experienced one or two of them in my time, and I know. How many times I've imagined myself in love, and then seen the man on the hunting field the next season and wondered what it had all been about. Be careful, Charlie. Don't be like your foolish mother. It isn't only Richard Blodmore who will hurt you—even if he doesn't mean to. His little Elena has a fine streak of jealousy in her. Be careful. Be very careful, my darling." And then she would be gone on her horse, refusing the offer of the Blodmore carriage and I would be left to see to the packing, and to ponder her words.

But I did more than see to the packing in those very few days when it was all arranged. Once I knew we were going and nothing would change my mother's mind, I made my own plans and kept quiet about them. I avoided ever being alone again with Richard; I seldom spoke at meals, and kept my eyes on my plate. I left the exercising of Half Moon to Andy—and why not, since Half Moon belonged to Clonmara and not to me. I was determined there would be no chance meetings with Richard on the shore, no gallops in the wet sand. I was always available when callers came to meet the new Lady Blodmore, and to make the introductions. I was quiet and self-effacing—and revolt and anguish raged in my heart.

And all the time, during the hours of the morning when the household still slept but the early summer sunrise gave me light to work by, I was carrying out a plan of my own. Before the keys of the household had been officially passed to Elena some of the best pieces were gone from the silver pantry—pieces Elena had never seen. In this I had the help and approval of Farrell. "Sure, wasn't it your grandmother's silver anyway?" he rationalized for me, sublimely indifferent to the fact that it had been in the silver pantry at Clonmara since it was made in the reign of George III. Also gone from the dust in the top kitchen cupboards where it had sat unused since the great entertainments my grandfather had given for his guest, the legendary Spanish Woman, was the three-hundred-and-twenty-piece Meissen dinner service. Systematically I went through all the rooms in this way, taking small items which seemed to me might have some value—pictures I had to leave because of their telltale marks on the walls. The main rooms I dared not touch, because Elena had sharp eyes and would remember, even though, in those early days, and until we should leave forever, she obviously struggled to control her impatience with us, her contempt for the chaos and mess into which we had allowed our affairs to slide. She knew she must make her life among the people who had known the Blodmores and after a fashion displayed an affection for us. It would not do to seem to be pushing us out. Her manner implied perfectly that she not only had all the time in the world in which to reorder Clonmara, but there was all the money too. She made it clear that she would neither pry nor interfere, and I played upon this, taking full advantage of it to add to the store of things I was gathering in the attics to be taken away and sold. I agonized for a long time over the books in the library. I knew some of them were valuable—my grandfather had made reference to that—but which? Once again I breathed little sighs of remorse for the wasted years when I had learned nothing.

I hesitated also over the locked gun rack in the passage that led to the small sitting room. My mother was well known as a markswoman; my grandfather in better times had had several guns made in London just for her use. There were his own guns also, handmade and expensive. I wanted to take them, since they really could be said to be personal property, but it would mean asking for them, and I would not let Elena Blodmore hear me ask for anything from Clonmara; the request stuck in my throat. My mother would have demanded them, but she seemed to have forgotten them. She was making a play of grandly renouncing everything at Clonmara. "We've just got the clothes on our backs," she would say to the company gathered in the little sitting room. She seemed perfectly indifferent to the enmity she earned from Elena with such words.

Farrell not only kept watch for me when I was on these missions, but he helped pack the boxes and said he would arrange for a cart to take them discreetly to Dublin. He expected a little share of the proceeds, of course, but this wasn't discussed. Hadn't he a cousin with the very vehicle, and didn't he know a man . . . I didn't know how much money I could realize from the sale of these things, and I felt I would probably be cheated, as thieves deserved to be; but I kept telling myself that whatever I got, a few pounds or a few hundred, they really belonged to my mother and me. I was fighting my own battle against what I considered the injustice of those hated words in the dictionary: *primogeniture* and *entail*.

"Ah, sure, and aren't they yours by right, Miss Charlie?" Farrell kept saying, soothing my and his own conscience. "And hasn't yer new man plenty of money, that's his wife's, to buy more. Sure, wouldn't he be turning it out in any case, and buying new stuff in its place? Everything new, that's what m'lady says. New curtains and carpets and beds and the Lord knows what. There's even talk that she's thinking of one of those new motorcars. And isn't there a butler coming from London, says she, and I'm to be under him—*me*, that's taken care of everything in this house since your grandfather was a boy. If I were younger, I'd be off, but I'm too old to be looking for a new place. And there's to be a French chef coming from London as well, and Cook is leaving. She'll be no scullery maid to a French chef, says she. Ah well, 'twas bound to change when your grandfather went. So take what you can, Miss Charlie, and good luck to you. They'll never miss it. What they don't know won't hurt them. Well, if I were a younger man I'd be coming with you on this great journey to Spain . . . the Earl, God rest his soul, would have wanted that. He'd know you'd be safe with me. . . ."

It was Nanny who refused to be left behind. "Lady Blodmore tells me that in Spain every young lady like Miss Charlotte has someone to be with her all the time. A du—a *duenna,* it's called," she added triumphantly. "I'll be that. I'm still useful for something. Besides, hasn't himself, Lord Blodmore, paid me five years wages and the price of some new clothes?"

"To be rid of you, no doubt," I snapped. I was feeling the strain of what I was doing, and the worry and uncertainty of what we were about to undertake. For the moment I was unable to bear the thought that Nanny must come too, unable to bear more than the burden of my mother, who was alternatively sharply decisive, then completely passive, willing to listen to the latest suggestion and act on it, or plunging headlong on her own way. Once the interview with the solicitors was over, the decision to go taken, the arguments with Richard Blodmore finished, my mother let herself slip into a mood of gentle melancholy. Rarely had I seen her so beautiful as in those few days that were left to us at Clonmara, her eyes misting constantly with tears, and then her mouth parting in a bittersweet smile. While my mother played her farewell scenes to the hilt, I did the packing and through the solicitors made the hasty arrangements for the passage to Gibraltar. "Let's get the heartbreak over and done with," my mother would say to friends who came to call. It couldn't have been easy for Elena Blodmore to listen to such talk, but my mother didn't seem to realize or care that she could be making our path in Jerez a lot more difficult because of it.

In the stables the atmosphere was different. The new Spanish horses were still a wonder and a source of pride to all the lads, especially to Andy. There was reflected pride also in the fact that Lord Blodmore was a rider, a skillful rider with a knowledge and interest in horses that might be said to equal the dead Earl's. He would be a worthy successor as Master of Hounds. There was bustle and whistling in the stables, and the horses were groomed with an ardent desire to please the new master and stay in his employ. So it was all the more of a shock when Andy came to me and asked if he might go to Spain with us.

"It'll be strange for you and Lady Pat without a man around, Miss Charlie. To tell you the truth, I've had a notion to travel this long time now, and indeed I was thinking of America. . . . But with the horses they have in this Spanish place, it seems I might do just as well there."

I looked at him for a long time. "You're lying to me, Andy. You no more want to go than we do—especially not now when there's a bit of money at Clonmara and you'll have good horses to look after. Tell me, Andy—*he's* done it, hasn't he? Lord Blodmore?"

I got it all out of him. Andy was thirty years old and he had never been able to afford to marry. He was very fond of me and my mother, and it would be a pleasure to accompany us and see us settled. He had Lord Blodmore's promise that once that settling in had been accomplished he might return to Clonmara, with a secure job and increased wages. When that time would be Lord Blodmore hadn't exactly specified, but it gave Andy a dream to hold onto. His wages would be paid for as long as he was away. More than that, there was the promise of a cottage to be built on the edge of the estate where his mother might live with his two brothers and one sister— a cottage and a few acres to go with it to grow vegetables and keep a cow. There was to be work on the estate for his two brothers, and for his sister in the house. The cottage and the acres were to be his own, free and clear. It was an unbelievable gift to a landless Irish peasant who had heard too many tales of the time of the Great Hunger, who feared its return and the dispossessing landlord. He had it in writing from Richard Blodmore, along with the promise that it should be legally cloaked so that none of his fellow workers would know that it was an outright gift from Blodmore; it was to be an unexpected "legacy" from some relative in America. It ensured that his own family would not have to emigrate. It had needed all of this to make him commit himself to the exile he dreaded. I knew that Richard had selected Andy with great care, and possibly at a sacrifice to himself, because Andy was the best there was at Clonmara. Another bond was forged between me and Richard in the gift of Andy's patience, endurance, and devotion.

When I learned this from Andy I went and sought Richard Blodmore out. "Come," I said. "I have something to show you." And I led him, wordlessly, to the attic where Farrell and I had packed the boxes ready to be taken away. "Don't blame Farrell," I said. "He only did it because he couldn't refuse me. You see, this is what I am. A thief! And you give me Andy! Look here—the Blodmore silver, even with the crest on it. We tried, Farrell and I, to pretend that it belonged to my grandmother, but it's been here since Clonmara was built. It belongs here, and I was going to sell it for whatever I'd get. The china, ornaments—they all belong at Clonmara. And I have become a thief.

"You see, you've wasted your feelings on someone who isn't worth them. And you give us Andy! What have I got to give you?—not even honesty. But I've been honest in one thing. I do love you. I would have stayed if I could. If it were possible. But for once I think my mother's right. We might have ended up hating each other, or worse, becoming indifferent. I couldn't risk it. You—you couldn't still love a thief, could you?"

"I love you, Charlie," was what he said.

He slumped in misery against the wall, surveying the rather pathetic assortment of boxes. Suddenly Farrell and I seemed very amateurish thieves. "If I had money you'd have had that, and a good deal more. I've managed the few arrangements I've been able to make—your mother's bit of money, Andy, the rest—by going very carefully over the estate books and seeing where we can be more economical and efficient. I've borrowed to do what's been arranged so far. It has to come out of the estate eventually. The money to be spent on improvements at Clonmara is, of course, Elena's. There are strings attached to it. The Marquesa saw to a very scrupulously worked-out marriage contract. She wasn't going to give any man a completely free hand with her niece's money. The Marquesa is very knowledgeable about money. So you see, Charlie, while Elena is rich and Clonmara will benefit, I'm still a poor man—will be until the estate begins to throw off good profits again. I have to see you and your mother go like beggars, and I can do nothing about it."

"You've done more than you know."

Then, over Farrell's protests, I put back everything I had taken in the place it belonged. No part of Clonmara was ours any more—and I was no longer a thief.

So it was Andy who was saddled up and waiting behind the Blodmore coach on the morning we left. We were to get the mail boat from Kingstown, and at Liverpool connect with the P. & O. steamer to Gibraltar. It had all happened in barely more than two weeks, and now that the moment had come I felt a sweat of panic upon me, a fear clutching at me. My mother and Nanny were already helplessly in tears.

Elena had risen early—a difficult thing for a Spaniard who infinitely preferred staying up late—to say good-by. The letters of introduction were thrust into my mother's hand. There was no sign of Richard.

"He has gone riding, I believe," Elena said. She strove to but could not quite keep a trace of satisfaction out of her voice. I guessed what she might be thinking. Her husband was not present to bid good-by to this unruly little hoyden he had appeared to admire, and the keys of Clonmara were firmly in her hands at last. There would be no more drunken scenes in the little sitting room. In a very short time every trace of the scandalous reign of Lady Patricia at Clonmara would be erased. If she believed that, I thought, she would learn that legends die hard in Ireland—she who should know that her own aunt was still a legend here.

I heard myself murmur stiff words to Elena. I even tried to thank her, for what I didn't know. A great coldness had come on me; I could say nothing to try to soothe the tears of my mother or Nanny; it did not seem possible that either of them could be experiencing anything half so savage as my own pain—but I suppose they were. I was not only leaving Clonmara but there was not even a word of farewell from Richard to ease the going. Just as well . . . just as well, I thought. Let it hurt badly now, perhaps it will hurt less later on. If he was now riding on the shore, then leave him be, and leave me be also— leave me to try to regain my hold on pride. Peace was gone. It rode with Richard Blodmore wherever he was. The carriage started; the oaks and beeches planted almost two centuries ago to line the avenue of Clonmara slid by. Forever in my memory I would name and count every one of them; in that sense this short ride from the house to the gate lodge was never to end.

He was waiting by the gate lodge. He was astride the great white stallion, Balthasar, on which he had first appeared in what now seemed an unerasable dream to me. And on a leading rein was Half Moon. He murmured

70

some words to Andy and slid from the stallion's back. Andy took his place in the saddle and took Half Moon's rein. The three of us in the carriage were dumb as he thrust his head in the open window.

"I have telegraphed ahead for the mail boat and the steamer to accommodate the horses," he said. "You will need good horses." Then he went to where he had left them by the lodge wall and brought to us the canvas bags that held my grandfather's best guns and the ones made especially for my mother. "The Westly-Richards, and the Winchester 1897," he said. "They all say you're a great shot, Lady Pat, and you'll surely be invited to Doñana for the hunting."

Then he half bowed over my mother's hand and raised it near to his lips without actually allowing them to touch it, in a gesture I came to know as typically Spanish. He barely glanced at me, but his words were for me.

"If you need me, send word. I'll come."

Dimly, as the high green hedges of Ireland slid by, as my mother leaned further and further out of the window to catch the last glimpse of him standing there in the road with his hat off, I heard her say in a choked tone, "The horses, Charlie—the horses! Only a gentleman would have given us the horses. . . ."

CHAPTER TWO

1

It was almost three o'clock in the morning, and still a fierce heat lay on the land. Only the heavy dew brought relief, a sense of freshness. I would have liked to hang my head from the carriage window and let that dew fall on the caked dust on my face, but I was too tired even for that effort. From the few dim lights we had seen clustered as we topped the last rise after leaving Puerto de Santa María, we knew we must be very close to Jerez, but not even that knowledge could cause any of us in the stuffy carriage to straighten our backs or attempt to brush the white dust from our clothes.

"Mother of God, do you think there'd ever be a cup of tea at the end of it?" Nanny demanded. No one answered her. My mother and I had given up trying to answer the same querulous demand ever since we left Gibraltar. "And isn't it famished I am."

Andy silenced her for us, as he had tried to do through the past two days. Riding Balthasar abreast of the carriage, and leading Half Moon, his words cracked from the height above us. "For the love of God, will you hold your tongue, woman! Haven't I a mind to put you off here and let your own legs carry you. And good luck to you!"

Nanny heaved herself around in the corner of the carriage, and the old springs protested. "The devil take you!" she muttered, and was mercifully silent for a while.

Since we left the steamer two days ago in Gibraltar—that brief voyage now seemed a sort of sparkling dream of teas and waltz music and attentive men that faded as the liner steamed out of Gibraltar and was lost in the fierce dazzle of the Mediterranean in the summer sun—we had been following first the coast road that skirted the formidable mountains, the Sierra Blanquilla, and then had taken the road that plunged through the two mountain ranges, with now the Sierra de la Plata on our left, bypassed Cádiz, and taken the road inland to Jerez. The carriage and the driver the shipping agent had hired were both old, and the man had not a word of English. The bright talk between me and my mother which we tried to keep up in the first hours of the journey had died away, withered in the heat and dust, dried on our dryer lips. We had spent one miserable, sleepless night in an inn along the road, an inn whose food we found difficult to eat, where we were afraid to drink the water, and the wine was rough and did nothing to ease our thirst. We had taken fleas away with us from the inn, and a dread of what lay ahead. We had hoped to make Jerez by the second evening, but at the height of the afternoon heat, when every soul on the landscape seemed to disappear, one of the bony, sway-backed carriage horses cast a shoe. It took five hours to get it to the farrier and back; it was after dark when one of the harness traces broke. Andy helped the driver mend it from the assortment of worn bits of leather the man carried. Andy then had called a halt at a cantina and bought bread, a strong-tasting hard sausage, cheese, and the rough local wine. We had all eaten ravenously, even Nanny, though with the usual protests. The driver grinned at us as he ate; the events of the day seemed to be entirely normal to him, I thought.

He was being paid for the journey to Jerez and back, and it didn't seem to matter to him when we arrived. He remained persistently good-humored, and I found myself grinning back at him. If we had been in Ireland, by now I and the driver would be good friends, and if one substituted the heat for the usual Irish rain, the two journeys might have had a similar pattern. I laughed aloud at the thought, and Nanny glared at me. "The sun's got her," she pronounced.

The laughter had died in the long hours still to be traveled on that rutted road, in that poor, bone-shaking carriage. The very countryside, I thought, had a formidable presence—the high bare crags of the sierra, the glimpses of the pounding Atlantic as we turned the corner northwards at Tarifa, the herds of goats cropping already almost bare ground, the occasional patches of lush growth, wheat, alfalfa, sugar beets, vineyards, the olive groves of silver-gray—all an austere beauty which nothing in Ireland had prepared me for. The bones of the country seemed to show through, presenting a lean but aristocratic face. We passed through Puerto de Santa María, where, I remembered, Richard Blodmore had said the vines producing the sherry grape began. We got lost looking for the road that led to Jerez, circled the huge bull ring several times before we found it. Then the dark stretch to Jerez itself. "There'll be bandits about, I'll be bound," Nanny muttered.

We took no notice of her. The outlying houses—they didn't much resemble the cottages of Ireland—began to come closer together. Lights showed in a few cantinas but we did not stop. Even Andy was finding the day in the saddle under the sun more than enough; he urged the driver on. But still it was almost three o'clock when the first paved road of Jerez rumbled under the wheels.

"And now," my mother said, "we have to find the house—and not a word of Spanish between us." Then she voiced the same thought that had been nagging at the back of my mind all day. "I wonder if the telegram the shipping agent sent from Gibraltar really got here, and if

74

it made sense to anyone? Well, Blodmore did say there was a caretaker. But I wonder if he can read?"

The answer seemed to spring from the darkness at us. We had passed through some sort of arch which appeared to signal the beginning of the town proper, and almost immediately there were shouts from two young boys who rushed at the carriage waving lanterns. I heard the word "Drummond" repeated several times, and "Plaza de Asturias," which was where the house was. The sudden shouts and lights upset Balthasar, who swerved violently. For a sickening half minute I thought Andy was going to be thrown as he struggled to hold the great horse and keep Half Moon from being injured. Only a superb horseman could have done it; once again I silently blessed his presence, and Richard Blodmore. The two boys hastily retreated, and now came more hesitantly into the circle of light thrown by the carriage lamps. They eyed the big white horse fearfully as they gave their message in Spanish to the driver. Now the words "Doña Patricia" were mixed with "Drummond." Whatever they said, it pleased the driver. He leaned around from the box to shout to my mother and me; he gave his toothless grin and slapped the reins on the backs of the listless horses and began to follow the lamps of the two boys.

The town was dark, and mostly shuttered, though one or two cantinas were still open. We passed through broad streets and narrow alleys, through plazas where oleanders scented the night air, and palms rustled above our heads. There were massively decorated churches with belfries, tall elegant houses, fronting on plazas, whose sculptured outlines could be seen against the warm night sky. In one or two places the shutters were still open. In the poorer places children cried; in the richer areas we caught glimpses of crystal chandeliers and heard the sound of music and laughter, saw the movements of servants. Some places even had electricity. "A shameful hour to be up," Nanny said. "Wouldn't you think every Christian would be in bed, and oh, don't my poor old bones—"

"If you're so old you'll be no use to us," I said brutally. "You'll take the next steamer back to Ireland."

"And mightn't I do just that. What with some people getting too big for their boots all of a sudden, and giving orders. Lady Pat, I'm surprised you let this chit talk to Nanny this way."

"Enough!" my mother retorted. "I'll not bother to put you on a steamer, I'll strangle you with my bare hands if you so much as utter another word. Besides . . . I think we're here."

The boys, barefoot and wearing ragged clothes, had led the carriage into a small square, which was completely shuttered and dark. A fountain and the outline of a church were its only grace notes. The boys waved the driver on to the other side of the plaza. They stopped before the tall and closed façade of a house; the windows were all shuttered and turned blank faces to the silent, deserted plaza; they all wore grilles of wrought iron which completely covered them and bowed outwards, like cages. There were no lights, and the way was barred by an ancient iron-studded door. One of the boys banged with his stick on the wood. The sound seemed to reverberate in an almost endless emptiness within, as if it echoed on itself. Then there was silence again.

"*Can* there be anyone there?" my mother said. "No lights . . . nothing. And yet the boys were waiting for us. But it's so late. Oh, dear God . . ." Her weariness and uncertainty broke through. The boys started banging again. Balthasar pawed the ground restlessly. He wanted a stable, his oats and water. Even through my own exhaustion I was once again made aware of the breeding lines in him; like any aristocrat, he was certain his needs would be attended to. For two days he had been smelling the familiar smell of the country which had bred him. He knew what he might expect here.

At last they came—the muffled cries in the distance, the drawing of stiff bolts still far away. The boys beat more furiously, and called out. They were answered now by voices on the other side of the big door, and the sound of more bolts being drawn. Even then, only a small door within the big one opened, and a head was thrust cautiously out.

There was a rush of talk, in Spanish, answered by the boys. I guessed we had been expected for hours past, and they had all but given up hope. A man and a woman, shabbily clothed, of indeterminate age, emerged finally and came close to the carriage. They stared up at the three dust-streaked faces, clearly unsure which they should address themselves to. The woman bowed, the man took off his cap, twisting it in nervous hands.

"You are welcome, Doña Patricia. You are welcome to the home of your father." It was all said in Spanish, but the meaning was plain enough. My mother fell back against the old leather cushions. "Thank God . . . at least we're here." Then she leaned forward again. *"Gracias . . . mucho gracias."*

There were smiles now, smiles from the man and the woman, smiles from the driver and the two boys. No matter how late, we had arrived. There was another delay while together the man and the woman, assisted by the boys, struggled to open up both sides of the big doors. They gave grudgingly, on hinges that had long been without oil. The carriage moved forward, through the portal, and beyond it through yet another set of doors, and at last into a courtyard. There was an impatient whinny from Balthasar; Andy climbed stiffly from the saddle. The man was pointing to yet another archway which appeared to lead to the stables. The man opened the carriage door and helped my mother to alight with all the flourish of a great gentleman on a great occasion. He had clearly now decided which one was Doña Patricia. "This is my daughter, Miss Charlotte," my mother said with great distinctness, no doubt hoping he would understand. Instead he looked puzzled and worried.

"Char . . . Char . . ." He shook his head.

"Doña Carlota," the woman hissed, digging him with a sharp elbow. Comprehension broke on the man's face. *"Ah! Doña Carlota! Bienvenida!"*

For the first time in my life I liked the sound of my own name. "Doña Carlota indeed!" Nanny, having been placed unerringly as having a lower status, had been left to scramble out herself. "Nanny," my mother said, indicating her.

The two smiled, but briefly. Then astoundingly, the man said in clear English, "Ah . . . *si* . . . English Nanny."

"Irish!"

"Are you going to stand there all night arguing?" Andy threw in. "The horses, Lady Pat—the horses!"

The driver was now talking rapidly to the manservant. The upshot seemed to be an agreement that the baggage would be unloaded, the ladies escorted inside, and the carriage and horses taken to the stables. *"Pronto* [Quickly]!" The boys were scrambling about on the roof of the carriage like monkeys; the straps were undone, the trunks handed down. It was all accomplished with the maximum of shouts, orders, and counterorders. Once again I was reminded of similar scenes in Ireland. I licked my dry lips and found a smile for the woman servant, who was peering into my face. She jerked her head in the direction of my mother, who, crumpled and tired, still wore her air of regal authority. *"Bella . . ."* the woman whispered. My mother, I thought, like Balthasar, looked as if she expected only the best.

At last the bags were off, and Andy and the driver were escorted to the archway that led to the stables. Two lamps suspended from brackets illuminated a further space that seemed as large as this. While all this was being done, the boys started to carry the first of the bags through another great studded double door which led into a large hall. I hesitated just a moment, looking around me. Even in the dim light a feeling of decay hung on this strikingly handsome house. A series of arches formed a sort of cloister on three sides of this first courtyard, broken by the entry to the stable area. But there was evidence of rot in the wooden shutters which barred all the windows; in places the finely decorated stonework of the arches had crumpled, weeds grew rampant between the stones of the court, and the cracked marble basin of the central fountain supported its own colony of rank weeds. The beautiful hanging lanterns were rusting,

78

the glass in many of them broken. Alien vines twisted through the roses which climbed the columns of the arches. It was beautiful and sad.

"Charlie! Are you dreaming, Charlie?" My mother's voice. The woman beckoned and waved her lamp towards the hallway where the boys had vanished. The lamp flickered on frayed tapestry and a broad flight of shallow marble stairs. We followed the waving lamp into a long, wide passage beyond the stairs. The passage, I guessed, looked into the cloistered courtyard we had just left, but every window shutter was closed, and the smell of rot greeted us, an oddly damp smell in the warm airlessness of the night. We passed through two more sets of double doors, and by now I had lost my sense of direction. The shuttered windows had changed to the other side of the passage, so it was possible they looked out on yet another courtyard. The floor we walked on was black and white marble squares, cracked in places, dulled with a film of dirt. Little piles of leaves and curls of dust lay in the corners, as if swept there by the winds of winters long ago, and left.

"I'm thinking there might be a ghost or two in this place," Nanny said.

"Hush!" But I silently agreed with her.

Now the woman paused before another set of doors. All had been elaborately carved, but this one bore traces of faded gilt outlining an escutcheon. The woman straightened her apron, tried to tuck in the straying wisps of hair that escaped the cloth tied about her head. Then, with an attempt at a grand gesture, she flung open one of the doors.

"Las señoras, Don Paulo!" She bobbed a curtsy and hurried forward to light candles which were placed on a long, carved stretcher table of dark oak.

Everything in the room was dark. Only one window was unshuttered, and I caught a glimpse of stars in a dark blue night sky, heard the familiar rustle of palms as a slight breeze relieved the airlessness. Even in the heat, the embers of a fire still glowed in a great hearth surmounted by a carved stone mantel. From a high-backed chair a figure rose—rose slowly, as if he had been dozing there. As the light of the candles reached him, I saw a man dressed in a suit of fine black linen, a white linen shirt, and a black tie. His iron-gray hair sprang back thickly from a face that was darkly olive in complexion, with features whose leanness just escaped the look of sharpness. He had hooked black brows over eyes whose thick lids gave them a hooded, secretive appearance. Except for those hooded lids, he would have been strikingly handsome. He wore his air of command and position with ease, like his clothes.

He bowed, and came slowly towards us. Beside the chair an enormous hound had risen, stretching as if she also had been sleeping. She was brindle-colored, with a square skull, black muzzle, ears, and nose; her great size and breadth of build gave her an appearance of grandeur and nobility which was only slightly diminished when she cocked her head sideways to look at us with an air of great good nature. With a flick of his finger the man commanded her to sit. He then approached my mother, taking her gloved hand, which was gray with dust, and lifted it near to his lips in the gesture Richard Blodmore had used.

"Lady Patricia, allow me to present myself. I am Paulo Fernández Medina. On behalf of my family I welcome you to Jerez."

"*Enchantée*—no, that's French. Forgive me, señor. You will find us sadly lacking in Spanish. May I present my daughter Charlotte."

My hand was also taken and raised, as he bowed. "Miss Charlotte . . . my pleasure." He had no difficulty pronouncing my name. His English was very nearly accentless.

My mother was confused, as well as tired. "Your name again, sir?"

"Paulo Fernández. Husband of Lady Blodmore's aunt, the Marquesa de Pontevedra. Forgive this poor reception, Lady Patricia. There was very little time to prepare. Richard Blodmore's letter did not reach us until yesterday, and at the same time the telegram arrived here. Paco, of course, didn't know what to do with it. But there

80

is food waiting. No doubt you are very weary. I have given orders that rooms be prepared, but you must expect deficiencies. The house has been unused for many years."

My mother shook her head in confusion. "But you—you don't live here?"

A wintry smile touched his lips. It occurred to me then that he had given us no smile in greeting. "No, Lady Patricia. This house belonged to your father only. I have . . . I have my own house."

My mother looked at him in astonishment. "But you are here to . . . to receive us. It is after three o'clock in the morning! You have waited so long . . ."

He bowed slightly, as if to dismiss any idea of discomfort. "It is my duty—no, my pleasure, as head of my house, to receive you and welcome you to Jerez. The hour does not matter. Doña Elena has also written, telling us of your . . . your kindness to her. I hope you will not find us lacking in gratitude or manners."

The import of the words finally sank into my mother. "You are . . . you are, then, the Marqués de Santander."

"To you, Lady Patricia, and the whole of Jerez, I am Don Paulo. We are simple people here. We much look forward to visits of strangers. I hope you will have a most pleasant stay among us. I am always at your service." He turned towards the table where a tray and glasses and a decanter were set. "May I offer you a *copita*—a little cup, as we say here. In my opinion, this wine is among the best my bodega produces. . . ."

He poured four glasses, gravely handing one to my mother and one to me, and then, after only a fractional hesitation, he took one to Nanny, who had remained silent and in the background.

"Oh no, sir. I never touch it."

He shook his head and for a moment I thought his smile was genuine. "You will find . . . ma'am . . . that all of us here 'touch it.' It is our life. Sherry is the wine of Jerez."

My mother jerked herself upright. "Oh, forgive me. I

81

had forgotten. Marqués . . . Don Paulo, this is Nanny."

"Ah, another English nanny joins the ranks. You will find many here in Jerez. We all learn our first English from them."

"*Irish*, sir, if you please."

"Ah, how stupid of me. A thousand pardons. Lady Patricia, do sit down. A meal has been ready since ten o'clock, but still there will be a wait. In Spain there is always a short wait, which we fill most pleasantly with our wine."

The big hound went to sniff at my mother and then came to me. I put my hand on the silken ears, the great heavy folds of the muzzle, felt the wetness of her nose. My hand was rasped by her rough tongue. "Pepita, mind your manners!" Don Paulo said. She turned her head, and then, as if ashamed, her great body slumped down and her head went between her enormous paws.

"What breed is she? I don't think I've ever seen such a dog before. So beautiful . . . so gentle."

"She is a Spanish mastiff. Hardly more than a puppy yet. Doesn't know her manners. One of my sons gave her to me. You think she is beautiful, do you, Miss Charlotte?"

"She *is* beautiful."

"Then you shall have her. You can take her back to Ireland with you. She is yours. A remembrance of Jerez."

A frown came to my mother's brow, but then she smiled and held her glass forward to be refilled. "It *is* a marvelous wine. Somehow the sherry at home never tasted quite like this. . . ."

"Only in Jerez does the wine taste 'quite like this,' Lady Patricia. You must enjoy it in its home while you may."

My mother laughed. "Then I shall be enjoying a great deal of it, Don Paulo. There seems to be some misapprehension. You do understand that we have not come on a visit? We have come to stay."

My mother's hand remained where it was, as if frozen momentarily by the look that came and vanished almost instantly on Don Paulo's face. His lips curved upwards, in the semblance of a smile. "A visit may be any length you choose, Lady Patricia. It may last a short time—it may last a lifetime. In Spain, there is always time. But we are sorry to see our guests depart."

We hastily washed off some of the dust, and Don Paulo came with us to the dining room when we were summoned. The room, like the one we had left, was sparsely furnished in the same heavy dark oak; it had a similar carved mantel. We were served in a flustered, clumsy fashion by the manservant, Paco, while his wife, Serafina, brought dishes from the kitchen. Don Paulo refused food, just sipped his wine, and hungry as we were, it was difficult to eat under the gaze of those hooded, secretive eyes. Nanny for once sat with us; no other arrangement was possible that night, but clearly she wasn't comfortable. When the door leading to the kitchen opened we could hear the ceaseless talk of the driver and Serafina, the chatter of the two boys; there was laughter as the wine took hold. Everyone was obviously eating with gusto, and Andy was at the table with them. I realized then that Andy would be the first of us to learn Spanish.

There was fish, and chicken, and beautiful pale, fat shrimps, and vegetables we had never tasted before, cooked in a way we had never imagined vegetables cooked. It was delicious. "All done in olive oil," Nanny said, while refusing most things. She grimly ate bread and butter.

"Nanny," Don Paulo said, "you will get used to it. You must. Where would Spain be without its olives?" He spoke to her gently, as one would to a child. His colder, more formal tones were reserved for my mother and me.

At last it was all cleared away, and Paco poured port for Don Paulo. My mother signaled that she also would have her glass filled. I watched her apprehensively. I dreaded the results of the combination of fatigue and hunger and many glasses of wine. But Don Paulo did not linger. It was after four o'clock in the morning.

He rose. He was not as tall as I had at first thought. It

83

was his presence which was so powerful, I thought—though he had great breadth of shoulders and chest. How old he was I couldn't say; the dark eyes looked as if they had seen a thousand years, but there was great vigor in his body.

"I will bid you good night, Lady Patricia." Her hand was raised near his lips. "Miss Charlotte." He bowed. "Nanny."

A sense of panic seemed to penetrate my mother's dazed fatigue. She half rose from her chair. "But when . . . when are we to see you again, Don Paulo? There are affairs to discuss. . . . I was told . . ." She looked helplessly at me. "Oh, Charlie, you remember all the things the solicitors said we were to ask."

Don Paulo bowed with finality, cutting the conversation short. "I am to be found at the bodega most days, Lady Patricia. If not there . . . then some other place. Someone always knows. One does not hide very well in Jerez."

"But *when?*"

He shrugged lightly. "When you are rested. There is plenty of time."

He started towards the door, and Paco sprang to open it. Pepita, the mastiff, who had lain at his feet during the meal, rose also and went with him. Don Paulo turned. "Pepita, I have bidden you stay. *Stay! Quédate!*" He stared at the dog and pointed to my feet. "You will stay with Doña Carlota. *Pepita!*" The expression on the dog's face was as unbelieving as my own must have been.

"Oh no!" I said. "You can't have meant it, Don Paulo. I couldn't take such a wonderful dog from you. She is obviously devoted to you."

"Then she will show her devotion by doing as she is commanded. *Pepita!*" He pointed once again at me. "You will stay with Doña Carlota. Go now! *Go now!*" For almost a minute Don Paulo waited for his order to be obeyed. Finally, sadly, with only the faintest whine of protest, the mastiff turned and came to me. With a great grunt she lay down on the floor beside my chair. She received her commendation in Spanish from Don Paulo. "You will have to learn English, Pepita."

Then he was gone. Paco went ahead to light his way through the passages. We listened to the two sets of footsteps fading into the distance. Pepita whined again, getting to her feet once more. She went to the door, listening to the last sounds of her master. "How could he?" I said. "The poor dog is brokenhearted. How could he give her away just like that! Pepita . . . ! Come, girl. Here . . . Pepita." She responded to the tone of my voice, returned to me, gazed at me with her huge dark eyes which pleaded for affection, for some understanding of this separation from her master. I stroked the silken head, huge and splendid. "Good girl . . . good girl. He'll want you back, you'll see. In the meantime, you had best make up your mind to wait." I kept on stroking her, feeling the contact with the animal as a sop to my desperate, swamping feeling of homesickness. I thought if I stopped talking to the dog I might weep instead, and for my mother's sake I could not do that.

"It's my opinion," Nanny said, "that _that_ man would give away anything if it pleased him. He wanted to put you out, Miss Charlie. Upset you. He's the sort who'd give away his own children if there was something to be gained by it. Pity it's such a terrible dog. Ugly great brute, isn't it?"

"Pepita is a beautiful dog," my mother said. "And we don't need your opinion of Don Paulo, Nanny." She poured herself more port. "But obviously we are not exactly welcome. All this talk about a _visit_. This is our house, isn't it? Don't we own part of his bodega? And isn't there a vineyard? Why shouldn't we stay? That man can't drive us out. Come to welcome us, had he? Come to scare us off! That's what he'd come for."

I looked around the room. It was very large, and the candlelight did not reach to all its spaces. The walls were bare, showing patches of mildew. There were no curtains at the windows. "I wish . . . I wish it weren't so _big_. We'll need so many things . . . servants . . ."

"Listen to them." My mother jerked her head towards the kitchen. "We _have_ servants."

"We have very little money."

"We'll manage." She drank deeply. "There has to be good wine in the cellar. That Paco man didn't get *this* in a cantina."

Nanny gave a little whine, rather like the mastiff's. "I wish we'd stayed at home."

Distantly we heard the rumble of carriage wheels and the sharp sound of horses' hoofs striking cobbles. The sound died, and then we heard the crash as the heavy doors were thrown together and closed, the protest of the metal as the bolts were driven home by Paco. It left a silence that was unnerving. I thrust my glass towards my mother. "I'd like some port, please."

Nanny glared. "What next?"

"Next, Nanny, we'll go to bed. One thing at a time. Didn't Don Paulo say there was always time in Spain?" I laughed shakily. I realized I sounded like my mother. That frightened me also.

We were shown upstairs to rooms with big brass bedsteads, and Serafina brought hot water in Wedgwood jugs. Then with a grin of pleasure she beckoned Nanny in order to show her a large room, painted in flaking white. *"Para la Nanny,"* she said. *"Para los niños."*

Suddenly I understood. "For the children. It's the nursery, Nanny."

"Well then, Miss Charlie, you'd best be finding yourself a husband, hadn't you?" came the dry answer.

The beds were made up with linen sheets which bore yellow marks along all the creases, as if they had lain in the cupboard, waiting, for a very long time. Our rooms opened on yet another courtyard where the palm fronds rustled at the height of the windows. "Three courtyards so far I've counted in this place," I said despairingly. "Why did Grandfather have such a huge house? It must have stood empty all these years, and yet he never said anything about it. Just Serafina and Paco taking care of it— probably one of their parents before them. I hate the thought of opening all those doors. *These* rooms are hardly furnished, as it is."

My mother spoke with unexpected clarity as she halted on her way to her own room. "We'll only open each door as we come to it, my darling. Only one at a time. We've come to the land of sunshine and oranges and wine. And jasmine. Oh, Charlie, do you smell the jasmine?"

I sat down on the bed and stroked the mastiff's head; she thrust her face at me trustingly. She was prepared to wait, she seemed to say, until her master came to take her back. In the meantime, she was mine. Then at last, with a grunt, she sank down and put her head between her paws.

"Yes, we'd better go to bed, Pepita. It will all seem different tomorrow—today. Jasmine and oranges and wine. There will have to be a bit more than that. God, I wish I were back at Clon—" *I* stopped the words, even though there was only the dog to hear them. I must never say them; my mother must never hear me say them.

The dawn light was breaking over the tiled rooftops on the town before I laid my head on the musty pillow in its Irish linen cover. I seemed to sleep only seconds before the booming of the Angelus bell sounded, it seemed, right over my head. The notes were echoed by the bells of all the churches all across the town, deep, beautiful resonant sounds, shallow, brazen, discordant sounds, not one stroke matching another, as if every clock in the town was set at a different time. And through it came the homely familiar sounds of cocks crowing from courtyards and alleyways, from little pens near the houses of the poor and the stable yards of the rich. I sighed, and stretched, and so did the dog on the floor beside me. Then we both settled back into sleep.

I woke to the harsh bars of sunlight falling across my face through the wooden louvered shutters. For the first seconds there was total confusion; I had dreamed again of a great white stallion and a man on a distant shore, the opening of a gate that led to a rose garden. "Richard . . . ?" I sprang up and went and threw open the shutters, letting the full blast of the Andalucian sun fall on my face and neck and arms. It was strong and alien, far from that soft and misty shore. The dog touched my hand then, reminding me that it was late; she had been waiting, unfed and uncomplaining. I looked down at her beautiful, sad, square face. She was real, and so was the sun. I had to stop dreaming.

2

We opened only a few doors that first day, and closed them again, anxious to forget what we saw. Some rooms were empty, some only partially furnished. Some doors stuck so that it needed Andy's weight to push against them. Inside we found dust, sometimes a half-unpacked box or two. Serafina brought her mother, an old woman who inhabited one of the many rooms off the kitchen area; she had, it seemed, lived in the house when my grandfather bought it. Her eyes were bright with interest, and she produced a few words of English with pride. "He stay one year. He buy things. Then he go away. I stay. Serafina stay. He never come again, but he pay . . ."

We had given Serafina a little money, and she produced two cousins who began with her the immense task of sweeping, and beginning to wash all the marble floors. We listened to their incessant chatter, their laughter about things we could not understand. But the cousins would only stay a few days; we could not afford to keep them on full time.

"Though heaven knows we *need* them. But we'll have to manage just with Paco and Serafina. I suppose at this late stage I'd better try to turn my hand to a few things," my mother observed. "It won't hurt us to make beds and do our own rooms. We can't expect Serafina to do everything." I knew she meant well, and would try when she remembered to. But all her life she had been the sort who stepped out of her clothes and left them. Someone else, sooner or later, had always come and picked them up.

We selected a few rooms we would try to make presentable, as few as we could manage with. For the rest, the doors must remain closed.

"There's stabling for twenty horses, Lady Pat," Andy told her. "But it'll take more than a coat of whitewash to make the place fit again. There's repairs needed. I can turn my hand to a bit of carpentry, nothing fancy though. But it'd need a real team of men to do a proper job."

"Then you'll have to manage with whitewash, Andy," I said. "There's simply no money for anything else. Those two boys—Serafina's nephews, I think they are—they might stay on and give you a bit of help. We shouldn't have to pay them much."

"Pepe and Jaime," Andy sighed. "Just try getting rid of them, Miss Charlie. They're like fleas. They'll stay. I think they'd stay for the meals they get in the kitchen and a roof over their heads. Might as well be back in Ireland, for all the difference there is here. The poor have nothing. The rich . . ." His eyes swept over the marble expanse of the entrance hall, the curved marble sweep of the stairs, the carved wood of the banister and the big doors. "The Earl had some madness in him, buying this place. This is for the rich."

"He was fairly well off, then," my mother said. We talked this way now in Andy's presence. He had become part of our family, a link with home. "It was twenty-five years ago, remember, Andy. Before . . . before he began to send all the money he could spare to London—to make more money."

"I remember it," Andy said. "Five years old I would have been, and all the talk about him going to marry the Spanish Woman, and then him staying away so long and coming back without her. So much talk there was . . . and they've been talking about it ever since."

"Nanny remembers all that," my mother said. "She was a young nurserymaid then. When she wanted to frighten me she would tell me that if I weren't good my father would never come back again. What an age ago it seems. Times were good then. . . ." She sighed. "Charlie, go and ask Paco for the keys to the cellar. If I know my father at all, he laid in good wines as well as linen sheets. . . ."

I went, wondering how my mother expected me to find the Spanish for such a request. In time, by gestures and patience, I made him understand. He grinned and produced the keys with pride, apparently glad to show how well his stewardship had been rendered to the master he had never seen. He lighted a candle and gestured to us all, Andy as well, to follow him. We descended by a circular stair, narrow and dangerous, with moss on the walls and treads. Andy had lighted his own candle at the rear of the procession. We reached the bottom at last, and the two candles were tiny pinpricks of light in the gloom of an enormous room, circular in shape, whose ceiling the light of the candles would not reach.

"Agua," Paco said. He made motions with his hands indicating drinking and washing. Suddenly I understood.

"I know what it is! It used to be a cistern. They must have stored water here for the dry months. But look . . ." I took the candle from Andy and moved about the huge space. Rack upon rack of wine was revealed, dust-covered, the labels, where they remained at all, black with mold and mildew. "There must be thousands. Thousands and thousands. . . . Do you suppose it was here when Grandfather bought the house? It must have cost a fortune to stock it like this. At least twenty-five years it's been here like this, and no one's touched it. I suppose some of it's not fit to drink now. . . ."

Paco seemed to get the drift of what I was saying. He was beaming, and he made a slight bow, jingling the keys. He seemed to be trying to convey to us that his honesty had earned him a job for life. Undoubtedly our coming had caused a great disruption in the easeful pattern of his and Serafina's lives, but I guessed that, like Don Paulo, he expected us to go eventually, as my grandfather had done and then he and Serafina could sink back into the lassitude of the undisturbed days, with few duties and much time to spare. He seemed to be smiling already at the prospect.

My mother was trying to read some of the labels on the

bottles. "You know—I think Father has left us a small fortune in wine. Perhaps we could sell it . . . but for lunch, since this is the first day, we'll just have this Bordeaux, and perhaps this Chambertin for dinner." She gave a small laugh of pleasure. "What a feast! What luck! He always had such great taste in wine. . . ."

I sighed. We would never sell the wine. It would be drunk.

3

It was not yet eleven o'clock on the morning of our second day in Jerez, but the sun already beat like hammer strokes on us as we rode, and caused the people who walked the streets to seek the black shadows of the buildings. When it was noon there would be no shade, and the heat would be relentless. We rode, a rather improbable three, I thought, led by Serafina's nephew, Pepe, and followed by the mastiff, Pepita. I rode Half Moon, and my mother had claimed Balthasar; Andy had an undistinguished-looking, tired mare hired from a livery stable. We'll have to find him a halfway decent horse, I thought, watching him maneuvering the mare to keep close to the great stallion in case Balthasar should prove too much even for my mother's expert horsemanship. Have to find some way to exercise Balthasar and Half Moon outside the town. Have to find some sort of trap and a carriage horse so we can go about more easily. The thoughts ran on and on through my head. Have to . . . have to . . . And always the second thought following the first. Money. How were we to find the money?

"Have you ever seen such a blue sky, Charlie?" my mother called back to me. She sounded gay, excited. She had forgotten the disorder of the house we had left behind, the difficulties, the thousand things we lacked. We were going on a visit, and that fact was quite enough to make my mother happy.

"There had better not be any rain," Andy said. "Or it

could ruin the harvest. The grapes don't like rain at this stage."

"Andy—how do you know such things?"

"Oh—" He glanced back at me, his expression sheepish. "Oh, I listen, Miss Charlie. The old woman still has a few words of English. She must have worked with some family that spoke it all the time. But I listen. Sometimes I think I understand a few things."

"That's another thing we'll have to have," I said. "We have to have someone regularly to give us lessons in Spanish. Someone . . ."

"Oh, Charlie dear, my learning days are over," my mother answered. "Your poor old mother was never much of a brain, and what there was has been shaken out of me with all the tumbles I've taken off horses. You'll have to do the learning, my darling, and tell me what's going on. Only the nice bits, though. Besides, if what I see here is evidence, there are enough people who speak English. Enough to keep me going, any rate. . . ."

Some of the streets through which we passed were lined on both sides with the thick, high walls of the bodegas, all with the high, grilled windows open so that the air itself seemed saturated with the warm scent—scent was the only word I could find for it—of the sherry as it lay in its casks, breathing, giving out the essence of the sun and the soil that had borne it. The sight of the bodegas had surprised me. I had always thought of wine cellars as being deep in the ground, but these were long high buildings, built above ground. They stretched, whole streets of them, through the town, their walls painted with the famous names of the trade—Williams and Humbert; González, Byass; Domecq; De Terry; Duff Gordon; Osborne—and Fernández, Thompson. English, Irish, and Scottish names. No doubt half of them were owned by families who now mixed their names with the Spanish, but there was reason for my mother's confidence that more than a few would speak English, as Don Paulo did. I began to see that I would be taking my Spanish lessons alone.

We were on our way to the principal bodega of Fernández, Thompson. Pepe led us through the streets with a high head and a look of pride that somehow negated the ragged clothes he wore. Half consciously I had noticed how so many of the Spanish seemed to surmount their poverty, to cloak it with pride. They were willing, but not servile. It evidently pleased Pepe highly to be seen in the streets of his native town with two foreign ladies so splendidly mounted on such outstanding horses. I saw how often he glanced at my mother, now at the height of her almost outrageous beauty, with creamy skin smooth and silken, dark red hair that escaped entrancingly in little tendrils to touch her cheeks. His looks seemed to indicate that she was fully worthy of the horse she rode. His chest was puffed out as he passed acquaintances in the streets and called the way we were to turn, indicating with the stick he carried. He was for all the world like someone who proclaimed the coming of a queen. My mother loved it.

The main offices of the bodega of Fernández, Thompson were approached through a gate as handsome as any I had ever seen. We passed into a paved courtyard, with areas of carefully cultivated flowers and bright pots of geraniums placed in clusters. More bodegas were revealed—a whole row of massively built structures with the unvarying high windows, white walls splashed with purple bougainvillaea. In the paved passages between the bodegas grapevines grew on gnarled old stems, thicker than a man's arm. Andy led the horses to the shade they provided—they were trained on wires strung from one building to the next. "Look," my mother said, "there are actually grapes on them. They look too old. . . ." And up among the bright, thick leaves I could see the clusters of pale grapes. Before dismounting, I almost reached up for a cluster, and then stopped. Close to, they were small and hard-looking, as if they were not ready for picking, perhaps never would be. They were the fruit of old vines which had to scratch their existence from the tiny patches of soil along the bodega walls.

A man came to help us dismount. He seemed to know

93

who we were: it was almost unnecessary to ask for Don Paulo. The man ushered us, with many bows, towards a building deeply shaded by a colonnade. The heavy, ornate doors I had seen everywhere in the town were open; inside the dimness came like cool water after the aching glare of the sun. We were led past a row of offices whose half-glassed walls gave us a view of many men at work at desks. One or two lifted their heads and then frankly stared. My mother was something to stare at. We passed from this corridor through another open space threaded with vines, and then were shown into the deep quiet of what seemed to be a reception area. Here there were big carved velvet-covered chairs set on silken carpet; there were discreetly closed doors where I guessed the more important people worked. The familiar marble floors gave the impression of coolness, as did the silence.

"Momentito, por favor."

The man went and knocked at one of the doors, stepped inside, and spoke some words. Almost at once Don Paulo came out to meet us. If he had been engaged in work he gave no sign of it; he had the air of one to whom courtesy to visitors was more important than any work. At the sight of him Pepita flung herself forward with a yelp of delight and was sternly rebuked by her former master.

"Miss Charlotte, you will have to be more severe with Pepita. I told you she was barely more than a puppy and does not yet seem to have learned her manners. I trust you to bring her up properly."

I felt as rebuked as the dog. Don Paulo formally took my mother's hand, and then mine, and waved his arm towards the open door of his office. "You are welcome," the lips said. The hooded eyes said nothing.

His office was richly furnished. There were English mahogany glass-fronted bookcases, a leather-topped desk, which bore an elaborate silver writing set. But lest even the desk should suggest too much of a sense of business, he led us to the other end of the long room where big chairs similar to the ones outside stood about a highly polished table. Already, as if some silent message had been passed, a manservant in white coat and white gloves was setting out small, inward-curving sherry glasses; three bottles were placed on a silver tray. There was another silver tray bearing small pieces of bread spread with pâté and little tarts filled with shrimp and melted cheese. There were silver bowls of olives and nuts. It was all done with deftness and silence; no sense of hurry. It was as if Don Paulo had nothing to do except wait on the arrival of visitors, which couldn't have been the case.

"You will take a copita, ladies?" He was already pouring. Our agreement was taken for granted. "Would you try our local custom of drinking the sweet—the cream sherry—before the dry, the *fino?* It would be a pity if you left Jerez without knowing something of how we drink our sherry here."

"I like Jerez," my mother said. "I'm sure I shall stay."

He behaved as if she had not spoken. "We say here that the cream sherry, the *oloroso,* cradles the stomach, and we take it as our first copita of the day. From that one goes to the *amontillado*, which comes in the middle. After that, the fino, which we then stay with for the rest of the day. For us it is the greatest wine, dry, pale, delicate on the tongue." He raised his glass. "I salute your health, ladies."

Gravely we tasted the warm, sweet wine, dark and rich in color. I noticed that Don Paulo held the glass beneath his nose for a moment, swirled it slightly, drew in the bouquet, and then drained it almost in one mouthful. Already he was pouring the next wine, one lighter in color, less heavy, I supposed, to nose and tongue. That also went quickly. My mother seemed to have no trouble keeping up with him. I found my third glass filled with the pale fino before the first one was empty. In the midst of my unease, I still couldn't help thinking what a beautiful spectrum of color they made, lined up beside one another.

Don Paulo now held out the silver dish with its spread of small delicacies. "Do have some, Lady Patricia. We call them *tapas*. Tapa is"—he gestured with one of the tiny tarts—"our word for lid or cover." He held the tart so that it neatly topped the rim of the glass. "To cover the glass. We seldom drink without eating."

I didn't want to eat, but under the spell of that man's quiet voice, compelling, I both ate and drank. It all seemed a kind of madness. We sat in this splendid room, acting as if we had come only on a courtesy call, acting as if we had nothing to do but exchange pleasantries about local customs, and soft Spanish words. I cautioned myself that if it continued much longer we would be leaving with our business unstated, undone. There was a hint of sharpness in the heart of the last wine, the pale bright wine which washed over my palate with a cleansing purity. I straightened myself in the chair.

"Don Paulo, if you don't mind, we must discuss some business. . . . The matter of my grandfather's shares . . ."

A frown began and was swiftly erased. "Miss Charlotte, it is rarely my habit to talk to ladies about business." His tone was soothing, almost patronizing; one did not talk to children of business, either, he seemed to imply.

"Unhappily, we have no *man* to talk to you of business," I answered sharply.

He held up his hand. "Ah, but you had. Your solicitors wrote from Dublin. Everything could have been conducted by post. There was really no need for your journey here, although, of course, we are all most delighted to have you visit."

"The solicitors in Dublin had only the barest knowledge of my grandfather's business interests here, Don Paulo. They were not known until after his death. Lord Blodmore knew no details either. He tried to dissuade us from coming. He tried to make other arrangements for us."

"Lord Blodmore has been known to show good sense before this," the man said dryly. "And what may I tell you?"

"About my grandfather's interests in this bodega—the extent of them. We understand there is a bank here which received payments from this firm but did not remit them to Ireland." I was striving to remember everything Siddons had said, and repeating it parrot fashion, wondering if I would make sense of the answers. "We heard of a vineyard. My grandfather's affairs seemed to be in some . . . some disorder when he died."

"I'm not entirely surprised to hear it."

My mother's voice rose in protest. "Oh, but you mustn't judge my father by *that!* Who would have thought he would be killed? He was only fifty-seven. Yes . . . about fifty-seven. There seemed years for him to arrange everything. He just didn't have enough time. . . ." Her voice almost broke. "He was the dearest, kindest man . . ."

Don Paulo was filling her glass again. "Your love and faith do you credit, Lady Patricia. Not all children are so respectful." He raised his head and nodded towards the door. "Now, here is one . . ." I, seated opposite Don Paulo, with my back to the door, was aware of the change which had come over his face. He struggled against dropping his habitual expression of weary cynicism, struggled against allowing those hooded dark eyes to widen and display his pleasure; he did not quite succeed. "Here is one, a graceless rascal, who shows little respect for his elders, and none at all for their wisdom and experience. May I present my son Carlos? Lady Patricia Drummond. Miss Charlotte Drummond. I might have known he would find his way here quickly. Beautiful ladies draw him even more unerringly than a good horse. I'm sure, Lady Patricia, I do not offend you with the comparison. Our horses are as precious to us here as our wine and our ladies."

I saw a tall, slender young man, surprisingly young to be Don Paulo's son. He had dark, curling hair. His cream linen suit with a tastefully embroidered silk waistcoat gave him the air of a dandy, but he was perhaps the most powerfully masculine creature I had yet encountered. He emanated virility as Balthasar did. He bent first over my mother's hand and then turned to take mine. As he executed the gesture of kissing it, his eyes, dark as his father's, ran over me in a practiced, knowing fashion. Then he smiled, and for a moment it was possible to believe he thought me the only female in the world. He had an oval face, perfectly regular, beautifully defined features; his complexion was lighter than his father's but it showed his days in the sun. He had his father's good looks, but with an added grace. He was saying something, but I scarcely comprehended the words; in those first stunned moments of looking at him I thought he was the most beautiful young man I had ever seen. He revealed his perfect profile as he turned to Don Paulo.

"What a pleasure for our little town to gain at one time two ladies of such beauty. I can tell you, the heads were turning as you walked by our offices. . . ." Now he bowed to his father. "That is, of course, Father, why I had to find some business of pressing urgency to bring to you now." He presented a folder and laughed at the same time. "You did not tell me, Father," and his tone was heavy with mock reproach, "that we were so honored. I should have called at once. Probably there are a dozen ahead of me." It was a measure of his skill, I thought, that no one could guess for which of us he held his greatest admiration. It was a most superb blend of flattery and truth.

He took a copita with us, smelling it as his father had done, but drinking it more slowly. He drank only the pale, bright fino, the wine which I had already decided I like the best. He talked as he drank; he talked about Ireland, questioned us about Ireland, about Clonmara "where his father's . . ." For a time we all fumbled as how to describe the relationship of Don Paulo and Elena. Finally Carlos found it: "My father's niece by marriage." And then he laughed. "How ridiculous that sounds. Here in Jerez we are all something-by-marriage." Then he talked of England. "I had the good fortune to go to school there," he said, "and then Father dragged me back here to scrape a living out of the sherry business."

Don Paulo allowed all this recital. "I heard nothing but how hard they worked him there, how cold it was, how early he had to get up every morning. A spoiled young man, I'd say."

Carlos gave a slight shrug. "I shall never redeem my-
98

self in my father's eyes, I think. I work my fingers to the bone. . . . Don't you see, Lady Patricia, how my fingers are worked to the bone?" He extended long, infinitely graceful hands to her for her inspection.

She laughed back at him, enchanted. "You poor young man!"

He looked at Don Paulo. "Father, you *can't* deny me the pleasure of showing our guests through the bodega. After all, you have me do it for boring old men, so surely I've earned this privilege?"

Don Paulo nodded. "You may, Carlos. Who am I to stand in the way of a young man's legitimate pleasure?— especially since, Lady Patricia, he will tell the story of our sherry as well as it can be done. I trained him myself." He rose, as my mother did.

"I should be delighted to be shown through the bodega. I promise you, though, I'm very ignorant and stupid. I don't know anything except a very little about horses."

"Ah, horses . . ." Carlos echoed. They were off in pursuit of my mother's true subject, and his enthusiasm seemed to match hers. They had reached the door before he was aware that I had not stood up. He looked back at me. "Are you not coming, Miss Charlotte? Or shall we call you Doña Carlota? Much prettier, I think. Carlota suits you."

"We call her Charlie," my mother ingenuously volunteered.

His nose wrinkled in distaste. "That will never do. It sounds like a pet dog. Are you coming, Doña Carlota?"

I hesitated. My mother was spellbound by the charm and good looks of this young man, who seemed very sure of them himself. She had entirely forgotten the purpose of the visit. I had no doubt that during the tour of the bodega more beautiful fino wine would be drunk. They would talk horses and wine, these two, until the hour of the late Spanish lunch came around. The sun would grow fierce, and my mother would need all her strength to mount Balthasar again and stay in the saddle until we returned to that old dark house. Another day would have passed with no questions asked and no answers given.

"Charlie is a good name for a terrier, Don Carlos," I answered. I turned back to Don Paulo. "Terriers tend to hold on once they have taken their bite. You must allow me to stay a little longer. A few questions only . . ."

Carlos bowed, having first glanced at his father for his direction. "Then I shall have the double pleasure of taking you through the bodega at some later time. Promise me, Father, that the honor shall go to no one else."

He closed the door quietly. For a few seconds I could hear my mother's heels rap on the marble floor, and the sound of their voices, my mother's laugh, that infectious, uncaring sound I had listened to all my life. For the moment my mother was happy. And the business details could be left to me.

I looked at Don Paulo and I was frightened. His expression was wintry, without encouragement. What had made me think I could handle a man like this? I tried a weak joke. "Perhaps I should have said a bulldog, Don Paulo. They are the ones with the reputation of never letting go."

He did not smile. "You have a certain beauty, Doña Carlota. The bulldog is an ugly if endearing creature. But they say he has a heart that, once fixed, is never shaken. I wonder if that temperament is yours? Or are you like Pepita, there, who gives her heart to every passing stranger?"

The words chilled me. The gift of Pepita had not been made out of generosity but with a sense of contempt. He had given what he little valued, the affection of a hound who loved everyone. I felt I had collided headlong with the extreme of the Spanish reputation for pride, austerity in the midst of riches, and a streak of cruelty, as Richard Blodmore had warned me. I delayed a long time, growing more frightened, afraid to speak lest my voice should tremble. I would not betray my fear of this man. At last impatience broke through this façade of Spanish courtesy.

"Come, say what you must and be done with it. You will not leave here without answers, I can see. You are not like your mother."

I put my glass on the table and took a deep breath. "We had begun to talk, Don Paulo, before your son arrived, about my grandfather's investment in the bodega. We wondered if it was substantial or trivial. All we know is that the moneys paid by your bodega remained here in Jerez."

"The moneys due under that investment were paid into the Banco de Jerez. What happened to them after that is no concern of mine."

"Can you tell me then, Don Paulo, how my grandfather came to make such an investment? It was a surprise to us to learn of it after his death."

He looked at me coldly, as if he hated to admit what he now must. "Your grandfather, Doña Carlota, happened to come to Jerez—some twenty-five years ago—at a time when my own business was in need of money. All businesses experience such times. Selling shares in anything that concerns my family is not something that pleases me. But I regarded your grandfather as a gentleman, a possible asset to our business while having no say in its running. I thought of him as a possible ambassador of our wine. If one may be permitted—I saw him as a possible salesman for our particular sherries, rather than our rivals'. In those days Blodmore mixed in rather different circles than he was . . . was reduced to in the end."

"Any circle my grandfather chose to move in was the better for it, Don Paulo."

Again that touch of a wintry smile. "You are loyal, I see. As your mother is. I like that, Doña Carlota. Family loyalty ranks high on my list of virtues."

"I am not here to discuss virtues, Don Paulo. I have few to discuss."

He shrugged. "Then what am I to talk about? When the dividends were paid each year into the bank, that was the end of the matter as far as I was concerned."

I almost blurted out a question about the note that had come each year with its cryptic message: *She lives*. But a newly found sense of caution warned me. One did not show all one's cards to a man like Don Paulo. And I said nothing about the fact that Don Paulo had married the woman my grandfather had been expected to marry. No, one did not say such things. Not yet.

My silence seemed to needle him. He took up the conversation again. "A number of times, Doña Carlota, I offered to buy back the interest your grandfather owned in the bodega. He did not respond. After we had news of his death, I repeated my offer to your solicitors. Again there was no response. Now you are here asking questions. I can only tell you that out of your grandfather's share of the original bodegas—the business as it existed at that time—he took the good times and the bad times of the sherry trade. When we had the scourge of the phylloxera in 1896 and our vineyards were destroyed, no one had any profits. No one. Have you any idea, Doña Carlota, how long it takes before a vineyard will produce its first usable grape? In some cases four years. If a man is wise he will wait five years. Five years is a long time to keep plowing money into the earth with no return. Five years we took before we had a harvest from our devastated vineyards, and many are not replanted to this day. To tend the young vines—to tend the vines at any time, is both a duty and an honor for the viticulturist. It all, however, costs a great deal of money. Those were lean years in Jerez, and we are now just beginning to emerge from them. We had the stocks of our bodegas, of course, but we could not sell off all that we had—there would have been nothing from which to replenish the solera. So we waited, and tended our vines, and no one grew very rich in those years. Nor did your grandfather's bank account wax very fat. However, you will find it all in order, every dividend scrupulously accounted for. The years we paid no dividends are the empty ones, when we had no profits. The state of your grandfather's bank account will be communicated to you by Don Ramón García, who is head of the Banco de Jerez. I myself will send a messenger to him."

He leaned back, and his words were slow. "And now, Doña Carlota, I would like to renew my offer to buy back those shares. I will make a handsome offer—well above their market price. Though their market price will be hard to determine, since it is still a privately held company. But the offer will be handsome. Enough to make the return to Ireland much easier, your settling down again more pleasant. I will even—I will even take that monstrous ruin of a house off your hands. It would cost a fortune to repair it, but the ground it stands on has some value. Perhaps as a site for a new bodega . . . That needn't trouble you. Instead of a ruinous house, you will have the money to buy in Ireland . . ."

"The vineyard?" I murmured.

His lips stretched thinly. "You are greedy, Doña Carlota. The vineyard your grandfather bought is worth nothing but the value of its albariza soil—the soil which produces the sherry grape. It was one of the vineyards never replanted after the phylloxera scourge. Why should I buy such a thing? There is plenty of my own albariza land which is not yet planted in vines. I could expand in many directions, and will do so as conditions of the trade permit." Then he waved a hand as if granting a sweet to a child. "But so—if you insist. I will buy the vineyard."

I shook my head then, and smiled. I was no longer so afraid of him. For some reason he wished us gone, and the knowledge gave me a sense of power. "But that is not, of course, for me to agree to, Don Paulo. Is it? It is my mother who owns these things. You must make your offer to her."

He gestured as if dismissing me. "You think I am a fool? It is *you*, Doña Carlota, who will make the decisions. You are hardly more than a child, but you are older than your mother. You will accept my offer, I am sure of that."

"My mother appears to like Jerez. She says she will stay."

He nodded, and his eyes almost closed. "Very well, then. Play your game if you must. My offer stands. My bodega is for *me*—for me and for my family. We want no outsiders."

I rose. "Then may *I*, Don Paulo, see the bodega? I am anxious to see where my—my mother's interests lie."

He considered for a moment, staring at me silently,

gently swirling the last of the wine in his glass. He rose. "Come—I will show you the bodega."

"Carlos . . . ?"

"*I* will show you the bodega, Doña Carlota. You will have the best guide in Jerez."

4

We walked through the passageway laced with the overhanging vines, and the heat smote us. He led me to one of the big open doors of the nearest bodega, and I paused for a moment, my eyes unable to focus in the dim light. I became aware gradually of the huge space about me, and the quiet. It was a vast building, vaulted in arches, which rested on thick pillars, almost like a church. There was a smell of wood and wine and damp. We walked on a cobbled pathway between piled rows of dark butts all with chalk markings on them in symbols I couldn't understand. Both the cobbled path and the earth underneath the butts was damp, but the butts were raised from the earth itself, resting on stout wooden beams.

Don Paulo stopped in the middle of the bodega, his eyes sweeping upwards to the high roof, to the barred windows high in the walls, which were shielded, on the side where the sun hit, by grass blinds like mats rolled down. He had taken a stick with him and he pointed, left and right, up and down, at all the intersecting rows of butts.

"The smell," he said. "The smell is like nowhere else on earth. That is our wine as it soaks through the oak casks. The wine has to breathe, so we leave it only lightly stoppered. We bring all our wine from the vineyards and collect it here in the town itself. Down here it matures best. It likes its own company. It breathes through the wood itself, and through the bunghole. We never completely fill a butt so that a large part of the wine within it is exposed to air. There are few ways to be miserly in the making of sherry. The casks are oak, and those in which we ship our wine abroad are snapped up by the whisky distillers, because the sherry-soaked wood gives their maturing alcohol color and flavor. We call the butts which stay here permanently in the bodega *madres*—mothers. They have the quality of age and are very valuable."

His speech had become slower, the tone almost ruminative. The antagonism that had bristled between us in his office seemed to have been left behind. Now he was talking as a man talks of something he loves, as if the wine were a person, someone precious, of individuality. Glancing at him as he talked, it seemed to me that his face and eyes had assumed almost the same expression as when Carlos had entered his office. I began to sense that this man who could appear so coldly reserved, detached, could also be capable of great and perhaps terrible passions. His wine was one of his passions.

He pointed to the butts stacked about us, reaching high over our heads. "The solera system makes our wine different from any other. We have no vintage years in sherry. Instead, we strive to achieve a uniform wine, one which does not vary in quality, age, or character, whichever of the broad groupings of fino, amontillado, or oloroso it happens to fall into. What we are doing is moving and mixing our wine in a sort of perpetual cycle.

"A solera consists of a number of casks stacked in tiers or, as we say here, scales. Here"—pointing with his stick from one side of the aisle to the other where the casks were stacked three high—"is an example of a solera of six scales. This bottom one, the first scale, contains wine ready to be sold. This is the real solera, the other scales we call *criaderas*—nurseries. The scale above the solera has butts containing wine about a year younger, and the one above a year younger still. Over here are the fourth, fifth, and sixth scales. The sixth scale will hold the wine which is about five years younger than the wine in the first scale. The wines of the different scales are always of the same kind and, whenever possible, they come from the same vineyard. The number of scales for the finos must be larger than for the more full-bodied amontillados and olorosos, because the full-bodied wines

105

vary much less from year to year than the finos. The scales of the solera can run from four to seven.

"When we draw off wine to sell from the bottom, the first scale, we take an equal amount from each cask of that scale. Then we top up the ullage with the wine drawn from the second scale, and this amount is then made up with wine from the third scale. And so on, right through the fourth, fifth, and sixth scales, if the solera requires that many scales. In the bodega we call this 'running the scales.' Wine, of course, changes as it matures, usually gaining more strength, body, and color. By using our solera system we compensate for the change produced by age. We refresh and rejuvenate the older wine by blending it with the younger one.

"I've used a rather simplistic example of the solera, Doña Carlota. It is easier for the newcomer to understand the solera if we stand here and say, 'We draw off the wine from the lowest scale and top up from the scale above it, and so on. . . .' It is easier to picture it happening that way. But in reality we often separate the scales of the solera which belong to one another. The lowest level is ideal for maturing the finos because they need a lower temperature—so you might find the third and fourth scales of a particular solera in the two bottom tiers in another part of the bodega. We might put a criadera of oloroso on the third tier, because it likes a higher temperature to mature. The various scales of our very important soleras are often divided between different buildings because of the hazard of fire destroying them all."

He paused, his eyes moving over the dark butts with their white markings. When he spoke again his tone was musing. "I have often thought, Doña Carlota, how wonderful it would be if we could apply the solera system to ourselves. Think, as we aged, if we could draw on the young for refreshment and invigoration. We feel we *should* be able to draw on our children for these qualities which we begin to lose, but mostly what we end up doing is merely envying them—which is useless."

"Surely," I ventured, "the young have a callowness you'd hardly want to mix with your own maturity, Don Paulo."

"Age without youth dies," he answered. "Perhaps you will still be here in September when we harvest our grapes, and press them, and bring in the liquid from the pressing to the bodegas. We call this liquid *mosto*—must. It is not then wine. Even as it is brought to the bodega it goes into a state of violent fermentation. The fermentation is natural—quite spontaneous. The must froths and bubbles—it boils, and sometimes, although we leave room for this when filling the casks, it overflows, bubbles over. This to me is the excitement, the strength and enthusiasm of youth. Some people describe the smell it has then as nasty, and it is certainly undrinkable. So youth has its bad qualities, but we older ones observe, and smell, and mark and classify, trying to eliminate what is undesirable and to encourage that which we think will make great wine. Some we see are only fit for wine spirits or for vinegar. We call them, *mostos de quema*—musts for burning. But for me all the tumult of youth is there in the must as it comes to the bodega. It is an exciting time. The must quietens a little in about a week, as youth settles down a little, but it still continues to ferment. We keep it only very lightly stoppered—youth will have its fling. It is during this second, quieter fermentation that the must begins to develop the individual characteristics which will distinguish it in later life. Then when winter comes to Jerez in December or January, the fermentation stops. The must, which up to then has been an opaque and yellowish liquid, becomes clear. The lees settle to the bottom of the cask. This is when we say, 'The wine falls bright.' Then, and not before, can we begin to tell what type the wine may be.

"And so, Doña Carlota, youth has turned the corner. The young wine begins to indicate whether it will be fino or oloroso."

He clapped his hands together and called out some order in Spanish. Almost at once a man appeared, as if

107

he had been in waiting for the summons. He brought with him something Don Paulo called a *venencia*, an object which looked to me somewhat like a candle snuffer. It was a small, cylindrical cup made of silver, on a black flexible whalebone rod, finished with a decorative silver hook. The man also carried stemmed sherry glasses, perhaps ten of them, between his fingers.

Don Paulo indicated one particular butt, and the man hastened to remove its wooden bung. With a swift movement Don Paulo plunged the silver cup through the hole. He took a *copa* from the attending man. Holding the venencia high, he poured the liquid in a long, steady stream which fell, miraculously, it seemed to me, into the narrow neck of the sherry glass. It was a gesture of great flamboyance and skill. "Only the smallest sip," he said, handing it to me. "You will not like it. It is last year's harvest." The wine was slightly muddied, thin and acid to the taste.

He took me in this way through the scales of a solera of finos, rinsing with water and then plunging the long venencia, taking a fresh glass each time, and each time pouring with that marvelous accuracy. Year by year the wine grew better, to smell and on the tongue, until finally, having begun with the youngest, we reached the oldest scale of the solera where it had attained the delicate, topaz perfection of the fino we had drunk in Don Paulo's office. "The finos we have to keep in a cool temperature —so we water the floors. The olorosos may be stored at a higher temperature—though, unless they are in need of more sweetening, we keep them in the shade."

We moved across to another bodega. Pepita had followed us through all this, moving constantly between us, not seeming to know which of us she should look to for her commands. Don Paulo studiously ignored her.

By now I was becoming familiar with the structure of the bodegas, the great height and the thickness of the walls bringing down the temperature many degrees. They were beautiful buildings; their whitewashed walls were often stained with mildew, holding their treasure of dark

108

silent waiting casks, where the wine lay breathing, living, maturing. "The 'cellar instinct,'" Don Paulo said, "is almost as important to the sherry shipper as his 'nose' for his wine, or his decisions about where to plant his vineyards. Wine here in Jerez develops better when stored in bodegas on the south or southwest of the town—possibly because of the moisture and aeration of the breeze blowing from the sea, but that again is scientifically unproven. I will not talk to you about alcoholic strengths, density on the Baumé scale, and all the rest of it. It is technical, and you are here to enjoy the wine, to carry back with you memories of how we create our unique product. If that has been accomplished, it is enough. . . ."

The quiet was one of the abiding impressions I had of the bodegas. There were workmen about, carrying out their various tasks, and each bodega had its *capataz,* its foreman, who had a position of high responsibility. I saw casks being rolled along the aisles, wine being siphoned off the butts into jars, then added to the next scale of the solera. "We never hurry with this process," Don Paulo said. "A jarful at a time. This method distributes the new wine evenly with the old, and there is no jet of pressure to stir up the sediment." But in the midst of their tasks there was still the feeling of quiet in the bodegas. I walked at Don Paulo's side and felt strangely at peace.

"Sherry," he said to me as we crossed yet another of those vine-threaded passageways between the bodega buildings which bore their own special name of *almizacates,* "is the special gift of God. Everything here about us in Jerez is exactly right for it—soil, climate, ferments, and fruit. But the special gift is for *flor.* I will not bore you with attempting a scientific explanation of what no one has yet exactly defined, but the flor is the flower of the wine, the spores of the yeast which rise spontaneously to the surface of the wine twice a year and reproduce, then fall to the bottom of the butt again. It is called a flower, but actually it is a rather ugly-looking film. It appears on the wine in April and May and again in

109

August and September. It is interesting that these periods coincide with the budding of the vines and their blossoming, and also when the fruit of the vine grows ready for harvest. It is a living organism, and we do nothing to induce it—just keep our casks on ullage and our bungs lightly stoppered, so that the air may react with the wine in the cask. A sherry wine will produce this flor for about six to eight years. If the older wine is not blended with the new, younger wine, the flor will die, and so will the wine. Renewed with other wines, it keeps on breeding indefinitely . . . and so I think about the family. How good if we could keep on being renewed in this way. . . ."

We had entered yet another bodega. A few casks were stacked apart from the others, differently marked. Once again Don Paulo called for the venencia and the glasses. "We use the little venencia so that it goes straight and swiftly through the flor and does not stir up any sediment in the butt. . . . These butts should not rightly be here. Their true home is Sanlúcar de Barrameda, where the grapes are grown and they mature best. I keep them here for my own observation, just to see the difference in the way the wine will develop. What does it taste like, do you think?"

It was very pale, the palest of the sherries I had seen. I sipped, and hesitated. "It tastes . . . it seems to taste a bit salty."

I couldn't tell whether he was pleased by the guess or not. "It is called a *manzanilla* sherry," he said. "You are right. It is slightly salty. The grapes that produce it are grown quite close to the sea, and we say it has the salt taste of the sea in it. At Sanlúcar the bodegas are quite near the sea. The wine likes its own home."

The many small copas I had had in the heat of the day were beginning to take their effect. I had forgotten how frightened I had been earlier of this man. As he talked of his wine, he had talked of something he loved, and with love there is always a tenderness and a streak of vulnerability. My own tongue had loosened.

"It's all one family of wine," I said slowly, trying to pick my words, trying to express the impression that the

110

whole exposition of the solera, the atmosphere of the bodegas had had on me, "gathered into one home. But in my father's house there are many mansions. I suppose it means many rooms. The wines go off into their own rooms. The quiet . . . the cool with still the blazing sun outside. You bring the wines here to make the family— the young and the old. The grapes growing out there in the vineyards are like the unborn babies of the family. Here you prepare the nurseries for them. You will teach and train them by blending and mixing them with their elders. The strength is in the family . . ." I trailed off, embarrassed to find my tongue so loosened with this man. Why did I bother him with my half-formed thoughts?

He returned the glass and the venencia to the hand of the waiting man, who then seemed to disappear into the shadows of the bodega. He looked at me for quite a long time before replying.

"The family," he replied, ". . . the family is everything. And yet your family and mine, Doña Carlota, have not been blessed with many members. In *our* mansions there are many empty rooms. Women who have not produced sons. Men who could not get sons on women. Our criaderas have been scantily filled."

He took my arm lightly, the first time he had touched me, and led me down the aisle between the tiers of butts. We turned into the main aisle which led to one of the great open doorways of the bodega. Outside was the harsh, blinding light. Silhouetted against the light were two figures, my mother and Carlos. The light behind them seemed to give them an aura of enchantment; the young man, throwing a dark shadow, seemed older; my mother, with her slenderness, her upright carriage, seemed a young woman. Each held a copa and, unable to see clearly into the dimness of the bodega, they appeared unaware of our approach. They gazed at each other, their tones, as they talked, low and intimate. The wine they held shone brilliantly in the sun.

Don Paulo's words came as a soft whisper; I wasn't even sure I was intended to hear them. "And there— there is my hope for this family. He was born of a woman

111

to whom I was not married. He does not even rightfully bear my name. And yet he is all my hope."

We walked towards them. Pepita then seemed to decide where she belonged. She fell in beside me and stayed with me.

CHAPTER THREE

1

She was waiting for us when we returned. She was seated in what we called the drawing room, and Serafina had served her a copita, which she appeared not to have touched. She was thin, wiry, and dressed in black. "I am María Luisa Romero Fernández Gordon. I have a host of other names which I won't trouble you with. I have come to offer my services."

My mother poured a copita for herself and then sat down opposite our visitor. I refused the offered glass and stared in fascination at the woman. She was ugly in a quite remarkable way, an outstanding ugliness, with snapping black eyes that brightened her sharp, sallow face. Pepita came to sniff her, and she put her hand without hesitation on the dog's big head. "I see you have Don Paulo's dog. . . . Carlos will not like that."

"Services . . . ?" I said, to bring her back to the point.

"Exactly. You will need someone like me if you are to stay in Jerez. Otherwise you will make a mess of things. You don't know how things are done in Spain. You don't

113

know who anyone is. To survive, you must be shown the way. I can do it. I'm related to more than half the families in Jerez, and I know the facts and scandals attached to all the others. I am poor, unmarried, and ugly. I get shifted from family to family, moved around when someone needs something—a duenna, a nurse, a housekeeper. I am everyone's poor relation. Now I offer my services to you. You need me."

I blinked at the rapid delivery of the words in perfect English. "Services? We can pay nothing."

"I didn't mention payment. I am tired of being ordered about in a society in which an unmarried woman of my age is nothing—nothing except an object of pity and someone to be used. I know you can pay for nothing. I need a roof over my head, food. A dress now and again. In return I will teach you Spanish. I will give orders to the servants and see that you are not cheated of the little you have. Jerez society is already buzzing with the news of your arrival. In a day or two they will start calling, swarming around, seeing what you are like. You will need someone like me or you will make many, and probably fatal, mistakes. There are very few women like me in Jerez. Most of them are idle and stupid. They laugh at me and would ignore me except that they know I am clever, and they are a little afraid."

My mother poured again. She said, in a tone of gentle amusement, "You seem remarkably sure of yourself, señorita."

María Luisa nodded. "I am. I've learned to be. It is the only way I survive. I'm the last of six daughters, all of the others pretty and married. I was left with my foolish father, who lost his money—gambling, bad business ventures, thrown away on mistresses." She uttered the word without coyness. "Now, happily, he is dead, and I do not have to stay with him to be the dutiful daughter in his dotage. But I am tired of being passed back and forth among my sisters, like a chair to be sat on. I am jealous of them, of course. Four of them made very good marriages—that was when my father was able to provide dowries. By the time my turn came there was

114

no money, and who would look at someone like me who has no money?" She added, with a twisted smile, "They must have known how I was going to turn out when I was baptized. I was given the name of the ugliest queen Spain ever had."

My mother sipped her wine, leaned back in her chair, eyes closed. "I really don't know what to say." She waved her hand without opening her eyes. "Talk to Charlie about it. You will learn that Charlie is much more practical than I."

"That I know already." Our eyes met, and I experienced not a feeling of pity but a sense of relief. This woman, I thought, was quite merciless, not just with others but with herself. The pain that was revealed in her own description of herself was flawed by not a trace of self-pity. Only one doubt came to my mind, and I voiced it.

"Tell me—and tell me truthfully. Has Don Paulo sent you? Are you here to 'look after' us, at his suggestion? His command, perhaps I should say."

The smile again twisted the thin lips. "So you have his measure, have you? Then you are not a fool. Yes, he would have sent someone to try to 'look after' you, as you put it, if he had thought of it first. No, he did not send me. If he had asked me I would not have come. I have performed many thankless tasks in my life, but I have never been a paid spy."

"But surely to come to us for nothing—for the little you say you need—that isn't much better than thankless."

"You must let me be the judge of that. This is not a Spanish household. I was born a lady, and here I can be one, even if I run the kitchen. I am not a duenna or an old aunt sitting in the corner. I can use my wits to help you, and I need that. And besides, I *am* being paid. A little."

"Paid?" I started forward, and my mother opened her eyes. "By whom?"

"You have a friend. I knew him when he was here. A shrewd and clever man who never made the mistake of ignoring me. His name then was Richard Selwin—now Lord Blodmore. He was poor, with no prospects. But he

115

was handsome, and that makes a vast difference. He was permitted to practice his charm, use his good looks. And although he always had to borrow his horses, he was a good rider. They used to lend him horses just to have them exercised. He was invited to make up the extra place at dinner tables. Clever . . . he used his opportunities. Of course, they were careful that he should know he would not be acceptable for one of their precious daughters. He understood that, and they were comfortable with him. No one seriously thought he would ever inherit from Blodmore. When he did, he was brought back here to Jerez and given the greatest prize of all, Elena.

"I used to admire him," she went on. "I used to watch to see how he would maneuver in a situation. He was more than a little of a cynic, and he knew exactly how he stood with these people here. We were almost two of a kind, and he recognized it. Whenever there was a really big party, an affair that one has to ask even the family old maid to, he always sought me out. He saw that my glass was filled, that my plate was not empty. He used to encourage me to talk, and some things I said made him laugh. Sometimes a little group would join us, and he made me feel clever and witty. A few times—a very few times—I knew what it was like to be a center of attention. I owe those times mostly to Richard Selwin. I haven't forgotten, and he hasn't forgotten. He wrote to me as soon as he knew you were coming, and made his proposition. I think he hopes you will not stay, but if you do, you will need help. Do you agree?"

I knew the question was directed at me, but I could not answer. Suddenly Richard's presence was in the room, like a light that dazzled me and which I could not escape, a hand which held me, still; it was a strange revenge of love that I had said he would never open the gate to the rose garden without remembering me. There was going to be, it seemed, between us, more than remembering. I might have persuaded myself, in time, that there really was nothing to remember, except that he kept reaching out to me. Those brief minutes on the shore, in the library, might have faded; I might have lost the early

116

summer scent of the rose garden, except that the tangible results were here with me—the annuity to my mother, Andy's presence among us, and now this strange, dynamic woman in our midst.

I gestured to my mother. She smiled, relieved, happy. "I think you will be a *great* help to us, María Luisa. Now, you will have a copita with us, won't you? It's been quite a strenuous morning. So much to try to remember . . ."

I knew both relief and dismay. María Luisa would be a help, as Richard had known. But she was one more added to the little circle, this small family which was growing up around us. I counted them off—my mother and Nanny, helpless, those two, like children; Serafina and Paco, needed, but also needing to be watched, which was what María Luisa had warned us of; the nephews, Pepe and Jaime, needed also, as one always seemed to need young boys, but these would in time grow to demand more than boys; Andy . . . My thoughts ran on and on. It now seemed a frighteningly large group, though there had been more at Clonmara. But Clonmara was home, and one knew how to deal with things at home. I looked at María Luisa again; María Luisa knew how to deal with things in Jerez, and that was her function. Richard Blodmore had once again sent a gift, not a showy gift, like Balthasar and Half Moon, but perhaps one much more valuable.

2

María Luisa barely touched her wine during lunch, which in the usual Spanish fashion wasn't served to us until almost three o'clock. She also ate abstemiously, I noticed. By now arrangements had been made for Nanny to have her meals in a room near the kitchen. "I can't eat with the family, Miss Charlie," she had said. "But I'm not going to eat with those chattering monkeys in the kitchen, either." So when Paco had cleared the last of the dishes, and the port had been placed by my mother's hand, María Luisa drew her chair closer to the table and leaned forward.

"I should tell you about Don Paulo," she said. "The man is very powerful in Jerez, and he is now related to you—however loosely—by marriage. He is anxious to buy back your share of the bodega—" I had already told them that; there seemed no reason to keep the information from María Luisa. "To know at least a little of his history will help you. . . ."

The story spun out into the hours of the siesta. "The Fernández family have been nobles since before the time of Isabel and Fernando, but they gave their greatest service to the Crown at the time the last of the Moors were driven out of Spain, and so their estates were principally in Andalucía, gifts of Their Catholic Majesties. Unfortunately, most of Andalucía is regarded as the poorest part of Spain, and estates had necessarily to be large to pay. Titles the Fernández family have—a string of them. The Santander title, which Don Paulo uses, came for service when the French were being driven out of Spain, and it was earned while fighting with Wellington. Some marriages at certain times brought money into the family, and some only brought more noble blood, and perhaps another title, which they didn't need. They may once have been rich when the gold was flowing into Spain from the Americas, but in the last hundred or so years they've fallen on hard times. They seemed to have the unhappy knack of marrying a girl with a good dowry or a fine estate, and somehow the dowry was spent or the estate lost. Don Paulo followed his heart when he married the first time—can you imagine such a man following his heart, or even being in love?—and the girl had little money. They say she was very beautiful, and she brought a dowry of poor mountain land as bare as if the goats had grazed it. They had one son, who died as an infant, and one daughter, who died when she was about seventeen. Don Paulo's wife died at the birth of the daughter, and everyone expected him to look for a marriage that would bring money, which he needed. His sherry business needed new capital. But he did nothing, made no move towards finding a new wife. He just carried on, growing his vines, trying to build his business. Perhaps no woman with a suitable fortune was available, and he had lost his romantic notions of love matches. He had mistresses, of course—most men have—but he didn't marry."

"You seem to know a good deal about him," I said. "But this first marriage must have been before you were born."

She shrugged. "What have women to do in a place like this except to gossip—to pass on stories? Especially if one is plain and is always left in the corner talking to the old aunts. And don't forget—one of my names is Fernández."

My mother nodded sympathetically, but being left in a corner gossiping was a situation she had never experienced.

María Luisa continued: "So Don Paulo went on, putting as good a face on things as he could—Spaniards will do anything rather than admit we are poor. We wear better clothes than we can afford and never let anyone see the inside of our houses lest they discover we live off bean soup. Of course things weren't too bad with Don Paulo, but still he was not a rich man. His treasure was in his vineyards, his nose for sherry, and his daughter Mariana. Now I do remember *her*—she was just a few years older than I, but even to me she looked like something from a fairy tale. She was quite uncommonly beautiful, and accomplished. She was, and did, all the things that men find delightful in women. She was never one of your bland little beauties without a brain in their head or a word of sense to throw to anyone. A good musician, a rider, several languages. Oh, Don Paulo guessed early what her value would be, and he squeezed out money for her education. She was being groomed for a high place, and that could only come through marriage. *She* would not be permitted to give her heart away, as he had done. Or if she did it would only be her heart, not herself, unless the two went together in the right place. I don't know about her heart, but her hand was going in the right place when she was betrothed to the eldest son of the

119

Duque de Burgos—a grandee of Spain, with money to match his titles. The young man had come down here to hunt at Doñana in company with the King. He met Mariana, who was then only sixteen. But he would hear of marrying no one else but this angel. He was prepared to wait forever for her, he said. They say there was much discussion and dissent, because he had been expected to marry a royal princess. But he was a young man in love. . . . In the end his father had to give his consent to the betrothal." María Luisa shrugged her thin shoulders, indicating that the ways of lovers were inexplicable.

"And then the Marquesa de Pontevedra came to her estate at Sanlúcar, which is just across the river from Doñana. She only came in the hunting season, and we in Jerez saw little of her. It was the first time she had visited here since the deaths of her brothers, and her inheritance of the titles and estates. Visiting all of *them* could have made a decent year's pilgrimage, believe me. They say she came to please her English lover, who wanted to visit Córdoba and Sevilla, and to hunt at Doñana. At least we called him her English lover. He was, of course, Irish. Lord Blodmore."

My mother set down her glass. "And *we* called her the Spanish Woman. It was easier than remembering all the titles. She made an enormous impression in Ireland. They haven't forgotten, to this day. I remember my father was counted the luckiest man in Ireland because it seemed she would marry him. She was *rich* . . ."

"You well may say it, Lady Patricia. She was rich. I wouldn't doubt that she is even richer now. Pontevedra was the only title she used, though there are others. She has Hapsburg blood in her, as well as Bourbon. The title has the right of descent through the female line, so she had it all. Oddly enough, she would have made a much more suitable match for the Burgos son than little Mariana Fernández, but these things seldom work out logically once you admit the fact of someone falling in love. Then, too, the Marquesa was a little older than he, but whoever heard of that stopping a suitable match? Oh, she had it all. Estates in Catalonia that the family had had for generations, and of course that led right into owning a large part of the industry of Barcelona. She owns whole avenues in Madrid, and a palace there. The estate in Galicia is said to be the size of a small kingdom. Her father bought heavily into Río Tinto mines—the family owned large parcels of land in Huelva Province, as well as their holdings around Sanlúcar."

"She was not beautiful," my mother said musingly. " 'Handsome' is a better word. Tall. Very regal. I remember being a little bit afraid of her when she was at Clonmara. What a funny, small place she must have thought Ireland. But she must have liked it. She stayed the whole summer . . ."

María Luisa took up the telling. "So Lord Blodmore followed her to Madrid, and came with her to Sanlúcar. People said she was in love, this woman who had so much money and a great deal of power. But she could not give herself easily. She could have had almost anyone, but she fell in love with the Irishman. It is hard to imagine a woman like that marrying for love. Money and power seem to marry each other. In her terms, Blodmore had little of either. She brought him here to parties in Jerez and didn't seem to care that people knew they were lovers. They visited everywhere together. All doors were open to them. She took an interest in the sherry business —she had vineyards and bodegas of her own in Sanlúcar. It was through her that Blodmore invested money with Don Paulo. Blodmore seemed at home here in Jerez. He seemed to enjoy himself. He issued many invitations for people to come to his place in Ireland. By then we here had begun to think that it would be yet another estate of the Marquesa de Pontevedra's. We were used to *her* commanding everything. But Blodmore seemed to hold back from her just a little. He was used to *his* way too, and she wanted everything from him. They seemed to enjoy each other's company so much, those two, but there were stories that they also quarreled fiercely—and then made it up again. Neither seemed quite willing to bend completely to the other. But still, we thought they *would* marry. Such talk it caused. I remember it all so well."

María Luisa paused to sip her wine, savoring her next part of the tale. "Then—suddenly everything was changed. Blodmore left the Pontevedra estate at Sanlúcar. He came here to Jerez, stayed for a few days in an inn, refusing all invitations. The next thing we knew he had bought this house and moved into it, all within a day or two. He lived in only a few rooms of it, employed few servants, and went nowhere, saw no one. He went riding—alone. He seemed to us like a man gone mad, fallen into melancholy. We had thought him temperamental, excitable, but this behavior was more than strange. It could have been a lover's quarrel, we said, more serious than any other. But the gossip was that the Marquesa had finally decided not to marry him, had cast him out as a lover. We guessed he would not accept the decision and was waiting here in Jerez with the hope she would change her mind.

"Then Don Paulo announced that he and the Marquesa had married—married secretly somewhere about the time Blodmore left Sanlúcar. It caused a sensation. No one had any notion that the Marquesa paid any special attention to Don Paulo. He had been invited to Sanlúcar to join the hunting parties which went over to Doñana from Sanlúcar, but while Blodmore was about the Marquesa had eyes for no one else. It seemed just possible that Don Paulo had caught her in the aftermath of a quarrel with Blodmore and she had chosen capriciously to show her power, to show that she could marry whenever and whomever she pleased. I will tell you Don Paulo was counted the luckiest man in Spain. All that money!—and a woman whose titles exceeded his own. But there could have been little time for celebration— for him to rejoice in his good fortune. The word came that the Marquesa had contracted smallpox. Don Paulo and his daughter Mariana were there at Sanlúcar. No one can imagine why he did not send Mariana away from Sanlúcar immediately—why he risked having her exposed to the infection. So careless . . . so careless of the Marquesa in the first place. It was possible to be vac-

cinated, though people were afraid of that still. But yet
. . . when her beauty counted for so much . . . But
Mariana stayed, and the news came that she had contracted the pox and then, very shortly afterwards, that
she had died. There were so many confusing stories at
the time . . . she was alive, she was dead . . . that she,
in fact, had contracted smallpox first and infected the
Marquesa." María Luisa shrugged. "When people like Don
Paulo and the Marquesa do not wish to talk, few dare to
question them. The triumph of Don Paulo was in ashes.
They said he truly loved Mariana. No one could ever
say with certainty that he had loved the Marquesa. His
only child was dead, his beloved child—and his marriage
to the woman who was responsible for that death was
only begun. What is that English proverb—Marry in
haste . . . ?"

". . . repent at leisure," I finished for her impatiently.

"Yes, that's it. At leisure. It almost seemed to us here
that Don Paulo had no marriage at all beyond a contract.
The Marquesa recovered, unmarked by the pox. She
went to her castle at Arcos with Don Paulo, and no one
saw them for some time. The tales were that she had
left . . . that she was back again. No one knew the truth
any more, so any rumor had credit. The bodega saw very
little of Don Paulo in those days. It was the only time he
had ever been known to neglect his business."

"And my grandfather?"

"Still in Jerez. Shut up in this place like a recluse.
Boxes of books coming, a few bits of furniture bought.
What he hoped to achieve by staying, no one could
imagine. It was as if he had had an illness, a terrible
shock, and could not shake it off. But time passed, and
one day we realized that he was gone. He had kept so
much to himself, he could have been gone for months
before anyone noticed. A servant or two were left here.
And the house just settled down to its dust and spiders,
and has remained so all these years. To tell you the truth
—though no doubt you can deny it—we thought him
perhaps just a little mad."

My mother sighed, and reached for the port again.

"You would not be the first to suggest that the Blodmores are just a little mad. Perhaps that was why the Spanish Woman—the Marquesa . . . Oh well, what does it matter? My father missed his chance, and Don Paulo took the prize."

"*She* took Don Paulo," María Luisa corrected. "We have never considered it much of a marriage. There have been no children. When they see each other it is like a formal engagement. When the Marquesa comes to this part of the world she generally stays at her *palacio* at Sanlúcar, while Don Paulo remains here at his house, Las Fuentes, in Jerez. When it is required, he will go to Madrid to be with her if it is some great court occasion. He is at Sanlúcar when she brings her guests for the hunting at Doñana. For the rest of the time she lives a life of complete freedom. Tales drift back. She travels. Paris for clothes, the London season, shooting in Scotland, gambling at Deauville. They say she still takes lovers—at her age! That could be just talk, since she seems to live a quieter life now, to stay more often in Spain. Her private life has been the subject of scandal, and the Church frowns on her—and yet what can they do? She supports so many churches on her estates. She gives handsomely when asked for help. Most importantly, she has the tacit consent of her husband in whatever she does, so the Church shuts its eyes to the scandal and takes the money."

"And Don Paulo permits it all . . ." my mother mused.

"He doesn't care, I believe," María Luisa countered. "Apparently it was no love match right from the beginning. But Don Paulo has himself profited mightily." She tapped the table with a long finger. "From the Marquesa came the money with which he expanded his vineyards and his bodegas until he became the greatest of the sherry growers and shippers. With money borrowed from her he has expanded in many directions. He began to irrigate his farm land, making it more fertile. He began to breed bulls and experiment with new strains of cattle. He grows wheat, olives, sugar beets—a hand in everything. He has ventured beyond Spain to make more money. He is said to be heavily involved in railways in South America. They even say he has profited from the opium trade in China. With the Marquesa's money he has become a rich man in his own right—and by doing that has entirely reversed the history of the Fernández family."

"The Marquesa *lent* him money—or gave it? I thought a dowry was the husband's to spend."

María Luisa gave a dry laugh. "I doubt the Marquesa would *give* money as well as herself. In fact, soon after their marriage Don Paulo accepted as his partner in the bodega a distant cousin of the Marquesa's—Don Luis de Villa Thompson—who was living here in Jerez and, apart from his own sherry business, was managing the Marquesa's estates at Sanlúcar. I would say she imposed the partnership on Don Paulo to protect her own interests. And I would judge that every peseta borrowed from her has been repaid with interest by Don Paulo. She is lavish with her money, but no fool."

I was remembering the events of that morning, the walk through the bodega, the strangely yearning love Don Paulo had evidenced for his son. "Carlos . . . ?" I said. "Don Paulo himself told me he is illegitimate."

"All the world knows that. Not only Carlos but his two half brothers, Ignacio and Pedro, who have yet different mothers, one supposes. While the Marquesa was enjoying herself all over Europe was Don Paulo supposed to live like a monk? He has acknowledged his sons, given them his name, and the Marquesa has countenanced it. Perhaps because their mothers are unknown. The Marquesa has had no rivals in importance or position. Probably the mothers were peasant girls from one or other of the estates, grateful that their children should be brought up as gentlemen, and perhaps a small pension, or a few hectares of land for the family. There is even the story that the mother of Carlos was a gypsy, though gypsies do not readily give up their children. So . . . in spite of the barrenness of the Marquesa, Don Paulo has his sons. It is evident that Carlos is the favorite. Between them, Don Paulo and the Marquesa will arrange a good marriage for him, even if his mother is a gypsy—or whoever she is. There was even some talk that the Marquesa's niece, Elena . . . but I never believed *that!*"

"Don Paulo has so much," I said, "and yet he still wants the small piece of the bodega my grandfather owned. What can it matter to him?"

"To a man like Don Paulo the fact that an outsider, Blodmore, who almost succeeded in winning the Marquesa, should own even a tiny fraction of his business must be like a bur under the saddle. Don Luis he must tolerate because it is a family arrangement, and advantageous. But Blodmore . . . think of it! Rivals all those years ago, and Blodmore was permitted to buy shares in the bodega at a time when Don Paulo must have been desperate for money. Blodmore was probably only the first of those Don Paulo was searching for to invest with him—invest but have no say in running the bodega. And only a few weeks later, by marriage to the Marquesa, all the money he needed and more was available. Yes, it must rankle. A bur under the saddle. I think perhaps he would like to wipe out the memory of Blodmore."

"But he will not succeed," I said. "The Marquesa has married her niece to Richard Blodmore. So the Blodmores are with Don Paulo however he dislikes the fact."

My mother drained the glass and did not reach to refill it. "Yes—he has the Blodmores with him still. Are *we* burs under the saddle to him, do you think? Then perhaps I shall hang on here a while yet. The longer we stay, the higher he will push his price. We might come well out of it yet, Charlie. Yes, we will wait. We will take our time. . . . Perhaps what happened twenty-five years ago will serve us very well. Perhaps this is precisely what my father had meant to happen. All these years he held on, when he must have been tempted so often to sell. So we also will bide our time. . . . It's pleasant enough here, isn't it, Charlie? And now that we have María Luisa . . ." By now she was almost talking to herself. "Perhaps for once in my foolish, rash life I will do the wise thing. Don Paulo may learn that the Blodmores are not quite as mad as we seem. . . ."

And I was thinking of the enmity that had been revived each year between the two men. In my thoughts I was back

126

in the library at Clonmara with Richard Blodmore's low voice translating the words that kept it alive. *Ella está viva.* There were some things even María Luisa could not explain.

3

It is possible that we would have managed, somehow, without María Luisa, but at times I didn't know how. Her sharp eyes were on everything, missed nothing; those thin fingers poked and pried and fixed and manipulated; her tongue, even in the mellifluous Spanish which I didn't yet understand, made acid and biting comments, gave orders to Serafina and Paco which they obeyed without question. Yes, it is possible we would have managed, but not nearly so well.

In short, we were organized by her. I tried to learn the way she did it, but it was a skill born of age and experience, and a lifetime spent, as she put it, "talking with the old aunts." If there was anything she didn't know, she would soon make it her business to know; if there was a cheaper way to do something, she would find it. How she worked, that woman. For her, the Spanish siesta hardly existed. She was impatient with the requisite hour or so when everyone rested in the heat of the day, and she would spend her time writing notes to herself, juggling strings of figures, making lists of things to do. It was from María Luisa that I began to feel that I might learn to do more than ride a horse.

First of all we made the dining room and the room where we had first met Don Paulo immaculate. "Leave the rest to the dust and spiders until we need them," María Luisa counseled as she waxed the furniture with her own hands. "We must have somewhere to receive." She had the supreme assurance of a born lady who did not fear to soil her hands—but equally she would have died before letting any other than members of the household see her so engaged. Together she and I combed the house for what little in ornamentation it would yield.

The bedrooms were stripped of their little pieces of china so that they might make a show for visitors downstairs. A crystal chandelier was moved from the principal bedroom where my mother slept, washed with great care, and hung in the drawing room. "What a pity Lord Blodmore did not buy more once he started," María Luisa commented. "To set up house here was madness, but at least he might have finished his lunacy."

Daily there were Spanish lessons. At first she tried to insist on my mother's presence, but even María Luisa's determination faltered in the face of my mother's good-natured sloth. María Luisa shrugged. "Oh well," she admitted, "what does it matter, after all? A woman as beautiful as that . . . the men will forgive her anything, and the women will be jealous in any case. So they will all practice their English on her, and she will pick up a little Spanish, a few words. She soon enough learned how to ask Paco to bring the wine. . . ." Then she pointed her sharp finger at me. "But you, Carlota, *you* must learn. You are young. You don't have a bad mind, but a lazy one. I think this Ireland of yours must be a very relaxed place. Oh, I know what everyone says about the Spaniards—'mañana, mañana . . .' But for most of us, if we want to eat, we must work. And so must you—for different reasons."

So I struggled with Spanish genders, and with the complications of Spanish etiquette, the impossible conundrums of Spanish names. "It is simple," María Luisa said. "First the father's name, and then the mother's name, and then the father's mother's name—"

"For heaven's sake. That means you have to *know* who everyone's mother was and who the father's mother was, and who the mother's father was . . ."

"In good society," she answered, "one *does* know."

From somewhere she produced the legendary little seamstress who could turn a sow's ear into a silk purse. "Your clothes," María Luisa said, "are a disgrace. You are clothed like a girl in a schoolroom. Your mother has not noticed that you have grown up." The woman toiled late into the nights to produce dresses for me, dresses María Luisa said I would be fit to be seen in, simple

128

dresses that cost little money but, with María Luisa's eye for line and detail, were surprisingly effective. I was startled by the new being that emerged in the mirror, someone older, with an unfamiliar touch of style. María Luisa clung to her own eternal black. "I did not come to spend your money," she said. "There's always someone to be in mourning for—the father of a third cousin, one of the old aunts." She snapped her fingers. "A fresh ribbon now and again, a bit of lace. People have stopped looking at me a long time ago. It's better that way. But for *you*—this is your time to be looked at!" So she sent to Seville for muslins and dimities and taffetas, and beautiful green cloth for a new riding habit.

"Lord, Miss Charlie!" Andy exclaimed. "I hardly knew you! A fine lady you've become!"

My mother was pleased. "Why, darling, you're going to be a beauty! What that color does for your eyes—and we must try a lemon rinse in your hair." Then she looked pleadingly at María Luisa. "When the señorita has finished with Charlie's things, do you think I could have a dress or two? Nothing extravagant, of course . . . I wouldn't want to spend a lot of money. I had such terrible dressmaker bills in Dublin. Poor things—I never have paid them. It's wicked, isn't it, how people like me go off and leave their bills unpaid? We should try to pay something on account. Perhaps Richard Blodmore . . ." And then her expression stiffened. "No! We must not ask any more from Richard Blodmore. We are too much in his debt." Then she sighed, looking at my new finery.

"A few dresses for the warm weather, Lady Patricia," María Luisa conceded.

"But this is *hot* weather now!"

"Wait until August," was the answer. "August is like a taste of hell."

So María Luisa polished and dressed me, like the crystal chandelier and the few ornaments the house contained; then she produced an ancient landau, hired cheaply from a livery stable, and two horses. Andy turned his nose up at all three, but he set to work to brush and groom and trim, to paint, and tack back the pieces of frayed upholstery. "You'll never make beauties of those two," he said, eying the horses, "but with a bit of decent feeding, and a good rubdown every day, they'll not be such a disgrace." He worked eagerly and well, and the boys, Pepe and Jaime, worked with him. I loved to hear the sound of his whistle in the stable yard. It was like home. And then I would remind myself not to call it "home" any more. I was never going home; I would never see Richard Blodmore again. I kept saying those two things to myself over and over, and still I didn't believe them.

The horses of Jerez excited our admiration and envy. It wasn't just the riding horses, but the carriage horses as well. The Andalucian horseman had developed his own style which came out of the country itself, and the needs which the horses served. They used a much heavier, higher-backed saddle than we were accustomed to—though we saw plenty of English saddles as well—because the horse had been used on the Andalucian plains so long as a work animal among the cattle. "It is obviously easier to stay in a saddle like that all day," my mother said. "I must have a saddle like that for Balthasar. And I should get some trousers and ride astride. Just imagine, Charlie —the bloodlines of these horses go back to 1579, someone told me—I don't remember who. . . ." For all of us the sight of the carriage horses was a daily treat. They pulled every imaginable sort of vehicle; beautifully matched horses, two, four, in harness, and the style which until now we had never seen of five-in-hand, three horses leading, two behind. The drivers we thought were almost as magnificent as the horses. They knew themselves the sight they made in their Andalucian dress, the short jackets, the round hats, the high tassled boots, and they enjoyed it. The harness for the carriage horses was often embellished with silver, and there was, to us, the delightful custom of adding small clusters of woolen balls, in different colors, to the harness, which bobbed with the horse's every movement. The effect was one of gaiety and charm. "Oh, Charlie, aren't they just beautiful! Have you ever seen anything like the way they turn, so smoothly? Oh, I'd love to have a go at driving a team like that. I see some ladies do. . . ." The last was said wistfully. We had seen ladies mounted on the box with an attendant coachman. My mother would drag her eyes reluctantly from that vision of splendid arrogance and beauty to the sight of our rather poor little pair pulling our old landau. "Ah, well, we have Balthasar, and Half Moon, and I've not yet seen anything finer than Balthasar. . . ."

One of the first things María Luisa did was to arrange our visit to the bank. Don Ramón García greeted us with grave courtesy and evident appreciation of my mother's beauty. He held her hand an unduly long time. Me he looked over with interest, and gave María Luisa hardly a glance. He had been seeing her all his life, and, as she said, people had almost ceased to see her. She didn't mind; those who were invisible as well as clever could do almost anything.

We drank copitas with Don Ramón, and talked anything but money for more than half an hour. We talked horses and hunting and how we did it in Ireland. He told us of the wild boar hunts at Doñana, the culling of the great deer herds in the autumn. He was not, he said, indicating his bulk, a great sportsman himself, but he had an eye for a horse—and a woman too, I thought. He was a fair shot, he said, and that started my mother talking about my grandfather's guns, and how he himself had taught her how to use them. He remembered my grandfather. "Oh, I was very young. Just begun in the bank under my father. We do most of our business with the sherry shippers. A remarkably fine gentleman, Doña Patricia. A great horseman . . ."

He would have gone on, and so would my mother, but María Luisa brought them to the point. "Don Ramón, the money situation, if you please. Lady Patricia cannot carry on here long if she has no money, can she? She must order her accounts—know exactly how much she may spend."

For a banker he gave a marvelous impersonation of a man who has an aristocratic disdain for money. He could

131

hardly bear to mention it. And I almost laughed aloud at the thought of my mother ordering her accounts. It was such a lovely little game we all played, and yet, as in everything, the money was of deadly importance.

He rang and ordered the ledgers brought in, as if he had not known in advance that we were coming. Beautiful books, they were, bound in fine red Spanish leather and tooled in gold. In such books, I thought, they would post, those clerks in the outer offices, whether one had assets or debts. I thought the debts should have been in black-bound books—but debts were always posted in red ink. There had been a lot of red ink in the life of the Blodmores in the past twenty-odd years.

Don Ramón turned the books on the desk for our scrutiny. My mother's brow wrinkled in puzzlement. "See, Doña Patricia, here in my own hand—a young boy all those years ago. This is where Don Paulo makes his first payment of a percentage of the profits of what he shipped that year. Lord Blodmore was very fortunate he made that investment. It has not given him a great return, but it has been consistent and steady—growing a little each year—except for the time of the phylloxera, and no one— *no one*—in Jerez earned money in those years.

"However," and here his face creased, as if he didn't like to give bad news, "Don Paulo might have needed money then, but he was, as ever, no fool. He gave your father, Lord Blodmore, only a small percentage of the bodega, and the produce of certain vineyards which he *then* owned. It did not include an interest in future development. In effect, the profit was to be paid to Lord Blodmore and was not to be used to reinvest as more vineyards came into production and more bodegas were built and filled with wine. What Don Paulo has done is to organize his affairs so that there are several companies within the organization. If Lord Blodmore had been able to gain a percentage of the total, he might have made a good deal of money. No one—least of all Don Paulo, I believe—could have known that within a few weeks he, Don Paulo, would marry the richest woman in Spain and have no need for partners such as Lord Blodmore. Don

Paulo was glad to take your grandfather's money then. In a very few weeks he had no need for it. After his marriage, with the loan of money from the Marquesa, Don Paulo began an enormous program of planting vineyards and building bodegas. Lord Blodmore remained forever outside that great expansion. His share was limited to the then existing assets of Fernández—excellent, but small."

His finger traced once more the columns of figures, which now I strained to see and understand. My mother leaned back in her usual attitude of belief that someone would do the understanding for her. "For reasons he never chose to explain, Lord Blodmore made no withdrawals from this account in all these years, except to authorize payments to the people who took care of his house here and the one at the vineyard. They were very modest sums. He spent no money on repairs. . . . And, of course, the interest on the capital sum we added each year."

"Just as well he made no withdrawals." My mother suddenly woke from the sort of dream, like a spell, which the memories of the Spanish Woman seemed to cast on her. "It would have followed everything else to the money men in London. It would have been spent. It would have bought a few more horses . . ." She gestured swiftly, impatiently. "Don Ramón, please show the figures to Doña María Luisa. She has our complete confidence."

The ledger was turned towards her. The black eyes studied the figures for a few minutes while we waited in total silence. Finally she raised her head, looking questioningly at my mother.

"Can we live on it, María Luisa?"

An almost imperceptible nod. "With prudence—touching the capital sum hardly at all, since it is one of your few assets, Lady Patricia—with prudence, we may live off the profits paid in annually." Don Ramón was already nodding his head. I knew my mother would be sorely tempted to put her hand on the accumulated sum, and there would be a short burst of fine horses and new dresses. But she had been frightened. Or perhaps the weight of both María Luisa and Don Ramón were too much for her. She did not protest.

She rose to her feet. Don Ramón sprang to his. "Don Ramón, I thank you for your gracious hospitality and your time. You have kept my father's trust faithfully. For that my daughter and I owe you double thanks."

He bowed low, and actually allowed his lips to touch her hand. "Forever at your service, Doña Patricia. If there is the smallest way I can be of assistance . . ." He, like so many others, had almost literally been swept off his feet by her beauty, her wonderful presence. He rushed to open the door. While he was bowing my mother through the bank's outer offices, I glanced at María Luisa's face. It was thoughtful, as if she were already planning how best the money could be used, and how far Don Ramón's offer of help could be extended. "It depends, of course . . ." she said in a low tone to me, as if thinking aloud, and as if I were the natural companion of her thoughts. "It depends on how well the money continues to come from Fernández, Thompson. We had better start lighting a few more candles for good harvests. . . ."

We were escorted to the newly painted landau, which put on a brave show but would deceive no one. I suppose it was about then I began to think our life in Jerez had begun.

We attended Mass at the church across the plaza, Santa María de la Asunción, and at the Collegiate Church. María Luisa bowed to everyone, and the bows were returned, along with stares. We were inspected and appraised. Among the "old aunts" of María Luisa's acquaintanceship, and among some of the elderly gentlemen, the name of Blodmore was murmured, and old memories revived. They inquired where we lived, and the address also stirred half-forgotten thoughts—the old questions about why Blodmore had so precipitately bought the place, and so swiftly left it to take care of itself, were revived.

They came to call, the old aunts and the elderly gentle-

men, some young matrons and the young girls they
chaperoned. María Luisa's sisters came. There were eager
questions about Clonmara and how Doña Elena liked her
new home. Among the young ones there were questions
about Richard Blodmore, whom they had known as Richard Selwin. The answers to these questions came painfully
and stiffly to my lips. I could often feel my mother's
eyes upon me as I answered, and she was herself unusually
restrained. The talk of Clonmara hurt her; even to think
of Richard hurt me. So the eagerly gossiping ladies and
the elderly gentlemen of Jerez got little enough information on either subject.

In our turn we repaid the calls. Some of the houses
could truly be described as "palacios"; others were smaller.
Some were richly maintained with great, wonderful gardens; others showed the kind of benign neglect and lack
of money which our own house betrayed. We visited old
ladies in mansions behind half-closed shutters and high
walls, and others in suites of rooms built around small
courtyards in the middle of the town. They were all, I
thought, gracious and hospitable, eager to practice or
show off their English, glad of new faces in their society,
anxious to know every small thing about us, barely con-
cealing their curiosity and asking questions that probed
as deeply as politeness allowed. There was much speculation, I guessed, about my mother. To be married and
living apart from one's husband was unusual in that
society where women often seemed the chattels of their
husbands. Her beauty was commented on, admired, and
her impetuous nature gave promise of more delicious
gossip to come. As women do everywhere, they licked
their lips and waited.

Pepita was with us wherever we went. When we drove
she walked beside us. "Big as she is," Andy said, "she's
still a young one, and she needs the exercise to develop
properly." She waited, like a lady, in the landau while
we paid our visits. Nanny regarded her with repugnance,
María Luisa with tolerance tinged with dismay at the
amount of money it cost to feed her; my mother adored

135

her, as she adored most animals and young things. For me, she had become a sort of companion of my heart. She was always at my side, slept by my bed, listened to my whispered longings for times that were past and things that were gone. Her beautiful, sad face regarded mine in a patient effort to understand what I said. Even in the short time she had been with us she seemed to have grown still bigger, until at times she appeared to me like a young lioness. She gave me something on which to focus my love. I knew this, and knew I asked too much from a mere animal. But she gave, and wanted to give. And I took, and tried to give back.

We grew used to the rhythm of life—the strangely late mealtimes, the siesta. As the days passed the younger men began to present themselves in my mother's drawing room. As the hot days gave place to warm evenings, they came, either singly or in pairs, escorting a sister or a cousin who had already visited us. "I don't know whether they come for you or your mother," María Luisa said to me, "but neither of you is eligible. Lady Patricia is married . . . impossible. *You* have no money. A young man in Spain may fall in love, but he rarely marries for love only. The families see to that."

It was very hot; no breeze stirred the warm night air. The visitors and the late supper had made me tired and irritable. I was tired of the exhausting dance my mother and I tried to perform to a strange music. I snapped at María Luisa. "You think it's only in Spain that happens? It is all wrong—and cruel. Every place. Without money, a girl doesn't have a chance."

Her sharp eyes seemed to soften, a thing almost impossible to imagine in María Luisa. "And you think I don't know *that*? Who better than I?" She patted my hand lightly. "Try not to think too much of it. Sometimes . . . who knows? Who knows what may happen? Go to bed now, *querida*. . . . Be fresh for what tomorrow brings."

I watched as she went to blow out the candles that remained. For her, the time for hoping was past.

Protestingly, María Luisa took us to visit the house at the vineyard. "There is nothing there. The vineyard houses are not places to live. They are for the foremen, the managers. Oh yes, there are some rooms for when the owner takes a fancy to visit, but no one *lives* there. And in the case of the Blodmore place . . ." She shrugged. "Who knows what we will find? Paco has had a cousin living there for these past twenty years. Merely to keep the gypsies out. There are no vines. He tends a few patches of vegetables, keeps a few goats, a cow, some chickens. They live rent free, with a tiny sum provided from Don Ramón at Lord Blodmore's bidding all those years ago. And the roof leaks."

But we went. Andy drove the landau with María Luisa and Nanny in it; my mother rode Balthasar and I Half Moon. Pepita walked beside us. Word had been sent ahead by Paco, but still we carried food and wine with us. "A picnic in the country," María Luisa said. "Better to treat it that way, and you will not embarrass Paco's cousin and his wife." She had odd kindnesses in her, as well as great practicality.

I was growing used to the countryside around Jerez—the low sweeping plain of Andalucía that rose in gentle slopes where the vines were spread in long straight rows and hid the ripening grapes with the thick roughness of their leaves. Where the soil was not suitable for grapes there were olive groves, and sometimes cork trees, red where their bark had been stripped. The unrelenting sun always seemed to cast a spell over me, so that it was a sort of dream landscape, at once gentle and fierce. I would turn my eyes away from the slopes where the vines grew, and there, somewhere off in the distance, I would catch the black outlines of the sierra breaking the haze of heat. Sometimes the dark wings of a vulture stooped and hovered, and then the bird sped off to its mountain eyrie. The tinkle of the goat bells rose on the air; the goatherd would lift the ragged brim of a wide hat to us. And out of the dust a fine carriage would appear, with liveried driver and footman; polite hands would be waved to us, a few words called to María Luisa. The contrasts were so sharp, and cruel. Great wealth and poverty dwelt side by side. And when I was sometimes critical, I would remember Ireland. I remembered what I had said to María Luisa. "It is all wrong—cruel. Every place."

I reacted to the vineyard house with a passion that surprised me. It sat there, on the top of a rise, the gentle swell of the land undulating about it, looking to other rises above other vineyards also crowned with their own white houses, against which the purple bougainvillaea flamed. I held Half Moon quiet for some minutes while the others rattled into the courtyard. A light breeze fanned the sweat on my forehead and neck, and in the sky pushed tiny, puffy clouds before it, so that the shadows ran across the vines, light and dark, dark and light, like the swell of a sea, like the ripples on a pond. A stab of homesickness swept through me. I rode Half Moon into the courtyard and dismounted without help from Andy.

A smiling youngish woman, the second wife of Antonio, cousin to Paco, showed us through the house. Her name was Concepción; she was dark-eyed and had once been beautiful. The child she carried on her hip and the young ones about her skirts had wearied her beyond her years. But she was proud of the simple things she did to keep the vineyard house presentable. The tiled floors were polished, the whitewashed rooms were clean. There were a few pieces of lovely, simple dark oak furniture, also polished. Great sweeping chimney breasts gave the rooms character. There was a marvelous simplicity in that place—bare, austere, with clean, uncluttered lines. It was the first time I had been aware of beauty of quite that character; it was the first time I was aware of something which was, at its heart, truly Spanish. A feeling of love for the place swept over me, and the wave of homesickness receded.

"It's beautiful," I breathed to María Luisa. "I should like to live here."

For the first time she stared at me completely without understanding. "You are mad," she said quite simply. "I

138

have told you no one lives in their vineyard house. Only if you are very poor, and then you don't count. It is a plaything—a place for short visits, for picnics. You would have no company here . . . no society."

"I wouldn't care," I muttered, and went on to walk the dim shaded rooms, to re-emerge into the aching glare of the courtyard with its stone-faced well and row upon row of clay pots brilliant with scarlet geraniums. The children played here, and they trooped about me as I went once again to the great arch and looked out over the vineyards. It was easy to see where the land my grandfather had bought began and ended. On each side the demarcation line was plain. His land was overgrown with scrubby brush. If any vines still existed, they bore no fruit. Small patches about the house had been cleared, and Antonio farmed crops of corn, alfalfa, beets—there were rows of tomatoes, cucumbers, peppers; chickens scratched the stony ground, goats were tethered to browse what they could from the brush; there was a lean pig in a pen. But beyond, where the land was tended, there was orderly beauty. The long straight lines of vines were trained on their low trellises, the ground between them hoed and clean of weeds. I stared at it a long time, and then put my hand down and gathered some of the soil that nourished this pale grape from which the wine was sprung. It was strangely grayish white in color, this albariza, and seemed full of small, sharp stones—curious soil from which to gather such a harvest. I think it was at this moment that I was first aware of the desire to see this ground cleared, to see the straggling brush give way to the ordered vines, to see the pale grape grown on this, our own land. It was madness. I let the soil dribble back from my hand to where it had come from, and shrugged. The children, who had been silent, watching me intently as I scrutinized what was their home and their only horizon, began to laugh softly, from shyness. We could exchange few words, but dark eyes looked into mine and smiled. I smiled back and went to join the others for lunch.

139

A snowy, darned cloth was spread on the table in the big main room, and clay bowls of the delicious cold soup they called gazpacho were ready. Hard-boiled eggs were set on coarse platters decorated with grape leaves; dishes of olives were at hand, and a board of *manchego* cheese, and slices of hard, dark ham. It was Concepción's contribution to our "picnic." She showed me a bedroom, windows hung with plain white cloth and a bedspread of yellowing lace, where I could wash my hands. The towels were coarse, and so was the soap. She looked at me anxiously. "Thank you—you are very kind." I was trying out my Spanish, and she beamed in appreciation.

We had a full, leisurely lunch, Nanny grumbling gently, continuously, in the background. By now Andy was perfectly at home in a Spanish kitchen. He knew enough words to make sure he wanted for nothing. My mother liked it here, I thought. She seemed gently contented to eat quietly and drink her wine, saying little. A drowsiness stole over us. Concepción came to clear away the dishes, and through María Luisa indicated that there were beds enough if we wished to take a siesta. We did.

A bluish dusk was creeping over the landscape as we rode back to Jerez—there was the first hint of dew in the air, the nightly, soaking dew that the grapes needed. I felt a pang of regret as we descended along the track, my grandfather's ragged acres on one side, the rows of vines, patiently tended, on the other, until we reached the road that led back to Jerez. Concepción and Antonio had stood to bid us good-by, their children gathered about them. "Go with God," they called. Now all I could discern of the house I loved was a vague shape against the skyline, the faint glow of an oil lamp. Pepita had been put in the landau, and now my mother urged Balthasar forward, urged Andy to a quicker pace; for her the somnolent pleasure of the day of the picnic was over. She hastened towards the lights of the town, and wondered aloud if we would have visitors that evening. I sighed, and no one heard.

140

We may have brushed Don Paulo's path many times, but we never saw him. He did not visit our house again, and we were not invited to his. "Las Fuentes it is called," María Luisa said. "Now *there* is a palace for you. It is furnished with fine pictures and statues. Everything is velvet and silk, silver and crystal. His stables are the equal of another man's mansion. I wish he would call again, and then we might visit him, but few people go there without invitation. He is available at the bodega, as he always says, but it is a privilege one does not lightly take. His three sons live with him. They say they fight like a bag of cats for their father's favor. I wonder how long it is now since the Marquesa de Pontevedra visited? . . . It seems her husband's home is hardly good enough for her. . . ." We grew accustomed to that lively mind of María Luisa's filling us in on the details of life in Jerez. She had a natural affinity for gossip but was generally able to sift fact from rumor. We sipped our copitas and listened, while everyone and everything was dissected; we were entertained, sometimes spellbound.

"If you had been born in England, María Luisa," my mother said, "I believe you would have been a writer—a lady novelist."

"If I had been born in England—if I had been born a man—I would have been Prime Minister!"

She almost persuaded me it was the truth.

Sometimes in the salons of acquaintants we came across Carlos. He was deliciously charming, smiling, flattering both my mother and myself with the same words. I thought his gaze flickered over me with more than a little interest, but it might merely have been the new clothes. He introduced us to his two half brothers, Pedro and Ignacio. They were all markedly different, Pedro having something of his father's broad, impressive build; Ignacio was lean and dark of face, with clever, intense eyes. "Ignácio is the accountant of the family," Carlos said disparagingly. "He knows how to keep his nose in the company books."

"And you don't?"

He laughed. "It is far more important to keep in my father's good graces. Other people can keep the books."

"And Pedro—what does he do to keep your father's favor?"

"My brother Pedro cultivates his nose!" He laughed at the expression on my face. "I mean he spends his days in the *cuarto de muestras*—the sample room. That's where we keep samples of all wines we export or sell in Spain. So when a customer writes and says he wants so many butts of such and such, which he may want to bottle under his own label, we know exactly what we must send him. It's also the place where we sample the musts and fix the price to be paid to the vineyard owner, and where we decide what category a wine belongs in—and keep sampling it to see how it develops. My father has the most famous nose for sherry in all Jerez. At least no one disputes that claim to his face. It is Pedro's ambition to please him by being a nose. Myself—I think noses are born, not made."

"And have you a nose?"

He laughed with charming arrogance. "Dear Carlota, I have everything. At least I make my father *think* I have everything. That's what's important. The truth may be something different. It's what one can make other people believe that's important. But yes—I have a nose. We all spend our apprenticeship in the cuarto de muestras."

It was a rather frightening cynicism in so young a man; once I would have turned away from him in scorn, but now I didn't do that. He had, in a sense, reached out to me, breaking through my shyness, breaking through his own custom of charm and good manners, to show me a side of him that the circumstances of life had scarred and roughened. Sons of different mothers, brought up away from those mothers, they all fought for the favor of the man who had fathered them. They had been brought up with silk and velvet, and under the whip of that man's power. For a moment, behind the bragging arrogance, Carlos had betrayed the lack of security that his birth had given him. Illegitimate—bastards, all of them—none was first in the eyes of the law; they must fight to be first in the eyes of their father. And did they also seek, through their father, the favor of that unseen woman, the Marquesa—childless, and with a huge fortune to bestow? In claiming to have so much, to have "everything" as he had said, Carlos had revealed the poverty of fear and insecurity.

Most vividly of those first weeks I remember the dance. María Luisa was excited when the invitation came. "It is from Luis de Villa Thompson."

"Who?"

"You have met him," she said impatiently. "He is Don Paulo's partner at Fernández, Thompson—the one I told you of—the distant cousin of the Marquesa de Pontevedra who was put into the Fernández bodega to look after her interests. But he has money in his own right, and vineyards that are not the property of Fernández, Thompson. Oh well—you will sort it out in time. *That* is not so important. What is important is that this is the first invitation to a formal gathering. Very important for you. I must see about a dress. . . ."

"Will Don Paulo be there?"

"For a time, I would think—yes. It would be an insult to Don Luis to stay away."

So María Luisa squeezed out the money for pale green silk, and a dress was made. "You should wear your mother's pearls, but she will want to wear them herself. But then, young girls look best with flowers. . . . You will have to make do."

My mother wore emerald silk, an old ball gown refurbished, and María Luisa wore her usual black, but lace this time, to mark the occasion. "The same lace dress I've had for years. It goes everywhere." A relic of her former state was displayed in a black lace fan, its ends inlaid with mother-of-pearl; a little cameo dangled from a black ribbon on her neck. "One has to make an effort," she said, shrugging it off. But there was the faintest flush of excitement in her sallow cheeks as we set off.

I suppose it was because it would be the first and, in a way, the last ball for me that I remember it so well—or was it the composite of all the balls I had dreamed of and had never attended, and the ones I would attend in the future, when everything had changed? But I was young, I had a new dress, and I knew I looked well, even beside my mother. I was curiously innocent, and for a few hours I forgot Richard Blodmore.

Don Luis greeted us. I did remember him then from some other occasion when we had merely exchanged small courtesies. I should have remembered him better. He had the long, thin face one sees in some Spaniards; he was not handsome, but his deep brown eyes were well set, alert and kindly. With this darkness, he had the strange combination of graying hair that had once been gold. There were lines deeper than his age in a sensitive face, but he was no longer young. He was tall, lean, and seemed to have permanently hunched shoulders, one of which appeared higher than the other. He greeted us with an expression of gentle pleasure and presented us to his wife, a much younger woman, hardly more than a girl, wearing an overelaborate dress and diamonds. She was too thin, and her face was peaked with fatigue. María Luisa had said to us on our way to the party, "So sad for Luis. This is his second wife, and not a child between the two of them. Of course they say it is the fault of Luis. . . . He is not *macho*. But no son, and a good deal of money to leave . . . well, it is a pity. This girl, this Amelia he has married. Not a good choice. She hasn't the spirit to rouse any man when . . . when there are difficulties. A whining, miserable little thing I remember her as, even as a child. Always with a cold, or falling over and howling for her Nanny. The Nanny has gone to live with her and Luis. But it will be, I think, a miracle if there is a child for the Nanny to bring up. They say Amelia has taken to going to Mass every morning and lighting candles. May God hear her prayers. . . ." But she clearly thought the situation beyond God's interference.

It was a wonderful party. Every woman looked beautiful to me that night; every man was handsome. The fans waved, the tongues savored the gossip and the delicious food. The men looked closely at me, and it did not seem rude, merely flattering. I was happy because my dance card was filled almost at once. Carlos came to my side and claimed the supper dance.

"Be careful," María Luisa whispered to me once when I retired to the room where the ladies had left their wraps. "Don Paulo is here, and watching."

"Let him watch. Carlos is a man, and will make his own choice."

"Carlos is Don Paulo's son. That is more to the point."

What point, I didn't quite see. It didn't matter. I was happy. I danced, and laughed, and forgot to be overshadowed by my mother. She also danced every dance, and never once retired to the sidelines where the young matrons thought it proper to be, where the old aunts gossiped. As I swayed in the waltz with this man and that man—not all of them young but, to me that night, all of them clever and distinguished, I knew why my mother would never sit on the sidelines. I did not want to myself, and I vowed I never would. "You are very brilliant tonight," Carlos said to me. "You have opened up—like a flower."

"Yes," I said happily, and meant it. Everything seemed both true and possible that night.

The garden of Luis' great house was lighted by lamps in massive wrought-iron stands and, for this evening, by Chinese lanterns strung through the trees. I missed the dance after supper to walk with Carlos along the path to the artificial lake where an ornamental fountain played, the whisper of water welcome on that warm night. "The Moors loved the sound of water," Carlos said. "And we have it wherever we can. Someday you will see—and hear—the gardens of the Alhambra of Granada."

Swans, made restless by the unaccustomed activity, the lights, and the sounds from the house, glided like wraiths on the other side of the lake. Mixed with the white swans were some rare black ones. They and their progeny had inhabited the lake so long that the house was known as Los Cisnes—The Swans. They seemed so much a part of their majestic setting. There was no moon; the warm dark blue of the sky made an almost unreal backdrop to that extravagant blaze of stars, as if it also was something arranged especially for that grand party of Don Luis'. Carlos kissed me, as I knew he would. I found myself liking it, which was something I had not known before the moment it actually happened. He kissed me in a practiced, experienced, and deeply sensual way. With him there was no fumbling, no hasty movement, and I did not pull away from him. In time we drew apart gently, and walked on, without speaking.

After the circle of the lake we came back to the house. Two great sweeping arms of staircase curved down to the garden. As we approached, the whole throng of guests began to appear, crowding down the stairs, coming onto the balconies that overlooked them. Behind the opened shutters the chandeliers blazed, but the servants were bringing more lights, a chain of lights to set about a small area of raised platform between the house and the lake. More servants came with tiny gilt-painted chairs, and the guests moved down to take their places in a wide circle about the platform.

"We will stay here," Carlos said. " 'La Llama' is going to perform. She is the greatest exponent of flamenco in all Spain. She was born quite near here. . . ."

In an almost desultory fashion a short, slight man mounted the platform. He was dressed in very tight trousers and an elaborately embroidered jacket; his soft boots seemed to be studded with silver. He carried a guitar, and almost as if it made no difference to him whether or not he was there at all, he placed his foot on a stool and plucked a few languid notes from his instrument. And then, as if she came out of the night itself, the woman appeared. She wore her dark hair pulled back in the classic style, a carnation placed in the low knot at her neck; her dress was flame-colored, tightly fitted to just above the knees, and falling in a great cascade of frills below that. She was neither young nor old, not particularly beautiful;

146

but she carried an air of immense authority. On the instant of her appearance the chatter among the guests died. In silence she stood on the platform, commanding those all about her. She waited—it seemed an age—before the first smallest movement of her arm; very slowly it rose behind her head, her body arched backward, and then for the first time in my life I heard the dialogue of the castanets with the guitar, knew the subtle, wild, passionate magic of the dancer's movements, the rap of her satin heels on the bare boards, the interaction between herself, the guitar, the castanets. The rhythms grew wilder, and faster; she had us hypnotized, spellbound. I felt again that wonderful surrender to something strange but yet familiar that I had known at the vineyard house. I felt tears prick my eyelids as a weird, oddly mournful and harsh sound broke from her lips. I felt I came close to the soul of this land in the form of this woman in the dress of flame.

She held us silent and still for time almost beyond my reckoning, transfixed. Then she finished with savage abruptness, breaking off almost in mid-gesture, leaving the platform without a backward glance, vanishing into the darkness around the side of the house, and disdaining to return to acknowledge the wild applause that marked her departure. There was a magnificent arrogance in her leaving.

"Will she come back?"

"No," Carlos said, and I knew from his tone that he, the smooth cynic, had been as moved as I, as filled with wonder and sadness. "She is La Llama, and she knows she is the best. She is a gypsy, of course. All the great ones have been. She is a queen among her people, and she will never mix with us. . . ."

His voice was almost husky, as if filled with unshed tears. All through the performance he had held my arm, and only then, as he gradually relaxed his grip, I knew how tight and tense it had been. The sudden rush of blood brought a tingling sensation along my arm. Involuntarily I shivered.

"Come, you are cold."

"How could I be, on a night like this?"

"It is La Llama. She does it to us all." Now he placed his arm under my elbow with only the lightest pressure. "To us all. . . ." But listening to the swell of talk that broke from the crowd which flowed up the stairs, I wondered if all of them had been caught in quite the same way, if all of them were fighting that inexplicable lump in the throat, as Carlos was. And then I remembered María Luisa's words. "They say his mother was a gypsy. . . ."

We were last up the stairs. At the landing where the two curving arms met, I was aware of a figure, a waiting, almost brooding figure. Don Paulo, wonderfully impressive in evening dress, a ribbon of some order worn across his chest, and the star of the order gleaming in the soft light, was standing there. He seemed a figure of great power; almost, he gave off the same air of authority and arrogance which had belonged to the dancer. We moved up the last few steps towards him.

He bowed. Without thinking, I dropped a half curtsy, as if it were his due. I felt Carlos' grip tighten once more on my arm. Carlos inclined his head to his father, and in total silence we passed on.

From that moment, for me, the party was over.

The next day my mother insisted that we go in person to thank Doña Amelia and Don Luis. "It is not necessary," María Luisa said. "A note will do. . . ." But my mother, like half the town, wanted to relive the party, so we went. Doña Amelia, her nerves frayed, and pleading a headache, had retired, leaving the great salon of the house to her husband, leaving a small host of servants to hand around the teacups. We saw the same faces as the night before, but now they wore the wilted look of those who had danced or played cards or gossiped until dawn. The crowd was so great that it overflowed into other rooms, rooms that at dawn had been heavy with the mingled perfume of the ladies and the pomades of the gentlemen, rooms that had seen a small drift of lost handkerchiefs, and fans carelessly left on chairs, glasses on the mantels, tiny gold-rimmed plates with pieces of cake

148

from which only a polite nibble had been taken, rooms where the gentle strains of the music had been a world removed from the passions La Llama had aroused. Now all these rooms were immaculate, and shaded against the afternoon heat. The passion was gone, spent.

I put my cup down and pushed open one of the long windows, and the shutters protecting it. I was at the top of the double curve of the staircase. Below, the lake with its fountain glimmered in dull stillness; the swans had sought the shade cast by overhanging trees. All the color was washed from the garden by the glare, as it had been washed from the visitors by the exertions of the night before.

"How do you find it, Doña Carlota?" The tone was gentle, even slightly hesitant, as if he did not wish to intrude.

I turned. By daylight he seemed older; the sunlight harshly carved the downward lines of his face. I was once again struck by how deep-set his eyes were, how intelligent, intent.

"Beautiful . . ." I could not find the bright, easy reply to him. "But last night . . ."

"Ah, yes. Last night . . ." Don Luis came nearer. The hunch of his shoulders seemed more pronounced, as if he also was tired. "One should hold the dream of such things." He did not try to specify what things. "Especially when one is young. Youth makes so many things possible. . . . Will you come in from the sun now? I hate to see that marvelous complexion at risk."

I took his arm. Together we strolled through the now emptying rooms. As much as with Carlos the night before, in these moments more of the child, and of the girl who had been, gave place to the woman who was to come with such swiftness.

5

I encountered Carlos several times in the next few weeks; he neither avoided me and my mother, nor did he especially seek us out. He brought us glasses of wine as they were served, passed cups of tea, was polite, charming, and slightly distant. He did not come to call at our house. I found myself looking for his face among our visitors, and feeling a sense of disappointment when I did not find it.

"I heard about him—" María Luisa had started to say when my mother mentioned his absence, and then she checked herself.

"What did you hear?" I demanded.

She kept her eyes on her sewing. "I heard Don Paulo was displeased by the attention he paid you at Don Luis' party. I even heard that he had been ordered to stay away from you. But *that*"—she snapped the thread off sharply —"that could be only the merest speculation."

He sat with us, though, for a few minutes one day as we watched the polo at the club on the outskirts of the town. I had never seen it played before, nor seen the swift, sure, tough little ponies which were ideally suited to the sport. "It was brought back to England by officers who had served in India in 1871, I think," he said. "One of the González family, the Marqués de Torresoto, saw it played there, brought some polo sticks back to Jerez in 1872—and we've been playing it ever since."

"One needs a lot of ponies to play it," my mother observed, as she watched the players changing from one pony to the next, which was held ready. "It's very hard on the legs, isn't it—all that stopping short from a gallop, and quick turning?"

"Yes, one needs a lot of ponies. Fortunately my father has an interest in the game and doesn't mind providing them for me." He laughed without self-consciousness. "I could never do it out of *my* salary. Look, you must excuse me, please, Lady Patricia. It's my turn to play now. . . ."

He was gone, quickly mounted, and the next game began. We watched until it finished. Carlos changed ponies a number of times. He rode cleverly, and had an eye for the ball; because of him, his side won easily. After the match he went off to change, and we didn't see him again. "Awfully hard on the ponies' legs," my mother said again; she wasn't quite certain she approved of the game.

The weather grew hotter. The days seemed almost unbearable, and the nights airless. I grew bored with the round of small visits, the sound of small talk. "You are drooping," María Luisa said, and prescribed a day at one of the beaches near Puerto de Santa María. It seemed a long, tiring way to go when at Clonmara we had had the sea beside us. But we went. It was hardly a success. The breeze and the water were fresh, but the journey both ways was too long and too hot. There was no shade, except what our parasols provided. Sand got into the food. The only one who was enthusiastic was Pepita, for whom I threw sticks into the water until I was sweating and tired. "We should have gone to the vineyard house," I said. I knew I sounded like a spoiled and sulky child.

"There will be a little excitement when the harvest comes. There are always a few parties to celebrate . . . and then there is the *corrida*—the bullfight. They say this time they have engaged Antonio Pérez, who is one of the greatest matadors—"

"I will not go," I said. "I can't bear the thought of bullfighting."

"You will go, even if you don't watch—or don't let yourself see," María Luisa said. "Everyone will notice whether or not you attend. We know what you English say about our bullfighting—that it is barbaric. But what do you think we think of your fox hunting?"

"Foxes have to be killed," I snapped at her. "And quite often the fox gets away. There's a sporting chance."

"And there's a sporting chance that the matador will be killed."

"But the bull is *always* killed." I stamped off and left her.

The heat hung heavily, and so did the time. I did what I could to fill it. I accompanied María Luisa on her visits to the market. Andy went with us to carry the baskets of food we bought. María Luisa was a keen shopper; she welcomed my presence because it gave me practice in

151

Spanish and sharpened my sense of money and the feel for a bargain. There was a market quite near the Plaza de Asturias, and so we always walked. Pepita protested at being left behind, but she was too big to manage easily among those crowded stalls, and I was always fearful of her picking up some decayed meat. I knew now that the Plaza de Asturias was in a section of the town that was running down. It was true that there remained some big houses nearby, but they were almost all occupied by families who María Luisa said could not afford to move to the big new houses now appearing on the outskirts of the town, houses with large gardens like those of Don Luis and Don Paulo. So I knew now that Don Paulo's offer to buy the house and perhaps use it as the site of a bodega had been only part of the bribe to buy us out of Jerez altogether. No bodega owner, building anew, would have chosen to build here, so far from his other bodegas, where the access was by narrow street or alleyway. He would have chosen the empty land on the south of the town, and reserved space for more bodegas, so that his business, as it expanded, could be run efficiently. Don Paulo, I thought, had offered to buy this house simply to get us out, and perhaps in time it would have become a tenement, where many families lived, and children played and fought in what once had been elegant patios, and washing would have been strung from window to window, as we saw all about us as we walked to and from the market. No, this was no longer a desirable *barrio;* fashion and money were moving away, and the poor moving in.

I found I was as impatient as María Luisa with the siesta time, and quite unable to sleep. I opened the boxes of books my grandfather had bought; they were in English, and smelled of mildew as I handled them. I found myself now more interested in the English poets than I had ever been at Clonmara, perhaps because I found the passages my grandfather had marked—most particularly he had seemed to love the descriptions of the English countryside by Wordsworth and Tennyson. There was a much-thumbed edition of *The Rime of the Ancient*

Mariner, and I read it for the first time. I felt very close to my grandfather then. Had he too been restless, sleepless, homesick under this alien sun? My curiosity was roused by a book on clocks—I couldn't remember that clocks had been of particular interest to my grandfather, but I had heard someone say that Don Paulo had a particularly fine collection of clocks, and I wondered if perhaps the book had been a gift from him in the days when my grandfather was a welcome investor in the firm of Fernández. So I whiled away some of the dead hours of the afternoons by studying the illustrations, learning a little about the mechanisms, marveling at the beauty and complexity of some of the designs. There were hanging clocks, lantern clocks, bracket clocks, long clocks, mantel clocks, clocks with plain faces and clocks with beautiful faces. They came in as many shapes and varieties as people. They began to amuse and fascinate me, and they ticked off, in my mind, the long hours of the Spanish afternoons, ticked off the listless hours of my growing boredom, ticked off the hours of my mounting frustration.

Tick-tock, tick-tock. I sometimes heard myself say that as I walked the corridors of the big house at night to the beat of an imaginary clock. The heat grew worse, and sleep seemed to have deserted me; I lay awake, and thought too much of Richard Blodmore. And then I walked to try to escape the thoughts. Always Pepita walked with me, puzzled by these nocturnal wanderings, but happy to accompany me. Sometimes I went and sat outside in one of the patios, where there was the illusion if not the reality of coolness. I had learned to hope there would be no rain in these last weeks before the harvest because rain at that time might mean disaster. But yet as I turned my face upward to the unyieldingly bright sky I thought longingly of the "softness," which was what the Irish so often called our misty rain. Sometimes at night I went and visited the horses. Andy always left the half doors of the boxes open so that they might have more air, and they turned in their stalls to greet me. For these private, secret visits I saved the sugar I kept for them, not neglecting the two very ordinary carriage horses, which, as Andy had predicted, had responded to good feeding and regular grooming, and, while they would never cause a head to turn, especially here in Jerez, at least they no longer totally shamed us. They were docile, placid creatures, who enjoyed their sugar treats all the more because they had never had them before. But always the first, the biggest helping, went to Balthasar; it was his right, his due. He turned his beautiful white head to me, looking with the dark eyes that seemed unnaturally intelligent and knowing, and a ripple of recognition and anticipation seemed to run through the big frame. He took my offering of sugar like a king a gift of state, and then I was permitted to move to the next box, where Half Moon waited her turn. I talked to them quietly in the dimness, talked to them of anything that came to mind, but what came to mind most was the memory of that first day on the strand at Clonmara. "Do you remember how it was?" I whispered. "Do you remember how we raced? The sound of the sea? Do you remember . . . ?"

And so some of the lines I had learned from my grandfather's books of poetry came back, and I whispered to Balthasar and Half Moon of how the Ancient Mariner saw his homeland again.

> "Oh! dream of joy! is this indeed
> The lighthouse top I see?
> Is this the hill? is this the kirk?
> Is this mine own countree?"

I would go back to my bed and sleep fitfully, and wake unrefreshed as the bells of the Angelus began their clamor across the town.

Then came the night when I discovered that I was not the only one who came to feed sugar to Balthasar, who talked to him in soft, low tones. The moon was brilliant, and it was sliding towards the horizon and towards dawn; the stables cast their own thick black shadow, and for a moment I did not see the figure beside Balthasar's box. I had frozen in an instant's fear as I saw that both halves of the door were open. Balthasar was gone?—no, the great white figure was there, standing quietly, as if mesmerized. I heard the low words, the Spanish words I could not understand. And then from the shadow of the box the figure of a man emerged. He gave a final, lingering caress along Balthasar's neck and prepared to close the bottom half of the door. "Andy?" It was not Andy.

"Carlota!"

Carlos. As I had never seen him before. Gone were the slightly dandified clothes. He wore plain black trousers and an open-necked white shirt. He could have been the gypsy they said his mother was; his hair was tousled and curling; neither his eyes nor his lips were smiling. There was a streak of melancholy in him I never suspected before.

"What . . . ?"

"What am I doing here?" he said for me. "I come quite often to visit Balthasar. I like to come alone, when others are not about to observe and report."

"But how? The gates are always closed."

He shrugged, and for the first time smiled. "Do you think such a little thing could keep me out? The *front* doors are closed, to be sure, but in an old place like this what is truly secure? I know at least three ways I can get in here—shutters which are not quite secure, the gate in the stable wall there—and there's always the way by the jacaranda tree. . . ." He pointed to the old tree whose boughs overhung the high wall.

"But *why*?"

"Because Balthasar was once my horse. The finest horse in Jerez. A gift from my father. And given—no, *taken* from me by my father to pay a debt to Richard Blodmore. Exchanged at the chess table because my father lost to Blodmore. If Blodmore had lost, the forfeit was to have been the finest Irish hunter in Blodmore's stables. I think my father actually would have liked to have the horse that killed your grandfather, but we heard that he also was killed. So my father took from me the best thing I ever

155

owned and gave it to Blodmore. One of the few creatures I have truly loved . . . as I might have loved Elena, who was also given to Blodmore."

My heart was twisting with misery. "I don't think Richard knew Balthasar was yours, Carlos. He wouldn't . . ."

He shrugged. "He may have known. He may not. It makes no difference. It is the sort of thing my father does —the sort of gesture he makes. The way he gave you Pepita. I had given *him* Pepita. A gift he throws away. As it was with Elena. At one time there was the thought —the possibility, that Elena would be my wife. Not that we loved each other. We had hardly met. But still . . . My father would have liked the marriage. *I* would have liked the marriage. Then the Marquesa de Pontevedra, my father's wife, appeared in Jerez, and Richard Blodmore was bidden to come. Then he and Elena were married. I heard my father make no protests. Elena was handed over, as Balthasar was, as Pepita was. . . . That is the way my father is. If it would serve his purpose, or the purpose of the woman he is married to . . ."

He drew in a deep breath, and for a while did not speak. He laid his head against the neck of the great horse. "I did not know I could actually *love* a horse until this one was gone. Or perhaps . . . perhaps I don't really love, but I am like my father. What is mine is mine. To possess, to hold, to give away. As I choose. . . .

"Someday, I shall make a decision which is my own, not my father's. I will act as he has always acted—for himself." His hand went up to stroke Balthasar's neck; the stallion responded by nuzzling his shoulder in a rare gesture of affection.

Suddenly the restlessness that had simmered in me for weeks boiled up so that it could not be checked. I longed to be free of all of this—this house, whatever enmity bound my grandfather and Don Paulo together, even past death, the vain longing that bound me to Richard Blodmore. All of it seemed to find expression in the sight of the dark head of this young man laid against the head of the white horse. I sought the only respite I knew, the form of escape that had always been my way.

156

"Carlos, will you ride Balthasar again? Shall we ride out—out beyond the town, while it is still cool? Before the sun is up?"

His head came around sharply, a look of incredulity on his face. "Carlota—would you? Would you do that with me?"

"Saddle up Balthasar and Half Moon. I'll get dressed. We must be very quiet. Andy sleeps over the kitchen. But the front doors are now oiled, and open very easily. . . ."

He moved like a shadow toward the tack room. "I'll be waiting."

The horses' hoofs made a great clatter in the courtyard, and I expected to be challenged by Andy or Paco, but no one appeared. The doors opened as easily as I had predicted—we left them slightly ajar against our return. Pepita followed at our heels. I had put on only the skirt of my riding habit and an old cotton shirt left over from the Clonmara days. My hair hung freely down my back. I felt lighthearted, almost like a child again, released from all the weight of these past months, happy in a way I had not been since my grandfather died. The gloomy oppressiveness of the house was left behind, and with it most of my caution, the last grains of good sense running like sand from an hourglass. The streak of recklessness which was in all the Blodmores was uppermost in me now. I did not recognize at that time I was being truly the child of my mother, as she was the child of her father. That knowledge would come later. For these magical moments of first light the strictures of such people as María Luisa did not exist. I was not born of a race of people who had ever been careful.

Carlos knew all the twisting back alleys of the town, and we were soon beyond it. We set out on a road I had never been on before, away from the vineyards. Here the country rolled to grassy hills. There was no one about. Not even the hard-toiling peasants were astir at this hour. "The road to Arcos," Carlos said. The walking stride of the horses was lengthening as they felt the freedom of the empty, open road. Together we urged them into a trot. It was brightening rapidly. We passed a place where, behind a well-made fence surmounted by barbed wire, a number of black cattle grouped together in a grove of eucalyptus trees. I could make them out only vaguely in that light. "One of my father's bull ranches," Carlos said. "Those are the cows—the mothers of the brave bulls." He turned and flashed a smile at me, the engaging smile he used so often, but never before had I seen it without its veneer of politeness.

"Do you know that we have trials with the female calves to test their courage before breeding them with a bull of a proven line? The mothers are often fiercer than the sons. If the mother is brave, there is an excellent chance she will bear a brave bull." His smile came again. "The female, you see, is always the most important, even if we men never admit it."

I laughed, delighted with the idea. And then suddenly the restlessness I had fought these last weeks would not tolerate even the fast trot of the horses. It demanded expression, total release. I urged Half Moon on, and she responded with the eagerness that all this time of sedate walking through the thoroughfares of Jerez had stored in her. She was as tired as I was of the restrictions, the politeness, the small gestures. Her stride lengthened, and broke to a canter. I felt the wind of movement in my face. It had a sweet freshness to it, something longed for. I let her out finally into a full gallop.

Carlos held Balthasar only a little longer. Then with a cry he let the stallion have his head. Very soon he was level, and then past us.

Was I, for a few instants of time, back on the shore beside Clonmara? Was it Richard who passed me on the great white horse? I wasn't conscious that I thought at all of him in those moments. The sense of freedom was intoxicating, both sharp and sweet. I kicked Half Moon to greater effort, and she pursued her stablemate as if there was a chance that she might catch him. But it was Balthasar's country, the place of his breeding. He suited the firm going of the dirt road, as the mare had suited the wet sand beside Clonmara. He was a long way ahead before

Carlos began to slow him. In Balthasar too the restlessness of these long dull weeks had been brewing.

He was standing still, sweat on his white coat, when I finally reached them. Pepita came panting behind. Carlos had slipped from the saddle and was waiting for us. Wordlessly, he helped me dismount, and there were no questions to ask as we drew aside from the road and entered an unfenced grove of eucalyptus trees like the one where the black cows had grouped.

The horses had had their longed-for gallop and were satisfied. We walked them for a time through the trees. The strangely pungent scent of eucalyptus in the early morning hung about us; the white trunks were like wraiths in these last moments before the sun rose. Still without saying anything, I surrendered Half Moon's reins to Carlos. He tied both horses, and then he took me in his arms.

I had always supposed the first time I loved there would be confusion and bewilderment, because I did not know quite the way it all should go. Too often I had seen animals mate and had thought that with me also it might be something hasty, over and done with quickly. But it was different. Carlos made it different. We had no wide, soft bed. The ground beneath us was hard, and the dried edges of the fallen eucalyptus leaves were sharp. But Carlos was in no hurry, and at any moment I could have stopped it; but I did not. I wanted his love—I was desperate to have the loneliness driven from my own soul, and I believed he could do it with his body. I accepted the first terrible pain as the price of our unity, the oneness that would end all my longings. I felt the thrust of him within me, and through the pain, its beauty. For a time I was lost in him, all of me submerged, giving and taking in equal measure.

At last he lay spent beside me, his hand brushed the long hair away from my face. "Carlota . . . my little brave one. Your first time and you are already a woman, a wonderful woman." He kissed me with great tenderness. "You are like the mothers of the brave bulls back there, those beautiful, strong, wonderful creatures. When you have sons, *they* will be brave bulls, my Carlota."

Later, before Carlos untied the horses, he took from his belt a thin, leather-sheathed knife. "Look, Carlota . . ." He was carving something on the tree. "With the finest Toledo blade I sign our names." The black and gold handle of the knife flashed in the sun, the thin steel blade cut readily into the white bark. I watched, fascinated, as the symbol took shape. "Two C's intertwined," he said. "Whoever owned this land does not know that now it belongs to us. Our brand is here as long as this tree stands."

Andy was waiting for us by the open doors when we returned, his face sharp with concern. He held the note I had left; it would have been madness to take the two horses without a sign to him because, like all grooms, he rose early. I had dashed off the words: *Andy—back soon—Charlie.*

Typically, Carlos didn't attempt any explanations. His father's son, he seemed to ignore Andy's presence. He slipped off Balthasar's back and handed the reins to the groom. He kissed my hand. "A miraculous morning, Carlota." And then he walked across the plaza and into a side street.

"Miss Charlie . . ." Andy began. There was a tremor in his voice which could have been anger.

"It's all right, Andy. We were very careful with the horses."

"And I'm wondering if it's very careful with yourself you've been, Miss Charlie. Lord Blodmore charged me to take care of you, and this young—"

I almost flung myself down from the saddle, and threw the reins to him. "Oh, damn Lord Blodmore! Damn him!"

The tears slid down my cheeks as I sped back to my room. Richard Blodmore was back with me. My morning of wonder was gone, destroyed by him. And I had to ask myself, after I had washed and put on a nightgown, and lay weeping between the sheets, if it had indeed been Richard Blodmore, and not Carlos, I had pursued as I urged Half Moon to catch up with the white stallion.

CHAPTER FOUR

1

The rain held off through those next weeks. "Any day now they will begin to harvest," María Luisa said when September arrived. Preparations were made for the celebration of the harvest, *la vendimia,* under the patronage of San Gines de la Jara. A special Mass was said at the Collegiate Church, and a *lagar,* a shallow, square wooden box, was set up on the steps of the church for the ceremonial treading of the grapes and the blessing of the first must which ran from the lagar. I was with my mother and María Luisa on the steps of the church when the four solemn, burly men, called *pisadores,* wearing very short trousers and their special nail studded leather boots, the *zapatos de pisar,* trod the first grapes, leaning on their wooden shovels. After a while the must began to flow from the lagar, the skins, pips, and stems held back by mesh strainers. Jugs of the must were passed around; it smelled rather unpleasant, tasted green and sharp. "Not drinkable, of course," María Luisa said, "but one must take a token sip. It is not yet wine, but they are saying the must this year is a good quality, and the harvest will be plentiful."

All of Jerez seemed to be there. For the first time for more than a month I saw Carlos in the crowd which eddied and moved and spilled over into the plaza before the church. He did not make his way toward us, and I told myself that he had not seen us. I told myself that, and only half believed it. For these weeks there had been no word from him, no note, no gesture. The only time I had been to the stable yard in the hour before the dawn it was Andy who waited beside Balthasar's box. "Good morning, Miss Charlie. Will you be riding out this morning? If you are, I'll just saddle up and go along with you—just to see that everything's all right, you know."

"No, I'm not going out, Andy. Just can't sleep, that's all." But I wore the skirt of my habit and carried my riding crop. I never knew if Carlos had come again and Andy's presence had deterred him. I had waited, day by day, for some message from him, and as the days passed, and none came, I tried to tell myself that it was as well. What we had done was madness. I had taken a young man and tried to use him to assuage the loneliness in the center of my being. For a time, a very short time, he had done this, but now the loneliness was greater than before. I hoped Carlos would not come, would not send a message to meet him, and yet I prayed he would. It was like a blow to see him across the packed steps of the church, to see his face which seemed to be turned deliberately, steadily away from mine. For him, I told myself, I had been a girl to enjoy for only one mad moment in the dawn. That was all. I did not love Carlos—how could I when I loved Richard Blodmore? But I desperately needed the reassurance of a sign from him, a gesture.

It was Sunday, and we went that afternoon to the corrida, my mother and I protesting, and María Luisa insisting. She had found places for us in one of the boxes in the top tier. "It belongs to a cousin—there are seats to spare. You *must* appear." She hustled us up the long flights of stone steps. "Sit at the back if you don't want to see, but say nothing." She greeted effusively all the various cousins, introduced us to those we hadn't met. Two of her sisters were there, and they patronized her. For a time my mother was happy. The whole bull ring was wild with the mood of the *feria*. We and all the gentry of Jerez were on the shady side, *la sombra;* on the other side, *el sol,* the workers and peasants sat unshielded in the merciless hammer blow of the three o'clock sun. We gossiped with those in the box, and witnessed the blossoming of the beautiful, many-colored silk shawls, with their delicate fringes, on the rails of the boxes all around the arena. "It is like a garden suddenly growing in front of one's eyes," my mother said. She had had several copitas, and the dread of what she might see had been blunted. "Charlie, aren't the mantillas charming?" The ladies had brought out their high combs and draped their lace mantillas from them. Some, the younger ones, wore a carnation behind one ear. Suddenly everything that was English about the town had been submerged in its essential Spanishness. They might bear English, Irish, and Scottish names, but these were Spaniards about me.

The old joke that the bullfight was the only thing in Spain to start on time was repeated, and we laughed. We witnessed the full ceremonial of the occasion, the march of the *toreros,* their suits of light flashing in the sun. From the height of the box it was colorful and romantic, and one did not think of the bull. The band played, the crowd applauded its favorites. It was nothing but a game, I thought. It would soon be over. The black hats of the fighters were raised to the president in his box. The men and the horses retreated to their places behind the *barrera.* The bugle sounded, gates were opened, and the mighty power of a great black bull was unleashed into the ring. The men who played him first with the stiff pink capes seemed puny and insignificant. The thundering might of the animal would defeat them. It could be no other way, I told myself.

I managed to stay in my seat all through the time when the bull and the mounted horsemen, the *picadors,* fought it out, the men with their long pics seeming to have the advantage as they strove to wound the animal to bring down the neck muscles, to lower the great head. But then I saw the wicked horns pierce the padded blankets which covered the horse's side. The horse and man went down. There was a wild scramble to distract the bull away from the horse and the fallen man. It succeeded, but not before the sand was red with the mingled blood from the horse's side and the blood that streamed from the bull's neck. The man and the horse were taken away, the president signaled again, the bugles blew, and the *banderilleros* came on, each taunting the bull, enraging him with their cries of *"Toro! Toro!"* The barbed shafts, so prettily decorated and so cruel, penetrated and stayed. They waved sickeningly as the bull moved, more slowly now, but still a great black menacing mass. The head was down, at an angle, María Luisa whispered to me, where the matador might hope to pass his thin sword straight through the neck and cleanly to the heart. But first, to show his courage and skill, he must play the bull alone in that suddenly emptied space, his helpers gone, safe behind the barrera, the man and the bull facing each other, with the chance that the man, as well as the bull, might die.

There was too much blood; I had seen enough. As quietly as I could, but with urgency, I pushed past the chairs of those around me, blindly seeking the entrance to the box. Out in the deserted corridor behind the boxes, I listened to the waves of sound that came. *"Ole! Ole!"* And then the waves of nausea could be held back no longer. I found myself vomiting repeatedly, almost uncontrollably.

It was María Luisa who came. I felt her arm about my shoulder, her handkerchief wiped my fouled lips. "It is too much for you? I would not have thought you so weak-stomached." She fanned my face and produced another clean handkerchief, this time wiping the tears of shame and weakness. Then she stopped, and the fanning stopped. "What is it, querida? You are too pale . . ." She left me, and in a minute was back with a glass of wine. She stood with me as I sipped it. The cheers of the crowd still deafened me, but she leaned in close, and I heard her quietly spoken words.

164

"But it is not just the bull, is it, querida?"

"Not just the bull? It was the blood . . ."

"You have seen blood before. It is not just the bull-fight at all, is it? *Is it?*" she insisted.

All her years of watching young girls, young women, were in that question. And yet it was gently said. The thing that troubled me most in the last two weeks was also in the question.

"Perhaps it is not the bull, María Luisa."

For only a moment she leaned back against the wall and her shoulders sagged. Briefly she closed her eyes, then they snapped open, black, resolute. "We have a saying here in Jerez—'The girls and the vines are difficult to guard.' I have been remiss. However, we will say, for the moment that it is the bull. We will go home, you and I. Your mother will find plenty to escort her. We must think. We must make sure. Yes . . . I will make some arrangements."

The next day Andy drove us to the office of Dr. Miguel Ramírez. "Do not be afraid," María Luisa said. "He is discreet. An old friend. He never talks. A good man . . ."

She remained in the room while he made his examination. She was silent most of the way home. "Now you must tell me, querida. Who is it?"

I could not lie to her. I had no defenses. She had not raised her voice in anger or disgust. She might have been speaking as if I had broken something valuable, something prized, which could not be replaced, but for which act I did not merit scorn or punishment. And then it occurred to me that that was precisely what I had done.

"Carlos," I said. "It was not his fault. I did not resist him. I *wanted* him."

"I did not speak of fault, querida. So . . . it is Carlos. You see now why, although the world laughs, we watch our young girls so carefully. The blood runs hot. So . . . Carlos . . ." Then she sighed. "Child, you do not make things easy for me. You might have chosen other than the best-loved son of Don Paulo." She let out a sharp, harsh little laugh. "Well, now I must really set out to earn that money Lord Blodmore sends to me. We must have you married."

"But I cannot *force* him. I could not endure that kind of marriage."

"A marriage there must be, querida. And to Carlos. If it kills me I will make arrangements. Yes . . . I will make arrangements. Say nothing to your mother. She would not blame you—but she might not be . . . discreet. Yes, I must make arrangements."

It took several days and several meetings with Carlos. "He resists . . . and yet he is willing to be persuaded," María Luisa reported. "The harvest has fully begun, and they work long hours at the bodegas, checking in the must from the vineyards, taking in the grapes from the growers who do not press their own, seeing that all the tallys are in order. I had to wait two hours today before seeing him and then it was the siesta. . . . I had to keep out of the way of Don Paulo . . ."

"Do not see him again," I said. I had been ill each morning, and feeling faint, and trying to keep it from my mother. "If he needs persuasion, then it just can't be. I *won't* be foisted on him. I'll leave—I'll go back to Ireland."

"To what?" María Luisa said sharply. "To take your child back to Lord Blodmore? Carlos' child? It will not do. No, be patient. Be calm. Carlos twists and turns, and does not know what to do. I'm certain he cares for you . . . but there is Don Paulo . . ."

"Yes," I said, "there is always Don Paulo. Even though Carlos is illegitimate, he might be expected to make a far better marriage than *me!* Don Paulo's favorite son . . . he must be expected to go much further and much higher."

"You will do him honor," she answered fiercely. "Whomever his other sons marry, you will bring the most credit to his house. Life is not lived in a day. You have your years ahead of you to prove your value. But better light a candle or two," she added, "that the child will be a boy."

She came next day, her face grayish with exhaustion,

her thin body sagging with weariness. "It is done. He has agreed, and the arrangements are made."

"What—?"

"Don't question. Just do as I say. Other matters will sort themselves out in time." She smiled thinly. "They always do."

2

Andy had the landau, its hood up, waiting before five o'clock the next morning. A faint mist which the rising sun would burn through lay over the town. I had made only one of the arrangements of that day myself. Balthasar and Half Moon were hitched to the back of the landau. Pepita lay across one seat. Pepe ran beside us, wide-eyed with wonder at what this secretive, early morning departure could mean; he had only minutes ago been shaken out of his bed by Andy.

We drove to the Church of Santa Catalina. It was tiny, hidden among the squares of the old part of Jerez, unnoticed by me before this. Pepe was left to hold the horses; we found the side door of the church unlocked. Deep quiet and shadow greeted us, and a musty smell. A sleepy acolyte was lighting candles before the altar.

An old priest came to greet us, his faded eyes gazing at me with interest. "This marriage will be blessed by God," he said in careful English. "I will hear your confession, my child."

Since we had sinned by loving unwed, Carlos and I must confess, receive forgiveness, so that we might receive the sacrament of marriage. I wondered how all of this might have gone if my grandfather had chosen to bring me up as a Protestant. Even María Luisa might have foundered on that rock.

I had so little, and so much, to tell the priest. He listened in an absent-minded fashion, probably not understanding too much of my rush of English. His manner seemed to imply that the lusty passions of young people were a gift of God, to be taken for granted. That we sanctified our passion with marriage was all that the Church required. I was relieved, and when it was over, and he had given absolution and his blessing, I ventured a question. "Will Don Paulo be angry with you, Father? He is a powerful man."

He considered the words, framing his reply slowly. "I am too old to fear the wrath of any man, my child. I am too close to the wrath of God, should He be pleased to consider only my sins, and not my few virtues."

I smiled at him. For the first time in many days I also did not fear the wrath of Don Paulo.

Carlos was late, but at last he came. I could see the visible relief in María Luisa's face, the way she let her shoulders sag in weariness while Carlos, in his turn, withdrew to make his confession. "It is almost done," she whispered, the words meant perhaps only for herself. *"Gracias a Dios."*

We were married before the bells of the Angelus sounded. We went to the sacristy to sign the register, María Luisa and Andy being the witnesses. I wondered how she felt about putting her aristocratic name beside the childishly formed writing of a stable hand from Ireland. But no matter; she trusted him as Richard Blodmore had trusted him, and she was lady enough to bring him up to her level.

"A small matter of interest, Don Carlos," the priest said as we rose from the table after signing. "A long time ago . . . I remember this marriage was also celebrated very early in the morning." He took a much older leather-bound book from a tall cupboard, turned the stiff pages until he came to what he sought.

"Your illustrious father, on a momentous occasion . . . a happy coincidence you have chosen the same church, and that I should be the one to join both the father and the son in the holy sacrament."

He pointed to the page, blank except for two names, two names so special that they deserved the space to themselves, as if they were royal.

I saw the signature I remembered—*Santander*. And then, scrawled slantingly upwards across the page, so that

168

no other name could be written there, just a single name. This was no anxious writing of a nervous bride, as mine had been. There was pride, authority, and great arrogance in that word, and in the large ink blot that finished it, as if the writer had been impatient to be done with the business. I stared at it. *Pontevedra.*

The Spanish Woman.

Outside the church, where the early Mass-goers stared at this little, unexpected assemblage, Carlos went at once, automatically, to rub Balthasar's nose. I went to his side. "I have brought him for you. It was the only wedding gift I could make." I did not add that I was not entirely sure that Balthasar was mine to give. But Carlos loved Balthasar, and if I had to steal to give him, then I would do it. My mother would forgive me.

Carlos looked down at me, and his smile had the warmth of the sun that was beginning to touch the high roofs about us. The look of anxiety he had worn was vanished. He seemed taller, and already older, as if he could take whatever consequence our marriage that morning would bring.

"Carlota, you do me great honor. Both by this marriage and by your gift." It did not sound like one of his usual flowery compliments.

We were going to the vineyard house. I was grateful for the refuge. I did not want, at this moment, to return to the house in the Plaza de Asturias, nor could we go to Don Paulo's house. Later in the day Carlos would return to the bodega and confront his father. "But first I will eat my wedding breakfast with you, querida."

I wanted to ride Half Moon, but Carlos insisted that we both ride in the landau and that Andy drive us to the vineyard house, Andy then returning with the landau and horse to my mother. "I will not risk my child by having you ride, Carlota. Remember—you are to be the mother of a brave bull." He said it proudly before the others, and made me proud also. So many of my thoughts, selfishly, had been for myself; I had thought so little of the child. I suppose it was from that moment I began to love it, and a new emotion opened for me.

So María Luisa, still looking tired, but treading with a sprightly step, set off to walk back to my mother's house. At her side was Pepe. Pepe seemed not quite sure of what had happened, except that it was something of great importance. Why else would the son of Don Paulo be abroad at this hour of the morning? He gave a little anticipatory skip, no doubt at the thought of the marvelous gossip he would have to relay, as he followed that black-clad figure from the square. Andy urged the horses on, and the white stallion and the mare followed. On the seat across from us, Pepita yawned. Carlos took my hand. I wanted to whisper my gratitude, my thanks, but he did not seem to expect it, and something beyond my usual impulsiveness warned me not to express it. A marriage had begun, and neither of us must be too humble before the other. The blood of our separate, proud families would mix; I was beginning to understand that pride was not only a desirable quality in a Spaniard but a necessity of life. I must not only be proud and brave, but I must also be the mother of brave bulls.

Along with all else she had managed to arrange, María Luisa had taken time to send a message to the vineyard house to except me and another, early that morning, and to prepare accommodation. Carlos' name, of course, had not been mentioned. A look of astonishment swept across the faces of Antonio and Concepción as Carlos sprang down from the landau. Though they must rarely have gone to Jerez itself, like all country people they seemed to know the names and faces of the rich who ruled their lives. Carlos spoke to them too rapidly for me to understand, and then broad smiles spread on their faces. Even if Don Carlos was a bastard offshoot, he still was of the house of Santander, and through that allied to the even greater house of Pontevedra. It was evident from their expressions that they thought their simple little Irish miss had brought off a great coup. Antonio reverently received Balthasar and Half Moon into his care, and Concepciòn, with many curtsies and apologies for the humbleness of the arrangements, led us inside. They did not know, of course, that the marriage had not Don Paulo's approval, and that this tumbledown vineyard house, in the midst of the fields of brush was all Carlos and I had between us.

María Luisa had packed a basket to furnish our wedding breakfast—cold chicken, ham, cheese. From the cellar of my mother's house she had packed another basket with bottles of some of the greatest vintages we possessed. Obviously, she had reasoned that Carlos must not be too rudely thrust into the poverty that might be our lot. In the first days the wine would help. It did help. Most of all, I thought, it helped me.

Carlos was quite unself-conscious about his intention of taking me to bed at once. Had he not married me? Such things did not have to wait for conventional hours. Thrusting the glasses and plates aside when we had eaten, he led me to the bedroom Concepción had prepared, the bedroom with the big brass bedstead, the white cotton curtains, the yellowing lace spread. There he undressed me with expertise and a show of tenderness, buried his dark head between my breasts. Then he made love to me in such a way that even the lingering thought, the desire, for Richard Blodmore was driven from my mind. The sheer maleness of him carried its undeniable stamp; there was no need for him to be rough or swift or brutal, but he would have his way. And I found myself responding as I had never imagined possible, urging him on and on. I did not recognize the cries that came from my own mouth; it was as if some hitherto unknown person, locked inside me, had broken out. I cried for more and more, and then at last Carlos burst into laughter, lying beside me, spent, the sweat bathing our two bodies.

"Truly, Carlota, it is a bull you need. Our nights will be interesting ones, querida." Then he was quiet a moment. "But we must be careful—gentle. The child. We must not hurt the child."

171

"But not yet," I answered, wondering where I got my knowledge. "There's lots of time yet."

"Time . . . yes, time. For a moment we have all the time in the world. We hold it in our hands, like you the child in your belly."

"Then kiss me, and say it's all right."

He did, and it was.

He went to wash then, his naked body astonishingly beautiful in the diffused light which came through the closed cotton curtains. Then he dressed, and kissed me good-by. "I must attend to the day's work at the bodega. And I must see my father." Searching his face, I saw not the least sign of apprehension.

I parted the curtains a little to watch him ride Balthasar down the road between our brush-choked earth and our neighbor's beautifully tended vines. He was erect, and himself like a king. Then I went back to bed, to smile a little at the beginning, then to weep a little for my lost love, Richard Blodmore. Then I slept, peacefully, all the rest of the morning.

But when I woke the thought came, like a rain cloud over the vineyards, that now I was irrevocably committed to Carlos, to Jerez, to a life in Spain. There would be no return to Ireland for me. I must not even dream about Clonmara.

He returned quite late that night, his clothes dusty from the ride. Concepciòn had slaughtered one of her precious chickens and cooked it in a delicious sauce. She put it on the table and then left us alone.

He drank some wine, talking of nothing in particular. The harvest was good, the volume greater than last year, the expectation of the quality of the must was high. Yes, it would be a prosperous year for Jerez. They would make the wine, and all it needed was someone to sell it well. He seemed to talk all around the subject, and at last I had to ask him.

"Your father . . . you told him?"

"I told him, Carlota."

172

"And—?"

He was thoughtful, and sipped his wine several times before he answered. "He seldom shows his anger. But one knows it is there, all the same. I am his beloved son, and I will always be his beloved son. But I am foolish and mistaken. I have made a mismatch—" The blood of shame rushed to my face, and gently he reached out his hand to cover my mouth so that I should not interrupt. "I told him truly that I had made no mismatch. He expected great things of me, and I have achieved them. I have married you, Carlota. You are my wife. No man, not even my father, may say such things and expect me not to strike back."

"But how? How can you strike back at Don Paulo?" I felt helpless and afraid.

"Through the only weapon I have. His love of me. He tries to hide it, but he loves me. That old man loves me, and sees his future in me. Already one can sense—can know—his longing for the child. I threatened . . . I threatened that I would leave Jerez. That I would go north. Perhaps to Madrid. Perhaps even to London. I am certain that I could find employment in the sherry trade there, though not with the firm of Fernández, Thompson. I threatened to take you—and his grandchild—away." Carlos smiled at me, but his face was weary, as if he did battle all over again. "He did not exactly crumble, my father. He is not that kind. We made a formal arrangement. I am to stay on at the bodega. I shall receive my salary, but nothing more. It means a little time of waiting, only, Carlota. In time he will come around. He is rich, querida. And he is growing old. He will not live forever. He desires to live to see his grandchildren flourish. A man like that lives to pass on his vineyards to his grandsons. You will give him his first grandson. And one day he will die, and then perhaps *I* shall be rich!"

"Carlos, how can you talk like that? He is your father!"

His features twisted, and he no longer smiled. "I talk like that, Carlota, because all my life that man has told me what to do, what to think, how to act, to *be*. Today I

173

am my own man. Today I have married my woman, without asking him if I might. I shall have *my* son, and he shall not be just the grandson of Don Paulo, Marqués de Santander. I do not know who my own mother was, and he will never tell me. She was of no account, it seems. But *I* am of account. I receive no favors from him. I expect none. When he chooses to give, it will be because it is my right, not because I beg. We shall be poor, Carlota. I shall not now have all the gifts it has pleased him to shower on me. So, I will do without. I am no man if I cannot do that. You've heard the rumor that my mother was a gypsy?—you must have. Everyone says it—particularly my half brothers, Pedro and Ignacio. And if that is so, then I am also my mother's son. I spit on him and his money. I spit on the alliance with Pontevedra, and on everything he had planned for me—or perhaps what *she* had planned. *That woman!*" He stopped, and sipped his wine again, refilled his glass. The lamplight made his dark eyes seem unnaturally bright, and then I suddenly realized that he struggled against unshed tears. The words he had used were brave and defiant ones, but had they been true? Perhaps he was as fearful as I was, and would not say so. Perhaps he did love his father, and would not say that either. The interview between father and son must have been painful and bitter, and I was inexpressibly grateful because he still declared his pride in me. Carlos could not be humble, no more than his father.

I trembled, and shivered, even in the warmth of the night; he reached for my hand. "Come, querida—to bed."

It was as beautiful as it had been that morning, but something was gone that we might never know again. In the passage of that short day we had both grown in experience. I was a young girl no longer, and Carlos had won his freedom, for which he had paid. The shadow of Don Paulo was with us that night, and would be with us many times in the future. We slept clasped in each other's arms, as much for comfort and reassurance as for love.

174

The carriage arrived quite early the next morning, not long after Carlos had left for the bodega, almost as if the coachman had waited to see him go. The doors of the carriage bore the crest of Santander, the horses were as fine a matched pair of bays as I had ever seen, the harness silver-decorated and flashing in the sun. There was a liveried coachman, and two footmen, whose gold buttons bore the same crest. Antonio and Concepción and the huddle of children were awed into complete silence. A footman handed me a note which bore the now familiar signature. There was no term of address, just the brief script. *I trust you will favor me with an interview. It would be best if you came in my coach, as we have some further traveling to do.*

I dressed quickly, but with care. Of course, as yet, my condition did not show, so I wore one of the gowns María Luisa had had made for me, a pale green muslin, a plain straw hat trimmed with a black ribbon, gloves and a parasol. A real Jerez lady, I told myself I looked, as I peered into the age-spotted mirror. The face that looked back was older than yesterday's face, and much older than the face that had been reflected for the last time in the hall mirror as I walked down the stairs at Clonmara. I welcomed what I saw; I felt that today I would need the scant wisdom of every day I had ever lived.

We drove to Jerez, not to the bodega, but to Las Fuentes, the mansion of Don Paulo, to which neither I nor my mother had ever been invited. It was grander, even, than the mansion of Don Luis. It reflected not just the money of the sherry trade but the money of all the many enterprises which María Luisa had said that Don Paulo had invested in with the help of the Marquesa de Pontevedra's fortune. The house sat on a slight rise and got its name, Las Fuentes, from the four fountains, each set at a different level, which sent water spuming into the air and cascading down to the lowest pool. The shrieking of peacocks greeted our arrival. There was a variety of exotic ducks; flamingos paraded their thin pink legs. All this Carlos had left for the poverty of the vineyard house. No wonder he had hesitated; I had already forgiven that hesitation. Now I understood it.

I was not, at that time, to enter the house. Don Paulo came to the carriage and took his seat opposite me. Immediately the carriage started to move again.

"Where are we going?"

"We are going, Doña Carlota, to Arcos—to Arcos de la Frontera, where my wife, the Marquesa de Pontevedra, has a castle."

"But why?"

"That, in due course, you will discover."

Then the hooded eyes seemed to close even further, as if he were some kind of lizard, waiting patiently, motionless, for the unsuspecting insect to come within range. I felt helpless, mesmerized, and the sweat on my body had little to do with the heat of the morning.

It was a long drive to Arcos—or it seemed so then. We passed the place where the black cows stood, sheltering in the shade of the trees. Then we passed the eucalyptus grove where my child had been conceived. Even in the extremity of my nervousness I gave it a secret and loving greeting. I thought that, apart from Clonmara, it was the place on earth I would most like to own, and then dismissed that too as an impossible dream.

The twin hills of Arcos de la Frontera rose spectacularly from the gentle swell of the country we had been traveling. On one side of the town sheer cliffs fell to the river, the Guadalete, and the plain below; I saw, through the heat haze, what seemed to be the crenellated walls of two castles, one dominating each peak, both with square towers brooding over the plain. Vultures flew beneath them and found resting places among the crags. Everything of the might and majesty of Old Spain was there, frowning with a kind of holy menace. I had imagined such places existed only in the illustrations of fairy tales.

I felt a nervous twist of my stomach, and fought against nausea.

I began to understand why, on that long journey, we had only two horses as we began to ascend the ever narrowing streets of the town; a coach and four would never have negotiated the twists and bends. The two footmen had got down to lighten the load. Once I felt a sickening lurch as one of the horses half slipped trying to gain purchase on the worn cobbles. Instantly one footman was at its head, the other lifting the harness pole to help it recover. We were in deep shade between those tall white buildings, and yet the air was stifling. Then abruptly we were in a large, flat plaza, with one open side which seemed to vanish into air; only a thin railing guarded against the drop to the river below. The sun was blinding, harsh, brutal. The carriage circled the plaza and stopped at one corner.

"Here we must walk. The horses can go no farther." I felt the reluctant touch of Don Paulo's hand on my arm as I got down, and my flesh seemed to creep. I walked beside him, silently, as we moved up a twisting lane between stone walls, where windows with barred grilles stared down upon us. At last we came to the massive doors beneath a Gothic arch, surmounted by two crests. We were expected and had been observed. A small portal within the gates opened to admit us. The man who greeted us wore a different and even more splendid livery than the servants of Don Paulo.

There was yet another steep twisting lane between buildings before we gained the garden courtyard of the castle. The place itself was built of lovely yellow stone, which had, in the distance, made it seem to merge into the golden rock of the cliff face. It seemed very ancient, and as if parts of it had been built at different periods. Three wells were placed about the courtyard, and I heard the cooling trickle of water. The winding way we had come to gain the castle courtyard had brought us the view, once again, to the second castle perched where the cliff curved, and which commanded yet a further stretch of the river and plain below. Half the town lay between them, but they stared at each other, twin guardians of the rich and beautiful countryside. I no longer wondered that it had been part of the frontier between the Moorish and Christian kingdoms. Whoever held these castles held the plain.

Involuntarily I had halted. Not for anything would I have admitted my breathlessness, since Don Paulo himself had kept up a sharp pace, but the place itself compelled me to stop—to stop and wonder at it.

Here Don Paulo could continue his silence no longer, as if his pride in his country and its harsh beauty could not be contained. "It is Moorish—parts built in the seventh century. We drove the Moors from it and held it for the Christians. At Granada we finished the Moorish conquest under Their Catholic Majesties, Isabel and Fernando, and Spain was restored forever to Holy Mother Church."

From anyone else, in any other place, it would have sounded absurd. Here, it was perfectly suited.

We were taken to a long vaulted room whose windows, in massively deep recesses, looked down on the cliff face, the river, and the wide plain. Now the vultures swooped beneath us. We were brought copitas by a servant, but I asked for water. Don Paulo's eyes were on my shaking hand as I drank. The intense silence was unnerving; we waited, and he did not speak again. The height and deep shadow of the room made it seem cool, like a church. Even with Don Paulo's eyes on me I could not repress a shiver.

She came at last. She was very tall, and slender; as she moved down that long room, it might have been a young woman who came towards us, but when she came into the light from one of the windows her hair was not golden but silver-gilt; her face had begun to show the marks of age. I had the impression of bright, cold blue eyes. She wore black—not María Luisa's kind of black, with ribbons and lace. It was a gown almost medieval in its fashion, as if she were a woman of no century at all. She seemed to wear no adornment until she raised her

178

hand to Don Paulo, and then the fire of emeralds and rubies and diamonds flashed.

Don Paulo took her hand, but his lips did not quite touch it. "You are well, Marquesa. I see that."

"Very well, Santander."

A greeting between people who have known each other a long time but are still strangers. "Interesting that I should have decided to come to Arcos at this time. Events have outrun you, Santander. It is not like you to be so careless with your possessions. I thought you had learned to take care long ago."

"We will not speak of that."

"Indeed we will not," she agreed. She had thrust beneath his guard and scored a point. She evidently enjoyed it.

"I have brought Doña Carlota—now my son's wife—as you requested."

"As I requested, yes. Now you may leave us, Santander."

He looked outraged, then stifled his reply. He shrugged. "As you wish. There is nothing to be done now. Impossible for the marriage to be annulled. As I said in my letter, she is with child. Carlos has reached his majority, and I have no doubt that Lady Patricia would say she had given her consent. It is better to leave matters as they are. Carlos has made his own bed . . ."

"Leave us, Santander!"

I waited in agony as he walked the length of the room and closed the door. As formidable as he was, at least he was familiar. Now I was alone with the Spanish Woman of legend at Clonmara, the Spanish Woman of one summer twenty-five years ago.

She gestured for me to be seated. Was it some sort of cruelty which made her place me so that the light fell directly on my face, so that nothing could be hidden—while she remained standing, her face in shadow?

"So . . . you are Blodmore's granddaughter." As I did not reply she was forced to go on. "So . . . you took away Don Paulo's son, his beloved son, Carlos, for whom he had such plans. How he must hate you—as he hated

179

your grandfather!" Suddenly a laugh, an almost wild but still mirthless laugh broke from her lips. "What a blow! Did you guess what you were doing to him? After all these years yet another Blodmore comes to break his heart."

"I didn't know . . ." My lips trembled; I felt ill, and prayed I would not disgrace myself by being sick on the magnificent oriental carpet of that grand and ancient room. "I *don't* know. It wasn't planned." Then life seemed to snap back into my flaccid limbs. I straightened my back. "It wasn't planned, you know. Carlos and I just happened . . . just happened to become lovers." The words were said. I wasn't ashamed; I would not feel shame about what had seemed so right.

" 'Just happened . . .' " Did that harsh, commanding voice soften just a trifle? "How fortunate for you. Many men have said they loved me. I never knew. Who would not say they loved the fortune and position Isabel de Pontevedra had to bestow? And none of my lovers gave me a child!" It was a primitive cry of anguish and anger, almost incredible coming from a woman of her age and position to someone as insignificant as myself, a stranger. She went on. "I did not feel barren. No doctor ever told me I was barren. But no man was able to give me a child. I might have had Blodmore's child—but I didn't. And you—in a few weeks you are with child and you have married Carlos. How quick you Irish are, when it suits you. I remember Blodmore was quick to want me, to take me when I permitted it. I lingered in Ireland all one summer because of Blodmore, and then he pursued me to Spain. He wanted to marry me—did you know that?"

"They still talk, at Clonmara, of the time you were there. They call it the summer of the Spanish Wo—Lady. They expected my grandfather would marry you. They said he was infatuated with you."

"Infatuated with my money! He—"

"My grandfather was not like that! I *know* it. And he didn't need your money. Not then. He had enough. Oh, he wasn't *rich,* like you, but there was as much as he wanted from Clonmara. He didn't have the taste for grand things. All he wanted was his horses, and Clonmara. It was only after he came back from Spain that he began to try to get money—any way he could. Doing foolish things. Making mad investments. No one ever knew what happened to him while he was in Spain. Did you think he wasn't good enough for you—wasn't rich enough? Was it you who made him so mad for money that he lost everything? Was it to try to impress you that he bought that absurd big house in Jerez? He had the money to buy that then, and to lend money to Don Paulo, who *needed* money. You say my grandfather was your lover, but you *married* Don Paulo."

She half turned from me; her hands went to her face in a gesture of rage or pain; I couldn't tell which. All I saw was the flash of the jewels on her long fingers. The sun made a halo of the fine silver hairs that stood out about her head. It was possible she had never been a beautiful woman, but she would always have commanded attention.

"You Blodmores! I loved him—and I didn't trust him! I loved no other man, but I was right not to trust him. I knew the difference between passion and love, and I held off. I held off, and I lost him!"

I thought she had not meant to say so much. I thought she had meant only to satisfy some curiosity about me, to torture me a little with her questions, but something about me had put her in disarray. Was I really so like my grandfather at times, as they said I was, that I had unnerved her? "I loved him," she had cried. Such words would not have come easily from the Marquesa de Pontevedra.

"*You* lost him, Marquesa? I cannot believe that. You could have had him at any time, I am told. You need never have left Ireland."

"I had to try him, and I lost him! His precious Clonmara! I had to show him how much else I had to give him. I took him on a tour of all my estates in Spain. Clonmara was nothing beside what was mine. But you Irish are so careless—so indifferent to anything besides

181

your own little world. Yes, perhaps he really didn't care for more than he already had, but I had to show him what was *mine!* I made him woo me—and I hoped he'd win me. I played with him, but too long. I lost him. He proved not to be the mouse to my cat's game. I lost him."

"How could you have lost him? And why do you blame me now? And why do you say that another Blodmore had come to break Don Paulo's heart? Don Paulo married you. *He* won you. How could anything my grandfather did have broken Don Paulo's heart?" Once more I experienced that weak trembling. She was more than I could deal with; my inexperience was too deep in the face of her complexity.

"Because," she said, "Blodmore took the thing that was dearest to Santander's heart—the thing that would have raised him above others. Something dearer to him than Carlos, more precious—more precious, even, I think, than his beloved vineyards."

She was silent for a time, studying me. I did not dare to speak, to question any more. She compelled me, utterly.

With an abrupt, almost impulsive gesture she turned. "Come! It is time you knew. You will live here among us, and you will know. But you will never, *never* speak of what you have seen this day. You will know how Blodmore betrayed me, betrayed Santander, and ruined his own life. If things did not go well for him it was no more than he deserved. . . ."

She was hurrying away from me, down the long room. I went after her quickly; somehow being left there alone seemed worse than anything she could tell or show me. I sensed that something in me had thrown her off guard. The moment might never come again, if, indeed, I should ever see her again.

We went out into the courtyard once more, crossed it to a separate wing of this three-sided building, whose fourth side was the open sky and the sheer cliff face. She never once looked back to see if I followed. She was accustomed to obedience. But even she had to pause and knock at a door, and wait there until a small window in it was opened and her identity established. Then the door swung open instantly, and the woman on the other side curtsied deeply. The Marquesa swept past without even a glance at her.

"Where is she?"

"She works at the loom, Marquesa."

I followed her to a room that was almost the equal in size to the one we had left; but here the handiwork of the Moors who had built it was much more evident. There were pillars and arches here, each decorated with delicate filigree in their stonework; there were portions of the room which still retained their original tiled walls, laid out with the brilliant mathematical jigsaw that I had been told was the hallmark of the long-ago inhabitants of this world, they whose religion prohibited the depiction of any image. Here the windows seemed larger and the light poured in. At our entrance a woman, in the plain dress of a servant or a companion, rose from where she was sitting, working at a lace pattern laid out on an embroidery cushion. With a gesture the Marquesa dismissed her; she went swiftly, softly, on slippered feet.

Close to one of the great window alcoves a girl sat at a large loom, her hand skillfully throwing the shuttle, while her feet worked the pedals. She was working something in silk which in many respects resembled the tilework about her, but the colors were rich and bright, unfaded by the centuries. Her hair, the color of straw bleached by the sun, but as silken as the threads she handled, lay on her shoulders in soft curls. She was slightly built, and her hands were very pretty as she worked the shuttle. She was dressed in white, a young girl dressed in what seemed to me to be the fashion of many years ago.

"Mariana?" The Marquesa's voice now was soft. The movements at the loom stopped. The head turned slowly.

It was no young girl I looked at. Her hair was not bleached straw-colored, but white. The woman had remarkably deep blue eyes, the color of the wild violets that grow in the ditches of Ireland, but they were strangely expressionless. If she had lines in her face it was impossible to see them for the deep encrustations on her skin. Her face was scarred and pitted so that I could

183

hardly discern any features. If she had ever had beauty, all that was left were the violet eyes.

She looked from the Marquesa to me, and for an instant some sort of recognition seemed to come to those blank eyes. She opened her mouth, as if to speak, and then closed it again. The blank, glazed look returned.

"Mariana, will you not show us your children?" The words were said first in Spanish, then repeated in English.

Obediently, like a puppet, the woman rose. I felt a sense of horror grow in me as the effect of that strange figure in her young girl's dress and white hair worn in ringlets about her ravaged face began to work. I felt my stomach lurch, and once more fought against nausea. I expected her to summon the companion to bring the children to her, or to lead us to a schoolroom, or playroom, but all she did was to walk to the farthest end of the long room. We followed.

Beyond the last arch, which was more elaborate in design than the others, the filigree of its stone so light it seemed to have been spun as lace, there was a step which raised this part of the room. There was no window here; it was slightly in shadow. A brazier stood in the middle, ready for winter use. It would be easy to imagine some caliph receiving here, in the privacy of this deep recess, emissaries and advisers, their whispered voices far removed from the others in the room. Or had this been the place for the favorite of the harem?

It was no such place now. Six cradles stood there, their flounces of lawn and lace falling to the floor, their hoods decorated with gay Moorish patterns and hanging silken balls. But if there were infants lying in them they were strangely, uncannily silent. There was no sound of breathing, nor any movement of a tiny fist towards the balls. I peered into the nearest, and a wax face, a perfect angel's face, looked back at me, white, pink-cheeked, blue glass eyes as expressionless as those of the woman. I looked beyond it to the next cradle, which was empty. In the next was an unbelievably lifelike form turned on its side, a wax hand laid under a cheek, as if it slept peacefully. Then, in the corner, on a silken oriental rug, three wax dolls sat upright. They seemed to smile sightlessly at each other. All were dressed in exquisite clothes, fine linens and laces, many petticoats. The wax hand of one was extended towards a ball that lay on the rug between them. Another doll was on hands and knees, as if crawling towards the ball. They were a uniquely perfect example of the wax-worker's art, and they struck me as coldly as a sigh from the grave.

I was taking in more. The alcove had been fitted with small, elaborately wrought cupboards, some of them decorated with Moorish designs, some of the finest marquetry. Mostly their doors stood open, displaying the contents of the shelves. Babies' clothes were there in abundance; tiny garments of silk and lace, some outdoor garments of wool, embroidered in Moorish patterns, as if this waxen tableau, dressed and with their jointed limbs rearranged, might be taken out for an airing when the harsh winter winds tore at the castle garden. There were bonnets with ribbons, and little knitted socks to put on their wax feet. Some of the clothes had faded or yellowed with age; many were quite new. The Marquesa moved among them, touching them, feeling the various fabrics. When she spoke, her voice was more gentle than I imagined it possibly could be.

"You care for them well, Mariana. Your children flourish."

The blank, ravaged features turned towards her, the lips twisted, but she did not speak.

"Mariana dresses all her children herself. Shawls and caps and dresses and petticoats. There are no more beautifully dressed children in the whole of Spain."

Those delicate, pretty hands pressed together, then they smoothed the ruffles of her white silk dress. Gently she touched a cradle, and set it rocking, adjusted a sheet about the shoulders of the sleeping infant. I caught myself then . . . I was beginning to believe that these really were children.

Unable to bear it any longer, I turned and ran down the length of that room of Moorish splendor, opened and slammed the door behind me. The companion waited there. Looking at my face, she made an exclamation of concern and led me to a chair. I bent my head between my knees, struggling to control the faintness that threatened. In the heat I shivered violently, as if I had come from a place of horror.

We sat in the courtyard, in the deep shade of a tree that must have struggled for centuries to grow in that rocky place. Perhaps I had experienced a period of unconciousness. I seemed hardly to remember how I got there. The collar of my dress was unbuttoned, and the Marquesa was bathing my face with a damp cloth. Finally she pressed it into my hand. "You are better? Drink some wine!" I was both ordered to drink the wine and feel better. The Marquesa would have little patience with those who grew faint, nor would she for long have continued to bathe my face.

"You saw her—that poor demented woman who plays with her dolls as if they were children? Who believes they *are* children. Your grandfather married that woman. That woman is Lady Blodmore. She is also the daughter of Santander."

I sucked in the dry air, and brought the wineglass once more to my lips. The words didn't make sense. The woman seated beside me was mad. As mad as the poor creature playing with her dolls.

"You don't believe it? Neither did I—for a time. Neither did Santander, until he was forced to believe it. That woman—she was promised, betrothed to the eldest son of the Duque de Burgos. She was to make the greatest marriage in Spain, bring great honor to Santander. He guarded her well, but he also trusted her well. He brought her to stay at my palacio at Sanlúcar, so that we could go over to Doñana for the autumn hunting. And I had brought Blodmore. The two came together. They became lovers under our eyes, and we did not see it. She was seventeen, he was thirty-three. They were married secretly, and the girl, Mariana, was with child. Except for that, Santander could have moved swiftly to have the marriage annulled, with a good chance of success. Blodmore was Protestant, and they had defied the laws of the Church

186

in not seeking permission. But the girl was already pregnant, and Santander did not know which way to turn. He did not inform the Duque. There was still hope, but little hope because the girl was madly in love, and even if the marriage had been annulled, she swore she would tell the Duque herself, that she would never give up Blodmore or her child."

"And you?" The words came out weakly.

She shrugged. "I was a woman scorned. Cheated. This little chit of seventeen had taken the man I wanted. In my own house they had become lovers. From my own house they had stolen away to be married. By a Carmelite friar. Santander made certain the man was silenced. No—he did not have him killed, though Santander is capable of it. The friar was sent to an enclosed order in the far north of Spain. For twenty-five years he has not spoken to another in the outside world. The page bearing the record of the marriage has been removed from the register at Sanlúcar. Such things we were able to do, Santander and I. The rest—the rest was the hand of God."

I was coming to life again, strength returning. "Was it the hand of God which caused you to marry Don Paulo?"

She looked at me, the anger now evident in that pale, thin face. "I do what I choose. *God* does not tell me what to do. I married Santander because I chose to do so." She had no need to say she had done so in a passion of rage and jealousy against my grandfather and the young girl, Mariana, who had taken him from her. I wondered again at the fashion in which these waves of passion seemed, in their season, to rule our lives. My grandfather, my mother, myself—all swept away, all caution, prudence, and reason gone. And this woman beside me—for all her power and position, for all her habit of command—it had been sheer blind jealousy, the need to revenge herself on my grandfather, which had impelled her into a marriage that had been one of convenience only.

"We separated them at once, of course. Santander was for sending the girl away to my estate in Galicia until the child was born, putting it out that she had been ill and

187

must recover her strength before her marriage. Blodmore, poor fool, was ordered from my house, and took himself to Jerez and bought that place to begin to prepare a home for Mariana. A feeble, hopeless gesture . . . He should have known I would not let him have things so easily . . . he should have known."

I thrust at her, growing angry now, "María Luisa told us that Don Paulo's daughter died of smallpox—which she caught from you—at that palacio at Sanlúcar."

The pale face flushed. "Do I *look* as if I have suffered smallpox?"

"Some people are not marked. *She* is marked."

"The smallpox came from a stupid maid who had been in contact with some sailor in Cádiz. I, of course, had been vaccinated. . . ."

I did not believe her. People like the Marquesa never supposed they would fall victim to the diseases of the common sort. I wondered if, twenty-five years ago, vaccination had been a routine practice unless there was an outbreak which drove people in fear to seek protection. A girl and a sailor from Cádiz . . . it easily could have come that way, but it was possible the Marquesa had been the first to contact the illness. No one but these two, the Marquesa and Don Paulo, would ever know with certainty.

"Mariana contracted it. She was very ill. We expected her to die. It would have solved a lot of problems if she had died. No one should have been able to sustain the fever she suffered and still live. But she lived. Every day Blodmore came, begging admission, and every day he was sent away—for his own protection, he was told. She recovered very slowly, her face marked, as you saw. I did not believe the child could still have survived within her, but the doctor said it still lived. When she was able to be moved we brought her here, away from the humid air of the coast. She came in a closed carriage, and no one ever saw her leave Sanlúcar or enter here. I brought women from the north to care for her, and told everyone she was a young, distant cousin, in need of a long rest, and the sun of Andalucía. By then it was evident she was to bear a child. It came at barely seven months. It lived for two days, then died. But the fools had stupidly allowed her to see the child. They allowed her to hold it. In her weakened condition her mind spun fantasies— what fantasies, who knows? But the dead child was too much for her poor mind. When it died she wept and screamed for it, until, in desperation, someone snatched a doll from one of the children of the castle servants here, and put it in her arms. Then she was quiet, and comforted. Since then she has known nothing else, appears to want nothing else."

"But my grandfather—you *cannot* have kept him away, when she was so ill, when the child was born."

"When a living child was born we admitted him. It was his child. A son. His heir. We admitted him to see Mariana. The smallpox that had taken her beauty must have been a terrible shock to him, but I have to grant him that he never faltered. He began to make plans to take her and his son back to Ireland. Then the child died, and her reason went with it. Once again she suffered high fever. Childbed fever. Once again we expected her to die. It would be better if she had. Blodmore stayed here, went to her bedside frequently, but in her fever she did not know him. For weeks it dragged on. And then the fever receded. She is strong, like her father. She survived. Only once did she look at Blodmore and know him. Her poor weakened mind associated him with her suffering, the loss of her child. There was hysteria and, once again, fever. The doctor forbade him to see her. He waited. For months more he waited in that house in Jerez. Then, when he was once more admitted by the doctor, Mariana had regressed to her own childhood. She knew her father, she knew me because by then I was as familiar as her attendants. She knew her dolls. She did not know Blodmore. Since she shrank from strangers, she shrank from him. She seemed to have some memories of her former beauty, because she would sit before her mirror, pulling at the craters on her face, as if to tear them away. She seldom spoke. Several times Blodmore tried to draw from her some memory of him, but there was none. His time in her life

189

had been brief, and it was obliterated. All she wanted was her child again, and another child was what she never could have. Even Blodmore was defeated in the end."

The harsh but nervous laugh broke through again. "Oh, I have to admit that he behaved well—he behaved well *then,* when the damage was done. He would have taken her back to Ireland with him, hideous and feebleminded as she was. He would have taken her to live in the house in Jerez, if she had wanted that. But still she shrank from him, cried for her father, and her child, and wanted no part of him. In the end he recognized that it would have been the greater cruelty to take her from here.

"So he returned to Ireland and never came again. Each year, Santander tells me, the profits from Blodmore's share of the bodega are deposited with the bank to be used for her needs. Santander, of course, refuses them. So Blodmore went back to Ireland, with a living wife who was no wife. Some stubbornness or sense of remorse held him back from trying to have the marriage annulled. Over this point he would certainly have encountered Santander's opposition. It would have been a terrible thing, a public scandal, with repercussions reaching very far. To the world, Santander's daughter is dead. Blodmore agreed to let it be so."

I was thinking of the single sheets of paper, one for each year, bearing the Santander signature. *Ella está viva. She lives.* Only his death had released my grandfather from the vows of his marriage. The living shell of it remained here, in this castle at Arcos, under the bright Andaluz sky.

"He greatly wronged us—me and Santander." She was speaking now quite softly, after a long pause. Perhaps she had been letting me ponder all she had said, letting me see how it had marked our lives. "He died without an heir, and his beloved Clonmara went to Richard Selwin. And *I* brought Richard Selwin back here, and offered him Elena and a large dowry. In the end, my blood, the blood of my family, will inherit Clonmara. And now *you* have come, and the Blodmore strain is back with us once more. You will bear Santander's first legitimate grandchild—who knows what other by-blows are around? This is the child of his beloved Carlos. I decided that you should know what it is you have done, what weight lies on your shoulders. *I* had chosen to have Blodmore, but with one look at a wide-eyed girl he lost all that I could have given him."

"He loved her. He *must* have loved her!"

"He lusted for her. It is as simple and as common as that. Your family seems to make a habit of these kinds of hasty marriages. Blodmore's first wife—utterly unsuitable, but it didn't matter to him. He wanted her. He got her."

"He loved my grandmother. I'm quite certain of that. I'm certain too that he must have loved Mariana." I would not stop defending him. I knew now the agony he must have endured during that year of exile. I loved him more. "If . . ." I said, "if he had been allowed to have Mariana after they had been married, everything would have been all right. Yes, I know . . . Don Paulo was more ambitious for her, but with my grandfather she would have been happy. He would have taken her back to Clonmara and the child would have been healthy and would have lived. There would have been other children, living children, not wax dolls. My mother would have had brothers and sisters. But you separated Mariana and my grandfather. You threatened that poor girl with annulment, with bearing her child in secret. You deprived her of her husband's presence, the very sight of him. All to satisfy your own jealousy. You married Don Paulo to show that you could marry any man by lifting your finger—Don Paulo, *her* father!"

"You go too far, girl! I did not ask you here to—"

"And I did not ask to come. I did not ask for the knowledge you've forced on me. Is it to have still more revenge you've brought me here? It's useless, you know. You can't reach into the grave. He's dead! He died among those who loved him. He died doing the thing he most loved to do. He is buried where his heart lies. *That* you can't touch!"

"So . . . the mouse stirs and squeaks and pretends to be a lion. Believe me, girl, you will know . . . you will

191

know what you have done! You will know it, and say nothing—nothing to anyone. Not to that drunken fool, your mother. Not to that vain, charming weakling, your husband. Not to that long-nosed nobody, María Luisa. You are a Blodmore. You have his blood. They tell me your own father is a scoundrel. Your mother is a disgrace. *This* is what you bring to Santander! Twice in his life you Blodmores have struck to his heart. How he hates you! Live with the knowledge, girl. Do not think you have rights—you have *no* rights in this family. We owe you nothing. Think of this feeble-minded creature here, and know that you owe us everything. Live to repay it. But repayment will take a lifetime. It will take all the energy and dedication you possess. Although Santander loves him, in my opinion Carlos is a poor sort. But you have married him and you will—you must—be the perfect wife, whatever treatment he cares to hand out to you. You will not run off as your mother did. You will stand by your promises. You will measure up to *our* standards now. You will do as *we* say."

I rose. "I will do what I believe is right. I think I had better leave, Marquesa. The sun is hot, and it is a very long way home."

I was striding across the courtyard when her voice reached me again.

"You will eat before you go, girl. You will eat for your child."

I turned slowly. "Yes. Yes—you are right, Marquesa. I will eat for my child. I will have a healthy child, you know. We Blodmores are strong people."

And before their eyes, in total silence, I ate a huge lunch. I drank wine, and had my glass refilled by the hand of Don Paulo. No servant was present to wait on us. It was entirely private. The Marquesa's eyes seldom left my face, nor did Don Paulo's, and yet I felt strangely liberated from the fear of them. They had told the worst there was to know; no longer did some unknown enmity haunt me. That morning I had been pale and trembling and nervous; many times I had wanted to be sick. That stage of my pregnancy seemed to leave me. I remember

I strode from the Marquesa's presence, having thanked her for her hospitality, and received no reply. I strode down the steep slope to where the carriage waited, refusing Don Paulo's arm. On the drive back to Jerez I sat erect and did not once reach for a handkerchief to wipe the sweat from my forehead. It was as if a rod of iron had been thrust into my back. For my grandfather's sake I would have to be all the things they did not expect me to be; I would have to find strength where I had not known it existed. And I would love my child, shield it from them, if I could. I pondered the story I had heard, the living witness to it I had seen. *Ella está viva. She lives.*

My mother was at the vineyard house when Don Paulo's carriage finally took me there. She swept me into her arms.

"Oh, my darling! María Luisa only told me today! Yesterday she said you were visiting. I didn't notice . . . Charlie, it's true—you're going to have a baby?"

"Yes, Mother. A baby—a child."

Carlos was there, in the background, letting my mother have her way for the time being. "Oh, Charlie—oh, Charlie!" And she held me tighter.

Then her head came up. "But darling, I've been waiting all day. All day you've been gone . . . with . . . with *him!*"

Very gently I disengaged her arms. "Yes, Mother. Don Paulo was kind enough to send his carriage for me. He took me to see his castle at Arcos. It is like a fairy tale, Mother. Sometime perhaps you'll see it."

"I have never seen the castle at Arcos," Carlos said. "Except from the outside. It really belongs to the Marquesa de Pontevedra."

I took off my gloves with great care, smoothing them. "Ah, yes. The Marquesa. I met her. She is in residence. A . . . a great lady."

My mother fell back, a little nervously. In Carlos' eyes I saw the dwindling of that look he had always until now given me, the look of affectionate indulgence one might give a playful kitten—or a young child. What came to replace it I was not exactly sure, but I knew that our period of uncritical acceptance was over. We had not had even the brief honeymoon young lovers are entitled to. Something had been stripped from me that day which could never be replaced. I was scarred and pitted with the wounds my grandfather had inflicted, and had had inflicted on him, like the face of the woman in the castle.

Ella está viva.

CHAPTER FIVE

My first son was born after a labor that was agonizing but mercifully short—so short that it was easy to forget it. Carlos took both things for granted; the first and most important thing being that the child should be a son; secondly, that I should produce him with as little fuss as possible and that I should recover my strength in hours, rather than weeks, which was the case with most gently bred ladies. He waltzed the baby around the room in his arms, pausing to kiss me on the forehead.

"But you are not like other women, querida. Did I not tell you that you are the stuff of the brave bulls? This afternoon my father will come to visit his grandchild. You will be ready to receive him." It was spoken not as an order but with the simple assurance that nothing else but obedience was possible. I was only a woman, after all.

Nanny, however, asserted her rights. "Don Carlos, that child is a few hours old. You'll make him sick swinging him all over the place like that."

"Nonsense, Nanny," Carlos said. "The child is as strong

as a horse, already. And look, he does not mew like a kitten. He laughs! You see, already he knows his father."

Carlos was always to be a winning father to his children, in the moments he remembered he was a father—always affectionate, laughing, taking little responsibility for the way they grew up. The discipline would not come from him but from Nanny, myself, and María Luisa. He expected obedient, intelligent, well-behaved children, but he didn't want the bother of helping them to become those things. My mother, as she watched this proud waltz around the room, seemed to want to carry it on herself. "He is wonderful! Beautiful! A son—oh, Charlie dear, a son!"

There was a little catch of heartbreak in her sigh of pleasure. How desperately sons had been needed in our family, and in the family of Don Paulo. And of us Blodmores, only I knew that my grandfather had had, at last, a son, the son he had longed for, the child who had lived and died in two days in that castle on the rock of Arcos. I nursed my healthy, laughing infant at my breast, and sighed myself, but with gratitude. "He has the eyes of the Blodmores," my mother said.

"Better for all of us, Lady Pat, if he looked exactly like my father." But Carlos still smiled, proud and satisfied. There would be plenty more, his manner implied, who would look back at the beholder with the dark eyes of the Fernández family.

Yes, it was all over successfully, but the months in between had not been so easy. I had kept it easy on the surface, as much as I could. The very fact that the baby had been born here, in the house in the Plaza de Asturias, had been against my wishes, but good sense had made it inevitable. I had wanted to be at the vineyard house, the place I loved. Carlos' pride had forbidden it; he needed a palacio, even the ruin of one, for his son to be born in, and besides, when the time came I would need the midwife and doctor quickly. I had longed for the peace of the place that had become my beloved refuge, the ministering hands of Concepción, the smiles of Antonio. It had been inevitable in the months of our marriage that we had come to stay more often at the Plaza de Asturias than the vineyard house. The journey each day, to and fro, had been too long to make to the vineyard house—Carlos had had nowhere convenient to return for the long, late lunch and the siesta. During the rainy months of the winter the roads were bad, and the track up to the house on that albariza soil had become dangerously slippery. My mother, driving out one day in a ramshackle dogcart she had acquired, had almost overturned trying to get the horse up the slope on which his feet could find no purchase. She had ended by abandoning the cart and leading the horse up to the house, the two of them liberally caked with gray mud. "Charlie, the first spell of dry weather I'm going to send Andy out here to move you into town. It's downright dangerous."

"I'm perfectly all right," I said. "I like it here." It was true. The house still enchanted me. The big light white rooms, almost bare of furniture, the fires that Concepción kept constantly replenished, the deep quiet and tranquillity that surrounded me—all of these, I thought, were good for the child.

"*You* may be all right," my mother snapped, in a rare mood of peevishness. "But what if you have an accident and harm the child?" She had been more shaken by her experience than she admitted. She sat and drank freely from the brandy she had brought with her.

"The child . . . yes, the baby." The child was all-important. It was the reason Carlos had married me. If I did not give him a healthy child the fault would be mine.

"Besides," my mother added, "Carlos has been staying too many nights at the Plaza de Asturias—or *supposed* to be staying. He comes to supper, then he goes out 'for a little visit' he says. You'll have to watch him, Charlie. You'll have to *be* there." She wasn't very subtle in her hints of what I already suspected. But when Carlos married me he had made no promise of absolute fidelity—and especially to a wife who was heavily pregnant.

So reluctantly I had returned to Jerez to live, to await the birth of the baby. As much as the vineyard house itself, I missed the daily inspection of the small venture I had persuaded Carlos and my mother to let me undertake. Really, it had needed only my mother's permission and the help of the little money she could spare—the land and the vineyard house were hers—but it would have been unthinkable to begin anything of the sort without Carlos' permission and seeming advice. He gave it grudgingly, with a shrug of his shoulders, no doubt thinking of better ways he could use the money. We seemed always to be scraping for money, and what I proposed would take many years before it yielded us a return. But what I had dreamed that first day I visited the vineyard house, the dream of seeing the rough land cleared and the orderly rows of vines planted, had its small beginning. Antonio had hired some labor to begin to clear the first few hectares of land. I had pegged and marked out the land on the slope that went down to the main road, the land nearest our neighbor, whose rows of well-tended vines and beautifully tilled land had first roused my envy and ambition. Carlos had agreed, as had my mother, as one gives in to the wayward whim of a pregnant girl, in order to keep her happy. But I watched the fires that autumn that marked the first clearing of the brush, choked in their smoke, and dreamed that I was beginning to plant a vineyard for my child.

After I was forced back to the town, on the dry days during the winter Andy would drive me out to see how the work progressed. The land had been intensively plowed in October, too late, everyone said, for that work, but I was too impatient to wait until next summer, for August, when the *agosta,* the first deep tilling of a vineyard, should properly be done. The soil had been broken to a depth of about sixty centimeters—I was learning to count this way now—by working with a narrow hoe. We had then to wait until enough rain had fallen during the winter—between twenty and thirty centimeters was needed—and this usually had come by January. Andy would never let me walk up to the house when the ground was wet—it was true that the albariza became extremely slippery in the wet weather. As the winter ended and I was growing heavy with the child, the land was leveled and marked out in what they called the *marco real* system, based on the square, the distance between each plant and the next kept at a strict one and a half meters. It was not as economical of the land as the other way, the *tresbolillo,* the triangle, but it meant that a man could work along the rows and reach across the whole width of the lane as he moved. It was my neighbor, he whose immaculately tended vineyards had given me the desire to try for my own, who advised me in all this.

I found to my delight and comfort that the land belonged to Don Luis. Carlos showed so little interest in my tiny, infant project that I took it on myself to visit Don Luis. His seamed, sensitive face lit up with interest when I told him what I was trying to do—and how little money there was to do it with.

"You shall have the advice of my foreman, Mateo. He lives at the vineyard house closest to yours." When I told him there was no money to pay for a specialist in viticulture, that Antonio's knowledge must suffice, he shook his head. "A badly planted vineyard will cause nothing but regret. When it is ready for production, in five years' time, you may, if you're lucky, see twenty-five years of excellent harvests from it—and some even go to forty years. It is essential that you do it properly from the beginning." He smiled at me. "I almost envy you your project. The land has been lying fallow all these years. The strength has gone back into the soil. Mateo will be thankful you are no longer growing a crop of weeds, whose seeds will blow into his soil. You will have good harvests, Doña Carlota."

So it was under Don Luis' eyes that the first vines were planted. We planted in the marco real system on his advice. "There's an old saying in Spanish agriculture about leaving plenty of room for growth. *'Retírate de mí que daré por tí por mí.* Get away from me and I will yield for both of us.'" He also advised me on selecting the stock, which for this vineyard was Berlandieri x Riparia, a purely American stock which had replaced the native vines after the phylloxera destroyed them. Before the new vines were planted the fertilizer was brought in esparto grass bas-

kets, about twelve kilos for each hole dug. By the time
I had paid for that, I knew I could not pay for the plant
stock also. It was then Don Luis offered me my first loan.

"I'm sure Carlos would not permit it," I said, and still
I longed to accept, because if I did not, the work would
stop and the new vineyard go back to brush.

"Carlos need not know. Carlos is a . . ." He hesitated,
just perceptibly. "Carlos is an intelligent young man, but
very easygoing. If you do not bring him your problems he
will not look for them. If he asks, say I managed to give
them to you at a very favorable price, since I was buying
many for myself. I will even make a bill of sale . . . the
labor of the men need not be included. We will bury that
item as firmly as we plant the vines."

"And for security? I have nothing to offer you."

"You have the best security. Your future harvests."

So, although I didn't own the land, I made myself
believe that I owned the harvests that would come from
it. I signed a paper for Don Luis, which was so obscurely
written I doubted any lawyer would have given it a
second glance. But it was enough for Don Luis and me.
We signed it, shook hands on it, and took a copita together. I felt both content and excited—happy.

"All this activity is bad for you," Nanny had grumbled.
"You should be quiet, and think of your child."

"That's what's wrong with most women," María Luisa
snapped. She was often irritable these days, trying to cope
with our tangled finances, trying to run our disorderly
household, trying to let us hold our heads up in the sharp-
sighted community which little escaped. "What Charlie
is doing may well be the best thing she could do. At least
she's *doing* something." When she was tired and her
guard was down, the name Charlie slipped out. Normally
she did not approve of it, but when she used it I felt her
affection break through the barrier of her formal manners.

"I hear that Don Luis' wife is ill," Nanny observed.

"Hear? Where do you hear such things?" María Luisa
demanded. "Who do you have to talk to?"

Nanny stiffened her back. "There are other nannies.
A lot of them. Most of the *good* families have them. We

200

meet. We meet when they take the children out. There aren't many have *my* experience." Since her total experience seemed to have been as a nurserymaid when my mother was a child, and then as a fully fledged Nanny to me, and neither of us had, by polite standards, turned out very well, I wondered what these other exiled nannies really thought of her. But it would have been cruel to deny her their companionship. At best she knew only the absolute minimum of Spanish words to insure getting her necessities. But the English, Irish, and Scottish nannies, who seemed to be prized by the families of Jerez, were valued partly for the very reason that they refused to learn any Spanish. The children in their charge, of necessity, had to speak English.

"So . . . so, Amelia is ill," María Luisa mused. "She always has been, more or less. Made a habit of it. I wonder what it is this time? It would be God's blessing if she were pregnant."

"It's not *that*," Nanny said. "*That* we would know."

Don Luis spoke to me of it one day when we drove out to the vineyard to watch the progress of the planting. The foreman—Don Luis' foreman, Mateo—had laid out the iron stakes which were to support the vines and was supervising the men hired to do the planting, adding the last of the fertilizer as each root was tamped into position. I noticed that Antonio worked beside Mateo with no sign of resentment at the other man being placed in a superior position. Antonio seemed to share my own dream, the dream of all the sloping land my mother owned one day being covered with the fruitful vines. By that time he would have learned a great deal about viticulture, more than he knew from observation and from hiring himself out as casual labor at the times it had been needed. He himself would be a foreman on the day the dream came true. Evidently he meant to be ready for it.

"You will have something to give your son, Doña Carlota," Don Luis observed as he came back from an inspection of the planting. "As he grows, so will the vines. By the time he begins his schooling you will have your

201

first harvest. By the time he is a young man the vines will cover all of your hillsides and reach right around to join my land again. Yes, you will truly have something to give your son."

I turned then and looked at the beautifully tended land, the mature vines pruned almost down to the ground, as was the custom here in Jerez, which belonged to Don Luis. I couldn't say anything, but he seemed to know my thoughts. "Yes, it is a pity I have no son—no child for whom I grow my vines. Well . . ." He shrugged. "We accept what God sends. My poor Amelia is not well. Did you know?"

I didn't want to confess I had listened to Nanny's gossip. I shook my head. "I'm sorry."

He sighed, and then gave the order to the coachman to proceed. The coachman, I knew, had instructions to move at a snail's pace. I was not to be bounced about; everyone understood that.

"Yes . . . not well. Not well at all. Something we don't understand. I brought specialists from Sevilla, and lately one from Madrid. They cannot understand it. They say they must have her in hospital for tests. They even talk of her going to London, or Vienna." He gestured helplessly. "I don't understand a thing they say, and I suspect they only talk that way because they don't have much idea themselves what might be achieved. Amelia, for the moment, refuses to go anywhere, especially as they can promise her no certain treatment, much less a cure. I can't say I blame her. She is wise in her own way, Amelia." He turned to me, almost pleadingly. "Would you not come now and take tea with her? She loves her English afternoon tea. She is always so anxious that it be done correctly. She would like your company. . . ."

From my faint recollection of the languid young woman I remembered from the evening of the splendid party they had given, I rather doubted that she would want the company of someone as insignificant, as socially muddled, as I was. And yet I thought Don Luis' request was genuine, and I would have done anything to please him. To my surprise Amelia showed pleasure

202

when she saw me, roused herself from the sofa where she had been lying, and came to kiss me. I didn't think it was because she particularly liked me, but she, like myself, sought to please Don Luis.

"And how does the vineyard go? It is the talk of Jerez, you know. Just imagine, you have been here only a few months, already married, planting a vineyard, and . . . and . . ." Primly she tried to avoid gazing at my swollen body. We were still playing the game that my baby would be born the decent nine months after my marriage to Carlos. But I knew that half the town was running bets on how much premature my child would be.

"Only with Don Luis' assistance," I said, accepting lemon tea in a beautiful Crown Derby cup. "Without him I would be floundering. But somehow . . . somehow I think it would have pleased my grandfather. I think, when he bought the vineyard, he truly meant to continue to work it. The old records show that it was a good producer before the phylloxera. . . ." I intended, I was determined, to bring up my grandfather's name whenever I could. It was an eternal irritant, I knew, to Don Paulo, and a blow at the Marquesa. My love for my grandfather demanded that he be recognized. I would never be quiet out of deference to the power of those two; I would be silent, for pity's sake, about what I had seen that day at Arcos.

Amelia clapped her hands in a pathetic gesture of gaiety. "Listen to her, Luis! Is she not something? Already talking about the records of the vineyard. I imagine she knows exactly how many butts it produced the year before the phylloxera. Very soon she will be in the corner with all you men talking of the last harvest, the next harvest, how many butts . . . and on and on." Then her little, pale face crumpled. "But you will have a baby also. Truly, you are blessed."

This was not the whining young woman of María Luisa's recollection. Along with her envy of my pregnancy, there was a gladness, for my sake, I thought, and still a forlorn hope that soon she would share my state. There was more sadness in the face of Don Luis; there was sadness, and no hope at all. I remembered what María Luisa had said of him. "He is not macho . . ." There was no woman on earth, however strong or well, who could cure that if it were indeed the truth.

I found myself going more frequently to visit Amelia; sometimes Don Luis joined us, more often he left us alone. It was a strange friendship we formed, with so little in common. But Amelia had lived nowhere but Jerez, and she was curious about Ireland. I could tell her only about Clonmara; until a few months ago, my world had been as narrow as hers. But she liked to hear anything I cared to tell her, facts and fantasies dragged up from Irish history. She surprised me one day by saying, "How different your country's story might have been if Philip's Armada had succeeded—aren't the Iberians and the Hibernians of the same race? England would have been Catholic again, and Ireland would probably be free. . . ." Then she threw in quickly, as if to get it over with, "I shall be going to Vienna soon with Luis. The doctors are talking of some sort of treatment. There is some man called Roentgen who has found some way of taking pictures of one's inside, and perhaps finding out what is wrong." She reached out suddenly and took my hand. "I'm so frightened, Carlota. I wish I were strong like you. They talk of things being wrong with my blood, but no one seems sure what to do. Will you pray for me, Carlota?"

I was not religious, and she must have known it. But I nodded. "I will light a candle for you every day."

She smiled, satisfied. "I will not be here when your son is born." This time she made no pretense of keeping up the fiction that my child's birth was still months away. "I would have liked to be godmother to him."

"You shall be."

She smiled, but without conviction. "Here—you must have this. Something to remember me by."

I gasped. From her dress she was unpinning a brooch of diamonds and rubies. It was the gift of Don Luis, and uniquely belonged to Jerez, since it was a tiny replica of the traditional venencia, the inner part of the little cup being rubies, representing the wine. "You *cannot!* It is from your husband."

"Luis would let you have anything I wished you to have. He likes us to be friends. He keeps saying he is too old for me, and that *you* need all the friends you can find. Is that true, Carlota? Do you really need me? No one else does."

"Luis does. I do." I took her cold thin hands in mine. "You will come back well, and you will be godmother to my child." Suddenly, here in the midst of the riches of this house, the Chippendale furniture, the Georgian silver tea service, surrounded by Wedgwood vases and pictures of horses painted by English painters, I was aware of the wealth I possessed, even though by these standards we lived in poverty. My body was healthy, and I carried a child. The little jeweled venencia seemed to be Amelia's tribute to that.

I showed it to Carlos that night, but he seemed to take no pleasure in it. "Are you sure it was Amelia who gave it to you? That mealymouthed whiner is a friend to nobody. Wasn't it Luis who gave it to you?"

"Jealous?" I said. "You think any man wants me the way I am?" I indicated the swollen bulk of my figure.

Carlos rose, thrusting back his chair angrily. "Jewels are *all* Don Luis can give a woman. He hasn't got anything else!" Then he left the house, not saying where he was going. He too often did that now that I was getting near to term. Moving into the house in the Plaza de Asturias had changed nothing. We dined with my mother and María Luisa, and had several rooms set aside for our own use, but Carlos was seldom there except for a token presence at mealtimes.

María Luisa was blunt about it. "All Spanish men are said to have mistresses," she said. "Carlos is young. He cannot be tied at home. Just be thankful he married you."

I tried to be thankful for that but it was not enough. The thought of other women hurt. What sort of women? I wondered. Married women—for the unmarried were guarded too well. Which women? Perhaps one of a class and sort I would never know. I spent sleepless nights on that thought, without an answer. Was it inevitable? I wondered if with Richard Blodmore it would have been inevitable. In these days of growing inactivity, while I waited, my thoughts often turned to Richard Blodmore. Sometimes I dreamed of the rose garden, and I willed him to remember me each time he touched its gate. The hurt that Carlos inflicted on me slipped away in the remembrance of Richard Blodmore.

During that time we attended the wedding of Don Paulo's son Ignacio in the Collegiate Church. It was not a good day for Carlos. All of fashionable Jerez was there, all resplendent in their finest clothes, showing off their best horses and carriages. The bride came from a family of French origin, settled in Jerez generations ago and reputed to be among the richest in the sherry trade. She was pretty, splendidly dressed, and displayed the security that only a fat dowry can give. María Luisa had done her best to see that I was well turned out for the occasion, but my vineyard had squeezed the budget dry. Carlos had complained about having to wear a jacket which he claimed had grown shiny at the elbows. It was an exaggeration, but he had been used to new clothes whenever he felt like them. He had been receiving his salary from the bodega, but neither my mother nor myself, and not even María Luisa, had so far suggested that he contribute to our household expenses. After all, my mother reasoned, it would be too bad to have to charge him for his food and wine, and how could we charge him for the rooms I also occupied? So Carlos kept his money and spent it as he pleased. He still played polo, but he nagged that he was obliged to play on borrowed ponies. It seemed Don Paulo was no longer prepared to support this particular extravagance: it had been done, of course, as part of the punishment for Carlos' rash action in marrying me, but it was only one of the many things that rankled. "I hate this penny pinching," he would say, and he was openly envious of the fortune that Ignacio would now control through his bride. "The accountant will have a busy time," he said bitterly. I could not face the reception at the bride's house, so I went home and left Carlos to enjoy himself in any way he could, unburdened by the presence of an ungainly wife. If it had been the marriage of anyone but a son of Don Paulo I would have stayed away. But I had promised myself, and my grandfather, that never again would I show fear or apprehension of the man. So I went, and endured it, and then dragged myself home. Only pride that matched any Spaniard's kept my body and head upright.

That night while Carlos danced, and undoubtedly flirted, at the reception for Ignacio and his bride, Margarita, I wept when María Luisa and I were left alone. My mother had also gone to the party. Her relationship to Carlos demanded that an invitation also be extended to her. María Luisa had shaken her head over my tears.

"Do not weep, Charlie. Never let a man see you weep. It drives him further away. Smile when he comes, and never let him see you weep." She brought me a glass of brandy and made me laugh. "You see what a treasure of wisdom some man has missed just because it pleased God to make me ugly? One day I shall have to ask God to pay what He owes me."

My son was beautiful and healthy, and so big that no one could have believed he was premature. All of Carlos' good humor and hope had returned. "Well, Ignacio's scrawny little bride will have to work hard to do better than that." Then he laughed loudly. "And so will Ignacio . . . so will Ignacio!"

He grew quiet, though, as the time for his father's visit approached. He had been at the bodega for a short time that day, doing nothing more than receive congratulations on the birth of his son, but his words dropped to nothing when he heard the sound of the carriage in the outer courtyard, and calls of Paco and the two boys, excited by the day's events and the visit of Don Paulo. Pepita, for no reason, suddenly shivered at the sound of the voices, the sound of the steps in the marble passages, and she crept close to the bed. I held my son proudly and protectively in my arms.

My mother entered first, her face flushed, but not, I

thought, from wine. María Luisa followed closely, two unusual patches of red staining her sallow cheeks. "The . . . the . . ." For a moment her sense of protocol deserted her. "The Marquesa de Santander y Pontevedra," she stammered. "The Marqués de Santander."

Carlos was bowing low over the hand of the lady who was his father's wife. If Carlos had ever been flustered, it was then. "You are welcome, Marquesa."

She took little notice of him, as if she already knew all there was to be known about him and he didn't interest her. She was dressed, as before, in black, and with jewels only on her hands. She swept towards the bed, bending low over my son, carefully examining the tiny, creased features, the features that, as yet, seemed to have no definite shape.

"Well, Santander," she demanded at last, "what do you think of your first grandson? Or should I say your first recognized grandson?"

Don Paulo took his time about crossing to the bed; he spent an equal time about examining the child. The Marquesa's hands were already busy, trying to unwrap the shawl that loosely covered the child. "He is all right?" she said. "There is no . . . no weakness?" Her tone was sharp, peremptory. I held the baby closer. We seemed almost to be tugging him between us.

"He is perfect. He is as strong as any baby less than a day old can be expected to be." The infant's eyes were already trying to focus on the flashes of light which sprang from the Marquesa's hands. His own tiny hand attempted to reach towards them.

"He is greedy, the little one," the Marquesa said. "Already he wants the best." She was suddenly good-humored, almost gay.

"He shall have it." Carlos was beside me, protective of us both in a way that amazed me. "He is as strong as a lion." Already his son had changed from a horse to a lion. He had started out as a brave bull. Carlos would expect much of him, I thought.

"And he has the eyes of a cat," Don Paulo said. "He has the Blodmore eyes."

208

"All young babies' eyes look like that," I said defensively.

"Not all children have the Blodmore eyes," Don Paulo answered, staring at me and then looking towards my mother. In this feature we both so much resembled my grandfather, and it offended Don Paulo.

"What will he be called?"

"Paulo," Carlos answered promptly.

Through the long day I had listened to Carlos' insistence that this, and only this, should be the first Christian name of our son. He would have a string of other names, of course, but Paulo would come first. I had been inclined to give way to him, anything to keep his good humor, even his favor, perhaps even to win a scrap of favor for the child from Don Paulo himself. Now these two came, thrusting themselves into my room as if it were they who were the new parents, though they had shown no concern through the long, tiring months of pregnancy. They came as if they brought precious gifts for the child; they angered me and stiffened my resistance.

"He shall be called after my grandfather. He shall be called John."

A cry of pure pleasure broke from my mother. "Oh, Charlie—how wonderful. How proud he would have been!"

"John . . . Juan . . ." The name sounded tenuous on the Marquesa's lips. "Juan—that is what I used to call him. Yes—the child's name shall be Juan." It was decided, not because I had decided it, but because the Marquesa had given her approval. All at once I did not want the name any longer. I could sense Carlos' confusion, as he looked from his father to this impossibly arrogant, overbearing woman. He waited to take a cue from Don Paulo, but none came. The habit of command had been too long abdicated where this woman was concerned.

"I shall be his godmother," she announced.

"I have already asked Amelia," I said coldly.

"Doña Amelia," the Marquesa said briskly, as if it were a matter of no consequence, "will not live to fulfill her duties as a godmother. A godmother, you know, has a very special place in a child's life."

At that moment, despite the sweet springtime warmth of the beautiful May day on which my son had been born, in spite of the blankets and shawls, I was cold. In my mind there flashed the remembrance of that fairy tale told to me long ago—which one had it been?—the one in which a sorceress, forgotten among the list of those invited to be godmothers, uninvited to the christening, had nevertheless come, and bestowed her unwanted, terrible christening gift upon the child. I saw the jeweled hands of the Marquesa upon my son, and I wanted, more than I had ever wanted anything, to snatch him out of her reach. But I had neither the strength nor the chance. Her mark was upon him already, her will proclaimed.

I loved Carlos at that moment. He moved closer, sat upon the bed beside me, put his arm about my shoulders, and thus embraced the baby also. As much as could be in the nature of someone so easygoing, he was stern.

He looked at his father's wife, the lady of legendary power and wealth who had ruled his life from a distance for so long. Everything that was masculine and brave in Carlos came out at that moment. He said: "I think my wife, Marquesa, has the right to choose the godmother. And if Doña Amelia . . ."

But I knew that Amelia was far away in Vienna, might never return. And how, I wondered, did the Marquesa know so much about her condition? How did she know so much about everything? Abruptly, the buoyant strength which had sustained me through the birth, through the day of joy and excitement, through this interview, drained from me. I felt depleted, as if all my strength had gone to my son. He would need every part of it if he were to fight this woman who had declared herself his godmother —and yet, if he were to fight the world, wasn't she a powerful ally to have with him? I could not refuse him that alliance. I felt my shoulders sag within the protective circle of Carlos' arm.

"It shall be. Doña Amelia will be represented by proxy.

You could not refuse her that? She is, after all, the wife of Don Paulo's partner, your own relative."

I bowed my head and silently begged my son's forgiveness.

Through a haze of weariness I heard her voice again. *"I* am to be a godmother by proxy. We have had news from Ireland. Richard Blodmore's first child has been born. A son . . . an heir for Clonmara."

The baptism took place six days after Juan was born. It was put forward because the Marquesa had decided not to remain any longer at Sanlúcar—which was where she stayed rather than her husband's home in Jerez. The child, they said, was healthy; there was no risk. The mother, however, was not expected to be present.

After they all had left in the carriages provided by Don Paulo, María Luisa carrying my son, I called Serafina and told her to help me dress. I took no notice of the protests. Gentlewomen were not expected to rise from bed for several weeks after childbirth—only peasants were back in the fields a few days later. I took no notice, pretended not to understand, but told Andy, who had been left behind, to harness the landau. "We will be there for the baptism, Andy." He understood.

I was supported by Andy and Serafina into the Collegiate Church. Around the baptismal font was gathered a splendidly dressed group. The fact that the Marquesa de Pontevedra was godmother to my child had drawn even the most reluctant guest, and many who had not been invited. I could not see my child for the crowd that surrounded the font. All I heard were his lusty yells of protest as the water was poured on his still tender forehead, as the taste of salt was put upon his tongue.

And now I heard that familiar voice answering the query: "Dost thou, in the name of this Child, renounce the devil and all his works, the vain pomp and glory of the world, with all covetous desires of the same, and carnal desires of the flesh, so that thou wilt not follow, nor be led by them?"

The voice, overriding every other sound, came suddenly

211

and assuredly, as if no thought of such things had ever troubled her soul.

"I renounce them all."

On the way out, helped by Andy, I lighted a candle for Amelia.

The christening gifts arrived the same day. From Don Paulo a beautiful, and from what I learned from my grandfather's book, rare carriage clock in a golden case: *To mark the golden hours of your life—Santander*. From the Marquesa came a three-year-old dappled gray pony, a beautiful animal, graceful and spirited, wearing red leather harness studded with silver. By the time Juan was able to ride him, he would most probably have turned completely white and be just the right age and size for the child. In the meantime, he had to be fed and exercised. Both Carlos and Andy were joined in their admiration of him. "Naturally," María Luisa said. "It is not they who will have to pay the feed bills—nor the Marquesa either."

PART TWO

Noon

CHAPTER ONE

1

Juan was only a little more than a year old when his first brother was born. We named him Martín Paulo Carlos. When the next son arrived, born after almost the same frighteningly short period, he was called Francisco Paulo. Each time the Marquesa appeared and assumed her self-appointed role as godmother. She seemed to sense almost to the hour when the births would take place. Each time she was in residence at her palacio at Sanlúcar, would come temporarily to take up residence with Don Paulo at Las Fuentes, and would appear at the Plaza de Asturias within hours of the birth.

"It's not decent!" María Luisa exclaimed. "Barely time to make you presentable."

By now it was taken for granted that I would produce my children with ease and that they would be healthy. The christening ceremonies had become almost a boring ritual with Carlos, except that each time he became surer that the birth of male children was as important to the Marquesa as to his father. Each time there were handsome

214

christening presents, and presents on the name day of each child, elaborate, expensive presents which generally were of little interest to the children. "She might try, for a change," Carlos remarked, "giving some shares in her Barcelona concerns, or Río Tinto. *That* would make more sense." The little dressmaker was now a permanent fixture in our house, busy each day making up the lengths of cloth which came from Seville and Madrid at the Marquesa's orders. "I must have my godchildren presentable," she said.

"Then the seamstress will have to be paid," María Luisa insisted. "And since she is so busy making unnecessary clothes for small children who grow out of them, we also need an assistant seamstress to do the ordinary household mending. Sheets have to be patched, Marquesa—in this house, sheets have to be patched."

This was said during one of the Marquesa's visits. She had a habit of descending on our household unannounced, and the children were turned out for her inspection. She agreed to a small salary for the first seamstress, and partly paid for the assistant. A laundress was engaged full time so that the children's clothes should always be immaculate. María Luisa was jubilant. "The only way to deal with the rich is to *demand* things. Otherwise they don't notice you have to struggle—or pretend not to. The rich are usually very mean with their money, except when it comes to spending it on themselves." She even, to my mortification, got a small additional stipend for Nanny.

"Nanny is our responsibility," I had protested. "We brought her here, and Richard Blodmore paid her—"

"And would you have Richard Blodmore go on paying for the Nanny of *your* children? That won't do! And Nanny stays on here now because she is needed by us. The Marquesa will not have it said that her godchildren do not have a proper Nanny. But she complains about Nanny's accent. It isn't English enough."

"It will do," I said. "It was good enough for my mother and myself." I know I snapped at her, and afterwards apologized.

She softened, as she so often did when we were alone

215

together. "It's all right, querida. I understand." She pulled off the little steel-framed spectacles she had taken to wearing. "It's not been an easy time, has it? Three children in less than four years. Always pregnant, or about to be pregnant, or getting over being pregnant. That woman, descending on you, wanting to run your life, but not willing to pay for it. Giving expensive gifts that we can't sell for fear of offending her. Spoiling the children. Criticizing your mother—yes, I know Lady Pat is something of a trial, but she is *our* trial. How she behaves is no business of the Marquesa's. . . ." Then she put her glasses on again and once more bent over her recipe book. With María Luisa it was always a recipe book or an account book, and both were used in trying to manage a growing household on a tiny budget. We had reached the stage that, when the yearly dividend from the Fernández, Thompson bodega was paid into Don Ramón's bank, we were already several months in debt against it. I think it was only the knowledge that the Marquesa had stood godmother to our children that saved us at times. People were always willing to lend money, at good interest rates, of course, where they smelled even more money. Perhaps they presumed what Carlos had hoped for—that the christening presents had taken a more tangible form than expensive but generally rather useless toys or trinkets. It was a matter of interest and speculation in Jerez that the Marquesa de Pontevedra displayed no interest at all in the children that Don Paulo's other son, Ignacio, had produced. And she had sent only a token wedding gift when the third son, Pedro, was married. Jerez was betting on the chances of my children being remembered handsomely in the will of the Marquesa, especially the oldest son, Juan, who was clearly the favorite. The Marquesa was not an old woman, it was true, but she was not young. Someday she would have to name the heirs to that part of the vast fortune which was not tied to the title. True, these children of mine were no blood relation to her, and she had cousins of every degree scattered through all the noble families of Spain. Yet Jerez was remembering the time, now almost thirty years ago, when my grandfather had come with her to Sanlúcar and a marriage had been expected. Those with very long memories even declared that my son Juan, as he grew older, bore a remarkable resemblance to the handsome Earl of Blodmore.

Because the power of patronage was so great, Jerez was even forgetting the scandal of my hasty marriage to Carlos and the untimely arrival of a child who clearly had not been premature. At least, if Jerez was not forgetting it, they chose now to overlook it. The godchildren of the Marquesa de Pontevedra could not be ignored, so I must be accepted along with them. The knowledge of our poverty, despite all María Luisa's careful managing, was common. We were invited to most parties, and had to refuse many of them because it was impossible to return them equally. A few times a year we in our turn gave little parties to whom we invited only those we could not leave out. María Luisa pared the list down to the bone, and the cost down to the last peseta, but still they cost too much. "I thank the Lord for the cellar Lord Blodmore laid down. Without it, we would be undone."

Between ourselves, though, we never talked about the fact that my grandfather's cellar was also causing problems for my mother. As titular mistress of the household she had access to it whenever she pleased. María Luisa had had the best wine placed on the highest racks where she could not easily find it, but she seemed to care less and less for the quality of what she drank. By the time of the siesta, too often she went off to her bedroom with the deliberate, upright walk of someone who has drunk too much and knows it. She snored softly through the afternoon hours and was ready and brightly expectant for the first copita of the evening to be served. My mother now seemed to hark back to the past more often. Dates became confused. In her mind, every birthday of Juan's recalled the death of Edward VII, which had occurred in the month Juan was born—and that led back to memories of her one London season, the balls, the race meetings, the triumphs she had had, the attentions of Edward, who had then been the Prince of Wales. She would always stop,

217

though, when it came to the point when she had been taken back to Ireland because of those attentions. I wondered, sometimes, if her runaway marriage might not have been the outcome of her frustration and disappointment at that time. The parallel in my own life was rather frightening. Could we Blodmores do nothing prudently and in the right time?

She was, as María Luisa said, a trial, but she was our trial. She was a loving, carelessly spoiling grandmother to my children, playing with them, helping Nanny bathe and dress them, singing to them, and never with a single word of Spanish.

"I can't ever remember her doing anything for me," I said to Nanny. "I didn't know she knew how to bath a baby."

"Nor yet she does, Miss Charlie," Nanny said. "Haven't I to be keeping my eye on her every second to see that she doesn't let the little one slip down into the water and drown his self? To tell you the truth, Miss Charlie, I could be doing without her help. She's more like another child to take care of, but one I can't give orders to . . . she being Lady Pat."

And yet, for all that her little "habit," as it was politely termed in Jerez, was known, she was still popular and still invited about. The fact was that she was still beautiful, still graceful, and still sat a horse in a way that wrung the admiration from even the most demanding Andalucian horseman. The men admitted, though reluctantly, that in the exercises of the High School of Equitation she was very nearly the match of any man among them, and they boasted that they were better than anything seen in the famous Spanish Riding School of Vienna. Around Jerez she acquired an affectionate nickname among those who were too humble even to address her. They called her *la dama del caballo*—the Lady of the Horse. With Balthasar and Half Moon she displayed the patience she showed towards her grandchildren. No time spent schooling them was wasted for her, and I thought they were her happiest hours. She had the gentleness that some Spaniards lacked; she was never in a hurry, and she had the courage that even Balthasar recognized and responded to. She learned the exercises of the Haute École, and trained both horses to them, though generally only stallions had the strength for the more extreme demands. But she enjoyed training Half Moon on the short rein and the longe rein, enjoyed introducing her to the exercises of the piaffe, a cadenced trot on the spot, the passage, which we called the Spanish trot, and the passade. These they called the "Schools on the Ground." Only Balthasar was able to progress to the higher art, the "Schools Above the Ground," which are all based on the piaffe. With him she actually achieved the levade, the courbette, and that heart-stopping movement of the capriole, when for an instant all four legs were off the ground, the forelegs tucked in towards his chest, the hind legs almost out straight with his belly. The stable yard whose size Andy had deplored proved big enough to accommodate these training exercises, and every morning, before the first glass of wine, my mother worked there for several hours. As soon as they were able to, my children demanded to be taken to watch Granny work her horses. They sucked their thumbs and were infinitely patient and interested as she was. It was hard for me to understand the extreme discipline that gripped my mother during those morning sessions, and then watch her come to lunch and the first of a long succession of copitas.

The schooling stopped during the hottest months. "The darlings need grass and shade and trees," my mother wailed. "Where are they to find them?"

They were found on the hacienda of Don Luis on the road to Arcos. Like Don Paulo, his partner Luis was also a cattle breeder and a breeder of bulls; he had olive groves and his cattle grazed under the productive cork trees. He had smiled and shrugged when he heard my mother's first protest that she could not accept such generosity. "What is two more among so many?" So Balthasar and Half Moon had summers of freedom when they never felt even the touch of a halter. Then when the grape harvest was past and the weather became cooler, they came back to Andy's stables and the work began again. During the summer months they lost some of the polish my mother had put on their training, but they were healthier and more eager.

My mother had made a sensation, during one exhibition of horsemanship, organized for charity, by appearing in the traditional dress of the Andalucian horseman, wearing the short jacket, the round black hat with its rolled brim over a spotted blue headcloth, and the matching sash about her slim waist. She rode as they did, with the right hand tucked disdainfully inside her frilled shirt, controlling Balthasar only with the knees and the left hand. She wore black trousers and the beautiful Andalucian boots with their swinging fringes. Some of the ladies were scandalized, but the men, once they were over the shock, applauded. Courage was admired, however it was displayed.

During those years Half Moon was bred to Balthasar. Her colt was a lovely graceful creature, but showing strongly Balthasar's strain of stamina and nobility. We called him Rodrigo.

"You are not the only one who breeds well, Charlie," my mother said, gazing with rapture at the thin-legged creature following his mother through the pasture at Don Luis' hacienda. "I think we may not geld him. Perhaps he will turn out to be as great a stallion as Balthasar." She was wearing the black trousers and the elaborately decorated and tooled leather *zahones,* the protective chaps which the horsemen wore on the outer sides of the legs. It was now her daily uniform, as much as a riding habit had been at Clonmara. Little lines were now appearing about the corners of her eyes because she went so often without a parasol in the sun. But the red hair remained as red as ever, the eyes their extraordinary light green. Some women said the red hair was not quite its natural color, but the men, if they noticed, didn't care. She could still, whether on horseback or dressed in silk for an evening party, draw a crowd of males about her. "But I'm a granny now," she would protest, and continue to flirt, and to drink just a little too much.

While she delighted in her grandchildren, she was

bored by my seemingly endless pregnancy. "Why, Charlie, if you don't stop it you'll forget how to ride! And you always had such a pretty seat on a horse, and good hands. Ah, well—one can't have everything at the same time. . . . Perhaps we should start charging stud fees for Balthasar. . . ."

Did her mind run that way because Carlos' proof of the vaunted *machismo* was so evident? Did she equate him and Balthasar? No longer did she warn me to hold Carlos close, no longer did María Luisa caution me against turning a tearful face to him. We were long past that stage. His infidelities had to be taken for granted. He was always carelessly good-humored, loving with his children, absent-mindedly affectionate with me—and always, from the first, unfaithful. He meant no personal insult to me by it. It was just the way he was made. It was not in his nature to couple with one woman for life. In that, indeed, he was like the stallion. He enjoyed love-making, to me as well as to other women. He was never brutal in the act; he was tender, considerate, imaginative, and all it meant to him was the casual satisfaction of an impulse. I do not think he ever loved me, but he liked me, and I had to be grateful for that. As I had never wholly loved him, I could not offer any reproaches, even unspoken ones. I wondered if he ever sensed that, beneath the passionate nature he enjoyed so much in bed, the underside of me was barely touched at all? Our love-making was physical and nothing more, so my heart was not wrenched by his infidelities. He could not know, and did not care to know, that feeling I had within me, that capability to love with more than my body, had been given to Richard Blodmore, who had done no more than kiss me and hold me briefly in his arms. So it seemed there was almost an unspoken pact between Carlos and myself. The heart of neither one of us would break for the other.

There was a conflict, openly, though, over the ownership of Balthasar. Carlos bitterly resented my mother taking the stallion over for training in the Haute École and riding him in exhibitions. I had made an impulsive gift of the stallion to Carlos on our wedding day, a change of ownership which my mother totally ignored once Balthasar was back in the stables at the Plaza de Asturias. There was, however, no getting past my mother's attitude, and so, since I could not ride myself for much of the time, Carlos reluctantly took over Half Moon. Then my mother began to train her, and also insisted on the summers being spent out on grass. So Carlos bought himself a handsome little mare, not an outstanding animal, but a very good one. He simply handed me the bill. We couldn't pay it, and I saw María Luisa's lips go white as she saw the figure. We looked for something we could sell, and there was nothing. There were the expensive presents the Marquesa and Don Paulo had given to the children, but the absence of any one of them would have been noticed and given deep offense. Amelia, coming to call on the day I had had the bill for the mare from Carlos, found me deeply dejected. She got the story from me, and she was indignant.

"Men—they're all the same! Except Luis, who must be a saint. Let me talk to him—I'm quite sure he would advance the money—"

"No, I couldn't! Not Luis. He's been so generous about the vineyards. I couldn't be more in his debt."

"Then let me—No! Carlota, don't refuse me. I have money. I never use up all my dress allowance . . . and lots of other things. Please, Carlota, let it be just between us. I've never been allowed to help anyone before. I've never had a friend to help, in fact. It would be a kindness. . . ."

I felt the tears of weakness, shame, and relief running down my cheeks. I blew my nose mightily and scrubbed my face with Amelia's dainty handkerchief. "How did you ever get mixed up with such a terrible family as this? We have brought you and Luis nothing but problems."

"You have brought us a family, Carlota. *That* we cannot buy."

So I accepted a loan, with no idea how or when it would be repaid. I insisted on writing a promise of repayment for Amelia, which she accepted with a shrug of

222

indifference, as if she might toss it in the wastebasket as soon as she got home.

I had, in my own fashion, marked the birth of my sons. Before I became pregnant with Martín I had consulted with Don Luis and I had borrowed more money from him, with his encouragement. The next section of fallow land was plowed at its proper time in August and made ready for the winter rains to soak in before the leveling and planting in January. By that time I was quite well on with my second pregnancy and thought of the vines being planted for this child, as the first had been for Juan. Don Luis had wanted me to take more money, so that more land could be put into production, but I had not dared. Only María Luisa knew the size of the present debt to him, and I knew that any show of an excess of money being spent on the vineyards would encourage Carlos to further extravagance. "It is uneconomic to plant in small pieces," Luis argued. I had to refuse him. We seemed to be in debt everywhere, and it frightened me. "I must wait," I told him. "I am one season on with the first vineyard, one season nearer a harvest with which I can repay you." My worst nightmare was that when the vines came to maturity we should have several seasons of poor or bad harvests, when not only would I lose money on my own venture, but the money paid by Fernández, Thompson would be less. I knew that the sources of our extra financial help puzzled Don Ramón—we were already borrowed to the hilt with his bank. But I think he supposed that some assistance came from Don Paulo, or possibly the Marquesa. I let him think it. With Carlos we kept up an elaborate pretense that the money was squeezed somehow from María Luisa's budget. He didn't care to inquire into the details; to discover exactly how we managed, how we lived at all, might oblige him to acknowledge unpleasant facts. There might even be a suggestion that he should contribute towards our expenses. He simply reasoned that three extra children ate little enough, their clothes were provided by the Marquesa's generosity, and they required nothing further spent on them. So long as no one troubled him with the details he seemed content—no, he seemed almost anxious—to remain ignorant. It appeared to me that he took just the barest amount of interest in his work at the bodega to satisfy his father. He was always a good representative for the firm of Fernández, Thompson, ready to drink and talk with those who came to buy, ready always to take the enjoyable journey to London to sell. He always returned from London in high good humor, with presents for all of us and new clothes from his tailor. "A breath of fresh air," he always said. "I enjoy London. . . ." His English was kept honed and polished, and he knew that if he should bring home some English traveler who had come to Jerez to buy sherry, he would be received at our house without question, and without that slight frigidness of etiquette which seemed to plague many Spanish ladies. María Luisa would rush to the cellar to plunder once more the stocks of good wine, she would somehow contrive some delicacy from the kitchen, and we would put on a good front. It brought business to Fernández, Thompson, for which Carlos got the credit. It didn't hurt, as Carlos saw it, to have an Earl's daughter to introduce as his mother-in-law. He had a handsome brood of children to show off. There was even Balthasar, if the caller was interested in good horseflesh. Before visitors Carlos would talk jokingly about "my little businesswoman" when the talk came around to the vineyard project I had embarked on, and there was the added eccentricity of my being accompanied, wherever I moved, not by a lapdog but a huge Spanish mastiff. Carlos made a joke of this too, though at other times he declared Pepita a nuisance. But on the whole, though he grumbled continually about lack of money, Carlos appeared to enjoy life as only those of his nonchalant disposition can. Nothing seemed to worry or disturb him for very long. His quick bursts of temper, though sometimes savage, were soon over, like summer storms. Mostly he smiled, hoped for money in the future from his father, and possibly from the Marquesa, and asked not to be troubled by the minor, boring details of domestic life. So when I made my private arrangements, indulged my passion for the vineyards, I did it without too great a sense of guilt.

Along with the births of my children, I marked the seasons and the years by the work done in the vineyards. The tasks and demands they made seemed endless; in this way too they were like my children, my family. The preparation of the new ground in August, the agosta; the leveling, marking out, and planting about January; the *cavabién,* the second tilling in March; the *golpe-lleno,* the third tilling in May to catch what weeds had been missed in the cavabién and stop the soil from hardening; the *bina* in July, a fourth tilling, held to be very important in Jerez not only to destroy weeds but to make the soil impervious to the heat of the summer and help it retain the moisture the vines would need through those next months; then the *desgrama,* the weeding in August of the first year of the vines, to get rid of anything that had survived the agosta.

For me there was yet no harvest, so we would go on to the *deserpia,* the first tilling of the agricultural year after the harvest. It began when the grass had started to grow after the first autumn rain. We dug square holes to expose the soil to the air and to absorb the rainfall. Then came the *desbraga* in December, when we dug a fifteen-centimeter trench around the young plant and cut the surface roots, which prevented the vine from getting too thick at ground level and produced a uniform thickness higher up to allow for grafting; the unwanted shoots from the last year were also pruned.

However far gone in pregnancy I was, I still came to the vineyards each year in the August of their own first year when the vitally important grafting, the *injerta,* was done. It was then that the buds of the native vine, mostly the Palomino and the Pedro Ximeniz, were grafted onto the American rootstock. The grafts were done at ground level, the graft bound up with raffia, and the earth heaped up around it, so that the whole hillside looked as if it were the unbelievably neat work of busy moles. "The earth holds out the cold of winter and the east winds," Antonio said to me, proud to be displaying his knowledge. He was now almost as fanatical as I about the work of the vineyards. All his life, as had Mateo, he had been associated with the vines, but it had carried little interest except as a way to earn money. The responsibility had never been his, the heartache if the vines failed had never troubled him except as it affected the prosperity of the whole district. Until now he had never looked forward more than one season at a time. Now, like myself, he must wait four or five years until our first harvest; he must wait with patience the long years until the vineyards returned the money and the toil that had been poured into them. One day he would be the true foreman of whole hillsides of vines that belonged to Doña Carlota; he was as impatient for that day as I.

The most heartbreaking task was when we went over the ground of a newly planted vineyard in October, examined all the vines to find and mark those which had failed and must be replaced. This was called the *repaso*. As much as fifteen per cent failed in the early years of the vineyard. I was appalled to see this but Don Luis, with the philosophic attitude of a man who has lived his life with the vines, shrugged. It was always so. I was stunned, and at times frightened, by the amount of work that had to be done. I had undertaken so lightheartedly what I did not understand. Luis smiled. "That is what youth is for, Carlota. If you never dare, what can you win? We all worry—we learn to live with it. But also here in Jerez we have the saying 'The colt and the vine—let someone else breed them.' And yet we go on. . . ."

I could not have gone on without him. His foreman, Mateo, was now my friend, as was Antonio. Mateo was a broad squat barrel of a man, always grinning at me with eyes half closed against the sun. Unlike Antonio though, he seemed to find it amusing that I should want to concern myself with the problems, the endless difficulties and labor of starting and cultivating a vineyard. He had lived with such backbreaking labor, under the cruel heat of the summer sun and the rains of the winter, all his life. He knew and cared for nothing else. But I—I was a stranger, and a lady. Why did I come out in the August heat and in

226

the cold winds to view the vines? He indicated that it could safely be left all to him; he and his men, and the anxious Antonio, would see it all through. Did I not trust him? he wanted to know. Did I not trust the word and experience of Don Luis? Better stay at home and have my babies in comfort and peace. Those who insisted on planting vineyards were mad, but by such madness he had lived all his life. So he grinned, and he shrugged.

My own worry, my excitement, my impatience, became infectious. I did not dare, in Carlos' presence, to talk about the vineyards—better to let him think of it as some harmless hobby, almost a whim of a perpetually pregnant woman who had to be humored. Occasionally he came to inspect the vines, slapping Antonio good-naturedly on the back and praising his growing expertise. He knew there was some loose arrangement by which we used the laborers from Don Luis' vineyards, and that María Luisa and Don Ramón between them somehow found the money. But Don Luis, as an older man and his father's partner, was not to be questioned. If the arrangement suited him, it must be all right, Carlos probably thought. So beyond these few visits he did not bother about the vineyards and I did not bother him. It was Amelia who was my confidante. I found myself leaning more and more on her, and she responded with growing closeness. She had made her journey to Vienna, had traveled back in a leisurely fashion to Jerez—had seen Paris and London with Luis. She had brought back many new gowns, and presents for us all, especially for her godchild by proxy, Juan. She would talk little of the time in Vienna. "I am no better—and no worse. They don't know what it is—or have no name to tell me." She shrugged. "If Luis knows, he does not tell me either. They say I am anemic. It is strange to eat, as I force myself to do, and sometimes not have the strength to put one foot in front of the other. I take all the disgusting medicines, they do more tests, and then they murmur about too many white cells in my blood—and they can do nothing." But her journey away from Jerez had altered her subtly. She dismissed her role as an invalid im-

227

patiently. "I will do what I can. I will live every minute there is." She was interested, as she had been from the beginning, in my vineyard project. She approved of Luis' financing a large part of it. "I hope he does not charge you interest, because he enjoys it more than anything else. Luis loves his vines. And his heart is with anyone brave enough to start out on that path. And a woman, too. . . ." She knew little about the business of viticulture, and until now had cared little. And then, as I began talking of the unending work demanded, naming each one of the tasks, she began to know them as well. The third year, in August, in the little cool that the morning hours gave, she insisted on being driven to the vineyard to watch the grafting. Mateo bowed almost to the ground when she made her appearance; until now she had been the unseen wife of Don Luis, a great lady who was said to be ill with some mysterious illness that did not get better or worse. We were driven up to the house, and Concepción gave us breakfast. Amelia walked through the bare rooms, surveyed the courtyard bright with bougainvillaea and geraniums, drank Antonio's own rather crude wine, and smiled. "I should come more often. It is quiet—and yet everything is growing, and full of life. It is clever of you to have discovered that, Carlota. It gives you something, doesn't it? . . . something besides Carlos and your family." She looked at me sharply, and she seemed almost to know the unspoken dream of my heart. Did she, in some mysterious way, know that these vineyards were an attempt to replace the emptiness, the part that was left vacant by the absence of Richard Blodmore? I turned away from her.

"I name each section for my children. Next year's planting will be named for you, Amelia."

She had been standing beside the window, and now she lifted the cotton curtain and gazed down the long, even slope, across to the vineyard house her husband owned. "Luis also loves the vines. He also tries to put them in place of what he cannot have." She dropped the curtain. "I wish before I die I could give him a child. Of all things, Luis would like to have a child."

"You will not die, Amelia. Not for a long time. And as for a child—you are still very young. There is plenty of time."

"There isn't plenty of time. This thing in my blood, in the marrow of my bones, cannot be resisted forever. It seems to be quiet now, but I know it will come again, and be worse. When I am so feeble, any illness could take me. I am prepared for it. And as for Luis . . . My dear Luis is not like other men. As weak as I am, I still might bear him a child if only he could give me a child." She walked to the table and drank swiftly of Antonio's raw wine. "Since we have married, Carlota, there has been no possibility of a child. It seems I have not in me what is required to rouse such a man as Luis. . . ." Her hand trembled so violently that when she put the glass down it crashed against the edge of the table, broke, and the wine spilled.

"Carlota—I am still a virgin!"

The intensity of her despair was in her voice. Pepita, who loved Amelia, lumbered across the room to her and thrust her big head under Amelia's hand. This expression of uninformed sympathy from a dumb animal seemed to undo the tight knot of her self-discipline. I watched, heartbroken for her, as she sank down on her knees and put her face on the shoulder of the big dog and wept.

2

We hardly noticed when the first talk of the possibility of war began; certainly we paid little attention to it. Those who traveled back and forth to London for the sherry business, along with the gifts they unwrapped, also brought out tales of the Kaiser's army, of the Kaiser's new navy, which he seemed to want to play with like a little boy; they repeated the talk of the solemn men who didn't like such things, said they were bad for business, and wrote letters about it to the London *Times*. There was some nostalgia for King Edward, who had seemed to be able to keep his German nephew, the Kaiser, from being too insufferable. It all seemed very like the travelers' tales that were brought back to Clonmara when anyone had been abroad, just something to talk about. We listened and tended our vines in our little corner of the world that seemed so untroubled. And so it came to the peaceful autumn of 1913, the last year before the world was turned upside down, and we were invited to visit the Marquesa de Pontevedra at Sanlúcar, and to be among the party that would cross the Guadalquivir each day to join in the autumn culling of the deer herds in the preserve of Doñana.

We dared not refuse. Only Carlos was anxious to go, but then he was not of a nervous disposition. He saw it only as a mark of favor. My mother seemed a little flustered. The Marquesa was one of the few people who ever seemed to unnerve her; but still she was excited, as always, by the prospect of a party. She began to look out all her dresses, and begged María Luisa for the money for some new ones. She cleaned the guns that Richard Blodmore had given her and went out to Don Luis' hacienda to get some target practice. Despite her drinking, she still possessed her uncannily true aim, which she seemed to have inherited from my grandfather. She was delighted with her success and looked forward as much to the shooting as to the social life.

I thought there was more than a touch of malice in the Marquesa's invitation. It wasn't possible that she knew of my feeling for Richard Blodmore, but she must have guessed how we felt about his possession of Clonmara; she must have known that Carlos and Don Paulo had once thought of the possibility of Elena as Carlos' wife, and Elena had been given to Richard. So she had blended her wine with bitter grapes when she informed us that the gathering at Sanlúcar was to mark the visit to Jerez of Lord and Lady Blodmore and their two young sons.

For once I was not pregnant. Francisco had been born a year ago, and I had been mercifully free since then. I had resumed the shape I had almost forgotten I possessed. When I took out my habit the waist was even a little loose. "You look peaked," María Luisa said. "Having

three babies so quickly cannot be good for any woman."
I looked at my face in the mirror and it seemed the face
of a woman, not a girl; even my hair had darkened, as
if one day it might be like my mother's. I wondered how
I would appear to Richard Blodmore, and how he would
appear to me. Would we look at each other and wonder
what had possessed us in those mad moments at Clonmara? Would he appear to be as settled into domesticity
as I did? Would it all seem a useless, foolish dream, the
image of a man and a girl on a shore and in a rose
garden? I told myself that that was how it would be.
There were memories, but faded ones. I must expect no
more. But still I fussed as the seamstress took tucks in the
habit, and agreed when María Luisa decreed that I must
have some new dresses. "Nothing but babies for three
years . . . you need something to brighten you up." So
she juggled the books a little, deferred paying some bills
for a while longer, and was satisfied that neither I nor my
mother would be a disgrace to our house.

Don Luis and Amelia had also been invited. Carlos
had told us with delight that neither of his half brothers
had been invited. Some of the grandest names in Jerez
society were to be there, as guests of either the Marquesa
at Sanlúcar or of the Duque de Tarifa at the Coto
Doñana. It was the custom of King Alfonso to join the
hunting party each autumn at the Palacio de Doñana. It
was one of the few times that the Marquesa made herself
available to Jerez society, and Don Paulo would be there
in his seldom executed role as her husband, the official
host of her gathering.

I both longed for and dreaded the first breath of
coolness in the air after the heat of the summer. October
would bring the tremendous migration of birds from
northern Europe to winter in Doñana's marshes. I would
see, Don Luis told me, if I was lucky, the beautiful
Spanish lynx and the imperial eagle, the true monarchs of
Doñana. I would see the wild boar, the herds of red and
fallow deer.

There were vipers in Doñana, Amelia said; I must be
very careful where I put my foot, I must be wary. I must

not stray from the party; I must not get lost. These were the beauties and dangers of Doñana. Only my mother knew the other danger to me. While I helped her pack she touched my hand briefly. "It won't matter seeing him again, will it, Charlie? I mean . . . it's all over now, isn't it?"

"Yes. All over."

3

So it was among many other people that I saw Richard Blodmore for the first time since he had come to the lodge of Clonmara to bid us good-by and give us the final gift of Balthasar and Half Moon. We were gathered in the grand salon of the palacio of the Marquesa at Sanlúcar. There were many guests, greeting each other, talking about the prospects of the weather and hunting, who had died, married, or been born since they last gathered in that place. There was talk, noise, laughter, the sound of glasses clinking, the sound of a guitar lost in an alcove. I looked across the room and saw Richard Blodmore, and everything else faded and went out of focus. The sounds fell to a low-pitched hum; for an instant every movement seemed to halt, the outlines of things, of both people and objects, grew blurred and went flat. All that had dimension was the figure of Richard Blodmore; only he seemed real. All around him had a fuzzy, dreamlike quality.

He saw me at the same time, as if he had been compelled to turn in my direction. He moved towards me, a strange, sharp movement in that unmoving, almost noiseless crowd.

"Charlie!" How loud his voice was. Surely everyone would turn and stare at us. "Charlie . . . ?" he said again. It was as if I woke from a dream. The sounds, the noise, the music, the movement was restored. And I knew I had been wrong. It was not all over.

"How . . . how is it at Clonmara?" I managed to say.

232

"Clonmara misses you, Charlie. The roses flourish, but they seem to have no scent. I miss you, Charlie."

Wildly dangerous words to say in the midst of this gathering, but they told me that for him it was not all over either.

4

Doñana is a wilderness on the edge of the Atlantic; it is like no place I had ever imagined on earth. It is desert and forest; it is marsh and dune and sea. It is the haunt of the soaring imperial eagle and the crawling snake, the fleet beauty of the fallow deer and the brute ugliness of the wild boar. It is the last domain of the Spanish lynx. In summer its wetlands are baked to a seamed, cracked nothingness, and in winter the sun is blacked out by the flight of a hundred thousand birds. It is earth and high heaven.

It was the place next to Clonmara and my vineyards that I loved best; it was the place where I knew finally that I could truly love no other man than Richard Blodmore.

About ten days in all we spent there, crossing the Guadalquivir River each morning from the Marquesa's palacio at Sanlúcar. This was the first time I had seen Doñana, and in the years to come I would visit it in every season of the year. But this year it was the autumn. The rains had filled the marshes—the Spanish use the word *las marismas,* which seemed to me better to convey the dreamlike quality of the landscape as it looked now with the winter green covering the mud flats. Wherever I looked there was an unbroken surface of soft, waving green, green that teemed with the wild life that lived off it, and yet it was life that was rarely seen. A deer crouching in its cover would suddenly be flushed—a flash of white, the roar of guns, and then the mad whirring of wings as birds beat their way to safety. Sometimes the sky seemed stained pink with the color of flamingos in flight. There was blood and slaughter; there was the tranquil beauty of navigating the marshes in a *cajón,* a flat-bottomed skiff, fastened to the tail of a muscular marsh horse who traversed the shallow water with ease, as had been done at Doñana since there had been men and horses, time out of mind.

And for those few terrible, precious days, there was the sight of Richard Blodmore.

We had little time in each other's company; we were only briefly alone. And yet, whether the men shot birds in the marshes, or deer and boar in the dry sandy areas among the pine and the cork oaks, we each seemed never for an instant to be able to forget the presence of the other. I would think of Richard as we rode, my eyes searching the ground and sky, mindful of the warnings and directions given by the guides who had lived at Doñana all their lives, and whose fathers and grand-fathers had taught them the ways and the secrets of the wilderness; I would think of Richard as I was obeying the commands of the guides, watching for the game, and I would turn and find his gaze on me, and know what he had been thinking. Most days we lunched at the Palacio de Doñana, the palace which the dukes of Medina Sidonia had built for their hunting, and which it had been the pleasure of many Spanish kings to visit. Protocol was imposed by the presence of King Alfonso, even in that relaxed setting, but wherever I was in that gathering, I would find Richard was briefly at my elbow, a glass of wine in his hand for me, a murmured greeting. We often managed to cross the river morning and evening in the same boat, but there were always half a dozen others with us. At times the tension grew until it was almost unbearable. It seemed to me impossible that the others around us didn't know what we, with all our senses, were silently telling each other.

Once when the party stopped to rest and have the English afternoon tea the Marquesa provided, we walked alone in the area of the sand dunes. These are the small mountains of Doñana, shifting dunes which with infinite slowness move year by year, engulfing the forest of pines which lie behind them, engulfing and moving on, leav-

234

ing behind the ragged, burned skeletons of the trees, gaunt against the sky. The dunes are high, and from their top the only sight is of the Atlantic. From the Guadalquivir, Columbus had set out on his third voyage to the New World; these dunes may have been his last glimpse of Europe. I shivered a little at the thought.

"You're cold," Richard said. "We shouldn't have come up here. The wind's too strong."

"Yes, cold," I agreed. "I seem always to be cold when you're near me. Out there, on the marshes in the sun, I'm cold. Part of me aches so much, like an old wound when the damp crawls in. Why does it have to hurt so?"

"When it ceases to hurt, you don't feel anything."

"I'll be numb then—or dead. I don't want to be dead, Richard. But I can't imagine life just going on this way. There's Carlos . . . and my children. I love my children, Richard. I'm fond of Carlos. But if he were gone tomorrow, for some reason—I wouldn't miss him. He isn't essential to me. And I keep believing you are . . . and still you're no part of my life, and never can be."

He put his arm about me and turned me to face him. The wind blew strongly in from the sea, the aftermath of a storm the night before; the sand was whipped on the top of the dunes like the spray of the sea itself. The waves crashed against the shore with a hollow boom. It was not like the feeling when we had first seen each other on the shore at Clonmara. What might have been a quick, swiftly fading infatuation had only matured in the time between. There were lines on Richard's face which had not been there before. My own body had borne three children. We were older, but the conventional wisdom of forgetting, the prudence of putting behind what was behind, had not come. The girl on that loved, familiar shore in Ireland was a woman now, wholly committed to this man, as we walked this alien wilderness with the Atlantic thundering near our feet. Both of us had built our lives about other people, and we would not recklessly abandon them. But I knew as surely as if I spoke for my own soul that Richard Blodmore belonged in his inner core to me. Did I sense a kind of blasphemy in that? I had been

235

taught that I must love only God in this way, before any other creature. But for me God was distant, unknown. And Richard stood by my side, real, human, beloved.

"I *am* part of your life, Charlie. I always will be. I'll never let you go." He held back my hair, which the wind whipped into my eyes. "I have no rights to you—except that I love you. I will go away and leave you here. And you will stay. We'll each bring up our families, and we'll always think that each child might have been the child of the other. And to think I was the one who didn't believe it was possible to fall in love. Romantic love didn't exist. Perhaps it doesn't, but if that is so, then I know that obsession does exist. I think of you every day. And I've grown almost to hate the scent of roses. . . ."

We resumed our walk. What did we say to each other? Very little, I think. We made no plans for the future, for there could be none. We did not talk of Richard coming again to Jerez, or of my visiting Ireland. There was no sense to any of it. This was an irrational, illogical love, with no hope of consummation. Yet it possessed us both. It was dangerous, and hurtful; and it was real.

We had turned back and were walking towards the place where we had crossed the steep height of the dunes to the beach. We saw the figure of a woman standing there, the wind holding her skirt close to her body. Even from a distance we knew it was Elena, and we did not know how long she had been standing there, if she had witnessed that moment when we paused and briefly lived in each other's arms.

As we came near she called something which the wind carried away. "She is probably telling us that the party is leaving," Richard said, as if it didn't matter.

"She knows," I said. "She knows we love each other."

"Yes—she knows. She's known since the first day at Clonmara. And I think she would prefer that I had a dozen flesh and blood mistresses living on my doorstep. Those she could have fought. She can't fight a spirit, a phantom, someone who haunts the rose garden at Clonmara but is never seen in the flesh. For me, there are ghosts of you in every corner of the house, and she knows

236

it. She's had her own disappointments, but we might have made a reasonable marriage if it hadn't been for a young girl who did nothing more than pass through my life, hardly more than glimpsed. Men like me, of my age, are not supposed to fling their hearts away like that. To me it seems I had no choice. It just happened. There is nothing Elena can do. She is a good wife, a good mother, a good housekeeper. If she indulges her very considerable passions, she is very discreet about it. She knows that she is beautiful, and she also knows that for me she hardly exists. Many women could fill her function. But none can fill yours. It doesn't seem fair, does it, Charlie? But I can do nothing about it."

"What you dream, Richard, is always better than reality. In time you would have grown used to me—even bored with me. The sort of love we feel now doesn't last when you meet it over the breakfast table every morning."

"Yes, but we never have. That's what Elena can't fight. Neither of us is quite real to the other. The dream lives, even if I sometimes wish it would go away and leave me in peace. . . ."

Peace. There was no peace. There would be peace for neither of us. The woman standing on the dune gestured to us, summoning us. Then she turned and disappeared down the steep slope towards the pines. The high angle of the dune was empty and windblown. It was almost as if she had never been.

The ten days of the Marquesa's gathering at Sanlúcar seemed endless. At night Carlos snored gently beside me, contentedly filled with the Marquesa's superb food and wine. He had been good-humored, pleased to be among that company, and not once had those flashes of ill temper marred his charm. He seemed determined to prove to his father, and to the Marquesa, just how well he could behave, how at ease and how gracious he could be, how he could win smiles and laughter even in the presence of the King. He shot as well as he rode, and that made him outstanding—and therefore happy. He was gentle

237

with me, and kind, and even paid me compliments on my new dresses. "A real beauty you've become, Carlota. Having children suits you. Your mother will have a rival soon." It was said teasingly, but with good humor. I thanked the basic simplicity of his nature that he did not seem to suspect my preoccupation with Richard. And with Elena he seemed equally offhand. He talked with her, even flirted a little, was often seated next to her at dinner, and yet I did not think her presence affected him strongly. Carlos had not been made to waste himself on hopeless causes. He had once wanted Elena, and she had been taken away from him. It was over and done with. With Carlos passion ran swiftly, but it did not seem to run deep.

I was aware of the extraordinary effort my mother made during those days. She had counted her copitas as carefully as María Luisa counted our money. She had been delighted to be allowed to shoot among the men, and she had gained new admirers for this skill. She still drew a small crowd of men about her, but she was quieter than I had ever known her. Perhaps she, like all the party, felt the dominating presence of the Marquesa, a hovering presence that seemed to create about it the small hush of awe which a sighting of the imperial eagle or the entry of the King could compel. There were certainly some among the party, both at Sanlúcar and at the Palacio de Doñana, who regarded the Marquesa's position as almost level with the King's, those with long memories who knew her Hapsburg blood as well as her Bourbon ancestry. Certainly a sense of the history of both these ruling houses lingered in the palacio. Stories were told of famous hunting parties of the past, the most spectacular of which must have been times when Felipe IV had been entertained by the Duque de Medina Sidonia. The story was told again of the time Goya had stayed at Doñana and had painted his mistress, Cayetana, Grand Duchess of Alba, as the immortal naked Maja. It was a place where romance and legend were woven into its being, and none of us was immune to its spell. Even the sadness which seemed to overhang the

238

marshes was part of the legend of the woman, Doña Ana, wife of the seventh Duque de Medina Sidonia, who had given her name to this silent wilderness, she who was said to have spent her whole life in prayer for the soul of her scandalous mother, the Princess of Eboli. From his retreat here with his wife, the wretched seventh Duque, never a sailor, had been forced to take command of the great Armada which Felipe II sent against England. To Doñana he had returned to die and be buried beside his wife. That, at least, was what the legends said. At Doñana it was easy to believe them.

The Marquesa seemed part of it all. She hunted and rode like a man, her slender athletic body seemed that of a woman much younger. She commanded, and was obeyed, and even the strength of Don Paulo's personality seemed to pale a little in her presence. I found myself avoiding her gaze whenever I was in the company of Richard, lest she of all people, should guess the tumult of my soul. And I wondered, as I observed my mother, trying so desperately not to disgrace us by any unseemly behavior, if the Marquesa had brought us here particularly to observe Lord Blodmore and his wife, to see their healthy infant sons, so that we would know all the more surely how completely lost Clonmara was to us. Beside all the splendors of Dōnana, and the Marquesa's palacio and estate at Sanlúcar, Clonmara seemed a poor enough place. But had she wanted to thrust home to us how finally it had passed into the sway of her influence? It was her money which had married Richard to Elena, her money which now restored Clonmara. With her actions she seemed bent on a curious revenge on the man who, thirty years ago, had preferred the daughter of Don Paulo to the great Marquesa de Pontevedra. In the midst of all the festive meals, the conversation, the laughter, the guitar playing, in the midst of the wild boar hunt, the shooting, the silent floating on the marshes, I think she meant me to remember that rejection. She meant me to remember the woman with the ravaged face who lived on the rock of Arcos with her dolls. The Marquesa had not planted dolls at Clonmara but live, healthy children. I could not be the only one who was aware that Elena, as her closest blood relative, would inherit the title of Pontevedra, if perhaps not all of the great fortune that was spread over Spain and beyond. And through Elena, Richard Blodmore's older son, Edward, would inherit the title of Pontevedra as well as the earldom of Blodmore. That would have been the same inheritance which would have gone to any son born to a marriage between the Marquesa and my grandfather. After thirty years the Marquesa appeared to have settled the score.

Amelia was not strong enough to accompany us during the day's hunting, but she was present at all the evening entertainments. On the last night at Sanlúcar we sat alone for a few minutes before any other member of the party came down to dinner. She said to me in a quiet, calm voice, "You did not tell me, Carlota, that Lord Blodmore was in love with you."

I turned away from the fire and looked at her directly; with her gaze steadily on me, I could not attempt to deny it.

"I didn't believe he still could be in love with me. We . . . we don't know each other. It's all . . . all absurd. It shouldn't be." And then the sharp thought came. "Does it show? Has anyone noticed?"

She shook her head. "Only those who know you very well, Carlota. I have plenty of time to sit and watch . . . to sit and think. Sick people often see things healthy people are too busy to notice. And you love him also. What will you do?"

"Nothing," I said. "We will do nothing. He will go back to Ireland. I will stay here."

She nodded. "I thought it would be that way. You are not wild, like your mother, Carlota. But still, you are a little mad. I think all the Blodmores must be a little mad. But be careful of the Marquesa. She has sharp eyes."

Don Luis joined us then, and the conversation went to the day's hunting, the change in the weather to rain, the journey back to Jerez the next day. The dispersal was beginning. I sat through dinner almost silent, trying not to look towards Richard. I avoided talking to him the whole evening and was thankful when it was time to go to bed. I lay awake, trying to will myself not to think of Richard and Clonmara; I thought of my children and my vines.

Lord and Lady Blodmore came to pay a courtesy call on my mother the day before they left Jerez. I was at the vineyard house and missed seeing them, something I was thankful for. I found my mother alone in the drawing room, surrounded by the tea things which Serafina had not yet removed. The fire was dying in the hearth, and I busied myself rebuilding it. The decanter of brandy was close by my mother's hand, and it was half empty.

"It's all right, Charlie," she said quickly. "I didn't have anything to drink while they were here. I did all the right things. Asked the right questions. Elena told me all about Clonmara. The changes . . . they've enlarged the stables. They've built a new summer house, and cleared out a lot of the rhododendrons and laurels. Richard seems to be a good Master of the Hunt. That's important for the Blodmores, isn't it, Charlie? We would have hated someone who couldn't be a good Master to take over. He's turned out better than I expected. He's . . . he's *steadier*. But he looks sad. He looks older than he should. Such a handsome man. . . . Elena said they were going to buy a motorcar. I hope it doesn't frighten the horses. . . ." The bright chatter faded. I straightened from my task of building up the fire and looked at her. A film of unshed tears stood out in her eyes. It was unlike her to weep.

"Mother . . . ?"

Her face seemed to crumple and to age; suddenly she was no longer the bright beauty of the drawing rooms and the hunting field but a woman of forty who needed the ease the brandy gave her. "Oh, Charlie—I can't help it! I'm so homesick! I try to make the best of things here, but it isn't home. It just isn't home, Charlie!"

I cradled her head against my breast and rocked her as I rocked my children. "Hush . . . it's all right,

Mother. You do so well. Really well. I know it's hard at times, but you do so beautifully. . . . We all love you. . . ." I let her weep, and I continued to say the things that might bolster and support her. I could do nothing to promise a release from the longing for home, because it was in my heart too. And I couldn't let her look up and see the tears in my own eyes.

CHAPTER TWO

1

I went back to my vines and to my children. In them I found some relief from the aching sense of loss that the sight and presence of Richard had renewed to an almost unbearable degree. The promise of the vines and the children were my hope for the future, the reason I lived from day to day, but looking still to the years ahead. Without them, the future would have loomed only as a vast, empty waste.

It was not even the same with Carlos after the time at Dõnana. I grew impatient with him because he was not Richard, and he, sensing that I was no longer so pliant, no longer the girl who had been grateful for the fact of marriage, no longer so manageable, so willing, so amiable, grew moody, and, for the first time, a little sullen. He was demanding of me physically; his love-making grew more passionate, less tender. Perhaps it was my fault. If I let thoughts of Richard flow through me as I lay in Carlos' arms, could I blame him if he tried to impose himself more fully on me, to shake me out of the kind of blankness that fell on me when we now made love?

"What is it, Carlota?" he demanded. "I don't please you any longer. You try to draw more from me. Well, then—you shall take more." And his love-making would become wild, and sometimes cruel.

"Damn you!" he shouted at me once. "You're not even thinking of me! You're thinking of something else—or some other man. Is that it, Carlota? Some other man?"

I was foolish enough to laugh at him. "Some other man? What a fool you are, Carlos! How could there be some other man? Every second of my day is taken up with caring for the children, the house, the vineyards—"

"And I say, 'Damn them all!' *I* am the most important thing in your life. Never forget it! If I should find that you took another man—if you *preferred* another man, I would kill him! Yes, I mean it—I would kill him. And then, perhaps, you also, my soft clever little Irish beauty, with your pale skin and your green eyes. Yes, I might kill you too."

Then he withdrew from me with savage abruptness, as if I were a woman who had been raped and was no longer wanted. But I could not blame him. He had sensed the emptiness within me. He reacted as most men would, with anger and frustration. And I no longer had the simplicity or the guile to charm him back. I let him go.

I was much occupied with my vines that year. There were all the endless tasks which a vineyard required, the regular cycle of hoeing, weeding, pruning, fertilizing. I had planted new slopes that January, and as I had promised, I named that new section for Amelia. She drove out to inspect it.

"My vineyard," she said. "Something of mine left after I am gone."

I looked at her in astonishment. "But you are the wife of Don Luis! And he has almost as many vineyards as Don Paulo. Surely all his vineyards are yours also?"

"Yes," she said. "He is very kind. All he has is mine. But no vineyard bears my name."

244

"But this is a very humble vineyard, Amelia. Well planted, well cared for, thanks to Luis. But still quite insignificant."

"But still my own," she answered. She stood at the entrance to the courtyard of the vineyard house. "I can count the years of your life here in Jerez, Carlota. There"—pointing directly in front, where the track led down the road—"that is Juan, your first-born." She moved on a little farther on the outside of the house. "And here, on this slope, is Martín. And from there is Francisco." Now she moved to the back of the house and pointed. "And there I begin. The very youngest vines, just planted. Many will perish, but most will live. That is Amelia."

That was the spring when I committed what I could only think of as a mad extravagance. I had the soil dug close to the house and had vines planted against all the traditional methods of the vineyards. They were to grow up posts and be left virtually unpruned. The posts would have lateral beams extending to the house itself, so that when the leaves came in the spring, and achieved full growth in the heat of the summer, the walls of the house would be shaded by a pergola. As winter came, the leaves would curl and die and drop, and the walls would receive the needed warmth of the winter sun. The grapes the vines bore might never be edible, but they would hang there, like the symbolic grapes which hung from the vines which grew in the almizacates between the bodegas at Fernández, Thompson. Perhaps I was, after all, being merely practical, even if somewhat wasteful of labor and materials. But Amelia knew at once what I intended. "Your house will have green shutters, Carlota, shady and cool." Then she gave it the name that stayed with it through the years. *Las Ventanas Verdes.* (The Green Windows.)

2

The months went by, marked for me by the traditional tasks of the vineyard. My life was shaped by the vineyard

245

as the pruning was shaping the vines themselves. On the advice of Don Luis, I adopted the pruning system known as *de virote,* which meant that we left a shoot with no buds at a height above the head of the vine from which the branches have to grow. This ensured we would have no grapes until the fifth year, but Don Luis told me the wait was worth the time and extra money. In Jerez the vines are pruned by the method known as *vara y pulgar,* stick and thumb; the *vara,* the stick, is left with seven or eight "eyes" which produce that year's grapes; the *pulgar* is a small shoot which will become the vara of the next year. The pruned vine grows close to the ground, receiving the benefit of the sun by day and the warmth of the earth by night.

The blossoms came in May, a green blossom which got lighter and became yellowish as they faded; the grapes appeared in June. Before the flowering we started to prop up the branches so that the shoots should not touch the soil, which would have meant the loss of the crop; in July we propped up the branches again so that the weight of the grapes would not drag them down. If the grapes touch the soil during rain they will rot. To lift them up meant also that the warm air could circulate about them.

So much to do, even more to learn. I was in despair at the cost of it. We sprayed two or three times in May with copper sulphate and treated the vines with sulphur to prevent the oïdium, the mildew. It seemed we were never free of the need to till and till again—the deserpia, the cavabién, the golpe-lleno, and the fourth tilling, the bina. There the tilling might stop, and in many of the vineyards it did. But Don Luis recommended that we go on to the *rebina* in August when the earth was baked to a point that in some places it developed wide cracks. The rebina took out any weeds that grew after the bina and helped with the ripening of the grapes, which then would contain more sugar. Luis quoted me a saying of the district: "He who tills the vineyard in August fills his bodega with must." So that year, the year of my first harvest, I borrowed more money so that I could employ laborers for the rebina.

By now I could hardly sleep at night worrying that there would be rain and the crop ruined or diminished. I bored everyone with the talk of the harvest to come. Carlos grew not only bored but impatient.

"For pity's sake, Carlota, stop it! What do you think I hear at the bodega all day? Do you think I want to come home to hear the same thing at night? For centuries we have done this work. We've had good harvests and bad harvests. Too much rain, and not enough rain. We have thousands of *aranzadas* in cultivation from here to San-lúcar—you have a toy vineyard! You can play with it as if it's a toy, attending to every vine as if your life depended on it."

And I snapped back at him in Spanish an adage I had learned from Mateo. *"A la tierra, no se le puede engañar."* (You cannot deceive the land.)

"Oh—you've become the expert now, have you? Well, perhaps we can expect your help at the bodega when it comes to classifying and blending the wine!" He slammed his glass down and left the table. Later we heard him leave the house; it was very late and he was very drunk when he returned that night. As he stumbled to the bed he fell across Pepita, who, as always, lay at its foot. There was a yelp of protest from her, and then a stream of curses in Spanish. Perhaps he drunkenly aimed a blow at her, because a low, warning growl followed; the sound frightened me. "Pepita—quiet!" I called. She subsided again with a sigh, as if she understood that one must occasionally suffer fools and drunken men.

"He thought he married a lapdog and now he finds a terrier," María Luisa observed the next morning. "Be careful, querida. And do not be too clever."

My mother cut in. "Let her be as clever as she can. Let her learn what she can. God knows, we could have done with a little more cleverness at Clonmara. There we starved the land to find the money to try to make more money. And the land didn't forgive us. We took from

247

it, and we didn't give back. And it took its own revenge. Richard Blodmore told me that they are draining the big north pasture. More than eighty acres in that. It used to be a fine meadow at one time—great fattening land, until the old shores crumbled and it went boggy. Now he's putting it back into good heart. . . ."

She had fallen into the habit of talking of what Richard was doing at Clonmara as if it were something done for us. I wished she would not. The time before we had first-hand accounts of what was happening at Clonmara had been more peaceful. It had been a happier time before she began to blame my grandfather for what he had done in his zeal to make money so that we could be provided for. But then, she hadn't the searing knowledge of the woman living at Arcos; she didn't know the reason why this house had been bought, why the vineyard had been bought. She didn't know the true reason why we were in Jerez at all.

So while I worried about my harvest, the events of the world outside passed me by. I only dimly heard the reports of the assassination of the Archduke Ferdinand, heir to the Austro-Hungarian Empire, and his morganatic wife, Sofia, at a place with the unpronounceable name of Sarajevo. When that happened in June I was busy arranging for the propping up of the vines; in July, while the embassies of the world hummed with activity, I thought only about how I could find enough workers for the harvest I expected in September. If I ever saw a news-paper, I don't remember paying much heed to the stories of the ultimatums passing between one country and another. Few people in those days knew who was in alliance with whom, and for what reasons, and why anyone should go to war over them. In Jerez we were concerned with our vines, and coming hopes of the harvest. At the end of July, Austria declared war on tiny Serbia, a country I didn't know existed. I was trying to get enough baskets for the grapes of the harvest, and enough grass mats to lay out the grapes for ripening and sweetening in the sun. August was our vital month. There must be no rain; the grapes were swelling and thickening on the vine. I read, with a faint sense of disbelief, that in swift succession in early August Germany declared war on Russia and then on France. Belgium was invaded. On August 4, when I returned from an inspection of the vineyards, taken there and driven back by Don Luis, he said as he handed me down from the carriage and waited for Popita to jump down, "Be prepared for bad news."

I didn't understand him. I ran inside. My mother and María Luisa were in the drawing room, my mother drinking brandy. "These Spanish papers, they don't tell you anything," she said.

María Luisa shrugged. "What is it to us? We will not go to war."

"War? What war?"

My mother raised her glass to me. "England, my darling, is about to declare war on Germany—so that means Ireland too."

I could only, stupidly—not yet shaken out of my concern about the harvest, how much must I would be able to send to the bodega, how much I would be able to repay on my loans—question, "Why?"

"Why? Good question, Charlie. Every woman in the world who knows about it must be asking that question now. Something the men have arranged. They're great arrangers, the men. This time they've arranged a little war. Just to keep everyone busy."

She was drunk, of course. And yet something very calm and cold at the center of what she was saying bore into me.

"What will happen?"

"For us, Charlie, probably very little. But the men we have known, all the sons of the fathers we knew, all the boys you went hunting with, will probably go off to war. They'll probably take their own horses." She waved her glass at me. "How do I know—I don't even know if men go to war on horses these days. Perhaps those motorcars have taken over. But how will they pull the guns without horses? Believe me, Charlie, Clonmara will sell every horse it can spare. I only wish we had a whole stableful

249

to sell here." Then her face crumpled. "But I would never sell a horse for war, Charlie—never. I would never sell a horse for *war!*"

I sat in silence for a while, thinking about what she had said. "Will . . . will everyone in Ireland go to war?" It was still a strange and far-off thing to me, this war.

"Every able-bodied gentleman will volunteer immediately," my mother said. "The others, the ones like Andy's brothers, will go because they've always fought in England's wars. They were here in Spain with Wellington, they were in the Crimea, they fought the Boers—when Uncle Bertie got killed. They've been fighting for the English for centuries, when they weren't rebelling against them."

I went and poured a brandy from the decanter. I took a long gulp at it before I asked the question whose answer I already knew. "Do you think Richard . . . do you think Richard Blodmore will go?"

"Very likely. It would be expected of him."

Now María Luisa broke in. "But your husband, Lady Pat, is already a soldier. He is already in it, isn't he, if war comes?"

I swung around to look at her. "My father?" It was perhaps the first time I had consciously thought of him as a person, with a job to do, a role to fill.

"Yes, darling—your father. Funny—I hadn't thought of him myself. He's with the 87th Regiment, King's Own Artillery. Or something like that. I could never get it straight. But he was always riding a horse—how can he be in the artillery?"

"Guns," I said. "They pull guns with horses."

"Oh yes, that's it, of course. Of course . . ." She sipped her brandy in silence and said little the rest of the evening.

Next day we knew that England had declared war on Germany. We were safe and quiet here, in our little far left-hand corner of Europe. Spain had no obligation to anyone, and so long as ships could ply from Cádiz, we would sell our sherry.

"In any case," Carlos said, "it will be over by Christmas."

So I brought in my first harvest to the distant, the very far distant, sound of guns thundering over the lowlands of Europe—the lowlands which once had been an important part of the great Spanish Empire.

3

The harvest began early in September and for those who had large vineyards, continued for almost a month. It is a time of agony for the vineyard owner to know when to begin to cut the grapes. If he cuts too early there will be less sugar and therefore less alcohol; if he waits he risks damage from rain. I waited until Don Luis began his own harvesting—but the vineyard next to mine was only one of many he owned, and he went from one to the other, the different varieties of grapes requiring different times of harvesting. There was also his work at the bodega to attend to, so when I saw him, it was briefly. I felt lost without him, the reassurance which his experience gave me. "Don't worry too much about rain," he said. "If it rains, stop harvesting and wait until the grapes dry. If they are properly staked and do not touch the ground, they are safe." I believed him, but still sent Nanny to the church across the plaza to light candles and pray that it would not rain.

That year I did not have the additional expense of building one of the high, rough watchtowers that go up in the vineyards when the grapes grow ripe for picking, places from which the grapes are watched night and day against thieves. One watchtower on Don Luis' property also looked over my land. "The men will watch for both of us," Don Luis said.

The grapes were cut and placed in baskets of woven olive branches. Each basket held about twenty-five pounds of grapes, and it needed sixty basketfuls to make a *carretada,* about the measure, Mateo told me, to make one butt of must. The grapes were carried to the space in front of and around the vineyard house and laid out on esparto grass mats to dry. They stayed there from twelve

251

to twenty-four hours, covered at night with another grass mat for protection from the dew. Then they were carried to the lagar to be pressed.

It needed four men to tread the lagar, and they began their work about midnight and continued on until midday the next day, so that they rested through the hottest hours of the afternoon. I had two teams of men for this, and for as long as they did not sleep, neither did I. This was no festive occasion, such as I had seen on the steps of the Collegiate Church. It was hard, continuous work. One carretada at a time was tramped between those muscular legs clad in short trousers and the nailed boots. The two lagars at Las Ventanas Verdes were old, and had had to be repaired, as well as thoroughly cleansed. The pisadores worked steadily, solemnly—working one side of the lagar at a time, leaning with their right hands on their wooden shovels. For them the vendimia meant only hard work and little gaiety. The boots they wore were an important item; the pips and stalks of the grapes were trapped between the nails, and not damaged, and a soft layer of grapeskins eventually formed over the soles so that the hard pips and stalks of the grapes would not be broken. Unbroken, they could not release their tannin, which could give the wine a harsh flavor. Before the treading started, the grapes were sprinkled with three or four pounds of gypsum, which Mateo told me considerably improved the quality of the must.

I was bewildered and fatigued. I had seen various stages of these processes of the harvest and the production of the must before, but never had it been my grapes and my must. I stood there, hour after hour, watching the pisadores slowly becoming besplattered with juice, watching the flow of the must from the lagar, filtered first by an open-mesh basket to take out the stalks, and then through a sieve to get rid of the skins and pips. The precious, though rather evil-smelling, liquid went into a waiting tub.

The second pressing was obtained by piling the pulp of the grapes into a sort of cylinder around a seven-foot-high steel screw fixed permanently in the center of the lagar.

The pisadores worked with their wooden shovels piling it up. Almost everything that touched the grapes was wood, lest the taint of metal contaminate the must. Again gypsum was sprinkled to give consistency to the heap. This heap they called the *pie* and they wound a long tape of esparto grass around it, both ends fastened to wooden blocks. One block was attached to the lagar at the bottom of the pie, the other at the top. The top one dovetailed into another piece of wood which fitted around the central screw. Mateo called these two pieces *marranos*— pigs. They were separated by a metal washer from the big nut which rotated on the screw. This was called the *marrana,* the sow. I understood why when I heard the grunting noise it made when the great screw, fixed to a massive steel handle more than two yards long, was turned. When this turned, the juice of the second pressing squeezed through the esparto grass band and down through the opening into the tub.

Any romantic notions I still had of the harvest were gone. At first this second pressing was quite easy. Two men, called *tiradores,* could manage it easily. Then it grew harder and harder, and two more tiradores joined in, two pushing, two pulling. It became impossible to turn the screw continuously. The men had even to tie their wrists to the handle for fear of slipping; I watched those huge muscles strained to the limit, and knew what a fall might mean. To watch them do it yet again was agony, but they did it, rebuilding the pie, pressing it once more. The grapes were forced to yield all they could give, and the men had to work through the night to take the must from them. This then was the end of all the long months of labor in the vineyard, under the rain and the broiling sun, the planting, tilling, pruning, propping, spraying. This was the cost of the bright wine in our glasses. The sweat of the men, their straining muscles, the almost unbearable smell of the must—I began to think it was too much to pay for the smooth, golden liquid.

Since this was a small vineyard, and we could afford to waste nothing, they pressed the pie yet again; they called this the *espirraque*. It was used as fertilizer, or as pig food. It seemed to me a hard way to get food for pigs.

The must from the treading and the first pressing went into butts. This would go to the bodega and eventually become wine. The must from the second pressing would be vinegar, or low-strength wines, which would eventually be distilled. The must was funneled into casks; the funnels also had sieves so that no skin or pips would go in. Then, after about six or eight hours, the miracle of the fermentation began—the violent, spontaneous fermentation without which there can be no wine. One of the reasons for working at night, Mateo told me, apart from its being cooler, was that the fermentation came more slowly, and the slower the fermentation, the better for the wine.

I watched, exhausted and appalled by what I had witnessed in the hours of only one night. "The better for the wine," I repeated. Now I said it dully, fatigue and concern having taken away the edge of my pleasure in this, my first harvest.

The butts were only partially filled to allow for the turmoil of the bubbling fermentation; they were fitted with a cane tube to prevent the must from overflowing. I saw them loaded onto carts to start the journey to the bodega. I watched them, the first butts of must from my vineyard, start down the track to the road. It had cost so much, in money, toil, hope, and time. It would never, at this stage, pay for itself. I looked back at the men straining in the lagar and wondered how money could ever pay them. But men had planted vineyards for hundreds of years, had tended them, and lived to extract their precious liquid. Whatever my feelings now, I was irrevocably committed. My legs ached from the treading, the tannin of the grapes burned my skin, my back broke from laboring at the screw of the lagar. I had done none of these things, and yet I had done them all. My blood was in that wine, and the wine was now in my blood, its violent fermentation was an excitement I craved. I would live for the next harvest, in hope and dread.

And when the men rested in the hot hours of the afternoon, I rested also. But exhausted sleep brought only dreams of harvests, more and more harvests. When I woke I was bathed in sweat, as if I had been straining at the screw of the lagar.

It was often Pepita who wakened me. She had come with me to the vineyard house but had to be confined indoors, unless I walked her on a chain, because she was in heat. She hated the enforced imprisonment of these times and begged to be taken out. So before darkness fell I walked her. Because of the man in the watchtower— they called it a *bienteveo,* meaning "I see you well"— one didn't move about the vineyards at night. Pepita endured the long days of the vendimia as best she could, as we all endured them.

My small vineyard would yield no more grapes, even though the men went back a second and a third time to find the grapes at their exact state of ripeness. We were pressing our last carretada. I had seen little of Don Luis during this time, but Mateo had been constantly at Las Ventanas Verdes, then hurrying back to oversee the operation at his own vineyard house. He had been busy for both of us; the yield of the vineyard seemed to belong as much to him as to me. But he took his added burden cheerfully. Don Luis was a good employer, and had obviously bidden him, and would pay him, to help out the novice on the adjoining ground. So he advised, helped, made decisions, and yet gave me the sense that I was still mistress here.

But he was, faithful to Don Luis' instructions, at Las Ventanas Verdes, overseeing the loading of the butts onto the cart, with another eye on the last pressing from the lagar, when Carlos arrived.

Carlos also looked weary. No doubt the days of the harvest are anxious times for all who deal in wine, however remote they make themselves from the actual business of growing the grapes and providing the must. Without the constant stream of wagons bearing the must to the bodegas, there would be nothing to fill the butts scoured and cleaned and prepared to receive the new wine. The quality of the must had to be judged, even though in the making

255

of sherry there is no such thing as a vintage. The true character of the must would not emerge until the second fermentation was over, during the cooler weather, when the wine fell bright. Only then could it be classified and take its place in the solera. That was work for later days, and for the experts. But while the harvest was being brought in the men of the bodegas worked as long as the carts brought the must in. It had to be examined, checked for volume, the price decided. The butts had to be stored, given their place in the bodega, even though that would be a temporary place.

Least of all, in the days of the harvest, did they want trouble from wives who didn't know that their task was to stay at home and see that everything there ran smoothly.

So Carlos, after the four days it took me to bring in my small harvest, came to Las Ventanas Verdes.

He found me in the courtyard of the house, watching as the last must ran from the lagar. He had slipped off his horse and was beside me before I knew it. There had been so much noise, so much to do, I didn't hear the new noise.

"So, Carlota . . . and how has the harvest gone?"

I was deceived. I took it as a natural greeting.

"Well enough. We have all worked hard. I don't know yet what price I'll get for the must, but it will . . ."

I stopped. His face, burned by the summer sun, lined with weariness, had contorted in anger.

"Do you think I care what you will get for your miserable few butts of must? For four nights you haven't been at home! Look at you! You look like a scarecrow. You are a disgrace . . . a disgrace to any man!"

I looked down at my dress, splashed and stained from the pulp of the grapes. I put my hand self-consciously to my hair; it was rough and straggled over my eyes. Even my hands seemed rough; they had caught too much of the sun and the freckles stood out on them. I knew I looked hardly different from the women who joined the men cutting the grapes.

Carlos continued: "Do you suppose I enjoy the laughter at the bodega when another of your carts comes in with the must? The laughter about the madwoman who labors like a man, who leaves her children to take care of themselves while she takes care of her few little grapes—who leaves her husband to look after his own needs . . ."

I could not help it. Perhaps it was the sun, the work, the worry. I said what I had never wanted to say to him. "And aren't there plenty of other women to take care of your needs, Carlos? You haven't missed a *woman* during these days. You have plenty of women. It's only a wife who isn't at home—and that hurts your pride. Well, let it hurt—"

We had spoken in English, so the words were not understood by Mateo and Antonio, who were standing close by, or by the tiradores who had stopped the pushing and pulling at the screw of the lagar in fascination at this unexpected entertainment which had come their way. They all stood, slightly openmouthed, amused that the gentry quarreled just as noisily as peasants. I think they even guessed what the quarrel was about. But they were all motionless and staring at the instant that Carlos lashed out with the full power of his arm and struck me across the face. I hadn't braced myself for that, and I found myself sprawling on the hot flagstones of the courtyard. For a moment I lay there, the breath knocked out of me. Than I sat up and put my hand to my lip; it came away smeared with blood, and I could taste blood on my tongue. I spat out the blood with all the gusto that any peasant woman would have used. Through lips that were already swelling, I said to him, "Go back to your women, Carlos. Your scarecrow of a wife will return when her work here is done. Not before."

I sat there in the sun, dazed, feeling sick. Carlos, for the moment, did not want to continue the argument. Perhaps he was regretting the blow, though he had most perfectly demonstrated the admired machismo before this group of workers. I heard his footsteps on the flagstones, the movement of the horse's hoofs as he remounted. He called to me, "You will come home. I shall expect you."

"Expect me when you see me!"

He jerked angrily at the horse's mouth, and as he clat-

257

tered through the archway he nearly ran down Don Luis, who stood within its shadow. We listened to the dying sounds of the hoofs on the hard soil of the track. Don Luis came forward, bending over me, lifting me under the arms. "Back to work!" he shouted to the gaping men. A moment later the grunting noise of the marrana began.

He supported me around the waist as we went into the house. Concepción had appeared—she may have seen and heard the whole event—and she brought brandy and glasses to the big room. Don Luis poured for us both, dismissing her. I was surprised to find that my hand trembled as I accepted the glass from him. I wasn't afraid, and I didn't yet feel the pain. I was angry—probably as angry as Carlos had been.

"If I were half a man," Don Luis said, "I would have pulled him from his horse. I am dishonored, as well as you."

I stretched my grazed, dusty hand across the table to cover his. "There can be no dishonor where none is admitted, Don Luis. I admit no such thing. You are the finest man I know."

For a moment he covered his face with his hand. And from the room where she had been shut up Pepita howled her protest. It was as if she knew every movement, every word, that had passed in the courtyard. She seemed to howl her protest that she hadn't been there to prevent it.

I stayed with Don Luis and Amelia until the swelling and bruising had gone. I knew that all Jerez must be talking of the quarrel, and possibly enjoying it. I spent my days resting in the shade of Amelia's beautiful rooms. Her maid massaged oil into my hair to counteract the dryness and dust of the vineyards, washed it, and brushed it until it shone. I had scented oil in my baths, and scented cream on my hands. Amelia produced two lengths of lawn and her seamstress made them up. "The color doesn't suit me," was all she said. She was very thin and pale and languid in those hot September days; she lay on her chaise most of the day and made only a small effort to walk in the garden at dusk with me and Pepita.

There seemed to be a special communication between her and the dog; Pepita seemed to know Amelia's failing strength. As they walked the big dog kept thrusting her nose under Amelia's hand and then running around to her other side, nudging her as if trying to give her support. One day I found Luis watching this. "If only—" he said. "If only Pepita could give to her what she needs. . . ."

The dinner gong was sounded, and Amelia and the big dog turned on their circuit of the lake and came back to the house.

I received my payment for the must from the bodega. It seemed such a pitifully small sum to reward that enormous effort, and all of it was owed to Luis. I had my account books with me and I studied the figures anxiously, putting aside sums for an extra gift to Mateo and Antonio, putting aside what would be needed for the planting of a new slope, one that would rise from the hollow and up the ridge, and beyond the next hill. When it was planted it would be the first time I would not be able to see all my vines by walking the perimeter of the house.

"Perhaps," I said to Luis, "I should stop. Wait until the rest of the vines have come into production before I plant further. I have almost no money left to repay you. It is barely the interest on the debt." But I knew if I stopped I would have wasted the money spent in August on the agosta, the deep tilling of the new slopes.

"If you are so cautious you will never make your fortune, Carlota. One has always to be in debt. It is the first rule of making money."

"I'm not so certain about that." I was thinking of how my grandfather had plunged again and again, always borrowing on the next year's income from Clonmara, never free of the specter of bankruptcy.

"That is how it is done, I assure you. And as for collateral—your vineyards are the best I can have."

So I signed yet another note and added the total in the account books. It was bigger than before, as if the year's

259

harvest had never been. I didn't dare think of what would happen if a harvest should be poor, or fail entirely. "No, do not think of it," Luis said. "You were born to be lucky, Carlota."

Looking around me, at the disarray of my life, I wondered how he could say it. And yet as Amelia struggled to get through each day, hardly able to drag her skeletal frame from one room to the other, it seemed I was indeed lucky. "I must go home to my children," I said. "I have been, pampered and cosseted here. I have lived like a duchess. My children won't know me when I get back."

Amelia's thinly transparent face glimmered in the dimness of the room. "I wish you didn't have to go." By mutual agreement we didn't talk of Carlos. "I feel there isn't much time left now."

"You're not worse," I said, and was instantly shamed by the lie. She had seemed to hold the illness at bay for so long, but now it gained rapidly on her, and the flesh fell from her frame. Doctors had come and gone. Luis talked of taking her to Morocco for the winter. "I think I would rather stay here in peace," she said. She did not know that one doctor, whom Luis had merely introduced as a visitor to Jerez, had been brought from Vienna. He had talked, Luis told me, of the multiplication of white blood cells. "She may live for quite a long time," he had said. "But the smallest infection may be fatal."

So Luis tried to guard her from infection, and she shrugged off the precautions. "You cannot hang a curtain between me and the world," she said. "If someone sneezes in the same room I may catch cold. And if I take care I may live to be a hundred."

So I returned to the Plaza de Asturias, and the household hardly seemed to notice. My children came to greet me as if I had been gone only for the day—except Juan, who now could count, and who had counted the days. "Next time you go to the vineyard, Mama, you will take me. I am old enough to work now."

"Yes," I agreed. "You are old enough to work."

Only María Luisa looked at me with her little sharp

sideways glance. "The town thinks you are very kind to be such a friend to Amelia. It cannot be easy for a healthy young woman to spend so much time with an invalid. But you look well, querida."

"I have rested," I said.

"And Carlos has waited," she answered. "He has waited with a patience I did not expect of him."

Carlos returned from the bodega that evening, and he smiled at me as if there had been nothing to forgive on either side. "You look well. Your visit to Amelia has done you good."

I was wearing one of the new dresses. My hands were smooth, my hair was shining. "There is a little supper party at the Garveys' tonight," he added. "We will go, perhaps. . . ."

We went, and played cards, and someone played the latest music that had come from London. We talked of the war, and how it might affect shipping between Cádiz and London. Everyone said it would all be over by Christmas, even though by now all of Belgium was gone and the Germans were fighting on French soil. Carlos paraded me through the rooms, bowing and smiling, his hand possessively through my arm. He had decided to laugh away whatever tales had spread about the scene at the vineyard house that day. A wife had been unruly, and he had handled it in the only way a real man could. It was all over.

He was once again that night the tender, delightful lover of the early days of our marriage. He took pleasure in me, and seemed to strive to give me pleasure; and for his sake I also tried. I think he was deceived, as I meant him to be. He stayed at home every night for more than two weeks.

"You have frightened him just a little, querida," María Luisa said. "But do not play too strong a hand. When he is in a rage he loses caution." She bent her head again over her sewing. "It makes one wonder if those stories of his mother being a gypsy were true. . . ."

CHAPTER THREE

1

We planted the new slopes in January. The weather had been dry, and Amelia was able to drive out to watch the work. She sat for an hour in the warmth of the winter sun against the south-facing wall of Las Ventanas Verdes. Antonio had carried her from the carriage, and Concepción had wrapped her in a rug. I had brought out the best wine the cellar at the Plaza de Asturias offered. We drank it quietly together, saying little. Amelia held up her face to the sun, as if trying to draw strength from it. I watched the steady progress of the men working the rows, under Mateo's direction, he marking out with a chain where each root should go, distributing the iron stakes which would hold them steady, seeing that each was firmly trodden in and fertilized. The immemorial work of the vineyard.

Suddenly Amelia spoke. "The wine tastes good, Charlie." It was the first time she had ever used that name; I hadn't even been aware she knew it. "It tastes better out here, in the air—in the sun." It was a red, full-bodied burgundy; strange how one sought to tempt her to eat and drink things that seemed life-supporting —red rather than white, meat rather than the delicate shrimp she preferred. Her eyes were not on the working men but on the slope of the vineyard which had been named for her. Now, in winter, it was nothing more than straight rows of dark, leafless roots thrusting up their vara y pulgar, stick and thumb, indicating the future twisted and gnarled appearance they would assume in their maturity. Now it looked like a burned landscape; impossible to imagine the lush greenness it would wear in the summer.

Suddenly she said, "Be very kind to Luis, Charlie, please. He will be lonely. You, the children, the new vineyards—they give him interest. He is fond of Juan, I know. You must take Juan to the bodega to visit him. You must let Juan show him how he rides his pony."

"He will not be lonely, Amelia. . . ." Then the words faded; it was useless, hypocritical, to protest that she would be there to keep him from being lonely.

She smiled absently. She had been a pretty young woman when I first saw her, but her illness had seemed to drain that youthful attractiveness. Now, as she sat there, her face seemed suffused with a kind of radiance, which gave her an unearthly beauty. She still stared at the blackened stumps of the vines, and we both knew that she would never see the green shoots of spring.

"I do not think Luis will marry again. Two failures are enough. Poor man . . . Such cruel jokes life plays on us, Charlie."

The sun seemed to slip at that instant, and the first shadow appeared in the deepest hollow between the slopes. She gave a slight shiver. I called for Antonio to come and carry her back to the fire in the big room. I had wanted her to go to the carriage and start the journey home, but she ordered Antonio to put her down in the chair by the fire. "We will finish the wine, Charlie."

And so we did in the room that Amelia's hand had subtly transformed. She had made what she called "little presents" to Las Ventanas Verdes. Nothing too grand or ostentatious for the basic simplicity of the house—Moorish rugs, a brilliant hanging for the wall, some vivid pieces of pottery, some clay figures from Mexico which dated from before the Spanish conquest—things that I suspected were much more valuable than she claimed. Some extra chairs had come—heavy dark oak, which suited the house, a great carved dresser to display the pottery. She had brushed aside my protests. "I must have *something* to do when I'm in Sevilla between consultations with the doctors. Please, don't refuse me. It is the first time I have ever had the interest of buying things for a house. Luis' first wife furnished Los Cisnes so completely that there has never been anything for me to do there. . . ." So now as the firelight flickered over her pale face I saw her look around and take pleasure in what she had accomplished. The sun slipped further down, so that now only the very tops of the vineyard slopes were lighted by it. Watching it, we finished the wine.

Two days later, at six in the morning, Luis sent a message that she was dead. I went and found her, with lighted candles about the bed, looking so peaceful, so beautiful, that all the ravages of her illness were wiped away. Luis sat quietly, watching her. "It's you, Carlota," he said, without even turning. "See how lovely she looks."

I dropped to my knees beside her and touched her smooth, cold hands. Then I turned and placed my hand on Luis', as it rested on the arm of the chair.

"Shall we pray for her?"

He smiled a little and shook his head. "The praying is over, as her life is over, Charlie." Now he also called me that name. "No—do not let me see you weep. You do not weep, Charlie. You have always been so strong. You gave her strength. Did you know that you gave her strength? I don't care what the doctors said . . . about how soon or how long it would be until she died. All I am sure of is that she lived longer because she drew strength from you. You will give your strength to many people, Charlie. Give me a little of it now."

He rose and led me from the room. In that dining room he ordered the servants to open the shutters to let in the growing sunlight of the winter morning, and he ordered coffee to be brought for us both. I wondered what would be said in the town about us sitting here, talking of the vines, the war, horses, all the everyday things of our lives, while his wife lay dead in a room upstairs. But I did not care. It was what Amelia had foreseen, had wanted. It was his loneliness which needed the small comfort of my presence.

In her will Amelia left me what seemed to me at that time to be quite a large sum of money, and she also left me the pieces of jewelry which had been Luis' gift to her and which did not belong by descent in his family. I was stunned, and a little shocked.

María Luisa shook her head. "They will say you were her friend for what you could get from her. I know it was not so, querida, but that is what they will say."

"I didn't know she had any money of her own to leave to anyone."

María Luisa mentally riffled through her formidable knowledge of the town's interlocking relationships. "She was the granddaughter of Manuel de la Riva, and *he* was the son of Tomás de la Riva y O'Neale. There was money. Her own."

There was also a long oak chest, a very old chest which Amelia had found in Seville. Luis said she had wanted me to have it—and its contents. I went through them with him, a painful and sad task. It contained an odd assortment of things. There was a collection of lovely fans, some surprisingly good water colors Amelia had made of the lake and the black swans in the early days of their marriage when she had been stronger. "I had them framed, but she decided they weren't good enough to hang. She had so little confidence in herself. . . ." There was a heavy brass book stand. "That was a present for Las Ventanas Verdes—it arrived from Sevilla the day before she died." There were a few elaborately bound books of Spanish poetry. "I will make an effort to read and understand them properly," I promised Luis. There was a tiny, beautifully wrought pistol, with ornamentation in silver and mother-of-pearl, laid in a velvet-lined marquetry case, with its own compartments filled with silver bullets. "We saw it in a shop in Vienna. It seemed to amuse her, though heaven knows why. I doubt she ever fired a weapon in her life. I remember in those days I was grateful for anything that distracted her. We got this petit point bag in Vienna, too. I don't remember her using it, though. And here are some porcelain models of the White Horses of Vienna—the Lipizzaners." He was unwrapping them from cotton wool to show me. "She meant to have a cabinet made to display them, but she seemed to lose interest— perhaps she couldn't find the right place in this house to put it. And here are some tapestry bellpulls from Paris. All little pieces of Amelia's life, Carlota. She put them all together in this chest for you. Her book of recipes—though I don't think she ever used it. She said our cook didn't pay attention to them. Her first communion veil, and the prayer book—her father has written in it, see." He handed me the exquisite little volume, bound in vellum with a stiff edging of gold, and a golden clasp. "When you have a daughter, they can be for her first communion. . . ."

Then he closed the lid of the chest, as if he were unable to continue. "How, I wonder, am I to go through the rest of her things, her clothes, her shoes . . . ? They should be given to some charity, but I don't . . ."

"María Luisa," I said. "María Luisa will do all that. Trust her. She is very tactful, and very discreet. Nothing will go where it will not be needed and appreciated."

He nodded. "One has a need of the María Luisas of the world. What a pity we don't more often tell them. . . ."

I had the chest taken to Las Ventanas Verdes. I knew that was where Amelia had meant her little personal treasures to be. As I began to distribute her things about the rooms I was aware of a terrible sense of desolation and loneliness. I was also aware that I had never had a friend of my own age before Amelia—and there could be none to take her place. Remembering Luis' remark about the María Luisas of the world not being told of their worth, I wondered if I had ever properly told Amelia what she meant to me—or had I even known it until she was gone? But I had named a part of a vineyard for her, the only gift I had to give.

The quarrel with Carlos started when he learned of the money Amelia had left me. He seemed to assume that part of the money would be for his own use. "The whole household needs money," I protested. "I must save something for the children."

"The Marquesa will take care of the children. You have only to ask."

"I will *never* ask anything of her."

He shrugged. "No matter. There are plenty of other ways to use the money. The children don't need it *now*. I have a few gambling debts—trifling, but still one does not like to owe one's friends. And that tiresome tailor in London has been dunning me for money. I shall not give him any more of my business, but it would be better if the matter was settled. . . ."

"There are *my* debts," I said. "What I owe to Don Luis. For the stock, labor—oh, a number of things."

He looked at me darkly. "I see—she has left you money only so you may pay it back to her husband. A fine legacy! And how much do you owe Don Luis?"

I didn't dare tell him. I had told so many lies about it in the past, pretending that more came to my mother from her interest in the bodega than was the fact, that we had sold a small piece of property in Ireland—property which did not exist. I had not been able to reveal to him the extent of my debt to Don Luis. So now I named half the sum.

"Well, pay him back! No man should be allowed to say that my wife is in debt to him! It is a humiliation for me!"

"But he does not say it. He never mentions the debt."

267

"It's well to be so rich he can overlook a debt of that size. *Pay him!*"

He left, and I did not see him for two days. Then he returned full of good humor. I had no idea where he had spent those two nights, or if he had even shown himself at the bodega. The reason for the good humor was evident. He was riding a wonderful mare, almost black in color, not big, but so beautifully proportioned that all her movements seemed sheer perfection. As the two of them moved about the stable yard, demonstrating her walk and her trot, they were two beautiful creatures seemingly fused together. When Carlos was entirely happy with the animal he rode, it would be hard to find anyone to equal his horsemanship.

"She is beautiful, is she not, Carlota?" he called to me. "Her name is Carmen. I got her from Domécq . . ." I gasped. This was the talked-of Carmen, the fabled mare that everyone said Don Jaime would never part with. Whatever persuasion Carlos had used, the mare was now his. But the animal could not have changed hands for a small price.

"I have sold the other mare—she was nothing beside Carmen, was she? Now I give you back Balthasar—formally. Carmen is your real wedding present to me. And I have acquired four polo ponies. I knew you would agree that it isn't right that I should have to beg a mount from other men. . . ."

So now I understood that between the purchase of Carmen and the polo ponies, the settling of his gambling debts and his tailor's bills, there would be almost nothing left of Amelia's legacy. Whatever feeling Carlos might have had about my owing money to Luis had been swept away in a fit of jealousy and self-indulgence. He bitterly resented his poverty and my lack of a dowry. He was simply taking what he regarded as his by right, taking it as the price of peace between us. I was certain that Amelia had left me the money so that the debt on the vineyards might be cleared and money provided for future planting and for labor. Now Carlos had taken most of it. Perhaps he had even done it with the thought that I would be forced to

268

give up the vineyard to settle my debts, and my refuge from him would be gone, my little base of independence destroyed. I watched him show off Carmen, and himself, to the whole household, servants and family, who had come to the stable yard to look and admire and applaud, and the feeling of rage in me was so great that I trembled, and had to go inside, away from the sight of him and the mare, and all it represented. Never, I thought, never—no matter what, would I let Carlos take the vineyard from me. I would never give it up.

"I'll never give it up," I said to Pepita. "Never—never!"

The same week, by letter from Ireland came the news that Richard Blodmore had joined the British army at the outbreak of war, was commissioned, and already stationed in France. The letter did not come from Elena. Perhaps she wrote to the Marquesa but she didn't write to us. The news came, along with a great deal of local gossip, from one of our neighbors at Clonmara. "Spiteful old goose," my mother said of Lady Sybil Wereham. "She thinks we're all too safe and cozy here in Spain. Wants to shake us up a bit. Write back to her, Charlie. Find out what other news there is."

At her dictation, since no one else could translate her idiom, I wrote back. It was the beginning of a long and terrible sequence of letters, sometimes many months apart, which related to us the course of the war, but more particularly the devastation it caused among those we knew, some of whom we also loved.

"Harry Lake was killed at Mons," I read. That had been as long ago as August, when I had been living through the last day before the grapes were to be harvested, and had ordered Mateo and Antonio to begin the agosta to prepare for the new vineyard. "Lord Blodmore, I hear," the letter went on, "is stationed somewhere near Ypres, though one isn't supposed to say such things. I suppose he was involved in that terrible battle there where they used poison gas. But Elena says he is all right. I expect you people in Spain feel quite detached from this. All the places around are selling their horses. The demand is quite unbelievable. . . ."

"Don't read any more, Charlie," my mother said. "I don't want to hear about the horses."

So I took to writing to Lady Sybil, and anyone else like her who I thought might spare a few minutes to write back. Never once did I directly inquire about Richard Blodmore, but always, I hoped, there would be some spinoff of gossip which would carry his name.

In those days I grieved for Amelia, and I prayed for Richard Blodmore. One morning, at the side entrance of the church across the plaza, I almost knocked over Nanny, who was coming from the first Mass. "Why—it's you, Miss Charlie! I've never known you to go to Mass except on Sundays and Holy days."

"Perhaps I have a little more to pray for now, Nanny."

She looked at me closely, her face puckered into a frown; her eyes squinting as if she sought to read in mine whatever wisdom had grown there. Then she patted me on the shoulder. "That's right, dear. Prayer never went amiss. And you've a woman's troubles to bear now, haven't you, Miss Charlie?"

She went slowly on her way back across the plaza to the house, and I went into the church. I lighted two candles, one for Amelia, who would have understood, and one, with a sort of smothered apology, for Richard Blodmore. I had always believed that one couldn't make bargains with God, and so prayer had to be entirely disinterested. How could I ask Him for the safety and life of Richard Blodmore? I looked up at the statue of the Virgin, at whose feet the candles burned. The Spaniards always talked of her as if she were far more important in the scheme of things than Christ, her son. "One woman to another," I said aloud in English. "Would you help?" The calm, grave face looked sightlessly down at me. I was reminded of those waxen faces of the dolls in the castle at Arcos. Why pray where there was so little faith? That time, I turned away, but often I went back to light candles—always one for Amelia and one for Richard Blodmore.

270

That summer Andy married Manuela, a niece of Serafina. I was a little taken aback when he came to me to announce his intention, and then I stifled my exclamation of surprise and made it one of pleasure. "I'm so glad, Andy. I'm so glad you won't be . . . be alone, any more."

He shrugged, and smiled shyly. "Might as well make up my mind to it, Miss Charlie. There's no going back any more, is there? I mean—we'll never go home again, will we?"

I shook my head. "No, Andy, *we* won't be going home. But you . . . you know you're free to go, if you want."

"I've settled, in a sort of way. Can't see what I'd be going back to. Lord Blodmore, when he was here, made a point of seeing me and saying there was always a place for me there at Clonmara, but I knew he'd rather I stayed here with you and Lady Pat. My mother and sister are nicely fixed in that cottage he settled them in. But my brothers enlisted in the British army. Things can't be so good if they've got to do that. Couldn't see myself enlisting in the British army, somehow. And there's Manuela. I wouldn't like to leave her behind, but somehow I don't sort of see her in Ireland. I doubt it'd suit her."

I nodded agreement. "I doubt it too, Andy." And my heart was breaking. This seemed the final severance of the link with Clonmara, the admission that none of us would ever go back.

We gave Andy a splendid wedding reception in the courtyard of the house in the Plaza de Asturias. María Luisa was furious with me for the expense incurred. "Must we use such good wine? You don't realize what you're doing in inviting *all* Manuela's family. They will all come, I do assure you—down to the last third cousin twice removed. Food for them all, and wine. You must be mad!"

"Perhaps. But Andy is family, María Luisa. We would want him to feel proud before all his new Spanish relations, wouldn't we?" I was thinking of my own hurried, secret marriage, the wedding breakfast shared only with Carlos. Andy deserved more.

She shrugged, as if resigning herself to a lifetime of dealing with such foolhardiness. "You Blodmores—I suppose I must expect such madness."

"Not all the time, María Luisa. Just some of the time. And we do love Andy."

She looked outraged. "You love a stable hand!"

I nodded. "That has to be the truth. How else could I put it?"

She sniffed. "Next you'll be saying you love a dried-up skinflint old spinster called María Luisa."

I laughed. "And next you'll be saying you love the crazy Blodmores, who give you nothing but trouble. Not even the Marquesa de Pontevedra could *pay* you enough money to stay on with us if you didn't love us—and forgive us for a great many things."

She lowered her head over the sheet of paper on which she had been worriedly doing her calculations. "There never was a love that wasn't helped by a little money. And are you going to be godmother to all Andy's family?"

"You cynic!"

She looked up. "There must be someone in this household who doesn't see everything in terms of either vineyards or horses. . . . Thank the Holy Mother I never fell in love!"

3

She appeared at that moment of Andy's wedding feast when everyone was just drunk enough not to notice her presence, much less recognize her. It was, of course, María Luisa who first saw that dark figure hardly emerging from the deeper shadow of the arch. The lanterns were lighted all around the house, but the light was soft. A great deal of wine had been drunk, and my mother had reached the stage when she thought she could join in the *sevillanas*. With the natural looseness of a born horsewoman, she

272

could readily fall into the rhythm of the dance. She was wildly applauded.

"The Marquesa!" María Luisa hissed.

I went to her. "I heard you were giving a wedding feast for your servant," she said. "I heard all were invited."

"All are invited. But it is a wedding celebration for our friend."

I was furious with her intrusion. She had the unhappy habit of appearing when she was least wanted, without warning or invitation. No one knew she was now in residence at Sanlúcar—or with Don Paulo at Las Fuentes. And even if we had known, it would have been unthinkable to invite her on such an occasion. The Marquesa was a person who did not wait for invitations, and did not heed them when they were sent. She lived by her own clocks and at her own whim.

Now she nodded, and her mouth twisted wryly at the spectacle of the courtyard set with tables, the decimated hams and chickens, the spilled wine, the group of musicians, somewhat drunk themselves, the colorful swirl of the dancers.

"So . . . And where are my godchildren?"

"Our children are too young for this, Marquesa." Now my mother held the center of attention, that lithe body swaying in perfect time with the rhythms, as if she had danced to them all her life. The Marquesa studied her for a moment longer; then turned to me.

"Where are they?"

"In their nursery, of course."

I led her along all the passages of the house, up the stairs to come to the wide, long room, with its flaking white paint, its children's clothes hung to dry on a rack, the toys neatly disposed on the shelves, Juan in a bed, Martín and Francisco in their high-sided cots. Nanny dozed in a chair by the window, the top buttons of her dress undone because of the heat, her head nodding to one side. A night light burned on the mantel. At the sound of the door opening, Juan's head popped out from the sheets; he was fully awake, his eyes bright.

He recognized her at once. "Tía Isabel!"

She held out her arms. "My little one!" He sprang from the bed, perhaps knowing that in her presence there was little chance of his being chastised. He was tall for his age, and his thin nightshirt was a long way above his bare feet. He was five years old, and trying out life with all the eagerness of an intelligent, willful child. He had never lost the dominance, the sureness that had come to him with being the first-born. He had never been jealous of the arrival of his brothers; they had seemed very secondary to himself.

Nanny started out of her doze. *"Master John—"* Then she stopped, heaved herself to her feet and sketched a curtsy. "My lady . . ."

"There's my good boy." The Marquesa bent and embraced him. "And why are you not at the party?"

He glanced quickly between me and Nanny. "They said I was too young."

"Never too young to learn to be a man," she replied. "Juan, will you escort me to the party?"

"My lady!" It was an exclamation of outrage from Nanny.

She made a sweeping gesture with her hand. "Just a little time. Quickly, Juan, put on your trousers and shirt. Here, I'll help you. . . ."

She had no notion of how to help a child to dress, but with Nanny complaining almost inaudibly, Juan was dressed, not in his everyday clothes, but in his best black, tightly fitted trousers, frilled shirt, and red sash. "There now!" the Marquesa pronounced. "You look the grandest gentleman in Jerez—in Spain. Will you take my arm?"

The tall figure leaned to allow his short arm to link in hers. They set off along the corridor and down the stairs.

Nanny's outrage broke through. "Miss Charlie! . . . It's a disgrace! Master John should never be allowed into anything like that down there—" She nodded her head contemptuously in the direction of the noise. "At his age! Ruined, he'll be. Spoiled—spoiled so no one will be able to manage him. . . ."

I shrugged, helpless, sad, angry. "Stay with the two

little ones, Nanny. I'll try to get him back to bed as soon as I can."

When I returned to the courtyard they had merged into the dancing, swaying groups, that tall, black-clad figure with the fire of her gems on her fingers, and the small, handsome, winning boy. She had dressed for the evening in the grand Spanish manner of long ago, with the high comb in her hair and the black lace mantilla falling back from it. In the soft light she appeared almost young, her body moving to the rhythms as easily as my mother's had, but with a great deal more sophistication and knowledge of what the gestures meant. She led the little boy on. He had witnessed the dance many times, but this was his first time to try it with an audience, partnered by a great lady. It was as if he were mesmerized. He followed her gestures, her movements, as if obeying an invisible command. He was totally in her control.

Gradually the happy, laughing crowd of Andy's wedding feast realized who was among them. They fell back, allowing room for that strangely matched pair. The identity of the Marquesa was whispered among them, and more and more left the dancing area, going back behind the tables, dropping their voices, clapping, somewhat timidly, to the rhythm. On the other side of the courtyard I saw Carlos, smiling. Finally the pair were left alone, the tall lady in black and the small boy. People had stopped talking. There was no laughter.

She had ruined Andy's wedding feast. And she had made a great stride in winning my son.

CHAPTER FOUR

1

The dead heat of the summer months came on us, the somnolence of the long hot afternoons. In July we completed the bina, in August the rebina. This was the second year I would harvest the first vineyard, the first year for the second; more workers were needed, more money to find to employ them. As the vineyards grew, so did their needs. I began to wonder if it would ever be possible to make money from tending the vines.

Luis kept pressing loans on me, offering them gently, more as suggestions of what needed doing in the vineyard than an outright offer of money. I continued to pay the interest, and I hoped after the harvest I might be able to pay back part of the loan.

"Patience is everything with the vines, Carlota. Those who look for money only had better look elsewhere."

"There are plenty of rich people in Jerez."

"There are those who've lost everything, too. Look to fortunate marriage and other interests for the money. But yes—it's true. Money has been made in sherry. Before the phylloxera the vines from our own rootstock produced for a longer period than the American rootstock. So the initial, almost crippling expense of planting a vineyard was something a man might have to do only once, perhaps, in his lifctime. So long as he cared for his vines they produced for him. It needed money invested in other places to survive the phylloxera, Carlota. Think of it— every vineyard in Jerez to be replanted, and some, like your grandfather's land, until you started, have never seen a hoe to this day. Those are the families who just quietly folded up and are not heard of now. The ones who sold their big houses or, if they couldn't sell them, just closed them and drifted away—the sons went out all over the world looking for whatever way they could to make a living, perhaps, with luck, to make a new fortune. The girls generally stayed here, living very quietly, in a few rooms in the town, being very careful with their money, never marrying because there was no dowry, waiting for their nieces and nephews to return from all parts of the world to see Jerez for the first time, waiting for their brothers to make fortunes and rescue them from their quiet poverty. . . ."

Luis often came to the vineyard house. He always knew from Mateo when I was there, and I would watch him ride down the track from his own vineyard house towards us. By the time he arrived the tray with the glasses and decanter and the tapas was set. He would sit and talk, very quietly. I saw him so much at ease in those plain white rooms to which Amelia had added her small bright pieces of decoration, and I thought of him alone in the splendor of his own house, empty without Amelia. He was, of course, still in official mourning for her, and there were no parties to brighten those big silent rooms. He was a little grayer in the months since she had died, as if the effort of being cheerful for her had drained him. He liked just to sit and slowly sip his copita, and talk. María Luisa shook her head over those visits of his to the vineyard house. "People talk."

"Then let them! I promised Amelia."

"Promises like that are easy to give and a problem to keep."

"He is lonely. He comes only to talk for a while."

"Then he should come here to the Plaza de Asturias. He should visit his cousins. He has dozens of cousins. He has the comradeship of the bodega. They all gather each day in the *sala de degustación* . . . it is not the *men* of Jerez who are lonely."

"He likes the vineyards best, María Luisa. It is where his heart is."

"Then take care that his heart doesn't linger too long at Las Ventanas Verdes!"

I shrugged, and decided it didn't matter. His friendship was precious to me; he was someone to talk to as I had talked to Amelia, someone to whom I could confess my worries, the small problems of our daily lives. With María Luisa I got companionship of a kind, but always with the cautionary tales which were part of her character; with my mother I got no relief at all, only the worry of her own problems which she brought to me, and then laughed away with the aid of a bottle of wine. I continued to write her letters for her and to wait with dread for the answers. Some of the men we knew were dead, many were wounded. "Peter Brennan will never ride again," Lady Sybil wrote. "Poor fellow lost a leg right at the thigh. I don't see how even *he* could sit a horse again after that. He never was a man to hang on by the reins. And do you remember young Dick Fitzgerald?—he would have been just a boy barely graduated from his pony when you left. He was killed at Artois. Richard Blodmore was mentioned in dispatches. Gerry Purcell is missing . . ." The roll call went on remorselessly. I saw the hunting field at Clonmara shrink. Anyone young enough to serve was gone. Even the women, those who were unmarried, had gone, many of them to serve as voluntary aids in hospitals; some had volunteered for factories in England, some, we learned with shock, were ambulance drivers. "I didn't think there were any women who *knew* how to drive," my mother said. "*That* has to be Sybil exaggerating." As we moved towards the autumn of 1915 Lady Sybil wrote, "We'll hardly have any hunting at all this winter. People have given up their horses, except just what's essential. Blodmore's hunt is under a temporary Master, who isn't any good—but that's not so important because it's not thought patriotic to keep hounds now. One has to set a good example, you know. It *matters* here. . . ." The implication was that in our disinterested, neutral country no such sacrifices would be understandable. She wrote nothing of the rumble of discontent under the patriotic surface. The Irish continued to join the British army in all ranks, and no one thought it strange. The war had indefinitely postponed Home Rule. "And a good thing, too," Lady Sybil wrote. "Perhaps by the end of the war that nonsense will have been forgotten. How on earth these people think they can run their own affairs when no two of them agree on anything . . ." My mother read over the letters many times, speaking the names aloud, remembering. "Oh, Johnny was a beautiful dancer. I can remember . . ." She actually took to reading the English newspapers which arrived in batches, reading the war news, trying to find out where the warfare actually raged. "Only such a few little miles, Charlie, and they've fought back and forth over it since it all began. I don't understand it. *We* were supposed to be so good at soldiering. But then . . . there was the Boer War. *That* took much longer than anyone expected. Didn't turn out very well, either. Poor Uncle Bertie . . ." She sighed again over the death of the man who was supposed to have inherited Clonmara, married, had a son, and kept us all there. Then one day as she read I heard her give a little choking cry. "Charlie!—it's Thomas's regiment. It's been stationed somewhere near Rheims."

"Thomas who?"

She looked across at me. "My darling, I'm talking about your father. He's with the 87th Regiment, King's Own Artillery. Terribly unfashionable regiment. They've never done anything very distinguished, I'm afraid. I didn't even have the sense to pick a man from a smart regiment. Do you suppose he's still riding horses, or have they all switched to lorries?"

My father meant nothing to me. It was the name of a man far less real than any of those mentioned in Lady Sybil's letters. "I expect they still use horses, Mother. I read that the lorries got terribly stuck in the mud last winter." That was all he meant, my father. A man in an undistinguished regiment hauling guns out of the mud by the brute labor of horses. I spoke of this, however, to Luis the next time we met at the vineyard.

"Poor Carlota—you've not had much love from men, have you?"

"My grandfather—"

He shook his head. "Too distant, and gone too soon."

"But Carlos . . ." I protested. And then I also shook my head. "But we don't have to pretend about Carlos, do we, Luis? Carlos doesn't love me, except in bed. Perhaps he's not capable of loving a woman any other way." Then I flushed because I was too close to Luis' most sensitive point, the point of pride and wounded masculinity, the feeble virility on which so many doubts and aspersions had been cast in that close society of Jerez. Everyone acknowledged that Luis was the best, the kindest of men; it was as bad as saying openly that he was no man at all. To cover the hurt I might unintentionally have offered him, I told him then of the man I truly did love, that love which had never been consummated and was based, physically, on such fragile things as a few embraces, a few words spoken in private, the looks we exchanged. Yet we both felt that this love was like solid bedrock in our hearts.

"So I *do* have a love, Luis. And I have our friendship. I have my children, and I have my vineyards. I am richer than anyone knows, except you."

He nodded. His sun-seamed face was serious as he studied the wine in his glass, holding it forwards slightly so that the sun caught its rich color. "I would have wished more for you, Carlota. No woman like you should have to love at such a distance . . . with so little hope. While Elena and Carlos both live . . . and each child born to either of you binds the bonds of each marriage tighter . . ."

"We have never thought of breaking those bonds, Luis. Neither of us could live with the responsibility of what we would leave behind. It is not particularly noble. It is common sense."

"It is very uncommon sense, Carlota. It is a tragedy that the times were out of joint by such a fraction. If Richard Blodmore had not returned here to Jerez instead of going at once to take up his inheritance . . ."

"Then it would have been a fairy story, and I am now too old to believe in them, Luis. Life is what it is. . . ." I shrugged, and poured more wine for him. I had told him as much as I dared, and it was sweet relief to have done so. But I could not go further. I could not tell him that the Marquesa had brought Richard back to Jerez expressly for the purpose of marrying Elena. It had been the one way she could reach back through the years to hurt the descendants of the man who had dared to cast aside her favor. I could not tell even Luis about the woman who still lived with her family of wax dolls in the castle of Arcos.

The harvest was over, a good harvest for me. The vines had yielded well; we were busy through several weeks of September bringing in the grapes, treading them in the lagar, extracting the last drop of the must to the squealing of the marrana. I saw many butts of must go off to the bodega in the carts, and the price was better this year. I paid the interest on the loan to Luis, and when I tried to pay him back some of the principal he gently reminded me that not all my land was yet under cultivation. I protested, and yet I agreed. I had fallen into the error of thinking of it as my land, and I loved it. And I made the mistake of letting Carlos see that I loved it. It seemed impossible that he could be jealous of anything but another man, but he was. He extracted payment for my pleasure in something beyond himself. He simply presented me once again with fresh gambling debts and the stabling bills for his polo ponies.

It was the price I must continue to pay for peace between us. This harvest there had been no such scene as had occurred the first time I stayed at the vineyard house. I spent most of September there, and a great deal of the time the children were with me. He did not knock me to the ground, threaten, shout, did not even object in words. He waited until payment was due from the bodega. Then, smilingly, he handed me an account of what he owed to his gambling friends and the bill for a new and flashy harness for his black mare, Carmen.

I looked at the sum, choked back my rage, and paid.

With the cool weather my mother brought Balthasar back from Luis' hacienda. She began once again the exercises of the High School with him. Half Moon was again in foal by Balthasar, and Luis insisted that she be given the freedom of the *campos*. Andy was slightly put out by this arrangement and rode out each day to see how she did; but finally, grudgingly, and perhaps because the headman at the hacienda was distantly related to Manuela, he acceded to the arrangement. "But when her time is near I will be there," he vowed. Perhaps he was so vehement about it because Manuela was pregnant, and for the first time Andy saw the cycle of life and birth, which he had witnessed intimately all his life, in a different and personal fashion. He was immensely proud and happy at the thought of a child. "Boy or girl, Miss Charlie, it'll be called Charlie."

"Do you want a son, Andy?"

He shook his head, and his face was strangely beautiful at that moment. "What God sends, Miss Charlie. I want a healthy child, and Manuela to be all right. That's all I want."

I envied him to be so free of dynastic obligations and needs. Manuela should be a happy mother.

2

The interference of the Marquesa in our lives continued, insistent, pervasive, and, because of Carlos, impossible to reject. She now quite often appeared in her husband's

house, Las Fuentes, a thing almost unknown, María Luisa
said, before our time. She came to be near our children;
Sanlúcar was too far for casual visits. We got accustomed
to the infuriating highhandedness with which she would
send around her carriage with orders that the children
were to come to Don Paulo's house for the *comida*. Nanny,
furious with the break in routine, would bundle them into
their best clothes, change her uniform, and go with them.
I was never invited. On her return, Nanny's face would
be heavy with wrath and frustration. "I pray to the Holy
Mother for patience, Miss Charlie! That woman—I beg
your pardon, the Marquesa—is ruining them! Just ruining
them! She bids me wait in another room while she eats
with them. Very unsuitable stuff they eat. Francis was sick
on the way home! All over his best suit. And she has the
cheek to complain to me that they don't know their table
manners! She lets them behave any old way, and yet she
complains when they take advantage. And take advantage
they do! Every child does. It'll take me days to get them
settled down again. . . ."

"Was Don Paulo there?"

"Yes—he always comes directly back from the bodega
when *she* is in the house. I heard one of the servants say
so." It was the first time Nanny had ever admitted to
understanding a word of the Spanish which flowed about
her. I wondered how accurate the information was, but I
would not ask Carlos. "Don Paulo," Nanny continued,
"eats with them. Can you imagine a man like that with
three young children spilling things all over the place, and
shouting and carrying on? It sounds to me as if they
turn into a pack of larrikins as soon as they get with *her*.
Showing off. Shouting. Well, she does them no good, I can
tell you. They come back here and turn up their noses at
nursery food. Every time there are new toys for them.
Now she's promised a whole set of trains and tracks
ordered from London. To be set up at Don Paulo's house,
of course, so they have to go there to play with them.
Imagine sending for toys for children from London when
there's a war on. Well, there are no rules for some people,
that's all I can say."

She was right about there being no rules for the Marquesa. No rules of manners or tact. The first news I had of a tutor for Juan came through Carlos. Don Paulo told him at the bodega that the Marquesa had secured the services of one of the young Fletcher cousins—the Fletchers were a long-established sherry family in Jerez—who had been invalided out of the army as a result of being gassed, and sent to his Jerez relations to recuperate in the Andalucian sun and air. He had, Carlos reported, a double first from Cambridge in history and mathematics. Juan was very fortunate.

I went myself to protest to the Marquesa. She was not then at Las Fuentes, so I had the long drive to Sanlúcar. After keeping me waiting for an hour, she consented to see me.

"It is impossible," I said at once. "We cannot have this man as a tutor for Juan."

"And why not?"

"To begin with, I haven't even met him. He may be totally unsuitable."

She laughed at me, unpleasantly. "I think, Doña Carlota, that I am a better judge of that than you. You are young, inexperienced. What do you know about bringing up children?"

"What do you know, Marquesa?"

The thrust brought an unaccustomed flush to her face. If I had hoped to be at all persuasive, I lost that hope now. She did not forgive such things.

"I am a woman of experience, Doña Carlota. I have been about the world, and I know these things. Your children need to be taken in hand. They are good children, intelligent . . . but they lack polish. That Nanny is, after all, just an ignorant Irishwoman, hardly more than a peasant. Do you expect to leave the teaching of your children to *her?*"

"We will teach them. Myself, my mother, María Luisa."

Her laughter was openly scornful. "*You* will teach them! Your mother—that fool! And you are almost as ignorant as the Nanny. What have you seen except a backwater of Ireland? Oh no—my godsons shall have much better than you!"

I had to accept the insult. There was too much truth in it to invite argument. "And you think that this young invalid man, just because he's a Fletcher and has a first in history and mathematics from Cambridge, is suitable? Do you not think he will find tutoring a small boy a very boring task? Surely he is looking to better things than that?"

"At the moment we take what we can get. When the war is over I shall have the pick of tutors, experienced with children, willing and anxious to come. Young Fletcher will do. It may be a boring occupation, trying to bring himself down to the mind of a five-year-old, but I am paying him to be bored. Paying him very well."

"And you think the money will somehow make him into a suitable person to mold Juan's character! What will he talk to him about—ancient Greece? Will he start him on Latin?"

She waved her hand in dismissal. "At least he will not talk to Juan eternally about horses! Or the fairies in Ireland—or the prospects of the next harvest, which, I think, is about the extent of the conversational range in *your* house. This young man speaks no Spanish, and I have forbidden him even to try. Juan must learn everything in English. His accent must be corrected. Now he speaks with an Irish accent, and constantly tells me of how the wicked English stole Ireland from its rightful owners. For the great-grandson of a Protestant earl, whose title was conferred by the English Crown, that is rather an outlandish view to hold."

"It happens to be the correct one, *historically*. Perhaps this young man's broad education will allow him to concede that."

She raised her eyebrows in sardonic amusement. "You also? I can see that someone like Edwin Fletcher is badly needed in your household to counteract these rather dangerous ideas. I have arranged for him to tutor Juan for four hours each morning. If it does not inconvenience you, he will lunch with you, and then return to his cousins' house. It will do Martín and Francisco good to hear his conversation."

"We do not normally eat lunch with the children. They are under Nanny's care."

"Then it is no wonder their manners require correction. I suggest you make the arrangement that all should eat together. Your kitchen can surely stretch to that—or are you afraid of the excesses of your mother being too closely observed?"

I got up and left her, but not before I heard the cruel laughter that followed me. As I climbed into the landau I held my head high for Andy's sake, but acknowledged defeat. There was that unhappy grain of truth in everything the Marquesa had said. I was as hungry for the good of my children as I was for the good of my land and vines. Education for them was like fertilizer for the soil. I could not pay for both.

So the young man called Edwin Fletcher entered our household. I was prepared to dislike him, and was terribly conscious of the deficiencies in my own education. After all, as the Marquesa had brutally pointed out, what had we three women among us experienced except a backwater of Ireland and this small conservative town in Spain? Carlos, at least, had had his time at school in England, his many visits to London and Bristol, but Carlos was too impatient to tutor his children, even if he would give them the time. So Edwin Fletcher had to be accepted with what grace we could muster. Nanny's revolt against the children joining us at lunch was hard to quell. "It's not *done,* Miss Charlie!" Her only experience of life in a big house had been at Clonmara, which had not been the best example of how a house should be run. How did she know such things? The gossip circle of the nannies of Jerez was as far-flung as that of the old aunts. I wondered what embellished tales Nanny told to her friends to make life at Clonmara seem much grander than it had been.

At first all the things I had feared from Edwin Fletcher seemed to be true; he seemed to be aloof, supercilious, with no particular liking for children. The Marquesa must indeed have been paying him handsomely to take this position; it was obvious that he needed the money. Not all the Fletchers were rich. He was thin and tall, with a pronounced stoop, and a dark drooping mustache which suggested that he attempted to hide a weak mouth. But the sight of him, the way he moved and walked, brought its own reaction of pity. Under the sun tan he had rapidly acquired here, his skin seemed gray, his face was strained. He had an air of fragility. Sometimes he went into terrible spasms of coughing and seemed to struggle for air. At such times he was embarrassed and profoundly apologetic. Carlos, who had perhaps feared a rival at his table, dismissed him with a shrug. "An academic milksop!"

"One, however, who has served his country," my mother said.

"Oh, we have become very patriotic, haven't we, Lady Pat? I wonder how your good husband is faring as he renders his patriotic duty? I suppose he really has to try, doesn't he? These Regular Army men have got to show that all the years on the parade ground produce *men,* don't they?"

I very soon saw that what appeared to be aloofness in Edwin Fletcher was purely shyness; he was grateful for the hospitality of his Fletcher cousins, grateful to be in Spain instead of languishing in an England which had no further use for him. He was grateful, also, for his salary. To my surprise he appeared to want to work for it, even to trying to cope with Juan's waywardness, his short span of concentration, his insistence on breaking into Spanish at every opportunity. It was true that Edwin Fletcher had no special affection for children, but he was prepared to substitute patience. In time Juan sensed that he would not, could not, wear down this thin, ill young Englishman, or provoke him to the bursts of temper which characterized his father's behavior. He was a gentleman, not a servant, and could not be ordered about. Gradually the two drew together. Juan's efforts to interest Edwin Fletcher in horsemanship equaling Edwin's efforts to interest Juan in the rudiments of English grammar. They seemed to come out roughly even.

287

But one thing above all others made me see Edwin Fletcher as a friend—his open and unaffected admiration for my mother. "What a perfectly splendid lady!" he said of her once as we lingered over coffee while my mother took the children back to Nanny in the nursery. "So beautiful. Such great spirit. And I hear all round Jerez that no one is her equal on a horse. . . ."

He did not despise us, then. In terms of his learning, we were very ignorant, but he knew how to see merit in other terms. My mother had a gift of compassion, and it was she, more than any of us, who helped Edwin over his distress and embarrassment when the fits of coughing shook his gaunt frame. She could be sympathetic without seeming to pity him. "We are all of us wounded in one way or another, Mr. Fletcher," she once said to him directly. "It just shows with some people more than others. That's the only difference."

When he left us to make his way back to the Fletchers' house, María Luisa made a great bustle about getting out her account books, slamming them down on the table with unusual noise, grumbling about bills unpaid, prices rising and rising and our income not at all. I knew it was not the prices or the unpaid bills which so much concerned her. She was used to them.

"María Luisa, what *is* it? It's not the bills—I know that."

Her lips puckered sourly. "You have a new favorite, I see. *He* could do your accounts very well for you, I'm sure. Squeeze out a few more pesetas. After all, isn't he supposed to be a mathematician, or some such thing?"

I put my arms around her and tried not to laugh at the absurdity of Edwin Fletcher wrestling with household economics. "María Luisa, how could we live without you? Our lives would fall apart, and you know it."

Her eyes dimmed. She took off her glasses and rubbed her eyelids. "Oh querida, what a load you have on you. Look at all of us! Look at all of us seated here about this table. And now another. *And* he is sick, and he will lean upon you as we all do. And look—already he is half in love with you in his stiff English way." She reached

288

over and smoothed back the stray wisps of hair from my face. "Yes—querida, I'm a selfish, jealous old maid. I want to be first in your life, as if you hadn't all the others." She shook her head. "Why can't you ever have things the easy way? Always the hard way for you, Carlota. Never the calm, sensible, easy way. What is it in you that must always make things so hard for yourself?"

I didn't even try to answer her. I just closed the books she had spread on the table and stacked them neatly.

"It is time for the siesta, María Luisa. And one more around the table isn't so very much, is it?"

But she had frightened me, just the same. I didn't want to count the numbers around the table.

3

It was Edwin Fletcher, with myself and Juan, who witnessed what happened that sharp, frosty morning in December when my mother's life was almost ended.

Edwin had looked gray and exhausted when he arrived to start lessons with Juan. I suspected that his sometimes choking struggle to breathe often left him sleepless. I urged hot coffee on him, and when he had drunk it I suggested that we take a walk to the stables to watch my mother working with Balthasar. The growing strength of the morning sun would warm him, I thought, perhaps help those tense and tired muscles to relax. Juan was delighted at the prospect of a half hour's freedom from lessons. He adored his grandmother, and he displayed an inordinate pride in her accomplishments as a horsewoman.

As we walked the corridors of the house, and through the first courtyard, we talked of the war. I had become reliant on Edwin to interpret the bare facts of the news which reached us. "It's a stalemate," he said. "And a very bloody stalemate at that. The whole British-French offensive has failed. We are just about in the same places we were at this time last year. And the British have used gas for the first time. . . ." I had kept my pace at a slow stroll because I had noticed that Edwin could not manage anything faster without gasping for breath. Pepita and Juan raced on ahead, returned to us, and then raced off again. Edwin paused for a moment by the old cracked fountain, holding his face up to the sun. "I can hardly believe it's December. Thank God I'm not in England. I don't think I could cope with the fogs yet. . . ." He rarely mentioned his illness, and never talked of his own experience of the trench warfare where it had its beginning. "I wasn't a gallant soldier," he had once said. "I just served my time. The gas rolled over us, and that was the end of it for me."

He still gazed up towards the sun, as if he could never have enough of it. "How long do you think it can go on—the war?"

He lowered his face, looked at me, and shrugged. "Now that our masters have committed us to this unbelievable blunder, this sort of dreary slaughter could go on indefinitely. We will go on, I'm afraid, until one or the other side is too exhausted to make another effort. But don't look for victory. We will just fall down in the mud and sleep like the dead." His tone suddenly sharpened. "And watch for trouble in Ireland when it's finally over. All those likely Irish lads have become very handy with weapons. Such expertise doesn't go to waste. You think you've had troubles in Ireland before this. Just wait until this lot gets back from the war and finds things aren't any better, and that England's still trying to hold on there. You should write your cousin, Lord Blodmore—"

I tugged at his arm and pointed to the archway leading to the stable yard. Juan, who had been jumping about in the crisp morning air, had stopped, and seemed frozen into his posture. Pepita gave a few sharp barks. Then Juan turned to me, his voice thin and shrill with fear. "Mama! Mama!"

I ran, leaving Edwin behind. I could hear my mother's voice, calling, pleading; I could hear Balthasar's voice, his deep whinny, the furious thrust of his breath through his nostrils. And I could hear Carlos' voice, angry, shouting

290

commands—Carlos' voice with a note of fear I had never heard before.

Carlos was in Balthasar's saddle when I reached the arch. He rarely, if ever, mounted the stallion these days, not since he had bought Carmen. He seemed somewhat jealous of the relationship that had grown up between my mother and the stallion; he tended to belittle her achievements in the exercises of the High School. I think he begrudged her the praise won for her and Balthasar.

I will never know exactly what had taken place before our arrival; it was never possible to find out. I am certain only of what I saw. Carlos was in the saddle, but the stirrups had been looped up as they are when certain of the High School exercises are performed. I didn't know whether my mother had permitted him to mount or he had demanded it, but it was certain that Balthasar did not want him in the saddle and was determined to be rid of him.

The great stallion was rearing on those huge, mighty hind legs, lunging, pounding down with the terrifying forefeet, rearing again, his voice sounding like a trumpet of wrath. With no stirrups, Carlos had only the grip of his knees and thighs, and he was doing what a rider does only in fear, he was holding on by the reins, tugging at the stallion's mouth, using his whip in a way that was intended not to control but to punish. Balthasar's white flanks were streaming with blood where Carlos' spurs had sunk. It couldn't last. The horse was stronger than Carlos, and he was in a sweat of fury. One great last lunge, in which he assumed a savage, crude variation of the classic capriole, was too much for Carlos' precarious balance. He came off, over the stallion's head, landing with a heavy thud on the hard ground.

It was not the end. Carlos' use of the whip and spurs, perhaps his very presence on his back, had infuriated Balthasar. Those mighty, slashing forefeet came down again. I heard the awful impact as one foot struck Carlos' arm. Then the stallion reared again, and Carlos lay directly beneath him. The cries from my mother, the screams of rage from Balthasar had brought Pepe and Jaime running, but they, like us all, seemed frozen. Andy was nowhere in sight.

My mother's commands had no effect. I doubt that the enraged horse even heard them. Hatred was in his own cries. My mother, as the stallion reared again, did the only thing she could do. She leaped for the bridle, managed to loop both her hands through it, and hung on. Her weight jerking Balthasar's head around was just sufficient to deflect the aim of the stallion's forefeet. He just missed coming down on Carlos' chest.

Still my mother hung there, and once again Balthasar rose. The devil seemed to be in him, and he meant to kill the man on the ground. But my mother had given Carlos just enough time to recover; he rolled over, got to his knees, and then, staggeringly, on his feet. He retreated, backed away, seeking the safety of the wall where the stallion could not have maneuvering room. Still Balthasar followed. By now I was beside my mother, had grasped the reins. Pulling on his mouth might only further inflame him, but there was nothing else to do. Still the stallion kept lunging. I too was off my feet, swinging wildly. Then I managed to get my hand under the halter, and my mother's strength gave way. The last toss of the stallion's head threw her sideways, and her hands slipped and released their hold. She was thrown in a heap against the wall where Carlos cowered.

I don't remember how many times I was lifted from my feet. But other hands joined mine in trying to control Balthasar. Jaime and Pepe had taken courage at last, and tugged on the other side of the halter. Edwin was there; all his fragile strength added to the others to try to hold the horse and quiet him. Paco had arrived and managed to overcome the fear he had always shown of the stallion, and he joined us, grasping the first piece of the harness he could lay hands on. Gradually exhaustion took us all, even Balthasar. At last the rearing stopped, the back legs gave a few last savage kicks, and then he was still, still and trembling, continuing to cry his anger and distress, frothing at the mouth, his coat lathered with sweat. We stayed, all five of us, not daring to move, trembling like the horse. I murmured the words my mother used to him, saying them over and over, trying to soothe and calm the animal.

But Pepita, who had early in her life been disciplined to remain quiet and move slowly when around horses, now gave a few unearthly howls. She and Juan were beside my mother's crumpled body.

Finally one of the boys moved to open the door of Balthasar's box, and with great caution and gentleness we began to lead him to it. I kept talking to him all the time, wishing Pepita would stop her howling. But I daren't raise my voice lest it startle Balthasar. Juan made it worse with his high-pitched screams. A few more times the stallion turned his head towards the place on the other side of the yard where Carlos had propped himself against the wall, and his great bellow rang out again. Paco looked as if he might be about to loose his hold and run. All of us kept as far away as we could from those terrible hind legs, with their power to kill or maim. At last he was in the box. Inside, as always in any stable Andy ran, there was clean water and hay, clean straw underfoot. I did not dare enter with him to secure his head to the ring. Better to leave him alone until the anger had cooled.

With the half door finally secured, I ran to my mother. Juan knelt beside her, and now he wept with terror, his face streaked with tears. Edwin was bent over her; he could say nothing. His body was racked with spasms of coughing. Carlos had moved away from the wall. He was holding the arm which Balthasar's hoof had caught, and he was deathly pale. Slowly he came to join the group about my mother.

The side of her head had struck the wall, and blood ran from it as she lay there, unconscious. I knelt down and loosened her stock. Juan's wild shrieks had turned to sobbing pleas. "Granny! Oh, Granny! Mama, is she dead? Why won't she answer?" He put out a hand as if to try to shake her into life.

"Juan—no! Don't touch her! Granny's not dead!" But I was feeling for a pulse. The blood still ran, gushing as head wounds always do. It had already stained her blouse and jacket. I looked for where I could get help. "Paco—bring towels, anything to wrap around her head. And blankets." Edwin's coughing made further help from him impossible. I said to one of the boys, "Run for Dr. Ramírez. Bring him at once. If he's not at his house, see if you can find Dr. Gordon. He's staying with the Domecqs. Don Manuel Domecq. Bring him at once." I called across the yard to Paco, who was about to enter the house, "Send Doña María Luisa."

She was beside me in no time. "Shall we take her inside?" she said as we eased a towel under my mother's head and held another against the wound. Deftly María Luisa tucked the blankets about her body. "It's cold, Carlota. She should be warm."

"I don't dare move her until the doctor has seen her. We'll need a door—something firm like that, to carry her on." I said to Jaime, "Tell Serafina to fill hot-water bottles. Edwin, go inside. Take some wine. You *must* stop coughing. You'll kill yourself . . ." The bright blood still flowed, darkening further the red hair, soaking the towel and staining the earth.

At last, as we waited, I looked up at Carlos. His arm obviously was broken, and he bit his lips against the pain. He stared down at my mother and then into my own face. I saw pain and shock; as his eyes moved from my face to my mother's, and back again, I thought I read, not concern, not worry, but hatred.

Then he spoke. "The animal shall be destroyed."

I gave the towel I was holding into María Luisa's hand and I got to my feet. I walked away from the little group and drew Carlos with me. Then I turned to him. "If you do that I shall take the gun you use on Balthasar and I will kill you. I swear it!"

He left me. He did not falter at all as he walked from the stable yard into the first court. His splendid jacket from the London tailor was dusty, and the sleeve that covered the arm Balthasar had broken was almost ripped away. Juan looked in bewilderment from his retreating father to the still form on the blood-soaked ground. "Papa!" and then, "Granny! *Granny!*"

4

She remained unconscious for a long time. Dr. Ramírez supervised her removal, on a borrowed stretcher, to her room after he had cleaned and stitched the wound. Much of the famous red hair had to be cut away. Dr. Gordon arrived, full of deference to the local doctor, but clearly interested in the case, and Dr. Ramírez welcomed a consultation. Gordon was an old man, a cousin to many of the Gordons who lived in Jerez, and he had come to escape the winter in Edinburgh and to shake off the effects of overwork and flu. He had been long retired, but the war, with its enlistment of younger men, had forced him back into practice. He had a special interest in neurology, which was why he had offered himself.

"Quiet, rest, and patience," was what he told me. "It's a bad blow, and one never quite knows how severe the injury may be. Now if we had some modern hospital equipment we might take X rays. There may be a hairline fracture. But still, such things usually heal themselves. . . ." He shrugged, a gesture of helplessness. "Dr. Ramírez tells me there's a good man in Sevilla."

The man came from Seville, but there was little he could add to the advice. In her moments of consciousness they tried testing her with little things. Could she see the doctor's finger? Where? How far? They put things between her fingers to feel. Was it wool, silk, paper? She answered listlessly or not at all. The man from Seville waited for a day but could spare no more time. "Bring her to me when she's able to travel, if you think it's necessary. These things so often look after themselves. A bad blow, and time and rest heals it. . . ."

We had three nurses, but either María Luisa or myself

295

was with her all the time. I remember the gentle snoring of the nurse in the chair about two o'clock in the morning when my mother opened her eyes fully and looked at me. She said, quite distinctly and firmly, "Charlie—what about Balthasar? Is he all right?"

"Perfectly all right. Andy's been exercising him every day."

"Tell Andy I'll expect him to be in top shape when I get about again." And then she closed her eyes and slept.

Andy came to see her the next day when she had a long, lucid spell. I had to order him to get a smile on his face before he entered the room. "Everything's just grand, Lady Pat. Balthasar's looking a treat. And Half Moon's in grand shape. Sure, it'll be a better foal, even, than last time."

Outside he said to me, with tears unashamedly in his eyes, "If I'd been there it would never have happened. I'd just ridden out to Don Luis' place to see if everything was all right with Half Moon. God knows what made Don Carlos—"

I stopped him. "Only God knows. And we'll leave it that way, Andy."

He inclined his head towards the closed door. "Will she be all right now? I mean—eventually?" All the household, and therefore the whole town, knew that she slept a great deal, had periods when she seemed barely conscious; and when she was awake she talked, and her speech was rambling and unclear. Then there would be brief and blinding flashes of lucidity, when she demanded to know about Balthasar and Half Moon. "Andy will keep watching her, won't he, Charlie? And what's the news from home?"

Dr. Ramírez came daily and, with his permission, Dr. Gordon. The two had struck up a friendship. I thought they almost seemed to enjoy the daily consultations. It gave them a chance to meet and exchange medical gossip. I arranged to have copitas and tapas served in the drawing room when the consultation was finished, and left them to their medical talk. There were more exciting things to discuss than one injured woman, who would probably be all right. I knew that it had been arranged that when the war was over Dr. Ramírez would visit Edinburgh and see what progress had been made with the treatment of shell-shocked war veterans.

Dr. Ramírez had, of course, another patient in our house—Carlos. It had been a multiple fracture of the right arm. Carefully set, it was mending well, Dr. Ramírez told me. Carlos was young and healthy. Breaking a few bones did not mean permanent injury. He was careful to say no more, to make no comment on the reason for the injury. He made not the slightest connection between my mother and Carlos, as if their injuries were totally divorced. He was the soul of tact.

That did not stop the rest of the town from making its own comments. Edwin Fletcher might be as discreet as he pleased, declare to everyone that he had arrived when it was all over and he knew nothing; but Pepe and Jaime had been there, and Paco invented and embellished what he had not actually witnessed. The town seemed to know more than we knew. Rumor was hotter than the truth, and moved swiftly.

When my mother was pronounced out of danger I received a visit from Don Paulo. María Luisa came to my mother's room to whisper to me that he had come. I should go and tidy my hair, change my blouse, before going down to him. I remember thinking how much in awe I had been of him in the past, and it seemed as if that time had been too long ago. Too much had happened. I neither changed my blouse nor tidied my hair.

"Is it true," he said directly, "that she saved my son's life? There are all kinds of stories, and I can get nothing from Carlos except that the animal threw him. The horse was also responsible for Lady Patricia's accident. It is dangerous, and should be destroyed."

"It is true Balthasar threw Carlos, who should not, I think, have mounted him. It is true that if my mother had not hung onto the halter and reins Balthasar was ready to trample Carlos, and could have killed him. It is true

297

that when my mother finally let go she was flung against a wall. But the horse was maddened. No one had ever used spurs and a whip on Balthasar. His flanks were streaming with blood. Carlos actually hit him across the head with the whip. You know the birch twig my mother uses—you've seen it. That is merely to guide his steps as they practice, to get the rhythm. Carlos does not say why he mounted Balthasar that morning, and my mother cannot say. It is, as yet, beyond her. We do not excite her with things like that. It would probably be better if it was never mentioned again."

"But Carlos was beneath the stallion's feet and your mother risked herself?"

"That is what I saw. So did Edwin Fletcher. Unfortunately, so did Juan. Perhaps even more unfortunately so did the boys, Pepe and Jaime—and Paco. I cannot make bargains with them not to talk. It only increases the talk."

He nodded. "You have asked Carlos yourself?"

I shook my head. "I have asked Carlos nothing. He has volunteered nothing. He has not seen my mother since the accident. Even if he asked to see her, I could not, as yet, permit it. She must not be excited."

"She will, however, be quite well in time? I mean—there is no permanent damage?"

"Ask the doctors, Don Paulo. 'Wait and see,' they tell me. 'Wait and see.' "

Against all the traditions of Spanish courtesy, I terminated the visit. "You must excuse me. I do not like to leave my mother alone too long."

He nodded. There was just the faintest trace of humility in the formal raising of my hand towards his lips. "You will indicate to your mother my profound gratitude. I could not easily have borne the death of my son."

"I told you, Don Paulo, we do not speak of such things. Nor will we."

He bowed and left. He still walked with all the outward pride and arrogance of before, but it occurred to me that for the first time in many years he was a man with a debt, and the debt was owed to a Blodmore.

She recovered; that is, she grew strong again, and was up and able to move about just as before. But she was not the same. The hair they had had to cut away grew back, but in a great swath of startling white from the temple where the wound had been inflicted. She observed it in the mirror as if it were on another person, and she did not attempt to cover it with the dye she had once used, so that all through her lovely hair long silver strands appeared. Her lack of concern over it worried me. I would have welcomed a return of the old vanity.

Every one of the characteristics she had displayed before was still there, but in an exaggerated degree. When she talked, she talked far too much. And in between, the spells of silence grew longer. Her span of concentration was short. She would pick up a newspaper, flick its pages, and lay it down. "Was there any news from home today, Edwin?" she would ask. She really meant was there any fresh news from France, any victory she could celebrate. We did not tell her of defeats. Edwin would patiently explain some minor movement on the Western Front only to have the question asked again an hour later. He never gave the slightest indication that he had said it all before. "Poor boys," she would sigh. "Let's drink to them."

The drinking also increased, and yet we did not know how, out of compassion, to stop it. Sometimes she complained of bad headaches, and lay in her darkened room for several days. Dr. Ramírez called to see her from time to time, and Dr. Gordon, who had lingered for the winter in Jerez, became one of the family circle. He had unlimited time to observe her.

"There has been some permanent damage, but not to the nerves which control the movements. You see, she is still perfectly co-ordinated. But these fits of absent-mindedness I don't like. . . . Nor the headaches."

"She has always been absent-minded."

"When it suited her, I think. Now she really *forgets*.

The headaches may be with her for the rest of her life. It's hard to say how much the brain may heal itself. If you took her to London they might be able to operate, might be able to help her. But neurosurgery . . ." He shook his head. "We haven't touched the surface of it yet. One only resorts to that in extreme cases where the patient is on the point of death, or is violent—a danger to others and herself. This is not so with your mother. It is perhaps better to leave well enough alone, and hope that time may yet help her."

Carlos observed her sullenly one night as she sat in the drawing room, a decanter of wine by her side, staring into the fire. It was one of the few nights he had spent with the family since the accident. He did not like even to sit at the table with my mother. This night he had drunk more than the usual amount of wine himself.

"She's crazy," he said. "Look at her! She hasn't bothered to change her dress or brush her hair. Sits there like a drunken old fool spilling her wine, and she doesn't hear a word that's said to her. She's crazy. There's talk in the town that all you Blodmores are crazy in one fashion or another. She should be put away. She should be in Nuestra Señora de Mercedes."

I rose and went over to him, speaking very softly so that she would not hear. "Be quiet! No one in this house will ever say such a thing again."

"But she is crazy. And I don't like my children being with her. God knows what she might do to them one day. These crazy old women . . . no one knows what they take into their heads to do."

"She is a danger to no one. And I'll see *you* in Nuestra Señora de Mercedes before she will go there." I straightened, looking down on him, which he didn't like. "You have no pity at all, do you? No remorse. You were the cause—"

He cut me short, his voice rising angrily. "Enough! I've had enough of things being hinted at—things implied. It was something that happened because your mother is a stupid, tiresome, interfering, drunken old woman. I would have been perfectly all right on Balthasar if she had not

300

taken it into her head to goad him into a tantrum. After all, he *is* my horse. He has been, right from the beginning. Don't tell me he doesn't know who is his master."

"Try riding him again, Carlos. You will find out who is master. If I do not kill you for vile insults to my mother, Balthasar will surely do it for me. Yes, I'd like to see you try to mount Balthasar again."

"You'd like to see me dead, you mean?"

"Yes!"

He cursed me in Spanish and left the room. After a long time María Luisa spoke. "That was not wise, querida. Words spoken like that are never quite unsaid. Even if you apologize—"

"Apologize! I will never apologize. Why should I? It is the truth, and he knows it."

"He will leave you."

"I wish he would, but he won't. He would lose his children. He would lose his hopes for what he may yet have from the Marquesa and his father. He made a bad marriage, but he must live with it. Unfortunately, so must I. . . ."

Silence fell once more. I moved to the fire and stood staring into it. Things had not seemed quite so bad until anger and passion forced them to be put into words. Any pretense of affection was over between Carlos and me. Since my mother's accident I had been sleeping a good deal of the time in her room on a cot bed. The nurses had left, but María Luisa and I did not think it wise to leave her alone. She had once risen in the middle of the night, lighted a candle, and upset it; the blanket had begun to burn before I woke. So I slept there, and on the nights when María Luisa took over I slept in an adjoining room. The house still had plenty of empty rooms. It was one thing we did not lack. At first I had made the excuse of Carlos' arm still being in plaster to avoid our bed; later I made no excuse at all. We spoke only in the presence of the children and when it was strictly necessary. I had fallen into the trap of so many marriages. I now did things "for the children." I cautioned myself, as I watched the flames, that they must never be made to bear the burden of that feeling. The guilt was not theirs. It was mine. It had been my mistake, and therefore must be my guilt.

Then I turned and looked at my mother. Silent tears streamed down the face that now looked so much older than its years, still a beautiful face, but so terribly altered. I went and knelt beside her. "Mother . . . Mother . . . !"

"He said I would have to go to that . . . that place." I knew what she meant. We had once visited Nuestra Señora de Mercedes together, with our small annual donation. I could remember the frightened silence which had descended on my mother when the Mother Superior insisted on showing us about the institution. "You see," she had said quietly, "it is quite a beautiful place. The Marquesa de Pontevedra has been most generous in helping us. The restoration of the cloisters—the ceiling in the chapel. All done through her kindness. And she sends linen each year for the inmates." There was no doubt that our connection with the Marquesa was the reason for her cordiality. Our donation would never rate such special attention. "Come, let me show you."

There had been a long white room, with bare tables, where women clothed in shapeless gray garments worked at sewing linen sheets. "These are the most fortunate ones. The quiet ones. Unhappily, some are rather more violent, and must be kept under close watch. Would you like . . . ?"

My mother shrank back. "Please, Mother Superior . . . I have promised my little grandson I shall take him to a birthday party. Perhaps some other time. I wish there was more we could do . . ." She was hurrying towards the great outer door that led from the cloister; the last steps were almost at a run. When we were back in the landau I saw that she was trembling violently. "That place . . . that terrible place," she murmured.

Now she repeated the words. "That terrible place. He wants to shut me up in that terrible place." She grasped my arm with astonishing strength. "Promise me, Charlie— *promise* me on your oath that you'll never let me be sent to that place. Or any place like it. Promise me you'll kill me before you'd let that happen. Do you swear it, Charlie? Do you *swear* it?"

I brushed the tears from her anguished face. "I swear it, Mother. Never—*never.*"

I remained kneeling beside her rocking her like one of my children. The room was still save for the sound of her harsh sobs. "That terrible place . . ."

That night, after I had seen my mother to bed and María Luisa had arranged the cot to her liking, I went to the room next door, the room that had become my own.

There, at what hour in the morning I do not know, Carlos appeared. Pepita's low growl told me of his presence. Automatically I silenced her, thinking of my mother sleeping so close, and María Luisa.

"Well, mother of my brave bulls, shall I get another on you?" He was drunk.

And then he raped me.

CHAPTER FIVE

1

Spring came, as it does in Andalucía, with a blanket of wild flowers that grew in all the places which during the heat of the summer seemed to be a desert. Along the sides of the roads and in the fields they grew, the small purple iris, the scarlet poppy, the sunflower; the violet flowers of the periwinkle appeared shyly in odd places. A white magnolia bloomed in our courtyard, the Judas tree displayed its pink against the soft blue sky, the jacaranda dropped its petals into the stable yard, jasmine appeared against old walls and scented the night air. The vines began to put out shoots.

"It is heaven," Edwin Fletcher said. He was forever stopping to bend and smell some blossom. "Things smell different here." It was as if he was trying to overcome the lingering smell of the gas that had nearly destroyed his lungs. He might revel in it all, but his health seemed little improved. He was still unnaturally thin, and fits of coughing still shook him. "You should drink more sherry," María Luisa advised. "This town is full of healthy old people who've taken their copitas all their lives as they have taken their religion." Edwin had enough regard for María Luisa's intelligence to be able to laugh at her ambiguity. So we moved a table into the courtyard where the sun would be warmest in the half hour before lunch; we sat and drank our copitas, and Edwin talked with the children, as the Marquesa had bidden him, but he did not talk of going home. Martin had now become his pupil for a few hours each day. Books suitable for their ages kept arriving from London. In spite of his efforts to remain true to his promise to the Marquesa, Edwin was learning Spanish. It was impossible not to. When he received the primers in reading from England, he went to Seville to secure similar ones in Spanish. "I'm no schoolmaster," he confessed. "I don't know how to teach them to read in one language and not in their own." It was strange to see this man who had that unusual double first from Cambridge sitting in the sun-warmed courtyard studying the primers with the large type face and the childish pictures. He made his own vocabulary list and studied it each day. It amused Juan to give him tests in spelling—Juan not realizing that he himself was learning the English translations of the words at the same time.

When we were alone, out of hearing of my mother, Edwin and I discussed the events of that spring in Ireland. The Easter Rebellion had sent a wave of shock and fear through England. The story of Roger Casement landing by German submarine had reawakened the old fear of invasion through Ireland. There was public clamor for the execution of the leaders of the rebellion. "They will make martyrs for Ireland," Edwin said, "and the Irish have always loved and fought for their saints. *This* insurrection has been put down, but I think it has not ended this phase of the Irish struggle. I think this time it will go on. . . and on. Your homeland could be ravaged. Once the war is over, if England has any strength left she will turn her attention to Ireland, and then God knows. . . . I wonder how Lord Blodmore feels about it. It must be an uneasy position to be part of the English Ascendancy now."

305

"The people will remember my grandfather," I said. "They will remember that he stood with Parnell and the Land Leaguers. There is a fund of good will for the Blodmores that Richard may draw on. . . ."

He nodded. "It could be so. Of necessity, the Irish have developed long memories."

The spring also brought another advance in my mother's condition. Balthasar, after the accident, had been sent to stay permanently on Luis' hacienda. My mother went one day to visit Half Moon's new foal, which promised to be even better than the last. Her delight in the sight of her beloved horses imbued me with a sense of new hope. I was almost about to put a question to her when she forestalled me.

"Why, Charlie, is there a saddle I could borrow? I do believe I'd like just to try a little canter on Balthasar."

Andy, who was hovering nearby, nodded. He went out every day to the hacienda to exercise Balthasar. The stallion was neither too fresh nor was he dangerous. He had greeted his mistress, and the sugar she brought, with whinnies of delight.

So she had a short canter through Luis' spring-greened pastures, through the flowers, through the fragrant scent which the eucalyptus have at that time of the year. When she returned to the paddock to unsaddle, her face wore the sort of radiance which belonged to the old days. After that, Luis sent his trap every morning to collect her from the Plaza de Asturias, and she had her ride on Balthasar, Andy at her side. Never again did she attempt the exercises of the High School. She lacked the concentration and the ambition for that. Perhaps the memories of that dreadful morning could not be faced. But occasionally, from sheer exhilaration and perhaps a desire to demonstrate his own skill, Balthasar, without urging, would fall into the step of the passage, or the extended trot. I saw him once or twice simply stop, and begin the piaffe, the trot on the spot, that marvelous movement when all four feet seemed simply to float above the ground. My mother showed no sign of fear when this happened, just pleasure in the intelligence and beauty of her beloved animal. She appeared to remember only the good things of the time before the accident. There was praise and sugar for Balthasar, and apparently no black memories. Her pleasure reminded me of a little girl with her first pony.

That spring Andy's first son was born. He had had his wish of a healthy child, and an easy time for Manuela. The child was not, however, called after me. That would have meant he would be called Carlos, and we did not even discuss the possibility. Instead he was called Patrick John, after my mother and grandfather. Andy always called him his full name in English, but for his mother and her family he was Patricio.

And that spring I also became certain that I was going to have another child, a child who would be the hurtful fruit of the night Carlos had forced himself upon me. This time I did not tell anyone but kept the bitter knowledge within me, turning sour like wine in an unclean butt.

To forget about the child, whose coming I would disguise as long as possible, I turned my attention once more to the vineyards. Neglected through the worst period of my mother's illness, I turned to them for the kind of pleasure and comfort she had from Balthasar. I stared out over the greening sweep of the slopes and knew, momentarily, a little peace.

2

During the winter the last of the land my grandfather had bought was planted out in vines. It was the first time I had not watched every part of it, known each plant, almost, and grieved when some of them failed, as some always did. So it was the time of the golpe-lleno, the third tilling of the vineyards in May, before I was able to visit Las Ventanas Verdes for more than a few hours. I planned to spend some days there with only Pepita for company. The house in the Plaza de Asturias could carry on without me; María Luisa would keep a watch on my mother, Edwin Fletcher would be there to teach and, in a sense, to entertain the children. Carlos would go about his own pursuits, as he always did.

I was received with affection by Concepción, with a mixture of pleasure and concern by Antonio. Since the time of my mother's illness he had been left virtually alone in the running of the vineyards, and although Mateo was ever present with advice, the responsibility had borne heavily on Antonio. We both seemed to have aged in those few months, I told him. We laughed together, I drank a glass of wine with them both, and I told Antonio I would walk with him to inspect the vines the next day. I had my dinner of stewed chicken, sat by the fire with Pepita for a time, and went to bed to sleep the sleep of restfulness which had not been possible since that terrible day in December. The silence and sweet air of the vineyards were all about me. I lay in those moments before sleep in the big brass bed which had been my marriage bed and tried to give my thoughts to my baby, the child whose coming I did not want, but for which I must somehow find love. I told myself that I must spend as much time as possible during this pregnancy at the vineyard. The child, I reasoned, would grow like the young plants. A grafting would take place, as it did with the vines. The native stock would be grafted to the foreign roots. The soil would give character, the sun would give sweetness. I would think of this child as the one who had been transformed by the soil, as the plants were. It would be the child of the vineyards. In this way I could forget Carlos.

The next day was one of pure pleasure. The sun was warm but not too hot. Antonio had done his work well. Everything seemed well tended, the vines looked healthy. I ate my lunch at a table in the courtyard, and Concepción's children played about me. They played fearlessly with Pepita, and she took their pats and the occasional tug at her ears with good-natured tolerance. She looked at me as if to indicate that children, like the flies of summer, were just something to be put up with. "You will soon have another one to guard, Pepita," I said softly to her in English.

Concepción and I exchanged gossip. I talked about my mother and how well she did, how she went every day to ride Balthasar. I found Concepción knew almost as many details of her illness as I knew myself, and had a few embellishments to add. It was always the way. Nothing could be kept hidden. She was as careful to avoid the mention of Carlos' name as I was.

"The señora looks tired. It has been a great strain. You should rest here for some days. It must be difficult to have that very clever man, Don Edwin, always at the table and have to talk to him. But they say he still reads books for little children. But how fortunate the señora is to have him. The Marquesa provides well. How fortunate to have an education. . . . No doubt the Marquesa will see that they all go to school in England. It is the custom. . . ." Then she bustled to clear the dishes, perhaps to cover a faint note of wistfulness which had appeared. I watched the merry, tumbling children in the courtyard, their number almost one for each year Concepción had been married. Like their parents, they would be lucky if they managed to write their own names and, very slowly, read the headlines of a newspaper. I understood the wistfulness; I knew it from Ireland.

After the siesta I brought out the books; the books I had meant to study carefully during these few days at the vineyard, the books that told my story of profit and loss, debt and solvency. I had many new figures to enter, and I was fearful of the final tally. Then I realized my mistake. What I had brought with me were the household books María Luisa kept at the Plaza de Asturias. The vineyard books remained back there. I shrugged, and then I smiled. The thought of profit and loss could be postponed for a few days. I could blame the magnificence of the fine Spanish leather binding, which demanded that major enterprises, as well as petty household accounts, should be posted in equal state.

I smiled and called to Concepción to bring some tea. It would be a holiday—a holiday away from the dreaded books, away from the cares of my family. It would be a holiday among the beloved vines, and time in which to learn to know my new child. I took down one of Amelia's books of poetry and began painstakingly to try to translate it with a sense of its rhythms. Much of it still evaded me, so I read just for the beauty of the Spanish words.

Along with the tea, Luis appeared. He bowed over my hand, and his eyes lighted with pleasure as he saw the book. "I was visiting the vineyard, and Mateo told me you had come. Things are better at home, then?"

"Better, yes. My mother seems happy, though—well, you understand. She may never be any different. But thanks to your goodness, she has a daily source of happiness in riding Balthasar."

"My dear Carlota!—I have nothing to do with it. I merely stand on the sidelines and wish I could help."

I got out of my chair and went and called to Concepción to bring our best fino. Then I took my friend's hand. "My dear Luis. Please don't think us unaware, or ungrateful. My mother rides each day out of your goodness. We have Balthasar and Half Moon on your land, and although we pretend to pay for a stable boy to look after them, we know that is mostly a pretense. They use your fields, your stables. Half Moon's first foal is still there, and now the second one. We had planned to sell both of them—the yearling is splendid, and so is the new colt. They would have brought a good price. A price that might at least have paid our feed bills with you, the stableboy—all the rest of it. But since my mother's— since my mother's injury, she seems to need them. She sees them as a hold on the past. I cannot imagine what it would do to her if the two young ones were sold just at this time."

"Sell them! You are mad, Carlota! They represent the sort of capital that the vineyards do. They are the beginning, possibly, of a great bloodline. After all, Balthasar is descended from our great Andalucian Arab, Tabal. Half Moon comes from the finest Irish strain. You would not, in the bodega, sell your wine before it matures. So don't sell your stud before it is begun."

"But I owe you—"

He gestured me into silence. "Owe! What is it to owe a

friend? In friendship we are all in debt. But let me convince you about Balthasar and Half Moon. About the importance of breeding. We have a charming, fanciful legend here in Andalucía . . ."

Concepción brought the decanter and the glasses. I poured our copitas. The shadows had fallen across the vineyard slopes and a small cool wind blew from the east. I went and lighted the fire, watching the small dry sticks burn, then the solid logs catch. I returned to my chair and leaned back, longing to hear the story, ready to be entertained.

"A fanciful legend," Luis repeated, "that the five main branches of the Andalucian Arabic are descended from the mares of Mahomet. The tale goes that the mares were all kept from water for four days, and then taken to a river and released. All rushed to the water except five, who obeyed the command to halt. From these five mares our great horses are bred."

I laughed with him. "I must remember to tell my mother. She will be enchanted." I listened as he talked seriously about leasing land from him for a stud. We did not talk about where the money would come from. It must, of course, come from him.

"Think of what interest and occupation it would give your mother. Think of her pleasure in her beautiful foals. With her knowledge and eye for a horse and its temperament, the best would be kept for breeding, and the rest sold to support the stud. It could be a life for her, Carlota—life that will be denied if she just shuts herself up at the Plaza de Asturias." Another thing, which we did not mention, was the hope that it would distract her from drinking; it would keep her busy for many hours of the day, and when she was busy and interested she didn't think about wine and brandy. Luis knew this as well as I. But still I held back. Studs were a notoriously precarious business. A broken leg and the destruction of a great sire or dam could mean the end of a whole year's profits and the future hope of profits. Sickness could run through the whole stable. The tasks and costs of feeding and caring for horses were as endless as the tasks of the vineyard.

But Luis was right when he reminded me that Andalucía was recognized as one of the world's great breeding places of horses, and the Carthusian strain was famous and valuable. The thought excited me. Ireland had spawned so many horse breeders, successes and failures. The challenge and the taste for the risk of it were in my blood.

We sat there, talking about that and other things for a time. And as the dusk began to fall we toured, with Pepita, the top of the slope where the house sat. My vines which had been grown as a sun shield had thickened and done well. We looked over the slopes of the vineyard where the pruned and shaped vines were beginning to take on their covering of green. "Although so much in debt," I said, "I am sad that the land is now all planted. There will be no more agosta, no more selection of the plants for each kind of soil and position, no more marking out and planting. I should be glad because now the labor will be less, and I may expect a full harvest. But not to be able to think, Next year, if all goes well, I shall plant this slope . . . It will be something missing from my life."

"Why should you stop?" Luis asked. "There is plenty of albariza soil around Jerez still not under cultivation for the vines. So much that was never replanted after the phylloxera. Around Puerto and Sanlúcar . . . more and more. Why stop?"

"How nice to be rich, Luis," I laughed. "There is only the question of money. No—don't start again. Already this afternoon you have me dreaming of a stud. Now you would have me start to plan on being a major grower of grapes for sherry. Even dreams must end, Luis."

He sighed. "A pity. When you stop dreaming, your youth is over."

"I promise, then, not to stop dreaming, Luis. But let it stay a dream."

He smiled that unexpectedly gentle, beguiling smile, touched my cheek lightly with his fingers, took my arm, and we returned to the house.

Concepción herself came to inquire if Don Luis would

be staying to eat dinner with me. She seemed to take it as a point of pride that he should stay. She was a skillful cook and could make a piece of tough beef, stewed gently with her own blending of herbs, into something that would have graced Don Luis' own table. The cupboards always yielded cheese and a little fruit. There was the wine I brought out from the Plaza de Asturias. She liked to make the table look pretty with Amelia's pottery candlesticks and a few grape leaves. It was almost a command to Luis to stay, and he did.

"I accept gratefully. It is a long, lonely table in my own house."

So we ate together, and caught up with the gossip of the town. There had been so little time since my mother's illness to talk. We talked about the war, and the stalemate on the Western Front, the situation in Ireland, and I confessed that almost everything I knew of both subjects came through Edwin Fletcher.

"Ah, yes—the young Fletcher." The meal was finished. Concepción had cleared the cloth, left brandy and port, and some nuts, built up the fire, and asked if there was anything else we required. "Leave a lantern for me, Concepción, if you please," Luis said. "I must make my way back to my own house, and then ride into Jerez."

"You will need no lantern tonight, Don Luis. The moon is as bright as day." Then she nodded. "But Antonio has it ready for you, if you need it." She withdrew.

"The young Fletcher," Luis continued; "does he have plans to return to England?"

I shook my head. "Only when he must. He will never go back into the army. They have discharged him. And England is not a good place these days for those who are forced into a kind of idleness. He cannot work a full day yet, so that would prevent him taking any employment in England. Besides, the Marquesa is very persuasive with her money, and the Andalucian sun is more than anyone can pay him. I think he's not strong enough yet to take the climate in England. Particularly the damp . . ."

313

"And so you have one more to care for, Carlota. How we cluster about you."

"*We?* You have no dependence on me, Luis."

"Then what am I doing here?"

"As a friend I value highly. As a . . ." I hesitated, and then plunged on. The thought of the expected child had been so much with me since coming here; I was feeling rested, and at peace, so much more ready to accept this child, to love it. As I had once told Luis of my love for Richard Blodmore, so now I found myself telling him what no one else knew. "Luis, there is to be another. In the autumn I will have another child."

He turned his face fully to me. "Fruitful, always, Carlota. A blessing, this child."

I shook my head. "I have not been feeling so. Only since I came here have I been able to think of it calmly. A child must be loved, Luis. So far I have not been able to love it. . . ." I did not say any more, dared not. I could not say that this child had been forced on me, and that since that night my door had been locked against Carlos. Even to Luis I could not say such things.

"You will love your child, Carlota. It is not in you to deny love. . . . Not to the helpless, and those in need. All those who come within your reach are drawn in. I do not have any fears for this child. I wish . . ."

He did not finish. From where she lay at my side, Pepita rose and gave a low growl. She had heard before we had the noise that suddenly erupted in the courtyard, the clatter of the horse's hoofs, the orders given, the loud, impatient voice. The peace was gone. It was Carlos' voice.

We heard Antonio's voice, and Concepción's, the unbolting of the doors, the hard ring of boots on the tiled floor. The door of the sitting room was opened quickly and crashed back to hit the wall. Carlos stood there and looked at us in silence for a moment. I recognized the signs of too much drink and the dreaded temper aroused. He carried a saddlebag which appeared to be heavily loaded. Behind him, holding a lamp, Concepción stood with a look of pleading on her face, as if to beg forgiveness for having to admit him. "Shall I take the bag, Don Carlos?"

"You can get out. And tell Antonio to unsaddle. I'll stay the night here." He slammed the door closed by kicking it. The saddlebag he simply dropped to the floor where he stood.

"Well . . . well. Our good and true friend, Luis," he said. "How convenient to find you here with Carlota. It saves me another journey. But then it does not surprise me to find you here, you and Carlota being such good friends." He strode to the dresser, took a glass, and poured brandy for himself. "I'm happy to see the best brandy is being served. After all, one does honor to one's true friend with the best one has."

"Have you come all the way here to say just this, Carlos?"

He turned and came to stand before us; he raised his glass with elaborate ceremony to both of us, and then drank deeply. "I'm a good deal more interested in what *you* have been saying."

I shrugged, trying not to let the fear that grew in me show. There was no predicting what Carlos would do or say in the heat of anger and wine. "The usual things. The war . . . the vines . . . the horses."

"Ah, yes. The vines and the horses. The same stimulating conversation that goes on at every meal in our house. What a pity you haven't the learned Mr. Fletcher to give you some additional points on the conduct of the war and what is going to happen in Holy Ireland." He drank again, and paced the length of the room. As he walked, he saw Amelia's poetry book on the dresser. "Ah, poetry, is it? *That's* a change for you, Carlota. I didn't know you read Spanish that well. I thought your Spanish was confined to the language of the stables. But no doubt Luis here has done the reading . . ." He threw it down so that it fell open with the slender, beautifully bound spine turned upwards. I saw Luis' mouth tighten, but as yet he said nothing.

Carlos drank again. "Can you imagine, Don Luis, how boring the company at my table is? I am surrounded

315

by dreary women and milksop men. I swear my sons are turning into girls before my eyes."

"Carlos, please . . ."

"Carlos . . ." He cruelly mimicked my tone, and went to the dresser for more brandy. "Whining women—that's all I have day and night. At least I used to have a bed companion, but even *that* is now denied me. I might as well go and live with the Carthusians."

"Go any time you please," I said, and instantly regretted it. One did not talk like that to Carlos when he was in this mood. His face darkened.

"Oh, so you're independent of me now, are you? I was all right to marry when you had gotten yourself with a brat, but now I've served my purpose, my time, I may be dismissed. After all, you've a plentiful supply of money. What do you need a *man* for?"

"Carlos, this is not something to discuss before Luis— before anyone."

Luis got to his feet. "Carlota, I think Carlos is not quite himself. No doubt he wishes to see you alone, but I think I will stay a little longer." The mild-mannered man was gone. His tone was cold, and unshaken.

"Stay!" Carlos shouted. "Stay as long as you please. After all, don't you *own* this place? Isn't even the roof over my wife's head owned by you? Can she dare throw you out?" He turned on me. "A few days at the vineyard, you said. A few days of rest. Did you come here to discuss your vines and your mother's horses? Or did you come to discuss some future plans? Have you any more schemes—ambitious plans on which I am not consulted? After all, why consult me? Why consult me when there is the rich and capable and helpful Don Luis to serve you?"

"What are you saying? I don't like riddles."

"Riddles, is it?" He put down his glass and overturned it. Then he went to pick up the saddlebag. We watched as he carried it to the big center table and undid the straps. I already guessed what was in that bag, and I was sick at the thought. The books, those familiar volumes bound in red morocco, tumbled out as he upended the bag. The candles flickered wildly. At the noise, Pepita growled again. I put a hand on her.

"There are no riddles, Carlota. It is simply that you are in so-called debt to your good friend Luis here for more money than you will ever see."

"Those books are mine, Carlos. My personal property. Private."

"Private? What is private between husband and wife?" he said. "Is not your property mine—and your debts my debts?" He was flicking the pages of one of the volumes, the newest one. "So unlucky for you, Carlota, that you took the household books with you, and that dreary drudge, María Luisa, has always to be so busy balancing her columns. How unlucky that I ventured to inquire into my wife's affairs!" He slapped down the book. "And what do I find? My wife is in debt to Don Luis for thousands of pesetas. No, not thousands—hundreds of thousands! By the evidence of these books he owns this vineyard, he owns its produce for years to come, he owns the horses. For all I know he may even own the clothes on your back. I took that stupid bitch, María Luisa, and shook it out of her. Your mother's income does not begin to pay for this expenditure. Nor does Don Ramón's bank extend such credit. No—only a very special creditor extends such loans. What puzzles me is that you bother to record it at all. Why not just take the money and put nothing on paper? Why go through the farce of pretending you have paid the interest—"

"Enough, Carlos! I lend my money where I choose. These are as sound investments as any man can make. Your own father would see that! He's been in debt in his own time. Even to Carlota's grandfather he's been in debt. The share of the bodega Lord Blodmore left to Lady Patricia is evidence of your father's need for money. But he made the mistake of selling a part of the bodega. I have only *loaned* Carlota—"

"You think me a greater fool than I am, Don Luis. How will this miserable little vineyard ever pay off these sums of money? For twenty years the harvests of this land will be owed to you. By the time everything is paid off the vines will be exhausted and it will be time to start all over again."

"You speak about debts," I said. "What of your own? What of the debts I have paid for you?" My fear was lessening as my anger grew.

"Debts? My debts? And why not? Didn't Amelia's will cover my trifling debts and give you a large surplus? And what of the jewelry she left to you? *That* could have paid your debts and mine as well. Or did . . . ?" Now he looked at Luis again, and a slow, insinuating smile grew on his lips. "Or did you demand that your wife make such a will, Don Luis? It would have been a convenient way to give Carlota more money, money which did not have to appear in these books. Respectable money. Money the town would say was a touching return of a great friendship. Were you really friends, Carlota? I always doubted it. What would a person like you see in a sniveling fool like Amelia? Why haven't you sold the jewelry? You never *wear* it. A little prick of conscience, perhaps? Was your wife forced to make these gifts, Don Luis? A woman who is sick and weak will do almost anything to keep a few people about her. She would have signed anything you told her to sign. Are there any other arrangements you two have made, I wonder? Am I the only one in ignorance? Did that marvelous friendship cover a lot more? I wonder if the whole town hasn't been laughing behind my back? No—*that* couldn't be the way of it. Everyone knows about Don Luis. Perhaps there is no more to it than quiet, cozy evenings like this. Does he just sometimes hold your hand, Carlota? Kiss you chastely, like a brother? *That* would not be beyond him, surely. There must be some return for debts as large as these—"

Now Luis moved close to him. He said in Spanish, "Insults to myself I can bear. Coming from such as you, they are nothing. But insults to Carlota are something different. Insults to my dead wife are not tolerable. You are a corrupt and ignorant fool!"

Luis hit him with great force across the face. Carlos had not been expecting the blow, and his head snapped back, and he staggered until his body came up against the table.

One of the red-bound volumes crashed to the floor. Beside me, Pepita was on her feet, tense, her body quivering.

Carlos recovered himself quickly. "No man strikes me and ever forgets it." He started towards Luis, but Luis went to meet him and hit him again. Carlos, surprised that Luis would go on the attack, gathered himself together and swung a blow, which Luis ducked neatly.

I stood up, and still hesitated. To interpose myself would further inflame Carlos. "For God's sake—"

Carlos' face was flushed and furious. He had obviously expected no such skill in Luis, and his drunken rage made him nearly incoherent.

"All right, old man—so you wish a fight of it. You'll have it. I have no intention of rotting in jail on your account. I had simply intended to make sure you canceled every last peseta of debt my wife says she owes you. But now I want more than that. I shall carve you up a little, so that when you shave every morning you will remember me."

It was then he produced the knife, the Toledo blade with the black and gold damascene handle, the knife with which he had carved our intertwined initials on the eucalyptus tree an age ago.

To my horror Luis actually laughed. "So you really are born of a gypsy! You fight with a knife." He made it sound amusing.

With a cry of rage, Carlos flung himself toward Luis. Luis side-stepped again, but the knife caught the sleeve of his jacket and ripped through the cloth. Luis grabbed the hand which held the knife, deflecting it away. But it was true. Compared with Carlos' youth, he was an old man, a strong and wiry man, but still twenty-odd years older than his opponent. He was lighter and more agile than Carlos, but in the end his age would defeat him. And the knife was no idle threat. At that moment Carlos broke from Luis' grasp and the point of the knife slashed across the other man's cheek. The blood poured out.

It was then I screamed and flung myself towards Carlos, grasping and trying to hold the hand that had the knife.

"Carlos—you are mad!"

He paused just momentarily. "And you too, you little bitch!" Reason wasn't in him any more. He was not now thinking of the consequences of his act. Rage and jealousy had gone too far. With his left hand he slapped me across the face, and then when, with the shock of the blow, I dropped my hands from his arm, I felt the sharp bite of the knife in the flesh of my shoulder.

I must have screamed again. I must have called something. Perhaps I gave a command, but I don't remember it. Perhaps it was the blow across the face rather than the knife wound which roused Pepita. With that terrible low growl she flung herself at Carlos with deadly purpose. This was no fight that she understood. All she could have known was that I had been attacked by a man she had known all her life. But there never seemed a question of where her loyalty lay.

Her size and strength were formidable. And she had no fear of the knife. She put the full weight of her body into the spring she made against Carlos, and he could not take the force of it. He fell, and in an instant her teeth were at his throat.

He struggled and tried to roll away from her, but the huge paws clamped down on his chest. Unearthly sounds came from Pepita, the low, awful rumble in her throat, the sound of an animal going for the kill. Carlos slashed at her with the knife, and her body received terrible wounds. But still she didn't give up. It seemed only seconds but she had found the vulnerable place, and Carlos' collar and shirt front were already soaked with blood.

"Carlota! Call her off!" Luis cried.

I tried. I think I tried. I think I called her name. I put my hand on her collar and pulled. But did I hesitate just that few seconds too long? Did I actually call a command to her to halt, or did I say nothing? Pepita had seen me attacked, and she had tasted blood. She had herself been slashed by the knife, and what do we know of the mind of a wounded animal? At last, though, she responded to my tugs at her collar and let go. But she still stood there, gazing down at him, growling, the blood from her own streaming wounds mingling with Carlos' on the floor. Carlos rolled over and lay limply.

"Pepita—go!" She grunted, and moved her big body over to the chair where I had been sitting. Then she slumped down, her gaze still fixed on Carlos.

Luis knelt over him. Carlos had let the knife fall. There was no sound from him, not a groan. Shakily I brought the candle to his side.

It was then Antonio and Concepción arrived. They stood rooted by the door for a moment, then Concepción went swiftly to Carlos. "Mother of God!" She raised her face for a moment, looking from me to Luis, and then, finally, at Pepita. She bent over Carlos again. "He dies!"

His throat and face were a fearful sight. His shirt was no more than a bloody rag. And still the blood pumped. First Concepción used the shawl she wore over her nightdress to try to stanch the blood, but it was a useless gesture. Antonio had run and brought towels, and they did nothing but soak up the blood. I could feel the tears of shock and anger burning on my face. I could feel the warmth of my own blood as it ran down my sleeve. Then I began to feel cold, and deathly tired. Luis held a towel to his face. The seconds went to minutes, and still Carlos bled.

Concepción looked up at me. "If he does not have a doctor to sew him up, he will die. I cannot stop the blood."

"I will go," Antonio said.

I thought, wearily, of the time it would take to saddle up, the time the journey would take into Jerez, even using Carlos' good horse, the time for the doctor to get back here. It was again a useless gesture, but one that must be performed.

"I'll help him saddle up," Luis said. I think he knew as well as I did the hopelessness of the whole thing, but he knew that it must be done.

"Tell him also to bring Don Paulo."

Then I went and sat weakly on the chair close to Pepita. She panted loudly, and she had, in the natural way of animals, already begun to lick at the many wounds she bore. I could hear the sounds from the courtyard as Antonio saddled up. Luis returned with a lantern, and once more knelt by Carlos. Now I could see his face better, and it was a strange, ashen, unnatural white, where it was not smeared with blood. Pepita had obeyed the instincts of all her kind too well, and had sought, and found, the jugular vein. I sat and waited there while Concepción and Luis did what they could. Pepita was as terrible a sight as Carlos, with one eye gouged and her broad chest scored and slashed a dozen times. Carlos had fought hard for his life and made her pay. The seconds of the lives of both of them ticked off.

Luis came to me at last. "I think he is dead."

I went and knelt again by him, trying to feel for a flutter of a pulse. The bleeding had stopped, and Concepción had closed his eyes.

I got to my feet with difficulty, Luis helping me. I don't think it was the bleeding from my wound that weakened me, but the thought of death, the ending of life, not in peace, not in a moment of happiness, as it had been with my grandfather, but the ending of life in violence.

I touched Concepción's arm. "Try to make him clean before his father sees him." She nodded, understanding.

I spoke softly to Pepita, and she made a heroic effort and managed to get to her feet. She followed me to the bedroom, and I placed her on the rug before the fireplace. I lighted the fire that was always laid, but in this weather seldom used. She must have been feeling the cold of shock and loss of blood; she held her muzzle gratefully towards the warmth. Then I went and got our best brandy, the finest distilling of the finest sherry Jerez gave. I cut up clean sheets and got warm water, so I could bathe and soothe her wounds; I covered her with a blanket against the chill which shook her. I opened her mouth and forced a good measure of brandy down her throat, and she took it, trustingly.

Then I went and got the tiny pistol in the velvet case that had caught Amelia's attention in Vienna. It was small, but I thought it would serve. I cleaned and oiled it, and loaded the chambers. It was more than a lady's

322

toy; it was well made, and designed for use. I could only hope that it now did its work and did not explode in my hand.

I sat for a while on the rug beside Pepita, waiting for the brandy to take effect. I drank two measures of it myself. Her head was on my lap. I noticed that some blood still trickled from the wound on my shoulder; it mingled with hers on my skirt. The time was passing, and I did not dare to wait longer. I could give into the hands of no one else what must be done; the act should not be carried out in the spirit of vengeance.

The brandy was working. Her undamaged eye drooped. I bent and kissed the top of her silken head.

"Pepita—dear, good friend . . ." With great effort she raised her head and turned it to look up at me, and that deep trusting look almost unnerved me. For me she had given the most she could give. I met that sad, afflicted gaze, and then I killed her.

The face of Don Paulo was terrible to see as he looked at the face of his dead son. At first he stood away, as if he did not believe what he saw. Then he went closer. Finally he knelt, as we all had done, beside that still form. For a moment I thought I saw the shoulders heave, as he bent over Carlos. It was over quickly. He rose to his feet stiffly, disdaining the hand of Luis.

He turned and looked at me, a face with the look of death and vengeance in it.

"The dog will be destroyed."

"It has been done."

Even as I said the words the pain began. I had felt too much pain that night, the pain of fear and loss, the pain of violent death, the pain as I had killed a beloved friend, the physical pain inflicted on me by the knife wound. The hatred in Don Paulo's eyes was the last pain. I stared at him for only seconds longer before he seemed to waver before my eyes, like the flickering candlelight. I must have lost consciousness standing on my feet. I did not feel the pain of hitting the floor.

Dr. Ramírez stayed with me all night but he was not

able to stop the hemorrhaging, not able to prevent me miscarrying the child, Carlos' last child. That life also vanished that night, the child I had promised to learn to love, the one who would have been the child of the vineyards.

3

I was too weak to attend Carlos' burial. The doctor would not even permit me to leave the vineyard house, so María Luisa spent her time between one place and the other. My mother was not able, alone, to receive the callers who came to offer their sympathy at the Plaza de Asturias, so María Luisa had to stretch her energies to both places.

I begged her not to come so often. "Concepción looks after me well. The doctor comes each day. I am growing stronger."

"I worry, querida. There are things you do not know."

"Don't worry." I don't know why I said that. There was much to worry about. I guessed from the agitation in María Luisa's manner that some strange tales had been told of what had happened here the night Carlos died. It was true that he had died from the terrible wounds given him by a savage and powerful dog. The dog was dead. But it had been necessary to stitch a knife wound in my shoulder and the long gash on Luis' face. Dr. Ramírez had had to make a report to the police because of the nature of Carlos' death. I didn't yet want to know what that report had said. But I heard, just the same.

I had been sleeping through the afternoon, made drowsy by the drugs Dr. Ramírez had given me. The curtains and shutters had been closed against the strong light. At first I did not see her when I woke in the dimness of the room. Then a small movement of her hand brought the familiar glitter of the jewels.

"You sleep peacefully, Doña Carlota."

"Marquesa . . . ?"

"I have come, of course, because Don Paulo, in his

grief, might make some move to destroy you. He might try to hurt you and Luis. If not to punish you, then to blacken what is left of your reputation. He sees, at the moment, no further than the loss of his son, which has been a terrible blow to him. He is not yet able to consider the position of his grandchildren, my godchildren. Whatever happens, they must be protected."

She rose from her chair and came to stand at the end of the bed, gazing down at me. I felt helpless, like a mesmerized animal.

"You Blodmores . . . perhaps there really is the streak of madness in you. Only you could get yourself into such a tangle of lies and foolishness. The entrapment of Carlos into marriage in the first place . . . it began there, and it has gone on ever since."

I tried to turn my head away from her, but her eyes compelled my gaze. "I cannot argue now. I am not well."

"No one suggested that you argue. I am here to tell you the facts."

"I know the facts. Carlos is dead because he attacked Luis and me. Pepita is dead because she defended me."

"You sound as if you grieve more for your dog than for your husband."

I made no attempt to reply.

"Luis and I arranged the story we gave to the police. The dog went berserk, attacked Carlos, who tried to defend himself with his knife. You and Luis intervened to help Carlos, and in the struggle both were wounded. As you said, Carlos is dead and the dog is dead. There is no other story."

"That is not what happened."

"You think I don't know it? You think Dr. Ramírez doesn't know it? But that is the official story. The police are prepared to accept it because Don Paulo does not dispute it. Who cares what people may say or think? No one can prove anything different. As you know, Luis is a kinsman of mine. He and Don Paulo are partners in the bodega. If they stand together, no one can shake that unity. And they will stand together, for all our sakes. It has been arranged."

I lay quiet. Thoughts still came slowly, as they had done since that night. Despite the growing heat of the afternoon I was cold. I said at last, "Concepción and Antonio know different. They know Carlos arrived here drunk, and that a quarrel broke out almost immediately. Anyone who ever knew Pepita would laugh at the thought that she went mad and attacked Carlos unprovoked."

"Let them laugh. Stranger things have happened. All that Concepción and Antonio will say is that Carlos arrived here to spend the night. They went to bed, were awakened by the noise. They found Carlos dying, and later you yourself shot the dog."

"But that is not all they know. They know different from that."

"I have told you that is all they will *say*."

"How do you know that is all they will say?"

"Because I have arranged it. Because that is what they have agreed. That is what they have already told the police. They listened very carefully to my suggestions. They are decent enough people, but little educated. They have dreams for their children. That is ordinary enough. Dreams that they will be educated, have their chance to make their way in life, give their parents some comfort in their old age. I have not been so stupid as to offer them money outright. They would not be able to conceal that. But if I choose to be generous in aiding the advancement of their children, then that is entirely my business. There are many workers on my estates for whom I do the same thing. Loyalty is more surely bought that way than with money."

She spoke the truth. She had found the way. "Concepción has said that Carlos arrived here to eat supper with you and Luis by arrangement. It looks better that way."

Yes, it all looked better that way. A little manipulation of the facts, a little rearranging of the truth. Concepción and Antonio would see no harm in it. The harm, the danger, the scandal would only come if they spoke the whole truth, and even speaking it would do no one any good. It could not restore Carlos' life; it could only bring more grief to his father. Yes, I understood very well why they would fall in with this plan. After all, it would save the reputation of everyone concerned. The only reputation which would be lost was Pepita's, and what did a dog matter, they would say.

"One further thing. The honor of Don Paulo of course demands that your debts to Luis should be paid in full. This has been done."

I struggled to sit up, and failed. "How do you dare!" I whispered. "Those were *my* debts, freely entered into. This house and the vineyards are the security against them. I have faithfully paid the interest. In time the debt itself would have been paid."

"Not soon enough to satisfy Don Paulo. He cannot allow anyone to know how deeply his daughter-in-law was in debt to another man, even such a man as Luis. It means, of course, that this vineyard now belongs to Don Paulo."

"That is not possible. It belonged to my mother, willed to her by my grandfather. It cannot be taken over without her consent."

"That consent has been given. Your mother is a sick woman, but she listens to reason. She signed."

The whole weight of my body sank into the bed. They had taken it from me. They had managed to wrest my beloved vineyard from me. It was mine no more. My poor, sick, tormented mother had been frightened into signing something she did not understand. I remembered the look of hatred on Don Paulo's face as he stood over the body of his dead son. We, my mother and I, who represented the Blodmores to him, had struck him a mortal blow. He must have known by his act that he had begun, at last, to have his revenge. My mother had saved Carlos' life, and I had been the cause of taking it. He could forgive neither thing.

"So I advise you to behave as you should," that calm voice went on. "You will observe a year's strict mourning. You may receive discreet callers, but you may not appear at any entertainment. You will wear black. Don

327

Paulo, as your nearest male relative, will exercise a grand-father's control over anything that touches your children. You and María Luisa between you will attempt to control your mother's unfortunate habits. Otherwise we must insist that she have stronger discipline."

What did she mean? How had they come to have this power over us? I thought of my mother's fear of Nuestra Señora de Mercedes, and I remembered my promise. I thought of how I had killed Pepita so that no one else should do it.

Weakness swamped me, and I could make no reply to her. Between them, she and Don Paulo had taken everything from me, my children, my vineyard, everything that gave me hope. I could look at her no longer. I turned my face into the pillow, accepting defeat.

From the doorway I heard her say, "It is a pity you lost the child. Another grandson would have done much to re-establish your standing with Don Paulo. Yes—a pity you lost the child. You should have been more careful."

My mouth pressed against the pillow so that she would not hear me cry out. By his last act, in dying, Carlos had finally stripped from me the thing he most resented, my little shred of dignity and independence. I was the creature of these two now—Don Paulo and the Marquesa; my mother, myself, my children, all helpless except to do their bidding. I was trapped by events which had begun long before I was born.

CHAPTER SIX

1

The town was kind—perhaps it was also wise. If in private there was speculation about exactly what had happened the night Carlos died at Las Ventanas Verdes, no one seemed to attach any blame to us. Don Luis was so well established that nothing could touch his reputation. The town closed ranks to protect its own against outside gossip, and that protection extended to me. That Don Paulo had suffered a terrible loss they acknowledged, and if they were not entirely convinced that it was the same with me, at least they made a good show of it. When I was well enough to return to the Plaza de Asturias, all the acquaintances who had called to offer condolences immediately after Carlos' death came once again, wearing black, to offer them to me. The miscarriage, the recurring horror of that whole night permitted me little sleep, and I had lost weight. The ladies exclaimed sympathetically over my appearance. María Luisa nodded sagely. "You look well in black, querida. You have the complexion for it." I thought she was about to say, "you play the part well," but she never actually spoke the words.

The Marquesa made her appearance at the Plaza de Asturias the first day I was there. Her presence set the seal of family closeness upon our shared loss. She sent over from Don Paulo's house a beautiful Georgian silver tea service, and a tea set of Crown Derby arrived from Sanlúcar, which she never took back. She also sent her chef and several servants from Sanlúcar for those first weeks, and stocked the larder with all the ingredients we would need for those dainty teatime sandwiches and little cakes so beloved by the ladies of Jerez. Silver cake stands were passed about the drawing room, silver spoons tinkled against bone china cups, while the Marquesa presided over the tea pouring. It was made clear that I was as yet too weak to undertake such tasks, and of course, my mother could not be trusted with them. So the Marquesa sat there in her black, with only the famous jeweled rings for relief, and her presence slightly awed even the most talkative Jerezana lady. I realized that not only was she presenting a picture of family solidarity, but she was also shielding me from unwanted questions. She kept me seated on the sofa beside her, and she encouraged me to remain silent.

So the weeks wore on—dead, slow weeks in which the true heat of the summer gathered force and smote us. Everyone in the house was listless. The Marquesa, satisfied that it was now safe to leave us, departed for her estates in Galicia, in the cool green northwest region of Spain. But she took her hostages with her. She took my three sons, saying that the Andalucian summer was too fierce for them, that they needed cool green gardens to play in, green fields to ride in, that they should not have to spend the summer in a house of mourning, trapped in the heat of the town. So they went, accompanied by a flustered and awe-struck Nanny, and Edwin Fletcher went with them. We were alone, three women in black, in a dim, shuttered house.

To give myself some activity, I rode with my mother each morning, while it was still relatively cool, to Luis' hacienda to see Balthasar and Half Moon. A gentle canter in the dry brown pastures was our day's only activity. We were back at the Plaza de Asturias by eleven, and the whole empty day stretched before us. The Marquesa had briefly played with the idea that Balthasar and Half Moon and their progeny should be moved to land belonging to Don Paulo, but then realized that the move might be unsettling to my mother, and also that it might signify disapproval of Don Luis and give cause for gossip, so she left things as they were. "But you will be most circumspect in your meetings with Don Luis. Do not forget that the town must believe that he was the guest of yourself and Carlos that night at the vineyard. You must not be overly friendly with him. You must never see him alone."

So I lost my friend, as well as all the rest.

I think I moved mechanically, with perfect decorum, through those months. I was ashamed at the relief Carlos' absence brought to me, but within my own heart I did not deny it. I ached with fierce longing for the vineyard, which was now barred to me, since it belonged to Don Paulo. I missed Pepita almost in the way I missed my children, and I felt a vague shame in this also. Her love had been so uncritical, her big body had been ever present at my side. Unlike the children, she made no demands; I had had her unexacting, unquestioning love, and I missed it.

I missed Luis, as I missed Amelia. In one last visit I had taken from Las Ventanas Verdes all the lovely, bright gifts she had made to the house; I took her chest full of treasures, and as yet had not the heart or the energy to distribute them through the house in the Plaza de Asturias. They belonged to another place, another time.

I also missed Edwin Fletcher. I read the English newspapers diligently, read the news of the war, which did not grow better, and missed being able to question him on points I did not understand, on matters of policy which seemed meaningless to me. During those months when the heat had Andalucía in its grip and the grapes ripened, the battle of the Somme raged. We read that for the first time the British used tanks, and I tried to explain to my mother what a tank was, and what it could do that a horse could not, but I wasn't sure myself. It wasn't until November that the battle petered out in rain and mud, and the Allies had advanced only about seven miles along their front. The cost to the British was four hundred thousand lives. Inevitably some of those names in the casualty lists were known to us, others were those of friends. I took to hiding the newspapers from my mother and making excuses when she wanted them read to her.

Most of all, in those months, I missed the vineyards. The harvest was meaningless to me, though no one in Jerez was not involved in some fashion. But none of my must was delivered to the bodegas; the nights when I would have labored at the vineyard with the men who tramped the grapes in the lagar, I lay restlessly, uselessly, in bed.

The beginning of October brought the children back to me, and they were very nearly strangers. Juan seemed to have grown more than an inch, and Martín was not far behind him. Francisco was no longer a baby. They were full of tales of the marvelous times they had had with the Marquesa in Galicia, the other children they had met, the outings they had had. They all had new wardrobes. "I expect they grew so much," María Luisa said, to soften the impact of receiving charity. "Miss Charlie," Nanny said, "they are spoiled entirely. They never listened to me a minute. They would just say, 'Tía Isabel said we could,' and that was that. It's well for the lady that she doesn't have to deal with them all the time, as I have. *Then* she'd know that rules and regulations have to be obeyed. And now they'll just turn up their noses at everything here, just see if they don't."

"I'm glad to be back," Edwin Fletcher said. "The Marquesa lives in great state up there. She is the greatest landowner in the whole region, I'm told. There is the sort of castle that might be perched on the cliffs of Wales, and a garden that seems a thousand years old. Everything she looks at, she owns, and that seems to include people as well. And they are poor. They're different people from the Andalucian. They're harder, leaner. If they have a little money to spend, they don't spend it. They don't seem to drink their wine with enjoyment, when they have it. Yes . . . I'm glad to be back. . . ."

Later he talked, ruminating, almost, as he sat in the courtyard with a copita, speculating, knowing that I did not regard it as impertinent gossip, about the extent of the Marquesa's wealth. "It isn't just the estates. Spain has profited greatly by this war. The factories in Barcelona are booming. I learned she also owns coal mines in Asturias. Then there's Río Tinto . . ." He had had a summer to observe her, and while he appeared to like her no better, he seemed to have a rather grudging respect for her abilities. "Not that she made me her confidant, of course. But I got the impression that she makes most of the important business decisions for herself. She really controls her own money—and seems to do it well. I saw a lot of very respectful men coming and going, all taking their orders from her. She insists on personal supervision of her interests. The most important documents must have her signature. Yes—in all, a very interesting summer. But I'm glad to be back," he repeated.

Sometimes I wondered if my children were glad to be back. A few complaints filtered through to us. Once when Juan spoke sharply to Serafina, criticizing the way the food was cooked, my mother suddenly wrenched herself out of her wine-fogged state and actually slapped him. "Serafina is a person, Juan, not a slave! She has feelings . . . she does her best."

His cheeks grew flushed, and he pouted. "Well, the soup was terrible. All fatty . . . Tía Isabel—"

"I see, John," my mother said, "it has taken only a very few months to turn you into a snob."

"What's a snob?" It was an English word he didn't know.

"It's what you've become," my mother said, too weary for the effort of trying to explain.

"At any rate," Juan said, "*we* were the ones taken to stay with Tía Isabel. She didn't invite the children of Tío Ignacia or Tío Pedro." Those were the courtesy titles he gave Carlos' two half brothers, since they were also the sons of Don Paulo. "*We* are the favorites. And I am the oldest son."

I felt sick. He was so young, and yet he already knew the significance of the favor of the Marquesa de Pontevedra. He knew he was in competition, and he seemed to be winning. He knew whom he had to charm and beguile and please, and he had his father's skill at the game. The first innocence was lost.

2

In November 1916 the old Emperor Franz Joseph died in Vienna. When she heard the news my mother said, "I wonder if they are still breeding the Lipizzaner stallions for the Spanish Riding School? After the war, perhaps we will have to supply them again from here." She had strange moments of lucidity like that, and a knowledge of things I had not thought she knew. That winter we were invited to join several sewing circles among the ladies of Jerez, ladies who rolled bandages, knitted scarves, and a helmet-like thing called a balaclava, whose intricacies I could never master. These were little informal meetings in each other's houses, and so did not seem to break our observation of the period of mourning. We took our own turn at inviting the ladies to the Plaza de Asturias, and served them tea from the Marquesa's Crown Derby. She had also sent us some silver to replace that which had been returned to Don Paulo's house. "It will be useful," she had said, "and in any case I would have been giving silver to each of my godchildren when he came to set up house for himself." So her presence was there, even at our little sewing circles.

My mother tried valiantly on those days. She drank very little wine, and worked with her needles, but María Luisa, like Penelope, unpicked at night the disastrous chaos my mother made even of a simple muffler, and reknitted it. There was a real sadness and concern among the Jerezanos about the war. Hardly a family there was untouched by the ravages among the men on the Western Front. Most of them had cousins of some degree or another who served, and there was almost the same proportion of casualties as any wholly British family suffered. One had only to go through the list of names so common in Jerez—Gordon, Gilbey, Williams, Humbert, Harvey, Terry, O'Neale, Osborne, Mackensie. There was hardly one of them who had not some such name tacked onto his Spanish name. Letters were read aloud at those quiet sewing circles, and there was a note of sadness in most of them.

We had our own particular worry about the events in Ireland. The execution of Casement and other leaders of the Easter Rising had left a bitter taste. England, brutally mauled in the war in France, and in her losses to the attacks of German submarines on her life lines, also kept looking nervously over her shoulder, wondering if perhaps there could not be a back-door attack by Germany through Ireland, or if the Irish should get sufficient arms, a revolt might not engage them in a disastrous, debilitating struggle. I knew, listening to Edwin Fletcher talk, explaining to me things about my own country I had never realized before, that the old life in Ireland was gone forever. "Oh, there may be a semblance of it left," he said. "People cling to customs. But the Protestant Ascendancy is doomed, if not already gone. Finally Ireland will have her freedom, and that will be the beginning of the end for the whole Empire."

I found it hard to believe, when so many of those in the British army were Irish. And where had the Irish to turn for markets except to Britain? A total break between the two seemed unthinkable.

"Not a total break," Edwin said. "But Britain has waited too long. Ireland won't be content with Home Rule now. She will go for complete independence." Then he added something. "Is Lord Blodmore's title in the Irish peerage or the English?"

How ignorant I was. "I . . . I don't know."

And how little it seemed to matter now. The title meant nothing; his life was all that counted. Every batch of newspapers that reached Jerez brought a new nightmare until I had read every name in every casualty list. The heartbreak of finding the names of those we knew was clouded by the dreadful suspense until, by reading each list twice, I was certain his name was not there. And then began the long wait until the next batch of newspapers arrived and the agony began all over again. I told myself that somehow I would know if he were dead—the part of me that belonged to him would die also. But still I read the lists with fear and hope. Nothing seemed to happen. There were no victories, but defeat was unthinkable. And then in April 1917 the United States declared war on Germany.

In a rush of uncharacteristically wild enthusiasm, Edwin Fletcher asked my mother if he might borrow the drawing room for a small evening reception. Where he found the champagne I never knew. But more than a few of his friends and acquaintances turned up to drink it, and although the year of mourning was not yet completed, María Luisa said it would be quite proper for me to wear white lace on my dress. My mother, delighted at the thought of a party, happily put on a dress of brilliant green. It was sad to think of her as she had been the last time she wore it, at the height of her beauty. Those who gathered at our house that evening perhaps were reminded also, and also remembered the reason why my mother was as she was now. The specter of Carlos haunted us, even though we did not admit it.

We exchanged toasts, and we said the war would soon be over now, and we would sell more sherry than ever to England. Edwin was happily explaining the almost unrecognized economic might of America, the power that would now be available to throw at the Germans. The room buzzed with talk. My mother laughed happily, though she didn't quite understand why. Juan, who had been permitted to stay up, was correctly polite and unobtrusive. In the soft light, even the drawing room didn't look quite so shabby as usual. We seemed lighted with hope, and it cast a soft glow. I told myself Richard Blodmore, having survived so much, would survive until the end of this brutal business. He would live, I told my-self, and so would I.

In another month, I told myself, the blossom would be on the vines. What did it matter if they were no longer my vines? It was a symbol of the eternal cycle of nature, the force of life itself. I had won back land to give to the vines. I had three children. I had made my contribution to the force of life. For a few hours I was almost happy.

An extraordinary thing happened that evening. It was nearly time for the guests to go. Edwin had made it clear that it was a very informal occasion, and there was no entertainment—just a few friends raising a glass to the hope that soon Europe would be at peace. As the first of the guests began to come to say good night, suddenly María Luisa nudged me. "Look . . . !"

Don Paulo stood in the doorway only momentarily, his glance searching for my mother. Serafina, who carried a tray with glasses of champagne, offered it, and he accepted. Then he went to my mother. "A small celebration, Lady Patricia, Mr. Fletcher's note said. I am happy to see you looking so well." Then he turned away, caught sight of Juan, and bent to receive his grandson's embrace. With his hand in Juan's, he came to me. It was the first time we had looked on each other since the night at Las Ventanas Verdes. He raised his glass. "I hope we may soon have a true celebration of peace."

"To peace," I said, also raising my glass.

He drained his drink, embraced Juan once more, and left. It took a few minutes before the talk in the room started once again. I looked at Edwin Fletcher in puzzle-ment. "Of course I had left a note at the bodega," he said, "but I never imagined he'd come. It seemed only polite, but I hardly know him."

"Peace," I said slowly. "Perhaps one day there truly will be peace." And Edwin Fletcher knew I wasn't talking about the end of the war, not the war between the Great Powers. I looked at Juan, and knew again the power that rested in my children.

337

Our sewing circles continued—a year had passed since Carlos' death, and it was now permissible for me to accept invitations. They came slowly. Almost shyly I made my appearance at a few parties and found that my status had changed. I was still young, but I was widowed, and the widow of Don Paulo's son. So young men would take my hand, bow over it, and pass on. The feeling, never spoken, but still tangibly there, that the Blodmores carried bad luck with them seemed to grow. People were kind, but they did not want to come too close to us. It was as if Don Paulo and the Marquesa had wrought some sort of screen between us and other families. There was no telling what plans the Marquesa might have for me and for my children, and in the meantime it was better not to get too involved.

Life went on at its draggingly slow pace, and the agony in Europe did not end quickly, as we had hoped it would. Edwin Fletcher was almost at a loss to explain it, as were all the generals who actually made and executed the plans. "It will end through attrition, finally," he said. "From sheer exhaustion."

He had moved out of the house of his Fletcher cousins. "It is too much of a good thing," he said. "I would like to remain friends with them, but an eternal guest is no friend." So he took rooms in the town with two of the maiden ladies of a sherry family badly hit by the phylloxera whose fortune had never recovered. It was, of course, María Luisa who found the place for him. "The sisters Niña and Catalina Hernandos Delgado are kindly souls. They will dote on Mr. Fletcher and take good care of him. Besides, they need the money, little as it is."

Books came for Edwin as often as the unreliable mail would permit, books he had stored at his parents' home in England. He brought them to the Plaza de Asturias, ostensibly for him to read when he was free of tutoring Juan and Martín, but he often left them behind, and I knew he did it for me. I must have seemed shockingly ignorant to him, but he was too kind to point up the fact. I began to read. There was so much time, and so little to do. I noticed that most of the books were not of the level which would interest a scholar, and yet were too advanced for Juan, so he must have sent for his old schoolbooks especially for me. In a backhanded sort of way he was attempting to make up for the education I had not had. I tried; for his sake I tried.

"Things will change for women too," he said, "when the war is over. They'll have the vote. They've proved what they can do during this war, and it has been promised. . . . So, yes, there will be changes." He seemed to be, through these books, trying to prepare me for them.

"Things may change for women in England," María Luisa said, and shrugged. "But in Spain it will be as it's always been. Women will only have power when they have money and position. If they are like the Marquesa de Pontevedra, they already have their power and need nothing else. Or they have power through their men, the back-door way. They won't seek to change that. The María Luisas of the world will get along as best they can."

Edwin Fletcher had no answer to that.

Occasionally, at small gatherings, I met Luis. Less frequently he called at the Plaza de Asturias. We tried not to let our looks convey the feelings the sight of each other aroused. The memories of that terrible night were still sharp and vivid. We were locked in a conspiracy of silence, to which we both had agreed. I missed his close friendship, as I missed the vineyards.

"You are lonely, Carlota," he said to me once when we met at a party, and talked for a few moments when the music drowned our conversation to others.

I shook my head. "Not lonely, Luis. Alone. I miss you, my friend."

He smiled his gentle smile. "Some young man will pluck up courage soon—"

I shook my head again. "No young man, no man, young or old, will take on a penniless widow with three young children. Everyone knows Carlos made a mistake in marrying me. It will not be repeated."

339

"Time, Carlota . . . time. All things change with time."

Time was what I dreaded. It stretched before me, emptily. I only saw my children growing up under the dictates of the Marquesa. I saw us spinning out the days at the Plaza de Asturias, trying to make every penny do the work of two, trying to keep what little social position we had in the town, the position which, in truth, was dependent on the good will of Don Paulo and the Marquesa. I toyed with the thought of returning to Ireland when the war was over, and knew at once it could not be done. To do that would be to remove my children from the influence of the Marquesa and Don Paulo, and they would do everything they could to prevent it. I knew Don Paulo would welcome the departure of my mother and me, but he clung to his grandchildren. And if I should manage to get us all to Ireland—what then? Where would the money for the children's education come from? What would I do with my mother, bereft of her tiny but promising stud? We were back at the same place we had been when my grandfather died, but with three children to provide for as well, and my mother needing now as much care as a child. Whichever direction I looked I could see only the need for money, and our growing dependence on the Marquesa. I even looked far enough into the future to wonder what would become of me when my children were grown, their careers, interests, marriages taking them away from me. The Marquesa would direct all of that as well. I would try to shake the thoughts away when they crowded in. Life could only be lived, borne, if I did not try to look too far ahead. A day at a time. *Mañana* could be met when it arrived.

It was not in the casualty lists I found Richard Blodmore's name; the news came first in a letter from Lady Sybil. "Poor Lord Blodmore has been wounded—but I expect you know that. Elena has gone to England to be with him. They say he's lucky to be alive—a shrapnel wound to the face, I heard. He could have been blinded. It was at Passchendaele . . ."

He was alive, that was all I cared. But he had nearly

died in an action which had won the British no ground. From July to November the battle raged, and in the end the exhausted troops were unable to follow up the advantage won by the surprise attack of the tanks and the penetration of the German lines. They fell back, and gave up most of the miles they had won. Edwin crumpled the papers in fury. "Those fossilized generals! Will they never accomplish anything?"

But Richard was safe, and back in England. Then we heard that he had returned to Ireland. A long leave for convalescence. Perhaps discharge. But trained officers and men were getting fewer as the toll of casualties mounted. I rolled bandages and thought of him, and lighted candles with the prayer that by some miracle the end would come before he was sent back into service. I never thought about his shattered face. His life was enough.

3

The months slipped away. There was much talk, worried talk, in Jerez about the Bolshevik Revolution in Russia, the beginning of the civil war there. "They're worried," Edwin said, "because this country has a social structure rather like Russia. They're afraid of Bolsheviks —and when you see estates like the Marquesa's, you know why."

Then we were in the spring of 1918, and the gnarled, twisted black stems of the vines of Jerez put out their green shoots. The sun, so gentle in winter, began to have force. And the letter came from Lady Sybil Wercham that Lord Blodmore had been posted back to France. By July we were stunned by the news of the murder of the Czar of Russia and his family, and saddened by the accounts of the second battle of the Marne. "We *must* do it this time," Edwin said. "If the Allies and the Americans can just push together . . ." We had almost given up hoping there would ever be an end. The protagonists seemed now like two weary giants facing each other barefisted, too bloodied and exhausted to see that it must be all over. "Why don't they just stop?" my mother said with the simple logic she was sometimes capable of. "No one is going to win."

We listed the collapse of Turkey, the collapse of Bulgaria, and, after so many centuries of rule, the end of the Hapsburg monarchy. "When the eagles die," Edwin Fletcher quoted, "woe to the sparrows."

The papers had not reached us at the time the telegrams began arriving. "I don't understand," my mother said. I snatched the first from her, fearing it was news of Richard Blodmore.

DEEPEST SYMPATHY IN YOUR LOSS, BUT HOW PROUD YOU MUST BE OF HIS HEROIC DEEDS. LOVE, SYBIL WEREHAM.

"Who?" I said. "Who does she mean?"

The official telegram came only after a dozen others like Sybil Wereham's, all of them from people we had known at Clonmara. It had been sent to Clonmara and redirected to Jerez, probably by Elena.

THE WAR OFFICE DEEPLY REGRETS TO INFORM YOU OF THE DEATH IN ACTION OF LIEUTENANT COLONEL THOMAS DRUMMOND. THIS OFFICER DIED IN THE PERFORMANCE OF DUTY IN CIRCUMSTANCES OF EXTREME GALLANTRY.

My mother let the telegram flutter soundlessly to the floor. "Thomas—Thomas is dead! Your father, Charlie, is dead."

I picked up the telegram and read it. "I didn't know my father had become a lieutenant colonel."

"Neither did I," my mother said faintly. "Well, with so many officers killed, I expect he moved up rather quickly. But a hero! I always thought of Thomas taking rather good care of himself. He's survived all these years. I imagined he had got himself some good safe job away from the front lines. 'Extreme gallantry . . .' I wonder . . ." She didn't actually weep, but her eyes were bright with unshed tears. "Such a long time ago . . . I was mad, of course.

Quite mad to marry him. And he was mad to suggest it. But for a little while we were in love. At least I know *I* was in love. It all went so quickly . . . and he never saw you. His only child."

"I may not be his only child."

She looked at me sharply. "That's true. That's perfectly true. How do we know there isn't some woman, some children for whom this is terrible news? Some woman the War Office doesn't recognize. She is bereaved, and I . . . I'm a widow. We're both widows, Charlie. How strange. How strange it all is, suddenly. After all these years."

"If there had been another woman, surely he would have asked for a divorce? You could have been free a long time ago."

She shook her head. "Thomas wasn't like that. What he had he wanted to keep forever. He would have liked me to come back to him, submissive, asking for forgiveness. I couldn't have done it—ever. He also knew, if there was a divorce, I could never be remarried in the Catholic Church. It was a mistake from the beginning, and there never was any chance of repairing that." For a moment she pressed her hands against her temples, rocking a little. Then she rose and went to the sideboard and poured herself some brandy. "I think I'll go and lie down for a while. . . ." When she went, she took the brandy decanter with her. I could hear her muttering as she closed the door. "Extreme gallantry . . . Doesn't sound like Thomas at all."

When she was gone I sat for a while thinking of what my life might have been like if she had chosen to stay with Thomas Drummond, or to return to him, as he had demanded. I would have been one of those children born in India, sent back to school in England, or to live with my grandfather, sent away to escape the heat. I might have had brothers and sisters. We would have lived in a series of houses provided by the army. I thought that that might have been where the marriage had come apart right at the beginning. My mother would have been hopeless at accepting or adapting to the unwritten code for army wives. She wouldn't have known how to be polite to the major's

343

wife or the colonel's wife unless she genuinely liked them; she would have flirted with every officer in the regiment. There would have been no free and easy life such as she had lived as the only, beloved, indulged child of Lord Blodmore. No, I didn't think there would have been a place in the army for my mother.

I wondered if she wept a little upstairs with her brandy, wept for dreams that had vanished into cruel reality, wept for the memories of a romance gone cold, for the waste of youth. She couldn't weep for whatever my father had become, because she had never known that man. Nor had I.

Apart from other telegrams and letters from friends in Ireland, a letter came from the colonel-in-chief of my father's regiment. It reached us in Jerez at the time when it seemed an armistice was about to be signed. The October sun was warm and bright, and the air was filled with the characteristic smell of the new must in fermentation.

> *The tragedy of his death is compounded by the fact that he served for so long and with such bravery here in France, often exposing himself to enemy fire to lead his men. He insisted on leading where other, junior officers might have gone in his place. He seemed to have no regard for his own safety, but his whole effort was bent on trying to do what he could for his men. He kept morale high, and his personal bravery was an example to all. In the action at St. Quentin in which he lost his life, he personally carried four wounded men to safety beyond the range of enemy machine-gun fire, returning each time to that stretch of open territory under continuing fire. He was killed in a successful attempt to overrun a long-range gun emplacement which the machine-gun fire protected. His gallantry and dedication to duty were of the highest order, and should be so recognized. I have recommended to my superiors that his award should be no less than the Victoria Cross.*

A little later a packet arrived in Jerez containing the things which his batman considered were most personal to him. It seemed my father had been, or had become, a spartan type. There was very little of value, or anything that indicated softness. A gold watch, a pair of brushes, well worn, a single pair of thin gold cuff links, plain gold studs for his dress shirts—only the bare minimum that an officer would need. There were no photographs, no diary, no notebooks; there was a copy of the Bible which appeared little used. Perhaps out of tact other things had been omitted. But the package did contain a medal in a box, which Edwin identified as the Distinguished Service Order. "Your father made a practice of being brave, I see." I looked at the few personal things which survived the man, and they revealed nothing of his personality. "I suppose I should in fairness, send them to his father, if he's still alive," my mother said. "And there were brothers . . . but he still had me listed as next of kin. He meant us to have these if he were killed. . . . Charlie dear, you'll write to his brother, won't you? His name was . . ." Her brow wrinkled in the effort at concentration. "His name was Gordon, I think . . . or was it Russell? The eldest, I mean. There were other brothers. They weren't at all well off, you know. That was why Thomas had to make his own way in the army. He always said he reckoned to pay his mess bills by his winnings at cards. He had a very cool head in things like that. Funny he should have wanted to marry me. He *knew* I had no income. Perhaps he thought Father would settle something on me. . . ."

It was ironic to learn from the War Office that my mother would now receive a war widow's pension. His estate consisted of a few hundred pounds in cash and some shares in South African gold-mining companies and the De Beers diamond company. These he had left to me.

Don Ramón at the bank considered them carefully, his eyebrows raised. "I will make inquiries, Doña Carlota. I think these are very good shares. They don't represent a fortune of course, but they have evaluated many times since they were purchased. They should yield a small income. Always useful." He looked at me speculatively. "Quite obviously your father must have done a little more than soldiering when he served his time in South Africa during the Boer War. . . ."

My mother was in tears over this. "He *shouldn't*. There are his brothers. He must have nieces and nephews. I think he did it just to make me feel bad, to point up how badly I'd treated him."

"Perhaps I *was* his only child, after all."

She nodded. "Perhaps. Perhaps he knew more about us than we thought. Perhaps he didn't forget, the way I did."

But we never knew. As the silence of more than twenty years had been unbroken by a single letter, so it remained to the end. Apart from his will, there was no shred of evidence that he had ever thought about us, my mother and me. There was no last letter to accompany his personal effects, nothing that a man in constant danger of death might have written. There was no message to me. I had been born a stranger to him, and I had remained a stranger right to the end. There was a terrible sense of loneliness in his death which chilled me. For the first time, now when it was too late, I began to want to know him.

And the new thought came that because of him, because of the war widow's pension, because of the small income that the gold-mining and diamond-mining shares would bring, we, my mother and I, might be able to take some small step towards independence from the Marquesa. He had restored a little pride to us, and that was the greatest gift of all.

All Jerez, which had come to offer condolence at the news of my father's death, came again to offer congratulations when it became known that the award of the Victoria Cross had been confirmed. The newspapers containing accounts of his last heroic hour had by now reached the town, and everyone had read them. The Blodmore legend now took on another aspect. I was the child of an authentic hero, and my children shared in the reflected glory. My mother was utterly bewildered by it, and more often than not refused to talk to visitors about it. "How can I?" she asked of me. "How can I talk to them when I know nothing about him? How old are you, Charlie? I keep forgetting."

"Almost twenty-seven."

"Almost twenty-seven—are you? Then it's more than twenty-seven years since I've seen him. How can I talk about him?"

More than the questions of those who came to call, she was troubled by the questions of the children. Juan was stiff-chested with pride in having a grandfather who had won the supreme award. "I never thought about my *other* grandfather," he said, and it seemed logical. There was the barest shade of reserve in the congratulations Don Paulo offered. The man he had been able to dismiss as a rogue and a scoundrel, a man of no account whatever, was certified as a hero in the eyes of his grandchildren. Don Paulo did not care to share their veneration with such a man.

The Armistice had been signed while all these events swept over us. "It's only an armistice, not a victory," Edwin said gloomily. "We will probably have to fight it out all over again someday." Christmas came and the turn of the year. "I must go home when the spring comes," Edwin said. "I have to make a life back there." He had been answering advertisements in papers for the various teaching posts which were available. "More fool I that I didn't take something when the men to fill those positions were scarce. Now they will all be flooding back, all wanting the same jobs. . . . I let myself be seduced by the Andalucian sun."

Then the letter came from my father's colonel requesting that my mother should make the journey to England to receive personally the posthumous award of the Victoria Cross from His Majesty. It would, he wrote, be a landmark in the history of the regiment, which had never before had a winner of the Victoria Cross. The letter tactfully suggested that the regiment would be honored to pay any expenses which Lady Patricia might incur in traveling to England, and, of course, she would be the guest of the regiment, staying at his own house, while she was in

England. There was no mention of Lieutenant Colonel Drummond's Scottish family. It was evidently preferable that the daughter of an earl should go to Buckingham Palace to receive the medal than some truculent Scottish Presbyterian farmer.

My mother was at once in a panic. "Oh, Charlie, I can't! I just couldn't do it! I'm not up to that. Not any more. I'd make a fool of myself, and disgrace you and the children." She put a self-conscious hand to the white streak in her hair, as if emphasizing her diminished ability. "You know what I mean. . . . You understand, don't you, Charlie?"

I knew. Since her injury, she was physically unable to undertake any such task. I had seen her shake with nerves at small social gatherings, terrified that she might do something wrong, might, as she chose to put it, "disgrace" us. The ordeal of appearing at Buckingham Palace, of curtsying to the King, of attending the regimental dinner in her honor, would have been too much, even if there was not the added misery of having to do without her daily intake of alcohol. She could not stand before the King of England smelling of brandy; but without it she could not stand there at all.

"Charlie, you must go. Yes, my darling, you'll do it beautifully. They'll all adore you. After all, it wasn't *your* fault that our marriage came apart. They'll just see you as you are—young, lovely, and sweet, the daughter of their hero. Darling, do it for me! Do it for the children. Think how thrilled they'll be to be able to say that you went and received your father's medal. You have to do it, Charlie. I've let everyone down, but you mustn't. You hear me, Charlie. You have to do this for us all!"

I agreed; I had to. Juan, Martín, and Francisco would never have forgiven me if I had refused. María Luisa nodded. "It must be done."

The necessary letter was drafted and sent off. From Colonel Saunders came an enthusiastic response. The regiment would be honored. Their headquarters were near Winchester, and I would be their guest. Most tactfully it was suggested that if I should like a few days to visit

London after the presentation at Buckingham Palace, which was arranged for April, I could either stay at the London home of the Colonel's sister or at a hotel, whichever I preferred. All expenses, of course, would be gladly borne by the regiment.

María Luisa began to fuss about my clothes. "Wear gray with a touch of lilac to the palace," my mother said. "Black would be out of place, and hypocritical. You must have two evening gowns for the time you stay with the regiment. They will want to fete you. It's a very unfashionable regiment, darling—Thomas wouldn't have been accepted in anything better, even if he'd had the money. But I'd like you to look your best. Since you're going, you must do your best for us all."

The excitement in the town was intense. While cousins and second cousins had won military honors during the war, none had achieved the Victoria Cross. My itinerary and wardrobe were openly discussed. And behind the fans was a soft sigh of relief that it was I, and not my mother, who would go. For that short time I represented Jerez, its pride in its English connection; it was possible, in a backhanded sort of way, that I might sell some sherry, or at least get it talked about. It was regretted that my father had not belonged to a really first-rate regiment, like the Coldstream, or the Life Guards, but then, one mustn't look a gift horse in the mouth.

My mother wanted me to have everything of the best, the best that Seville could produce. I protested about the money being spent. The regiment, after all, would not pay for my wardrobe.

"Those shares, darling. You could sell those shares."

"No! He didn't mean them to be sold. I'm sure of it."

"Borrow against them."

"No!" But Don Ramón, falling into the spirit of the occasion, advanced some money against my mother receiving her new war widow's pension.

"You must pay for your own hotel in London," my mother insisted. "You must be independent to *that* degree. You owe yourself a few days there, darling, to be beholden to no one. So long here in Jerez, and no fun at all . . ." She was living, vicariously, the journey, the excitement, the nervousness. She was living it, but glad she didn't have to participate except once removed. She was gayer and brighter than I had seen her for a long time.

And then the Marquesa appeared. "You have no jewelry to wear," she said peremptorily. "You represent Jerez there in England. You must represent us well."

I was furious at her sudden appearance, unannounced as always, her calm assumption that her decisions would be accepted without question. "I have the jewelry Amelia left me."

She dismissed that with a single wave of her hand. "A few trinkets."

"I cannot wear jewelry to the palace," I pointed out. "It is a very simple morning ceremony when others will have medals presented. Many of them will be enlisted men."

"The regiment will give at least a dinner for you. There will be other invitations. I have written to our Spanish Ambassador in London. You must have a tiara and a necklace. These I have chosen for you. They are quite suitable to your age. I wore them myself when I was young."

"I cannot accept such things."

"It is not a matter of acceptance. It is merely a loan." Before the startled eyes of us all, she placed a velvet-lined box on the table and withdrew a delicately made tiara in emeralds and diamonds; the necklace matched it. "The emeralds my ancestors brought back from the New World," the Marquesa said, as if Spain still owned the Americas.

I saw the hunger in my mother's eyes as she gazed at them. Unable to help herself, her hands stole forward until she held the things, turning them to catch the light. "How beautiful," she said softly. "How lovely you will look in them, Charlie."

"I don't think I should—"

"You must, Charlie," she said. "I always dreamed of wearing such things. You will do it for me, won't you, darling? While you're in London you must have a photograph taken in them. And get a velvet frame. Then I shall have you as you are now, forever. This is the time, Charlie. It doesn't come again."

And so I went, dressed as I'd never been in my life, carrying the Marquesa's jewels, fully insured, she told me, and not worn for more than thirty years. The way she dismissed them indicated that there were things much more magnificent shut away in some vault. I was to take a P. & O. steamer from Gibraltar. It seemed a lifetime since we had disembarked there on that hot day almost ten years ago.

Edwin Fletcher was traveling back to England with me, taking up a post as research assistant in an economics study being set up in Cambridge. My children clung around us as the boxes were strapped on the carriage the Marquesa had lent for the journey. There were tears for Edwin Fletcher in Juan's eyes as he said good-by. "I'll be at school in England soon, Tía Isabel says. I'll come and see you, won't I, Mr. Fletcher?"

"Of course. And one day you'll come to Cambridge to take your degree." Edwin Fletcher did not seem as cheerful as a man should who has turned his face again towards home.

And then, just as we were about to leave, Luis came. He held out his hand. "A good voyage, Carlota. We are proud of your father's achievement." Then he drew me aside, away from the others. "Will you wear this for Amelia? If she had been alive she would have been more delighted than any of us." It was a large solitaire diamond ring which must certainly have come from the collection of his family's jewels. "Gems seem to fade when there is no woman to wear them. It's time this piece had its turn in the light."

I could not refuse him, though the ring was more than I ever wanted to wear. But when I looked at the ragged scar across his cheek I knew that the debts Don Paulo had paid off in money would, in truth, never be paid.

"My father's rather obscure regiment will think we are very rich, I'm afraid."

"They will know that you have good friends in Jerez,

351

that's all. I will see to your mother while you're gone. Have no worry about that. María Luisa knows she can call on me. Try to enjoy yourself, Carlota. Forget for a while the things you leave behind here. . . ." His glance indicated my mother, her hair in disarray, laughing with Edwin Fletcher so that she wouldn't cry, the three boys clustered about them, María Luisa examining every luxurious detail of the Marquesa's carriage, the courtyard with its cracked, waterless fountain, and all the evidences of poverty. "Put off our Spanish somberness for a while. Laugh and dance and flirt with all the officers. We make our women old by dressing them in black and shutting them in dark houses. It is time to stop praying in dark churches with only candles to light against the dark. It is time to fling open the windows."

4

Edwin and I parted at Southampton. He wished me good-by and I wished him good luck in the presence of Captain Carton, who had been sent from the regimental headquarters near Winchester with a staff car to meet me. I hadn't realized until I saw that tall, stooped figure turn and move through the crowd, and finally become lost in it, how much I would miss him. "My sons' tutor," was how I had described him. But as he walked away I felt as if I had suddenly lost a brother I hadn't known I possessed.

It was the first car I had ever ridden in, and the first time I had seen England, except for those few hours when we transshipped in Liverpool so long ago. Captain Carton seemed to find these two circumstances quite amazing. "It's all much tidier than Ireland," I said. "But then, Ireland is much poorer." I had almost forgotten quite how tender were the greens of the northern spring, how muted the skies. The noisy engine and the smell of petrol did not at all blend with the gentle curving beauty of the countryside. "The horses must hate these things," I said. And then I laughed. Captain Carton wanted to know what was so amusing. "I sound just like my mother," I said. "Yes, Luis was right. It's time to fling open the windows."

Since we were traveling with the hood down, he must have thought me quite as mad as he had probably heard all the Blodmores were.

There was a slight air of *nouveau riche* about the regimental headquarters. They had been established less than a century and seemed faintly self-conscious. I sensed that more men with money now joined the regiment than had been so in my father's early times with it. They would probably have come from rather minor public schools, sons of men who had made their way in industry and could afford to donate a new barracks wing, donate the regimental silver, splendid cricket pitches and rugby grounds. What they could not buy was tradition, and that was why my father's Victoria Cross was so important.

The car came to a halt before a Georgian house where the Colonel lived. Even the ivy seemed new and washed. Colonel Saunders was a lean, spare man, red-faced, unsmiling; his wife was plump and soft, wearing clothes that were frilled and laced so that I could not discern the outline of the garment. She clearly hadn't decided whether fashion would return to the prewar look or retain the wartime simplicity. I decided that my Jerez clothes would do very well. Probably we had more time there to study the fashion magazines from London. I was welcomed effusively. A family of creamy Pekingese dogs swirled around our feet, and one nestled in the lace of Mrs. Saunders' bosom.

"So good of you to come all this way," she said. "We are so happy you are here. It is a great occasion for the regiment."

We walked into the polished, shining marble hall. "I'm sure you'll be glad," Colonel Saunders said, "that you aren't quite among strangers. Your cousin, Lord Blodmore, has kindly agreed to come over."

He stood with his back to a long window that gave a view of a vivid green lawn behind the house. I couldn't see his face clearly, but the outline of his body seemed thinner and therefore taller; he seemed slightly stooped.

I hardly heard now the noise around me, the fluttering talk of Mrs. Saunders, the barking of the many small dogs. He began to walk towards me, and I to him. I saw then that the cheekbone where the shrapnel had hit was smashed; an attempt to repair it had not been successful. One side of his mouth was dragged upwards. The handsome man of my memory was gone. It didn't matter. Richard Blodmore remained, and I still loved him.

He held out his hand formally. "Hello, Charlie."

CHAPTER SEVEN

1

There was a kind of agony in being so close to Richard and yet not alone with him. We were in the same room, seated side by side, and yet we could not talk to each other. Mrs. Saunders or some other officer's wife was nearly always in attendance, as if I were some sort of royalty whose every request must be granted. That afternoon I met most of the officers' wives at a tea Mrs. Saunders gave. I talked about Jerez, and the life there, and it all sounded quite romantic and beautiful. The wife of the youngest lieutenant sighed as I described the bodegas, the time of the harvest, the beautiful horses, the countryside. "How wonderful it must be to live there." She reminded me of myself ten years ago. I looked across at Richard and marveled that my wildly romantic, impossible love for him was the only thing which had not changed in that time.

Elena was not with him. We managed to pace the Colonel's rose garden at the end of the clipped green lawn between tea and the time to go upstairs to dress.

"She didn't want to come," he said. "No—I don't think it was because of you being here. She just doesn't care that much. Not any more. She . . . well, I think she's been enjoying herself with Theo Wereham. Before that it was Simon Lawson. He was invalided out early and was around most of the war. We haven't been very close, and we grow further apart. It wasn't much of a marriage, as you know. At first she was jealous and possessive, and then she stopped caring. Now she can hardly bear to be in the same room with me. The very sight of me sickens her, I suppose."

I looked at him fully in the face. "I love you, Richard. For however long I live, it's never going to change."

His shattered features twisted still further. "Charlie, it's never going to work for us, you know. Carlos is no longer there, but Elena is, and she'll stick. There's no possibility of a divorce. She's Catholic, and she's determined to remain my wife . . ."

"Richard, don't you think I know all this? The Marquesa wishes you to remain married, and Elena will not oppose her, no matter what her feelings are. These years . . . have taught me some things. I know that one does not really choose where to put love, what person to love. It just happens. You're lucky if it happens with the person you eventually marry, and you're lucky if you stay in love with that person. My mother got the man she wanted, and see what happened to that. I told you before, it would have been a fairy tale if we had fallen in together at the right time. Life isn't that tidy. The ends don't come out even." The buds were forming on the roses in the Colonel's tidy garden; they all seemed to rise to regulation height. The whole place had the aura of beeswax and brass polish about it. "Tell me about Clonmara."

Elena's money had restored the house, he told me. For ten years he had worked on bringing the land back into good heart. He had managed to acquire several smaller farms which had been outside the entail and had been sold off by my grandfather. Now the estate was beginning to round out again. His sons had each been sent to boarding school when they were seven. They would go on to Eton. "They've been brought up as Catholics," he said. "Elena insisted on that, and I didn't care enough to make an issue of it. Perhaps for their future in Ireland it's a good thing. The Protestants in the south are hardly a force to be reckoned with any more, Charlie. England can't hold on there much longer, I think. But I think, too, that there'll be bloody battles before the Ulster thing is settled, if it ever is. So . . . I till and sow my acres, and I think of you, who should be there. It's not fair at all, is it?" Then he added quickly, "I never wrote to you after Carlos' death. I didn't know how to. I didn't know what to say."

"If you had, I couldn't have replied. Best leave it alone, Richard."

My fingers found one lone sucker which grew unsanctioned from the root of a rosebush. I bent and plucked it off. "And the rose garden?" I said.

"Just as you left it. I've learned how to take care of it myself. We still go on grafting from the same rootstock your grandfather planted. The locals think I'm mad. There are many better roses to be had these days, and nurseries to supply them. They still call it the Countess' Garden, and many of them are so young they don't even know about your grandmother and why the garden was made. They think it is Elena's garden, but she hardly ever goes there. For me, it's Charlotte's garden."

I thought of my bare feet on the soft grass that morning, the end of my robe soaked in dew. "You shouldn't hold onto things like that, Richard. There's no sense in it. And you're a sensible man."

"I used to believe I was. That was why I married Elena. That was an eminently sensible thing to do. Practical. Pragmatic. And look what all that got me. Clonmara would be better as I first saw it, half falling to pieces, if I could have had you there with me. So what if I keep the rose garden? And what if I ride on the shore alone, and remember? What else have I got?"

A gong sounded in the house and we turned obediently

357

to answer its summons. To watching eyes from the house we were just very distant cousins, admiring the Colonel's perfect turf, his budding roses, and catching up on family gossip.

2

We dined with the Colonel and his closest staff that evening, and the next day they drove me around the countryside. We visited Winchester Cathedral and had tea with the Dean, who was related to Mrs. Saunders. Richard and I were together all day, and yet never alone. I noticed that people tended to look past Richard rather than at him, the way they skirted around my Catholic upbringing when we visited the cathedral. They chose to ignore Richard's face as they ignored the fact that the Lieutenant Colonel Drummond had been separated from his wife for all but a few months of their long marriage. My mother did not exist, in the way Richard's injury did not exist. In the way that, when his untouched profile was turned towards me, it was possible to reconstruct what he had once been, I kept remembering my mother at her gayest and best and bravest. If they, these strangers surrounding me, had only known it, I believed my mother a match in courage to the man the King and the nation would honor with its highest award. And yet, from all the talk that flowed, still nothing emerged that gave me any more knowledge of my father. They used his name quite often, but they didn't talk about him, just the things he had done.

"Of course," Colonel Saunders said, "one might have tipped him for great things when he got the D.S.O. in South Africa. Damn bad luck he didn't survive the last do. He'd been in the trenches in France through the whole four years. Wounded twice, and went back each time. Needn't have gone back. He had an offer to go to the General Staff. Refused it."

I thought of the worn brushes and the virtually unread Bible. I thought I would like to meet his batman, but when I suggested it the Colonel said he had been injured

in the very last days of the fighting and had been de-
mobilized as soon as he left the hospital.

That night they gave a splendid dinner in the officers'
mess, and there was to be dancing afterwards. Senior
officers from older, better-established regiments had been
invited and had agreed to turn out to honor the occasion.
The Dean of Winchester was coming, and the Lord Mayor.
Some of the silver that graced the long table looked very
new, as if officers' families had dug further into their
pockets to put up a good show. In the display of silver
on the long sideboards I saw that some of the pieces had
sad little commemorations of fallen officers. Even among
the invited guests from other regiments there were few
young faces. "We lost almost all our young men," an old
general said to me. "Every year a fresh batch straight out
of school and basic training would arrive, and so many
of them lasted only a few months." He fixed his monocle
and stared at me. "You had a brave father. Hear you've
got three boys yourself, and you're widowed. Sorry. Hear
that part of the world you're in is very attractive."

I had asked for Edwin Fletcher to be invited, and was
startled to see him present in his officer's dress uniform.
I had never thought of him as a soldier. And Richard
wore his uniform, and a medal. I thought we hardly
recognized each other, their uniforms as little part of their
personalities as the emerald and diamond tiara and necklace were part of me. Edwin was placed at a table in one
of the adjoining rooms, which would be cleared when the
dancing began. The long main table was only for the most
distinguished guests. Amelia's ring glittered in the candlelight, and I knew that many of the women guests wondered where the jewelry had come from. It was generally
known that the Blodmores of Jerez were not well off. The
ring would fit only my little finger; Luis must have had it
altered to fit Amelia's growing thinness. At the last minute,
as I dressed, I pinned the little ruby-filled venencia she
had given me beneath a frill of lace. It could not compete
with the emeralds, but it represented Amelia, Luis, and
the vineyards we had created together. The dress had had
to be cut high on the shoulders, though low at the neck,

359

to hide the scar where Carlos' knife had ripped my skin. I viewed the faces of the distinguished strangers about the table, trying to remember each of them, every detail of uniform and dress, so that I could relate it to the eager ears in Jerez; I was startled to realize that I was quite desperately homesick, and it was for Jerez, not Clonmara.

I listened to the speech Colonel Saunders gave, welcoming me, mentioning Richard as though he had been a close relative of my father's, honoring my father's valor. The Drummonds of Scotland seemed forgotten. But again nothing of my father came through the words. There were no fond or funny reminiscences of times shared or times of danger lived through together. My father seemed to be a name in a book, a name that would go on the regimental roll of honor. If they had not, of necessity, worked closely together, I should have imagined that Lieutenant Colonel Drummond was a stranger, someone Colonel Saunders had read about.

I danced every dance, the partners changing all the time. I danced with Richard, and with Edwin Fletcher. "You look very beautiful, Doña Carlota," Edwin said, teasing me with the title and speaking in Spanish. "I shall write Juan and describe every single thing about it. Lady Pat, too." Then he added, unexpectedly, "I miss Jerez. I suppose I'll fall back into the rhythm at Cambridge, but it feels strange now."

When I danced with Richard we didn't talk at all.

When Colonel Saunders approached me for the dance I had promised, I felt I knew him well enough to ask if we might sit it out. He looked relieved. I think by then he had had a good deal to drink and didn't want the public scrutiny of the dance floor. Because the room was hot we sat close to an open window, half hidden from the dancers by a bank of flowers and ferns. He brought me champagne, and a mess orderly hovered just slightly out of earshot with a tray and a full bottle, so that our glasses were never empty. We sat silently, almost companionably for a time. I said suddenly to him, "My face aches from smiling. You don't mind if I don't smile for a while?"

"My dear young lady, you must do exactly as you please. You've put up with a great many pompous old bores like myself this evening. You've done us proud, very proud. Quite a sight, you are." I realized he was truly drunk. Just his soldier's ingrained discipline kept him completely upright.

"I've found it difficult, Colonel. I can't talk about my father, since I never knew him."

"No, you didn't. I remember your mother, you know. I was in Ireland with Drummond the time they ran away to be married. They nearly kicked him out of the regiment, but decided to smooth things over because it would have made things even worse for Lady Pat. Wasn't a bit surprised when she left him."

"You weren't?"

His speech was a little slurred. Captain Carton approached to claim his dance and was peremptorily waved away by his senior officer. He withdrew. The orderly refilled our glasses.

"Not a bit surprised. She was far too good for him. One of the most beautiful girls I'd ever seen. Only a girl then. Couldn't imagine what she saw in the fellow. Of course he was handsome. Had a way with the ladies, I suppose. But hardly a gentleman, and when I remember what Lady Pat's father was like I'm still surprised she couldn't tell the difference between one sort and the other."

"You mean my father wasn't a gentleman?"

He was drunk enough to answer. "No. Never was. Opportunist. Always an eye for the main chance. Played cards to pay his mess bills. Nearly always won. But no one ever found him out in cheating. Either he had the devil's own luck or he was far cleverer than any of us knew. Oh, what am I saying?—*of course* he was clever. If he'd the right connections he'd have made general in time. But insisted on staying in the bloody trenches."

He waved to the orderly, and the glasses were filled again. "We've got to go through all this, because, after all, he did get a V.C. But we all wish it had been someone else."

Despite the heat of the room, I felt cold. I had wanted

to know my father, and now I was hearing what none of the speeches or citations would say. "He wasn't liked, then?"

"No. That's the truth. Kept himself to himself except to play cards. No one ever refused to play with him because he was so damn good, and it was considered something to beat him."

"The men—the enlisted ranks. Your letter said he kept up their morale."

"And he did. Never let a thing go. They were spit and polish even when they were in the trenches. He would wrangle all kinds of things for them, little bits and pieces, anything that would make that hell a bit more bearable. He *cared* for them. But he didn't care for them as individuals, although he knew everyone's name. He cared for them as a fighting force. And, by God, he made them into that, even the rawest replacements they sent. You could always tell what sector of the lines Drummond commanded. Always in better shape than anyone else's. It was a nonsense that someone of his rank shouldn't have delegated more, but he insisted on keeping his finger in, even with all the other work he had to do."

"So he was a good officer?"

"He was a bloody fine officer. And as the men probably said, he was a right mean bastard into the bargain. No friends. No favors. And he was possibly the bravest man I'll ever know."

3

It was, after all, very simple. I went to the palace, escorted by Colonel Saunders and Richard, stood in a long line of those who were to be honored with various orders and decorations. The citation was read; I received the box containing the Victoria Cross from the King's hand; I heard him say something and could never remember afterwards just what words he had used, so I had to invent them to tell my children. I curtsied, walked a few steps backwards, and it was the turn of the next person in the line. There were those in wheel chairs, some on crutches, and those led by others because they were blind. There were also others like myself who had come to receive a posthumous decoration for a dead relative. There were no feelings of celebration; the whole occasion was touched with sadness.

We drank champagne with Mrs. Saunders and the Colonel at lunch. There was a sense of relief that it was all over. The regiment now had its V.C., and a small tradition called Drummond had been grafted to its pedigree. We stayed at Brown's Hotel, and that night the Colonel and Mrs. Saunders would attend a small reception and dinner given by the Spanish Ambassador. Richard was alos attending, as were a number of representatives of the sherry trade in London. The Colonel and the Spanish Embassy had co-operated to see that the presentation to the daughter of a Victoria Cross winner rated several paragraphs in most newspapers. There was added interest in the story that I had come from Jerez to receive it. A little more sherry might be sold because of it. It was too good an opportunity to miss.

Many invitations had come from London representatives of the sherry shippers. Mrs. Saunders beamed at me. "My dear, you could make a regular season of it. It would take you weeks to get through all these. And just think, you've never been in London before! Are you *sure* you wouldn't prefer to stay a little longer—with the Colonel's sister? She would be delighted to have you stay . . . such a nice house, a large one, in Mayfair. It would be no trouble, I do assure you."

"Everyone is most kind," I said. "But there is a lot to attend to in Jerez. I don't like to be away from my children for too long—especially now that Mr. Fletcher has just left." It was, of course, a fiction. I was urgently needed in Jerez for nothing. There was nothing María Luisa could not see to. The Marquesa's distant eye was on the household, and a new tutor had been engaged, again a relative of one of the sherry shippers, this time a Scot. The only thing I longed to return to was the ongoing work of the vineyards, and that was denied me. But the honor of Jerez and the family demanded that I should not seem to have too much free time.

"I shall stay just a few days, so I think it is best if I stay here at the hotel."

"And I shall make sure Charlotte sees something of London," Richard said. "How can she go home and confess to her children that she hasn't seen the Tower? She's been to Buckingham Palace, but she has to see the changing of the guard. There are presents to buy her sons . . ."

That was the first time I knew that Richard intended to stay on with me after the Saunderses had gone. The champagne suddenly came to life. Through a kind of blur I heard the Colonel saying something about my sons coming to school in England. "Must come and visit the regiment," he said. "Very glad to show them around. Who knows . . . one of them might take a fancy to join. Grandsons of the Marqués de Santander, aren't they? Now there's a great name to be remembered from the Peninsular War. . . ." The hunger for tradition was strong. But I knew that if it was the choice of the Marquesa to thrust one of my sons into the British army it would be into a regiment much grander than my father's. I smiled at the Colonel over the champagne. And my heart was alight with the thought that I should be with Richard for at least a few days. The luncheon party took on a rosy glow; I was almost able to forget the somberness of the scene that morning at the palace. It was a time to live—even if just for a few days.

I wore the Marquesa's jewels again that evening to the Spanish Embassy. I greeted those guests who should have been so greeted in very passable Spanish, giving them their correct titles, getting around the intricacies of the Spanish names. The Ambassador seemed pleased. He was an old friend, he said, and very distantly related to the Marquesa de Pontevedra, and that she had sent, in me, a most welcome ambassadress for Jerez. I wasn't sure if he meant the town or the wine. But whichever, the report would be favorable, I knew. I wanted it to be favorable for my sons, for my mother, for María Luisa. I saw many eyes on me that evening and I knew that the ten years since I had left Clonmara had changed me in a subtle fashion. I would never have my mother's beauty, but maturity had brought its own grace. And most of all I saw Richard's eyes upon me, and remembered he had loved the gauche girl by the seashore, the girl in her dew-wet gown in the rose garden. He had loved me without emeralds and diamonds.

And I knew that I would wait no longer to give him that physical love that we both hungered for. The hours of that splendid evening passed with aching slowness as I did everything that politeness demanded. I talked, and I didn't remember a word I said. I was complimented many times and the words meant nothing. All I knew was that Richard's eyes were upon me, and that we promised each other that when it was all ended, however many hours more we must wait, after ten years of loving we would finally give ourselves to each other.

Colonel and Mrs. Saunders bade me good night, and good-by, at the door of my suite. Richard had remained downstairs to smoke a cigar. The Saunderses would leave by an early train tomorrow. I must come again to England very soon, they said. I would be the welcome guest of the regiment at any time I chose, and the Colonel's sister, who had been a guest at the Embassy that evening, would be delighted to have me stay with her in London. I said my thanks, many times over, and was not impatient. After ten years there was no need to begrudge a few minutes more. I found myself inviting the Saunderses to Jerez, and then was horrified at the thought of revealing our true poverty. I was growing like a Spaniard, I thought, and it was this that I first said, laughingly, to Richard when he came.

He smiled. "You're more than halfway there, Charlie. You've got a strange sternness about you. You've got their dignity. You've caught some of their best qualities. And even asking the Saunderses is their sort of hospitality.

365

They can give everything, their last real, their last peseta, with supreme grace. And as for the rest, well, you're Irish, and a mad Blodmore. . . ."

"But we're both Blodmores, and at this moment there is no such thing as madness. There is only the inevitable good sense of something too long delayed. Richard, my love . . . It's almost worth having waited, because now I know what I have. I have you. I can love you as a woman, not a girl. Not an ignorant, trembling girl on the shore, or in the rose garden. Spain taught me that also. . . ."

I laid aside the tiara and unclasped the necklace. I put Amelia's great diamond aside, taking time to look at it and remember her. I remembered her anguished words. "Carlota, I am still a virgin." I was not a virgin, had not been when I married. But I was a new and a different woman when I lay in Richard's arms. We made love as if we had all the years before us. There was no haste, no desperate urgency, but the climax was an explosion of joy and sweetness. Parts of the few memories we had were shared in those moments—the wildness of the race by the shore mingling with the faint sadness of the rose garden. There was the assuaging of the great longing that days of Doñana had brought forth. I traveled the journey from a young girl to a woman in Richard's loving that night. I was reborn and renewed by his body that night. It was the first time, in loving, that I had known the spirit as well as the body. I gained, and grew. I woke, better, older, wiser, infinitely happy, in Richard's arms, as the first sound of the mingled traffic of the motors and the horses' hoofs began in the street below.

4

A week later Richard saw me off on the P. & O. liner from Southampton. It had been a week on which I must feed for the rest of my life, and even a few hours away from him the hunger was growing again.

I had gone sight-seeing in London only because he had

insisted on my having something to tell my children; I had bought presents for everyone. I had had the photograph taken for my mother. I had accepted the most important of the invitations from the sherry families, for it would not do to arrive back in Jerez and have seemed to have snubbed them. It seemed right that Richard was my escort; he was accepted as such. Perhaps there was talk about us because of Elena's absence, but if there was I did not care. I had done without for too long; I could not let the concern for convention eat away at the precious hours we had together. He lay in my bed each night, and I cursed the coming of the dawn, the sounds of the city waking.

"I love you, Charlie," he said each time as he left me. And then, "Don't go back to Jerez."

I thought about what he asked, but never seriously. Not to return to Jerez would be to abandon my children to the Marquesa, for I knew she would make sure that I never saw them again. My mother would be alone with María Luisa. Richard could not return to Clonmara, or his own sons. It was too great a price, and I could not ask him to pay it, nor could I pay it myself. It was too great a burden to place on our love. I knew I was reckless in my love for him, but I was not quite mad.

"Good-by, Richard," I said in the cabin of the steamer in Southampton, and I was ready to accept that it was the end.

"I'll come to Jerez," he said.

"Don't. It wouldn't be like this. We would never be together. Why do you want to make it harder?" and then I stopped his next objection by kissing him. "Go now—please go. I don't want to come on deck. I couldn't bear to see you standing on the dock and the water growing wider between us. You have always been a figure on another shore for me. . . ."

A figure on another shore. I counted over our times together as the ship plowed on through rough seas to Gibraltar. A feeling of frightening emptiness had overtaken me. I was no longer brave as I stared out to the Atlantic horizon. As we neared Cádiz I remembered us walking the dunes at Doñana, I remembered sharing the boat as we crossed the river each day. Pitifully little I had to remember, and yet I had had the whole man. A bond between the years and the events they held had been welded. We had been one flesh, and now we had to go on alone. The rock of Gibraltar thrust itself up. I was returning; the slow cycle of my life would begin again. I felt it reach out, and I could not resist. There were other things beside loving, though in those moments I wondered, in a panic-stricken way, if I could make them enough. And then I shut the thought and the memory of Richard into that separate compartment it had occupied for these last ten years. I would have to make whatever there was enough; it would have to be sufficient, because there was nothing else.

The presence of the Marquesa waited on the dock as we berthed. She had sent her very latest acquisition, a Bentley motorcar, and an English chauffeur, to collect me. Her hand was there, and I was under it once more. The illusion that I had ever been free to make a choice of not returning had been only that—a dreaming illusion.

CHAPTER EIGHT

1

The hurt grew less as I saw and embraced my children; the hunger was still there, but they gave me food of a different sort. I knew from the way they clung to me that my absence had been real to them; for a time they forgot to ask for their presents. I saw the look that lighted my mother's face, a brief return of the old beauty, as she emerged into the courtyard to greet me. María Luisa pressed me to her bony chest. "We have missed you, querida." From such things my comfort came.

Half the town seemed to file through our house in the next few weeks. I had to tell the story of the palace, the regiment, the sight-seeing over and over. I did not try to hide the fact that Richard Blodmore had been there. I let it be thought, though I did not say, that the Saunderses had been in London with us all through the visit. "The Colonel's sister lives there. Elena was unable to come." Half lies, but necessary. I brought greetings from the London partners to many of the sherry shippers. There was a pleasant round of the bodegas, to sit in the salas de

369

degustación, sampling their sherries and telling them of the reception at the Spanish Embassy, delivering the messages from their business associates. There was no strict need for it, of course. These people exchanged letters all the time. But it was an enjoyable courtesy. I took my mother with me and saw her pleasure in getting dressed up, but noting how slipshod that dressing had become, rather wild and disarrayed, like her hair. She was heroically careful about the numbers of copitas she drank on these occasions; the salas de degustación at the bodegas were notoriously generous with their hospitality.

I drove in person with Andy to Sanlúcar to return the Marquesa's jewels. She received me at once, and ordered tea to be brought. It was a fine day, so the long windows that looked down on the Guadalquivir were open; the sun poured into the room. The river traffic up to Seville was busy. It had always fascinated me to think that the gold and silver from the Americas had flowed into Spain at this point. The Marquesa in her black dress, her face in profile to the light, could have come from the seventeenth century, when the riches of the Indies had passed beneath these walls on the way to Seville. Perhaps her ancestors had sat in the same place and calculated what wealth those ships held that was theirs.

"You have done well," she said. "I have excellent reports from our Ambassador."

"Then there is no need to tell you more. You already know everything that has happened."

She turned her face, and her lips twisted into a thin smile. "There are a few details I am not acquainted with. It matters that we were well represented. You should, however, have been more discreet with Richard Blodmore. I do not care for my godchildren to be associated with any scandal."

"There is no scandal to be associated with," I said. I wondered how far her influence went. It would not have been beyond her to have arranged to pay the servants at Brown's Hotel to report to her. She had a mind which thought of such things. "It was pleasant to have Richard's company. Otherwise I was completely among strangers."

"Quite so." She poured China tea and handed the cup to me.

"I have brought back the jewels. They were much admired."

"So I heard. And Don Luis gave you a ring that belonged to Amelia."

"No. It was a loan. Just to be worn as I wore your tiara. I did not like to refuse him. Amelia and I were close."

"Do not get too close to Don Luis. He is not the man for you. It is possible, in time, that I may find the man for you. But it takes time."

I got to my feet. *"Find* the man for me! You are mistaken, Marquesa. If there is another man, I will find him."

She soothed me with a wave of her hand. "You must, by now, understand how these things are done in Spain. You are poor, widowed, with three children and a mother who only by the greatest charity can be called eccentric. It takes time, and a great deal of thought, to find the right husband for you—"

"How dare you! If I never have a husband, I swear he will not come by arrangement."

She turned fully, and now her aging face showed itself in a full smile. "That is what we cannot get from our young women in Spain. One demands that they obey their elders, and so the spirit to disobey is a rare commodity. You have it. You have given it to your children. It is something to treasure . . . to admire. And yet difficult to sell."

"Sell! You don't think I'm in the market for selling!"

"Your children are my godchildren. *That* is for selling if one chooses."

"I do not choose. Can't I make you understand? *I* will choose for myself."

That cunning smile reappeared; she seemed to be pleased, a rare event. "Yes, you are good. The trip away from Jerez has developed you even more. You are good at the task you have set yourself. There is much to be discussed—"

"Discussed? There is nothing you and I have to say to each other on this subject, Marquesa. If such a situation would arise, *I* shall decide. If I ever marry again, I will marry the man I choose."

She nodded. "Well for you that you can afford to be so independent. Do not count on my agreement, or my support, however dear my godchildren are to me. Think of your household. Think of your demented mother. Think of your children. Even . . . think of that miserable old maid, María Luisa. They are all better for my help and protection. Think well before you reject it."

I started to walk down the long room. Her voice arrested me. "Oh, and you may take the jewels. You have worn them well, and with credit. Take them!"

I walked back the length of the room. I thought of all that the sale of them might have given us, of all the things we needed, and would need. "In the sort of future you paint for me there will be little need for such adornment." I swept the jewel case off the table and as it spilled open the sun caught the bright lights of the tiara and necklace. "I am alone. I alone will make my decisions. Jewels do not buy me."

I walked out. I traveled back to Jerez with Andy, wondering what I was to do, wondering how I was to act. I had spurned a powerful ally. I had antagonized a woman who could be a powerful enemy. I was truly alone.

And it was the first day that I had been absolutely certain that I was pregnant.

2

I waited until after the bodega closed before going to Don Luis' house. I had sent no message that I was coming, so took the chance that he would be there, and alone. There had been no opportunity to return Amelia's ring, except when we had been in public, and I could not do that. He had visited us at the Plaza de Asturias, and I had seen him also in the sala de degustación at the bodega, but these meetings had been formal. There was so much more to say, to tell. My wearing of Amelia's ring had been only a symbol of our friendship—a friendship that had seemed to deepen despite the separation forced on us by Carlos' death. We had shared the horror of that night; it had forged a bond that nothing now would break. I wanted to tell Luis the things about the journey to England that could be told to no one else. I wanted to tell him what I had learned of my father, and I wanted to tell him about Richard Blodmore.

I had Andy harness up the little governess cart which the Marquesa had presented to Juan, and it was Juan's pony I used. Andy didn't like my going off by myself once darkness had fallen, but I told him I would be back in time for supper. It was better to go openly to Luis' house than try to hide in the darkness of the landau. I set off in the scented dusk to his house on the edge of the town. The big iron gates were open and lamps lighted. The night watchman saw my arrival and, remembering me as Doña Amelia's friend, greeted me warmly. Yes, Don Luis was at home, and alone. Don Luis would undoubtedly be happy to see me. It was good, he said, to have a visit from Doña Carlota again, and he hoped it would be more often now. He knew about my journey to England, and perhaps someday I would show him the great medal the English King had given my father. I promised I would, and I imagined he expected it would be something like the great jeweled orders that the Spanish grandees were given. It would be a disappointment for him to see that simple cross on its mauve ribbon in its plain box.

Luis greeted me warmly but a trifle shyly. The constraint placed on our friendship had taken its toll. He led me through the rooms that looked just as they had when Amelia was there, except that the touch of the fresh flowers she had loved was missing. All was polished and shining, but the rooms had a faint air of disuse. About to take me to the drawing room, Luis change his mind.

"No—come to my study. It's about the only room I spend time in now." Here his desk had papers spread across it, and a small pile of books; another package of books just unwrapped from their brown paper had come from Seville. There was a smell of cigar smoke in the air. There were many books in glass-fronted mahogany cases. I realized I had never been in this room before, and it reminded me strongly of the library at Clonmara. Without ringing for a servant, Luis himself brought a decanter and glasses from a side table.

"You would prefer a fino, I think," he said, indicating the sherry.

"I . . . I think I would like some brandy," I said. His eyebrows raised a trifle, but he made no comment, just brought another decanter.

"Now tell me . . ." he invited. "It was good of you to come especially to see me."

"To you of all people." I raised my glass to him, and then drank. "You used not to be so formal."

He nodded, and shrugged. "I used to see you more often."

"Yes," I admitted. "So much changed so quickly." I brought out the ring from my purse. "I enjoyed wearing it. I thought of Amelia. It wasn't like wearing the Marquesa's jewels. You probably heard about the jewels . . . ?"

He nodded. "There is little that's not talked about in this town." He touched the ring slowly but left it where I had placed it on the desk. "So, Carlota, you went to England. . . . It has changed you. You are older."

I found myself talking about the events of those days as they really had been. I told him about the regiment, and the revelations about my father that perhaps Colonel Saunders now regretted making. I told him about the sadness at the palace. And then, finally, after I had had my second brandy, I told him about Richard Blodmore.

He kept nodding as I talked. With a gesture he asked permission to smoke a cigar. I kept on talking as I re-called it all, things I had told him before—the time when we had first met at Clonmara, the time at Doñana, and now, the time when we finally became lovers.

The smoke swirled about him. "So this is the greatest change I see. I see an older woman, someone who is more

374

beautiful. You have the look of a woman fulfilled. I am glad Richard Blodmore has been able to give you that. But you are alone again. And being alone is harder now that you have learned what the sharing is like."

I got to my feet. I could make no answer to that. "I think I must go. It has been good of you to listen, Luis. There was no one else I could talk to. After seeing the Marquesa this morning, I had to talk. You were the only one. I was angry—very angry. I regretted allowing her to dictate how my life has been these last years. I regretted listening to her advice that I should not see you alone any more—for fear of gossip. And now she threatens to arrange some marriage for me. *That* I will not allow. I wanted to come to see you to return Amelia's ring, but I also needed to see you because it is the first step in making my own life. My children may suffer for my independence, but I hope I'll be able to make up to them in some fashion. There are many problems . . . there will be more. But I must take the solution of them into my own hands. I cannot live any longer in the shadow of the Marquesa and Don Paulo. That part of my life is over."

He had not risen when I did, as if he were reluctant to let me go. Once again he touched the ring lying on the desk. "But you are alone . . ."

I smiled faintly. "If you call the household I have about me being alone . . . children, my mother, María Luisa. Not so alone, really." Suddenly, without asking his permission, I reached for the brandy decanter and poured for myself. The decanter rattled against the glass as I tried to control the trembling of my hands. "And ever less alone, Luis. I am going to have Richard Blodmore's child."

I sat down again and watched his face, tried to read its expression through the haze of smoke, the half-closed eyes. For a time he didn't look at me directly—his long, thin fingers played with the ring as if he were fascinated by the refraction of light thrown out from its heart.

He spoke very slowly. "Will you go away? Will you go to England until the child is born? Does Blodmore know?"

I shook my head. "None of those things. If I were to go

away it would be to keep the birth a secret. My child would be given to someone else to bring up. I could never allow that. Not my child—and Richard's. No, I—and the family—will have to face it out here. In time Richard will come to know of its birth, and he must know that it is his child. I will beg him to do nothing. I wish he would never know, but he will hear, and he will guess. Perhaps the town will guess. I will meet all that when I come to it. It will do the child and the family no good to have Richard's marriage broken—for him to come and live with us when we can never be married so long as Elena lives." Now my voice also trembled a little. "Brave talk, Luis. I have only known since this morning. Dr. Ramírez confirmed it. I don't know how brave I'll be later on. I don't know what pressures the Marquesa may bring against me to take my sons from me. Through Don Paulo she might be able to take them from me because I will be judged an immoral woman. Can the courts do that in Spain? Can the Church? All this, no doubt, I'll discover. I have some months yet to think it out. Before I let that happen I will take us all out of here. . . . That could be a rash movement, since we have nowhere to go, but it may be necessary. Perhaps I believe myself braver than I am. I have time to think about it all . . . there are some months yet before others will know. You are the only person I have burdened with the knowledge."

He leaned back, and his face was almost beyond the range of the light thrown by the lamp on the desk. The lines in it seemed deeply etched. His mouth twisted, and the scar of Carlos' making showed white.

"If it is your decision not to go to Richard Blodmore, I have something I can offer you, Carlota."

I held up my hand in dismissal. "No money, Luis. I have not come for money. I came to talk, because I cannot yet lay this on María Luisa, and certainly not on my mother. I have not asked your advice. It is impossible for anyone to offer me advice when I must make this decision alone. I cannot—"

He silenced me by lifting his hand. He leaned forward

and his face came back into the light. It wore a look of infinite sadness, a look of pain.

"I can offer you and your child one thing, Carlota. I can offer my name—and therefore my protection. No court in the land—no pressure from whatever source—can take your children from you if I stand beside you—as your husband."

I shook my head. "You are kind beyond belief. Did you think I was hoping for that? I would not insult you, Luis. You are my friend—"

He shrugged. "Perhaps you see it as an insult to you. You, a beautiful, passionate young woman married to someone like me—someone who for a long time has been only half a man. I cannot be your lover, Carlota. You probably know that, as half the town seems to know or guess it. Knows it and laughs—pities me. I have borne the laughter and the scorn for a long time. I have been twice married and have no child. All I can do for you is to stand at the head of your household and offer you the protection which that gives. It is not enough, I see. You throw away the chance of some other marriage. A young woman has the right to think of a love, of being loved as she should be. *That* could not be my role."

"Luis, you do me the greatest honor . . ."

"But you do not accept. . . ." Again the bitter smile, the shrug that sought to cover the hurt. "Well, it was an idea. . . ."

I sat and looked at him for a long time. Then I stretched out my hand and took the ring again. I put it back on the little finger where I had worn it in London. "I accept. Let them say what they want to say. You gave me the ring before I left. Many people knew of it. It was your token of love. They will say we were lovers before I left. The child is yours, Luis. Who is to say different? Who can prove different? The town gossiped about us when Carlos was killed. They wondered. Well, let them assume that the gossip they made then had a basis in truth. Let them think back to that time. Perhaps you had bad luck with two wives who were barren, but not with me. The child will be yours, Luis. The child will be *yours!*"

A strange, dawning light was in his face; some color came to it, almost a look of expectancy. "Blodmore?— and what of Blodmore?"

"Richard shall never know. It is *your* child, Luis. I will swear it, before him or before anyone else. No one but you shall have a claim on it."

I moved around the desk and went to him. Quite naturally I found myself on my knees before him, my face pressed against his knees. When finally I looked up at his again I saw his face distorted through my tears.

"I thought I could do it alone. But I am grateful—"

He put his fingers against my lips. "There must be no such talk. We make a bargain, you and I, Carlota. You gave and bring to me the sort of wealth I cannot bestow on you. Let there be no talk of gratitude. We have made bargains in the past, and you always paid the interest on your debts. I trusted you, and I placed my trust well."

"The interest I can pay on this debt will be my fidelity, Luis. Let there be gossip, but you will have a true wife. And Richard Blodmore shall never know. Let him hate me, if he must, for rushing back to the arms of another man. If he thinks that way, then that is how he must think. I shall never tell him different. It is between you and me, Luis."

He cradled my face between his hands. "I fear I may shut you in a prison."

"Can there be a prison if one does not make it so? Can there be a prison built of love and tenderness and fidelity? What do I bring you? Only burdens. You make no easy choice for a wife, Luis. I bring you only a dowry of problems. But I can give what love can give. I can give you companionship by your hearth and at your table. We can talk of the vineyards again, as we once used to talk. . . . We can make a marriage of sharing."

He raised me to my feet. "You must never kneel to me again, Carlota. You do my house honor. The burdens you bring have the weight of a feather. The dowry you bring is beyond price. It is not something that could be written into a marriage contract."

I felt the press of his lips on my forehead. Then suddenly he was tugging at my hand, pulling me eagerly like a young man.

"Come, I'll order the carriage, and we'll go at once to tell your mother! And María Luisa! Through her the rest of the town will know very soon. Tomorrow I will inform Don Paulo that you have done me the honor of agreeing to become my wife. We will publish the banns . . ." He was running along the shining, deserted hall, calling to his principal manservant. "No, we will not wait to publish banns. These things can always be arranged. In a few days you will be my wife. Why should we wait . . . ?" It was a cry of happiness from him that almost broke my heart.

3

We were married in the Collegiate Church five days later with full ceremony. It was true that everything could be arranged if enough pressure was brought. Although very few people had been formally invited, half of those we knew in Jerez seemed to turn out to our nuptial Mass. The two principal witnesses who signed the register were Don Paulo and the Marquesa de Pontevedra.

Afterwards the carriages rolled up, unbidden, to Luis' house, which was now my home. It seemed, with true Jerez sagacity, the servants had expected such a thing, and food was produced and the wine was plentiful and well chilled. The Marquesa stood near us, greeting guests, but whenever she looked at me there was a kind of controlled rage behind her impassiveness. I had taken more than a small step beyond her control, and I think that she feared that my sons might slip from her influence. So she sought to exert it once more by seeming to have not only fully condoned this marriage but actively encouraged it. The about-face had been swift and complete, and, as was usual, Don Paulo had not opposed her will.

The occasion had a charming informality about it. Since no one had been invited, it was all right for everyone to come, as if paying an unexpected call. Protocol was not observed. Children came with their parents and romped through the rooms with my sons; young girls tried to escape the eyes of their mothers and aunts and vanish into the garden with the young men. It was a boisterous, almost rowdy affair, improvised, but wonderfully successful. While he was being congratulated by someone, Luis accidentally spilled wine all down my blue dress, one of the new ones I had worn in London, but which had never been seen before in Jerez. I looked at the ruin of my dress and shrugged. "Never mind—I was feeling rather hot." Then we laughed helplessly together, like old friends, or new lovers. The town looked on, and the rumors that had gone around at the time of Carlos' death were revived. The feeling grew, I thought, that this was no new arrangement but one of long standing. I had, they would think, waited a decent length of time since being widowed, and then married the man I had wanted all along. I took my cue from the expression in the faces around us as they watched us laugh and drink together. I would do this, and much more, to make everyone believe that this was truly Luis' child. If we could not be lovers, at least it would be known only to ourselves. The scorn and contempt Luis had suffered would be gone. This would have to be my one gift to him.

It was an almost unbelievable joy to learn that there was something else I could give. I undressed that night in the room adjoining Luis' which Amelia had used. I felt comfortable there, not a usurper; Amelia and I had been too close friends for her to have begrudged me this place, and I looked at the things she had used with affection. I felt mellow with the wine, happy, tired but relaxed. I had dismissed the maid who had wanted to fuss over me. I smiled at the image in the mirror as I brushed my hair. Outside the cicadas sang.

Without awkwardness I went then to Luis' room. He was already in bed, a book, which he was not reading, held in his hands.

"Carlota?" He half sat up. "Is there something wrong?"

"What should be wrong?" I kicked off my slippers and perched cross-legged on the bed. "I just felt like gossiping. What a good day it's been. . . . I've laid my blue dress with the wine stain on it away in tissue paper. I'll laugh every time I think of it. What a good party it was!—Jerez never went to a wedding quite like this one before."

"There never has been a wedding like this before. It was the most muddled party I ever saw, and the best."

I took the book from his hands. "Don't go to the bodega tomorrow, Luis. Let's take a picnic to the vineyards. I can sit in your vineyard house and look across at Las Ventanas Verdes and remember all the hours you spent there instructing me in caring for the vines. Remember how Amelia named it? Remember how she came there only a few days before she died? She loved it too, Luis."

Then I added quietly, "We do not need to remind each other of the night Carlos died. You have spent some of the worst hours of my life with me, Luis—and some of the best." I moved up the bed and slipped beneath the sheets, placing my head against his shoulder. I felt his body go rigid. "Oh, Luis, hold me. Just hold me like a child. I feel safe with you. No need to be brave any more, because you will take care of me. We have been such friends, and now we need never be parted."

"Querida . . . querida . . ." His body relaxed against mine; one arm slipped beneath me, while the other stroked my hair. "We will go anywhere you want. A real journey, perhaps. Not just to the vineyards, but a real journey together. You have had so few treats in your life, Carlota. Let me spoil you a little, as if you were my child. The way I hold you, as if you were my beloved child—my dearest companion."

"Your wife, Luis." I placed his hand against my breast.

What he had thought impossible was happening. I felt the sweat break on him, I felt the surge of his manhood against me. We clasped each other, but not like children. It was over swiftly, because for Luis it could not long be sustained, but we became lovers. The marriage was a real one.

It was a fact that Luis, in his happiness, could not help proclaiming. Not that he ever spoke to anyone but myself about it, but it was self-proclaiming in the way he bore himself, the ease with which he slipped into the new relationship with me. Before all Jerez he talked of the coming child, and from his talk no one could have doubted that it was his own child he looked forward to.

María Luisa smiled and shook her head. "You have been a sly one, Charlie. You have used some magic and transformed that man. Now he acts and talks like a man, and one would think there had never been a child born in the world before."

"It is his first child, María Luisa. When a man is over fifty and has given up hope . . ."

"But two wives and no children. It does not look so well for him."

I shrugged. "The first wife may have been barren. Amelia was ill before she married him. What does the town say, María Luisa?"

"The town thinks you are a seductress, and a shameless hussy—and a very clever woman. And Don Luis thinks you are the Madonna. And he struts like a man. For the first time he struts like a man."

I smiled, and cradled the baby growing in my womb. "That is good. That is very good."

We did not make the wedding journey Luis had suggested. I wanted to savor the first utterly peaceful period I had ever known in Jerez. My children had settled down happily in Luis' house. My mother and María Luisa stayed on at the Plaza de Asturias. My mother glowed in a kind of reflected happiness. "I will not be a silly old woman spoiling your time with Luis. You should be able to sit at your own table at nights, talk as you and Luis have always been able to talk. María Luisa and I do very well where we have always been. We are two old ones together, and we suit each other."

So I left it that way. I stayed quiet as the summer advanced towards another harvest. I stayed in the shade of Luis' garden, watching the swans on the lake, remem-

bering as if it were a far-off dream the first night I had
come to the party here, and Carlos had kissed me, and
Don Paulo had watched us. Sometimes I seemed to hear
the haunting flamenco music of the gypsy woman, the
mournful guitar. I thought of these things only occasionally as my children played about me or did their lessons
with the quiet young Scot, Ian Frazer. Perhaps the memories were more persistently invoked because Martín
seemed more serious and more determined than most
other young Spaniards to develop his evident skill with a
guitar. He sat with me very often in the garden and
played while I waited for my child. I tried not to think
of Richard Blodmore. I thought of my baby, and of Luis.
I wanted it to be his baby. Despite my love for Richard,
if I could have willed it, this would indeed have been
Luis' child.

But when our son was born, no man could have made
it more his own. The child had the light greenish eyes of
the Blodmores, as the other three did; he had the Blodmore cast of feature. My mother smiled over the cradle.
"He looks like my father. Will you call him Luis?"

"No," Luis said. "I think he could be called after Carlota's father. We shall call him Tomás."

When she was alone with me María Luisa adjusted her
glasses and examined him closely. "All Blodmore," she
pronounced. "He will grow up looking just like you and
your mother. Looks as if he'll have red hair, too—when
he gets a bit more." She gave a wicked little chuckle.
"And the town is saying that you snared Luis by being
able to give him a child. They do not believe this is
a premature baby, any more than they were deceived by
Juan. They remember the ring Luis gave you before you
went to England. They see everything, these people, and
forget nothing."

"Let them remember—it can do no harm." I said it
thankfully; Luis' reputation was safe. Let them think I
had seduced him. Let them think anything so long as they
did not think that Richard Blodmore was Tomás' father.
I knew I could trust absolutely the discretion of the Marquesa, if indeed she did know the truth of my relations

with Richard that brief week in the English spring. It was in her own interest to keep the established position, if she wanted to keep her own position with my children. If she wished to remain "Tía Isabel" she must accept this new situation. We were no longer poor and friendless. She was less needed, and so her own need grew.

She came, having for once announced her arrival and, quite humbly for her, suggested that she should again be godmother. I felt myself stiffen, and the words of refusal formed. But Luis merely smiled; he was always smiling these days. "Why not, Marquesa? You might as well have them all under your wing." I bit my tongue against the words that wanted to come. It was true that Luis had no close women relatives and that the Marquesa was indeed a distant cousin; there seemed no reason to exclude the Marquesa now from the position she held with the other children. I realized that it would appear better if this child did not seem different from the others. Anything that bound us together as a family was important, more for Luis' sake than my own. My independence had been stated the morning I crashed the Marquesa's jewels to the floor. It was possible that she believed I had known then that I would marry Luis, and that had been the basis for my display of arrogant confidence. If she had suspicions about Richard Blodmore, let them remain just that—suspicions. So long as the child continued to show such a strong resemblance to my mother and me, then no one could say for certain that he was not the child of Luis.

I nodded towards the Marquesa. "I will agree to whatever Luis wishes."

She looked at me sharply, knowing that never in the years of marriage to Carlos had I ever played the role of the submissive wife, although I had had to submit. So much had changed in the years of our unequal relationship. I was no longer a frightened young girl, and she had come, at last, to ask rather than command the favor of being godmother to my child.

So once again Isabel, Marquesa de Pontevedra, stood at the baptismal font in the Collegiate Church, an aging woman, but still erect and formidable, and swore, in the name of my son Tomás to renounce the Devil and all his works. I could have wept at the sight of Luis' face as the sacrament was administered; the mingled pride and love gave him a strange and moving beauty, his humped, uneven shoulders were transformed to an ascetic attribute, not a near deformity. And Tomás lusty screams as the water touched him gave the promise of rude health. Luis himself held the child for almost an hour at the reception which followed the baptism. The long lace robe flowed over his arms. It was a very unusual thing for a man to do in Spain; they loved and were proud of their children, but babies were women's business. But it was only with reluctance that he surrendered Tomás into Nanny's arms when she protested that the noise and excitement around the child were too much. Luis would have gone himself and laid the child in the flounced and frilled cradle if I had not held him back. "Your friends want to drink to your son's health with you. . . ."

"Ah, yes . . ." But his eyes followed the child carried away in Nanny's arms.

4

It was January when Tomás was born. By February I was able to ride out every day to visit the vineyards, to watch the work as I had loved to do. Luis owned a number of vineyard houses, but the one I went to most frequently was the one lived in by Mateo and his family on the rise opposite Las Ventanas Verdes. I often walked the slope to visit Concepción and Antonio. This could not now be forbidden me; although it was owned by Don Paulo, I was the wife of his partner in the bodega. Concepción and Antonio always greeted me enthusiastically, bringing out the best wine, urging a few tapas on me. I promised I would bring Tomás to show them when the weather was a little warmer. "When the blossom comes on the vine," I said. The evidence was plain that the Marquesa had kept her word of help to them and their children in return for their silence about the night Carlos died. It was there in small ways, but ways that counted. The roof over the whole house had been mended, the range in the kitchen was new, water could now be pumped directly into the kitchen, an almost unbelievable luxury for Concepción; piles of wood were heaped about the courtyard so that they could be lavish with fires. More important for them, their two eldest sons had been sent to live with a family in Jerez and were receiving instruction, along with other boys, from a curate. They would be able to read and write and add columns of figures, Concepción told me. They were assured of a place among the clerical staff in the bodega; that was a promise made for all their sons. If they showed ability, they could rise further. "They will not be field workers, my sons," Concepción said. "In good times and hard times there will be work for them at the bodega. They are even learning some English so in time they will be able to write the letters necessary to be sent. Vicente shows some ability with French, the curate says. He will go far." The boys walked the six miles every Sunday to visit their parents and their younger brothers and sisters. But it was not the same as it used to be. "It is natural, is it not, Doña Carlota? What interest can Antonio and I hold for them? They are good sons, but we grow apart. The Marquesa has promised a small dowry for the girls, so they will all find husbands. We will be secure in our old age. . . ."

That much Carlos' death, and the manner of his death, had brought them. No sudden riches, but a secure old age, with the children slightly ashamed of the parents.

Sometimes I would go to the Plaza de Asturias and join my mother as Andy drove her out to the hacienda to ride Balthasar. The foals of Half Moon and Balthasar had reached the point at which the best of them were now producing their own progeny. It was becoming a notable line, and the foals now brought good prices. The management of the prices, the expenses, and the stud book was something that fell to María Luisa. My mother cared only for her "darlings," as she called them. The buyers were as carefully selected as the sires and the

386

brood mares. She had been known to refuse a good sale because she did not trust the qualities of the man who wished to buy. "Some people are not fit to have a cat, much less a horse . . . or a child. Let him go elsewhere." María Luisa would sigh over the loss of a good sale, but my mother would never be shifted. "She is right," Luis said. "Why should she not be careful? Why should she not see that they are well placed? A horse that is well treated gives of his best, and the reputation of the stud benefits. Your mother has as good an eye for a horse as any man in Andalucía, and more than that, she has a strange influence. She is a calming force among the mares. To see her walk those paddocks among the mares and foals is a revelation. They seem to breed easily and well because she is there. They drop their foals easily." She had an uncanny knack of seeming to know just the hour when a mare was at her time. She would have Andy harness up in the middle of the night to drive her to the hacienda. If it was a difficult birth she was there on her knees in the straw beside the mare. More often the mare slipped her foal with ease, and the little creature on its spindly legs was out at pasture with its dam the next morning.

A modest prosperity now sat on the house in the Plaza de Asturias. There was the growing money which the sale of the horses brought, there was the war widow's pension from the British government, there was the money from the bodega. And that money no longer had to support me and my children. "We are, in a manner of speaking, rich," María Luisa said to me. "That is, we are not beggars, scraping along from loan to loan. Don Ramón has us posted in black in his ledgers. He pours us generous copitas when we visit the bank."

"But he always has."

She nodded. "You're right. Even the way your mother is now, she still fascinates him. He can't forget what she was once. He's growing old. He wants to remember the best things."

In a strange way my mother had carved her own place in the society of Jerez. Some might say she was mad, but then they quickly recalled that the accident which had

387

caused her madness had come about when she saved the life of Carlos. Others, with more kindness, simply described her as eccentric. She was a woman who drank too much at times but had a way with horses and children. Her strange habits were overlooked and forgiven, as if she were one of those who had been touched by God.

On the mornings when I went with my mother to the hacienda I would leave her when she returned to the Plaza de Asturias and go on to the bodega to wait there for Luis to be ready to come home to lunch. I knew it pleased him when I did this. He had grown rather proprietorial of me, showing off just a little that I was his woman, a young and good-looking woman who enjoyed the society of men, and yet waited patiently for him to finish his business and be ready for the late lunch and the siesta. I always waited for him in the sala de degustación. This was always the liveliest place in the bodega, where friends and customers of the firm were entertained and invited to "taste." When the serious business of ordering had been done, the men came here for their copitas. I heard many languages, and I often joined the talk when the visitors were English. It was a world of men, mainly, but I was accepted as if I had slipped in through a back door.

Another thing which gave me pleasure, and which I often did before going to the sala de degustación, was to walk through the bodega itself, the tall, vaulted buildings with the tiers of dark butts, which I thought, though I did not say it because it might have sounded blasphemous, were more beautiful than the cathedrals they so strangely resembled. I loved the quiet, the smell of the damp from the earth floors, the smell of the wine. It was almost as if age had a sound of its own there. There was, of course, constant activity—wine being transferred from one scale of the solera to another, bodega workmen examining the casks, racking the wine off its lees, taking samples to be carried to the cuarto de muestras, the sampling room, to be graded by the expert "noses" of the trade. I found it soothing and interesting to walk there among the tiers of butts, sometimes stopping to talk to the capataz, the foreman, or some of the workers, pleased that my Spanish was quite adequate to the task. And how they loved to talk, to explain. I got to know the foremen well, and they would produce the venencia and the glasses for me to do my own smelling and tasting. Perhaps they thought it unusual to see a woman there alone, interested, asking questions, but as the wife of Don Luis I could do as I pleased. One day, at one of these informal, unarranged smelling and tasting sessions, I found that a silence had fallen on the capataz. He couldn't get his tongue around the words he wanted to say; he stared past me, and I turned to see what it was that distracted him. The bulky figure of Don Paulo stood there.

"Well, have you come to take over the business as well?" he said in English. It could have been a joke, but it was not.

I shrugged. "I have some little time to wait until Luis will be ready. I like to walk in the bodega."

"Do you remember much about what I told you the first day?"

"A little. I know more about the vines. The management of the solera is new to me."

"That first day . . ." Then he stopped. That first day he had taken me through the bodega, I had met Carlos.

"Come," he said. "We will go to the sala de degustación. We will take a copa together."

I had often seen him in the sala when I waited for Luis, but never before had he himself invited me to take a copa. I hurried after him as he turned away and walked down the long aisle between the butts. Could age be mellowing that fearsome old man? Perhaps María Luisa was right in saying the old liked to remember the pleasant things.

A hush fell momentarily over the bodega members gathered in the sala when we appeared together. Old customers of course knew Don Paulo. He greeted them by lifting his hand in salute, but chose for us a small table where there were only two chairs. He called for the whole spectrum of the sherries to be brought, and glasses for each. We went from the richest oloroso, through an amontillado, to the marvelous tang of the fino. It was

389

extraordinary; I felt almost shy with him. We had never really held an ordinary conversation before, and we did not know how to talk, so we sat in silence. No one else approached, though normally the sala was a great place for socializing, for changing from one group to another, for introducing strangers, for making friends.

"And shall you give me a manzanilla, as you did the first day?" I said at last.

He called for the manzanilla, and that reminded me of Sanlúcar, where the grapes were grown. He raised his glass. "Here is a health to your new son." We tasted.

"Then my son will be of sharp and salty character, like the wine."

He stared at me a moment longer, and I was dismayed to see his aging, hooded dark eyes were bright with tears. He rose abruptly. "Good day, señora." He left the sala without a word to anyone about him. I slowly sipped the wine that had in it the taste of the sea. He had loved Carlos very much. He tried to forgive me for his death, and he had not succeeded. No doubt he feared that, with my marriage to Luis, his grandsons were being taken away from him. For the first time I felt pity for him. Beware pity, I reminded myself. He had not pitied me.

5

That spring Luis took me to the Fair in Seville. It was the first time I had ever been to that legendary event. Now Luis and I had our own *caseta,* our "little house" where we could entertain and dispense hospitality to all Luis' friends. They came from everywhere in Andalucía, and some even from Madrid. I thought it was his way of introducing me to a wider circle than I had known in Jerez. Everyone who could manage it always went to Seville to the Fair. Carlos had gone every year, staying with friends and claiming it cost him nothing. There had never been money for me to go; María Luisa had never been able to squeeze out enough to provide the new dresses. This time

I had more than I could wear. My children rode their beautiful ponies, gifts of the Marquesa, all of them, accompanied by Andy and another groom, through the passages between the casetas, wearing Andalucian dress, their saddles decorated with silver, silver on their soft boots. Juan was ten, Martín nine, Francisco eight; they were babies no longer, and would soon be young men. I was complimented on their good looks, their horsemanship, their manners. Luis talked of the day when Tomás would be old enough to join his brothers. I loved the parade of the young men on their horses, the perfectly gauged nonchalance of their horsemanship, the way their eyes went from one young girl to another, sizing them up, thinking perhaps of their looks and their dowries. The Fair at Seville each spring seemed to serve no real purpose except as a great social gathering which included all classes and every sort of person, from grandees of Spain to the lowliest gypsy. There was music and lights, horses, women, wine and food in one grand mix. I was bewildered and delighted, and also strangely tired.

Luis had planned that we should go on to visit Madrid for a few weeks before the hot weather came to the capital; the children were to go back to Jerez with their tutor, Ian Frazer. But when the Fair ended I asked for us to return with them. "I'm not feeling very well, Luis."

His face instantly clouded with concern. "What is it, querida? You are not well?" All kinds of memories of Amelia's illness must have flashed through his mind in those few seconds. "I shall bring a doctor at once."

We were alone in our sitting room. The hotel looked out over the wide beautiful avenues of the city. The Geralda dominated, as always. Seville was a place of sensuous beauty, and the orange trees truly grew on the streets. Our breakfast table had been set near the balcony, so that we watched the city slowly pick itself up after the week's mammoth celebration. I hadn't eaten anything, just sipped my coffee, and counted the few motorcars now to be seen mingled with the city's population of horses.

I slipped my hand over to touch Luis. "I have prayed, and lighted candles, as I used to do. There will be no need to call a doctor. I consulted one yesterday morning when you thought I was shopping. Luis, we are to have a child."

The expression on his face was almost painful to watch, the quick succession of joy, of fear, and then of doubt.

"Do not doubt it, Luis. Do not doubt me. I gave my promise. It is truly your child."

He buried his face in his hands and wept.

6

During that pregnancy I was guarded and cosseted as if I might break in two. At times I grew weary and impatient of Luis' concern, his hovering presence. He did everything he could to keep me either in the house or garden, and there was always a servant within call, so that I could not lift a book, or stretch for a fan, or pour a cup of tea. Luis tried to bring a nurse from Seville to be with me constantly, but I rebelled against that. He indulged me in every possible way, but there were still things forbidden to me. I was not to go to the vineyard house; the roads were too rough. It would be better if I did not go to the hacienda with my mother; I might be jostled by the mares and foals. I was sometimes sharp with him as he laid yet another stricture on me, reminding him that I had borne four healthy children, and then, very quietly, he would remind me of the miscarriage on the night Carlos died. For all his joy, he was dismayed that this pregnancy had followed so quickly after the birth of Tomás; I could not have had enough time to recover sufficiently. Seeing his face, alight with hope, and yet fighting back a terrible fear that this child also might be lost, I gave in to whatever he wanted. So much of his belief in himself as a man rested in the child that I could not deny him. But the months of waiting seemed longer and more tedious than ever before.

Something that lightened those months was the return of Edwin Fletcher. He had written and asked if he could come back as tutor to the children. "It is absurd," I said, giving the letter to Luis. "He is overqualified for such a position. He took it only as temporary work while he convalesced after he was gassed during the war. He has a brilliant mind, I believe, and there should be a great future for him. He will be wasted here . . . tutoring little boys."

"He does not seem to think so," Luis answered, tapping the pages. He read from them:

> *"England is very far from being the land fit for heroes that they promised us. I am homesick for Andalucía. I long for the sun. These winters half kill me, but there I know I shall be well. I hope I shall be able to get back my rooms with the Señoritas Hernandos Delgado. I hope Juan has not become so good a horseman that he leaves me completely behind. I miss Lady Pat. I miss you all."*

Luis recalled the coughing, the breathlessness, the fragility that no amount of Andalucian sun could cure. "Tell him to come," he said. "We should count ourselves lucky."

So he came, and now his salary was paid by Luis, not the Marquesa. He was a welcome companion for some of those months of waiting. He returned as if to a beloved place, to a beloved family, and there were presents for all of us, even for Andy, which was more than I thought he could afford, but no one could offend him by protesting. At Luis' request, he brought many books in English to stock the library shelves—not just books of scholarship, but the kind of fiction Luis thought might interest me, and help to pass the time. It was a suddenly empty house when they all, the three boys and Edwin, departed for the Marquesa's northern estates in Galicia for the worst months of the summer. "I would send you also," Luis said, "to escape the heat, if it were not for that long journey. It is too far, the trains too uncomfortable, too slow." What he did not add, but a fact that I knew, was that he feared my being out of his sight, as if the longed-for child might be snatched from him. For myself I would not have wanted to go. Even the coolness of Galicia would not make acceptable months of living under the Marquesa's eye and rule.

So I waited, with as good grace as I could muster. We did not entertain, and I did not accept invitations. Luis said the excitement, the noise, the heat of such occasions was not good for me. My mother and María Luisa came almost every day, and brought gossip of the town. I still wrote letters for my mother to Ireland. Through all the replies I searched for some mention of Richard Blodmore, but they were few.

> *Lord Blodmore,* Lady Sybil wrote, *has been very quiet since the end of the war. He does a good job as Master of the Hunt, and he's become a very successful farmer. But he's very quiet. Hard to shake a word out of him. Perhaps the effects of his injury are worse than we know. Such a shame. He used to be such a handsome man. Lady Blodmore is very dashing. . . . But we do miss you, dear Pat. How good the old times used to be at Clonmara. There never was such a man as your father. I miss him still. Perhaps it's just that I'm getting old, but nothing seems the same since the war, and this poor country is heading into such trouble. . . .*

"Yes, the old times at Clonmara," my mother sighed. "They were such good times. I wonder why anyone wants to change things? They were all right once." She saw everything in terms of the simple and indulged childhood she had had; she knew only that her father's tenants had been well treated by the standards of the times. She failed to see why it all had to tumble into the chaos that threatened. Edwin Fletcher tried to explain the complicated issues to her, the difficulties of establishing a united, but free, Ireland; but it was too much for her confused mind. She kept returning to the memories of her childhood. "We were all right then," she said.

My mother and María Luisa often came after the siesta, and at Luis' urging sometimes stayed for the evening meal. They would sit with me as I lay in the bed in what had been Amelia's room, María Luisa usually with a piece of needlework, my mother fluttering restlessly about, her concentration never focused for very long on any one subject. There had been only a few new pieces of furnishing introduced into the room since Amelia had used it. I had had the best of her collection of fans framed and they hung each side of the big gilt-framed mirror over the mantel. Her water colors of the lake and the black swans were on the wall facing the bed. I dismissed completely María Luisa's observation that it was a little morbid that I gathered the possessions of Luis' former wife about me. "Nonsense! Amelia and I were friends. It's perfectly natural. And these, in any case, she left as special gifts to me." Luis had found a beautiful Louis XIV corner cabinet, inlaid with Sévres plaques, in Seville. Here, at last, the exquisite porcelain models of the White Horses of Vienna found their showcase. They were depicted in all the classic exercises of the Haute École—piaffe, levade, courbette, pesade—all of them small masterpieces of the ceramic worker's art. They were a special delight to my mother, and she often opened the case and handled them. I was always nervous when she did this after she had had wine with lunch, but she was very careful, as gentle as she would have been with a live horse or a child. The bottom shelf of the cabinet also displayed the beautiful little gun in its marquetry box, surrounded by its silver bullets. I had never touched it since the night I killed Pepita with it. The first time the cabinet was in place, displaying its treasures, my mother clucked her tongue in disapproval when she saw the gun. "It's not been cleaned, Charlie." So next time she visited, she brought oil and cloths, and thoroughly cleaned it. "Such a pretty thing," she said admiringly. She also waxed the marquetry box, even polished the silver bullets.

"It's a pity, Lady Pat," María Luisa said, "that things in your own house don't similarly interest you. We have a few brasses that could stand your attention."

My mother pulled a face at her and laughed. "Oh, brass! What's that? We have nothing half as lovely as this. Besides, you know I always keep my own guns beautifully cleaned."

But she truly loved the White Horses, and I was tempted to give them to her, but didn't because they had come from Amelia, and Luis might have been hurt. Nor did I give her the little pistol. I no more wanted to forget Pepita than I wanted to forget Amelia.

The autumn months came, and I moved heavily now about the house, feeling grateful to obey Luis' and the doctor's instructions to rest. Through the wet months early in the winter I sat before the fire, and was often too listless to read a book. Edwin and Luis kept the children away from me for all but short periods. "They tire you, querida. Three rowdy boys . . . what can you expect?" Tomás was brought to me each day by Nanny. He was a happy baby, but too energetic for me to hold on my lap for more than a few minutes. "This one is full of sparks, Miss Charlie," Nanny said. "He'll be a bit of a handful later on. Give his brothers a run for their money. Now rest you, my lamb. You're looking tired. Come now, little Master Thomas. Kiss your mama. Look, he's worn you out, the little devil. . . ."

On a stormy night late in November, with the wind thrusting in from the sea, a month before the baby was due, I went into labor. It was not at all like the other times. This was not the intense but brief labor that had characterized the other births; it was slow, protracted, exhausting. I heard myself scream, and could not believe it was I. I saw, through a haze of sweat and pain, Luis' frightened face near mine, felt his hand clutch mine. "Courage, querida. It will come soon now." But it was agonizingly slow. More than a day passed, and the contractions went on. The doctor never left. Luis would not allow him. Another doctor came from Seville. I heard their murmured words when they thought their drugs had dulled my senses. "Another few hours we can wait, but no more. Then we must take it from her, or she may die, and the child with her."

I opened my eyes. "I can't die!" I screamed at them. "I must give Luis his son!" And then I screamed again as

396

another contraction gripped me. They were close together now. "Bear down now, there's my good lady," the nurse said. "Keep bearing down, and you'll soon have a fine child." They gave me ropes to pull on, and a cloth to clench my teeth against.

At last I heard it, the cry of a newborn child. A feeble, pitiful cry, like the mewing of a kitten. But a living cry.

Luis' daughter was tiny and fragile and beautiful. She did not, even for a few hours, have the red and rumpled look I had come to expect of all newborn infants. She was white and neat and her cry was only a feeble protest against the roughness of her journey into the world. When she was washed, Luis himself came and laid her in my arms. I had to guide the reluctant little mouth to my breast.

"She is perfectly formed, our child, querida. She is so beautiful it is hard to believe."

"I'm sorry it wasn't a son, Luis."

He smiled at me. "What foolish things you say, my Carlota. We have a beautiful daughter. She will be the queen of Andalucía."

When she finished feeding she opened her eyes wide, trying to focus, trying to gain some hold on this frighteningly harsh world into which she had been born. Her eyes were very dark, like Luis'. She was the only one of my children not born with the light greenish eyes of the Blodmores.

For a time she hovered on the edge of life, as if she had not the strength to grasp it. Her cry was a mere whimper. She was difficult to feed, and yet seemed hungry. It was torture to see how Luis hung over her cradle, hardly daring to breathe if she slept, putting out a finger tentatively to touch her tiny ones when she was awake. He would not leave her to go to the bodega. Only reluctantly would he leave her in charge of the nurse to try to get some sleep at night. He grew haggard; the scar was very white against the gray of his skin.

Then one morning I wakened to see the nurse bending over the cradle and the sight of the tiny arms beating the

397

air as if in anger. The cry was sharp and demanding. When the nurse brought her, she sucked greedily at my breast.

"Go and tell Don Luis," I said softly. "Wake him if he is asleep. Tell him she is well."

But it was still a fragile, light form, beautiful in her long lace robe as white as her skin, which the Marquesa held in her arms for the baptism. This was a formal ceremony, merely to receive her names and mark her entry into the Church. She had been baptized within an hour of birth because it had seemed so possible that she would not live. She received the water and all her names without a sound—Luisa, Isabel, Patricia, Angela, Milagro —which means miracle. She was, in truth, the miracle of Luis' life. She was the angel child. He possessed nothing more precious.

And for me, Dr. Rámirez told me that she would be my last child.

PART THREE

Spanish Twilight

CHAPTER ONE

1

Our lives settled into a quiet rhythm. At times it seemed almost too serene. I kept expecting some storm to sweep out of the sky at us; I found myself looking over my shoulder watching for the thundercloud, listening for the distant rumble. Very faintly it could be heard, but it was far away, and indistinct, a sound I could not quite identify.

On the surface I was busy; I had a family of five children, but with servants there seemed little to do except give orders. Nanny had as much help in the nursery as she asked for, and yet she was jealous of giving over the care of Tomás and Luisa to other hands. Edwin Fletcher now kept Juan, Martín, and Francisco at lessons full time. Juan was maturing quickly; he was by turns charming, boisterous, assertive, confident. His younger brothers looked to him as a natural leader, and he accepted that position without question. It was what he had been born to, his manner suggested. Tomás, who was just as assertive, was as yet too young even to interest much less challenge Juan.

Edwin Fletcher studied them with interest. "One day you may have to pull those two apart. They're born to scrap, I think. Be a good thing for Juan if Tomás was able to give him a run for his money. . . ."

Perhaps he used the phrase unconsciously. A run for money might be what it all turned into. Juan, as Carlos' son, had no money of his own, nor did Martín or Francisco. All they had was a natural hold on their grandfather's affections, and the special standing they had with the Marquesa. Juan by now knew that he ranked first among all of Don Paulo's grandchildren—and that included the children of Ignacio and Pedro. He fully understood the significance of being the favorite godchild. He had marked the fact that the Marquesa had not become godmother to any of the children of his father's half brothers. He knew also that Carlos had been the most loved son of Don Paulo. He was even beginning to hear hints and old stories of his great-grandfather Blodmore, the Irishman that the Marquesa had been said to have been in love with, at a time very long ago, a time that stretched back past his comprehension. He heard, as children always hear, recollections of the time that the Irishman had come to Sanlúcar with the Marquesa and had been expected to marry her. But instead she had married Don Paulo very suddenly, and Lord Blodmore had bought the house in the Plaza de Asturias which Juan's grandmother, Lady Pat, now occupied. He had begun asking questions about the place called Clonmara. It was a tangled, confused history, about which he was able only to build a sketchy outline. He would ask a question, and someone would answer vaguely. His interest would wane. What did it all matter? At his age it had all happened so long ago it belonged in the realms of the fairy stories he had once listened to so eagerly, the ones that invariably began "Once upon a time . . ."

What mattered was that he was the favorite, however history had woven itself to make him that.

But there was little Tomás, and even more important, it sometimes seemed, there was the tiny child, Luisa. These were the children of his stepfather and must, for that reason, be favored by him. And they were also the godchildren of the Marquesa. It dismayed me sometimes to see the evidence of these facts being worked out in Juan's young mind. Juan could easily remember the days of our poverty in the Plaza de Asturias, when the only good things came as gifts and favors from the Marquesa. But he had accepted the world of plenty, the beautiful house, the many servants provided by Luis, without question. He had seen what a provident marriage could bring. I noticed that he was very careful in his manner towards Luis, polite, respectful, as he was to Don Paulo and the Marquesa. He had learned very young how to use his charm, the charm and good looks inherited from Carlos. It was a rather frightening knowledge in someone of his age.

I had feared, at first, that our family would be split in two parts, both by the gap in the ages between Carlos' children, and the younger two, and by the knowledge that they were the stepchildren of Luis. But it was Luis himself who prevented that. He talked always of "my sons." He took care to spend time with the older ones, talked with them, rode with them. He was un-Spanish in his attitudes to them, in that he did not leave all their training to me. He involved himself actively in everything that went on in the house. He visibly relaxed, and that rather mournful face took on a look of peace, as if he had at last attained what he had waited for for so long. If anything he was too indulgent, too tolerant with misdemeanors. "You're spoiling them, Luis," I warned.

He smiled at me. "Love cannot spoil them, only harshness. Look how your mother breaks a horse. She does not ruin a tender mouth with hard hands. They are still so young, querida, and all too soon the world will take over and offer its own hard lessons. Let them be children while they can."

I could not quarrel with him over them. I could quarrel with him over nothing. His rather withdrawn personality had expanded like a cactus which soaks up rain after a long arid spell. "I have a beautiful wife," he said. "I have

402

a family. After so many years of quiet, this house now has life. Let me enjoy it, querida."

But while he could talk lovingly of his sons, it was evident that Luisa was a child apart. Her he worshiped. Each day on his return from the bodega he would go to the nursery to see her, as if to reassure himself that she really existed. He would hold her in his arms, in his lap, the way no Spaniard did with a young baby. Luis didn't care how he appeared to others. "Let them think me a foolish old man," he said. "Why should I worry? I have my Milagro, my miracle."

And the baby seemed to take it all as perfectly natural. She seemed more at ease with Luis even than with me. She learned to recognize him at a very early stage. Luis swore that her first word had been "Papa." He may have been right, since he seemed to hear a distinct word where the rest of us just heard some sort of gurgle. But there was no doubt of her response to him. Her quiet, calm, beautiful little face would light up at the sight of him. She was a grave, sober little girl, but for him she would laugh. He would pretend to toss her in the air, holding her very gently, and she would laugh with toothless gums. He would carry her about the house, Nanny hurrying to try to keep up; it was to Luis she took her first steps. If she had a childish fever, Luis himself was nearly ill with worry. Watching them together, I was aware of a fear, a fear of what might happen to Luis himself should something happen to her.

Because for all our care, for all the advice we took from doctors, she was delicate. It wasn't just the naturally slighter physique of the girl compared to her brothers. She seemed to go through the illnesses of childhood with alarming rapidity, and with each of them she took a long time to recover. What with Tomás would be a mild head cold, with her would be accompanied by a high fever. She was often in bed, listless, but not fretful. "Sure she's like an angel," Nanny would say, and kept on saying it until I asked her to stop. If she said it in the presence of Luis his face would grow gray with fear, as if the miracle

403

child he loved so might indeed become the angel spirit Nanny talked of.

But she reached her second and third birthday. She still was guarded against the possibility of every ill; in the winter she was not allowed out when the wind was cold; in the summer she spent every afternoon resting until the worst heat was past. In his garden Luis began to grow every sort of delicacy of fruit and vegetable which might tempt her appetite. She was never forced to eat food which she didn't want, but instead coaxed with something else. But Luis insisted on the cod-liver oil and malt, which she hated, and an abundance of orange juice, which she loved. But when she was ill she would accept the most foul-tasting medicine if it came from Luis' hands.

She was a princess in her little kingdom, and she soon learned it. But she never took advantage of this knowledge, as Juan did. I could almost have wished to see a childish tantrum occasionally, to prove she was like other children. But the usual faults and tempers of childhood seemed missing in her. She didn't even soil the tiny white dresses she wore.

"More like an angel than a child," Nanny would say, but out of Luis' hearing.

In only one aspect did the Blodmore blood seem to come through strongly. Luis had imported a tiny Shetland pony especially for her, and it was my mother, with all the family watching, who first lifted her into the saddle, showed her how to hold the reins, and herself took the bridle for Luisa's first ride around the ornamental lake. She returned, her dark eyes shining, her tinkle of a laugh carrying to us as we stood and watched. "Papa—isn't it wonderful? Granny says I can soon learn to jump just like her. . . ."

And Luis was torn between delight in her animation and dread of the times when she would suffer the inevitable falls.

"He's called Colonel, after Grandfather." She had, of course, been told many times by Nanny about her grandfather, who had won the great medal for bravery. She was yet another Jerezana who looked naturally to England as part of her heritage.

So my world was peaceful and serene, and my children were growing and flowering, like Luis' beautiful garden. I wanted for nothing in the world except the one thing I did not often allow myself to think of. But it was there, the thought, shut away in my memory, as if in a room locked and seldom visited—the thought of Richard Blodmore. No one, I told myself, could have everything. It was against all sense, all logic, to go on remembering and wanting the experience which I had so briefly tasted and would never have again. But it remained, the canker in the bud.

2

These years of serenity were also a time of growing awareness for me. Now that I had the leisure, and the urgent necessities of life did not press upon me, I began to look about me, to look at the far reaches of Spain, the world beyond our bodegas and our vineyards. At last there was time, and the money, to travel. Luis took me to Paris and Rome, Vienna and London. We never discussed the possibility of visiting Ireland. I was always, in the end, happy to return to Jerez. I came back with new insights that stimulated me but also disturbed me. I suppose these things would have thrust themselves upon me, whatever the circumstances, but now there was more time to ponder them, to ask questions. And, more often than not, it was Edwin Fletcher who answered them.

It was from him I got the books, in English, of Spanish history. Up to then I had seen Spain only as the power which had threatened England with invasion by the Armada, the land which had sent out those who had explored and conquered the New World, and brought the gold and the silver pouring back to fill the coffers of the King, and set him firmly on the pinnacle as Holy Roman Emperor.

This had been my picture of Spain, and the history books had not caught up with what had followed in the long years of decline.

"You were still toddling round, Carlota," Edwin said, "when Spain lost the last of her possessions in the New World. It was the dark night of the Spanish soul in 1898 when Cuba and the Philippines were lost to the United States. Spain once ruled half the world, and most of Europe. . . . Think how the British will feel when their Empire is stripped from them, piece by piece, as it will surely be."

I began to look closely at my own Andalucía to learn, as I did from talking with Luis and from the increasing trust he put in me, forgetting most of the time that I was a woman and these things were not supposed to be my business. Andalucía was an example of the great *latifundias*, the vast estates owned by people like the Marquesa and, to a lesser degree, by people like Don Paulo and Luis himself. We had always lived a privileged life, even in the days of the most stringent economies in the Plaza de Asturias. The peasants were without land, not only in Andalucía but all over Spain. We had seen, in our corner of the world, little of the disturbances which had rocked Catalonia and the Basque country. We read about strikes in the factories of Barcelona and the mines of Asturias, about bomb-throwing and convent-burning, and yet our little world, the world close about us, remained calm. It was Edwin who told me about the "Tragic Week" in 1909, when more than fifty convents and churches in Barcelona were burned, and in reprisal hundreds of people were shot by troops. All I could remember of July 1909 was that it had been the time we came to Spain, and my mind and feelings had been numb with misery and longing for Richard Blodmore. It was Edwin who pointed out to me the grim consequences of the final humiliation of the Spanish army in Morocco, where it had for years been trying to keep the tribesmen at bay. In 1921 an outpost at Anual was overwhelmed, and in the retreat some fourteen thousand men were lost. Even I, though, was aware of the uproar through the whole country as the incompetence and corruption within the ruling structure were made clear. There was a clamor for strong, effective rule, and in 1923 Primo de Rivera, the captain general of Barcelona, "pronounced" against the government. The coup succeeded, and Spain had a dictator, which most of the ruling class welcomed because he stood for the iron rule which upheld their position. We listened to his demands for a purified government, listened and approved. For us, in Jerez, it was the time of harvest, and we were busy bringing in our grapes.

The King, Alfonso XIII, whom I had met at Doñana, welcomed the dictator because he scorned the parliamentary system. We didn't know it then, though Edwin predicted it, that these coming years would be the last gasp of constitutional monarchy in Spain. We thought, we let ourselves believe, that the people would see the sense of Primo de Rivera's rule, that they would be satisfied with slow reform.

"You will see, Carlota," Luis said, "that this has all been a violent fermentation, like the must at the time of the harvest. It will fall bright, like the wine."

I made a note about the harvest that year, as I had been doing each year since I had planted my first vineyard. *Lean crop. Good quality.*

We did tell ourselves that it would be all right, but that was the year when Juan came home wiith his head bloodied after a fracas in front of the Collegiate Church.

"You wouldn't believe what they are saying, Mother," he told me as I bathed his slight wounds. "This Communist stuff. They're going to overthrow everything—and the Church is first. They're going to confiscate everyone's property. Take the land from us. Take the Church's property first. Every peasant will have land, they say. Every man will be his own master—so long as he does what the State tells him. They can't do it, can they? The army would never let them. . . ."

"I don't think they can do it, Juan. But perhaps there's a case for some of the things they say."

"They didn't think it could be done in Russia, either," Edwin said with a certain laconic detachment.

Juan looked from one to another in disbelief. "You sound as if you're in *favor* of that rabble!"

Edwin smiled. "Don't count me with them, Juan. Just don't forget I've been trained to see both sides. I wouldn't fight for them. I'd try not to fight against them. But if it comes right down to it, the historian gives way to the man. I *like* my privileges. Even the privileges a *poor* Fletcher has."

3

There were ripples on the surface of our seemingly placid world, but in Ireland there had been revolt and now civil war.

Richard and Elena Blodmore and their sons, Edward and Paul, came to Jerez after spending a summer at the Galicia estate with the Marquesa. People, now worried by what they had experienced and heard of terror and anarchy in their own land, pressed them for reports on what was going on in Ireland. As always it was too complex to explain simply, as we could not easily explain the Spanish situation to those who came freshly to it.

I wished Richard and Elena had not come, but they had. With Elena as the next holder of the title of Pontevedra, and the eldest son, Edward, to inherit after her, it was natural that the Marquesa wanted her great-nephew trained in the language and customs of Spain. There was no way of avoiding our duty to entertain them. For a time they were the focus of every party, the ones who brought the freshest news, and people were avid to hear it, even though it frightened them. The first reception for them was given at Don Paulo's house, with the Marquesa there as hostess, one of the few occasions she deigned to appear in the social life of the town. I watched her as she greeted the guests, Don Paulo beside her, then Elena and, beyond her, Richard. I knew, of course, that the Marquesa had the power to command Elena to come to Jerez, or any place else. It was the Marquesa's money which had arranged the marriage between Elena and

Richard; no doubt she held the purse strings for other favors as well. I thought of all the children now influenced by the sway this woman held, by the power of her money. She had been godmother by proxy to Richard's and Elena's sons. Almost as if she knew every detail of our lives and thoughts, she seemed to delight in playing each off against the other.

The lights were bright; the soft candlelight of the earlier era had given way, and we were all revealed more starkly than we would have wished. As I joined the line of guests who waited to be received, I looked at them all closely, critically, as I looked at myself in a wall mirror opposite. The Marquesa and Don Paulo were revealed as aged. How old was she now? I began to calculate her years. She had been twenty-five, they said, when she led my grandfather through the courting dance which had ended with his falling in love with another woman—no, not a woman, but that eternal child who still lived on in the castle at Arcos. The lights were harsh on the Marquesa's lean, lined, aristocratic face, gave added brilliance to the fabulous jewels she wore on her hands. In honor of the occasion she wore a necklace—not the emeralds and diamonds which she had wanted to thrust on me as a kind of tip for good behavior. No, these were rubies, and fit for an empress, but the light they flashed back into her face was unkind. Beside her, Don Paulo seemed indifferent both to her and to the whole proceedings. He seemed bent, folded in upon himself. People said he had never recovered from Carlos' death. It could have been true.

I greeted the Marquesa, and she gave me her thin smile. Don Paulo's lips twisted in some form of greeting, but really we said nothing to each other. Then I went on to greet Elena; she gave me a brilliant smile, murmured something about Clonmara, laughed at whatever it was she had said. She was wearing the Marquesa's emeralds, both the necklace and the tiara, and her manner made it clear that they were no loan; they were hers. She had accepted what I had flung back at the Marquesa, and she probably knew it. But they were hers, and she triumphed in them and all that the bestowing of them implied. My mother saw them at the same time. "Oh, Charlie—but they were *yours!*"

Quickly I placed my hand on my mother's arm and gave it a little shake. She didn't understand what was required of her, but at least she was quiet.

"Clonmara is looking quite lovely, Lady Patricia. Why don't you come to visit? All your old friends ask about you." Elena's smile was knowing, and contemptuous. My mother, despite our best efforts, looked a ruin. How had her hair tumbled down so quickly? And how had she managed already to spill wine on her dress?

But she caught eagerly at the name. "Clonmara?" Then she shook her head, and hairpins showered about her. "No—no, I can't go back again. It isn't my home any more. Father isn't there—I can't go back. . . ."

She would have gone on. She would have stood before Elena Blodmore rambling on, her haunted, weary face expressing all the moods that surged through her as she relived the past. She didn't care about the people lining up behind. She didn't know they were there. She blinked many times, and seemed to see Elena with new eyes.

"You!—you're the one who came, aren't you? The one who came and made us go away . . ."

I held her arm more firmly and tried to lead her on. She stood rooted, and Luis was nowhere in sight to help me. Then Richard Blodmore laid his own hand over mine on her arm.

"You remember me, Lady Pat? You remember me and Balthasar?"

Her eyes widened as she stared at him. *"Yes . . ."* she said, almost in a whisper. "But you were beautiful then! A beautiful man. What has happened to you? Did you fall from a horse? Did someone ride over you? Your face is smashed . . ."

She was talking about things other people didn't mention. Suddenly Richard took her other arm, leaving the receiving line, and led her away. She walked between us, her hair falling in wisps about her shoulders, her gown stained, her gaze upturned with horrified concern at

Richard. People parted before us. I could hear the talk start as we moved through. "Lady Patricia at it again . . ."

"Let's go and have something to drink, Lady Pat," Richard said. "Yes, you're right. It was a fall. All my own fault. A devil of a big bank it was, and I came at it the wrong way. Do you remember that big devil at the end of Malloy's Long Field?"

"Yes . . . yes . . ." She nodded eagerly. "How well I remember it."

He placed a glass in her hand. "Well then, you see, I was coming at it, and didn't have my wits about me . . ."

Perhaps unfortunate words, but they served. She was following every detail of a hunt that had never taken place, a fall that had never happened. She had forgotten all about the war, the war in which Richard had served and in which he had lost half his face. She had forgotten about the husband who had been killed, my father who had won the medal. She had remembered the emeralds, and now she remembered Malloy's Long Field. She lived every moment of the chase, she seemed to hear the cry of the hounds again in Richard's voice.

The excitement became too much for her. "Gone away . . . gone away!" she cried, echoing the huntsman's call. People were gathered around, listening openly. She gripped my hand, and the wine spilled from her glass down on her dress. "Oh, Charlie, won't it be wonderful when we're back at Clonmara again!"

My eyes met Richard's fully for the first time since we had parted at Southampton. The call of the huntsman's horn echoed in my own heart. *Gone away . . . gone away . . .*

4

It was the last afternoon of the Blodmores' visit. To-morrow they would travel to Gibraltar. This time Juan would go with them as far as London. In a week's time he would enter his first English school. He put a good face on it, but I could sense just a shade of apprehension in him, a certain stiffness that usually was totally lacking.

"I suppose my English really is good enough?" he said to Edwin Fletcher. In the last week he had asked that at least once a day.

"Your English is good enough. It's the slang that will trip you up in the beginning. You'll get the hang of it soon."

Edwin had been quietly against sending Juan to school in England. "They're rather barbaric places, really. They produce bullies and snobs."

"It is necessary," the Marquesa had said. Juan was already one year late in going there. We had held him back in Jerez because Don Paulo's health was giving concern, and a daily visit from his grandson seemed to help him. But now Juan must go, and in another year Martín, and then Francisco would follow him. It was a pattern long established in Jerez.

Now on this last afternoon we sat together in the garden and I thought, except for our clothes, we might have posed for one of those Edwardian photographs, with the table laid formally for English tea, a butler and a footman in attendance. The touch of Edwardian atmosphere was made stronger by the presence of the Marquesa, who still wore her black dresses to the ground and, out of doors, a large black, tulle-draped hat. A black lace parasol was propped against the side of her chair. As always she dominated the group, even though, because it was an exceptional occasion, Don Paulo was also present.

Richard and Elena were there, and their sons, Edward and Paul. My mother had come, with María Luisa. María Luisa's dress, like the Marquesa's, was unchanging. My mother's skirts were a little shorter, but she still clung to the old styles, although her slim body would easily have carried off the loose, shapeless form that fashion now favored. Elena wore her skirts shorter than anyone in Jerez had dared think of, and her still golden hair was bobbed. She wore lipstick frankly, had long painted nails, and smoked her cigarettes through a holder. She was the epitome of the new woman who had emerged through the war years. I thought the time she had spent in Spain must have been a severe strain. She had completely broken from the old Spanish mold in which we were still confined. That she did not like this man-dominated society was clear. She talked of driving cars, and how fast they could go, as well as riding hunters. She talked of visits to London when Richard did not accompany her. She crossed and recrossed her legs restlessly as we sat in the late-summer garden, obviously bored with the obligations of this family gathering, obviously looking forward to the release that the next day would bring.

Luis had stayed away from the bodega that afternoon to be present. I thought for him also tomorrow would bring relief. The presence of Richard Blodmore must have been almost as hard on him as it had been on me. He had been so considerate with me, so understanding of the stress the visit laid on me. He had never once asked me about Richard, about my feelings. But he knew them; he was there, at my side, at the very worst moments when Richard and I had to be part of the same gathering. Sometimes the pressure of his hand on mine had been all that had signaled his understanding; sometimes he had leaned to me and said softly, "All right, querida?" He knew that I had never allowed myself to be alone with Richard Blodmore, and Richard himself had not sought me out. No words were necessary.

All our children were there, Nanny in the background in case Luisa needed something or Tomás had to be restrained. They were a handsome lot, these children of mine. It must have given both joy and pain to Don Paulo to see Juan's extraordinary resemblance to Carlos. Except for the Blodmore eyes, Carlos would have looked exactly as Juan did at his age. Tomorrow's parting would hurt the old man perhaps even more than one could guess. Juan himself was strutting a little, possibly to hide his apprehension. He wore white flannels and a striped blazer. All of us, except the Marquesa and María Luisa, were dressed in white. Small Luisa, our baby, seemed the most immaculate of all. She sipped her lemonade, put it carefully on the table before daintily eating her thin sandwich.

413

She selected her cake with care, ate it without seeming to drop a crumb.

Elena's eyes had been on her. "That child," she observed, "is too good to be true." She stubbed her half-smoked cigarette into an ashtray which one of the white-gloved servants rushed to replace with a clean one. "Myself, I don't think it's natural. Not quite healthy."

The Marquesa turned her cold, glittering eyes on her. "The child is a delight to be with. She is more than healthy. It's apparent she has inherited Carlota's constitution." It was as if the Marquesa had flung a challenge at Elena.

Elena shrugged. "Oh well . . ." And her eyes deliberately went to my mother, as if indicating there might be some of the Blodmore inheritance which was wholly undesirable.

They had spent too much time together, these people. For two months they had been with the Marquesa in Galicia. It had been more of a command than an invitation. It had been an invitation which even Elena had not dared to refuse. Our children had been with them, and it was the first year Luis had consented to Luisa's going with them. Only the thought of the cool green rain-washed shores of that far northern coast had persuaded him; summer in Andalucía was a test of endurance for anyone, let alone a child as delicate as Luisa. So she had gone, and I thought to myself that it could have been a crucial time of testing and weighing for the Marquesa. Briefly, she had also invited Ignacio and Pedro, Don Paulo's sons, with their wives and children. Luis and I had begged off, and she had accepted our excuses. Perhaps she thought she already knew us well enough. But those weeks of a closely confined family life must have been a trial to the restless Elena.

No one knew what it had been for Richard Blodmore. That shattered face and the upward-twisted mouth defied reading. He smoked his cigarette and stared off into the distance, as if the movement of the swans on the lake was all that interested him.

"Well," the Marquesa said, "I hope it has been a peaceful time for you. Things have been very bad in Ireland."

Elena shrugged. "Oh, we haven't come through it at all badly. Richard is such a stick-in-the-mud. He just gets on with his farming and lets politics alone. I've often said he's too easygoing. He could have been leading the country if he'd put any effort into it. He should have been elected—"

Suddenly, out of a seeming torpor, Don Paulo raised his voice. "There is nothing wrong with a man tending his land and minding his own business. And since when could a member of the British House of Lords be elected to anything?"

"A member of the House of Lords doesn't even have a vote," my mother said. Everyone turned to look at her. It was one of her lucid days, days when her mind seemed to sharpen, when she seemed to know more than she should have known. There was no confusion this day. She knew exactly who Elena was, who Richard was and why they were there. She had not spoken of Clonmara at all. She had appeared to be watching her grandchildren and paying little attention to the conversation. All at once we knew she had missed nothing.

"And women can vote now, can't they?" she added. "Strange to remember we used not to think it mattered. Perhaps one day we'll vote here. But poor Ireland—what troubles she's had. It must be hard to see the state of the people now."

"The state of the people is no worse than it was. And no better," Elena retorted. "What good have they done themselves with all this strife? Oh yes, we have an Irish Free State now, and little Ireland is a member of the League of Nations—much good *that* will do them. But what we have paid for it! There's been nothing but bloodshed since the Easter Rising. They've got their Free State and their own Parliament, but they've had civil war. Those Sinn Feiners and the Republicans between them are dragging the country down . . . people assassinated, people ruined. Estates going to ruin. The best people leaving—"

"*We* have not left, Elena." Richard seemed to come out of his reflective trance. "Nor will we. We have a duty to stay. These are not times when you leave an estate to be managed by an agent. . . ."

Suddenly I noticed the Marquesa nodding her head, though I think it was a movement she had intended no one to see. Then she rose. "Come, children. We will take a stroll. Bring some sandwiches and we will feed the swans. . . ."

They rose eagerly, too long confined to their chairs by the ritual of tea. They were used to obeying the Marquesa, as everyone was. The tall, black-clad figure moved off with her graceful, swaying walk; as always, when one did not see her closely, she appeared still a young woman. My four sons and the sons of Richard and Elena crowded about her. Luisa ran ahead. Even though the young ones did not yet understand the power of her money and influence, they felt the power of her personality. We watched as she spread her hands. "Come, Luisa. Come, Tomás. Take Tía Isabel's hands."

The two young ones were joined with her. It made a striking composition, the solitary black figure in the midst of the summer-white children. The black and white swans drifted towards them, in anticipation of the food.

"Damn!" Elena said.

We turned to look at her. "Is there something wrong?" I asked.

"Nothing," she snapped. "Just a run in my stocking." But it wasn't that which troubled her. She feared that her sons had been excluded. She knew she had expressed the wrong sentiments when she talked about Ireland. To people like the Marquesa and Don Paulo, land was sacred, as was any inheritance. Something to be guarded and watched over. Like children. She stubbed out another cigarette.

"Would you care for a copita?" I asked.

For a moment she hesitated. "What I'd really like is a cocktail. That is, if your servants have ever heard of such a thing. You know, you make it with gin."

I called over the manservant and gave the necessary

416

instructions. The bottles and ice were brought, and Elena mixed her own drink. Don Paulo's eyes followed every movement. He viewed the bottle of gin with distaste.

"And what is this, the 'cocktail'?"

"Oh, it's something the Americans thought of. You should try one, Don Paulo. It's all the rage in London. Shall I mix it?"

He shook his head. "All my life I have lived for sherry wine."

I handed him the glass of fino. Luis had filled the glasses for my mother, María Luisa, Richard, Edwin, and myself. Elena had lighted another cigarette and was already sipping her martini cocktail. Then Don Paulo raised his glass.

"To the children."

We watched them walking back across the lawn. Luisa still held the Marquesa's hand. There was a late afternoon hush on the garden, and those white-clad figures seemed, for a second, frozen in time. Young and beautiful, they all were, but Juan and small Tomás seemed somehow set apart, as if something burned in them which the others had missed. It happened that the two walked side by side, though not as comrades. It also happened that at that moment I turned and caught the gaze of Richard. He stared at me for a moment and then looked back at the two. But as they came nearer I saw that he really looked at Tomás alone. I knew that he was wondering. He must often, through that summer, have stared at the typically Blodmore face, have counted the weeks since that April in London and Tomás' birth. And he was wondering still.

And I promised myself again, as I had once vowed to Luis, that he would never know.

CHAPTER TWO

1

Almost imperceptibly, after Juan left for school in England, Don Paulo and I grew closer together. I knew that part of him would always hate the Blodmores, and yet the Blodmore strain was in his grandchildren, whom he loved. He was aging visibly, growing weary rather than feeble, though his mind was as sharp as ever, and his authority at the bodega, whether it was in settling matters of business or in the art he had developed his whole life, that of blending and insuring the quality of the sherry, was unchallenged.

Perhaps our closeness grew because not only the vineyards but the bodega itself had now become one of the strong influences of my life. Almost daily now I went to fetch Luis home for our late lunch, and almost daily I found time for that walk through the bodega, where the dim light, the smell of the dampness, and the smell of the wine, had a strangely calming effect on me. The children used to laugh at this habit. "Mother's going to church," they used to say.

By design or accident, almost every day I encountered

Don Paulo. We often would pass with just a nod and a murmured greeting to each other, particularly if he had other men with him, customers or visitors to the bodega. But sometimes he would fall into step with me; we might wordlessly pace the long aisles between the butts. Our silent companionship was no longer uncomfortable. We did not feel a need to talk always. Because he knew my interest, sometimes he would call for the venencia and the old expertise of hand and eye and "nose" would be displayed. Whereas before I had known only the growing and tending of the vines, now, from Don Paulo, I began to learn of the wine itself. I learned only a very little, compared with his vast knowledge, and I remained humble about what I did know. I learned from him as he sampled the wine and graded it, though most often this was done in the cuarto de muestras, the sampling room, and there my presence as a woman and a distraction was not welcomed. Don Paulo was one of a number of men at the bodega with the title *catador*, taster. These men were said to have *la nariz del vino*, the "nose." Pedro had this ability and was proud of it. To these men fell the responsibility, once the wine had fallen bright after its fermentation and had been racked off the lees, of classifying it for its eventual place in the solera. A young wine does not immediately declare its character. For its first classification they used the symbol called the *raya*. After examining the young wine for appearance, bouquet, and sometimes taste, they would mark the casks with chalk. One oblique stroke, /, *una raya*, meant the wine had a clean nose and a reasonable body; two strokes, //, *dos rayas*, was a wine not altogether clean on the nose, or with some minor defect; three strokes, ///, *tres rayas*, was a wine that was not clean, or slightly acid, or very thin, and so was marked for distillation and called mostos de quema, musts for burning. I had also seen these casks marked with a stroke through the three rayas, ///, which indicated the gridiron of a hearth. The other grade, vinegar, was quickly taken away, lest it infect its neighbors. Later came the classification for type—the finos and the olorosos, and eventually the different types of sherries which fell within these two broad types. The finos would be stacked inside the bodegas to keep their temperatures down; sometimes the butts of olorosos were placed outside so that the sun would increase the sweetness of the wine. All were fortified with alcohol.

The activity about the bodega was constant, though not noisy. The big vaulted rooms seemed to impose their own sense of quiet and order. Don Paulo, though, often seemed to walk the aisles of the bodega for the reason I did—just for the pleasure it gave, or perhaps the reassurance of continuity it imparted. I liked to be with him when he worked and talked with the capataz or another catador. I listened to the terms they used to describe the wine: *limpio* (clean) or *sucio* (dirty); *verde* (green, unripe) or *maduro* (ripe); *delgado* (thin) or *gordo* (stout); *punzante* (pungent) or *apagado* (dull). They could have been speaking of people, and it seemed to me that the wine was often regarded in that fashion. The wine had a way of its own and could develop unexpectedly. Don Paulo or any of the catadores never spared the chalk in downgrading a wine if that was necessary, but there was also the pleasure of upgrading it if it showed more promise than expected. They worked with care, holding the glass always by the stem lest finger marks obscure the color or warmth from the fingers change the bouquet. They did a great deal of chemical analysis in the cuarto de muestras; they talked knowingly and technically about the chemical composition of the wine, about the Baumé scale used for measuring the specific density of the wine, the degree of alcoholic strength it possessed; they could write a chemical formula for any of the wines they produced. But in the end it was the feel for the wine, the recognition of its taste, color and bouquet, which was vital for the continuance of its quality.

I talked once with Don Paulo as we sat at the little table in the sala de degustación after I had been with him during one such session. "Do you remember the talk we had the first day—the talk about the members of the family all contributing each his own character, as the different wines do to the solera?"

420

"I remember."

"Well . . . I've noticed that sometimes a certain wine will come along and develop qualities that are not expected—sometimes strength and body, sometimes a lightness, a delicacy, and you blend these to produce the wine you need. But a family can't work quite that way, can it?" I shook my head, feeling for words. "We cannot say, 'Take a little of Carlos and add the sympathetic nature of Martín,' say. Nor can I blend my shy and earnest little Francisco with Juan's confidence and assurance. But if a family can only stand together, it still can represent the strength of the solera system. If we only could discard that which is frankly bad as you do the wine that is useless . . . What am I saying, Don Paulo? Do we mark our children too early in life, knowing that we cannot add one to the other in the way we do with the solera?"

He sipped his wine thoughtfully. "All my life I have thought in those terms, but a man is not a wine, nor is a woman. But in the blending of the two, in the development of what comes together, one may hope for something that will combine the best qualities of both. I had little hope for you when I first knew you. I marked you a gridiron. At times, to this day, you have a taste on the tongue which I find like vinegar. And yet, when I view you through the glass, when I shake and smell, sometimes you seem to come through as a *palma*." I knew enough to know that this was the classification given to the finos of highest quality, those with a particularly clean and delicate aroma. I bowed my head a little. I had never expected to hear such words from Don Paulo.

"Women," he added, "the best of them, generally come through as olorosos as they age and develop their quality. But you, if you carry out your duties properly, if you train your sons to what is right and what is their duty, may yet develop as the best of all wine, an old fino, the rarest and purest. Think of the wine, Doña Carlota, whenever you make decisions that will affect our family. What you add, what you take away, will determine how the wine will grow. Women, unhappily, do not think enough in terms of the wine."

He looked down at his glass, and the folds of the skin on his face and hands were very deep, and spotted with age. I wondered if at that moment the vision of all of us, the women, went before his inner gaze—the Marquesa, born to be a palma, but how did he grade her?—my mother, promising, but badly blended; myself, sometimes gridiron, sometimes palma. He had known bitterness from me, that taste of vinegar, and yet, in the children I had produced, he saw the hope of his old age.

In the stillness of the bodega, within the mildewed walls, the flor rose on the wine twice yearly, renewing itself, or being renewed by mixing with a younger wine. The fermentation could be violent. It was something nature gave to the wine in this, our particular little piece of country, and could not be imitated or manufactured. So it was within the family. The solera worked so long as the sight and the nose were right, the markings definite, the bad unhesitatingly rejected, lest it destroy the quality of the rest. But how could one reject the bad, the weak, the acid, when they were people, not butts of must? I could see no way to do that; love affected the nose and the taste.

The old man before me had seen and smelled only the good in Carlos, had loved the clear, bright promise of him. He could never accept a lesser marking for Carlos.

2

Juan returned from his first year at school altered, as we had expected he would be, but with his attitudes fined down and sharpened by his experience. For the first time he had lived in a world where his name and position were not known; he had had to prove himself. He had had to prove himself academically and at games. The experience had given him a little humility, or at least the appearance of it, but with no lessening of his own innate confidence. For the first couple of weeks before he went with his brothers and Luisa to join the Marquesa in Galicia, he went daily to the bodega when I drove to pick up Luis. And daily he walked the aisles of the "cathedrals" as I now quite openly called them, and always his grandfather walked with us. There was a great deal of sampling done—the old man trying to give the young one a lifetime's knowledge, but we all knew it was knowledge that could not be imparted in a few weeks, or even a few years. It was possible that Juan, like his father's half brother, Ignacio, would never develop it sufficiently. But each time they held a glass up to the light, shook the liquid a little, and smelled, I saw the hope grow brighter in the old man's eyes.

Juan then joined us at our special little table at the sala de degustación; we would drink across the spectrum of the sherry, from the most mellow, the richest, the sweetest, to the light delicate fino. Don Paulo would call for the best wines, sometimes to be drawn directly from a particular butt; then occasionally he would slip in an inferior one to see if Juan's nose and tongue wrinkled with displeasure.

"What tricks you play on me, Grandfather. Did you think you could put *this* one over on me?"

Luis would join us for one copita, and we would drive home in one of the splendidly equipped and turned-out carriages which it was Luis' pride to maintain. I remembered how we had admired these carriages in the early days, envied their owners. The sight of them still stirred me; I loved the paint glistening in the sun, the splendidly matched horses, wearing their harness decorated with silver and the many-colored woolen balls, the little bells that jingled with their movements. There were gaiety and brightness which were particularly Andalucian and lifted the art of coaching away from the austerity that characterized it elsewhere. But the standards asked of the horses and driver were as rigorous, and demanded as much training and practice, as anything connected with the horse always did.

That summer, for the first time, Juan was allowed to take the reins himself, but with José, the head coachman, always at his side, ready to take over if anything beyond Juan's capability occurred. Sometimes I would see them practicing in that unusual coupling of three horses leading and two behind, and every ounce of concentration Juan had was required to manage and turn this splendid and rather awesome rig. My mother took particular pleasure and pride in the skill Juan developed. And it pleased me to see that Juan's absence had made his fondness for his grandmother more marked. He was kind and gentle with her in a way he was with no one else. Very often, on his practice session with José, he would drive to the Plaza de Asturias and my mother would ride in the carriage, a parasol to shade her, her hair tumbling out from a large hat, happy even if just briefly, as only someone of her temperament could be. She loved all her grandchildren, but Juan, the first, was the favorite, and she couldn't hide it.

"We should have a motor," Juan said teasingly to Luis. "All the families of the fellows at school have them. Some of the fellows drive them themselves."

"What!" Luis said in mock horror. "And break your grandmother's heart! You bring those fellows at school down here to Jerez and let them see a way of life they can't imagine. Let them see if horses are as easy to manage as motors. Let them drink sherry where it is born."

Juan rather liked the idea; I could see that. He had a grand and privileged world to show off to his school-fellows. The Plaza de Asturias was only a shadow in the background, and Juan now knew enough to know that a rather mad old grandmother, if she were sufficiently aristocratic, and more especially if she had once been married to a war hero, was no great social liability. He was learning that eccentrics were something prized by the English. "Perhaps I shall," he said. "It would be a change for them. Perhaps we could visit Doñana. . . ." And then he added, "Did you know that Lady Blodmore had invited me—and Martín and Francisco because they'll be at school too by that time—to Clonmara for next Easter?"

"You'll miss Holy Week here," Luis said. Holy Week

424

was something very special, with its processions, more pageant then solemnity, rivaling, in a small way, the processions in Seville that same week.

He wrinkled his nose. "Oh well—that doesn't matter too much. All that carrying on, with statues and all that—well, it's a bit overdone, isn't it?"

I remembered what Edwin Fletcher had said about schools turning out snobs and bullies. Juan always had had the makings of a snob in him, more especially since he had learned that his own father had been illegitimate. I prayed there would not be the makings of a bully also.

I sat silently through the rest of the drive, thinking about that invitation to Clonmara. I was almost certain that it had not come because Elena herself wished it. Had Richard been the one to suggest it, or had the Marquesa? Was this the first of many times my children would be invited to Clonmara, and would the connection grow closer? The Marquesa had an obsession with the Blodmores, and still, it seemed, the desire to control Clonmara itself, which had been denied to her once. But there also persisted the thought that Richard himself had looked into the future, the future which seemed to indicate that one day Tomás also would be sent to England, and one day Tomás would be invited to Clonmara.

Was it Richard reaching out to touch, perhaps to hold, his son? Turning to look at Luis, I saw that he wore an expression of brooding gravity, and I wondered if the thought had come to him also.

3

The summer moved on and the heat took its iron grip on the land. It had been a dry winter, and the grapes lacked water; it would be a small yield at harvest time, though with luck a good quality. All over the region the earth had a brown and seared look, the animals were thin and listless, the grazing was sparse. Even the goats which wandered the verges of the road could find little to eat. Luis' prize herds of bulls and my mother's mares and stallions were being hand-fed by August, an expensive procedure which would take the profit out of the whole year's business. But with bulls and horses, as with the wine, one could not look at one year only. Don Paulo and I paced the bodega together, taking comfort from the feeding of continuity which the solera always imparted. We did not need to say to each other that endurance was not for one year only. The bloodlines of the horses and the brave bulls, the lifeblood of the solera, which was the new must, would continue.

The house was very quiet, not only because the heat caused a lassitude but because all the boys had gone to Galicia to the Marquesa, and Edwin Fletcher with them. Luisa remained. She had had a slight fever at the time they had been ready to leave, and Luis had refused to allow her to go. She did not seem to mind. She played quietly in the nursery with her dolls in the mornings, and I taught her the alphabet with building blocks. In the afternoon she rested in her shaded room; in the evenings Luis read stories to her. She moved quietly, always, and did not overexert herself. By now she had grown into a quite startling beauty, with lovely delicate features which were an intense refinement of Luis' own pale skin, and dark eyes fringed with thick black lashes.

I took her sometimes with me to the bodega. It was cool in the dim cathedrals, and she seemed to enjoy the place. Don Paulo looked down at her and said, "*This* one you will have to guard extremely well." And a ghost of a wintry smile crossed his face as he quoted the traditional proverb of the region which I had first heard on the lips of María Luisa. "*Las niñas y las viñas son difíciles de guardar.*" (Girls and vineyards take a lot of watching.)

The time of the harvest came. The whole town echoed to the sound of the wheels of the carts that brought the must to the bodegas, and that unmistakable and, to some people, unpleasant smell of the must in violent fermentation was everywhere. There was little time to talk in the sala de degustación, but there were always a few who

426

found time to come for their copitas, and it was there I heard the first vague rumor.

It sent me at once to Don Paulo's office, but he was not there. It was hardly surprising. As the carts with the casks of must arrived at the bodega, it would have taken a great deal to keep Don Paulo away from the scene. I found him at the entrance to one of the bodegas, the frantic activity of the harvest all about him, the sounds, the cries, the occasional arguments. The heat and the necessary tempo of the work frayed everyone's tempers. Don Paulo demanded to be consulted about almost everything, and I had to wait my turn. In fact there was no need for him to be there at all. There were plenty of men to take his place, younger men, but he seemed unable to sit quietly in his office while other men presided over some of the most exciting and difficult hours in the bodega's year.

"*Momentito, Don Paulo.*"

He turned to me. "What is it?" he answered sharply. "You can see this is no time for gossip."

"I hope it is only gossip. But there is talk of typhoid in Arcos."

"Who says so? I have heard nothing."

"A man in the sala de degustación. He came directly from there this morning. A few cases, he says."

"Probably just a few people with bad stomachs." But his face grew pinched. He waved away a man who came to him bearing a tally sheet. "In any case, they have their own wells in the castle. They need have no contact with the rest of the town."

"It is carried on food, remember."

"I will inquire."

And so I was dismissed. I returned to the sala de degustación to wait for Luis.

I did not go to the bodega for the next two days and so did not see Don Paulo. But the story of typhoid at Arcos was confirmed. Luis was in a panic about his daughter. "Should we send her north—to Galicia? You should go with her, Carlota."

"But they are all about to come back. The boys must

427

leave for school in a week's time. Their passages are booked, remember?"

"Yes . . . yes . . ." He was twisting his hands together. The harvest was always a busy and anxious time. It wasn't surprising he had forgotten the exact date they would leave. This time all three would go. He thought for a while longer. "We will get passages for you all. You will go with them, and take Luisa and Tomás. You will stay in England until the danger has passed."

"That surely is a little extreme, Luis. There are no cases reported in Jerez or Puerto—"

For once he was sharp and peremptory with me. "That is what I have decided. You will obey me in this, Carlota." Then his face seemed to crumple; suddenly he looked very old in his fear. "I'm sorry, Carlota. I did not mean . . ." He wiped the sweat from his forehead with his handkerchief. "If I should lose her through negligence, it would kill me also. I have to send her away, Carlota. You must understand that."

I nodded. "Yes, I understand. And I will go. I will have everything ready. I will telephone to the Marquesa in Galicia to send the boys at once—as soon as I'm certain we can get on a ship. We will go straight to Gibraltar when they get here."

"If there isn't a ship available from Gibraltar at an earlier time, then you could take one of the sherry ships from Cádiz. Not so comfortable, but it will do. I shall begin arrangements at once."

I thought it all unnecessary, but it would have been cruel to deny him. He would be in a fever of apprehension until he knew that Luisa was safely away from the danger. He was already on the telephone, asking for the shipping agents in Gibraltar. I went to Nanny and gave her instructions to start the packing. Her face puckered with anxiety.

"Typhoid . . . it used to run through the poor in Ireland every so often, and sometimes be carried to the gentry. And here . . . the heat, the flies . . . and shortage of water to wash properly." She glanced over to the end of the long room where Luisa was absorbed

428

in rearranging the furniture in her dollhouse. "And that wee thing there just couldn't stand such an illness."

A day later it was all arranged. We were booked on a sherry ship which was leaving Cádiz at the end of the week. I had sat by the telephone for hours waiting for the connection through all the hundreds of miles to Galicia. The Marquesa had offered no resistance to the new plans. "Sensible," she had said. And then, cautiously: "And what do you hear of the situation at Arcos?"

"I have not seen Don Paulo since the news first came, but he said he would see to . . . to it." We were careful what we said on the telephone with the operators no doubt listening all along the line.

"Then everything is in good hands," the Marquesa said, and hung up. A few hours later we had a telegram from her to say that the boys and Edwin Fletcher would start the long train journey south the next day.

"Only a few more days and she will be out of here," Luis said. "Then I shall breathe again. And in the meantime, Luisa will be tended by Nanny only. Every ounce of water is to be boiled, even what she washes in. She must have no milk. Nanny will prepare her food on the spirit stove in the nursery. She will not leave there. You have instructed Nanny about scrubbing her hands . . . ?"

"A hundred times a day." I smiled and placed my hand on his own sweating one. "Luisa will be all right. It is you I worry about, Luis. You have had so little sleep, and you eat nothing."

He smiled back. "I know. I make a fool of myself. But she is my life, querida. And in any case, I drink sherry. That's food enough, and no typhoid will live in it. . . . Come, let us have a copita together, and eat a little. Then I must go back to the bodega. Thank God there are no reports of anyone being ill in the town, but I have asked all the doctors to let me know at once if there should be any signs of it. . . ."

I knew he was now counting the hours until his precious child would be away, and safe.

That afternoon I had a telephone message from María

429

Luisa. She was abrupt, as she always was on the telephone. To her it was still a strange and unnatural instrument. She much preferred to write notes.

"Can you come over here, Carlota? Something rather strange . . . no, I'll tell you when you come."

In the heat of the afternoon I went to the Plaza de Asturias. A quiet lay on the old courtyard with its broken fountain. Times were more prosperous for my mother, but money did not extend to repairs of that nature. Besides, she always said she liked things left as they were. I could hear Andy whistling in the stable yard. I reminded myself that I must go and see him and Manuela and their three children before I left. None of the household here yet knew that all of us were going to England. I hoped the news would not upset my mother.

María Luisa greeted me quickly and kept me away from my mother's room, where she was resting. "I didn't want to disturb you, or her, but a very strange thing has happened, and I am not sure what to do. Perhaps I'm getting old. You have enough on your hands, and if I'd known you were weeping to go to England . . ."

"What is it?"

She sighed. "Rather one should ask, '*Who* is it?' She appeared out of nowhere a few hours ago. Got off a cart. Some workers had found her walking on the road some miles outside the town. She would say nothing to them except 'Plaza de Asturias' and one of them heard her say 'Blodmore'—or thought it was a word like that. So they brought her to the Plaza de Asturias, inquired at the church, and the sacristan naturally sent them here. He remembered your grandfather's name, you see. They wouldn't have taken such trouble about an odd woman wandering on the road, I'm sure, but, you see, she is very well dressed—or was. Her clothes now are in a terrible state, but it's plain to see she's no peasant. I suppose they thought there might be a few pesetas in it for them. So they got their few pesetas, and I—well, I got this . . . this woman."

"*What* woman . . . ?" I was growing impatient and, now, vaguely frightened.

430

She shrugged. "You may well ask, Carlota. *I* can't make sense of her. See if you can. . . . Perhaps I should have sent her to the nuns at once. But they're so feather-headed at times. Talkative, too . . ."

She walked ahead of me as she spoke, up the stairs to a room that was one of many seldom entered in this house. It had once been my room. The brass bedstead was still there, the few pieces of mahogany furniture, the old basket chair. The shutters were closed against the afternoon sun. María Luisa entered quietly and very gently pushed back one of the shutters halfway. The light streamed in. I saw, sitting in the basket chair, the figure of a woman, a woman with her straggling white hair tied in blue bows, wearing a dusty soiled white dress, a dress with many frills of lace, made in the style of many years ago. Her satin shoes were in tatters, as if she had walked a long way. She looked at me with those remembered violet eyes, looked at me blankly. And in her arms she cradled a wax doll.

The face had aged, but it was still the childlike face I remembered; the pockmarks seemed less noticeable be-cause the lines were deeper. Her cracked, parched lips moved, and I had to bend to hear the whisper. Only one word. "Blodmore . . ."

So close to her, I saw that she burned with fever, and yet her teeth chattered as she tried to say the word again.

I straightened, and looked at María Luisa. "I know who she is. And she has come from Arcos. You know there is typhoid in Arcos . . ."

4

Because she was who she was, we could not send her to the hospital or to be nursed by the nuns. We brought Dr. Ramírez, who confirmed that it was typhoid. "Who is this lady?" he said when he had finished laying out the medicines and drugs we were to use. I shook my head.

"We don't know. Someone some workers picked up on

431

the road. She asked to be brought here. They left her. She's . . . she's too ill to be able to tell us anything."

He didn't believe me, but I stared him down. "I had better send a nurse."

I was afraid of what she might say in her delirium, and so I refused. "María Luisa and I will take care of her."

"But you are going to England." He knew all our plans, as he was so often in the house to visit Luisa, whether she needed attention or not.

I looked at the poor creature lying in the big bed, tossing restlessly. Dr. Ramírez, after seeing the rose-colored spots on her chest and stomach, said she had probably been ill for at least a week, her temperature rising each day a little higher. When he had examined her, asked if she had backache, she had not answered, had not seemed to know that he even touched her.

"I can't return home now," I said. "I've been in contact with her. I might carry the infection to the household—to Luisa."

"Infection of typhoid is rarely carried directly. Go and bathe. Have them send clean clothes from the house. Burn the ones you have on. There should be no danger."

"I dare not. If by any chance I have become infected . . . No, it can't be. I could never forgive myself if Luisa should become ill."

He shrugged. "You are taking unnecessary risks staying here. A nurse would be more competent, more experienced. This is often dirty and disagreeable work. And for a stranger! Someone you don't know . . ." He began packing his bag. He knew a lot of our secrets, this man, and he had kept them all. He would ask no more about the identity of the unknown lady.

I had to play out the same charade with María Luisa, but she was more blunt. "You said you know who she is, but you choose not to name her." She flung her hands wide in a gesture of impatience. "And yet we have to take it on ourselves to nurse her. She may die on us—this lady from nowhere." She looked at me closely. "After all these years you can't trust me, querida?"

"I gave a promise long ago. I must keep it. I know she
432

is from Arcos. I can't tell you any more. Forgive me, María Luisa. But I gave my word. . . ."

She shook her head. "Strange . . . strange. For this we must sit up at night, perhaps catch this wretched infection ourselves. It is evident this is no ordinary woman. You know her, and yet I don't—I, who know *everything* that goes on in Jerez . . ." She shrugged. "Well, that is what the María Luisas of the world are for. We do what we are told, and ask no questions."

"You know it isn't like that."

"Yes, it is like that. Now let us stop this chatter and get to work. We must organize things. The others will have to be kept away. The servants . . . everyone." She had begun making a list. "Food we will prepare on the nursery stove. Water boiled. Plenty of clean sheets. We must wear aprons and tie our hair in cotton . . ." She muttered other things to herself.

"One thing, María Luisa. My mother must not see her. Tell her what you think best, but she must not see her."

She paused in her list-making. She looked carefully from me to the figure lying in the bed, her expression one of mingled disgust and compassion. "You need not worry. Your mother will come nowhere near her. It would be better, perhaps, if she were sent away. To the vineyard house, perhaps, or to Don Luis' hacienda. They will take care of her there. She has not been in contact with . . . with this lady. She should be quite safe. We must find some excuse for sending her. The less she knows about this lady the better. You know how she talks at times . . ."

After María Luisa had gone to start her preparations I stood looking down for a while at the pathetic and sad figure in the bed. She had been my grandfather's wife, had borne him a son. Even in her delirium she clutched the doll and would not be parted from it, though its clothes were as dirty and stained as her own had been. I knew that one of the first tasks, while we sat with her, would be to fashion some sort of nightgown for the doll from clean linen. I even thought it would be safer if we cut off its beautiful golden hair, but I shrank from that.

Then I went downstairs and wrote a note to Don Paulo.

He came at once, his face a mask of fear and worry. "We have searched for her night and day. No one knows where she has been. There is typhoid at the castle. The wells ran dry and they had to bring in water. All three of her personal attendants are ill—one is gravely ill and may die. The others—the ordinary servants—are not so vigilant and they are afraid to go near that part of the castle. The Marquesa is of course in Galicia, otherwise she would have instituted a much tighter control. I came too late. Before I had time to make the arrangements for the nuns to come in to do the nursing—before anyone knew Mariana herself was ill—she had vanished. She has never shown any inclination to leave the castle before. Quite the opposite. She shrank from contact with strangers. Why, in God's name, did she come *here?* Has she forgotten her father . . . ?"

He gazed down at the figure of his daughter in the bed but she didn't see him. Restlessly she turned on the pillow and fought with me a little when I wrung out a cloth and wiped the perspiration from her face and neck.

"I think the fever has made her remember the . . . the other time," I said. "She may be, in her mind, back in the time when she was so ill and she was kept from my grandfather. She has remembered his name, and remembered that he had bought a house here to bring her to. The doll she brought with her was his child. I am sorry, Don Paulo . . . it was so long ago, but I don't think the years in between exist for her."

He went and stood by the window, staring down into the dusty patio. He seemed hardly to be able to bear the sight of the woman in the bed. His hooded eyes were closed, as if he were in pain. Forty years lay between one event and another, the cataclysmic arrival of the Irishman into his world, and now this poor creature lying clutching her doll on the bed. Forty years was a long time to nurse a hatred, and Don Paulo was old.

"I was mistaken," he said finally. "I thought she had forgotten completely. They had so little time together, I thought it could all be wiped out. But it has endured to

434

this day. I should not have interfered with what happened, but accepted it. None of us can foresee the future, nor can we change what will be. Can one interfere with God? *You* came here as a direct result of that year when Blodmore was denied his wife. And then you and Carlos . . . I loved Carlos. This one here . . ." He nodded towards the bed. "How can one love a mindless child who is also nearly an old woman? But I am responsible before God for her. I do not love her, but I pity her. It would be as well if she died, but I am commanded by God's law to pray for her to live."

I accompanied him to the big doors that opened on the plaza. "You have been exposed to the infection. You have touched her, changed her clothes, bathed her. You cannot return to your home now."

"Not until the incubation period is over. Not until she is better."

"Or dead," he said. He started to turn away. "I will come each day to inquire. I will be as discreet as possible. To the world—to those who must know—she will be what she has always been at Arcos. She is a distant cousin of the Marquesa's. As few people as possible will know of her presence here. Your being here will be an unfortunate mischance, and you cannot leave for fear of infecting your children. The town will understand such things. It is all anyone will need know. . . ."

He walked across the plaza, a bent figure in his white summer suit and a wide-brimmed panama hat. He had not had himself driven here, and it was a long walk back to the bodega in the heat. He would do it each day, I knew, trying to avoid attention. But the town and its talk were ever present in his mind. The town . . . He had always been so careful, so clever in handling this situation. But could one hide the woman upstairs in the bed forever? And as I watched I saw him enter the church. I remembered his words. "It would be as well if she died, but I am commanded by God's law to pray for her to live." The stern God of the Spaniards was very much present in Don Paulo.

435

Over my protests Don Paulo sent a nun to help with the nursing. She came from a convent which had been the beneficiary of Don Paulo's charity for many years, and she clearly saw it as her duty to both pray and give practical help. She was old, silent, tired, and immensely experienced. She coped with the vomiting and the diarrhea without fuss, changed the sheets over and over again, took temperature and pulse, even sat and sewed a clean nightgown for the doll. She cut Mariana's hair and the hair of the doll at the same time. "There now," she said. "Now you'll both be more comfortable, won't you?" She asked not a single question about her patient, only asked Dr. Ramírez about certain symptoms. She had seen typhoid before, had lived through it herself. It was she who pointed out the rigid stomach of her patient and informed him of the first sign of bronchitis, which could lead to the complication of pneumonia. She was both tired and tireless. When she was not tending her patient she sat in the basket chair with her beads in her hands, her lips moving; she read her daily office from her book. With difficulty we got her to take periods of rest, but she was always ready when she was needed. She was called Sister Mercedes; she had been well named.

Dr. Ramírez brought and injected us with the precious anti-typhoid vaccine. "Your children have gone," he said. "Don Luis didn't give them an hour in the town. A sherry ship leaves Cádiz this evening."

It was only when the children were safely away that Luis himself came to the Plaza de Asturias. I made him stay outside and talked to him through the iron grille on the window of one of the long-disused rooms that looked out into the plaza.

"Carlota, this is madness! Why do you stay to look after this . . . this woman?" Don Paulo had been to see him, to explain my presence here. "You could get it. You could . . . you could die, Carlota." He was pained and frightened and anxious. He wore the expression of shock an older man suffers when he suddenly realizes that a younger wife might die before him. He had been through it with Amelia. He had not thought to suffer it again.

"I stayed because of the children. I could not put them in danger. Surely Dr. Ramírez has explained that to you! Now I must wait until the incubation period is over. She will be better soon. Then I will be home. We will go together to join the children in England. Together . . . as soon as the harvest is over." It was odd that at this time of extremity we had reached out to my father's regiment for help. Luisa and Tomás and Nanny were to stay with the Colonel's sister in London until we came. Meanwhile, the Colonel's sister was renting a house for us, was engaging staff. I was insisting that Luis should come with me. I was trying to tell him that I did not wish to risk another meeting with Richard Blodmore if he should decide to come over to London. I was telling him I needed his help, and he looked at me with grateful eyes.

"Yes, querida, that is what we will do. We will go as soon as you are ready. We will make a holiday of it. Take Tomás and Luisa about—show them everything. Together. I wish though . . ."

"What, Luis?"

"I wish you did not feel you have to nurse her. Is she so important that *you* have to do it?"

"She is just a poor, rather mad woman, Luis. A relation of the Marquesa's who's found her way here. Quite unimportant—and yet important in the way that anyone who comes to one's door is important. Would you have me look the other way, Luis? Pretend she does not exist? She is important to Don Paulo, because he places importance on all family ties. Would you have me be less than he?"

"You are the mother of children, Carlota. You are my wife. Your duty is to your own family first." He shook his head. "I don't understand this. Or Don Paulo. There is something I am not being told. Don Paulo is acting strangely . . . he is hardly at the bodega, and this is harvest time . . ."

I reassured him. I told the necessary lies, which I loathed doing, to him above all others. I was weary of it all—it had happened so long ago, and now it counted almost as nothing, except in the eyes and feelings of Don Paulo. Then I thought of my grandfather, and thought, too, that if things had been different the woman lying upstairs would have lived at Clonmara, would have given more children to my grandfather. My mother would have had half brothers and sisters. It was not nothing. It seemed almost like the hand of God that after forty years I was the one to care for her.

Luis gripped the bars of the grille with frustration and impatience. "If you say so, Carlota, then it must be. I have to charge you to be very careful. You have children . . . responsibilities." He made to turn away. "And look at this old place! The grille is ready to come apart in my hands. It's falling down!" He stood back and looked along the whole façade of the house. "I must either put it all in repair, or your mother must move out and come live with us. It's madness for her to stay on here. This part of the town, too . . . it's not suitable for her to be here any longer. This place is decaying, just like the rest of the area. What in heaven's name was your grandfather thinking of when he bought it, and just let it sit here?" He sighed, and shrugged, and tried to smile. "Well . . . you Blodmores, I'll never fully understand you. . . ." He saluted me briefly through the grille, blowing a kiss from his finger tips. "How absurd this all is. Anyone would think I was a young man courting his sweetheart—and a duenna sitting in the background. A grille between us! What next?" But he was laughing, and cheerful again. "I will come each day, querida. I will bring flowers. Too bad I no longer play the guitar . . . what a suitor . . . !"

I consulted with Sister Mercedes the next morning. "She is very bad, I'm afraid. I think it is time to send for the priest."

He came, the priest from Santa María de la Asunción across the plaza, bearing the Eucharist, an acolyte walking before him ringing a little bell to inform passers-by that the sacrament was being carried. Some, the older ones, fell on their knees. Many ignored it. María Luisa received him at the open door of the house with a lighted candle. We gave him a few moments alone with the sick woman, in case there should be a chance for confession, but she did not speak. Then we knelt as she was anointed and received the sacrament. During this time Don Paulo remained in the sitting room, kneeling. I found him kneeling still after the priest had gone.

"I try to pray, and my words are dry, like barren earth."

6

No one could say afterwards quite how it had started, or why. The Plaza de Asturias was bounded by a district where some of the poor of Jerez lived, those whose roosters and hens challenged the bells of the city's churches in the mornings. They lived in crumbling buildings too closely huddled together; they carried their water up long flights of stairs, their children cried in the night. There was never enough work, except at harvest time, and then, they said, the wages were too low. It was a time when such complaints were becoming vocal. At nights the cantinas sounded to the rumble of discontent. They talked much, Andy told me, of the landowners and of the Church, which was the greatest landowner of all. It may have started with an argument or a piece of rhetoric over a glass of wine. It ended, and that was all we knew, with a march whose target was the church of Santa María de la Asunción, across the plaza from my mother's house.

We heard the low murmur of their sound from the back rooms of the house, that frightening sound of a mob that has no definition. Andy appeared at once to report to us, coming only to the door of the nursery where María Luisa and I were cooking our meal. Everyone in the house had instructions to come no closer to us than that.

"There's some sort of disturbance, Miss Charlie. Speeches and such on the church steps. People throwing stones at the church door. Sounds to me as if a couple of them out there would like to burn it."

"Dear God," María Luisa said. "Has it come *here?*" We all knew what she referred to. Fresh in the minds of all of us were the stories of convent-burnings all over Spain, the rising vocal scream of anti-clericalism that came from a people who thought the Church too oppressive and too rich, saw the Church as guarding the long-established rights of the few over the many. But that it should have come here, to Jerez, seemed unthinkable. All that, we believed, was for other places, big industrial cities where the people went on strike for more money and better conditions. But what did the vineyards have to do with the factories of Barcelona?

"The doors are closed, Andy?—and all the shutters?"

He nodded. "Yes, Miss Charlie. But just say your prayers that they don't turn around and charge this way. Those old doors would give if a fly pushed them, and so would the shutters. Wouldn't say any of that grillwork on the windows would stand much handling, either. So rusty it'd come away in your hand."

"Andy, you know what you have to do. You can get out through the gate at the back of the stables." It was the gate where Carlos had once come in. "Take everyone. Manuela, the children, Serafina, Paco. Make them all go. They should go to Don Luis. At once. Don't wait to pack anything. If you go one at a time you'll mix with the crowd. They won't notice."

"And leave you here, Miss Charlie? I'll not do that! Manuela and the family will go. You both could go if you wanted to." Then he shrugged as he read the expression on my face. "I can see you won't leave *her.*" He jerked his head in the direction of the room where the sick woman lay. "Well, I'll get everyone off and do what I can to wedge a few braces against the front doors—not that *that'll* do much good." He directed another grim and exasperated stare towards the sickroom. "And it's not the best of all times to be having a nun in the house, if you don't mind my saying so."

"I do mind, Andy. She's an old woman, and she's never harmed anyone in her life. And perhaps we could stand a few of her prayers."

He indicated with a gesture that it was none of his responsibility, even though he made it his business. "We shall at least have one *man* with us," María Luisa said. "But we have a greater weapon. If it gets out of hand and they start pushing their way in here, just shout one word—*tifoidea*—typhoid! That will clear them quicker than cannon." She marched off to warn Sister Mercedes, who took the news with a nod and her usual unshakable calm, as if she had this and much more still to expect from life.

"God's will," she said. I stood in the doorway as she tried to take the temperature of the delirious woman in the bed. "For this one," she added, "God's will must soon be known. She is worse. When that godless rabble outside has cleared, we must send for Dr. Ramírez. Not that he can do much now. But at least we must be sure *all* has been done. . . ."

I lighted a candle and went through to the disused part of the house that overlooked the square. When I reached one of the front upstairs rooms, I snuffed the candle and with some difficulty, because of its stiffness, slightly opened one of the shutters.

It wasn't so terrible as it had sounded. A few hundred people, some with torchlights burning, had gathered in the plaza. But it was a small plaza, and the size of the crowd seemed intimidating. I became aware of Andy's worry when I realized once more that in size the façade of the house just about equaled that of the church opposite. Although the place was shabby and run down, and belonged to a woman who was known to be almost perpetually in debt, if the mob turned away through fear from the sacrilege of burning the church, this house was the next natural target. After all, debts or not, it represented the inequality of wealth and poverty in Andalucía, and through all of Spain. I listened to the chant that had become a distinguishable word. *Tierra!* Land! The eternal peasants' cry. They had no land; they wanted land. All their lives they and all the generations they could remember had worked the land of others, or they had toiled at something they could never own. Many times before they had demanded reform and reform had not come. Under the dictator Primo de Rivera reform had been promised, but there had been no action. In this house which was falling down around me, I thought of what riches my mother must seem to have, even though she was poor. But she owned this house, had owned a vineyard, had a stud in the country. Her daughter was married to a rich man. Her grandchildren were godchildren of one of the richest woman in Spain. I looked at those burning torches and fear gripped me.

It was over quite soon. The Civil Guard had been called. They came in lorries and on horseback. It needed so few of them to disperse the crowd. A few shots fired in the air. Some people falling, the others fleeing down the side streets that led to the barrio. There were shouts, orders, screams. The flaring torchlights were suddenly gone. I saw one fly through the air towards the street doors of the house, but it fell far short of its target—if in fact the house had ever been a target. The people were running, running. They had no weapons to turn and fight. The horses of the Civil Guard were reined in. The plaza was suddenly almost deserted. A few rapid commands. The Guard made no attempt to pursue the people into the side streets. They would stay just long enough to prevent them reassembling, to give a show of guarding the church. It had been nothing much after all. Just a little civil disturbance, of the kind that was taking place all over Spain these days—indeed, all over the world. This one had began quickly and ended quickly. I could imagine the talk there would be tomorrow through the town, and what the newspapers would say. Just a little firmness was necessary, and the people would do as they were told. In time there would be reform—in time, but not too quickly. They would say chaos came from too much haste.

But I had seen my first sight of hate and need, had heard the cry of anger. The crowd had been hungry for more than food. I shivered in the warm night air.

The Civil Guard had regrouped. I listened to the sound of the horses' hoofs on the cobbles. Those who had come by the lorries were gathering around them again. I saw the cigarettes come out, and the flare of the matches. And of those few who had fallen before the swift rush of the Guard, some had not risen. I saw four dark, crumpled shapes lying there below me, shapes indistinguishable as men or women in the dim light. The flaring torch that had been thrown towards the house had been extinguished. The plaza was now almost totally in darkness. I closed the shutter and fumbled my way back through the dark corridors of the house.

We had been expecting the commander of the Guard to come to the house; he would be inquiring if all was well. I told Andy to open when we heard the old bell clanging in the courtyard. I stood back a little as Andy opened up, prepared to warn the man that he or his men should not come closer. But when Andy slowly opened the big door it was not just the commander who stood there. Behind him four of his men were grouped, their rifles slung over their shoulders, and between them they bore the limp form of a man.

The commander recognized me as I moved out into the light. "Doña Carlota . . . a terrible misfortune . . ."

They shuffled foward. "He must have been caught here when the disturbance began. One of the anarchists, the anti-Christs, must have recognized him. They are like that—animals!"

The commander was admitting nothing. It could as easily have been a blow from one of his own men's truncheons as from the clubs some in the crowd had carried. Whichever it was, it had been a blow of tremendous power. Luis' skull had cracked under it, and he must have died very quickly, for there was little blood.

They moved forward into the courtyard and laid him on the stone bench surrounding the fountain, straightening his dusty clothes, one of them even crossing his arms across his breast. There was no talk of a doctor. They were very sure he was dead.

Then one of them, awkwardly, proffered a mangled bunch of flowers. "I found this by his side. My sympathy, señora. He was a much-respected gentleman."

I looked at the bruised blossoms Luis had come to the Plaza de Asturias to give me.

Sister Mercedes performed the task which was so often hers of washing him and laying him out. The terrible wound that had splintered his skull she covered with a large linen square tied about his head. It gave him a faintly rakish look, a look he had never had in life. I sat beside him and took his cold hand in mine, stunned, unbelieving. When María Luisa tried to take away the flowers I held, I resisted her. "Leave them. They were his last gift."

I had left the windows of the room open where he lay, and the false dawn had come, that silent time before even the first cock of the barrio had begun to crow, when Sister Mercedes came to tell me that the lady, her patient, had died.

7

There were two burials to attend. Luis' coffin was followed by half of Jerez after a solemn Requiem Mass had been sung in the Collegiate Church. The Civil Guard turned out to honor him. There were delegations from Seville, from all the sherry shippers, from every convent and religious order in the area, because he had been generous with his help. Four of Jerez's most beautiful black-plumed horses pulled the hearse. I could never forget how brightly the sun shone on the open carriages laden with flowers which had been sent. Along the route of the cortege the shops and cantinas closed. People jostled for space on the balconies above.

I lost Luis among all the ceremony of mourning that followed him. Don Paulo rode in the carriage with me, but I was still alone.

The other requiem Mass had been offered at the Church of Santa María de la Asunción across the plaza from my mother's house. It was very early in the morning, and only the few old women with their black dresses and shawls who regularly attended early Mass were there. There was only one carriage to carry Don Paulo, María Luisa, and myself. There was one wreath. I followed the body of my grandfather's wife to her grave with bitterness. Indirectly she had cost the life of Luis, and I found it hard to forgive. But she had been my grandfather's wife and must be laid to rest with dignity.

Anyone who was up early that morning in the town and who might have wondered about the identity and importance of the person who was followed by the Marqués de Santander and the widow of Don Luis would not have their curiosity satisfied. Later, when a stone was erected to mark her grave, the words told nothing. *Una Dama Desconocida*. An Unknown Lady. Even in death Don Paulo could not acknowledge his daughter, nor I the wife of my grandfather.

CHAPTER THREE

I went through all the motions of mourning that are demanded in Spain, but they meant nothing because Luis himself was not there to know them. I found myself talking to him at times, beginning to discuss something, and turning, almost in anger, to realize that he was missing. There was a great hollow at the center of my life, and almost the worst hurt was realizing that I had probably not managed to make him understand how important he had been to me. Perhaps I had not fully known it myself, and I cursed myself. I should have made him *know,* I said to myself, but I didn't realize . . . I kept thinking of that last bunch of flowers.

I looked at myself fully in the mirror one day after weeks of not noticing how I looked. I saw a thin woman with gaunt hollows at her cheeks. "A bag of dried old bones rattling together with nothing soft at the center," I said to the woman in the mirror. "You must have loved him, Charlie. Not the way you love Richard—but you did love him. I wonder if he ever knew? Too late to tell him now. No way to show it. . . ." I turned away from the stranger in the mirror. No point in looking there any longer. The face of Luis would not appear in it behind me.

I went to the bodega often, but never to the sala de degustación—that would have been too painful, and would have been unseemly in a newly widowed woman. But I found there some of the peace that had deserted me with Luis' death. Very often Don Paulo fell into step with me. We discussed the business of the bodega but little else. The talk had little meaning. We were simply companions to each other, reaching out in the only way we knew. "Most women go to church to pray," Don Paulo said. "You come here."

"What should I pray for?" I demanded of him. "That Luis come back? We know that cannot be. That he is in paradise? *That* must be certain. He was a good man. What should I pray for—tell me? For resignation? If I am resigned, then I stop mourning him. I will never stop mourning him. God, they say, never gives anything one asks for oneself. . . ."

"Come and have a copita," he answered roughly. "In my office." It was his way of offering sympathy, or was it, perhaps, a vain attempt to fill the gap? In his office we would drink a copita together, talk about the children, the state of the vines, the prospects for the harvest. We talked of politics—distant politics, the rumble we now heard through Spain; we talked of the Church, in which Don Paulo still believed, but more as a political force than a spiritual one, and we talked of Communism, which he abominated. We talked of nothing and everything. Sometimes I looked with amazement at the old man seated across from me and wondered if it were possible that, finally, we were growing to be friends.

But through bodega gossip the town knew of my walking along the aisles between the butts. They knew and they talked. "It's a pity, Carlota," María Luisa said, "that you cannot do your walking in your own garden at home. *That* anyone could understand. But at the

447

bodega . . . ? You know they are saying again that all the Blodmores are a little crazy."

"Let them say. I'll walk where I choose. I *like* the bodega. It calms me to walk there."

She shrugged. "Well, so long as it is only Don Paulo you walk with. Oh yes, everyone knows that too. You walk with your father-in-law, and talk. That's all right. When the year of mourning is up, just watch for the other men who will want to do the walking with you."

"Aren't two marriages enough, María Luisa? And don't you think they might not only be saying that all the Blodmores are a little mad, but also that they are more than just a little unlucky?"

"I never heard that the thought of perhaps a little ill luck trailing a woman ever kept off the men. Not when there is some money involved. The thought of money dissolves all sorts of fears, querida. They will be looking at you, and thinking that Luis left you well off. Even the young ones—the ones who haven't been married yet. You don't have to settle for a widower with children, querida. You could be attractive again, if you put a little flesh on your bones. If you would learn to smile again—that is, when the proper time comes. After all, you're only thirty-four. Not old . . ."

"Would *you* settle for just any man in order to be married?" I snapped at her.

She shrugged. "Well, since no one ever asked me, and there never seemed the remotest possibility of being asked, I can't answer." Then she paused and added slowly, "Perhaps I have become too content in my niche with your family, querida. Perhaps I am so long past hope that I forget what it is. But *no* . . . ! If I were you, I wouldn't settle for just any man." She nodded. "You are right, Carlota. You do not have to settle for any man who offers, or barter yourself away. . . ."

I ended the conversation because I was in danger of saying too much. There was only one man I would settle for, and him I could not have. There was a finality about it. I did not even answer the letter of sympathy, written with such excruciating care that the pain showed through

448

the conventional words, which Richard Blodmore wrote me. We seemed further apart than ever. I had two more children, and the memory of a husband I had loved, in my own fashion. Thirty-four, María Luisa had reminded me. It seemed young, and yet it was old. So much passion burned up with Carlos, so much tenderness expended with Luis, and the love that had belonged to Richard Blodmore all these years largely wasted, like the river in spate which rushes to the sea, leaving the dry land about it parched.

The terms of Luis' will had been precise. One third of his estate went to me, one third to Tomás, one third to Luisa. This gave me voting rights at board meetings of the sherry company of Fernández, Thompson; I would exercise these rights also for Tomás and Luisa until they came of age. My mother had signed a proxy which gave me voting control of the shares my grandfather had purchased so long ago. Don Paulo had nodded over all this speculatively. "You have become a small power among us, Doña Carlota. Be very careful how you use it." He did not offer again to buy my mother's shares. That ambition seemed to have left him.

I knew that Juan had been shaken by his exclusion from Luis' will. He and his brothers, Martín and Francisco, must now look to Don Paulo and the Marquesa if they were to have more than an ordinary position at the bodega. Perhaps Luis had foreseen this and known that it was probable that these three children of Don Paulo's most loved son would benefit from their special place in the affection of the old man, and from the possessiveness of the Marquesa over them. So he had given Tomás weapons of ownership to use against them when the time would come. Giving Tomás so much, singling him out from his half brothers, was Luis' way, after his death, of proclaiming to the world that Tomás was his son. No one, he seemed to say, could ever doubt it now, since he had not. Luisa's place, of course, was secure.

Luisa was too young to know or care about any of this. Her whole world had turned upside down with her father's death. She had returned from England and shrieked in

449

anguish at the reality of finding him truly gone. Nothing we could do for her seemed to comfort her for his absence. No indulgence was enough, no distraction would suffice for the loss of his undivided attention. She, who had always been so biddable, suddenly gave way to tantrums. She broke her toys and screamed with rage at trifles. She had bad dreams, and wept at night, and frequently I would take her, crying, from the nursery, to sob herself to sleep against my shoulder in the big bed where she had so often romped with her father. "Papa . . . Papa . . ." the suddenly querulous voice would cry. "I want Papa."

I began to take her with me to the bodega. Each day I would order out the carriage and the horses in their full festive harness, and we would drive there and walk the aisles of the bodega together. She would solemnly sip a tiny copita with Don Paulo, looking alarmingly like one of those beautiful wax dolls in the castle at Arcos. I don't know if the whole exercise did any good, but at least the walking tired her, the wine soothed her, and she was ready for the siesta.

She added something also to the life of Don Paulo. He had granddaughters—five of them—the daughters of Ignacio and Pedro. But beside Luisa, I thought, they seemed dull little girls who might have his affection but did not engage his attention. He saw the problems of Luisa's anguished longing for her dead father, and as she had charmed Luis, now the charm began to work on Don Paulo. He ordered toys from Seville and even from London. Some were successful, others not. Luisa had, at this time, no stock of politeness to cover what didn't interest her. But when she was pleased the smile that came on that grave little face brought a look of delight to Don Paulo which I had never seen before, not even in his dealings with Carlos or Juan. "With girls it is different," he would say, trying to excuse himself. "One may indulge them without ruining them." It wasn't true, of course, but I didn't argue. I granted that Don Paulo had been sincere in his judgment that he had been too harsh with his own daughter. It would have been cruel not to give him the relief of being excessively indulgent with Luisa. And anything that could turn Luisa's mind away from the aching loss of her father was welcome. Perhaps Don Paulo was making this effort with her in an attempt, in some way, to try to make up this loss. But it seemed to me now that we both, Don Paulo and myself, had become exhausted by keeping the score, tired of our animosities towards each other. If one looked back on it, it was a long and sorry list to tally—my grandfather's unsanctioned marriage to his daughter Mariana; my own marriage to Carlos; Carlos' life at the expense of my mother's grievous and permanent injury; Carlos' own death blamed on me; then the coming of Mariana to the Plaza de Asturias and so being, inadvertently, the cause of Luis' death. There was too much now to weigh in the balance, and I think in the year that followed Luis' death we decided to abandon the whole battle, like two opposing gladiators who realize that there can be no winner. We allowed ourselves, in that year, in the guise of helping Luisa, to become friends. I did not blame Don Paulo for the waste of time. He could be a friend of the woman in a way he could not have been a friend of the girl. I had had to grow up to him.

Luisa needed the male influence in her life. We were now a household of women. After the scene I had witnessed from the window in the Plaza de Asturias, I felt it no longer safe to leave my mother in such close proximity to the barrio and the focus of discontent represented by the church across from her door. So she and María Luisa, Andy and his family moved to Los Cisnes. Serafina and Paco resumed the duties of caretakers which had been so unexpectedly taken from them seventeen years ago. Peace and dust could descend on the house once more. I thought of how Serafina and Paco must have settled back into the kitchen on the first night after everyone had left. They hadn't expected seventeen years of the sort of turbulent existence we had brought them. They had expected us to be gone within the year. Instead of which I was now inextricably woven into the texture of Jerez life, and my children with me. I thought of the first night when Don Paulo had waited to give us what had seemed to be a welcome, but had really been some sort of warning. I thought of the stables where Balthasar had ruled, and had almost killed Carlos. I thought of my children being born there. For a time the old place had teemed with the life for which it had waited so long. My grandfather's intentions had been carried out, but not in the manner he had expected. Now it was deserted again and was sinking back into a dreaming state, and into decay.

"You should sell it," I said to my mother. In a sense, its purpose had been served, though only I knew it. Mariana had come there to die, to the home my grandfather had prepared for her. But I wasn't surprised when my mother shook her head.

"No—let it be." I didn't press her. Perhaps she thought of the other homes that had gone—Clonmara, the vineyard house. She wanted to keep something that was her own, even a moldering mansion in a no longer desirable part of town. I never mentioned it again, though María Luisa often pointed out to me the drain of keeping it in even minimum repair, the cost of Serafina and Paco, "eating their heads off and doing nothing." But she said that only to me because she thought she should. She had learned not to trouble my mother with such things.

The three boys had made their visits to Clonmara, and now usually expected to be invited there each Easter. They seemed to enjoy Ireland and were friends with the Selwin boys, Edward and Paul. Their bond, of course, was the love of horses, and they even spent a Christmas there, to get a taste of Irish hunting. I did not want them to go, and yet I could find no real reason for stopping them, especially since the visits were encouraged by the Marquesa. "But don't talk to Granny about it," I cautioned them. "It only upsets her. She remembers Clonmara in a different way. . . ." Yet sometimes she would talk of Clonmara to them with perfect good sense, asking about the changes—she preferred to call them changes, rather than improvements—and other times she would talk of it and the people she had known as if no time at all had elapsed since she had last ridden to hounds, following her father. There were the times when the boys learned to be silent, to let her talk. They had almost ceased to be embarrassed by her.

But Juan, after Luis' death, began showing more interest in remaining in Jerez. Perhaps it was that he saw his position threatened by Tomás, and by the sons of Ignacio and Pedro. Everything lay in the future for him; it promised bright. But it was only a promise. The future was not secured. He was torn one summer by the decision whether to accept the Marquesa's usual invitation to escape to the cool greenness of Galicia, or to stay and endure the heat of the Andalucian summer so as to begin to learn the work of the bodega. In the end he achieved his object by the diplomatic device of riding out to Sanlúcar to visit the Marquesa and putting the matter directly to her, asking her advice, appearing to rely on it.

"I told her," he said when he returned, "that it was time I began to learn from my grandfather. He has, after all, the best nose in the business. I shall never have a better teacher. She advised me to stay."

So when the summer heat descended on us it was Juan instead of Luisa who walked the aisles of the bodega with me, though he had not much time to do this. He was working regular hours at the bodega, filling in with whatever tasks were required of him, and learning what he could pick up along the way. He was dissatisfied. "I have hardly anything to do with the sherry. Mostly they send me round with messages from one office to the other. I file papers. I translate into English. I try to get into the sample room whenever I can, but Tío Pedro always finds a reason to get me out. . . ."

"That you must expect. He has two sons of his own."

"And Tío Ignacio has three. So we must all fight it out to see who can get what. If my father had been alive—"

I cut him short. "Learn what you can from your grandfather."

He nodded silently, and in some mysterious fashion he always seemed to know the days when Don Paulo and I met in the bodega, and he would contrive to join us. He listened respectfully to whatever Don Paulo had to say and he waited hopefully for the invitation to join us in the sala de degustación. If Don Paulo required his presence, then every other task was excused him. I knew that Ignacio and Pedro believed I contrived these meetings to advance Juan with his grandfather, and perhaps they were right. I knew that the meetings were happy ones for Don Paulo; I had begun to care for that.

It was now quite proper for me to appear in the sala de degustación once again, among the customers and visitors to the bodega, especially since I was accompanied by Don Paulo and my eldest son. It seemed to me that Juan began to eye with hostility any man who came near our table, especially if the man was unmarried.

"They will come sniffing round, Mother," he said. "When you marry again, you must choose very carefully."

"You expect me to marry again?"

"Well, of course. You're quite pretty, still. You're well off. You could do the family a lot of good by the right marriage."

I ached to slap that handsome, too worldly-wise face. "Mind your own business, Juan."

"I think it *is* my business."

A little coolness grew up between us after that. I was glad when the time came for the others to return from Galicia, and the three boys to go back to school in England. I had Tomás and Luisa to myself again. The harvest was over, the days were quiet. I wrote in my book for that year, 1927: *Very lean crop and poor quality*.

Edwin Fletcher, who as usual had spent the summer in Galicia with the boys and Luisa on the Marquesa's estate, came to me and suggested that he should get another tutoring position. I looked at him in surprise.

"Whatever for?"

He was slightly embarrassed. Even since his return from England after the war, after I had married Luis, his salary had been paid by Luis, not the Marquesa. "Am I of any use to you now? One small boy of seven and one little girl to teach. Is that enough? People will say I have become a parasite on you."

I rounded on him. "*You* are not going to desert me,

Edwin Fletcher!" Then another thought occurred. "Or perhaps you want to go? Someone else has made you a better offer. I'll match it."

"There has been no better offer. I haven't even got another position in mind. I just thought . . . well, maybe you'd like a governess instead."

"What rubbish!" I asked angrily, "Tell me, Edwin, has Juan been hinting anything to you? He talks in a pretty vulgar way of men coming 'sniffing' around me. Is that what's troubling you? You have to tell me."

His silence answered me.

"Haven't you got the courage to stay with us through a little gossip, Edwin? What can anyone say except that you come daily to teach my children?—a position for which you have always been overqualified. That you stay and eat lunch with us as a member of the family. You were a member of the family when both my husbands were living. Will you let the nasty hints of a boy upset all that? After all, aren't I properly chaperoned? My mother and María Luisa both in the house with me, a child hanging on my hand wherever I go? Everyone knows we are lucky to have your services. Are you going to desert me, Edwin? You are needed. Think of what it would do to Tomás and Luisa to have one more of the linchpins of their lives taken away at this time. They would grieve for you, Edwin. They need you. I need you."

He flushed deeply. "That is what the Marquesa said."

"You discussed it with *her*. That isn't fair, Edwin. She doesn't run this household."

"She brought up the matter. She has a long vision. She can see the dangers of my staying, and yet she thinks it is better, on the whole, that I do. That is what she *told* me. She had it all thought out."

"Perhaps you should go home for a time. Back to England. Have a holiday. It would clear the air, and your mind. If you come back, it would be because you wanted to, not because of pressure. After all, it's very selfish of me to say you can't go elsewhere because you're needed here. You might have other plans. I've always expected that one day you would marry . . ."

"Carlota!" He used my name this way only when we were in private. "Have you forgotten how long I have lived here in Jerez? How long I've been away from England? I've only lived this long because I've lived here, because I've had this dry air and the sun. Marriage, you say? Who wants to marry a man with no money and only one lung?—and that one none too good! Would any of the young ladies of Jerez have me? I think not. Even the poor and the plain would look on me as a pretty bad bargain."

"Then why are you talking all this nonsense about leaving us?"

"Because of *you* . . . your reputation. I would do anything in the world rather than hurt you. But even a devoted dog has feelings of his own. . . ." He broke into a fit of coughing which he couldn't control. He struggled to his feet and left the room. I heard his hurrying footsteps in the passage, and the sound of a door to the garden being opened and slammed closed.

"Oh, God," I said aloud. "Not Edwin. I can't stand it if anything happens to send Edwin away." But I realized the truth of his accusation. For too long I had placed him in almost the same category as María Luisa, reliable, patient, always there. A fixture in my life that I didn't have to think would ever change. "Even a devoted dog has feelings of his own. . . ."

At supper that night María Luisa said, "Is Edwin very unwell, do you think, Carlota? I came on him in the garden today, sitting down on the ground by the wall in the sun. He looked almost as ill as he did when he first came. Perspiration standing out on his face. Hardly able to speak for coughing . . ."

I looked around the table. Three women dining alone, as we always did. Tomás and Luisa with Nanny. Edwin Fletcher seated at the table of the Señoritas Hernandos. I was ashamed of all the years, of all the ways I had taken him for granted. And yet it was true. I did need him. "He takes these spells now and then, María Luisa. We mustn't forget that when he first came we expected he would die on us in the first months."

456

My mother looked up from her soup, face agitated. "Die? Who's going to die?"

"No one, Mother."

After that Edwin made a bid for some sort of independent existence. He bought a few hectares of land on the edge of the sierra near Medina Sidonia. "It's very poor land," he said. "I'll never be able to raise fat cattle on it. But it's the first place I've ever owned." He had a well dug, and began to build a very simple house. "Hardly more than a hut, but it will serve." Once a month he took four days off and went and stayed there alone. He began to move books there, and he said he was trying to write. "Just a few ideas I have about history. No one will ever publish them—but just the same . . ." He would come back from those spells away looking lean but somehow toughened. I began to envy him the freedom of his time alone. "The Señoritas Hernandos Delgado are very kind, but at times a little overwhelming. I like my rustic retreat." He had a war disability pension from the British government, and his savings. "It's my stake in the world, Carlota," he said. "I know I'll never go back to England permanently. I'll die in Spain."

I went on with all the things that Luis had left in my hands. I attended the board meetings at the bodega, only cautiously venturing any opinions at first, listening very closely to what was being said, trying to make sense of the financial statements, tending to follow Don Paulo's lead in everything, but determined that I must, in time, gain some independent opinions against the day when he would not be there and I must then face Ignacio and Pedro, and whoever else would be then on the board. Although I had not wanted to, at last I broke down and asked Edwin to explain the financial statements to me. "I can hardly read them," I said, "much less see where they're heading. It was simpler in the old days when I just had the vineyard. So many butts of must, so many pesetas, set against what I had to pay out for labor."

He sighed. "I studied mathematics, Carlota. That

doesn't mean I'm an accountant. I'm more used to theory than practice." Then he laughed. "This is where we people with theories always fall down. . . . But I'll try."

The bodega was a complex business in terms of what I had previously known, and it was a sometimes precarious business. The labor costs were increasing continually, and the sales had to be made abroad to keep pace. We carried the burden of the bad seasons and scrambled to make up in the good ones. I worried about exports now as I never had before. Sherry was an expensive wine to produce, and it had to compete on the market. I began to realize that, of the sherry shippers who were rich, most of them had other interests. And so I began to understand more fully Luis' concern with the breeding of his bulls, the careful experimentation with his cattle, the growing of sugar beets, the tending of his olive groves. If there was a loss on one enterprise in one year, there was a chance to make a profit on something else. Having made Edwin a party to the accounts of the bodega, I now opened the books of all the other concerns to him.

"Carlota, I'm not a businessman. I can read the balance sheets, but I can't take the risks for you."

"I'll take the risks, Edwin."

I also showed him the stocks that Luis had left me in other businesses, ones in which he had no active control but which yielded, mostly, a good dividend, money which was quickly swallowed up by the house, the family, the other expenditures. "I had no idea we cost Luis so much," I said. "I am very stupid and thoughtless. I would have tried to make economies. But Luis never said anything. . . ."

"Only a miser is incapable of enjoying money, Carlota. Luis did it the right way."

But when Juan returned at Christmas he saw what had developed, and he was resentful. "You might have waited for me, Mother. I have only another half year at school. Then I shall be here all the time to help. You could have waited."

"I thought you were going to Cambridge. You know Luis wished that."

"That was when my stepfather was alive. Now he is dead, you need a *man* here."

"We'll see, Juan. You would be better prepared for a career here if you had some years at university. I wish I had. . . ."

He gestured impatiently. "Well, women don't *need* that, do they? England's quite spoiled since women got the vote. They're forever sticking their noses into men's business."

"Women have always done that, Juan. But they usually managed to leave the men unaware of it. But England isn't Spain, and women here will be as they've always been, for quite some time."

"Then I shall take care to marry a Spanish girl."

He rode out with me when we went to inspect the bulls and the cattle, often giving advice where it wasn't wanted. But I kept silent. He had to learn sometime, and it was better if he made his mistakes with me. He was only a year older than Martín, and two years older than Francisco, but beside them he seemed a man. They followed his lead absolutely, as they had always done. When we rode together, my mother among us, it was always Juan who spoke for the three of them. I had to admit that he had an eye for the bulls. He rode among them skillfully, fearlessly. He had developed as a splendid horseman. He was brave, but he had the wisdom not to show off, especially among the men who rode with us, those who spent their lives in the saddle. When we sold bulls he was often there to help select and to cut them out from the herd. He spent a long time studying them and the cows. "We have to know which ones to keep back for breeding, Mother. If you sell off all the brave bulls you leave only poor blood behind. Don Luis had a reputation for breeding brave bulls. We must not let it down." Conventional wisdom, but at least he was learning.

He had been admitted to the company of the *garrochistas,* those who tried the young bulls from horseback to mark their qualities of courage. In this exercise two horsemen rode together with their long limewood bullfighting spears. The object was to tumble the calf with a

459

blow from the spear; it was a difficult maneuver which required not only good horsemanship but courage and steady nerves. The calf that regained its feet and charged the horse would be a brave bull. The *arcoso y derribo* was the only test permitted with the young bull calves, and it was the only guide for the bull breeder before sending the bull to the ring years later. The bull learns quickly, and too much knowledge is dangerous in the ring. I thought it strange that I could enjoy the experience of the breeding of bulls, and yet I still could not attend a bullfight without the old sickness and revulsion returning. I attended the corrida very seldom, and only on very special occasions, and half the time hid my eyes behind a fan.

When we rode my mother's stud, the years that had passed were visibly before me in the form of Balthasar. He was now very old, any part of him that had been cream-colored was perfectly white; he moved stiffly. And yet when he heard my mother's voice call him he would come at a trot across the paddock, his head lifted in eagerness, a whinny of affection to greet her. "Wouldn't it be kinder to put him down?" Juan whispered to me. "He suffers from arthritis. Look how his teeth are."

It was one of my mother's days of keen perception. She heard everything. "He can still trot. Sometimes I have come out here early of a winter's morning and seen him roll on the ground. He still enjoys his life. Why should I take it from him?" She gave him the sugar he craved. "He and Half Moon were founders of this stud. She is gone, but look what, between them, they have left behind. I sell my horses all over Spain, to England—even to Ireland. And that's like selling his own horse to a tinker. No, let Balthasar have the length of his days, whatever they are."

It wasn't good business, but in certain terms it made perfectly good sense.

The Marquesa came from Sanlúcar and took up residence with Don Paulo at Las Fuentes for the Christmas period. It was an unusual concession for her, who usually preferred to be alone at Sanlúcar. We all attended midnight Mass, and we were all bidden to Don Paulo's house the next day—all of us, even Edwin Fletcher. Ignacio's and Pedro's families were there. There was a great distribution of presents, and twenty-five were seated around the great long table. The Marquesa had brought her own chefs; the food and wine were superb. But a slight air of constraint lay on the party. The presence of the Marquesa tended to do that always, but on this occasion there was a distinct sense of competition for the notice of both her and Don Paulo. Like Balthasar, they revealed their ages in so many ways. The Marquesa was years younger than Don Paulo, but even with her one noticed a slowing of the movements, the deeper lines on her face. But the minds of both of them seemed only honed sharper by the passage of the years. They sat there and listened to Martín play his guitar after the dinner, sat and watched the dancing that followed; their eyes seemed to be summing up all of us, these second cousins, these half brothers and sisters. We were a motley mix. I sat quietly, and Edwin Fletcher kept away from me, dutifully going the rounds of all the daughters of Ignacio and Pedro, and their wives. My mother, careless after so much good wine, danced with wonderful grace with Juan. Ignacio came to offer me his hand. We danced decorously, and almost without a word. I had very little, ever, to say to Ignacio and Pedro. And then Juan silenced the musicians Don Paulo had hired, and produced a gramophone he had brought from England, and some jazz records. The Marquesa sat listening, as if it were her duty to be informed of everything that was happening in the world, even something so alien as this. And Juan tried to teach my mother the Charleston. One of Ignacio's girls went to the piano and produced her own version of jazz. She was quite good, Juan conceded. Luisa had slipped into the big chair with the Marquesa, as if it were her rightful place. Her face was flushed with the dancing. She was tired. I saw that the Marquesa held her hand, and, in the only maternal gesture I had ever witnessed in her, smoothed the dark hair back from her hot forehead.

Then the Marquesa went to the piano; her fingers were

stiffening, but she still could find the notes. Together we sang some Christmas hymns. Don Paulo's eyes glistened beneath his heavy lids, and I could not tell whether it was pride or tears that made them shine.

That winter Don Paulo was confined to bed with a chill that held on stubbornly. He did not appear at the bodega for many weeks. I missed him. The lofty buildings now were cold, especially when the levanter blew, and I was muffled up as I walked the aisles. I felt oddly alone, and although I seldom encountered them, the presence of Ignacio and Pedro pressed on me. I felt I had to hold on for my children's sake, and did not know quite how to.

I went frequently to visit Don Paulo. He was up, and sat before the fire in his room or, when the sun was strong, by the window. He was thinner, and rather feeble, but his head came up like a snapping turtle's when anyone suggested that he should take his time about coming back to the bodega. "Think they'll get rid of me, do they? Tell them there's a lot of life in the old man yet."

The Marquesa had come again from Sanlúcar to stay with him during his illness. This was so contrary to her custom that I wondered if he were not worse than anyone else knew. But one day when the first warm sun of April was touching the bodega's walls he appeared there again, only slightly slower in his walk. We paced the bodega again, went from one building to another, a long walk for anyone, a tiring one for an old man. He insisted on talking with the capataz of each bodega, and began to make plans for visiting the outlying ones in Puerto. He smelled a few samples of the must from the previous vintage, discussed their grading with the catador, called for some samples from the various scales of the solera. It was a virtuoso display as he insisted on handling the venencia himself, and not a drop was spilled.

We went to the sala de degustación together and took our places at our accustomed table. Everyone there came to pay his respects. The faces around him were pleased, or not, according to how they regarded Don

462

Paulo. It looked as if the old man would be there forever.

Easter came, and unexpectedly Juan returned home. He had only a few days to spend with us. Martín and Francisco had gone to Clonmara. The Marquesa had stayed on in Don Paulo's house, which surprised me. She did not care for the processions of Holy Week, and liked to save her energy for the Fair in Seville. There were arguments between her and Juan about his going to Cambridge. "Your education hasn't begun," she said.

"I want to stay in Jerez," he said, rather sullenly for him.

"You can stay in Jerez after you've learned the world outside it." I found myself in a strange alliance with the Marquesa. I needed Juan's support here in Jerez, and yet I needed the support of a man, not a boy. The Marquesa seemed to know it. "Do not," she said, "make your father's mistake of thinking he knew everything, when he knew only half of it. Take a year at Cambridge. Take a year or two in Madrid. Then you may be able to take Jerez."

"I can continue studying with Mr. Fletcher."

"I was not talking of scholarship." She tapped her long fingers on the arm of the chair. "I shall be very disappointed in you, Juan, if you decide against this."

That was the final word on the matter from her. She did not hold out a bribe or make any promises. She offered nothing except the certainty of her displeasure if her wishes were not obeyed. Juan raged and fumed, but now he did it in private. "Tío Ignacio's sons and Tío Pedro's two are not hounded and bullied this way," he complained to me. "She doesn't tell *them* what they must do. They'll be years ahead of me here at the bodega, sucking up to Grandfather—"

"Perhaps she doesn't *care* what they do. And as for sucking up to their grandfather . . . don't you do rather a lot of that yourself, Juan? Absence, they say, makes the heart grow fonder. Try it, Juan."

He lingered on after Easter, when he should have returned to school. "What does it matter," he said, "so

463

long as you write them? I've passed all the exams I need. I have a place at Cambridge. You can't say my reports haven't been good. . . . All I'll be doing this term will be a bit of extra reading, and Mr. Fletcher's a better tutor than any at school. He's given me a reading list to get through before I go up to Cambridge."

It was true he had been an excellent scholar, which had rather surprised me. It did not surprise Edwin. "He's always had a good brain, but not a deep one. He doen't love his work for its own sake, but for where it's going to take him. Ambition and a bright mind . . . If he were an Englishman he might make a good politician. But I'm not sure if that isn't insulting him." We laughed together, but perhaps the description was apt. I suspected, though, that Juan's hard work at school, his determination to get good reports, was to show his superiority to the sons of Ignacio and Pedro, who with Don Paulo's help had also been sent to school in England. They were all younger than Juan, and Juan seemed determined to be the pacesetter. When Ignacio had started to talk of sending his older son to an English university for at least a year when the time came, I knew that Juan's acceptance of Cambridge was guaranteed.

Was it, I wondered then, the politician in Juan which caused him, with the extra week he was taking off school, to decide to remain in Jerez when, after Easter, the rest of the family, headed by the Marquesa, set off for the Fair in Seville? It was an occasion that young men like Juan gloried in—the chance to show off their beautiful horses, to size up the suitable girls, to be admired and applauded, to get a little drunk and to flirt, all under the eyes of the girl's family, which made it respectable. There was so much gossip traded back and forth at Seville each year, the new faces examined and appraised, and matched to the possible dowries. Yes, it was Juan's natural place, and yet he did not go.

"My grandfather is not well," he said. "*You* are staying to be with him. I have only a few more days before I have to go back to England. I might as well stay here. Seville will keep for another year."

Jerez and the bodega seemed very quiet when everyone of any social pretensions had left for Seville. It was a week of wonderful weather, warm but not hot. Don Paulo was stronger. He walked the aisles of the bodega with more pace and confidence. He took Juan for several sessions alone in the cuarto de muestras. Here he could range through all the samples of sherry either shipped abroad or sold in Spain, and the way the customer's requirements were met as to the degree of dryness or sweetness. Here also the samples of must, at harvest time, were brought so that the bodega could decide on the quality and make their offer to the vineyard owners. When they joined me later in the strange quiet of the sala de degustación Juan's eyes were alive with excitement and pleasure.

"Grandfather says that if the harvest comes early in September and I've not already left for England, he'll let me in there when the samples of must are brought in, and try to grade them myself."

"Well, we've had the right amount of rain. The vines look good. It promises a good harvest. But you *are* going back to England in September, then . . . to Cambridge?" I wanted to hear it from his own lips.

He lowered his eyes, those greenish Blodmore eyes that ran through the family—he was looking unnaturally diffident. "Grandfather has persuaded me that it is the best thing to do. I'm doing it for him."

Politician—but glancing over at Don Paulo and seeing those dark eyes as skeptical as ever, I knew that Juan had a long way to go before he could match his grandfather in this sort of game.

"Well, let's drink to it then," the old man said. The servant came forward and poured the fino. We all held our glasses to the light, as we had grown used to doing, the color and purity of the wine as much a pleasure as its taste. *"La penúltima,"* Don Paulo said. In Jerez we never thought of drinking our last glass of sherry, it was always the last but one, the one for the road, and we called it la penúltima. It was a going-away salute to Juan.

We smelled, and sipped and tasted the wine against our tongues. The first was always the best of the day. I was feeling almost happy. The quiet of the bodega had soothed me, the news that, for whatever reasons, Juan would have at least a little time at university, the sparkling April sunshine that came through the windows of the sala, the glimpse of the green shoots which the old vines trained between this building and the next bodega had put out, all these things raised a spirit of hopefulness and renewal in me. It was like the flor appearing once again on the wine, the promise of a renewal of life. I thought of Luis and Richard Blodmore, but not with sadness. I looked at the color of the wine in my hand. It was a wonderful thing to have loved, to have been loved. It was a good thing to sit here in the spring sun in peace with the old man and the young man, and feel that I was the instrument of life that bound them. I smiled.

"Grandfather!"

I looked at Don Paulo. For an instant he had seemed to smile, but Juan's instinct was quicker than mine. He sprang to his feet and leaned over the old man. The thin lips twisted now, upward, as if he held them set against the pain. Then he whispered something. Only because the sala was deserted did we hear the words. "La penúltima . . ."

He died there in that sturdy oak chair only moments later. He had placed his glass carefully upon the table, and the wine was not even spilled.

"Grandfather . . . !" The cry of anguish from Juan was unheard, the dark eyes stared unseeingly at the green shoots on the vines.

The shock of his death was carried on to the will. He had left a third of his estate to the Marquesa, a third was divided between his sons, Ignacio and Pedro, and Carlos' sons, Juan, Martín, and Francisco, and a third, which by law he was entitled to leave as he chose, was left to me. The one portion of his estate which was singled out from the total was Las Ventanas Verdes, which he also bequeathed to me.

A soft gasp went around the room when this was read out. I had been invited to attend the reading, but I had assumed that it was only a courtesy, as Carlos' sons, in whatever proportion, would inherit a share of the estate. Now I felt all the eyes turned on me, mostly with hostility, some with outright anger. Only the Marquesa remained unmoved. It was probable she had already known.

We made the barest formality of drinking a token copita together, for the sake of giving the appearance of family solidarity. Pedro avoided me completely. Ignacio was already counting up how many shares—those left me by Luis, those I voted by proxy for my mother, those I voted for Tomás and Luisa until they came of age, those now left to me by Don Paulo—how many shares in all I controlled.

I said good-by to the Marquesa. "Will you be going now to Sanlúcar? You will be going to Galicia as usual for the summer months?"

"I shall go to Galicia, certainly. But I do not think I shall now go back to Sanlúcar. It is too far to come in here to Jerez every day. I shall be attending the bodega regularly. Don Paulo always expected people to take their responsibilities seriously." She was moving closer into our lives. Her words had carried through the room. We had been shocked by the reality of mortality. We had expected Don Paulo to go on forever, but he was dead. The prospect of the death of the Marquesa moved inexorably nearer. The power that her wealth would bestow, and the question of how she would choose to bestow it, hung like a tangible presence in the room. Now this knowledge that she would involve herself in the affairs of the bodega made everyone uneasy. This was no submissive spirit but a formidable will. A sense of fear edged in, and the knowledge of a battle joined. But no one could see the forces on the other side. No one knew this capricious woman well enough to know where she would decide, finally, to place the strength of her power.

Juan, who accompanied me to hear the will read, kept his outrage to himself until we were alone. "How *could* Grandfather do that! Leave it to you! *I* am the oldest grandchild. I am a man now. He could have trusted me.

That third should have been divided between me and Martín and Francisco, with the biggest share going to me."

I thought I saw jealousy as well as anger in his face. He didn't seem to care how he was revealing himself. "It was his will, Juan. That is what the word means. He had his reasons—"

"He could have left it in trust for me until I'm of age. But to leave it to a *woman*. He didn't even like you!" He added bitterly, "I thought he loved me, but now I know I was no more to him than any of Ignacio's or Pedro's tribe."

"He meant you to wait, Juan."

"Wait until that old woman dies?—if *she* leaves me anything! Wait until Granny dies. Wait until *you* die. I have only *women* in my world, and now I have to dance attendance on all of them! My shares will amount to so little I won't count as anything, unless the Marquesa . . ."

I recoiled from him. I thought I had already learned all the weaknesses in him, the things that could be expected and forgiven in a young, good-looking, rather spoiled young man. But here was a streak I had not touched before. "Perhaps," I said, "your grandfather intended patience to temper greed."

He did not rise to the insult. I think he hardly heard it.

"Now I shall have to go on paying court to that terrible old woman. I shall have to work like a dog at the university to please her. I shall have to do everything she says I must. I shall have to come and kiss her hand every day I'm in Jerez, and bring her flowers. I shall have to court her like a young woman. For how many years? How long do I have to live this charade? I'm better than all the others. Grandfather knew it. He must have known it. But he left all that to *you!* So I am pulled between you and that old toad, Tía Isabel. A world of women! Grandfather wouldn't have stood it for himself. But he expects me to stand it."

He was less than gentle as he handed me into the carriage. He sat brooding for a time, watching the familiar streets of Jerez, watching the long lines of bodegas with their strangely un-Spanish names lettered on them. At last he spoke as if he were talking to himself. "They say she married him on a whim. One day she married him just as if she had pointed a finger at the nearest man."

"That does less than honor to your grandfather."

"And to her, the damned old witch! Well, it was God's curse on her that she didn't have children of her own."

"If she had had children of her own, Juan, you wouldn't even be considered."

He looked at me and nodded, his eyes wise, disillusioned, and now calculating. "Yes—perfectly true, Mother. So I shall go and kiss her hand, and bring her flowers."

CHAPTER FOUR

1

They were busy, useful years, but for me they had a curious hollowness at their core. The daily round of our lives went on, each hour was filled, and yet as each harvest came and went I looked back on the year gone by and wondered what I had achieved in it, and often, with a sense of slight panic, wondered how the rest of the world and its events were shaping our futures, events which were totally out of our hands. I wrote for the year 1929: *Fairly plentiful crop, good quality,* but that was also the year of the Wall Street market collapse and its almost endless shock waves which spread through the world. Our exports of sherry from Jerez were good, but we never knew how much more we might have sold in the following decade if times had been better. The Marquesa's factories in Barcelona were hit with falling orders, and many workers lost their jobs. There were smaller dividends, not only from the bodega but also from the other shares Luis had left me and those which came to me as part of Don Paulo's estate. "Those with land need fear nothing," the Marquesa said with the assurance of someone whose family had been piling up their wealth for so many generations, in so many diverse fields, that a spell of decreased dividends was only a small matter which would correct itself in time. "The land," she added, "has always held its value."

That was also the year the University of Madrid and other universities in Spain were closed because of agitation from students and intellectuals for more freedom, and so Juan had to agree to stay on another year at Cambridge. Martín joined him there—he had never been as good a student as Juan, and only Edwin Fletcher's extra coaching during the holiday got him there. He resented having to return home during the summer to work with Edwin. He would have preferred, I thought, to go to Clonmara. But nothing interested him as much as his guitar. Every hour he was not studying with Edwin, its plaintive but sensuous sound was heard in the house.

The bodega, on the insistence of the Marquesa and myself, bought more albariza land that year, and the next January we started our planting of big new vineyards. "Chickenhearted," was the way the Marquesa dismissed the objections of Ignacio and Pedro. We were planting for the future, and yet the future seemed uncertain that January when Primo de Rivera resigned, his Assembly dissolved, and local government was restored. "The future has never been certain," the Marquesa remarked as we went ahead with our planting. All over Spain there were demands for a republic; King Alfonso was denounced as being responsible for the errors of the dictatorship, and anything else that was wrong with the country. When the censorship of the press was removed, we were buffeted with wave after wave of demonstrations and criticism. I read the denunciations of the landowners and the wealthy in the newspapers and realized, with a sense of shock, that they were talking about me and my family among the rest. My thoughts drifted to Clonmara when similar things had been said about our class, but then I had been young and heedless, every man and woman for miles around had a name and a history known to me, and everyone loved my grandfather. But Ireland since then had had a revolution and a civil war.

"Fools!" The Marquesa flung the newspaper across the desk at the bodega. "Don't they know they're going to cut their own throats?" Her holdings in Barcelona were threatened by the demand for Catalan autonomy, and in the north her estates and mines seemed threatened by the Basque separatist agitation. She didn't hold with unions or with strikes, and yet the demands were all there, now uncensored. I wondered, as I looked at the faces of the bodega workers, at the faces of the vineyard workers, what were the thoughts now behind their impassive gazes. What did Mateo think? What were the thoughts of Miguel, and José, and Rodrigo, whom I had now known for years as they moved about the tasks in the bodega? They were as courteous as ever, as hard-working. "Have they stopped to think," the Marquesa demanded of me, "who will provide the capital to nurse along those new vineyards, who will keep the others in production, if we do not? Who will buy the casks and pay their wages if we do not? Do they think they can run the place better by themselves?"

I had no answers for her. Edwin was philosophic. "Spain comes late to this, Carlota. She's really not yet in the twentieth century."

And the Marquesa and I pushed through the decision to start our own cooperage works to make the oak butts for the sherry, and to increase our distillation of brandy. Ignacio shuddered. "You will bankrupt us yet." But when the Marquesa and I voted together we held the balance of power.

In December came news of the mutiny of the garrison at Jaca and the demands for a republic. The mutiny was suppressed with difficulty, and martial law was declared throughout the country. This didn't last long, except in Madrid, but for us Madrid seemed a long way away. We were depressed, anxious, confused. The Marquesa reacted characteristically by declaring that all the family should come to Sanlúcar to spend Christmas with her, and that we should have some shooting at Doñana.

We gathered reluctantly, I thought. Only the authority of the Marquesa now held us together. With Don Paulo's going, there was not even the bond of blood between any of us. Ignacio was tense, as he always was in his dealings with the Marquesa; Pedro had not forgiven me for taking such a large part of his father's estate. Our children all mixed together, much of an age, the oldest of them young men and women now, looking at each other with speculative eyes. The youngest, and the only carefree ones, were Tomás and Luisa. Ignacio and Pedro now both had daughters of marriageable age, and they began to sum up my sons, their worth, their capabilities, and most of all their prospects.

The summons had also gone to the Blodmores, and Elena and Richard appeared, their sons with them. The young people seemed to perform an elaborate *paseo* before us, and the Marquesa watched them, her expression revealing nothing of her thoughts. She was over seventy now, arthritic, and leaning heavily on a stick. With the loss of that elegant, swaying walk, the last of her youth was gone, but the rings blazed on the age-spotted hands, as always, and with her gold-topped stick she appeared more formidable than ever. Each evening she would summon one or another of the young ones to her side, and they would endure a sort of trial by questioning. It must have been agony for some of them, the shy and awkward ones, those just striving for maturity. For the girls it was particularly hard, I thought.

"Say what you like," the Marquesa muttered to me. "Luisa has the most *style* of any of them, and she's only a child. I like style. She knows who she is, that child, and yet she knows whom she speaks to. She respects authority, but she will have her way."

Luisa had recovered her sense of balance with the years. She no longer cried for her father, but she often talked of him. He was a beloved figure, growing into the realm of myth and legend in her mind. "Do you remember, Mama, when Papa and I . . ." was often on her lips. Sometimes the memories were awry, and Luis was an idealized figure, the prince in the story in which Luisa was always the princess. But he had lived long enough to give her the priceless sense of being treasured, which never now seemed to desert her, and which gave her the confidence to face such personages as the Marquesa without shyness or a sense of awe. The early promise of beauty was every year more fulfilled; she had a lovely, grave, delicate face which would suddenly break into a radiant smile to charm whoever watched her; she had the complexion which had once been my mother's but was made more translucent by contrast with her dark eyes.

"If this monarchy isn't stupid enough to run itself out of the country," the Marquesa declared, "she could be a wife for a prince." I listened and shivered. I dreaded the thought of the Marquesa beginning to manipulate Tomás and Luisa's lives as she had done with my other three sons. These two young ones had a small measure of independence, and I realized I would have to teach them to use it.

Tomás, though, hardly needed to be taught how to assert himself among his cousins. He was almost eleven years old, but he, unlike Martín and Francisco, refused to follow where Juan chose to lead them. Perhaps it was the gap in ages, but more clearly it was shown to be his own idea of how he should go. He was tall for his age, and had the pronounced Blodmore features. I noticed the Marquesa's eyes often upon him broodingly. "That is how Blodmore would have looked at his age," she said, and her stick beat an agitated little rap on the floor. I looked at the aging face, the eyes sunken. I remembered the stories at Clonmara of the long-ago summer of the Spanish Woman, her style which had dazzled everyone, her willful pride which had caused her to lead the man she had fallen in love with on a chase half across Europe, and then to witness him fall in love with Don Paulo's daughter, who would have seemed to the Marquesa an unsophisticated child. I wondered if the old memories still hurt. The times when she called Tomás to her side she was particularly sharp with him, testing his humor and his good sense. But, like Luisa, he was not in awe of her; the potential power of her money had not yet touched him. It was a strange contrast to see how often and eagerly he sought out his grandmother's company. "Granny, you'll come on the shooting party tomorrow? Granny, you'll come in my boat, won't you?" My mother had somehow retained her expertise with a gun. She still oiled and cleaned and used the guns, which Richard Blodmore had given her. Tomás was proud of her skill and boasted of it to the Marquesa, who didn't like to hear it because she herself had given up the trips to Doñana. I noticed the Marquesa strove to distract Tomás from my mother, strove to command his attention, but he would not be commanded. He bestowed his favors and presence quite unself-consciously. He would bring the Marquesa a glass of wine, carry a cushion or book, see that she was comfortably placed wherever she was, but he did it as if he were unaware that every other young member of the party was trying to do the same thing. But when she wanted him, he was often not there; he was off on his own pursuits, or with his grandmother.

"Blodmore!" she said once in my hearing as she watched Tomás dancing with Lady Pat. They were a sight to watch, this tall child with his reddish-blond hair and green eyes, his cheeks still with the bloom of childhood on them, and the taller, aging woman, in the unfashionable dress, her graying hair escaping from its knot, laughing together as they danced, enjoying each other's company. "Blodmore. . . ." the Marquesa repeated. "Willful, wayward." I think she meant the words only for herself.

The presence of Richard Blodmore there was painful to me. He still had the power to stir me. I seemed to know, without having to see him, when he entered a room. The sound of his voice made me tight with apprehension lest I betray myself. I dreaded him and Tomás being in the same room; whenever I saw them talking I wanted to go and break in, invent some errand for Tomás to send him away. And yet I could not. To interfere in any way would have been to mark out Tomás, to turn eyes upon him, perhaps questioning eyes. But his likeness to my mother and grandfather was more marked than the few features he shared with Richard.

Because of my concern over Tomás, the days at Sanlúcar and Doñana dragged; because of my feeling for Richard, they went too swiftly. His effect on me was spontaneous and could not be controlled; it was the green shoots on the vine, the flor rising on the wine. I was renewed, but it still was a painful renewal.

I tried to avoid him without the avoidance becoming obvious, but one morning before breakfast, with the winter sun still unable to dispel the chill, he found me walking on the terrace above the Guadalquivir. The water was a frosty gray in the pale light. I had slept badly, and thought I would beg off the day's shooting across the river in Doñana. I had thought a walk in the cold morning air would invigorate me, but I was sluggish, and only shivered.

"Why are you out in the cold? Have you had coffee?"

His back was to the rising sun, and as it had been the day I saw him in England at the Colonel's house, I could not readily see the disfigurement. Then he turned and stood directly in the sun's rays, and the broken and twisted features were shown up harshly.

"No, I thought I'd walk—get some air. I . . . I didn't sleep well."

He was brutally blunt. "You slept well with me— once."

I turned on him in a kind of fury of frustration and love. "God, Richard—don't! It's past. It's gone."

"Are you saying you wish it hadn't happened?"

"No. I'll never say that. Or believe it. I'm grateful for loving you. For being loved. But we can do nothing about it. Ever. Why do you torment me? Can't I have peace? In God's name, can I never have peace from you?"

"While we're apart there'll be no peace, Charlie. I still wait for you. I wait for you on the shore—in the rose garden. Everywhere I look at Clonmara I see you. I wish I were rid of you. I wish *I* had peace. But there is none. I just keep on. I love. That's all. I live with some sort of wild hope that someday we'll be together. But when I see you here like this, with your children, I know it's only

476

that. Just a wild, unfounded hope. A wish. A want. A terrible wanting."

That was it—a terrible wanting. Nothing had come to take its place. "We can't ever be together, Richard. Things like that don't happen. Only when one dreams. So we must just go on . . . wanting."

"I still wait for the day you send me a message to come to you. I still wait, Charlie."

"That won't ever come, Richard. Each year there is more and more I must do for my children. The trust Luis placed in me has to be discharged. By the time they no longer need my help, you and I will have outgrown the wanting. It will be a memory."

"You deceive yourself about them needing you. Children grow up. Outgrow *you* . . . leave you behind."

"But now they need me. The young ones need me. When they are ready to do without me, I'll face what I must."

"Have you thought that *I* might need them, as well as you? One of them is *my* son, Charlie. Did you suppose I didn't know that?"

I denied it without an instant's hesitation. "No! That's not true. It is *not* true." I had given my promise to Luis. Not even for Richard would I break it. "Tomás is Luis' son."

"I'll never believe that, Charlie. Never."

"Believe what you like! Imagine what you like. That doesn't make it true."

I turned from him and walked swiftly along the terrace. As I fumbled with the handle on the door he called after me. His voice was clear and sharp, loud in the crisp morning air, as if he wanted the world to know what he said. "I'll wait, Charlie. I'll wait till hell freezes over."

I didn't go to Doñana that day. "I'm just tired, Juan," I said to him. "All women get tired now and again and, unlike men, we're privileged to say so."

He gave me the faintly patronizing smile of the superior male. "I'll take care of everything, Mother. And I'll see that Tomás doesn't get underfoot."

"I shouldn't worry, Juan. Tomás always does what the guides tell him."

"He shouldn't need to be told by the guides. He's in danger of being spoiled, Mother. You realize that, don't you?" Then he shrugged. "Well, school will knock all that out of him."

I nodded, wearily. "I suppose it will. A pity . . ." I didn't want school knocking anything out of him. He was far from perfect, but I wanted him left alone. I watched the boats cross the river. The sun was warmer now. They were setting out for a day's hunting as it had always been done at Doñana. Over the years I had been to Doñana many times—Luis had loved it as much as I did. We had explored it together at all seasons, sometimes staying at Sanlúcar, sometimes at the Palacio de Doñana itself. After his death I had continued to go there whenever I could. My children were still privileged to use this wild kingdom as their own, its beauty theirs, its animals theirs. They were the privileged few. For hundreds of years they and their kind had entered Doñana and taken what it gave. But they had also preserved it. Wealth had created it, and wealth kept it. The wild life fought out their life cycle safe from the encroachment of many, protected from poachers, because these few who could afford it preserved it. The birds came in their hundreds of thousands, because it was a wilderness, and they feared only their own kind, their natural enemies. Those who came with guns obeyed strict laws of preservation. But all around the edges of Doñana there was poverty and hunger, and some looked on the deer herds with angry, resentful eyes. I had known these forces at work before, in Ireland. It wasn't any easier to weigh them in the balance now.

2

Elena had not gone to Doñana either. She spent a good deal of time with the Marquesa; she seemed very confident of her position with the Marquesa, but at the same time she was careful. Like all the rest of the family, she had her interests to protect. She had been the Marquesa's protégée; she knew the rules.

She was sitting alone by the fire in the great salon when I entered. We—the Marquesa, María Luisa, and whoever else had stayed away from the hunting that day—would gather here for the still elaborate ceremony of tea. Elena was smoking a cigarette, gazing into the flames; she nodded in a detached sort of fashion as I came nearer.

"I'll be glad when I'm out of here," she said unexpectedly. Then she laughed. "Oh, don't look so shocked. For a Blodmore, you know, at times you're so deadly *earnest!* It isn't usually their style. Sometimes I can hardly believe it when I hear you going on about your vineyards and your bodega, how many hectares of albariza, how many butts for export. It all bores me to death. All this family business. All pretending to be so united, when all we're waiting for is for the old one to die to see how it's all carved up. There's so much more than a few butts of sherry to be parceled out. We're like the buzzards over there"—she nodded in the direction of the river and Doñana—"the way we circle about the old woman. I wonder how many more years? She might live to be a hundred."

I sat down opposite her. I didn't want the fact of standing over her to seem to give me an advantage. "Has it occurred to you that perhaps I *like* the vineyards—*like* the bodega? And as for the Marquesa, as you well know, she and I haven't always been friends. We are thrown together now because of the bodega business . . ."

She flicked the butt of her cigarette into the fire. "Oh, rubbish! You're no different from any of us. Your children know exactly how to play up to her. Your Juan has a head on his shoulders. He plays her like the matador with the cape."

"You both flatter him and insult him at the same time."

She shrugged. "Oh, don't let's get too intense about this. Sometimes you're more Spanish than the Spanish. The real matriarch. Your only care is your children. That's what you'd like everyone to think. But you're still in love with Richard, aren't you? And he's bemused into thinking he wants you."

"I prefer not to discuss Richard."

"You *prefer!* Well, talk about it or not, as you like. It doesn't make any difference to me. The situation's quite safe. I know you won't leave here. You won't leave your children and your nice cozy little world to go to him. And he will stick at Clonmara for want of anything better to do. Oh yes—we have a nice accommodation, Richard and I. I'm the perfect wife in that hole in Ireland, and then there's the flat in London, which is where I really begin to live. There, I do as I like. Richard doesn't care. He hasn't cared for a long time now. Almost from the beginning. Funny, isn't it, the way you got yourself into my life? You got Carlos. I was half in love with Carlos, and probably would have been completely in love with him if my aunt had permitted it. But she chose Richard for me instead—or rather she chose Clonmara. And then that cold fish, Richard, who I thought couldn't love anyone at all, fell head over heels for a silly little girl who didn't know anything except how to sit a horse."

She smoothed the folds of her tweed skirt thoughtfully, and looked across then at me. "Still tight-lipped, aren't you? Not saying anything. If you could just let yourself be honest. It's Richard you want, but you also want everything that's here, and anything the Marquesa cares to give your children. So you must wait for one before you can take the other. You've taken so much of this little world already, haven't you? And to think you came here a penniless nothing! You got Luis' money, and in some way that no one can understand you cheated the others of their share of Don Paulo's estate."

"It is a well-known fact that Don Paulo never favored me. In fact he not only didn't favor me, he was actively hostile to me. I married his favorite son. He had looked for a much better marriage for him."

"Yes—he hoped for me for Carlos, until Tía Isabel decided otherwise. Well, you won him over. He didn't leave you a third of his estate because he hated you.

You might say you won your way to him by producing a string of children. Well, that's a gift only nature can give. I suppose you thank God every day for the gift of fertility, especially in a family where it's been singularly lacking on both sides." She laughed crudely. "What a joke! All you had to do was lie back and enjoy it. And in the end, everything came to you. Through Carlos through Luis. And now you wait for what will come through Tía Isabel." She leaned forward. "Well, let me tell you something. You will never have Richard. I will never give him up to you. I will stay married to him as long as I live. This last thing you want you'll never get. And as for Tía Isabel . . . in the end, blood is thicker than water. She always meant to have Clonmara, though God only knows why. She wanted to dominate the Blodmores. Through me she can do both things. We will wait, both of us, and you will find that what I'm saying is true. Oh yes, you'll dominate the bodega, but who cares about that? I, of course, will have the title of Pontevedra and the estates, and Edward after me. The rest . . . all the rest of it will be mine. If you're honest you have to admit it—"

"What must Carlota admit?" The door had opened soundlessly at the far end of the long salon. The Marquesa stood there, leaning heavily on her cane, her face parchment-colored above her black dress.

Elena turned smoothly, apparently not in the least perturbed, though neither of us knew how long the Marquesa had been there, or how keen her hearing still was.

"Bullfighting, Tía Isabel. Carlota and I were talking about the bulls she sells for the corrida, and still she will not admit she hates bullfighting. I was asking her to be honest, just for once."

3

It happened that night, our last night at Sanlúcar. They had all returned from the hunting at Doñana flushed with the exhilaration of their sport, from a day in the crisp air, hungry and pleasantly tired. Dinner had been un-usually festive. We all had the sense of an occasion, the eve of a dispersal, and at the same time a chilling fore-boding that we would never gather here in this same fash-ion again. Don Paulo was missing, but his spirit remained; the Marquesa as usual dominated the gathering, but she appeared old and tired. The last night no outsiders were invited; it was an ingathering of the family, although of all of us there only Elena and her two sons were tied to the Marquesa by blood. But we were Don Paulo's family, and so hers.

To mark the occasion even Luisa and Tomás were al-lowed to stay up for the late dinner. There were many courses; the wine was drunk freely. In the salon after dinner when the coffee and brandy were passed around, and the men had come to join us, Martín produced his guitar. This was the one gift he had which made him different from the others. All of them were excellent horsemen, all of them, from time to time, plucked a guitar. But for Martín it had now become a serious under-taking. He hardly ever played flamenco, though when he did it was with a far greater understanding of the art than any of the others possessed. His passion was the classical guitar, and he and Edwin Fletcher spent much time transposing the works of the great masters into a literature for his instrument. I had a feeling that most of the young ones would have preferred flamenco, but they were forced into silence as Martín played Bach.

"You'd never imagine, would you," I heard Ignacio say to Pedro, "that he is the grandson of a gypsy?" I was meant to hear it.

The Marquesa, however, approved, and called for more. We listened to De Falla and Granados and Albéniz. At the end the Marquesa beckoned Martín to her. "You are much more accomplished than I supposed. Find out the best teachers. You shall go to them."

Her words caused a little stir through the room. Young men might play an instrument as a hobby, an entertain-ment. They were not expected to study it seriously. Where, everyone was wondering, did this fit with Martín's future in the bodega, or did the Marquesa mean to make him independent in order to study further? On the faces of Pedro and Ignacio I read the two opposite reactions, pleasure at the thought that Martín might be kept out of the bodega and give their own sons more chance for advancement, and concern that his unexpected gift made him stand too large in the Marquesa's esteem. It was the usual family situation, a step forward, a step back. The only thing that united us was the jostling for the Marquesa's favor, and watching her as she looked around after her announcement, I knew she was perfectly aware of this.

Martín then made a gesture to the preference of his audience with a popular *seguidilla,* all the young ones joining in to sing the *coplas,* the verses, swaying and tapping their feet to the rhythm. It all finished on a lively, good-humored note, all of us going to bid the Marquesa good night, and good-by, as we would be gone in the morning before she was downstairs. There were a few more bursts of song as we left the salon and started upstairs. My mother was one of the first, her body still moving a little to the remembered rhythm; Tomás' arm was under hers as they climbed the great wide staircase together. Then, who knew whether from too much brandy, or because she was still half dancing and the ancient satin shoe caught in a ruffle of frayed lace at the hem of her long dress, we heard her give a little cry, and she was crashing down the stairs. Tomás, who tried to prevent the fall, was pulled with her. They ended in a tangle at the bottom.

For a moment there was dead silence through the hall. Tomás stirred, and tried to move against the weight of my mother on top of him. Then everyone was about them, lifting. Tomás was on his feet, his face deadly white. "Granny—*Granny!*" For a while her eyes remained closed. Then she opened them, blinked several times, and said, "I seem to have been unseated." Very gingerly she began to sit up. I didn't want her to move, but she resisted me. "Oh, Charlie, stop fussing! What's a little tumble now and again? Just so long as you don't hurt the horse. Did I hurt you, Tomás? Sorry, old boy. I'll try to be more careful next time. Try to fall clear."

A servant was offering her brandy, which she didn't need, but which she still drank. By now she was sitting on the bottom step, her dress torn, her hair tumbled about her shoulders. But the color had returned to her face, and to Tomás' also. He was even starting to laugh, thinking it all a joke.

Elena's voice came clearly. "That old fool. She's quite mad—and drunk. She shouldn't be allowed near the children. She's a danger to herself and everyone else. Probably set the house on fire one night. She really ought to be locked up for her own good—"

"Elena!" Richard tried to silence her.

She shrugged off his protest. "Well, everyone knows she's been out of her mind since that accident with Carlos. She should be locked up, I tell you!"

The group around my mother fell back a little, not knowing how to cover the words. She had heard it all, and her face, which had been warming with color, went white again. Shaking away the hands that sought to help her, she grasped the newel post and pulled herself to her feet; she gazed at Elena with a pitiable look of fear and unbelief. Her first words were incomprehensible, a sort of gibberish. Then she managed to make sense. "You'd shut me up! You'd put me in that place—that *awful* place. I'd rather die than go into that place. . . ." I knew what she was talking about; the memory of the inmates of the asylum of Nuestra Señora de Mercedes she had once seen returned to her.

"Mother . . . it's all right. Let's go up to bed now."

As if through a fog she seemed to recognize my voice. "Charlie, you promised! You promised you'd never let me be put in that place."

"You never shall. I promise. Now—"

Elena broke in again. "Well, that's *your* risk, Carlota. Personally, I wouldn't want to have what she might do on my conscience."

My mother looked at her, her eyes widening, the look

484

of fear fading from them. "*You!* I remember you! You're the one who came and took Clonmara. You took everything! Stole it! And now you want to shut me up in that terrible place. Shut me away from everyone. Bury me! Well, you won't. I'll die before I'll be shut away, but I'll kill you first—"

She lurched towards Elena. The movement was so quick and unexpected that none of us was able to restrain her in time. Her hand tore at Elena's face, and when Elena staggered back her cheek was marked with a long, bloody scratch. She recovered herself quickly and retaliated with a sharp blow with her open hand across my mother's face. "You old maniac! You *should* be locked up!"

Richard interposed himself between them. "Elena—you shouldn't have touched her! Can't you see she's—"

"I can see she's mad, and dangerous. Now get her away from me—"

"What is this?" The Marquesa was standing in the doorway of the salon. "Have you descended to some sort of brawling now?"

A dozen explanations reached her at once. I didn't try to give any. I took my mother's arm, and with María Luisa on the other side we went slowly up the stairs. By the time we reached the top, silence had fallen on the group below once more. They stood motionless, gazing up at us. All that could be heard were my mother's words, repeated over and over, amid her strangled sobs. "You promised, Charlie. You *promised* . . ."

CHAPTER FIVE

1

Perhaps, in many ways, that was the last ingathering of the family. We would be together at other times, the same faces, the same people, but never again would we do it with the old sense that our little world was tight and immutable. Forces which we had long thrust to the background of our minds broke through. We carried on—we took in our harvests, we saw the musts turn into wine, the solera was renewed; we watched our children grow up, some were married and more children born, but never again did we have the old surety that this generation and the next would inherit the Spain of their fathers. All that was changed.

The new year, 1931, brought the King's announcement of the restoration of the constitution, and fixed the date for parliamentary elections in March. There was a popular demand for a constituent assembly, and in April the municipal elections brought an overwhelming victory for the Republicans. Their leader, Zamora, demanded the King's abdication. Two days later, on April 14, King

Alfonso XIII left Spain, but without abdicating. Zamora set up a provisional government, with himself as President. When in June the elections came, the Republican-Socialist Party had a huge majority. By November a committee of the Assembly declared the King guilty of high treason and forbade his return to Spain. The royal property was confiscated.

The only certainty we had then was that, no matter what happened, our world was changed and we could never return to the old certainties. I remembered the King at Doñana in that informal gathering which had come to hunt with him. I remembered the chair he had used, his signed photograph on the wall. We could not turn back the clock, undo the resentments and the injustices that had brought this about. Spain had moved too slowly; no one could make up the centuries in a few years.

We woke one morning in December that year to read that we were a democracy. Everyone would have the vote to determine who would go to the single-chamber parliament, the Cortes, which would sit for four years. The President was to be chosen by an electoral college, and no army officer or member of the clergy was to be eligible for this office. The constitution proclaimed complete religious freedom and separated Church and State. The Church was no longer to run the schools. Church property was to be nationalized. We were told that the government would have the power to take over private property and to nationalize large estates.

That day I walked the bodega in a daze of disbelief. I even went out to the vineyard house and looked down the long, orderly rows of well-tended vines. The workers were there just the same. Mateo came to greet me and said nothing about what was happening. I walked over to Las Ventanas Verdes and only there did I see fear and concern in the faces of Concepción and Antonio. In their way, they had as much to lose as any of the vineyard owners and the bodega owners. They had the jobs of their sons, the security of their old age. Concepción wept a little as we shared a copita in the sun in the courtyard. "They say it is for the people, but how will the people

487

just come in and run the vineyards, the bodegas? I don't understand. Does *this*"—she gestured to the house about her, the glimpse of the slopes beyond—"does this belong to the government now? And who will pay the wages?"

I had, of course, no answer. Nor did the Marquesa when I sat with her in the office at the bodega which had been Don Paulo's.

"Who indeed will pay the wages?" she demanded, tossing the newspaper down on the desk. She, of course, had more to lose than any of us. How many of Barcelona's factories did she own, or partly own?—and Barcelona was the capital of Catalonia, which had been given a measure of autonomy. And what of the estates in Galicia, which was known to be heavily Republican? Would they be taken away from her? How much of the output of the Río Tinto mines and the mines in Asturias would she be allowed to keep? "We shall soon have to have the priests as permanent guests in our homes—that is, if they allow any priests to stay. Or if they don't shoot them all."

Juan had now completed his time at Cambridge and put in a year in the London office of Fernández, Thompson. He was back home and had taken his place permanently at the bodega. He now exercised his right to vote the small number of shares which had become his under Don Paulo's will, and he resented the fact that, shared out among so many grandchildren, they had been watered down to comparatively few. He resented, at the same time, that I should vote so many.

"Have you thought, Mother, that now I'm of age it would be better if I handled your affairs at the bodega? There is no need for you to go there so often, or concern yourself with its affairs. Women do not usually—"

"I have no need to be told, Juan, what women do and do not usually do. My place here has always been different from most women's. The town is used to it."

"Now that you have sons old enough . . ."

"We'll talk of it later, Juan. When I'm old."

"As old as the Marquesa, I suppose," he said as he turned away.

That was the year Martín had gone to Paris, enrolled

488

at the Sorbonne, and found himself a teacher of the guitar. He had followed for a while the travels of Segovia and taken some lessons from the master. Martín seemed at last to have emerged from the shadow of Juan and become his own man. *I'll come back to Jerez someday, Mother,* he wrote, *but for the time being I want to taste the world, and listen to music.* He talked of going to spend some time in Vienna. I showed the letter to the Marquesa. She nodded her head. "Just as well. He will like it better here when he knows what the rest is about. I don't expect he'll ever be a great, much less a famous musician, like Segovia. But let him try his wings . . ." And she insisted on paying his expenses. Unlike Juan, who seemed inclined, though with a little more eye to prudence, to repeat his father's extravagances, Martín lived modestly. *It's too conspicuous to have more to spend than other students,* he wrote. "Ah!" the Marquesa exclaimed over that letter. "Here we have either a budding Republican or the beginning of a wise man." She looked forward to Martín's letters, and I always took them to her; it seemed to me that she lived again a little of her youth as he traveled the cities of Europe. "He will be worth talking to when he returns," she said. "Not a village boy any longer. We should be looking to see whom he should marry. Though it's difficult to know whose fortune is secure these days."

"Perhaps we shall just have to let Martín choose for himself, and leave the fortune to chance. Who knows, he may bring back a little Bohemian from his travels."

She looked outraged. "He will not go *that* far!"

Francisco had followed Juan to Cambridge, and then into the London office. He remained as he had always been, a faithful follower of everything his eldest brother said and thought. They formed a sort of alliance, feeling that their solidarity made them a stronger force at the bodega against the influence of their father's half brothers.

"There's a nice little civil war shaping up there," María Luisa commented. "And so much still depends on how the Marquesa disposes of her estate. *If* they leave her any estate, that is."

It was Tomás who gave the heartache, and perhaps

the most promise. He had been sent off to school in England the September after the last gathering at Sanlúcar. He had returned eagerly for the Christmas holidays, persuaded the Marquesa to open up Sanlúcar again so that they could go each day to Doñana. But he didn't go to hunt, except the necessary culling of the deer herds. More often he stayed alone with a guide, his binoculars on every living thing that moved, bird and beast. He had saved his money and bought himself a camera; he taught himself how to develop his own film. A record of Doñana began to emerge. He marked the sightings of the imperial eagle and the Spanish lynx; he studied the old notebooks of previous visitors to Doñana, and warned that the numbers of these rare creatures were dwindling. He wanted stricter controls in Doñana. "You do not own Doñana," the Marquesa reminded him. "Nor do I. You go there only as a guest."

He nodded, unhappy. "I wish I were rich enough so that I could buy it."

"Places like Doñana are rarely for sale."

He knew his way about the bodega; when there, he left off his formal suit and his formal manners and joined the workers at whatever they were doing. Some of them didn't like it; those with Republican sentiments must have seen it as some sort of extra privilege which this sprig of Don Paulo's tree had taken to himself. But after a while they forgot who he was and just let him learn, which was what he wanted. "Perhaps he has the nose," the Marquesa said. But I think she said it more to upset Ignacio and Pedro than out of any conviction that this raw boy had any particular gift except curiosity and the ability to get along smoothly with the workers.

"You should keep him more in check, Mother," Juan said. "I see him eating with the workers, and sometimes talking like a peasant. It doesn't do. It makes things more difficult for the rest of us."

"Times are changing, Juan. Perhaps Tomás is wise to learn how a peasant thinks."

But he shook his head, refusing to believe that Republican ideals could triumph. "It would be the ruin of Spain," he said simply. "We cannot let that happen."

"Then *you* go and get yourself elected President!" Tomás shouted at him. "See what you can do for Spain!"

"But they say Mr. De Valera will soon be elected President," my mother objected, proud to show that she was following the conversation.

"That, Granny, is *Ireland*. You're getting your Republicans mixed up." Juan had less patience with his grandmother these days. She was no longer a romantically eccentric figure but an untidy, aging woman who drank too much, whose mind was too often clouded, and was hardly to be trusted alone. She merely nodded at him and smiled. "Ah yes, Ireland. When shall we be going back, I wonder?"

Nanny, who divided her time between acting as a substitute duenna for Luisa when María Luisa could not do it, and as a sort of unofficial guardian of my mother, snapped awake out of a doze at the sound of the word. "Ah, Ireland! Wouldn't it be grand if we could go back, Lady Pat? Go back to Clonmara. There never was a place like Clonmara."

"Stupid old biddy," Juan commented as he left. "She's getting too old to know what she's doing. She should be pensioned off. She'll be talking about the fairies next. It isn't right to let Luisa listen too much to her. She'll be getting fanciful notions."

But I thought there were few fanciful notions in Luisa. She was the perfect child she had always been, calm, serene almost, in an oddly grown-up fashion; and she grew more beautiful. She was clever, and took care with her studies, even the subjects which interested her least. In this she was the opposite of Tomás, who could show brilliance where his attention was completely engaged and utter indifference when it was not. Luisa and Tomás seemed to form the same sort of alliance as Juan and Francisco, except that Luisa was irked by the restrictions placed on her because she was a girl. But she seemed to please everyone without effort. She even took an interest in rather old-fashioned styles of needlework because it gave María Luisa pleasure to teach her. "Rich you are now, child," María Luisa said, "but you never know when it may be a blessing to know how to sew a fine seam—or stitch on a plain old button. Look at your poor mother there. She always has been hopeless—and helpless."

"I think Mama is very capable," Luisa said, and rattled off what she counted as my accomplishments, my spheres of influence—the bodega, the vineyards, the bull ranch, the farms, even my mother's stud, which was now largely left to me to manage, my mother only going there for the pleasure of looking at her "darlings." "Perhaps one day I shall be like Mama, and be able to see to everything."

I thought that times had indeed changed in Jerez, in Spain itself, when a daughter like Luisa could display pride in a mother who had once been considered more than faintly scandalous. Perhaps there were more things on people's minds these days than to drag up old memories of the girl who was thought to have seduced and captured Don Paulo's favorite son. People had long ago stopped counting the months between my marriage to Luis and Tomás' birth. I tried to see myself as the town must now see me, the one had become the friend of Don Paulo, who appeared to have formed an alliance with the Marquesa. To some of the younger ones I must have seemed as much a part of the established old order of things as the Marquesa herself. I stood for a traditional way of living in a world that threatened to turn itself upside down.

The Marquesa had now moved permanently to Las Fuentes. Less and less did she travel to Sanlúcar, though a retinue of servants was kept there awaiting her pleasure. It was ironic that only after Don Paulo's death did she take up the residence of her husband as if it was her home. That summer, for the first time since I had been in Spain, she made no plans to travel to the estates in Galicia. "I'm getting too old for that sort of journey," was all she said. But I wondered if even such a formidable courage as hers might not be daunted by the hazards of the long journey in these troubled times, and by the thought of the

Republican sentiments which would await her there. Although she hardly ever talked of the disturbances, the riots, the strikes, I think she took them hard. Hardest of all, I guessed, for her to bear was the fact that the King had been driven from his own country. The declaration of the Assembly that he had been guilty of high treason in the mismanagement of the country was almost as if we, the nobles and the landowners, had been condemned with him. She, Isabel, sprung of both the Hapsburg and the Bourbon dynasties, was aligned by history and fate with the deposed monarch. She could only wait and watch the events that swept the country onward to what none of us could truthfully predict. She was quite powerless to change anything. I thought it was the growing knowledge of this, more than her actual years, which made her now appear an old woman.

But she still enjoyed the privileges of her position. She had taken to visiting the bodega regularly, and always Don Paulo's empty office awaited her. "I enjoy keeping Ignacio and Pedro out of it," she had once said to me spitefully. "And who knows, if I turn my back, *you* might have it." She seemed to share my enjoyment of walking the bodegas. Quite often she would be driven, with me at her side, to one end of the long row which housed our treasury of sherry, or would pick one at random. "Might as well let them all see me—let them know there's still someone from the old days in charge," she said. She would walk the aisles with me at her side, slowly, her stick making a dull tapping on the ground. "I wonder can it survive?" she asked once, a question which she didn't expect me to answer. "The anarchists would blow it all up and then say the aristocracy was depriving them of their wine!"

She had also adopted a custom which I had begun. Each day she was at the bodega she would appear in the sala de degustación. Her arrival there would bring every man to his feet, though there were some murmurings that, between us, she and I were turning it into a women's sewing circle. Customers and visitors were brought forward to be presented. She was all graciousness as she sipped her copita, extending her hand, still unabashedly displaying those magnificent rings on the old wrinkled fingers.

2

It was the spring of that year, 1932, just when the vines were putting out their new shoots, that we had the message from Tomás' school that he was missing. The Easter holidays had been too short to allow him to return to Jerez, and he had gone to Clonmara. This had been much against my will, but I had not dared to oppose it, lest it seem to single out Tomás too much from his half brothers. They had all in their turn visited Clonmara; there seemed to be some sort of agreement between Elena and the Marquesa about inviting them, as if it were the Marquesa's will that they should get to know it well, and Elena had acceded to her wishes. Two weeks after he had returned to school Tomás disappeared one Wednesday afternoon, sports afternoon, when he had not been missed until time for prep. The school sent a telegram to Jerez. They had tried to telephone, but it was one of the many times the telephone system was not working. At the same time that they sent the telegram to me, they had also telephoned Clonmara. Richard, in response, was on the first boat to England the next day.

He telephoned me from the school. "Tomás left with only a little money. He couldn't have drawn it all out from the bursar without attracting attention."

"But he *left*? You're sure of that, Richard? He's not . . . not . . . ?" Not what? I couldn't think; I didn't want to think. Nothing could have happened to Tomás.

"Well, of course the police are making inquiries. They've already searched the woods around here. Today they're dragging the pool at the old gravel quarry. They've made inquiries at the local railway station, but no one remembers seeing him take a train. Of course it's only a five-mile walk to Burston, and that's a major junction.

If he went there he could have taken a train to almost anywhere in England, providing he had the money."

"My mother says she sent him extra money at Easter. He said he wanted to buy special attachments for his camera. He probably didn't tell them at school about it. Richard, he didn't *want* to go back. I know that. It isn't the school. He just didn't want to be away from here. I thought he'd get over it. After all, it's his first year. I thought he needed time to settle down . . ."

"Charlie, I'm trying everything. The London office . . . the routes to Ireland. He doesn't know England that well."

"He's tough, Richard. He knows the land very well. He knows how peasants live. He could last a long time on a little money." I was gnawed by the thought that in these depression years a young boy on the road, a boy speaking perfect English, able to take care of himself, would attract little notice. The country was full of men and boys walking the roads, earning a few shillings here and there, moving on again in the hope of the next few shillings. That would be Tomás' style. I did not let myself think of the woods and the gravel quarry.

It was Edwin Fletcher who made the suggestion. "Have them try the sherry shippers in Bristol. It's nearer than London. They go directly to Cádiz, most of them."

I sat up all night trying to contact Richard by telephone at the hotel near the school. About four o'clock in the morning we finally made contact. There was a long wait while the night porter went to bring Richard to the phone, and I had to beg the operators, in Spanish and English, not to cut us off.

"Try Bristol, Richard," I shouted into the phone. "Try Harvey's. Try every sherry firm who ships into Bristol. For God's sake, Richard, *find* him!"

I thought he answered, "I'll find my son—" but the words were distorted and blurred, and then the line went dead. I was left weeping, and then María Luisa, who had waited up with me, was beside me with some brandy.

"Why, María Luisa? *Why* would he do such a thing?

If he has done it, and now I pray God he has. The alternative is unthinkable."

"He's different from the others, Carlota. He is not shaped the way they are. He does not conform. Be brave, querida. You will hear."

We did not hear. Richard went to Bristol, and then to London, and none of the sherry shippers knew anything about Tomás. Ten days later, when we were sitting down to a supper none of us would eat, he arrived at Los Cisnes. He was lean, dirty, and cheerful. "I'm sorry, Mama. I just couldn't stick it. I'm Spanish. England isn't for me."

He had spent four days searching out a ship in the Bristol docks which was bound for Cádiz with a load of machine parts. He had got a few hours' casual employment helping to load it. It wasn't legal to employ him, but when he spoke English to the Spaniards, and Spanish to the English, each had assumed that he was in some way connected with the other. He looked dirty enough to have been a Spanish peasant employed by the line, or one of the millions of English looking for any sort of work they could find. When the ship sailed no one had realized he was aboard. They had found him, hungry and still cheerful, just a few hours out of Cádiz. The captain, who might have had no particular love for the sherry dons who ran Jerez, had simply let him find his own way to us, without sending a message that he was found. What did one boy more or less matter in a country where so many were looking for some way to scrape a living? Even if the boy did speak English, it was no proof he belonged to the family of Fernández, Thompson. And if he was not who he said he was, why hand him over to the police, who would beat the information out of him? The boy had given no trouble, had stolen nothing but the passage. He had some money on him, Spanish and English money. He was better off than most. Tomás had bought food in Cádiz and a ride with a man heading for Seville.

There was no way to punish him, none I would countenance. "Didn't you think how frightened I have

496

been? You might have thought of that, Tomás. That has been the worst of all. Sometimes I thought you . . . thought you dead."

He looked ashamed. "I thought of it. But if I'd contacted you from Bristol they'd have had me back at school. I wasn't going to have that. There was no way I could send a message from the ship, was there? They don't send radio messages for stowaways. I thought of telephoning from Cádiz, but that was too conspicuous. Mother, you must have *known* I was on the way home. Where else would I have gone? This is where I want to be."

The Marquesa thought she devised a punishment for him which turned out to be no punishment at all. "I have written to the Duchess. I have asked permission for him to spend the summer at Doñana, living with one of the guides. No luxuries for him. Let him work the way they do. Let him burn charcoal, watch for poachers. Let him broil in the heat there, and eat what they eat. Afterwards we will see about school. There are some rather strict ones, they tell me, in Sevilla."

He spent the summer at Doñana, and it hardened and toughened him as nothing else could have. He lived as a peasant, and learned things the Marquesa had not dreamed of. He had the luxury of his binoculars and camera, and a supply of film given by my mother. He went on compiling his schoolboy's record of Doñana; he was isolated, there were no parties, no entertainment, only a little guitar music, rough wine to drink and simple food. He was happy, he said later. He had helped teach a boy of his own age to read. Of all the other things he himself had learned we had only the sketchiest knowledge. But he had learned what it was like to be a Spanish peasant, and that was more education than any of his brothers had had.

"You may finally have succeeded in making a Republican of him," María Luisa said.

The idea of school in Seville was abandoned when, in August, General Sanjurjo seized Seville for the rightist movement. The revolt was quickly suppressed, but there were many who expressed approval of it. Jerez did not like the radical legislation of the new regime. They did not like it when they heard that the property of the rebels had been confiscated and divided up among the peasants.

"And a lot of good that will do them," the Marquesa scoffed. "What will they get when it is divided—the leg of a mule each?" But the idea of school in Seville was dropped. "He is wayward, that boy. Even in the strictest place, who knows what ideas he may get? Better get Edwin Fletcher back again."

Edwin had taken a post teaching the son of the Williams family, coaching him for entrance to his English school. I had wanted him to stay on with Luisa when Tomás went to school, but he had refused. "I would do anything for you, Carlota, and you know it. But I can't become a governess to a young lady, however much I love her."

"What shall we do without you, Edwin? *All* of us?"

"You will manage, Carlota."

But the Williams boy was ready for school in September, and so Edwin returned to Los Cisnes. He looked at the sunburned, hard, lean youth before him, the sun-bleached hair with its ragged cut, the powerful shoulders, the hardened hands. "Well, you've become a man while my back was turned, Tomás."

A wide grin split Tomás' face as he grasped Edwin's hand in a grip that made Edwin flinch slightly. "You'll take me back then, Mr. Fletcher? I've learned a lot of things at Doñana. I've dissected a few specimens; Granny had bought me a microscope . . ."

"I'm not much up on biology, Tomás."

"Then we'll learn together, Mr. Fletcher. You should hear the things that happened at Doñana! I rode bareback most of the time, you know. They taught me all kinds of things I couldn't have learned in England. I don't need all that fussy stuff, you know. Look, come up to the schoolroom. There's a lot to show you." Then he gestured towards his sister. "All right, Luisa. You can come too. You don't mind, do you, Mr. Fletcher? It's odd for girls to be as curious as she is, but she didn't even mind the photographs of the vipers at Doñana. And you'll be teaching both of us again, won't you? Luisa's awfully glad to get rid of that English governess she had. She was turning her into a sissy. I've got some lizards in solution. Come on, Luisa . . ."

They went off, the three of them, Edwin helpless between the two whom he loved most. I heard their voices fading off as they went up the stairs, each trying to outtalk the other.

María Luisa smiled faintly. "The Marquesa will have to be a little more ingenious in thinking out her punishments. The boy has been in heaven, and now he's telling Edwin and Luisa what the angels are like."

3

The political upheavals in Spain in the next years brought Elena Blodmore to Jerez a number of times, her object always that of persuading the Marquesa to leave the country. The granting of autonomy to Catalonia meant that the Marquesa's factories and business interests there were severely threatened. I witnessed one interview between the Marquesa and her niece on a day when she had arrived unannounced in Jerez and, not finding her aunt at Las Fuentes, came to the bodega where the Marquesa and I were in Don Paulo's office examining the latest balance sheets produced by Ignacio. The Marquesa was contemptuously impatient with her niece's suggestions. "I am not the sort to go into exile just because a few anarchists say they will take away my property," the Marquesa snapped at her. "Why should I leave? They can only take so much."

But the great radical rising in Barcelona, which was repressed by government troops, had spread to other cities. It indicated the growing impatience of the people with the slowness of the reform movement.

"They can take your life," Elena answered.

The Marquesa shrugged. "There is not much more of that to take. And God or the Devil will take it—which I cannot say."

"Come back to Clonmara with me."

"I thought you had a revolution of your own going on there."

Elena visibly fought her impatience. "All that's over. The country's going through a hard time because England raised tariff barriers, but no one's being shot out of hand. There aren't riots and assassinations any more."

But Elena was forced to withdraw. "Well, if you're murdered in your bed . . ."

María Luisa smiled when I reported the interview to her. "That one doesn't entirely get her own way with the old woman. She wants her at Clonmara because there she'll be completely under her influence. Of course, when Elena tries next time, she may succeed. The Marquesa is not now, and never has been, a loved personage. She smacks too much of the old days. She reeks of the aristocracy, and that can be dangerous in these days."

The Marquesa learned that fact on the night a mob burned Las Fuentes. It happened as spontaneously as the scene I had witnessed from the window at the Plaza de Asturias—at least it appeared to be spontaneous, but María Luisa darkly recalled the long-ago existence of *La Mano Negra,* the Black Hand, and then the terrible night in Jerez when a mob of more than four thousand sacked shops and killed the shopkeepers. "But that was 1892, or thereabouts. The trouble is that so many of these Andalucian peasants have gone to Barcelona looking for work, and the Marquesa is too well known in both places."

It must have been a desperate hour for the old woman when she fled Las Fuentes. The house was close enough to the outskirts of the town for the word to spread quickly of what was happening, and for the glow in the sky to bring more people to watch and possibly to enjoy. The Civil Guard was there quickly also, but not quickly enough to prevent one of the Marquesa's servants from being beaten to death. The Guard cleared a path through the riotous crowd for the old fire-fighting engines, but the roof of the house was well ablaze, and in the morning only the blackened walls were left. The Marquesa had been led away through the fields at the back of the house when the first of the mob appeared. She had resisted her servant's efforts to make her leave until the first burning torch crashed through one of the unshuttered windows on the first floor. She came to Los Cisnes, reluctantly, I thought. It galled her to be driven out, and perhaps even more it galled her to accept hospitality.

She was weary, dusty, but almost unshaken as she received a report later from the head of the Civil Guard. María Luisa had offered brandy and coffee, and the Marquesa even poured it herself with a steady hand.

"The furniture, the pictures, the tapestries—all gone. Don Paulo's collection of clocks, all gone. Those barbarians! What good does it do them? And my man, Alvaro, dead. He was a good man. He did his duty. A watchman all his life he's been. And for that he gets death."

The man listening to her nodded gravely. "We will find his killers. But there were guns among the crowd. The times are troubled, Marquesa."

"What times have not been troubled?" she almost spat at him. "We must resist."

So, finally, she came under my roof and, against all expectations, there she remained. "We are stronger if we stand together. If I go to Sanlúcar they will burn that. Perhaps they will burn it whether I am there or not. They tell me to stay away from Galicia, at least for the time being. I shall impose myself on you, Carlota."

We had little choice, but it made an uneasy household. She was immediately offered hospitality by Ignacio and Pedro, and a dozen other families in Jerez, and all over the country. "To go to Madrid is madness," Edwin Fletcher counseled. "There you will not have an easy night's rest. And if anything really serious starts, you could be trapped. Whoever seeks to rule Spain must have Madrid."

She settled down among us, but she was little used to a household of which she was not automatically the head. She had brought her own servants with her, and that created clashes between our own and hers. There were scenes with pans banged about in the kitchen and the odd dish hurled at the offending head. She was used to her

501

own chef, and he stayed on, which offended my cook. I called my staff and begged for patience.

"She is an old lady. Change is not easy for her," I said.

There was some muttering, and one or two left my service. I had a feeling they would have done so whatever happened. The country was rapidly taking sides, and we were automatically assumed to be of the far right. Perhaps some went out of their own conviction, in the belief that a Republic had no place for such as we. But it was possible that they went in simple fear for their own safety. A house that was likely to burn about one's head does not make for peaceful sleep.

Elena was back in Jerez as soon as she heard what had happened. She stayed with us at Los Cisnes. "*Now* will you come? This is no safer than Las Fuentes."

"There is no safe place in Spain, Elena, but that will not cause me to leave. We have trebled the guard about the house. They are armed."

"And you think the mob is not armed? Come to Clonmara."

"No," the old woman said. "Here I stay."

And she did, seated at my right hand at the dining table, resentful that she had not been given Luis' place at the other end. But that had been my mother's place since Luis' death, and I would not have it changed. So on most nights we were five women seated with Juan and Tomás about that long table, on which the silver still shone and the crystal gleamed. We were waited on by white-gloved servants. The violence and agitation all over the country seemed safely shut away outside those guarded walls, but it was an illusion only. My mother had by now completely lost track of the events of those years. She knew little and cared less that Catalonia was going to have its own elections, she knew nothing about the demands of the Basques. She didn't understand the new laws passed, or why the convents and churches were burned, why the priests and nuns were turned out and the buildings given over to secular use. But her delicate mental balance sensed the tension, and she herself grew more tense.

502

She drank more, and we did not try to stop her. Even the Marquesa concurred in this. "If it gives her relief, let her have it. Perhaps it is a mercy not to understand."

The Marquesa read the newspapers thoroughly each day and enjoyed debating their contents with Juan and Edwin Fletcher at lunch. She whooped with triumph when, at the first regular elections for the Cortes held in 1933, the groups of the right won forty-four per cent of the vote, while the left got only twenty-one per cent. "There!—the people have more sense than one sometimes gives them credit for. They know which side their bread's buttered on."

"They often don't have bread," Tomás commented.

"Ho, ho, my little radical!" the Marquesa answered. "Just look around you in the world and see that it has always been thus. Do they have more bread in Russia now because there is no Czar? They have less, we are informed."

But Tomás usually didn't join the arguments. He grew grave and silent in those years in which we watched a series of coalition ministries come and go, all more or less helpless and unpopular. Tomás worked hard at the lessons Edwin Fletcher set him, but without the spontaneous outbursts of boisterousness that had always made his company both a joy and a trial. He listened to the political arguments, read the newspapers, and said little. Each day he joined in the target-shooting practice which the Marquesa had established for her staff of guards, and for any other who cared to join. Edwin Fletcher was one of them; Juan, who had always been a good shot, practiced regularly, and challenged and encouraged Francisco, who was now back in Jerez, and who had a less keen eye than his brother. My mother joined sometimes, happy that she could still handle a gun and fire accurately, though she thought of it only as a test of skill, with no purpose of defense. She made a point of cleaning and loading her own guns; she was meticulous about returning them to the locked room where the household guns and ammunition were stored, and whose keys were held by María Luisa. We set up targets on the other side of the lake, as far from the house as possible, but still the noise reached us, and added to the tension that these days hung over most households in Spain.

Then one morning as we walked to the target area we found Luis' peach trees, which he had grown in a beautifully espaliered fashion on the wall of the vegetable garden, had been decimated. They had been hacked away from the wall and lay broken and already withered. The empty space of the wall had been daubed in huge black threatening letters. *Muerte*. Death.

Elena came again to Jerez after a series of crises had convulsed the country in 1934. A Catholic and monarchist party had formed a cabinet, and two days later Catalonia declared its independence. This rising was again suppressed by governmennt troops, and then came the insurrection of the miners in Asturias. We heard stories, and only half believed them, of the brutality with which these risings were put down. Elena, however, had access to uncensored reports in newspapers we never saw, and she was alarmed.

She came to Los Cisnes to argue with the Marquesa. "Will you *now* come?"

"Why should I? Aren't the right people back in control? What do I have to fear?"

Elena sighed with impatience. "Oh, don't you see? This government can't last. There's been trouble enough. There's much worse to come. There's nothing but anarchy ahead for Spain. You've no right to expose yourself in this way. No right!"

The old woman looked at her, her face cold with anger. "Who says what my rights are or are not? Since when, Elena, did you begin to give *me* orders?"

Elena left, dissatisfied and frustrated. Her last words to me were bitter. "She stays because you assure her it is safe. She's an old woman now, and she listens to whoever is closest. You've used your time well, Carlota, but she had never been anyone's fool."

"Only a fool would count her that, Elena. And I am no fool either."

The Marquesa continued to visit the bodega. In fact,

504

with the country in its present state of turmoil, she derived, it seemed, some pleasure from the relative tranquility of the place. But that was also the year in which I had to note in my diary, *Very abundant crop, but gathered by inexperienced workers. Strike in vineyards and bodegas. Musts of high strength*. We were not immune, no more than anyone in the country. When the strike ended we could no longer look into the faces of the bodega and vineyard workers and be sure they were friendly faces. And yet, I thought, we were all so dependent on each other. I watched the shoots begin to appear on the vines the next spring with a sense of deep depression and apprehension. It began to seem that Spain would never have a stable government. I looked at the new vineyards which the Marquesa and I had caused to be planted. We had invested in the future, but I no longer saw the future in clear and simple terms. It was ever more possible that it would not be a matter of battling only against the various problems of tending the vines, gathering the harvest, selecting and grading the musts, replenishing the solera. Forces quite beyond the ones we knew and were used to —weather, drought, and disease—might decree otherwise. As I feared the phylloxera and the oïdium, I feared the things that might come, either quietly or with violence, to steal the vineyards.

I was startled, on my return from such a tour, to find that Luisa was at rifle practice. I turned on Edwin Fletcher. "How can you let her? What ideas are you putting into her head?"

He shrugged and did not apologize. "Have you forgotten how old Luisa is? She is almost fifteen. To know how to handle a gun is no disadvantage in Spain these days. Would you object if she were learning to hunt deer in Doñana?"

"This is different. She is so young yet, Edwin. Do we have to make her afraid?"

"I hope no one, boy or girl, I've ever taught will not be able to look around them and see—make their own decisions. Ignorance breeds the worst fear of all."

"Leave her alone, Mother," Tomás broke in. "A girl

must be able to protect herself. Who knows when she might have to?"

I lay awake that night and thought of Luis, and his precious, his miracle child, Luisa. It would have grieved him to see her exposed to what she heard every day, to stand near that disfigured wall where his peach trees had been massacred. He had thought to make her life like that of a fairy princess. Nothing evil or painful was ever to have touched it. But there had been no fairy godmother at her christening to grant such a gift. Instead she had for a godmother a woman whose name was hated in many places, whose very presence among us placed us the more in danger. But my delicate little flower, Luisa, was learning to shoulder a gun along with her brother. Who could blame me if, in moments of weakness, I yearned for the simpler days that were gone?

4

Almost the worst heartbreak of those troubled years was the day Martín reappeared at Los Cisnes in the uniform of an army subaltern. We had thought him still in Paris, and I had written chiding letters to him, complaining of his long silence. "I've been in Morocco, Mother, doing my training."

"*You,* Martín! You are the last one to go into the army. You were made for—for music, for study . . ."

"I think if one would have the freedom for such things as music and books, one is going to have to fight for it. The army is the only organized force. Outside of it is only anarchy. There is going to be war, Mother. I want to know *how* to fight, and I want to fight with the army. I will not have the Communists telling me how my life is to go. Don't forget I've heard a lot of Marxist theory talked in the places I've been. We all must do this or do that. I prefer to choose. So I have chosen the army."

It was terrible. He was young and handsome, probably the most sensitive of my children. I could not imagine him pressed into the regimentation of army life; I could not see him learning to kill scientifically, being taught how it was done. I could not bear the sight of him in uniform. "Your father was a soldier," he reminded me. "Why should I be less than he? He left a great example for us, didn't he?"

The sight of the uniform alarmed my mother. She looked at him, trembling violently. "Why?" she asked again and again. But she could not understand the explanation. "The war is over," she said. "All over. They promised there would be no more wars . . ."

The Marquesa viewed him with pride. "You have become a man, Martín."

He spent his short leave in Jerez, and the night before he was to return I made a show of family solidarity by inviting Ignacio, Pedro, their wives, children, the husbands and wives the children had acquired, all to dinner at Los Cisnes. Because of the presence of the Marquesa there, they came, all of them. We went through the usual formalities. For once the cooks had worked in unison, inspired by the occasion, and the meal was splendid. I had searched the cellars for the best wine. Toasts were drunk: we drank to Spain, and there were tears in the eyes of many of the women as we drank a toast to Martín.

Afterwards, in the drawing room, when coffee and brandy were served, Martín, without prompting, brought out his guitar. He had acquired an old instrument, a very good one, mellow and true. It was as if he wanted to offer his own farewell salute to us. Unlike the time at Sanlúcar, however, on this occasion there were no restless movements from the younger ones, no tapping of the feet or snapping of the fingers and demands for flamenco.

He sat on a chair, wearing his uniform, his foot on a stool. Luisa sat on a low stool near him, her eyes never leaving him. What we heard then was what the years in between had made him. He no longer seemed a gifted amateur but an artist—a young artist, still being shaped and molded, but an artist. He played only Spanish music that night, ranging from the tunes of the troubadors to the music of the masters of our century. All the brilliant, exotic, grand, turbulent, troubled history of Spain was there in his fingers, and it held us all silent, spellbound.

When at last he played flamenco, still no one stirred nor moved. When he finished there was no applause; we were silent, awed.

Then he rose and walked over to me, holding out the guitar. "Take care of it for me, Mother, until it's all over."

He turned to his grandmother, who had sat through the music not touching the brandy at her side, her eyes, suddenly young and brilliant again, devouring Martín. "Granny . . . ?" When he spoke to her she lowered her lids and the unshed tears started down her face. "We'll go upstairs to bed now, shall we, Granny?"

It was then I felt compelled to speak to Nanny, to offer her a chance to return to Ireland. She was now nearing eighty, and she was indeed, as Juan rather ruthlessly put it, of not much use to anyone. But she looked at me with her old sharpness when I spoke of leaving.

"Well, I know I'm past my usefulness, Miss Charlie, but is that a good enough reason for packing me up and shipping me out?"

"But you're always talking of going back—back to Clonmara." I wasn't sure that Elena would receive her at Clonmara, but I counted on Richard's help in settling her somewhere on the estate.

"Clonmara, is it? Oh, Miss Charlie, I only talk about Clonmara to be humoring your poor mother. There's no going back for me. What's left to go back to? The old days are finished, Miss Charlie—except in your mother's mind. I'd be dead in a month if I went back. These old bones would miss the warmth . . ."

I had to point out to her the dangers of staying, make sure she understood. She merely shrugged. "Miss Charlie, it's the same for me as for Mr. Fletcher. I'll die in Spain. . . ."

5

In September we brought in the harvest, and yet another cabinet fell, that of Alejandro Lerroux. We had several more ministries in quick succession that year, none of them achieving anything, though promising much to the people. We waited for an army revolt against the Republicans. I wrote in my diary of the harvest, *Normal crop of good quality, average-strength musts.*

By Christmas Francisco had appeared in army uniform and was posted to the Canary Islands. By January 6 the Cortes was dissolved. We would have more elections.

When the elections came in February the parties of the left—Republicans, Socialists, and Communists—won a decisive victory over the parties of the right. The social reform program, the distribution of land, the anti-clerical movement were resumed. We wondered how long the army would wait.

A month later Juan joined the army and married Leonor, a young relative of general Queipo de Llano's, whom he had been courting for a year. It was a hurried, simple ceremony. There was no thought of a large, fashionable church wedding. There had been no such thing in Spain for years. We found a priest, and Juan and Leonor were married surrounded by ranks of the military. It was the final brand we had set upon us. No one could doubt where this family stood.

As the wine circulated after the ceremony, as the military men came to pay their respects to the Marquesa as if it were she who was the head of the household, I realized that María Luisa was absent, and so was Tomás. That Tomás was missing was not surprising; he was going through the adolescent phase when such affairs are either boring or irritating. He had no sentimentality over brides, and he couldn't imagine being in love. But María Luisa was the heart of such occasions. It was she who kept an eye on the trays of drinks being served, who motioned to servants when a glass was empty, who went back to the kitchen to see that the food on the long buffet table was kept replenished. It was her eagle glance that went over a servant's uniform, saw the spot on the apron or the grease mark on the white glove. But she, unaccountably, was not there.

As soon as I decently could I went to look for her. She

was not in her room, not in the kitchen, not among those who had spilled over into the early spring sunshine in the garden to view the famous black swans. I found her at last in the little room we used as a kind of household office, where the accounts were examined, the letters written. She lay full length on a sofa. Tomás was with her.

"What is it?"

Tomás turned with relief to me. "I was at the back during the ceremony. I saw Tía María Luisa was swaying a bit. She didn't look well. So I brought her here." I saw that he had also brought brandy, but she had touched little of it.

"When I got her here, Mother, she fainted."

I bent over her. "It's nothing, Carlota. Just the heat in there. So stuffy. So many people. We should have had more windows open."

It hadn't been particularly warm or stuffy. The big room had not been crowded. The slanting spring sunshine was now fully on her, and I saw, with a sharp stab of guilt that her face, which had always been sallow and thin, was now yellowish in color, and the skin was stretched on the sharply etched bones. She looked ill and worn, and I had not noticed.

"It's nothing," she repeated. "Just getting old, that's all. One gets funny little spells as one gets older. All the excitement and fuss of getting ready for the wedding—all the military people. One always feels one has to do twice as much for the military, as if they might downgrade Juan a rank or two if things weren't just right." She tried a laugh, which turned out to be a sort of dry rattle. Then she struggled to rise. "Now I'll just go and put my head into the kitchen. You never know when the Marquesa's people will take it into their heads to start running the place . . ."

I thrust her back against the pillows. "I'm calling Dr. Ramírez in to you." He was, of course, among the guests. Ramírez was now retired, but he would come if I asked him. He knew the family so well, he knew the personalities of each of us, and knew that it was wholly unlike

510

María Luisa to be here, lying on a sofa, when the house was full of guests.

She waved a hand which I suddenly saw had become clawlike in its thinness. "Oh, don't disturb him at a time like this. I've been to see him. I don't much care for the new doctor. It's just what I said—old age, querida. We all get our aches and pains. He gave me a tonic. It really is helping. But he says I can't expect to be skipping around."

"Why didn't you tell me? I'm ashamed—I haven't noticed."

She gave that same dry cackle. "It's charitable of you not to notice, Carlota. We old crows don't like people noticing such things. We like to pretend we're as good as ever. Once our usefulness is past, there's nothing for us. So you just leave me alone and continue not to notice, and I'll continue to pretend I'm indispensable to you all."

"You know you are." I fussed about her, making a play of loosening the lace at her throat, but it was already sagging from the fleshless bones. "Here, drink a little brandy, will you? And promise me not to go anywhere near the kitchen, or back among the guests. Tomás, you'll stay with her?"

"*What?* And have him miss all the fun out there!" María Luisa looked outraged.

"I'll stay—gladly. All those generals with big bellies make me a bit sick." I hadn't time then to dwell much on his remark. I had guests to think about, and the shadow of María Luisa being ill hung on me.

A few days later, without her knowledge, I visited Dr. Ramírez. He shrugged when I questioned him. "It's just as she says, Doña Carlota. She is not young. You must expect things to get a bit worn out, and we haven't found a way of putting in new spare parts, like these motorcars. I'll keep an eye on her. She doesn't like being fussed over, you know. The worst thing you could do would be to make her feel she wasn't being useful. That's all she's got in her life. She's devoted to you all, you know. Devoted. The family—God forgive me if I blaspheme—is her religion. She'd gladly die for any of you."

I left, not fully reassured. María Luisa went on as before, taking her "tonic," assuring me she was quite well. "Well enough for my time of life, querida." Her appetite was poor. "I'm not the first old bird to go off her bird seed," she quipped. But a nagging worry about her was one more thing which darkened those tumultuous and uncertain months. I noticed that Tomás was often at her side; he tried to tempt her to eat and sometimes she did, it seemed to me, just to please him. He was so gentle with her, and yet so irritable with the rest of us. He applied himself to his studies so that Edwin Fletcher had no complaint of him, but he sat silently through meals, not joining in any of the conversation. He listened intently to radio broadcasts of the political situation, read the newspapers avidly, and yet said nothing. Each day he put in target practice. "Preparing to be a soldier?" the Marquesa asked, and did not wait for an answer. And yet, when any of Juan's fellow officers called—he was stationed at Cádiz—Tomás absented himself. "Jealous, I wouldn't doubt," the Marquesa said. "Jealous of their uniforms, because he's too young to get one himself. Just watch him, Carlota. He'll be the next to go. . . ."

6

A joke began to filter through Spain early in July, after a nervous group of Falangists had seized the radio station in Valencia and announced that "a National Syndicalist Revolution" would soon break out. They were gone before the police arrived. Later, in Madrid, when the Prime Minister, Casares Quiroga, was told about the matter, he was reported to have replied, "So—there is going to be a *rising*? Very well, I, for my part, shall take a little *lie-down*."

It was perhaps the last joke before the tragedy.

Later we were all to know the sequence of events, but then it was a secret known only to the officers who planned the rising.

It began in Melilla, in Morocco, where Francisco was then stationed. There the colonels Seguí and Gazapo, on July 17, arrested their general, Romerales. The officers declared a state of war. There was violent fighting about the *casa del pueblo* and in the lower-class districts, but the workers were taken by surprise, and they had few arms. Those captured who were known to have resisted the rebellion were shot. Anyone known or suspected of having voted for the leftist Popular Front in the February election was in danger of execution.

Colonel Seguí telephoned his fellow conspirators in Morocco, and also General Franco, who was in Las Palmas in the Canaries. In the early evening telegrams were sent to the garrisons on the mainland of Spain giving the simple and long-awaited password—*Sin novedad*. (As usual.)

At a quarter past five on the morning of July 18, 1936, Franco issued his manifesto and Spain was gripped in the mortal coils of civil war.

On that hot July morning, all through Andalucía, as was the plan, garrison after garrison followed the lead taken in Morocco. Cádiz, Jerez, Algeciras, and La Linea were overrun by the army, the Falange, and, in most cases, the Civil Guard. Where there was no garrison, the Falange and the Civil Guard would act by themselves, declaring a state of war. Resistance there was, but it was crushed in the next few days by the arrival of the Army of Africa. Seville was in the hands of General Queipo de Llano.

But we knew it was not over. It had only begun. Madrid and Barcelona would fight; all over Spain, Republicans would fight. From Madrid the woman known as "La Pasionaria" broadcast, demanding resistance to the insurgent army and their sympathizers. I listened to the broadcast and remembered with what words she exhorted the women of Spain to fight with knives and burning oil, and how she ended with the words: "It is better to die on your feet than to live on your knees! *No pasarán*. (They shall not pass!)"

The old words used at Verdun were back again, and

513

became the rallying cry of the Republic. I, all my family, and all gathered around me were immediately branded the deadly enemies of that woman and all her kind. No matter how swift the victory of the army had been in Andalucía, we all sensed that a long struggle lay ahead, and we could not be sure of its outcome.

After the broadcast, Rafael, the *serrano,* our watchman, came to tell us that half the guards the Marquesa had hired had deserted, with their weapons. A chill wind seemed to blow through the corridors of Los Cisnes that hot July night.

"What is going on?" my mother demanded in anguished bewilderment. "What is going to happen?"

We soothed her, but none of us could honestly answer her.

CHAPTER SIX

1

Through all the confusion, through all the tight controls which the army had placed on the province, Elena and Richard Blodmore somehow made their way to Jerez and to us at Los Cisnes.

"We have come," Elena said to the Marquesa, "to take you out of here. Out of the country."

The Marquesa rapped her stick on the floor. "Never! I do not leave. That is final."

"This is only the beginning," Richard argued. "Germany and Italy will go for the right. Russia, of course, will try to intervene for the left. This is going to be much longer and bigger than you suppose at this moment." Edwin Fletcher nodded his agreement.

"We are safe here. The army holds Andalucía."

"The Republicans aren't yet organized, but they're a powerful force. Do you think they will be converted overnight because the army holds the garrisons? They *are* organizing. They're gathering in small bands now, which will get bigger and bigger as they get more arms. Did you know that German planes have been sent already? Do you expect Russia to watch that happening and do nothing?"

"Guns, planes, tanks—let them send what they want. I will not be moved. I stay!"

The argument raged for days. Richard was explosive in his frustration. "Look at you here! A houseful of women! You expect me to go away and leave you?"

The Marquesa laughed unpleasantly. "You could stay and defend us. Or don't you think the insurgent army's cause is the right one? Do you side with the Communists, who choose to call themselves Republicans?"

"I side with no one. I just want to know you're all out of here safely. Look at you—" He swung around the circle we made sitting in the drawing room—the Marquesa, stubborn and old and indifferent to threats or persuasion; María Luisa, impassive, saying little, her face sear and yellow, her body skeletally thin, appearing to think that the whole business was academic; my mother, bewildered by all the talk, not understanding any of the arguments Richard used, her eyes clouded by drink. The center and heart of Richard's plea must surely be Luisa, who sat among us. She was too young to leave to the strains and misfortunes of war. She should grow up as protected as Luis had meant her to be. I knew that if Luis had been here he would have ordered us all to go. Not for any consideration would he have allowed his precious daughter to be endangered. Tomás, for some reason, absented himself whenever the arguments started up again. He was sixteen, just halfway between boy and man, left with women while his brothers had gone to fight, and probably resenting it bitterly. He was sullen and unreachable, contributing nothing to the decision that had to be made.

Finally Richard turned to me. "*You,* Charlie!—surely you must see the sense of leaving. You owe it to your family . . ."

I couldn't meet his eyes. "I don't know, Richard. I don't *know!*" Then I forced myself to look at him directly. "Shall I leave the bodega in *their* hands? The vineyards?

516

Don Paulo trusted me. Luis trusted me to take care of things. Shall I go and leave it all? Can you answer that for me?"

"I can answer only that if things go wrong here there may be no bodega. There may be no vineyards. You may, for the sake of possessions that can be destroyed, destroy yourself, your children, your mother. . . . Have you thought that you may be killed? Think of it. I beg you to think of it."

"And the Marquesa, Richard," Elena said with an edge to her voice. "I am her only relative. You think I wish to leave her behind?"

"The Marquesa evidently will make her own decisions. I'm appealing to Charlie to see sense for *her* family."

"*Her* family. That's all you care about. That's why you've come. You think only of her. . . ."

My mother clapped her hands over her ears. "All this shouting—I can't stand it!"

No one took any notice. We were a family quarreling. "Why stop at us?" the Marquesa demanded of Richard. "What about the families of Ignacio and Pedro? Why not take all of us? Why not evacuate the whole of Spain . . . ?"

"Oh, for God's sake . . ." Elena cried.

It was hard to hear each other for the din we made with our own voices.

But a few of the things we spoke of got through to my mother's baffled, confused mind. "Clonmara?" she questioned, after Elena had spoken of going there to the Marquesa a dozen times. "Are we going back to Clonmara?" She turned to me, her face alight with memory and hope. "Is that where we're going, Charlie?" She brought her hands together in a gesture of pleasure, like a child. "Oh, won't that be wonderful! I'll ride again, and walk by the sea. And see all my friends. There'll be parties, the way we used to have them. We'll walk on the terrace, and in my mother's rose garden—"

Elena had risen and advanced towards her. "I don't know where you're going, Lady Patricia, but it isn't to Clonmara. If Richard wishes to take you out of here, he

517

must make arrangements for you. But the arrangements don't include Clonmara. Clonmara isn't yours any more. Do you remember that? Can you get it into your brain? Not yours! You're not going there. Forget your friends—they're all dead. You haven't any friends left. There won't be any parties. You won't walk on the terrace or on the shore—or in the rose garden."

Elena stopped to place a cigarette in her holder and light it. "You should know, since it seems to obsess you, that there isn't any rose garden any more. I had it dug up and replaced by herbaceous borders. This spring. I was tired of all those old-fashioned roses. Richard was upset—furious with me. But he's old-fashioned too. It was done before he knew it. So . . . not even the rose garden, Lady Patricia."

My mother got to her feet, her lips quivering. "My mother's rose garden! You dug up my mother's rose garden! How *dare* you! How dare you touch anything at Clonmara! My mother's rose garden! It was famous. How could you have dug it up? Who gave you leave?"

"I didn't need permission, Lady Patricia. Clonmara is mine now. It belongs to me."

"Elena!" I didn't want to look at Richard's face. He tried to silence her, but she persisted.

"Oh, Richard, be quiet! You don't listen to this madwoman, do you? What business is it of hers what happens at Clonmara? She has nothing to do with it any more."

Richard looked at me, his face flushed with what seemed to be anger and shame. "Charlie, I didn't—"

Elena seemed perfectly aware of the anguish she caused. "Richard was on business in London," she said. "It was a surprise for him when he came back. It was such a surprise, he was speechless." She laughed dryly. "It's quite an achievement, after all those years of marriage, to be able to surprise Richard. But that did it . . . believe me, that did it. He went into a sulk for weeks. I even had a row with Edward over it, who's become, I'm sorry to say, as much a stick-in-the-mud where Clonmara is concerned as Richard is. He's a real traditionalist, is Edward. He *likes* farming. He's grown just like Richard. Copies him in everything." She turned and looked at the Marquesa. "When it comes to Edward's turn to inherit Pontevedra you'll find an excellent estate manager."

"I'm glad to hear there are some who take their inheritance seriously," the Marquesa snapped. "But don't put me in my grave too soon, Elena. Don't—" She fell silent and looked beyond her niece.

My mother had drawn close. The talk about Edward and Pontevedra had not touched her. "My mother's rose garden . . ." In a soft murmur she repeated the words again. "Dug up . . . Gone! How did you dare?" She was carrying her wineglass and her movements were slow but quite deliberate as she tossed its contents into Elena's face. "You touch nothing at Clonmara, do you hear? *Nothing!* It never belonged to you. Never."

Elena moved with equal slowness. She took her handkerchief and wiped the wine from her face.

"I would be angry with you, Lady Patricia, if I didn't pity you. You are quite demented, you know. I've said before you should be locked up. But that is not my responsibility. Others must see to that. But there is one thing I wish would penetrate your poor, sick brain. You are never coming back to Clonmara. *Never!*" Then she turned and left the room.

My mother stood looking at us for a moment longer, her face twisted in her anguish. She spoke to me. "I've disgraced us again, haven't I, Charlie? I didn't have any right to. But *she* didn't have any right to dig up my mother's rose garden. But she can't have me locked up for saying that, can she? You wouldn't let her, would you, Charlie?"

I took her upstairs. Her protests dropped to confused muttering. "My mother's rose garden . . . *He* planted it for her. The rose garden . . . Who is this Edward who farms at Clonmara? Did my father give him permission? Why did he let her dig up the rose garden . . . ?"

After almost a week we had argued ourselves into an exhausted enmity. The Marquesa and I kept refusing to go, but I kept saying Luisa must. Richard would not leave us. Elena's voice was heard pleading, urging, cajoling the Marquesa; in the extremity of her frustration she tried forcing the old lady, beginning to pack luggage for her, asking for the key of the safe so that she could collect her jewelry. The Marquesa's refusal was as stubborn as Elena's insistence. It was clear that Elena did not care what my decision was. She did not care whether we stayed or left. She offered no sanctuary at Clonmara to Luisa. My mother she totally ignored. The Marquesa was her only concern. "You will be perfectly comfortable at Clonmara," she said. "You can sit it out in peace and quiet there."

"Peace and quiet are not things I have particularly treasured through my life. Privacy, yes. Safety . . . ?" The old woman laughed. "To live is to take chances. I'll take my chances here."

This lasted until the night when Tomás failed to appear for dinner. We waited, but the hour was already late. María Luisa sent a servant to his room and to the schoolroom, but he was not in either place. We ate dinner without him. Even the Marquesa was disturbed. "Doesn't he know it isn't safe to be roaming out at night? Not in these times. He's only a boy, but who knows . . . he could be taken for a man if he's in some doubtful place. People shoot these days and ask who you are afterwards."

"That thought can hardly be comforting to Charlie, Marquesa," Richard said.

She spooned her soup and said nothing. None of us ate much. Meals had come and gone that week, almost untasted. I looked along the table to María Luisa and saw that she made only the motions of eating. Her face was gaunt in the candlelight, her eyes far-sunken into her head. I reminded myself that tomorrow I would go once more to Dr. Ramírez. His tonic powder was having no effect. I would insist on a proper examination, a second opinion. Tomorrow—surely by then we would have settled our arguments. Tomás would be home safely. I would have time tomorrow.

María Luisa excused herself almost as soon as coffee

was served in the drawing room. Luisa was making the rounds, saying good night to us all; her lovely, grave little face seemed haunted by our indecision. "Carlota," María Luisa said, "I will go and talk to the guard. They must be especially vigilant that they do not make any mistakes . . . with the boy out at this hour, and everyone nervous. We do not want any accidents. Why don't you go to bed? You are tired. It's useless to talk further tonight. You will decide nothing. Go to bed. I'll wait for him. I'll wake you when he comes in."

"You should go to bed yourself, María Luisa. You need rest as much as any of us."

She shrugged. "We old ones don't get much sleep, whether we're in bed or not."

We sat almost silent over coffee. Richard poured some brandy which the Marquesa refused and the rest of us took. My mother then, within a few minutes, held out her glass to Richard to be refilled. He raised his eyebrows, questioning me, and I nodded. It didn't matter any more.

It was then María Luisa entered the room again, agitation making her step swifter than it had been of late. "I found this in my room, Carlota. I don't know why he left it there. It's for you."

I took the envelope and ripped it open.

Dear Mother,

Forgive me. I can't stay here, and I can't go away with you. I have made up my mind. I can't leave Spain. I intend to fight with the Republicans. I know it will take you a long time to understand why, but I hope you will. Please do not inform the Civil Guard. I have taken guns and ammunition, and if they come after me and find me, they will probably shoot me. I have friends to go to. I will be safe with them, and they need the arms. I love you. Kiss Luisa and Granny and María Luisa for me. Tell the Marquesa I fight for Spain. I don't want to leave you, but I have to. We will be together again when it's all over. Tomás.

Weak with fear now, I handed the note to Richard. I looked at María Luisa. "He left the note in your room because he had been in there to get your keys. He has opened the gun room. . . ."

We went and looked. Five guns were missing from the rack, the most modern, the easiest to get ammunition for. Grimly María Luisa locked the room again; the keys had been left in the door.

"My fault. I must indeed be getting old when I don't know better in these times than to leave the keys out of my possession. Without the guns, he would be just a runaway boy. With guns he is in grave danger. . . . My fault . . ." She shook her head and didn't hear our denials.

Richard had gone to Andy's quarters, and by now Andy was with us. He had slipped in quietly, past the kitchen, so that the house servants did not know he had come.

"His horse and the harness is gone, Miss Charlie. Three horse blankets . . . some leading reins, saddlebags." He nodded towards the gun room. Richard had told him about Tomás' note. There was no question of not trusting Andy with the information. Tomás meant as much to him as his own sons. "That's about as much as one horse could carry. He must have wrapped the guns in the blankets . . ." He looked at the circle of faces surrounding him. "Makes you sick to think of it, doesn't it? This whole area swarming with army and Civil Guard . . . God, Miss Charlie, why did he do it? Just a boy . . ."

Elena was the only one who spoke. "Yes, it makes you *sick!* This miserable little traitor in our midst . . ."

I turned away and dragged myself upstairs to my room, but not to sleep.

All the next day the argument raged with Elena. "The authorities *must* be told. It's criminal. He is going to give guns to the Republicans."

"The Republicans are still the elected government of this country, Elena."

"The Republicans are Communist scum, and so is he."

The Marquesa pounded the floor with her stick. "Be quiet, woman! You want the servants to hear? We do not need an informer. The boy is criminally mistaken, but we can do nothing about that now. We must give him time to reach his friends, whoever they are. They probably have some place . . . they say there are places where the Republicans are caching arms away from the military."

"You sound as if you approve," Elena said bitterly.

The Marquesa rapped her stick again. "You know that is not the truth. He is a fool, but he is only a boy. He is my godson. I detest his politics. But I care for his life."

"And what will we do when they find he is gone? Someone will notice soon. The servants talk . . ."

"Let them talk," I said. "It is more dangerous to inform the military than to let him go. This way, he has a chance. The other way . . . I have burned the note. We know nothing, you understand? Nothing, Elena. *Nothing!*"

I told the servants that Tomás was at Ignacio's house; they were arranging some special shooting practice, I said. I don't know whether I was believed, and perhaps, later, when the truth was known, Ignacio would make trouble about my lie. But I had to say something. I have to give Tomás time. It was his life. All through the day I could hardly bear to look at Richard's face. I thought that if he had been left to himself he might have wept in his agony. He said only one thing to me, alone, after he had read the note.

"Shall I go to search for him?"

"Where would you search? Where in God's name would you begin to search without rousing suspicion? He may still be somewhere here in Jerez. He may have headed for the Puerto, or for the sierra. Which direction would you start, Richard? You dare not *ask* after him."

He bent his head. "I should have taken better care of him. I should have known what was in his mind, and stopped him."

"His mind, I think, was being made up years ago. It was made up when he ran away from school. It was made up, finally, and forever, when he spent that summer at

523

Doñana. He may not have realized it fully himself—God knows, *I* didn't know it, and I should. But he has been bending in that direction for years. This is not a boy's silly bid for adventure. I'm certain he knows what he's heading into. He may be killed, Richard. And if he is killed, it will be fighting on the opposite side from his brothers. He knows that. He knows that *that* is what civil war is. He is older than any of us knew."

"I've failed you, Charlie."

I shook my head. "We've all failed him. Or else he is right and we are all blind."

We got through the day and into the night. The strain of pretending that nothing was wrong had told on all of us, and emotions were close to the surface. By using the same pretense that Tomás had gone to Ignacio's we had managed to keep the news from Luisa, but we knew she sensed that something was wrong, and by the next day she would know. The worst strain had been wondering if my mother might start to talk of it. She had been with us the night before when we read the note and examined the gun room. She knew that her loved Tomás was gone, but why he had gone, or to whom, she seemed not to understand. But she said nothing. All day she had been silent and withdrawn; perhaps she brooded as much over the loss of the rose garden at Clonmara, over the final ending of her dream of returning, as she did over Tomás absence. We had kept her and Luisa apart as much as possible. She had been sipping wine for most of the day, staring vacantly ahead of her, eating little.

Dinner was over; we were again seated in the drawing room; coffee had been served and I had dismissed the servants. Luisa bade us good night. She lingered as she kissed my mother, stroking her cheek for a moment. "Don't be sad, Granny. He'll be back soon. I know he will."

My mother roused herself for a moment, smiling. "Yes, child—dear child . . ."

When Luisa left us Elena burst out. "How long is this going to go on? Luisa guesses—if she doesn't know everything! You realize you are putting us all in jeopardy by failing to inform the military that he is missing? You need say nothing about the note. But soon enough—tomorrow, at latest, someone is going to know. You know how this town is. They will know he is not at Ignacio's, and then we shall be in trouble for failing to report him missing. They are bound to ask about the guns. They *know* there are guns here."

"Elena . . . that is enough! Leave Charlie in peace, if you can. She has as much as she can bear."

Elena turned on him. "Charlie!—she's all you care about, isn't she?—she and her wretched, traitorous son. We'll all be in trouble because of him. *I* don't care to be shut up in a Spanish prison because of him. You know they'd shut us up with the Republican scum, don't you? The military *rules* this town, and now we have a Republican traitor among us, and you are condoning it. It is your duty to go to them. At least it would protect us. Let them find him and shut *him* up with his Republican friends. We would be safe. We would have disowned him."

I hadn't realized how great her fear was. I had been so frightened for Tomás, frightened as the slow hours of the day ticked away that some terrible news would come of him, that I had forgotten the danger to the rest of us. I looked now at the Marquesa. She had not wavered all through the day. Tomás must be given his chance to get away, as much time as there was. There the difference lay between Elena and her. The Marquesa was not afraid. For the first time, along with my respect for her, I began to feel the unfamiliar stirring of love. Because she loved Tomás, cared more for his safety than her own. She did not approve of his actions, but she would keep him safe if she could. Now, when it was almost too late, I perceived what the relationship with this formidable old woman might have been, might yet become. She had been cruel in the past, but she had protected those she cared about. She had not disowned or denounced Tomás. Although he had offended against every feeling that someone of her rank, class, and age held sacred, still he had the mantle of her protection. Perhaps she was declaring in this action a love she had been unable to declare in any other way.

I thought of the years we had missed, this woman and I. The feeling I had developed towards Don Paulo had come late, but with this woman it had come almost too late. Suddenly I understood why it was to my house she had come when the mob burned Las Fuentes almost over her head. She had known before I did that the mutual respect we held for each other was indeed a kind of love. She had known love existed where I had not. She also knew that love was not some fancy thing to be taken up and put down. When it was given, by someone of her character, it was forever. I believed now that she had truly loved my grandfather and had never stopped loving him, even through her bitter hurt. And that love, in its various fashions and shapes, had carried on down the years. She had interpreted it as a trust placed with her to protect and defend all the Blodmores. She had done it possessively, in her harsh, autocratic manner, unable to believe that anything she thought right for the Blodmores could be less than right. Now, to the last of them, Tomás, she with her silence offered her love.

"We will not disown him," the Marquesa answered Elena. "We will inform no one."

The long wait was broken by Andy. He came to the drawing room himself that night, something he had never done before. He knocked and then entered without being bidden. He looked around and saw only familiar faces.

"Miss Charlie, there's news."

I sprang to my feet. "What news?"

He was looking around again, now a little uncertain whether he should have spoken. The Marquesa thumped her stick. "What news?"

"It was brought to me. I . . . I won't say how. Tomás crossed the river at Sanlúcar. They took him through Doñana. Now he's at a place near El Rocio. Shall I go and fetch him, Miss Charlie?"

I thought for a while. "Fetch him? I don't know if you can do that, Andy. He's not a child. He can't be dragged back if he doesn't want to come. And how would you do it? You'd need help from . . . from whoever brought you the news. You'd need to be met on the other side in

Doñana. You couldn't find your way through Doñana by yourself. And to go the other way, through Sevilla, is impossible. There are army checks all along the road. You'd have to have a pass, and a reason for going." I sat down again, the first hope gone, the misery of the decision still to be made. "I don't know what to do," I said. "I don't know what to do . . . If he were a few years younger, you could say he was a child and not responsible. If he were a little older, you'd say he was a man and had made his choice, as the others did. . . ."

"I could go," Richard said. "It would be a lot easier for me to go than Andy. I'm carrying a British passport and have a permit from the commander in Cádiz to travel. Juan's married into General Queipo's family, and I could use his name. I'd bluff my way across the bridge at Sevilla. Get to El Rocio somehow. Perhaps Tomás would listen to me, Charlie. I'd try to make him see sense. Try—at least *try!* It's not too late yet." He asked Andy, "Has the . . . the person who brought the message gone?"

"The person has gone, m'lord. It was only passed along, you know. People don't travel these days. I would have to pass the message back—that is, if you wanted to go through Doñana. Through Sevilla . . . ?" He shook his head. "I don't know how to pass anything that way. You see, they . . . they didn't mean me to know too much. They knew that Miss Charlie would be worried, and wanted her to know he was all right. But you see, m'lord, they know *I'm* not really for all this Republican business. They know this family is all mixed up with the military. They weren't telling me much, you understand, m'lord. Just that he was safe with them, and the way he'd gone. Perhaps . . . perhaps he isn't even at El Rocio any more. . . ."

Richard said, "I still think it's worth a try. If I left at first light . . . not much use to try it at night. They're more likely to be suspicious . . ."

"Richard—" There was something in Elena's tone which warned Andy. He looked quickly at me.

"Well, if that's all for the moment, Miss Charlie . . . You'll let me know if you want a horse, m'lord. There's Miss Charlie's car, of course, and the Marquesa's. Both have a full tank of petrol. But when that's gone, who knows where you'd get more in these times? A horse would be slower, but it might be easier. You'll let me know, m'lord. I'll wait up. No need for Manuela or anyone else to know anything about this. Fewer know, the safer it is." He closed the door softly.

Elena rose and went over to Richard. "If you try to go I'll find some way to stop you. I will *not* have our safety, our standing with the military, put in jeopardy for this boy. Think about it, Richard. Think about it. . . ."

She left the room almost as quietly as Andy had done. As we talked, planned, argued, I didn't notice that my mother had left also.

It was perhaps half an hour later we heard the sounds of the car outside. It was enough to alarm us, because the guards had instructions to allow no one to enter unless we told them someone was expected. We looked at one another in an agony of apprehension. I went to the door of the drawing room and opened it. There had been no sound of a bell being pulled at the front door but Elena was already there and had opened it. We heard the voices in the hall, hers and that of a man. As he came into the light I saw that it was Colonel Rodríguez, the officer commanding the troops now quartered in Jerez. He had been a guest at Juan's wedding.

"I came as soon as the orderly passed along your telephone message, Lady Blodmore." I understood then why he had been passed by the guards at the gate. No one interfered with the movements of the military these days. They would have been admitted as soon as the army car and its occupants had been recognized. One did not argue, either, with the military.

"It was good of you to come—at such short notice." She was closing the door behind him. Outside I had caught a glimpse of the car, the driver, and an aide.

Elena gestured him towards the drawing room. "I hope I can be of service. The Marquesa, perhaps . . . ?"

"It is a family matter, Colonel. A rather delicate family matter. I thought it rather better if you came here, than that we should go to your headquarters."

He smiled affably. I guessed that he rather enjoyed being asked to help with a family matter when the family was as important as the Marquesa's, a family with such good military connections, a family whose money might be called on to help provide what the army would need. "Good evening, Doña Carlota." Then he advanced to the Marquesa and lifted her hand. "I trust I find you well, Marquesa. And you, Lord Blodmore. These are troubled times, are they not? But we have it well in control. The government still refuses to hand out arms to the people, and so every day that passes we gain more territory while they vacillate. Did you know that General Franco and General Mola have set up a Junta of National Defense at Burgos? Ah, thank you, Lady Blodmore. . . ."

He accepted the brandy Elena had poured. He had been speaking English, rather proud of the fact that he spoke it so well. "Please be seated, Colonel," she said. She waited until he had done so, even offered him a cigarette and a lighter, waited until he had taken the first sip of brandy, rolled it appreciatively on his tongue, inhaled, and then blew out the smoke. None of us spoke all this time. I looked at Richard and saw that the old scars flamed on his cheek. There had to be some way to stop Elena, and yet there seemed none. The Colonel was here; he had been summoned for a purpose, and he would want to know it.

"There is something . . ." Elena began.

"No!" My mother's voice sounded almost a cry in the quietness of the room. "You have no business bringing the military here."

"I must do as I think best," Elena said. "Carlota, can you not control your mother? Pray excuse this, Colonel. Lady Patricia is often not quite . . . quite well."

He nodded sympathetically. Everyone who came to Jerez soon learned about my mother, learned the whole story, often distorted, about Carlos and Balthasar. But however mad this Irish lady was, she was still a member of one of the town's leading families, who protected her. Her "eccentricities" were always overlooked, even if they sometimes caused a laugh.

"Of course, of course," the Colonel said soothingly. He

rose to his feet. "There is no need for alarm, Lady Patricia. The army is only here to preserve the peace and order of this country. To stamp out the forces of anarchy who would destroy it. There is no need for alarm at all."

I saw it before anyone, because I recognized it. She had kept it in the fold of her long, old-fashioned skirt. She looked so strange, with her hair in disarray and her body swaying slightly as if she had had far too much to drink, that no one paid attention to anything else about her. But she held it in her right hand and I saw it. I sprang towards her, and the movement startled her.

"Mother! *No* . . . !"

But she had reached Elena before I could stop her. Amelia's little gun, the gun with which I had ended the life of my loved Pepita, was in her hand. The gun, which had lain undisturbed in its beautiful box for all these years, once again fired its silver bullet. Elena slumped in her chair. The shot had been fired at point-blank range, and it appeared to have entered her heart. I think she died almost at once. There was very little blood on the pale silk of her dress.

My mother looked down at Elena for a moment. Then she turned to the Colonel. "She was going to have me shut up, you know. She'd even dug up my mother's rose garden."

He stared at her, incredulity making his face vacant; his mouth hung open a little. Then he recovered himself, put down the brandy and cigarette, and bent over Elena. Richard was beside him, but it was the Colonel who took Elena's wrist to try to feel for a pulse. Richard held Elena upright in the chair while the Colonel bent to try to hear a heartbeat. A minute or more passed, and he straightened slowly. His expression was still incredulous. "Lady Patricia, are you aware of what you have done?"

My mother's face twisted in a terrible parody of a smile. "She's dead, isn't she? I'm quite sure she's dead. All my life I've been a crack shot, and she was so close." Then she laid down the little pistol on the table beside the Colonel's brandy and cigarette. With the kind of dignity a drunken person can assume, she walked from the room. Immediately, María Luisa followed her.

"Lady Patricia," the Colonel called after her. "Lady Patricia, I must insist—"

The Marquesa spoke. "Leave her go, Colonel, please. She will be confined in her room, I promise you that. You need have no worry that she will be permitted to leave this house. . . ." Very stiffly she got to her feet. "Colonel, may I have your arm? There are things I must say to you, things we must discuss. Will you come with me to another room? I cannot . . ." She looked at Elena in the chair, Richard still bent over her. "I cannot talk here. Carlota, will you come?"

It was an order, not a request, and the Colonel reacted to it as people had been reacting to the Marquesa all her life. He offered his arm, and she leaned on it more heavily than she needed to. I followed them, and closed the door on Richard and Elena.

We went to the dining room. "Carlota, another brandy for the Colonel—I will also have a little. My nerves . . ." She had never displayed nerves, but she permitted her hand to tremble a little as she raised the glass. "This is a most terrible thing."

"*Terrible*," the Colonel repeated. For a while he dropped into Spanish. "Marquesa, it is inexplicable!" He took a large gulp of brandy. "Being a military man, I have seen many things in my lifetime but nothing quite so bizarre as this. Two *ladies*—that little gun. Extraordinary! Was Lady Patricia fully aware of what she was doing? Did she know that that little gun, small as it is, could kill? Or was she trying to frighten Lady Blodmore? How could she have come by the weapon—in her state it is most dangerous. You have guns here. Do you leave them available to whoever wants to take them?"

The Marquesa raised her hand. "No, no, Colonel. We are not so irresponsible. The guns are carefully locked away. But who would have thought of this? It is, of course, a museum piece, as you saw. Jeweled—with silver bullets. It has never been used, to our knowledge. Something that Don Luis' second wife, Amelia, took a fancy to in Vienna many years ago and brought back here. It has always been in its own box, with its own silver bullets, in a display case which also houses some other works of art. That was all it was ever meant to be—a work of art. I'm afraid we have been most negligent in forgetting that it was also a true weapon and that Lady Patricia was knowledgeable enough to use it. That she *would* use it never occurred to any of us."

"But *why* did she use it?"

The Marquesa shook her head slowly, as if the answer was inexpressible. "How can we know exactly what was in her poor sick mind? You know, I think, Colonel, that Lady Patricia suffers these spells of derangement. At other times she is perfectly sane and lucid. It is all due to an unfortunate accident she suffered years ago, an accident which happened when she saved the life of my husband's son. Because of the debt we owed her for that brave act, we have tried to be very gentle with her, and never before, I swear, has she shown any inclination towards violence. It has been a sad cross for Carlota to carry, and she has done it with grace and love. She has been a good daughter to her afflicted mother. It is a . . ." Her voice broke. She pressed a handkerchief to her eyelids. "Forgive me, Colonel. It is a most terrible tragedy that Lady Patricia should have committed this act of violence against my niece. How shall we bear it . . . ?"

The Colonel looked in bewilderment from one to the other of us. "Lady Patricia said something about Lady Blodmore threatening to have her shut up. Was *that* why Lady Blodmore telephoned me? To come here to take Lady Patricia away? It is, of course, entirely outside my sphere of duty."

The Marquesa shook her head slowly. "None of us had any idea Elena had telephoned you, Colonel. It's true, she's been heard to say many times that she believed Lady Patricia should be confined, and it has been very upsetting to hear. She doesn't . . . didn't understand Lady Patricia as we did. Unhappily Lady Patricia must have taken her words far more seriously than we thought."

The Colonel threw out his hands in exasperation. "But why call on *me?* She said a family matter. You think she wasn't referring to Lady Patricia at all?"

I grew cold as I watched the Marquesa's face. Tomás'

immediate safety now depended on her. With amazement I saw tears appear in her eyes, where I had never seen tears before. "I'm terribly afraid, Colonel, that I may have been the unwitting reason for the tragedy. It is my belief that Elena had asked you to come here to speak to me personally about the situation in the country. To explain its seriousness."

"It is serious, Marquesa. Everyone knows that."

"Ah, yes—but you must understand that my niece was seeking to have me leave the country. She and her husband have been here for almost a week, and it has been Elena's whole concern to have me convinced that we—I, that is, am in serious danger. Myself, I said I had perfect confidence in the army and the forces of law and order. If people like me, Colonel, flee the country, what sort of example is that to others? I consider it my patriotic duty to stay. Elena, who, as perhaps you know, has not lived in Spain for many years, doesn't entirely understand—didn't understand how we feel here. We must stay to support you in this struggle, if we can. It is as simple as that."

He coughed. "Your sentiments do you credit, Marquesa. In the long term I see no possible outcome to the struggle but victory for the forces of law and order, but it is true that we need every sort of support. Moral and actual."

She nodded. "Quite so, Colonel. But I think Elena brought you here in a last attempt to make me feel that possibly people like myself were a burden. I can as easily contribute money to the cause from outside the country, and while I remain I place an unnecessary burden of protection on people such as yourself."

"If we cannot protect our supporters inside Spain, Marquesa, then we have lost already."

"I agree. That is the whole point. Elena could not see it—would not. This has been a week of severe strain on all of us, and for poor Lady Patricia I'm afraid it has tipped her delicate mental balance. She does not, cannot, understand what is happening. It is quite beyond her. But listening to these arguments all the week, she must somehow have confused Elena's arguments with her repeated statements that Lady Patricia should be confined. My

533

niece has not always been as sympathetic to Lady Patricia's condition as she might. She has spoken rashly—perhaps cruelly, in her presence. Lady Patricia has been very depressed and nervous these last few days. I begin to think she was afraid that Elena had some sort of power connected with the military, and when she saw that Elena had brought you here she thought you had come to take her away. It is my opinion that if we question her she will be able to give no rational reason why she committed this terrible act. She may actually have forgotten that she did it."

The Colonel was uncomfortable. "May I smoke, Marquesa?" She nodded and he took his time lighting his cigarette. "This is no matter for me, Marquesa. It is really no business of mine or the military's *why* this act was committed. It is obviously a matter for the doctors. But a crime *has* been committed."

"Exactly so, Colonel. It is a terrible problem. A terrible moment for me. Elena was my only close blood relative. She would have inherited the title of Pontevedra. You understand how I feel. Pity for Lady Patricia. Grief for my niece. I can hardly realize it yet. . . ." I listened, the sweat growing cold on my body as she embellished her role. "I am old . . . it has been a great shock. Carlota, a little more brandy, if you please, and for the Colonel."

By the time I had poured, Richard had come to the doorway. He had an air of infinite weariness about him; the shattered face, the upward-twisted mouth seemed grotesquely exaggerated. Perhaps the sight of him reminded the Colonel that he was dealing with a man who had been through years of a different war.

"My profound sympathies, Lord Blodmore."

"Thank you, Colonel. It's been a tragic mistake. Lady Patricia is so confused . . . Poor soul. She has never done harm to anyone before—"

The Marquesa broke in, "Precisely what I have been telling the Colonel, Richard. A tragic error. She has confused Elena's concern to make me understand the seriousness of the situation, to get me to agree to leave, with her too often repeated opinions that Lady Patricia should be locked away. And the unfortunate Colonel was seen as the instrument of that policy. Indeed, if one thinks about it, the Colonel might have been Lady Patricia's more natural target. . . ."

"Exactly," Richard said. "That can have been the only reason for her doing what she did. Yes, it might well have been you instead, Colonel."

I thought the Colonel paled a little at the suggestion. He drew hurriedly on his brandy and, with the glass empty, glanced hopefully at me. I poured again, and then filled a glass for Richard. Richard said, "To cope with the immediate details, Colonel—may I have your permission to send your car to bring Dr. Ramírez? There is, of course, no hope for my wife's life. She must have been dead a second after the bullet entered. But still there must be a medical man to examine her. . . ." He faltered. "I have left everything undisturbed. . . ." I took the brandy to him. "I ask, Colonel, if I may send your car because it is much easier for the military to move at night than a civilian. The doctor must confirm the death and the circumstances. I'm sure you will need—need everything to be in order."

"Naturally, it must be done correctly. Perhaps I should instruct my aide." He looked as if he would have been glad to be away from us all.

"Let me do it. Stay with the Marquesa. It obviously comforts her to have authority with her at this time. If you wouldn't mind?" He took the brandy I offered and drained it.

When he was gone the Marquesa started again. "You are the authority now, Colonel—as well as the principal witness. You must instruct the Civil Guard. There can be no question of a trial, of course. Everyone knows she has these . . . these spells. You cannot put a madwoman on trial."

"Equally, Marquesa, she cannot be permitted her freedom. You may, of your generosity, be able to forgive her the murder of your niece, but the law will say that, at the least, she must be prevented from doing the same thing again. If she feels herself persecuted, as is obvious from her strange remarks about Lady Blodmore,

535

who knows what she will do next? It is not, I repeat, a matter for the military."

"She must be confined, certainly, Colonel. The tragedy must never be repeated. It will need several doctors to certify that she is insane—doctors who have observed her behavior over the years. We have tried to avoid this extreme measure. She has an exaggerated horror of being 'shut up' as she calls it. But obviously her mental condition has deteriorated to an extent none of us realized. You heard that quite unrelated remark about a rose garden. Pure imagination. Poor soul. You should have known her when she first came to Jerez, Colonel. . . . What a woman she was *then*. . . ." It was hard to believe it was the Marquesa speaking.

The Colonel looked helplessly from the Marquesa to me, and then to Richard, who had returned and was standing in the doorway, slumped against the frame.

"What am I to do then? I cannot put her in jail. It would be unthinkable in the circumstances. The jails are overflowing with Republican murderers. Coming from a family such as yours, Lady Patricia would be in danger of being harmed—perhaps in danger of her life from them. And as for the usual places such unfortunates are sent . . . well, they no longer exist. The nuns have been driven from all their institutions. The Church is no longer permitted to engage in such charitable activities. Naturally, all that will be restored when we have established the proper order again, but in the meantime we are in a state of war and conditions are extreme. I can think of no place where I can reasonably send her."

"With your permission, of course, Colonel . . . after the doctors have given their testimony . . . after the facts have been noted and the depositions taken . . . after all that, I could pledge you that she would be put in a safe place of confinement where she can hurt no one. I have a castle—a fortress, really, at Arcos. Perhaps you have heard of it? There, I assure you, she would be quite safe, and unable to escape. You may satisfy yourself on all these conditions. We, the family, would be responsible for her until such time as conditions return to normal."

For a while the Colonel said nothing; he sat sipping

his brandy, smoking, trying to rid himself of this awkward problem. "Perhaps I should consult with General Queipo . . . though with all he has on his hands at this moment he won't thank me to trouble him with civilian matters."

"Need we trouble him, Colonel? *You* are in charge here. It is obvious that one cannot condemn a madwoman to death. Spain has not reached *that* point. It will be understood that my family bears enough sorrow in the death of my niece without the additional horror of such an action. No—it is unthinkable. Arcos, I believe, is the answer. . . ."

The old cracked voice went on, making the plans, smoothing the way. The Colonel was nodding, the smoke from his cigarette half obscuring his face. He seemed almost mesmerized by the Marquesa's voice, the compelling, undeniable logic of what she argued and persuaded him to. I slipped past Richard. He would remain there to reinforce whatever the Marquesa said, and Tomás' name would not be mentioned. But my mother . . . It couldn't have happened, and yet it had. My mother had killed Elena. As I climbed the stairs I heard again and again the terrible words of sentence for her crime. "I have a castle at Arcos . . ." My mother would take the place of the woman who had inhabited it before her.

I found her in bed, María Luisa seated beside her. She was propped up on her pillows, wearing a white lawn nightgown edged with lace. Her hair had been brushed and lay smoothly on her shoulders. It was now completely silver, and one could no longer see the white streak that had appeared so dramatically after her accident. In the soft light she looked beautiful again, and perfectly serene. She smiled at me. A glass with a little brandy left in it was on the table beside her. María Luisa gave me the chair closest to her. My mother stretched out her hand and took mine.

"There you are, darling. I've been waiting for you. Everything's going to be all right now, isn't it? She won't interfere in our lives any more, will she? She's gone, and we can have peace now. Only you won't let them shut me up, will you, Charlie? You always promised me that."

537

I stroked her hand. "You must try to sleep, Mother. It's going to be all right."

"Yes . . . all right. I know it will be all right. You would never let them shut me up. I'd rather die than be shut up." I sat there, holding her hand, in an agony of love and sorrow. I could not weep; I could say nothing. I thought of the promise, so often given and never, I had believed, to be honored. Gradually the pressure of her hand in mine relaxed. Her eyes were closed and she was breathing deeply.

María Luisa touched my shoulder. "Leave her now, querida. She is sleeping. She will not wake."

Outside in the passage I leaned against the wall. I was sweating again. María Luisa pressed her handkerchief into my hand and I wiped my face.

"What in God's name am I to do?"

Down below I heard Richard's voice in the hall, the Colonel's voice; I heard Dr. Ramírez' voice. Then the noise of the motor, and someone calling to the guards.

"So—the Colonel leaves, and Ramírez has come," María Luisa said. "What is going to happen?"

I told her quickly how the Marquesa had explained Elena's request to the Colonel and what the Marquesa proposed to do with my mother. "She believes she is doing the best she can—and I suppose it *is* the best. But it's the same as shutting my mother in prison. She will have no freedom. After what she has done, they will turn it into a prison, up there on that rock. She'll not ride again . . . not do *anything* again. She won't see her grandchildren. And I promised her, María Luisa. So often I *promised*—but I never thought it would be a promise I would have to keep. *Why* did she do it? She really must be . . . mad. There's no other word. She must be quite mad."

"I believe myself, querida, that she never had a saner moment. She knew exactly what she was doing at the time. She meant to prevent Elena telling the Colonel about Tomás and the guns, and she achieved that. We have imagined her sitting in a fog of drink, but she had heard and known everything. She knew Tomás was in danger.

538

She had to stop Elena. She told me she heard her speaking on the telephone to the Colonel's aide, asking for the Colonel to come. The gun room was locked, but she remembered where she could find a weapon. She was quite ready when the Colonel came. It is, perhaps, a mercy that it was not the Colonel who received the bullet. The military would hardly overlook *that*."

"But does she think there will be no punishment? Does she really understand that she has killed Elena? She hasn't just stopped her from talking about Tomás. She has *killed* her."

María Luisa shook her head. "That part I do not know. She expects to be looked after, as she has always been looked after. You know how quickly she changes. One moment able to understand everything perfectly. Able to plan, to see ahead. The next it is all gone. She is back in her fog. But she trusts and loves us, querida. And she counted on your promise."

"Which I cannot keep."

"It is kept, querida. I have seen to that. I told you she will not wake. That is the exact truth. She will not wake."

I gripped her arm, and she winced. "Please, querida. Not so hard." I released her.

"What have you done?"

"I gave her the medicine Ramírez gave me. All of it—in the brandy. She will not wake."

"That—that tonic? What can that do?"

"Morphine is a very powerful tonic, querida. It was for the pain. There is nothing Ramírez or any other doctor could do for me, except to give me morphine against the pain. More and more of it. In the dose I gave her, along with the brandy, it is lethal. She will never be shut up, querida. The promise is kept."

"The pain . . . María Luisa, what are you saying?"

She held up her hand as if to dismiss the question. "I have only a few more weeks, at most. Perhaps not even that long. A little lump in the breast." She shrugged. "Who wants to bother with such things? By the time I went to Ramírez there were other lumps, in other places. He said I should go into hospital. They could try. He

539

didn't hold out much hope. So . . . well, I am too old to let them start cutting me up. What difference would it have made for just a little extra time? I preferred to die in my own way, in my own time. So I took his tonic and delayed as long as possible the moment when I would have to take to bed. I forbade him to speak to you of it. But I am happy that, in the end, I have been able to serve you. I have kept your promise for you, querida. You have been my life, my beloved child. All these years . . . I was an old maid, and you gave me a family. You have loved me, I know. And I—I hope I have been, finally, of service."

I clasped her to me, careful now that I didn't hold her too tightly. She was so frail and thin; I could feel the fluttering beat of her heart, like a frightened bird one holds in one's hand. The tears were hot on my cheeks.

"How am I to lose you both?"

She gently disengaged herself. "Where there is love, querida, nothing is lost forever. I will go now and sit with her, and pray to God that He understands. He should understand the way love works, He should understand the way love goes, shouldn't He, Charlie? The things it is sometimes necessary to do out of love? Who but God would understand better? I do not fear His judgment." She turned the handle of my mother's door softly. "Do not tell the Marquesa or Lord Blodmore until Ramírez has gone. It would be his duty to try to revive her, and that would only be distressing and would not work. So let her go peacefully. In the morning she simply will not wake."

I stayed with the Marquesa while Ramírez examined Elena. The Colonel, she said, had taken the little pistol. Ramírez came into the dining room and signed the certificate in our presence.

"A most unfortunate business," he said. "And Lady Patricia?" he added. "May I do anything for her?"

"She is asleep," I answered. "You know how easily she sleeps when she has had a lot to drink. María Luisa is with her."

He closed his bag. "I will come in the morning
540

again. I will see her in the morning." I thought he looked at me very closely, as if he discerned too much in my too quiet words. But he said nothing more, asked no more questions. He had kept a great many secrets for this family. He would keep this last one until the morning.

When he left in the car the Colonel had sent back to collect him, I told the Marquesa and Richard what María Luisa had done.

After a long silence the Marquesa nodded her head. "It is well. It took great courage to perform such an act, but she has done all she could do for this family. She has done well."

2

I sat with my mother as long as she breathed. It was peaceful; there was no struggle. As María Luisa had said, she simply did not wake.

Then in the dawn I went down and found Richard and the Marquesa together. They were drinking coffee. The cigarette butts in the ashtray indicated how the night had gone. The Marquesa's personal servant, who had also waited through the night, brought fresh coffee. Although the day already promised heat, I shivered, and was grateful for the warmth of the liquid. Richard looked ill and tired and old. He was a man well on in his fifties. We were young lovers on the shore no more.

"I have told the Marquesa," he said, "that you and I will marry as soon as possible. I will take you and Luisa to Clonmara . . ."

I shook my head. "Marriage will come when it does, Richard. And you will take Luisa to safety—to Clonmara. But you know that I cannot go."

"Will you tell me, in God's name, why not? What will keep you here now?"

"I have sons, Richard. I have sons who fight on opposite sides of this war. My senses tell me that it will not be over quickly. My senses tell me the Republicans will resist the army to the last bullet and bomb, and it will be long and agonizing. Many will die. Perhaps some of my

541

sons will die. But while they fight, on whatever side, I must be here. I must hold the center. I am neither left nor right. I am their mother. This is their world, their home. I will be here to hold their inheritance for them, to guard it, to keep something of the good they remember, to try to keep alive what each of them believes he is fighting for. I can do it only here. Not at Clonmara. Clonmara must wait."

The Marquesa turned to Richard. "That is what I told you she would say. That is her answer."

He put his elbows on the table and his face was cupped in his hands. At last he looked up and directly at me.

"I will take Luisa, if that is what you want. I will take her to Clonmara and give her into Edward's care. You need have no fears for her. From Edward she will have kindness and concern. He will care for her the way he does for Clonmara. Both are safe in his hands. And I—I will come back here. I will come back. My instinct tells me to go now to look for Tomás, but the Marquesa has convinced me that *your* instincts are right. He cannot be dragged back against his will, and my very presence, if I should find him, might only lead others to him. He will probably vanish into the morass of this war. I cannot bear the thought that I may never see my son again, but neither can I put him into more danger. Oh, God, Charlie—help me!"

Before the Marquesa's gaze he put his hand out and reached for mine across the table. And from her expression I knew that she had never doubted that Tomás was Richard's son.

3

Richard waited only to see Elena buried, and my mother, and that was done swiftly and with little ceremony. I watched the coffins lowered into the Spanish earth and thought of how much of me now was buried here. My past was buried in the earth, with Carlos, with Mariana, my grandfather's wife, with Luis, whom I had loved, with Don Paulo, who had hated, and in the end given power to the

542